THE
EMBER
BLADE

THE EMBER BLADE

BOOK ONE OF
THE DARKWATER LEGACY

CHRIS WOODING

This edition first published in Great Britain in 2019 by Gollancz

First published in Great Britain in 2018 by Gollancz
an imprint of the Orion Publishing Group Ltd
Carmelite House, 50 Victoria Embankment
London EC4Y 0DZ

An Hachette UK Company

9 10 8

Copyright © Chris Wooding 2018
Map illustration by Neil Gower 2018

A CIP catalogue record for this book is
available from the British Library.

ISBN 978 1 473 21486 6

Typeset at The Spartan Press Ltd,
Lymington, Hants

Printed and bound in Great Britain by Clays Ltd, Elcograf S.p.A.

www.chriswooding.com
www.gollancz.co.uk

For Anna

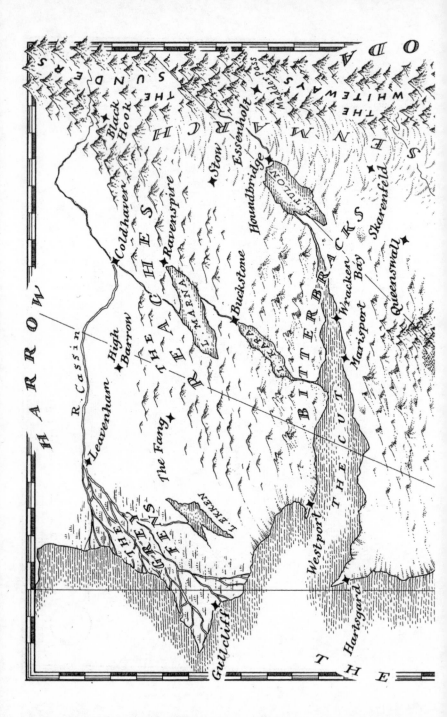

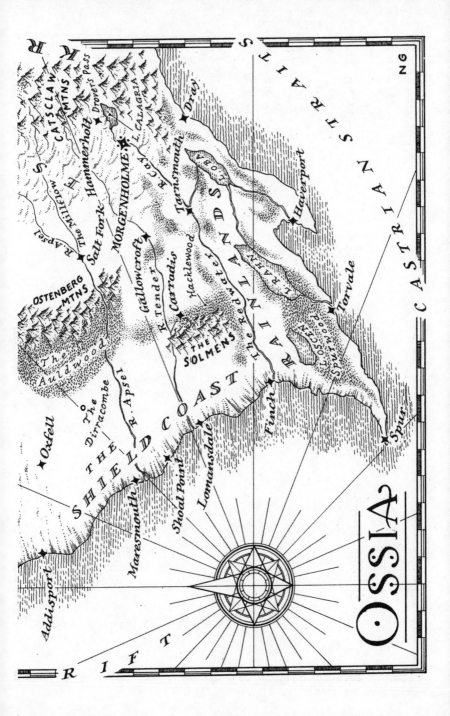

I

'Keep faith and hold fast, and we will free our land!'

Edric had said that, not three days past, as he stood on the battlements of the keep at Salt Fork and watched the enemy closing in. Side by side with his brothers and sisters, pride swelling his chest and angry defiance in his eye, it had felt like truth.

He knew better now.

The forest whipped and scratched him as he clambered up a muddy slope, breath burning his lungs and a cold fist of terror in his gut. Dirk laboured through the undergrowth in his wake, white with exhaustion. The older man was at the limit of his endurance; it was plain by his slumped shoulders and the vacant look in his eyes.

Edric hauled him the last few paces to the top, where Dirk bent over, pulling in air like a man near drowned. He scanned the forest fearfully while his companion recovered. The trees were loud with birdsong, dewed leaves stirring in the dawn light. There was no sign of their pursuers yet, but he could hear the Emperor's hounds through the trees.

'You go on,' Dirk said, raggedly. He had the flat stare of a dead man. 'I'm done.'

Edric had known Dirk for less than a season and liked him for none of it. He was a low sort, fond of drink, and spitting, and the kind of rough humour that made Edric uncomfortable. Edric was a frustrated young man with lordly blood, looking for a way to define himself; Dirk was an illiterate ironmonger with nothing left to lose. But Salt Fork had brought them together, united them in common cause. Even when everything lay in ruins, Edric wouldn't let go of that. He pulled Dirk upright.

'You'll run,' Edric said. 'And when you can't, I'll carry you.'

Together, they stumbled on.

He'd always known Salt Fork would be the end of him, but he'd dreamed a different end than this. Fifty of them had seized that town, fifty who dared to stand against their oppressors. Their act of defiance was to be the spark that would ignite the fire of rebellion in their people. He never expected to survive, but at least his name would be remembered in glorious song.

The bards would sing a different tune now. They'd sing of how the townsfolk's resistance crumbled as soon as the Krodan army came into sight, how the crowds threw open the gates and tried to arrest the men and women who'd led them astray, hoping to trade them for Krodan mercy. They'd sing of a shambolic escape through smugglers' tunnels, with the ringleaders fleeing for their lives as the soldiers marched in.

They'd sing of failure, and they'd sing it in the tongue of their overlords.

He'd seen Renn swallowed by the mob he was trying to reason with. Ella had died defending him, killed by a stone to the head. He didn't know if any of the others had survived; in the confusion, he'd lost everyone but Dirk. Perhaps there'd be a rendezvous days from now, some message left at a dead drop, but he wouldn't be there to read it. The Emperor's huntsmen had chased them through the night and drew closer with every hour. They wouldn't see another sunset, and both of them knew it.

A temple loomed suddenly from the trees, towering before them. The sight of it brought them to a halt. Its walls had been breached by the forest and a mossy cupola lay in ruins near the entrance. Balconied domes and soaring vaults had been gnawed bare by time's appetite, yet still it stood in testament to its makers, an elegant masterpiece from a lost world.

Dirk's legs shook and he fell to his hands and knees. Edric stared, wide-eyed. Exhaustion had drained him of emotion – even his fear had been numbed – but now he felt a sense of wonder which slowed his hammering heart.

Once, his people had been great. They'd led the world in art, theatre, medicine, architecture, philosophy, astronomy and the ways of war. Their empire had spanned the known lands, and Ossia had been the home of heroes.

But that was the past, and the past was long behind them. Their empire had faded centuries before. Ossia had been under a Krodan boot for thirty years now, longer than Edric had been alive. He'd never known true freedom, and so, in the end, he'd gone searching for it.

The collapse of the Salt Fork uprising and the long and frantic night that followed had shaken his faith. He'd cursed himself over and over for staking his life on a naïve dream of revolution. Yet here, before this silent monument, he found new strength. The blood of its builders still ran in his veins, and one day his people would cast off their chains.

'On your feet!' He hauled Dirk back up, though the man was a dead weight.

'Leave me to the worms,' he wheezed. 'The Red-Eyed Child comes for me.'

Edric pointed to the temple, where a dark doorway gaped amid a tangle of vines. 'If we must die, it will be with the Nine at our backs, in the house of our ancestors.'

'The Nine!' Dirk said bitterly. 'Where are they now?'

'They're still here,' said Edric, his jaw tight. 'This is their land. It is *our* land, and it will be again.'

'You're a fool and a dreamer, Edric,' Dirk said. 'I always thought so.' Then his mouth twitched at the corner. 'We needed more like you.'

The arrow hit Dirk with enough force to knock him to the ground. He fell face down, a thick shaft fletched with ragged black feathers in his back. Edric stared at him stupidly for a moment, dazed by the speed of his death. Then terror took hold and he drew his sword, backing towards the temple, searching the trees for the enemy. He found only stillness and an uncanny silence. Even the birds had fallen quiet.

Something was out there, a presence that iced his spine. The leaves hissed in the wind and the very forest seethed with evil.

He ran, springing up the temple steps two at a time, and reached the top before his leg gave way beneath him in an explosion of pain. He crashed down on the flagstones, sword skidding from his grip, clutching at his thigh where the barbed and bloody tip of an arrow poked out. Veins stood stark in his throat as he screamed.

Numbness and corruption spread from the arrow, tendrils of foulness worming into his flesh that froze and burned all at once. He tried to rise and screamed again as the shaft moved inside his leg. His head spun, and everything was suddenly dim and distant.

Through the fog that clouded his eyes, he glimpsed a soft red light inside the temple. A light in that long-abandoned place, where he'd seen only darkness before. He was seized by a desperate hope. Was there somebody in there who could save him? Here, in this sacred place, had the Aspects sent him a sign?

Gasping with the pain, he dragged himself inch by excruciating inch over the threshold.

The forest had choked up the windows and shadows clustered thickly between the columns. Overhead, birds shifted quietly in their roosts among the stonework, subdued by the same dread that had silenced the others outside. Statues loomed at the edge of the darkness, barely more than lumps, hands lost and faces smooth. He recognised them anyway. There was Joha, the Heron King; there was brutish, squat Meshuk, Stone Mother; there, jaws agape and straining at his chains, was Azra the Despoiler, Lord of War.

Edric offered a silent prayer to the Nine Aspects as he pulled himself over cracked flagstones, each movement sending fresh fire from the wound in his thigh. A set of steps led deeper into the dark temple. The source of the red glow was somewhere below.

There was no sound from his pursuers, but he dared not hope this ancient place could keep his enemies out. He focused on the next lurch forward, and the next, until he reached the top of the steps. The red glow illuminated the bases of the columns beyond but its source remained out of sight, hidden by the broken pieces of a toppled statue.

With dry mouth and trembling arms, he slithered down the first step, and the second. At the third, his elbow gave way and he went tumbling and sliding out of control. The arrow in his thigh caught on an edge and wrenched sideways, and the pain which followed drove him into the black waters of unconsciousness.

When he surfaced again, he was lying on his back at the foot of the steps, his head tipped to one side. Tears filled his eyes, wet red hexagons swimming there, glistening. He blinked and the tears slid free.

The source of the light was finally visible. It wasn't a sign after all, just the fading remnants of a fire left by some vagrant, or a wandering druid who'd sheltered here. No hope of help, then, and no reprieve. He watched as the glowing wood brightened in a faint breeze, and a peaceful, aching sadness soaked into his heart as he realised he'd reached the end of his road. It hadn't felt nearly long enough.

He turned his head and saw the man at the top of the steps.

To Edric's dimmed eyes, he was little more than a shadow, but the red light reflected from his round spectacles and made him look infernal, an imp from the Abyss come to carry him away. He was short and balding and wore a long black coat. When he spoke, his voice was breathy and damp; the sound of gentle murder.

'No more running.'

He stepped down into the light. He was fish-lipped, weak-eyed, with a pale, soft face and the look of a clerk about him. In other circumstances he might have appeared comical, but he had the double-barred cross on his shoulder, the hated symbol of the Iron Hand, and Edric didn't feel like laughing.

'I am Overwatchman Klyssen,' he said. 'Hail to the Emperor.'

Edric had dropped his sword on the temple steps, but he had a knife at his hip, which he drew and held before him. It was a feeble threat, and Klyssen ignored it.

'There will be others,' Edric said. 'Others like me. And we'll drive you from this land.'

'The folk of Salt Fork did not share your conviction.' The overwatchman raised his head, taking in the gloomy grandeur of the temple. 'We have made your highways safe and swift, brought order to your cities and given you the gift of the Word and the

Sword. We protect you against enemies who would slaughter or enslave you. Your farmers enjoy the fruits of their fields, your seamstresses sew in peace and your children want to be Krodan.' His tone became puzzled. 'When will you be satisfied?'

'We'll be satisfied when the last Krodan is gone from our land, when your thrice-damned god is cast down and an Ossian sits on the throne again with the Ember Blade in their hand,' said Edric. 'We'll be satisfied when we have our freedom.'

Klyssen lowered his gaze and the light made his spectacles red again. 'Ah. That you will never have. Because, in the deepest places where you dare not look, you know you are better off without it.'

'One day you'll eat those words from the tip of an Ossian sword,' he spat. 'Kill me, if you're going to.'

'You'll die, have no doubt of that. But first you'll talk. There is one among your companions I seek. You knew him as Laine of Heath Edge, but we both know that's not his real name.'

Edric lay in silence for a few moments. Then he began to chuckle, a pained sound almost like sobbing. 'He has evaded you.'

'For now.'

'Then hope is not lost.'

'I wouldn't say that.'

Klyssen motioned with his hand and three figures appeared at the top of the stairs, silhouetted by the light from the temple doorway. One was hulking and armoured, carrying a great hammer. Another was ragged and thin, holding a bow. The third was cowled and cloaked, with a gleam of metal where a face should have been. The sight of them was like a cold weight on Edric's chest. Here was the source of the nameless dread that had silenced the forest. It drained the courage from him, and fear made him babble.

'I can't tell you where he is. I don't *know* where he is!'

He became aware of an itch in his knife-hand, increasing to a burn. Something was writhing under his skin there, vile tunnelling worms that turned and coiled in the light of the dying fire. Horror and disgust choked him. His other hand flew to his face, where the skin had begun to blister, swell and ooze.

'We'll see what you know,' Klyssen said quietly, as Edric finally found breath to scream.

6

2

The cave was a triangular maw filled with shadowed teeth. Aren studied it warily, knuckles white where he gripped his sword.

'You think she went in there?'

Cade nodded from his hiding place, crouched behind a boulder, poised to flee. He had his knife in hand, but he clearly had little faith in it.

Aren glanced back in case their quarry had slipped around for an ambush. The green flanks of the ravine sloped steeply up to either side. At the top, sunlight slanted across the grass, but down here it was dimmer and the air was still. The ground was cluttered with rocks of all sizes, from pebbles to great boulders shaken loose by the march of ages, shaggy with moss and lichen. A shallow stream, ankle-deep and a few paces wide, splashed between them. Dank, scrawny trees drowsed nearby, with watchful crows in their branches.

They heard a sharp clatter of tumbling stones from the cave.

Cade sprang to his feet, ready to bolt. Aren caught him by his shoulder and pressed him back down.

'It's her,' Aren whispered, half in triumph and half in terror. Cade gave a low moan of despair.

Heart thumping, breath short, Aren stepped into the open and crept forward. When Cade showed no sign of moving, he scowled and gestured at him to follow. Cade slid out from behind the boulder, muttering darkly.

They were no longer boys and not quite men, adults in their own minds and no one else's. Aren was gangly but not tall, his body still finding its proportions. Cade had a heavier build, a clumsy, solid boy who moved without grace. Thick brown curls hung across Aren's brow; he had soft eyes, a flat jaw and a long, wide nose that split his face like the shank of an anchor. Cade had small features in a fleshy frame, a quick, restless mouth and the first dusting of a beard, the same muddy blond as his close-cut hair.

It was Cade who'd glimpsed their quarry first: a rush of movement, a thrashing in the bracken, a flash of haunch. Big as a bear, he told Aren, when he got over the fright. Just like Darra said she was. They'd tracked her into the ravine after that, and finally cornered her here.

Aren crept up to the mouth of the cave. Within was a chill, grey world of hard angles. Nothing moved. He was about to go further when Cade grabbed his arm.

'You ain't actually going *in*?' he whispered incredulously. 'Why don't we wait here?' Aren saw him struggle to think of a good reason. 'We can jump her when she comes out!'

Aren was tempted by the idea. Better to tackle the beast in daylight, where they could manoeuvre. But lurking in ambush felt cowardly. When Toven chased the draccen of King's Barrow into its lair and slew it, he didn't hide outside for hours first.

'No. We'll catch her unawares, where she can't escape from us,' he said.

'Oh, aye, that's a great plan,' Cade griped. 'Foolproof. And what if *we* want to escape?'

Aren went in and the quiet gloom closed around him. He kept the stream to his left, moving in a low crouch, his sword held defensively across his body as Master Orik had taught him. A splash and a string of curses told him that Cade had followed him inside, and that he now had at least one wet foot.

'*She was like a wolf, but like no wolf you ever saw!*' Darra had said, his eyes bright and earnest. '*A she-warg, high as your shoulder, broad as a cart, teeth like daggers! I saw her walking through the trees in Sander's Wood!*'

'*My brother saw her, too,*' Mya had said. '*Next day, three of my father's flock were gone, only blood and torn wool left to mark them.*'

Aren tried not to think of the beast's size, or her teeth, or the fact he wasn't one-tenth the swordsman Toven had been. Instead, he imagined the townsfolk cheering their return, the nods of respect from the Krodan honour guard, the pride in his father's gaze as the governor praised them. Best of all would be the sight of Sora's delighted face when he presented her with the she-warg's paw, a hero's token to his lady.

Ahead, the cave bent sharply to the right and the way was obscured by a bulge in the rock. The light from the cave mouth was feeble this far back, and Aren wished they'd thought to bring a lantern. Facing the beast in darkness wasn't something he'd anticipated. Perhaps an ambush *did* make sense. He'd always preferred the stories about clever Tomas to those of his mighty brother Toven anyway. Tomas won through wit and craft rather than force of arms.

But what if there was another way out of the cave? After all this time searching, he wasn't about to let the beast get away.

Staying close to the cold rock, he peered round the bend and saw a small underground chamber beyond. There was a jagged fissure in one wall, wide enough to squeeze through. The stream ran across the chamber and away down another passage. Nothing moved but the restlessly tumbling water.

'How's it look?' Cade asked.

'Come and see,' said Aren, and stepped in.

The darkness was pushed back by a thin shaft of daylight which cut diagonally across his path from a dripping hole in the ceiling. An assortment of slimy plants had found purchase along the stream's edge and glowed dimly there. He saw phosphor moss and riddlecap, and other moulds and mushrooms he couldn't identify.

Cade slunk in behind him. 'Don't much like the look of that horrible great crack in the wall,' he said.

As if in reply, they heard a furtive rustle of movement from the fissure, the sound of something unmistakably alive. They turned to face it together, with mounting dread.

'You know, I heard a tale about a cave hereabouts,' Cade murmured. 'A cave at the end of a ravine, with a little stream coming out of it. An old hermit lived there, rotten to the core, with a hook for a hand.' His voice dropped and he leaned closer, eyes like saucers. 'More than one traveller took shelter in that cave on a rainy night and never came out. He hung them up like meat. Story goes he died alone and hateful, but his shade walks here still, and the last thing you'll hear before he gets you is his hook, scratching along the stone...'

Aren gave him a flat look. 'You just made that up so you can go home,' he accused.

'Aye, I did,' said Cade, shrugging. 'Worth a try.' He picked up a rock. 'Shall we see what's in there, then?'

'Not like tha—' Aren began, but he was too late to stop Cade tossing the rock.

A maelstrom of thrashing wings exploded from the fissure. Aren yelled and swung his sword at the air as flapping creatures beat at his face. His blade clanged off stone and numbed his fingers, nearly jolting out of his grip. Cade capered about, slapping wildly at his own head, trying to dislodge a bat which had become tangled in his hair. Half-seen shapes darted past them, whirling in panicked circles before flurrying away towards the entrance of the cave, leaving the two boys panting and gasping in fright.

Cade rubbed his hands through his hair and looked at them in disgust. 'Flying rats. Ugh.' He spotted Aren leaning against the cave wall with his sword drawn. 'You get any?' he asked dryly.

'Next time you think you have an idea, why don't you float it past me first?' Aren said breathlessly.

'I ain't the one who just led us into a cave to face a she-warg without any lanterns.'

'No, you're just the one who followed him in.'

From the passage they heard a splash of water and an animal snort that set them rigid.

'Well, reckon that's me done for the day,' said Cade, heading off after the bats.

Aren grabbed him. 'No you don't,' he said, dragging Cade back to his side. Together they stared into the dark passage. Cade's fingers flexed nervously on his knife-hilt, his expression dubious. 'Sure you don't want to go for an ale at the Cross Keys instead?'

Aren slapped him on the back for encouragement. Cade rolled

his eyes and tutted. 'Go on, then. Let's get this over with. But I ain't going first.'

Aren had no intention of letting him. This beast was Aren's to kill. It would make a poor tale for Sora otherwise.

High as your shoulder. Broad as a cart. Teeth like daggers.

They trod quietly as they followed the stream deeper into the cave. The blackness thickened and they were forced to hunch over as the ceiling bore down on them. Just before they reached the limit of the light, they found a new passage leading off to the right. They heard another snort, loud and close enough that Aren jerked back and held out an arm to bar Cade's way.

The beast was right around the corner.

Cade's eyes glittered with fear and he grabbed Aren's elbow, shaking his head. But Aren gripped his friend's forearm firmly and stared hard at him. Now it came to it, there was no question of turning back.

'We strike together,' he hissed.

Cade wavered, but Aren wouldn't let him go.

'We can do it!' he said, and this time he saw reluctant determination settle on his friend's face. 'Aren and Cade,' he whispered, with a reckless smile. 'They'll call us heroes.'

'They'll call us *something*, that's for sure,' Cade agreed grudgingly.

'Are you ready? On my word.'

Cade nodded, but not without a look that made plain what he thought of being dragged into this adventure.

Aren listened. There was another grunt; the sound of the beast moving. He drew a breath, held it for a moment and then let out a cry, as fierce as he could make it. They plunged round the corner, blades raised.

Utter dark faced them. Utter dark, and no sign of their quarry. They faltered, not knowing where to strike, not daring to go onwards, and in that moment the beast was on them with a terrifying scream.

Aren and Cade stumbled back, sloshing into the stream as it charged. Aren slipped on a wet rock and his leg went out from under him. His head struck the wall, stars exploding before his eyes as he dropped to his hands and knees in the chill water. Pain sang from his shins and palms. Somehow his sword had jarred free of his grip. He cast around frantically in the stream but it was nowhere to be seen.

He heard Cade shout a warning, and he was swatted by the beast's hot, bristly flank, its musty stink filling his nostrils. He tried to wrap his arms round it, to wrestle it down rather than let it batter him, but the beast bucked and skidded in the stream, slamming Aren against the wall, its coarse fur scratching his face. Teeth gritted, he struggled to hold on to it.

'Cade! Stab it!' he yelled, though he couldn't see his friend through all the water splashing in his eyes.

The beast kicked, catching him low and hard in his gut, and his arms came loose. A heavy haunch slammed into his cheek, and then the beast was away, charging downstream, grunting and squealing frantically. The sounds faded as it reached the freedom of the open air, leaving Aren kneeling in the stream, bruised and winded, a dull ache in his belly and groin.

'Aren?' Cade hurried up to him. 'Are you hurt?'

He blinked dazedly, popped his eyes wide a few times to clear the fog in his head, then laboriously got to his feet. 'Where's my sword?'

'I don't know. You dropped it somewhere. There it is, in the stream.'

Holding the back of his head with one hand, Aren stooped to retrieve his weapon. His face felt hot, and not just from the battle.

'That was no she-warg,' he said at length. 'That was a wild pig.'

'Looked like one,' Cade said. Then, to make them both feel better, he added: 'It was a really *big* wild pig.'

Aren, sodden and dripping, saw the edges of Cade's mouth turn up, and that set him off. The two of them leaned on each other and laughed until tears streaked their cheeks. Eventually, Aren showed signs of calming down, but then Cade oinked at him and they were away again. By the time they were done, Aren's stomach hurt and Cade was in danger of fainting.

'Maybe best we don't tell anyone about this,' Aren suggested as they made their way out of the cave and into the sunlight.

Cade crouched by the stream, wadded up a rag from his pocket and soaked it in cold water. 'As if I would. They'd never let us forget it. Here, put this on your bump.'

Aren pressed the rag gratefully to the back of his skull. The laughing fit hadn't helped his headache much. 'So what do you think? Next time we try the east ridge?'

'You ain't *still* after that she-warg?' Cade said, amazed. 'Four times we've gone hunting for her now! That's every day I've had off work in the last two weeks! Can we at least explore the possibility that Darra's a liar and Mya's just gullible?'

'We'll explore that possibility,' said Aren, 'right after we've explored the east ridge.'

'There ain't no she-warg!' Cade cried.

'You give up too easily,' Aren said over his shoulder as he started to trudge up the ravine.

'Aye. And you don't give up at all.'

3

'Step, step, feint! Now parry, feint, thrust!'

Cade sat against the base of a dry-stone wall, eyes closed and face turned up to the sun, content as a basking cat. Bees droned lazily nearby and the breeze stirred the long grass of the meadow. In the dappled shade of a lone spreading oak, Aren jabbed and darted at imaginary foes, practising his sword drills.

'Are you even watching?' Aren demanded. 'I'm trying to teach you something.'

Cade cracked one eye open to look at him. Aren stood with a fist on one hip and his blade lowered, sweating in the heat. Beyond him, the fields spread down the hill to the coast, a patchwork of green and yellow dotted with farmsteads and speckled with sheep and cows. From their vantage point, Cade could see the Robbers' Highway snaking from the east and the Cross Keys Inn on the outskirts of town, where he and Aren had sucked down more than a few foaming ales under old Nab's indulgent eye. Shoal Point was a cluster of buildings along the coast, mostly hidden by a fold in the land. West of that there was only ocean, glittering bright enough to dazzle.

'I've been thinking,' Cade said at length.

'Have you now?'

'All this business with the she-warg... do you reckon Sora even *wants* a dirty great wolf paw?'

Aren made a quizzical noise.

Cade elaborated. 'If you were the highborn daughter of a rich Krodan family, wouldn't you want jewels and flowers and such?

I'm just saying she might be less than thrilled when you hand her a dismembered piece of a recently dead animal with the stump all crusty with blood.'

Aren opened his mouth to make a sharp reply, then shut it again and frowned. The question hadn't occurred to him before now. 'Well, obviously I'll clean the blood off first,' he said testily.

'It'll still smell pretty bad,' Cade said. 'What's she going to do with it, anyway? Wear it as a necklace? It'd put her back out if the beast's as big as we're told.'

A sour look passed over Aren's face. 'Do you want me to show you Master Orik's new drills or not?'

Cade levered himself up, satisfied that they wouldn't be exploring the east ridge on his next day off. Aren handed him the sword. It felt heavier than usual, but that was probably because he was feeling lazy.

'Ain't it a bit hot for sword practice?' he tried half-heartedly.

'Stop complaining. Come autumn I won't be here to teach you any more.'

Cade saddened at that, but he tried to make a joke of it. 'Just promise you'll send me the paws of any mighty wargs you slay. I'll have them, if Sora won't.'

'Ha! Get to work, you layabout!'

Cade let Aren demonstrate the new moves again and copied them as best he could, but his mind wasn't on the task. As a highborn Ossian approaching his sixteenth birthday, Aren would soon leave for his year's service with the Krodan military. Cade, a carpenter's son, wouldn't be joining him. Krodans didn't want working boys like Cade. They only cared about the sons of rich Ossians, who could be trained as loyal and useful servants of the Empire.

He had other friends, but they were the children of bakers, potters, fishermen. None were like Aren, who could speak fluent Krodan, who knew history and mathematics and etiquette and had a permit to carry a sword, even if he had to keep it sheathed and wrapped within town limits. In truth, Cade was a little in awe of the highborn boy, and secretly dreaded the day Aren realised he could do better than a dockside lad with little education and no particular skill in anything.

The year ahead loomed large and empty. He feared it would be a different Aren who returned, one he didn't know.

He made a passable effort at sword practice, enough to show his appreciation, but it was exhausting in the heat and he gave up as soon as he thought Aren would let him. He didn't like the sword much, and he'd never be permitted to own one anyway, but Aren always enjoyed showing off what he knew.

'Maybe it *is* a bit hot for sword practice,' said Aren. 'Do you want to learn some Krodan instead? I could teach you how to make a diminutive noun.'

'Why don't I tell you a tale instead?' Cade suggested, with an enthusiasm that verged on desperation. 'I've got a new one. You'll like it!'

'Is it a Krodan story?' Aren asked.

'Naturally,' Cade lied. 'Do I tell you any other kind?'

He wished his mother *would* tell him some Krodan stories sometimes, so that he could pass them on to Aren; but though she had a bard's tongue, she refused to recite the legends of their oppressors. Aren, on the other hand, loved anything Krodan, and said the old Ossian folk tales were for bumpkins. To get around the problem, Cade changed the names in his mother's tales and passed them off as Krodan. He suspected Aren knew, but the deception let him enjoy the stories of his homeland without admitting it to himself.

Aren settled himself by the dry-stone wall while Cade launched into the tale of Haldric – renamed Lord Merrik – and his companion Bumbleweed. It began with the hapless pair stumbling across a maiden bathing naked in a rock pool, a woman so fair she stole Lord Merrik's heart. But clumsy Bumbleweed stepped on a twig with a loud snap, and the alarmed maiden melted away as if by magic before Lord Merrik could introduce himself.

Against his companion's advice, Lord Merrik decided he had to find the maiden and marry her. So they went to see an old woman who told him that the maiden was the daughter of a kraken, and she only walked the earth one day every ten summers, spending the rest beneath the sea. Lord Merrik wasn't of a mind to wait ten years for another glimpse of her creamy skin, so they set off in search of her, finally reaching Joha's River in the sky – recast as a magic stream so as not to give the game away – where they learned to breathe water from a fish with scales of fire.

Suitably prepared, they descended to the depths of the sea where Lord Merrik challenged the kraken to a battle of wits, ably assisted by Bumbleweed, who'd happened upon all the answers to the kraken's riddles during their journey. When Lord Merrik won, he claimed the right to ask the kraken's daughter for her hand in marriage. The kraken granted his boon, but his daughter promptly refused, asking why she should marry a man who made a habit of spying on naked women in rock pools.

Aren howled with laughter as Cade aped Lord Merrik and Bumbleweed trudging dejectedly from the sea onto the shore, and cheered when Lord Merrik swore off women for ever and promised eternal friendship to Bumbleweed, who'd supported him faithfully through all his adventures.

'Your best yet!' Aren said when he was done, and Cade glowed, though he knew it was flattery, and bowed. Then he shaded his eyes and looked towards the sun.

'Best be getting on,' he said. 'I have to be home for supper, and Da will tan my hide if I miss it again.'

'"All things can wait but supper and lovers",' Aren quoted happily as he got to his feet.

'That's an Ossian proverb,' Cade said. 'Bumpkin.'

Aren shoved him down the hill.

4

By a wooded path on the edge of town stood an old boundary stone, weathered to a nub. There they paused while Aren wrapped his sword and scabbard tightly in burlap cloth.

'I'll bet you can't wait till you don't have to do that any more,' Cade observed. He was sitting on the boundary stone, tapping his heels against it and patting a rhythm with his hands.

'When I get back from my service they'll have to give me a full permit,' Aren said. It galled him to see the sons of Krodan highborns swanning about Shoal Point with their swords on display. He wouldn't feel a man till he could match them.

Cade drew his knife from his belt, the blade he used for whittling and cutting his meat, and studied it without enthusiasm. 'Reckon I'll have to make do with this.' He tutted. 'It'd be easier if we could all carry swords, like before the Krodans came.'

'Are you joking? You know what it was like back then. Drunken swordfights in the street, armed gangs in the alleyways, bandits on the road. It's not called the Robbers' Highway for nothing. It was lawless!'

'That ain't how my da remembers it,' said Cade.

Aren gave him a warning glance. 'Then he'd best be careful who he remembers it to.' He stood and secured his bound-up sword across his back with a strap. 'Ossians are too hot-blooded,' he said, matter-of-factly. 'We don't have the discipline the Krodans do.'

'In other words: we can't be trusted.'

Aren frowned. He didn't like it when Cade talked like that. It was dangerously close to sedition, which made him nervous. If you didn't report sedition, you were part of it.

'Come on,' he said, walking off up the lane. Cade sheathed his knife, slapped his thighs, slid off the boundary stone and followed.

The town square was filling up for the evening. Families gathered round tables in a smiling jumble of hugs and hails, kisses and back-slaps. Lanterns were being lit against the coming dusk, and a cool breeze carried away the heat of the day. Ropes of bunting and sheaves of shadowbane had been hung overhead, and children wearing spooky masks dodged and chased each other across the cobbles while old men watched from benches, smoking pipes and drinking beer from leather jacks.

There was celebration in the air, and with good reason. The fishermen had spotted hull whales breaching off Gabber's Bank. The ghost tide was on its way, and the festival began tonight.

'There's a mummers' troupe coming to town!' Cade exclaimed. He was studying the crier's board, where the town notices were posted.

'Hmm?' Aren was only half-listening, scanning the crowd in the faint hope of seeing Sora. As usual, it was only Ossians who thronged the tables. His countrymen liked to dine in numbers, and raucously. Respectable Krodan families ate at home, where it was possible to hear one another.

'Mummers!' Cade said again. He squinted in concentration, mouthing the words as he read them. 'They're doing *Podd and the Pot of Plenty*!'

Aren gave him a look. 'It's hardly *Breken and Kalihorn*, is it?'

'Dunno. What's "Breakfast and Kaliwhat"?'

'Rinther's masterwork about two feuding brothers?' Aren said, but all he got was a blank look. 'Rinther? Kroda's greatest playwright?' When Cade still didn't know what he was talking about, Aren gave up. 'He's famous,' he said.

'Ain't *that* famous, apparently,' Cade said. He caught sight of someone over Aren's shoulder. 'There's Mya and Astra.'

They crossed the square. Mya was loafing against a low stone wall, watching the festivities with lazy-lidded eyes, a shock of frizzy brown curls framing her calm face. Astra sat on the wall, long, straight hair tucked behind one ear, scratching at a wafer of paperwood with a stick of charcoal.

'Aren and Cade, Vaspis be my witness,' said Mya as they approached. She liked to invoke the Malcontent whenever she could; he, of all the Nine Aspects, was her god of choice. Aren thought she was just doing it for the shock value. 'Darra was sure you'd be devoured by now. Still after that she-warg?'

'We're in more danger from heatstroke than from any she-warg,' Cade said.

'Well, let us know if you find it. Astra's keen to get a sketch.'

Astra looked up at the mention of her name, only now noticing the boys. Cade had a habit of falling in and out of infatuations, and Astra was his latest. Aren could always tell because he smiled wider than normal at them, which was unfortunate as it made him look simple.

'What are you drawing?' he asked.

She tipped the wafer of wood to show him. There was a large dragonfly pinned to one side, next to its likeness in charcoal.

'That's really good,' said Cade and grinned wider, progressing from simple to witless. Astra went back to her work, barely acknowledging the compliment.

'Going to see the ghost tide tonight?' Mya asked Aren.

He grinned. 'The Torments themselves couldn't stop me.'

'Really? I heard your da was funny about letting you out after dark.'

'Where'd you hear that?' Aren said, as if the whole idea was preposterous, rather than embarrassingly true.

She shrugged. 'Heard it around.'

'Well, it's a lie. I'll be there. You can count on it,' he told her confidently. And he meant to be, assuming he could get past the servants. But he had a plan in mind for that.

Mya looked over at Cade. 'You going, too?'

'Oh, I don't reckon I will,' said Cade, affecting nonchalance. 'Need to be up early to help in the workshop.' He glanced at Aren and away, and Aren felt a stab of guilt. Cade wanted to go with him tonight, and without Aren he'd likely just mope at home. But there were some things even a best friend couldn't be part of.

They said their goodbyes and headed away from the square. Aren didn't take the most direct route, preferring to detour past the towering temple which rose above the roofs of Shoal Point a few streets away. If he was lucky, the priests would still be at evensong and he'd catch the end.

'I need to be back for supper soon,' Cade protested, guessing where they were going.

'We won't be long. Just passing by.'

'You never "just pass by".'

They emerged into a small cobbled plaza in front of the temple. Aren slowed to a halt and let his gaze travel up the façade. No matter how many times he saw it, his sense of awe never waned. The stern, imposing lines, bold geometric forms and strict symmetry spoke of strength, order and discipline. It came from another world than the narrow, winding sandstone alleys which surrounded it, buildings piled up higgledy-piggledy with their plaster cracked by salt and sun, joined by uneven steps and crowded passageways. An old temple to the Nine had stood there once, but it had been torn down and replaced when Aren was young.

Like all Krodan temples, it had two entrances, representing the two routes to the Primus's light. Above each, standing in an alcove, was a statue. One was a young man in robes, his face serene, an open book in one hand. The other was armoured, staring boldly out across the plaza, hands folded on the pommel of a sword resting point-down between his feet. Scholarly Tomas and brave Toven, the Word and the Sword, earthly champions of the Primus.

'I'm noticing a marked lack of "just passing by" and a sight more "stopping and gawping",' Cade grouched.

Aren ignored him. As he'd hoped, the priests were still singing. Their voices drifted hauntingly across the plaza, echoing and reverberant, a net of harmonies mystifying in their complexity. High voices soared above the tide of sound like gulls on the wind, then the basses rolled in, and the hymn swelled till it filled the sky. It was music of dazzling craft, and Aren found himself caught in its spell.

Ossia had no music like it. Only a few great works had survived the fall of the Second Empire, and they were dated now and rarely

21

played. His people favoured folksong to formal music, tunes for the inn and the campfire, sometimes bawdy and sometimes elegiac, but always intimate and inclusive. Aren couldn't deny they had a certain primitive power, that they tunnelled into his heart when he'd had a few drinks and conjured a yearning for times he'd never lived through, but they were childish compared to Krodan symphonies.

'Oh, Nine, they're at their bloody yowling again,' said Cade, rolling his eyes.

Aren suppressed a scowl of irritation. Cade worshipped the Nine and liked music he could clap and stamp along to. Aren influenced him in most things, but despite his best efforts, Cade had never shown the slightest sign of changing his mind about that.

'Young Aren! You're a little early for convocation. Five days early, in fact.'

It was Predicant Ervin, hailing him from one of the doorways at the top of the temple steps. He was an elderly priest, popular in the town for his light heart and easy manner. He wore beige and red robes – beige for parchment and red for blood – stitched with Krodan rays across the shoulder and chest. On a chain around his neck hung the sign of the Sanctorum, the blade and the open book, wrought in gold.

'I just wanted to hear the evensong,' Aren called back. 'Are you not joining in?'

'Alas, the Primus saw fit to give me the voice of a bullfrog with a mouth full of wasps. I fend off the Nemesis in other ways.' He brandished a twig broom. 'By sweeping the steps, for example. Noble work, if you can get it.'

'We all do our part,' Aren said with a grin. He noticed Cade edging anxiously towards the plaza's exit. 'But we should go. Even the Primus won't save Cade if he's not back for supper.'

'I'll see you both on Festenday!' said Predicant Ervin, raising a bony hand in farewell.

'Still don't see why I have to go to convocation,' Cade grumbled as they hurried away. 'I don't even believe in that stuff. Nor do half the Ossians in Shoal Point.'

'Maybe they're hoping that one day you will.'

Cade snorted.

They left the plaza and walked along the flagstones of Fish-mongers' Way. The shops were shuttered today and there was no market, but the beer-hall rang with Krodan voices singing the anthems of their homeland. Dim, distorted figures raised their tankards behind panes of bullseye glass. A wooden sign hung over the doorway, depicting two fighting falcons: the emblem of the Anvaal Brewery, advertising thick, dark beer from the heart of the Empire. Two soldiers stood guard outside, clad in Krodan black and white, their grim faces made statuesque by their distinctive angular helmets.

At the end of Fishmongers' Way, a knot of lanes and tiny plazas ran along the edge of the western cliffs, descending steadily towards the docks, beaches and coves beyond. Here were the hole-in-the-wall bakeries that sold morning rolls and pastries, single-room bars hidden upstairs behind rusty gates, crushed-together houses with sagging eaves where cats groomed themselves on tiny sills. To their left, gaps between the houses revealed a peaceful blue sea, the sun balled and red on the horizon.

Aren grinned. The sun couldn't fall fast enough today. When night came, the adventure would begin.

'Aren!'

His smile faded as he looked back up the alley. Standing at the corner were two young men. One was corn-blond, handsome and athletically built: the Krodan dream of vigour and poise. The other was less well favoured, with a long, pointed nose, pitted skin and ruddy hair. Harald and Juke, Sora's elder brothers.

'Still loafing about with the carpenter's boy, I see,' Harald said. 'I'm glad you're keeping company that befits your station. It's a habit you'd do well to nurture.'

Aren thought of a dozen insulting replies and said none of them. 'What do you want, Harald?'

The two Krodans sauntered up the alley. They were dressed in fine waistcoats and embroidered trousers, and narrow swords hung at their hips. By their attitude, they meant trouble.

'Do you remember what I said last time we spoke?' said Harald.

23

'I think you do. I feel we were very clear, even allowing for the remarkable dull-wittedness of you people.'

Aren felt angry heat rise up from his chest. It was an effort to remain polite. 'You told me to stay away from Sora,' he said.

'You *did* understand!' Harald said. 'And that wasn't your first warning, either. In fact, you've had several. Our father even visited yours to make his feelings clear.'

Aren said nothing, but he held Harald's gaze steadily, which was as much defiance as he dared.

Juke turned a disdainful eye on Cade, as if noticing him for the first time. 'Run along, eel-sucker. This doesn't concern you.'

Cade glanced at Aren, then back at Juke. He didn't move, though his feet shuffled as if he dearly wanted to.

'Are you deaf?' Juke asked.

'I can stand where I like,' Cade mumbled.

'Say your piece, Harald,' Aren said, bringing their attention back to him. Juke gave Cade a dangerous glare, but was content with that for now.

'What can I say that will make you listen?' Harald said helplessly. 'Has it escaped your notice that you're Ossian, while she is Krodan and cousin to a count? She may not have the sense to look after her own reputation, but it is our responsibility to see that she remains marriageable. And if you … *ruin* her, Aren, then I will be honour-bound to kill you, and neither of us wants that.' He cocked his head and sighed. 'I can only assume you find it all a little too complicated to grasp, so let me boil it down for you.' He leaned in close and dropped his voice to a menacing whisper. 'You will *never* have her,' he said, and shoved Aren in the chest so forcefully that he tripped over backwards and landed hard on the rough ground, skinning his elbows, his wrapped sword jarring against his spine.

Juke brayed with laughter as Aren scrambled back to his feet, teeth gritted and face flushed. He desperately wanted to plant a fist in Harald's supercilious mouth. They were both bigger and stronger than him, and they'd beat him hard, but it would be worth it to split that lip.

A lifetime of ingrained restraint stopped him. He was Ossian, and they were Krodan. If anyone reported it, the punishment would be severe.

'You'd love to strike me, wouldn't you?' Harald said with a smile. 'Look at you, clenching your fists. You people solve everything with violence. Luckily for you, we are more civilised.' He drew a folded letter from his breast pocket, its wax seal broken. 'We found this in her room. She never was very good at hiding things.'

Aren's stomach dropped as he recognised the letter. 'Give me that!'

'That's not going to happen,' said Harald dismissively. 'However, we *will* give it to our father if we ever suspect you've met with Sora again. He has the governor's ear, as you know. I wonder what will happen to your father when the governor learns he failed to restrain you?'

'That's mine!' Aren could barely force the words through a throat thick with humiliation and rage. 'It's private!'

'Not any more. Not when it concerns my family.' He handed the paper to Juke, who unfolded it. 'Perhaps your friend would like to hear some?'

'"Sora, my love, my only love",' Juke began, trilling in parody of a tortured romantic.

Just one punch. Just one. But his body wouldn't respond. He could walk into a cave to face a she-warg, but he couldn't hit a Krodan. Everything in his life had trained him against it.

'Stop it!' he demanded, and was appalled by how pathetic he sounded. Cade looked like he wished he could be anywhere else.

'"To be apart from you is agony",' Juke continued, holding the back of his hand to his forehead and wilting. '"I must—"' He stopped and snorted. 'You missed the accent over "agony". If you have to write in Krodan, learn to do it properly.' He resumed. '"I must see you, my darling! It burns my—"'

'Enough!' Aren shrieked.

Juke looked to Harald, asking with his gaze if he should go on. Harald stared at Aren coolly.

'I think we've made our point.'

Aren nodded, biting his lower lip. Juke folded up the letter and handed it back to Harald, who slipped it into his breast pocket and patted it. Aren stood slump-shouldered, looking anywhere but at his tormentors.

'Find yourself a nice Ossian girl,' said Harald, with unexpected gentleness. 'I know you love her, but it will pass. My sister's not for you.' He clapped Juke on the shoulder and they turned to go. 'No more warnings, Aren!' he called as they left.

Once they were out of sight, he became conscious of Cade eyeing him awkwardly. 'You alright?' Cade asked.

Aren bit back a sharp reply. He wanted to take out his feelings on someone and Cade was an easy target; but it wouldn't be the right thing to do.

'I think I'll just head home,' he said. Without further words of parting, he walked away. Bravery loved company, but Aren had long ago learned that shame was best borne alone.

5

'There's my boy, and not a moment too soon! Set the table, supper's ready!'

Cade did as his ma told him, laying out bowls, spoons and leather drinking jacks. Between the table and the stove there was little room to move in the kitchen, but they slid around each other with practised ease. The dusk leaked in through sheaves of green herbs hanging over the window, and the air was damp with steam and rich with the smell of rabbit stew. Walls of bare, uneven brick and cracked mortar were hidden by cluttered shelves, racks of spices and pans on hooks. It was hot and close and dim, and it was Cade's favourite room in the house.

To be in Velda's kitchen while she was cooking was to be a leaf caught in a storm, sent flurrying here and there, never able to settle till the tempest was over. His da avoided the room for that reason, but Cade liked to help. He enjoyed cooking, and he made an eager apprentice. While they braised and mashed and chopped, she told him stories, and sometimes had him tell some of his own. After a long day in the workshop with his da, it was always a relief to do something he was good at.

Velda bustled past him and ladled out the stew, hollering his da's name as she did so. She was a tough, round woman, tanned and salted by coastal life, who sold oysters on the docks. Her eyes were creased and kindly, her greying hair bound up in a kerchief, and despite her increasing years she was as bright and busy as a field mouse.

'Sit! Sit!' she urged him, and placed a round loaf of warm black bread on the table, wrapped in a chequered cloth. He took his spot on the bench as Barl came in from the back, a broad-chested man with a broken nose and a thick, tangled beard.

'Son!' He slapped a heavy hand down on Cade's shoulder. 'Where did you get to today?'

'I was hunting that she-warg with Aren again.'

'Mmm-hmm,' he murmured absently. His gaze skipped over Cade to his wife. He put an arm around her waist, kissed her quickly on the cheek and sat down. 'Rabbit stew!' he said with great satisfaction, betraying the real focus of his attention.

Velda gave Cade a smile as she poured weak ale from a jug. She'd heard him, and approved. She believed boys should have adventures while they could.

'Thanks be to Hallen, Aspect of Plenty, for this bounty,' Velda said, once she was seated. 'The Nine protect this house.'

They set to the meal, tearing up the bread and spooning stew into their mouths. Cade sought out tender chunks of rabbit among the potatoes and vegetables, and sopped up the thick, peppery stew with his bread, softening the hard crust before he crunched it down. He found a wonderful stillness in the midst of a hearty meal. He felt centred, entirely in the moment, his mind clear of thought. For that brief time, there was no need to speak, and no one expected a thing of him.

'Good, good,' Barl rumbled to himself when he was done. He sat back and took a pull of ale. Cade could tell he'd had plenty already by the glaze in his eyes and the slow way he moved. It was Jorsday, which meant he'd likely spent his day off in Finnan's tiny bar by the docks, drinking with the fishermen.

'Squarehead farmer up in the hills wants a wardrobe making,' Barl said, and burped. 'Krodan style. Ossian furniture ain't good enough for that lot.' He took another pull and set his ale down. 'That used to be Arrol's farm before they took it from him,' he added bitterly. Then he looked at Cade. 'We'll set to it on the morrow. I'll show you how to make duck-beak joints the way the squareheads like. You can mix up the varnish.'

Cade nodded and kept eating. He didn't want to think about tomorrow, about sanding and hammering, chisels and saws, splines and splinters. He had his ma's head for stories and her clever tongue, but his hands were hooves and there was none of Da's craft in him. No matter how carefully Barl taught him, he never got it right. Barl wasn't a patient man, but he was a persistent one. Every day he tried anew to make his son a carpenter, and every day Cade disappointed him.

If Cade had a brother, things might have been different. But he'd almost killed his ma as she pushed him out – a fact Barl never tired of mentioning, sometimes in jest, sometimes not – and Barl loved his wife too much to risk another child. So there was only Cade, and when the time came he'd have to take over the business, and that was how it was.

'There's a mummers' troupe coming to town for the ghost tide,' Cade said. 'It was on the crier's board. We could go and see them. After we're finished in the workshop, I mean.'

'That's a fine idea!' Velda enthused.

'As long as they ain't Sards,' said Barl. 'I won't stand to watch Sards. Filthy folk. If they ain't trying to sell you something that's broke, they're picking your pocket.'

'I don't reckon they're Sards,' Cade said uncertainly. 'It's an Ossian play – *Podd and the Pot of Plenty*.'

'Oh, I like that one!' his ma said.

Barl harrumphed, swigged his ale and said nothing.

'Aren says that mummers' troupes sometimes hire a carpenter to travel with them,' Cade said tentatively. 'To build and repair the stage, make props and such. Easy stuff. The carpenter gets to be in the play, too. Everyone in the troupe has to act. Sometimes they play the lead, even.'

'Mmm-hmm.'

Cade looked down at his hands, where he was knotting his fingers. 'I thought… well, I reckon it might be good experience for me. To really help me get a grasp of the basics. And I can make people laugh, I'm good at that. They might take me with them, if I asked. Just for a few weeks.'

Barl was silent. He took another slow drink, his eyes far away and full of thought. Cade glanced at his ma, who made an encouraging face. Da appeared to be considering what he'd said. Cade let himself hope, just a little.

'And another thing about Sards!' Barl snapped. 'They're so cursed secretive! Stick to their own, don't they? Whispering in their secret tongue. That ain't how honest people act. We should kick them all out, that's my view on it. This ain't even their country.'

Cade's heart sank and his gaze dropped to the table. His da hadn't even heard him. Cade had no love for Sards, either, but in some ways he envied them. They were the Landless, roamers who were unwelcome wherever they settled, but at least they were free to forge their own fates. He dreamed of the world beyond the walls of his da's gloomy workshop, a life where the weeks and years were not already laid out before him. Somewhere he counted for something.

But it was a fool's dream. He was a carpenter's son, and that was all he'd ever be. So the world turned.

'Cavin called by, looking for you,' Barl said. 'You never go about with that boy any more.'

'I was with Aren,' said Cade.

'Hunting she-wargs,' added Velda, with a glimmer in her eye.

'I wish you wouldn't go trailing round after that boy like a lost puppy,' Barl grumbled.

'I ain't *trailing round* after anyone,' said Cade, roused to indignation. 'He's my friend.'

'Aye, until he's not,' said Barl, sucking down the last of his ale. 'He's his father's son, and the apple don't fall far from the tree. Disloyalty's in his blood. Only one way an Ossian gets to be rich in this day and age.'

'Barl—' Velda warned.

'I'll speak my mind at my own table,' he said. 'And I call Randill a turncoat. Lickspittle. *Collaborator.* Just like all the rest who rolled over when the Krodans came, desperate to keep what they had.'

Velda pointed a stern finger at Cade. 'You ain't to repeat that outside this room. Not even to Aren. *Especially* not to Aren.'

'I ain't stupid, Ma,' said Cade, for whom the whole thing was a lot less serious than his parents seemed to think it was.

'And you!' Velda snapped at Barl. 'Hold your tongue. You want to bring the Iron Hand down on us?'

'Should I fear spies in my own house?' Barl crowed. 'Hiding in the stew pot, perhaps?' Made smug by his own wit, he put his jack to his mouth, and looked faintly puzzled when he found it empty.

'Not here,' said Velda, 'but loose words breed loose words, and when beer makes you bold, you're apt to say what you're thinking. One day you'll say it to the wrong person. And who'll run your workshop then?'

Barl scowled at that, but he didn't argue. He held out his jack and Velda filled it, satisfied that he'd got the message.

'That boy's a Krodan-lover, and he's the son of a Krodan-lover,' Barl said darkly. 'Mixing with his sort will only bring you trouble. Heed that, boy.'

'Aye, Da,' said Cade, but he didn't. After all, his da had never taken heed of him.

6

Aren leaned forward, his brow furrowed, hand covering his mouth, deep in thought. Master Fassen, seated opposite, watched him keenly, awaiting his next move. Between them on the castles board, two armies waged war.

The hexagonal board was divided into hundreds of smaller hexes, across which dozens of carved pieces were scattered, some of ivory and some of polished black stone. The castles which gave the game its name were unevenly placed around the board. The object was to capture and hold them while protecting your king. A broken line of blue counters, representing a river and its fords, meandered between them.

Aren's eyes flickered over the battlefield. He held two castles and had made gains by capturing a ford with a pair of giants. Master Fassen held the other four castles and was steadily pounding Aren's left flank with superior numbers. It didn't look good.

Aren picked up a swordsman and advanced it two hexes into enemy territory. The moment he released the piece, Master Fassen slid an archer into firing range and took it.

'You didn't think that through, Aren,' he chided.

Aren's tutor was a gaunt man, straight-backed despite his age, sober in dress and manner. He had large ears and a beak of a nose, a bare pate, bushy white sideburns and a solemn dignity that Aren thought particularly Krodan

'Perhaps I should reconsider my strategy,' Aren said. He sat back, regarding the board as if it were a puzzle he couldn't solve.

Night was thickening outside, the hedgerows and lawns silvered by starlight. Aren could hear the tinkle and rattle of the servants cleaning up in the dining room. Soon they'd be in to draw the parlour curtains and trim the lamps.

The hour after supper was for digestion and relaxation, when members of the household and their guests would gather for games, music and conversation. Nanny Alsa and Master Orik had also joined them tonight. She was embroidering a handkerchief and he was sitting in an armchair, drinking a glass of dark brandy and smoking a thin cheroot.

Aren picked up an ivory draccen, weighed it in his hand and mind, then flew it over the river to take one of Master Fassen's swordsmen. His opponent raised an eyebrow and slid a black knight through a gap in his lines to bump up against Aren's draccen. Aren tutted as the piece was removed.

'You must think three moves ahead,' Master Fassen advised. 'Know your intention before you act.'

Aren sat back again and made a show of thinking to satisfy the master. Everything was a test with Master Fassen, everything a lesson. But Aren's mind wasn't on the game, and he suspected his opponent knew it. He was thinking of tonight, of the first night of the ghost tide. He was planning his escape.

Master Orik cleared his throat in an unsuccessful attempt to draw Nanny Alsa's attention away from her needlework. He didn't live at the house but was often to be found here, and his interest in Aren's governess was evident to everyone except Nanny Alsa.

'Does your cheroot not agree with you, Master Orik?' Aren inquired innocently.

'Oh, it's quite fine,' said Master Orik, with a look that said Aren would suffer at practice tomorrow. 'A dry throat, that's all.' He sipped his brandy, glaring at his pupil. Nanny Alsa never raised her head, but Aren saw a hint of a smile on her lips.

She was pretty and apple-cheeked, with strawberry-blonde hair worn in buns over her ears. She'd cared for him since he was ten, after his previous nanny departed suddenly for reasons nobody had ever properly explained to him. He sensed there was a scandal there, but didn't care enough to pry as he'd never liked her much.

Nanny Alsa, by contrast, was all he could wish for in a surrogate mother. She was sweet and playful and loving, permissive when she should be and strict when necessary. She'd never raised her voice to him, as her disappointment was enough to shame him if he misbehaved; there was something in her manner that made people want to please her. She was liked by all and loved by some, but in the five years Aren had known her, he'd never seen any sign that she was interested in romance. Which made Master Orik's plight all the more amusing.

Aren picked up one of his giants and sent it stamping across the castles board. Master Fassen moved to counter the danger and Aren slipped an assassin over the ford. Master Fassen shifted a trebuchet to one of the raised hexes that indicated high ground. Doing so increased its range and put Aren's giant within reach. Master Fassen plucked the giant from the board.

'You are throwing your pieces away now,' said Master Fassen disapprovingly. 'This is very unlike you.'

Master Orik, restless and bored, got to his feet and went to the decanter to refill his brandy. He moved with a slight limp, the result of a leg wound sustained in the Krodan army. He still dressed like an officer, his jacket neat, trousers pressed and shoes shined, but he could no longer be one. Instead he taught swordplay to the sons of the rich, and his regret over his lost past was evident in the amount he drank and smoked. Though young, his face was ruddy behind his red moustaches.

He poured himself a new glass and straightened. 'Miss Alsa, if I might observe, you've been unusually quiet tonight, and full of sighs,' he announced, abandoning subtlety entirely. 'Are you troubled?'

She put down her needlework and sighed again, as if to prove his point. 'Your enquiry is kind, but it is nothing.' She spoke in Krodan; it was the language of the household, and everyone here was Krodan except Aren. Only the servants spoke Ossian, though Aren and his father sometimes did when they were alone. Randill had only learned the language of their occupiers after the invasion, and even thirty years later he still found his mother tongue easier.

Aren moved a piece. Master Fassen took it and Aren cursed, drawing a scowl from his opponent. He raised a hand in apology.

'Please, Miss Alsa, if you would speak of it, perhaps I could help,' Master Orik persisted.

'It is not a thing that can be helped,' she replied sadly. 'I grieve on a friend's behalf. I suppose you've heard of the recent events at Salt Fork?'

Aren's ears pricked up at that. Salt Fork had been the subject of hot debate among the locals ever since the news reached Shoal Point. Ossian rebels had seized a fortified town that stood at the junction where the Millflow joined the River Apsel. It was a vital link for river traffic, and for a time they'd snarled up transport in the region. Some thought them heroes; others called them mud-headed fools who threatened to bring the wrath of the Krodans down on them all.

Aren had been following the news with particular interest because his father was travelling in that region, and he'd been due back days ago. There had been no word to explain the delay, but that wasn't unusual. Likely he was simply held up by the chaos surrounding the uprising, but Aren couldn't shake the niggling worry that something worse had befallen him.

'Surely Salt Fork is a cause for joy, not grief?' Master Orik said. 'The rebels were crushed entirely.'

'By the grace of the Primus,' Master Fassen added piously.

'His will be done,' Aren muttered in automatic response.

'I am glad of the victory,' said Nanny Alsa, 'but I grieve at the cost. Rosa, the chandler's wife, is a dear friend to me. Her son was at Salt Fork.'

'A rebel?' Master Orik sounded disturbed.

She shook her head. 'A notary. But he lived in the town, and he was part of what happened. The Iron Hand have made an example of the mayor and the town's leaders for going along with the rebels. Now they are questioning even minor officials, seeking guilt. Rosa fears her son will be among those punished. He is Ossian; there will be no mercy.'

'Your generous heart does you credit, Miss Alsa,' said Master Orik. 'But you need not grieve. If he is innocent, he has nothing to fear.'

'And if he collaborated, he is not worth your tears,' Master Fassen said sternly.

Nanny Alsa picked up her needle again. 'You are right, of course,' she said quietly.

Aren used his last giant to capture a swordsman. Master Fassen moved another piece to flank the giant, thereby preventing it from moving. Aren deployed a knight to try to free it up, but Master Fassen managed to take the giant first. Aren tried to move his knight from danger, but Master Fassen intercepted it with his queen.

'A truly disastrous assault,' Master Fassen observed. 'You have lost almost all your major pieces. Perhaps you would like to concede?'

'Not just yet,' said Aren. He slid his assassin through the hole where Master Fassen's queen had stood, tapped it against the black king and won the game.

Master Fassen stared at the board in outraged astonishment, then up at his pupil. Aren grinned. 'There is no victory without sacrifice, Master.'

The master was still searching for a sufficiently tart reply when they heard hooves clopping in the lane and Aren surged to his feet. Horses approaching at this hour could only mean one thing.

'Father!' He hurried out of the parlour, through wood-panelled corridors, past paintings and busts of Krodan thinkers and generals. The servants were already preparing for the new arrivals as he scampered through the door onto the grand stone porch and down the steps to the forecourt. Two horsemen were dismounting in the moth-haunted lanternlight, one rangy and tall, the other broad-shouldered and squat: Randill and his Brunlander bodyguard Kuhn.

Randill heard Aren coming and turned to meet him with open arms. Aren crashed into his father and held himself there, to his warmth and wiry strength, breathing in the sweat-and-leather smell of him. It was a greeting of Ossian passion rather than stout Krodan reserve, the uncouth embrace of a peasant, but in that moment Aren didn't care.

Father was home.

7

Randill's arrival sent the servants into a frenzy. The ostler and his daughter hurried to see to the horses. Maids stoked fires to heat water for baths. Most frantic of all was the kitchen, where the cookboys ran hither and thither, in and out of the pantry, while the cook loudly bemoaned the lack of notice. A boy was dispatched to town with orders to get more bacon for the next day's breakfast, even if he had to wake the butcher to do it.

When Randill was away the house felt empty; his return filled the rooms with warmth. He'd barely entered before his steward assaulted him with a flurry of pressing matters that needed his attention, but he brushed them off and slung an arm around his son.

'There's nothing so urgent it can't wait till the morrow,' he said. He winked at Aren. 'Or at least till I've reached the bottom of a goblet of wine!'

Taking the hint, a servant hurried off to uncork a bottle of Carthanian red. Randill headed for the dining room, nodding at the greetings from his household staff, Aren grinning at his side. Kuhn loped behind them, scowling.

'And what of you, eh, my boy?' Randill asked. 'Getting into trouble, no doubt!'

'Nothing anyone's found out about,' Aren said brightly. Randill's laughter echoed down the corridor.

The masters and Nanny Alsa joined them in the dining room, which had been hastily cleared after supper. Grey velvet curtains were drawn across the tall windows and lamps hung on silver chains above the long, narrow table. Presiding over the room was a magnificent portrait of the Imperial Family, purchased at great expense from an artist in Morgenholme who swore it was painted from life.

The cook had whipped up a platter of cold meat pies, pickled fish, cheeses and fruit, plus a bowl of salted eel soup for Randill. Those who'd already eaten sipped wine or brandy and picked at sweet biscuits.

'Your business in the east went well, I trust?' Master Fassen enquired of Randill.

'Not particularly,' said Randill, fishing out a chunk of slippery white eel. Master Orik watched him through a cloud of cheroot smoke and looked slightly nauseous. Krodans had always found the Ossian love of eels repulsive, which Aren privately thought a little unfair, since one their own delicacies included boiled bull's testicles.

'Was it the Greycloaks?' Aren asked.

'Ha!' said Master Orik. 'Greycloaks! They call themselves resistance fighters, but they're nothing more than a rabble of disorganised thugs. Don't even have a uniform. How do you know who's on your side if you don't have a uniform?'

'I doubt they even exist,' said Master Fassen. 'A secret underground network? I say it's wishful thinking on the part of those who'd see us gone.' His brows gathered together. 'Though Salt Fork is somewhat concerning, I will allow. These rebels grow bold.'

Randill wiped his mouth and sat back. His face was all angles, hard and spare of flesh, but it softened when he smiled, and he smiled often. Aren had inherited his dominant nose and wide jaw, but his gentle eyes and fuller mouth came from his mother.

'Greycloaks or not, they were rebels of some stripe. My poor luck that we were close to Salt Fork when the trouble hit. I'd found an opportunity, some land I thought would make for good vineyards. We were coming to a deal when Salt Fork was seized, trade snarled up and the army came through. There was no business to be done with anyone after that.'

'But you were so late returning.' Aren tried not to make it sound like a complaint, but it came out like one. He couldn't help it. It wasn't his place to question his father, but he was disappointed that there'd been no letter, no word of explanation until now.

'My travel permit only allows me to use certain routes, and in avoiding the chaos round Salt Fork, we strayed too far and fell foul of a particularly … *diligent* official.'

Kuhn stopped eating pies and cheese for long enough to give a snort of disgust. Aren noted he avoided the fruit like it was poison. He was a squat, shaggy man, dark-haired and weatherbeaten, who hunkered jealously over his food as if defending it from potential thieves.

Randill gave him a faint smile. 'This particular paragon of efficiency kept us locked up until we could send word to the right people and get ourselves released.'

'They locked you up?' Aren was appalled. Now he felt guilty for mentioning it. No wonder there had been no letter!

Randill shrugged. 'He was just doing his job, I suppose.'

'Scribes and clerics,' Kuhn grunted. 'That's what's wrong with the world now. Time was you could ride from Ossia to the lowland coast and you didn't need a piece of paper to do it. Once, arguments were won with blades and bravery. Now it's who tells the finest lies in a courtroom. Used to be a man's oath was enough for truth, but honour's long gone, and we put contracts in its place.'

'Here, now!' said Master Orik. 'You Brunlanders needed some organisation. You barely knew how to lay a decent road before we came!'

Randill slapped a hand on Kuhn's shoulder, intercepting him before he could rise to it. 'Forgive my friend, Master Orik,' he said. 'It's the curse of Brunlanders to speak plainly.'

'True,' said Kuhn resentfully. 'We never did learn the trick of keeping our mouths shut so as not to discomfit our masters.'

There was an awkward silence in which Randill gave Kuhn a hard stare. The Brunlander held it as long as he dared, then looked down at his plate.

'Anyway,' said Randill, once satisfied that his authority had been asserted, 'Salt Fork is over, the rebellion put down. Let us be glad of that.'

Aren was glad of it indeed. It had made him uneasy to see the suppressed excitement on the faces of his countrymen when they spoke of Salt Fork and the Greycloaks. Their appetite for treason angered him. But he saw now that he need not have worried; it was an empty dream they entertained. They wished for revolution, but they weren't willing to inconvenience themselves to get it. They wanted someone else to shed the blood for them.

'Tell me what I've missed,' said Randill, in an effort to restart the conversation and restore some levity to the room.

'Aren just beat Master Fassen at castles,' Nanny Alsa said, with a mischievous glance at Aren.

'Is that so?' Randill cried, delighted. 'And I thought the old twig was unbeatable!'

Master Fassen bristled and smoothed his sideburns with his knuckles. 'Old twig!' he muttered.

'How did you do it?' Randill asked Aren.

'I owe the victory to Master Orik, actually,' said Aren. Master Orik looked up from his brandy glass in surprise. '"To overcome your enemy, you must first understand him."'

'Ah, yes,' said Master Orik, though he still seemed bewildered to be getting the credit. 'That's so.'

'A strange idea to teach a boy learning the sword,' said Master Fassen, 'when his only goal is to spear the object of his attention with a length of polished steel.' His tone made it clear what he thought of the fighting arts.

'Not at all!' said Master Orik. 'If you see only the enemy, you do not see the man. People are more than just enemies and friends, opponents and allies. Does he hate you? Then he may reach too far, swing too hard. Does he fight to defend his family? Then he may be careful, or desperate. Does he seek death, or fear it? Know his heart and your blade will find it all the easier.'

'I presume you didn't beat Master Fassen by stabbing him through the heart, though?' Randill said to Aren. 'That would be a cheap victory.'

'I should think he didn't!' Master Fassen spluttered. He was beginning to feel picked on, and it was hard on his dignity.

'Master Fassen scorns the weak mind and despises the lazy and inattentive,' Aren explained. 'I threw the last three games to persuade him I was both.' He knew he shouldn't go on, but he was unable to resist. 'Eventually it made him lazy and inattentive himself.'

'Well, that's too much!' Master Fassen exclaimed, red-faced. Randill roared with laughter, Master Orik choked on his cheroot and even Nanny Alsa had to hide a smile.

'You've got your mother's gift,' Randill told him. 'She could see right through people, knew what made them tick. One look at someone and she had them figured out.'

'Would that he applied half so much craft to his studies,' grumbled Master Fassen.

While they'd been talking, a servant had slipped into the hall to stand by Randill's chair. Now he leaned down and whispered in Randill's ear.

'Of course. Send them in,' said Randill.

The servant motioned to the doorway, where the cook and one of his boys were lurking. They came to stand before the table, beneath the portrait of the Imperial Family. The boy, a mop-haired youth with a large brown birthmark on his cheek, looked nervous.

'Apologies for interruptin',' said the cook, 'but the boy has something I think you'll want to hear. Tell 'em what you told me, Mott.'

'I been to town for bacon,' Mott blurted. 'I was in the square, and a rider comes thunderin' in, all done up in fancy livery. Says he's an Imperial messenger, says they've been sent far and wide to announce the good news!'

He stopped breathlessly, anxiously awaiting a reaction. The cook clipped him round the ear. 'Which is ...?'

Mott's face cleared as he realised he hadn't actually told them the good news yet. 'He says there's to be a royal marriage! Prince Ottico is marryin' Princess Sorrel of Harrow less than five months hence, on the last day of Copperleaf, um, I mean Deithus,' he added, belatedly remembering to use Krodan months instead of Ossian.

'Hurrah!' cried Master Orik, surging from his seat. 'I'll drink to that!' He held his brandy glass aloft, waiting for the others to join him.

Nanny Alsa clapped her hands. 'What wonderful news!' she declared.

'And that ain't all!' Mott went on. 'As his weddin' gift, Prince Ottico's to be made Lord Protector of Ossia! The Emperor's givin' him the Ember Blade! Thirty years it's been gone, but the Ember Blade's comin' back to Ossia!'

Aren straightened in his chair. All his life he'd scoffed at the tales and superstitions that surrounded the Ember Blade, yet the thought of it still rang some distant chord in his soul. That sword was the symbol of Ossia itself; he couldn't help but feel its significance.

'Has it been thirty years?' Randill asked faintly. His eyes were distant; the news had struck him as it had his son. 'Yes, yes, you're right. Thirty years since Queen Alissandra fell. How the years have flown.'

'Thirty years,' said Kuhn grimly. 'And now the Ember Blade comes back in the hands of a Krodan.'

'That's enough, Kuhn,' said Randill. He sounded weary and sad. 'That's enough.'

He got to his feet. Master Orik was still standing with his glass held aloft, arm trembling, unable to drink or to sit down without a humiliating loss of face. Randill raised his goblet. It was the signal for the others to rise and do the same; all but Kuhn, who remained resolutely seated.

'To the royal marriage,' Randill said, and they drank. Master Orik gulped his brandy down with obvious relief. 'Now, you'll have to excuse me. I'm tired from the ride and a hot bath is calling.'

They said their goodbyes and he walked from the room, ruffling Aren's hair distractedly as he passed. Aren watched him go, a concerned frown on his face.

Master Orik poured another slug of brandy into his glass and raised it again, tottering only a little as he did so.

'To the health of our good Prince Ottico!' he slurred.

'Oh, sit down, man!' snapped Master Fassen.

8

After his bath, Randill retreated to his study and his papers. Aren went to find him there, bearing a tray with two crystal glasses and a silver jug of golden sweetwine.

He entered quietly so as not to disturb his father's thoughts. The study was full of cosy shadows cast by candles and wall-mounted lamps. Unshuttered windows let in the sea breeze; thin curtains stirred beside a desk piled with documents. There were shelves containing maps and records and a few valuable hidebound tomes, and on one wall hung the symbol of the Sanctorum in brass and gold: a downward-facing sword resting across an open book, its pages like wings to either side of the blade.

Randill sat in a wooden armchair of Krodan design, its high, straight back decorated with bold symmetrical rays. He was leaning forwards with his elbows resting on his knees and his hands clasped, staring intently into the darkness of an unlit hearth. Several letters lay open on a side table.

Aren watched him from the doorway. Perhaps it was the vacant chair at his side, or his pensive manner, but his father cut a haunted figure tonight. Randill had still not noticed him, which Aren thought strange. It was normally all too easy to break his concentration, and the servants knew to be stealthy when he was working. He showed no sign of stirring, so Aren walked across the study, carrying the tray before him. 'Father? I brought you—'

Randill jerked violently at the sound of his voice, then lunged out of his seat towards Aren, fear and hate in his eyes. Aren went rigid with shock. Halfway to his feet, Randill checked his attack;

Aren saw recognition dawn on him, and his face crumpled as he sank back in his seat. Aren's gaze switched to the letter knife in his left hand, which he'd snatched up to plunge into his son.

'Father?' Aren said tremulously. He was still holding the tray level. The dainty crystal glasses had wobbled but not tipped.

Randill pinched the bridge of his nose and closed his eyes. 'Forgive me,' he said. 'You startled me.'

Aren's mind was blank. For an instant, he'd seen a cornered man, mad and desperate. Now his father looked weary beyond his years.

'I brought some sweetwine,' Aren said, dully. 'It's Amberlyne.'

'Thank you,' said Randill. Aren placed the tray on the table and retreated in confusion, but Randill caught his arm in a gentle grip.

'Sit with me awhile, my son,' he said. 'We've been long apart, and I've missed you.'

Randill's voice calmed him a little. There was the man he knew. Still wary, he drew up another chair as Randill poured the wine.

'Who did you think I was?' Aren asked. The words came out unbidden, but he had to know.

Randill gave him a wry smile. 'Perhaps I thought you were the Hollow Man.' He handed one glass to Aren. 'You remember him, don't you?'

Aren remembered him well. It was difficult to forget the nightmares he'd suffered as a young boy on the Hollow Man's account. But that was just a tale to scare children, and it angered him that his father would try to palm him off with such fictions. He took a glass and stared at it resentfully.

Randill saw it and sighed. 'I don't know who I thought you were,' he said. 'For a moment, you seemed an enemy. A robber, perhaps. I am more tired than I thought.'

Aren was reluctantly content with that. He glanced down at the letters on the table and wondered if they were the cause of his father's upsetting behaviour, but enquiring into his private mail would be to pry too far.

Randill raised his glass in salute, and they sipped. The complex, delicate taste of Amberlyne flowed over Aren's tongue, now sweet and nutty, now creamy, now sharp. Randill let out a breath of satisfaction and Aren relaxed a little more.

44

'There truly is no wine like Amberlyne,' said Randill, admiring the contents of his glass in the lamplight. 'One thing our people can still sing about.' He looked over at Aren. 'Soon you'll be the one travelling, eh? Your military service.'

'I'm ready for it, Father,' Aren said.

Randill chuckled. 'I've no doubt you are. Master Orik tells me you've been working hard, and that what you lack in natural talent you make up for in persistence. Your other tutors tell me the same. They say there's no student more dogged than you.'

'You're being kind, Father. I know what they say. I try my best, but the lessons don't seem to stick.'

'Well I know that pain,' he said. 'I was the same. No boy was beaten more often than I.' He grinned, and Aren grinned back, warmed by the wine. 'I gave up on my schooling, chose the life of the blade instead. Likely I'd have died of it if I hadn't inherited our family's lands. Not you, though. You keep going. You force yourself onwards, no matter how unpleasant the task.'

'There is no great honour in working hard for what you want,' Aren said modestly, deflecting the praise as Krodan etiquette dictated. 'The Primus teaches us that. Diligence and persistence bring all things to a man.'

'So they say,' Randill replied, but his smile became strained and fell away. 'Would that the world were as simple as priests see it.'

'Father ...' Aren hesitated, afraid to ask the question, afraid of an answer he wouldn't like. 'The wedding ... I saw how it affected you. Aren't you glad?'

'Glad enough,' said Randill. 'It's a canny match. Our nervous neighbours to the north have a formidable army and grave concerns that they might be the next country swallowed up by the Third Empire. A match between the last two royal families on the continent will stabilise the region and present a united front against Durn. They executed their own royal family not ten years past, and neither Harrow nor Kroda want anyone getting any ideas.'

'But ...?' Aren prompted.

'Ah, my son. Fifty-five years I've been alive, you know. I've lived longer with Krodans as our rulers than without. But for twenty-five years I had the freedom to go where I pleased. The Nine held sway over this land, and we all spoke Ossian and nothing else. I saw the reigns of two queens and a king in that time, but only ever one Ember Blade. A sword of rarest embrium that showed red like fire in the rays of the sun. You know they named Embria after the Ember Blade? Did they teach you that in school?'

'They did, Father.'

'It's more than a sword. There's something of the divine in it. We believed it was a sign of approval from Joha himself. Every Ossian ruler since the Reclamation had it in hand when they took the throne, and whoever held it was *meant* to rule. Even in our darkest days, when we had tyrant kings, or weak ones, or mad... Even then, people believed that the Ember Blade would find its way to the right hands, guided by the will of the Aspects. We didn't know it, I think, but all our faith was in that sword. Our dreams for what we might one day become as a people. It was the last piece of the old empire that wasn't crumbling, or forgotten, or dead.'

Aren had never heard his father speak this way before. He'd always been guarded when discussing the past, careful not to say anything unfavourable towards the Krodan regime. The passion and longing in his voice made Aren uneasy, but they also made him understand.

'And now it returns to Ossia in the hands of a Krodan,' Aren said, echoing Kuhn's words at the dinner table.

'We've lived well these thirty years,' said Randill. 'Life has been good under the Krodans. But it's still hard news to bear. I'd thought it locked in some dusty vault, or on display in the Emperor's palace in Falconsreach, far from here. I'd thought never to hear of it again.'

'Perhaps...' Aren ventured. 'Perhaps it *has* found its way into the right hands. After all the turmoil of the Age of Kings, perhaps this is the stability Ossia desires. Perhaps Prince Ottico *is* meant to rule?'

'Ha!' Randill's laugh was humourless. 'If the Nine really guide its destiny, I doubt they'd place it in Krodan hands. Not while the Sanctorum starves their temples of funds, arrests their druids, makes mock of their teachings and all but outlaws them entirely.'

'Father...' Aren warned. This was getting too close to sedition.

Randill held up a hand in apology. 'Forgive me,' he said. 'I suppose the old gods are no easier to cast aside than the Ember Blade was, much as we might try. We learn the world in our youth and believe that is how things are. To unlearn it ... Well, I wonder if we ever really do. And, sometimes, if we should.'

'What happened, Father? When the Krodans invaded. Did you fight them?'

'I did,' he said, bowing his head. 'We all did, for a time. Until the Ember Blade was lost.'

'And then?'

'Then I compromised,' he said. 'It was that or die.' He looked across the table. 'Do you recall the day you came to me and asked me to take on Master Fassen? You said you needed extra lessons to keep up with the other boys.'

'I recall. I was ten. I had just been shamed by Master Klun in front of the whole class. I was supposed to recite the Lay of Valan Saar, but when I stood up to speak, the words disappeared from my mind.'

Randill nodded, as if to himself, and said nothing for a time. Aren wondered if that was the end of the conversation. Then Randill stirred, leaned over the side table and laid a hand on Aren's.

'I never told you how proud I was of you that day,' he said. 'I don't tell you enough. You're all that is good in me, all I have left of your mother. Whenever I think of the choices I've made, the things I've done, I think of you, and I know I took the right path. For had I done otherwise, I would not have such a very fine son.'

The unexpected praise took him off guard, and Aren felt his eyes prickle with the threat of tears. But there were shadows in his father's words; they thrummed with secret meaning. What choices? What had he done? He wanted to ask, but wasn't sure he dared.

Randill took his hand back. 'I am sorry,' he said. 'I am not myself tonight. Let's breakfast together in the morning. I promise you a new man then.'

'Of course,' said Aren. He put down his glass, which he'd hardly touched, and awkwardly got to his feet, not knowing if he was relieved or disappointed. By the time he reached the door, his father was staring into the empty fireplace again.

'Father?' he said.

'Hmm?'

'Is everything alright?'

Randill turned his face towards Aren and smiled wanly. For the first time in his life, Aren saw the lie in his father's eyes.

'Everything is alright,' he said. 'Hail to the Emperor.'

9

The house creaked and ticked like a living thing in the deep of the night. Aren stepped out into the shadowy blue quiet of the corridor and eased his bedroom door closed behind him. The servants were mostly abed, but Aren was far from sleep.

He slipped along the corridor in his socks, carrying his boots under one arm, alert to every sound. If all went well, no one would ever know he'd gone, but if caught, he'd be punished. It was the one rule his father was very strict about. He had to be back home every night, and he wasn't allowed out after dusk.

It galled him to be treated like a child. Other boys his age were allowed to run free till late. Randill was usually understanding and reasonable, but in this matter he wouldn't be swayed, and Aren had never been given a convincing reason why.

Well, he was a young man now, a boy no longer. And there were more important things than following another man's rules, even his father's.

The lamps were still burning in Randill's study, yellow light leaking beneath the door. He passed by silently. His father's strange behaviour had filled him with unease, curdling his excitement about the night ahead; but that was something to worry about later. Right now, he had to escape.

His hand went to his pocket, touching the brass key there. It was a key to the servants' door, copied from one he'd stolen from the maid. He'd bribed the locksmith's apprentice to make him a duplicate and returned the original before its absence was noticed. It had given him pangs of guilt for days afterwards – petty theft and deception were not the acts of an honourable person – but then Cade reminded him that the heroes in his stories were always stealing swords, or magic rings, or maidens, and they were still counted as heroes. That made Aren feel better. Sometimes it was necessary to do something ignoble in pursuit of a noble goal.

Down the stairs he went and through the moonlit parlour. The castles board had been cleared away and the room returned to order, but the stale smoke of Master Orik's cheroots lingered.

The low murmur of voices came to him from nearby. He pressed himself to the wall and peered through the doorway into the corridor beyond. The ostler and the steward were walking away from him, talking quietly by the light of the candles they carried. He waited for them to move out of sight then nipped into the corridor, where he came face to face with Nanny Alsa.

Both of them jumped, each as surprised as the other. She was wearing her nightgown and was standing in the doorway of the buttery holding a scone drenched in honey.

For an absurd moment, Aren considered running for it. Nothing could be allowed to prevent his escape. He opened his mouth to make some excuse, but Nanny Alsa raised a quick finger to her lips. It dawned on Aren that she was carrying no candle. She'd been sneaking around in the dark as well.

'I did not see you,' she whispered with a smile, 'if you did not see me.'

Aren grinned.

'Enjoy the show,' she said, then slid past him like a spectre and was gone.

Aren gave silent thanks to the Primus for the luck that brought him a governess like Nanny Alsa. She remembered what it was to be young. Staying out late on the first night of the ghost tide was virtually a rite of passage in Shoal Point. Aren had always been frustrated in the past, but he wouldn't be tonight.

He reached the servants' door and let himself out, then locked it behind him, slipped on his boots and scampered across the grounds. The curtains of the house were mostly drawn, but he didn't feel safe until he'd passed out of sight of the windows and was well away down the lane. There he stopped and took a moment to exult. He let the cool wind from the sea blow across his face and listened to the trees stir and the animals rustling in the grass. The lane was bathed with calm, steely light, and the freedom of the world was his.

He heard a low, mournful groan from beyond the cliffs, like a giant of old stirring in its sleep. In reply came an eerie, far-off, whistling cry that conjured a vision of some spectral eagle flown out of the Shadowlands.

The ghost tide was here. Spurred by the sound, he hurried on.

The route he chose took him parallel to the cliffs, but he was careful not to get too near the edge. He didn't want to see the sea until the moment was right. Instead he followed the brambled lanes that wound through fields and sloping pastures.

The Sisters were close in the sky tonight. There was pale, bruised Lyssa, bright and smooth, brushed with streaks of pastel blue, green and pink. Nearby was baleful Tantera, black and swollen, riven with glowing red cracks. The Hangman stood station in the west, outshining the neighbouring constellations, and to the north a dim, glowing smear could be seen, speckled at the edges with uncountable stars. The Path of Jewels, or Joha's River, as the Ossians still called it.

When he was little, Aren had looked up at Lyssa and imagined his mother looking down on him. She'd been named Lyssa, too, and to a young mind that had profound significance. On nights when there was no moon, or on blood moon nights when Tantera took lone watch and painted the land red, he'd wake distressed in the small hours and scream for his father. His mother might not have been there to comfort him then, but his father was a rock, strong enough to cling to in a storm.

Tonight, that rock had fractured. He'd never thought of Randill as a person, only as a parent; a force of authority, not a fallible man. Randill had never shown him worry or weakness before, so Aren had somehow assumed there was none to be found. Now, for the first time, he doubted him.

He tried to dampen those thoughts. They scared him. His father was just tired, he told himself. But the memory of their conversation gnawed at him.

Perhaps I thought you were the Hollow Man. You remember him, don't you?

The Hollow Man. Aren hadn't thought of him for years. A dead man who walked the land, searching for a soul to replace the one he'd lost. There was a great scar across his neck where his throat had been cut. 'If you ever see the Hollow Man, you run,' Randill had told his terrified son once. 'You run and you don't stop. For he's come to kill you.'

Why had his father mentioned the Hollow Man tonight? Why, for that matter, had Randill tormented him with it at all? In all other ways he was so protective and warm, yet he'd given his son nightmares for weeks, and he'd done it more than once. Aren distinctly remembered overhearing Nanny Kria, his first governess, complaining that Randill was frightening Aren to death with nonsense. What had inspired such uncharacteristic malice?

When he was older, Aren had told Cade about the Hollow Man, and Cade had been fascinated. He'd never heard the legend, and he prided himself on collecting tales of shades and bogeymen. So Cade went to his mother, who seemed to know every tale ever told; but she'd not heard of the Hollow Man, either.

A group of giggling figures crossed the lane in front of him and went forging off through the long meadow grass. They were heading for the coves, where most of their friends would be gathering. Aren was aiming for higher ground, where the tallest cliffs reared above the waves. He was heading for the watchtower.

At last it came into sight, and in his excitement he forgot all about his father and the Hollow Man. It was a broken fang against the clifftops, lit from below and behind by pearly light, its ancient bricks mortared with shadow. Only the side that faced the sea still stood, narrow and alone, looking out to the west and the islands of the elaru beyond the horizon. The rest of the tower had crumbled until it was little more than a ring of stones barely higher than a man, surrounding grassy piles of rubble and the fragments of arched doorways. This wasn't the craft of Old Ossia, the long-lost empire of his ancestors, but a poor copy, clawed from the ground in the brutal centuries that followed when Ossia was driven back to ignorance, savagery and war.

He headed up the hill, following the overgrown road on the landward side where stones laid in another age still rested in the dirt. As he neared, he spotted others slipping towards the ruin in the moonlight.

He found at least two dozen inside. Groups of friends drank wine and joked among themselves while couples walked arm-in-arm through the tumbled remains, the stars bright above them. Despite their number and their high spirits, laughter was quiet and voices low. There was something forbidden about this place, something delicious and frightening that discouraged disturbance. Or perhaps it was simply the magic of the night that quieted them, and the plaintive cries coming from the sea.

His eyes were covered from behind and he felt a warm body press up against him. 'Who could it be?' wondered a voice in his ear.

'It can't be Sora,' he replied with a smile. 'She's such a good, obedient girl. Definitely not the sort to sneak from her home in the dead of night against her father's wishes.'

Sora gently nibbled his earlobe. 'I have heard that love makes girls do the strangest things.'

Aren had to suppress a shiver of delight. The heat of her breath against his cheek burned away his patience in an instant. 'Let me see you, then, if it really is Sora and not some shade sent to torment me.'

The hands left his eyes and he turned. There she was, laughing in the moonlight with that look she had, half innocence and half mischief. The sight set off a cascade of joy that spread out from his chest, leaving him stunned, empowered, amazed. He was helpless before the force of first love. There had never been any girl like her in his life, and there never would be again. He knew with dizzying certainty that she was the one he was meant for, that he'd marry her and they'd spend their lives together.

She was a Krodan blonde like her brother Harald, hair cut to the line of her jaw, with wide-set grey eyes in an open face that suited mirth and play, and a broad, toothy smile. Some distant part of him knew that she wasn't considered one of the great beauties of the Empire – not even the prettiest girl in Shoal Point – but that didn't matter to Aren. In his eyes she had no equal.

For their rendezvous she'd chosen a light, floaty dress of emerald green, now dirtied at the hem and entirely at odds with her stout walking boots. Elegant *and* practical; he marvelled at her cleverness. He reached for her, to bring her to him and kiss her, but she danced away, tut-tutting.

'Where is your restraint, my wild Ossian boy? Kisses, is it? I thought you lured me from my bed to show me mysterious wonders.'

Aren's grin was tinged with frustration. He wanted her lips against his, but she'd have her game first, her teasing and flirting. She'd make him wait. She'd said once that the chase made the catching all the sweeter, but all things being equal, Aren would rather cut straight to the good part.

'Well, then,' he said, holding out a hand. 'Will you walk with me, my lady? I hope you'll find the spectacle worth your while.'

'Why, he's a gentleman after all,' she said and laid her hand in his. Just the touch of her palm made his heart quicken.

They ambled among the stones, making their way unhurriedly through the crumbling outlines of forgotten chambers. Walking with her hand in his, he felt a foot taller. That she should have chosen him, of all the boys of Shoal Point! Nobody appeared to be paying them particular attention, but he imagined secret envy and grudging respect in every glance that came their way.

'They say this is where Kala of the Dawnwardens watched for the elaru fleet coming from the sea,' he said, eager to show off his knowledge. For once, he didn't mind telling an Ossian tale. 'King Angred the Maimed had been told that the elaru were preparing to invade, but he was bewitched by a silver-tongued elaru ambassador who convinced him that the true danger came from the Harrish to the north. He sent his armies to the Harrish border, but the Dawnwardens knew better and set Kala here to watch. For thirty days and thirty nights she waited, and on the thirtieth day she saw the sails of the fleet just as the sun was setting. She took to her horse and rode non-stop night and day to Morgenholme to tell the king.

'The king realised his mistake and sent his armies to the coast. Everyone believed it was too late, but when they arrived, they found that the Dawnwardens had raised all the local garrisons and held back a force of elaru ten times their number, keeping them pinned along the coast until reinforcements could arrive. The elaru were driven back to their ships and fled, and the invasion failed.'

She clutched his arm. 'That's so exciting! Were the Dawnwardens great heroes, then?'

'They were an order of warriors, adventurers and scholars who swore allegiance to the Ember Blade. Sometimes they acted as an elite royal guard, trusted with the most sensitive and dangerous missions, but they operated in secret, too, always looking to the good of the realm. Their true loyalty wasn't to any ruler, but to Ossia itself.' He looked up at the seaward wall, rising above the ruins, strange white light glowing through its narrow stone windows. 'Yes, they were great heroes. Back when we had any.'

Sora pursed her lips and frowned slightly, the way she did when she was thinking. Aren found it unbearably charming – but then, he found everything she did unbearably charming.

'I have heard of the Ember Blade,' she said uncertainly. 'You lost it when Ossia fell.'

'It was captured,' Aren said, 'by a Krodan general called Dakken, and taken to Kroda with the other spoils of conquest.'

'And what about the Dawnwardens? Where were they?'

'There have been no records of their deeds for two hundred years. They belonged to another time; they are nothing but stories now.'

She sniffed. 'Petr says that when the Ember Blade was captured, the Ossians all gave up.'

Aren tensed at the mention of Petr, a Krodan boy altogether too sure of himself who spent more time in Sora's company than Aren would like. 'That's true.'

'But it's just a sword,' she said, puzzled. 'Petr says the Krodan army would *never* surrender just because someone took a sword away.'

Aren was unable to keep the pout from his voice. 'Well,' he said, 'perhaps that's why you won.'

'You're jealous!' she teased. He scowled. 'Oh, don't be. Petr's a loudmouth. You're the one I'll marry.'

'If your father and brothers allow it,' Aren said sulkily. Just the mention of another boy had made him peevish and obtuse. 'You know Harald and Juke warned me off again today?'

'Ha! They barked at me, too,' she said, waving a hand. 'What a pair of sneaks, stealing a letter from their sister's room! How very mature of them.' She smiled at him wickedly. 'But I'm the better sneak. They told me I couldn't go out tonight, but I slipped past them anyway!'

'They knew you were meeting me?' Aren asked in horror.

'They suspected. But they didn't see me leave, and what they don't know won't hurt them. Oh, here are the stairs. Let's go up!'

A set of precarious steps climbed the curved interior of the seaward wall. The stone was much eroded and in places there were alarming gaps where a chunk had fallen away. Aren, however, was less alarmed by the steps than by Sora's last comment. It was as if she didn't realise how serious this all was, or what might happen if they were caught. He was risking more than just a beating tonight. If Sora's father spoke with the governor, the consequences would fall on his father, too, and he dreaded to think what they might be.

He took her other hand and turned her to face him. Suddenly, he needed to know if she was truly his, if she'd wait for him to return from the army. He wanted to spill his thoughts to her, confess all his insecurities and share his growing fear as he began to comprehend the enormity of the future bearing down on him. A year apart, unable to see or touch her. A year not knowing what she was doing or who she was doing it with. He'd avoided thinking about it for a long time – ignoring difficult questions, Nanny Alsa had once said, was a particular talent of his – but now he felt as if a terrifying void yawned at his feet.

She saw it in his eyes and put a finger to his lips. He was a man, not a boy, she said with that gesture. This wasn't a night to be faint-hearted. Not if he wanted his kisses.

So he swallowed his fears, relieved and hurt all at once, and led the way up the stairs.

The stairs were broken off partway up, ending in empty air and stars. To their left was a doorway, which led onto a balcony that ran around the outer edge of the seaward wall. It was little more than a wide ledge chewed by the years, its parapets long fallen. Moonlit figures sat along its length, their legs dangling over the three-storey drop to the turf below. They'd braved the heights for a view that stretched fifteen leagues in every direction. From the watchtower, it was possible to see the whole spectacle.

Aren and Sora stepped out and joined them, and Sora's eyes widened as she saw the ghost tide for the first time.

The very sea was aglow. All along the coast, strange aurorae curled and slid like slow ribbons beneath the waves. Where the water met the shore, in the coves and against the cliffs, the glow gathered to a blinding intensity. The docks were ablaze with it, rickety jetties and moored boats made dreamlike, floating in liquid white light.

Further out were the hull whales, vast barnacled monsters so encrusted they seemed more stone than flesh. They jetted clouds of water, rolled over with a splash of fins. Occasionally one would surge up from below with its mouth agape, scattering the ribbons of light into tiny shreds. Then they'd crash down and sink, and there would be calm, and the ribbons would slowly re-form.

It was the whales that Aren had heard on his journey here. Great bass creaks deep enough to feel in the breastbone; strange, irregular popping noises; eerie howls and screeches that set his nerves on edge. They were supernatural sounds that brought to mind the wild, ancient places where things from the world of the dead were said to hold sway.

No wonder the sailors of elder days thought the ghost tide was the spirits of the drowned dead returning to land, herded by Joha's whales. It was the hope of every Ossian to return to the earth when they died, where the agents of Sarla, Lady of Worms, could break down their bodies and return them to the green cycle of life. Those who went to sea prayed to the Heron King, Aspect of Sea and Sky, to deliver them back to Sarla if they should sink. The ghost tide was proof that their prayers were heeded.

Aren didn't believe in the Nine, in Sarla or Joha or any of the rest. He followed the light of the Primus and scoffed at the ignorance of his forefathers. But standing here, faced with this inexplicable majesty, it was hard not to feel the spirits of the old world reaching out to him, or the gods of his homeland like tall shadows at his back.

He turned to Sora, intending to remark on the view, but the words died in his throat as he saw the tears in her eyes. She reached out, took his face in her cupped hands and brought his lips to hers at last.

IO

Diligence. Temperance. Dominance.

The credo of the Sanctorum. Aren gazed across the classroom at the plaque above the blackboard. *Diligence. Temperance. Dominance.* Persistence and self-control led to victory.

If only it were that simple with girls.

The master's voice had become a background drone to the turmoil in his tired mind. The board was covered with letters and numbers and lines, but Aren had lost their meaning. He tried to pay attention, but his thoughts kept skating away.

It had been three nights since the ghost tide began. Three nights in which he'd hardly slept, and when he did, he woke violently, his heart pounding. Once, he dreamed the Hollow Man entered his room and stood next to his bed while he lay paralysed. The Hollow Man tipped his head back and the scar at his throat parted like a wet, red mouth. Aren had jerked awake, whimpering like a puppy.

There had been no word from Sora, and no sign of her in town. The silence worried him. Had he offended her somehow? Had she fallen ill, perhaps? Had her brothers found out about that night?

He blinked the thought away for the hundredth time. *Concentrate*, he told himself, and focused on the blackboard again where Master Bilke was pointing his rod at an equation. He was a short, plump Krodan with huge bushy eyebrows and tufts of grey hair that stuck out over his ears, giving him the appearance of an angry owl. The other dozen students were dutifully scratching on their slates. Aren made a half-hearted attempt to look busy, but he found his gaze drifting back to the credo again.

Diligence. Temperance. Dominance.

Everything had changed when the ghost tide arrived. His father had been a new man in the morning, as he promised, and for the last few days he'd been as warm and attentive as ever. But Aren wasn't fooled. It all felt false now, all of it a front. Uncertainty had spread through him, causing him to question things he'd never questioned before.

Sora, for example. His night with Sora had been everything he wanted. She was dazzled by the ghost tide, and their time together had been full of kisses and professions of desire. Yet after they parted, he was plagued with doubt. They talked of love, marriage and children, but never of concerns, fears or problems. He wanted to know how they'd overcome her family's opposition to their union. He wanted to make plans for their year apart. But somehow it was never the right time to talk about the difficult realities of their relationship. Somehow she made it that way.

He was beginning to wonder if Sora was taking all this as seriously as he was. The idea threatened him with such torment that he hardly dared think it.

'Aren!'

Master Bilke's voice jolted him back to the moment. With sudden horror, he realised that an answer was expected of him, but he didn't know the question. The other boys turned towards him one by one as the silence stretched out.

'Well? Stand up!' said the master. Aren shot to his feet, grateful for a task he could accomplish. Master Bilke tapped his rod against an equation on the blackboard. 'Solve for b, please.'

Blood flooded Aren's face as he stared witlessly at the blackboard. He was lost, and everyone in the room knew it. Some of the students smirked; others wore pity on their faces. He didn't know which was worse.

'Come along!' barked Master Bilke. 'I've just told you how to do it!'

Aren's mouth was dry. He swallowed, opened it, shut it again. 'I ... Master Bilke I—' he began, and was saved when the door to the classroom burst open and there was Cade, of all people, sweaty and panting. Aren had never been so pleased to see him.

'How dare you, boy!' Master Bilke roared, with a face like he was about to expel a pellet. 'Get out of my classroom!'

Cade didn't even glance at him. His eyes found Aren's, and they were full of fright. 'You have to come!' he gasped. 'They've arrested your da!'

The world closed in on Aren and the heat of humiliation cooled to icy shock. The master, the other students, even Cade faded away to insignificance as the meaning of those words sank in. He scrambled out from behind his desk, fled the classroom and ran for home.

He remembered little of the journey back. It was as if he'd entered a tunnel, and outside was nothing but a hazy blur, strange noises, shapes without form. All he knew was the motion of his body, the pain in his muscles as he sprinted through streets and down lanes. At one point, he might have heard Cade calling his name as he laboured in pursuit, but there was no question of slowing down for him. His mind was a blare of senseless panic and disbelief. It couldn't be. It wasn't real.

If he could get home, somehow he could sort this out, make it right. He just had to get home.

There were a dozen townsfolk gathered outside the house when he arrived, Krodan and Ossian both, drawn by neighbourly concern or ghoulish curiosity. They parted for him as he pelted up the drive from the road. Waiting by the front steps was a black carriage drawn by four black horses, with a double-barred cross on the side: the sign of the Iron Hand, the Emperor's most feared investigators.

His steps faltered and he stumbled to a halt before it, blanching with dread. The Iron Hand didn't trouble themselves with minor felonies or local squabbles, they dealt with threats to the Empire. When the Iron Hand took someone away, they didn't come back.

A Krodan woman reached out as if to comfort him. Her husband pulled her back, his eyes cold, his expression detached. If the father was an enemy of the Empire, then what of the son? Better to be safe than to be tainted by association.

At that, Aren gritted his teeth and straightened his spine. Curse them all, then. Curse the faithless who thought his father condemned. They'd be ashamed when this was over, when this misunderstanding was cleared up and justice was done. Randill was a good man and loyal to the Empire. That was as true as the moons in the sky. Whatever had happened here, he was sure his father had done nothing to invite the wrath of the Iron Hand.

But maybe *he* had.

He dared not follow that thought to its end. Clutching his ribs where a stitch jabbed him, he lurched past the onlookers, up the steps to the porch and inside.

Nanny Alsa was among the servants gathered fearfully in the corridor. She tried to stop him going into the dining room, but he threw her arm off and pushed past, almost falling through the doorway. Rough hands caught him and he was hoisted to his feet by a man wearing the livery of the Iron Guard, the soldiers of the Iron Hand.

'And you must be Aren,' said a small, bespectacled man with moist, fleshy lips, in a tone of weary disdain. He wore the long black overcoat and the double-barred cross of a watchman: one of the Emperor's inquisitors.

Aren struggled in the soldier's grip, but he was held fast. The room was busy with armoured men. There was another watchman wearing an identical overcoat, who was otherwise the opposite of his companion: tall and blond, with stern, well-proportioned features and a swimmer's shoulders. At the centre of it all was his father, grey-faced, manacled, resigned. He had the look of a man who'd arrived at his own grave.

'It's a mistake! He hasn't done anything!' Aren shouted, unable to understand why his father had submitted to this treatment. 'Get off me!' He pulled an arm free of the guardsman who held him and was rewarded with a clout round the head, hard enough to rock him. Before he could recover, a second guardsman restrained him and he was held fast.

'Klyssen! Leave him be!' Randill cried, roused to anger by the sight. 'He's no part of this.'

Klyssen, the first of the two officers, studied Aren with reptilian calm. 'Thank you for coming, boy. You have saved us the trouble of finding you.' He motioned to one of the soldiers. 'Take him.'

'No!' Randill snapped, desperation in his voice. 'Your business is with me! Not him!'

'You are a traitor, and he is the son of a traitor,' Klyssen said coldly. 'He will be dealt with accordingly.' He waved at the other watchman. 'Harte, go with them.'

The guardsmen began dragging Aren out of the room. 'Father!' he screamed, and the sound jolted Randill to action. His eyes hardened, he twisted, and suddenly there was a knife in his manacled hands, stolen from the sheath of a nearby soldier. Quick as a snake, he plunged it into the throat of the man he'd taken it from. Before anyone could react, he spun and slashed the face of another, opening his cheek to the bone.

Then everything was chaos, the crash of armour and the ring of drawn blades as the soldiers holding Aren dropped him to the floor and piled in. Aren landed hard, knocking the wind from him, and he struggled to his elbows, gasping. A guardsman reeled back from the fight, a hand to his face, blood seeping through his glove. Nanny Alsa was shrieking out in the corridor. Klyssen, alarmed by the unexpected violence, shrank against the wall of the dining room, keeping well clear.

Aren saw a blade flicker and another Krodan soldier staggered away, clutching his throat, blood soaking his uniform. For an instant, he was the Hollow Man, a vision of gargling death come to claim him. Then he crashed against the dining-room table and collapsed.

All at once, the tangle of soldiers parted and Randill was hauled to his feet by Harte, with the point of a knife pressed firmly under his jaw. The watchman stood close behind Randill, his hair mussed and his teeth bared from the savagery of the fight. Guardsmen seized Randill's arms, but he'd lost his weapon now and wasn't resisting any more.

'You are a traitor to the Empire and a murderer,' Harte said. He looked at Klyssen, eyes glittering with defiance. 'Under the circumstances, I think we can skip the trial.'

With that, he drove the knife home.

Aren saw the light in his father's eyes go out. Randill sighed, one long breath that carried his life with it, and he dropped in a pile of meat and bone at Harte's feet.

Aren screamed.

He was still screaming as they dragged him down the corridor, hurling curses and fighting the whole way. They struck him across the face more than once, but it did nothing to quiet him. Nothing they could do was worse than what had already happened.

'Get off him! You're killing him! Get off!'

It was Cade, angry and sweaty and out of breath as he shoved down the corridor past the servants. That broad face loomed in his vision, his cheeks red and his hair damp against his forehead. 'Aren! What happened? Where are they taking you?'

Aren stared at him without comprehension. His words were just noises. In the shock of Randill's death, nothing connected.

'Out of the way, vermin!' snapped one of the guardsmen. The ostler grabbed Cade by the arm and tried to pull him aside, but Cade's feet were set and he was rooted like a tree.

'You can't take him!' Cade cried, but he was yelling in Ossian and the soldier was yelling in Krodan, and in the heat of the moment neither understood the other.

'Out of the way, I said!'

'He's done nothing wrong!' Cade shouted. His protests were cut short as a guardsman slammed the pommel of a sword down on his head, behind his ear, and he crumpled like a sack.

Aren heard Klyssen's wet voice from close behind him. 'Interfering with an overwatchman of the Iron Hand is a crime,' he said, for the benefit of the witnesses. 'Take him, too.'

Aren tried to look over his shoulder as he was dragged out, but he couldn't see his friend as he was hauled onto the porch. The crowd numbered three dozen or more now. They stared in silence as he was manhandled down the steps, tears and snot and blood across his face, rage and grief written there.

Then he saw her. And he knew that what he suspected all along was true, why the Iron Hand were here, why his father had died.

Sora was in the crowd, hands to her face in horror. Standing with her were her brothers and her father, a hawkish man with a stony expression. Her trip to the watchtower had been discovered. Her father had spoken to the governor about the impertinent Ossian boy who was harassing her, and how Randill had failed to control him. They'd trumped up a charge of treason to remove the problem. Suspicion was enough to seize their lands; even a man as rich as Randill could do nothing about it.

They were only Ossians, after all.

'No more warnings,' Harald had said. But in the arrogance of love he hadn't listened.

The soldiers shoved him inside the black carriage and tipped Cade in alongside him, unconscious, blood splayed across his cheek like a spidery red hand.

'No,' he whimpered. He shook his head and kept shaking it, his eyes fixed on Cade. 'No, no, no.'

But all the denials in the world couldn't dent the truth. The enormity of what he'd done threatened to swallow him whole.

It was his fault. All of it.

The door of the prison carriage slammed closed behind him with a sound like the doom of all dreams.

I I

Dusk lay red on the hills as the druidess laboured up the grassy rise, her hound loping at her heels. She walked with a splintered staff of lichwood and lightning-glass, planting it in the ground before her, but she was not old, and her legs were strong from the passage of many leagues.

She wore sturdy boots and scuffed leather trousers. A tatty patchwork cloak made of the stitched-together skins of rabbit, fox and stoat flapped about her as she climbed. She clicked and clattered with charms of bone and wood and metal, and carried a great pack as if it were no weight at all. Her hair was long, black and filthy, falling to either side of an oval face with dark eyes and a serious mouth that turned down at the edges, lending her an air of intensity and purpose. That face was smeared with streaks of stark white and coal black, as if for camouflage, or for war.

Her name was Vika-Walks-The-Barrows, and she was late.

The journey had been long and unforeseen diversions had delayed her arrival, Krodans chief among them. They delved deeper into the wild places than ever before. Once, they could have been relied upon to stay near roads and cities, clinging to the apparatus of order like fearful children to a mother's apron. They were lost without their rules and routines, and shied away from nature, which didn't respect their laws. But they'd become bolder in recent years, and she'd encountered them several times on her way through the hinterlands: camps of engineers plotting new roads, workmen building settlements, surveyors scouting for minerals to exploit and forests to log. Her lip curled in anger at the memory.

Near Salt Fork, she'd unwittingly walked into the path of the Krodan army, marching to quell the rebellion. She'd been forced to hide out for days, moving from place to place while the forests swarmed with scouts and foragers gathering supplies. After the rebellion collapsed, huntsmen were unleashed to seek out fugitives. With them came something else, something that the forest itself recoiled from. Three beings that wore the shape of men, but which were not.

They almost caught her as she sheltered in an abandoned temple, but the animals warned her of their approach and she fled, leaving her fire behind. Later, she glimpsed them through the trees: one an enormous pile of tarnished black armour with a great hammer in his hands; one ragged and thin, carrying a brutal-looking bow that was all spikes and points; the third cowled and moving like a whisper, with two thin blades in his gloved grip and a metal mask covering his face. The mere sight of them turned her cold, and she stayed well clear.

It wasn't her they hunted, thankfully. Their targets were two fugitives from Salt Fork. She didn't linger to see what happened to them, but she doubted the outcome was good. Instead she was forced to hurry on, through forests still thick with Krodans. At one point, the huntsmen picked up her trail, perhaps believing her a fugitive like the others. It took every trick she knew to throw them off; but she knew a lot of tricks.

Now, at long last, they'd reached their destination. Too eager to wait, her companion hurried off through the bracken and gorse towards the crest of the rise. She was a shaggy grey wolfhound bitch named Ruck, longer nose to tail than Vika was tall. Vika followed in her wake, full of grave thoughts.

Maggot's Eve had come and gone five nights since. She hoped Hagath had waited for her, though it was a faint hope at best. Too many meetings had been missed these past years; news wasn't travelling as it should. Now, more than ever, it was important the Communion be maintained, but she feared the druids' habitual solitude would be their undoing. Every year, there were fewer of them. Everywhere she went, temples were left to ruin and sacred sites abandoned. It was rare to encounter fresh druidsign, and when she did it spoke of ill things, of restless, angry spirits and turmoil in the Shadowlands. The Primus grew in strength as the Aspects waned, yet still her gods were silent. The elders had to act; a Conclave must be called. But she'd heard nothing.

Perhaps Hagath would have news to cheer her. At the least, he'd have left druidsign to indicate his next destination, so Vika could catch him up. She was in sore need of company and hope.

But hope crumbled to ashes in her breast as she reached the rise where Ruck waited, and saw what lay beyond.

Before her lay a wide hollow, a dent in the hilltop flanked by steep rising slopes and backed by a cliff. She stood at its eastern edge, with the rolling hills behind her and the long shadows of dusk upon them. The sun, weak and low amid thin layered clouds of gold and blood, was just visible above the cliff. Warm light glowed along the rim, but the hollow lay in a summer twilight.

It was called the Dirracombe – *Hirn-Annwn* in the tongue of the druids – and it was said that the first humans, descended from the giants of old, paid fealty to the Nine here in thanks for seeing them through the Long Ice to the spring. They raised ten great stones in worship: one for the Creator, and one for each of the pieces into which he broke himself when he birthed the universe. The Nine Aspects: each an individual yet each a part of the same being, nine sides of the same unknowable god.

Those stones had stood through the mysterious millennia before written history, which men called the Age of Legends. They'd endured the rise and fall of empires, keeping silent watch as the land suffered cataclysm and barbarity, and emerged from the ruins forged anew. But they didn't stand now. After more lifetimes than Vika could imagine, the ten pillars lay toppled.

Ruck whined at her side as she stared, horrified. When she'd last visited, three years ago, the pillars stood proud and grim along the shore of a kidney-shaped tarn, a small mountain lake like a mirror turned to the sky. The tallest, carved for the Creator, had stood in the lake itself. Its shadow reached across the water every dawn, touching each Aspect in turn as the year ran its course, like a giant sundial.

Now that pillar was a broken stump, poking from water grown thick with weeds. The other Aspects lay in pieces, shattered where they fell, hidden among the heather, bramble and vine that sprouted unchecked around them.

Three short years, and the Dirracombe had fallen. Nobody tended it now; no pilgrims came any more. It was already being reclaimed by the earth.

How had she not heard of this outrage?

Dazed, she walked into the hollow, Ruck trotting uncertainly at her side. The pillars had been weathered by the years, and the gods were mere bumps and grooves hinting at form. Yet there was still a sense of them, their presence heavy in the air. There was half of a snarling face that had to belong to the Despoiler, Azra, Aspect of War. Nearby was the voluptuous earth mother, stone-skinned Meshuk, Aspect of Earth and Fire. They'd existed so long, she'd thought them eternal. Now she was no longer sure.

How could you let this happen? she asked the Aspects. *Why did you allow it?*

But the Aspects, as ever, kept their own counsel.

She scanned the hollow for signs of Hagath, but if he'd been here, he hadn't lingered. Ruck sniffed at something in the grass, raised her head and gave a sharp bark. Vika drifted over, still stunned by the force of the blasphemy surrounding her. She knelt down and picked up the coin Ruck had found in the dirt.

It was a Krodan guilder. On one side was a vertical sword laid across an open book. On the other, the likeness of the Emperor in profile. She scraped the dirt from the Emperor's face with one cracked thumbnail and looked down at him. It was proof enough for her, if proof were needed. The stones had been pulled down, destroyed with forethought and purpose, at the order of the Sanctorum.

They are erasing us, she thought.

She dropped the coin and walked to the shore of the tarn. It was summer, and warm even in the shade cast by the cliff, but she pulled her cloak about her nevertheless. Ruck hung back, sensing her mood, as she looked down into the water. A painted face returned her haunted gaze.

It's true, then, what the Apostates said. Our gods have abandoned us. This land is forsaken.

The fire crackled and snapped at the edge of the tarn, its flames reflected in the black water. Vika sat cross-legged before it, eyes closed, Ruck slumbering nearby. On the ground near the fire was a small black pot from which wisps of steam arose. Night had fallen beyond the circle of light and the sky was sprayed with stars.

She had been still for an hour or more before a rat grew bold enough to investigate her. It slipped along the water's edge, sniffing the air, drawn by the intriguing smells from the pot. Keeping the fire between itself and the wolfhound, whom it recognised as an enemy, it scurried through the dark and into the shadow of Vika's knee.

Her hand shot out and she snatched it up by its throat. Lifting it quickly, she held it before her eyes, its paws scratching the air.

'Thank you, little one,' she said, and broke its neck with one quick twist.

Ruck raised her head and watched with mild interest as Vika slit the rat's throat with her knife and drained its blood into the pot. As it trickled out, she muttered prayers of gratitude to Ogg, Aspect of Beasts, and paid her respects to the little animal that had given the gift of its life. When there was no more blood to be had, she tossed the body to Ruck, pulled back her sleeve and drew the edge of her blade along her skin, among dozens of old scars. She let a few drops of her blood run into the pot, then wrapped a rag around the cut.

Swirling the pot to mix it, she bowed her head and murmured ancient words in Stonespeak before drinking the bitter, salty draught. That done, she settled herself again, cross-legged, eyes closed. Ruck snorted, crunched down her rat and fell asleep.

Who is here? Vika asked in her mind.

She'd searched the site for druidsign but found none. Hagath hadn't been here, and it was too much to hope that he'd also been delayed. Hagath was the most reliable of her contacts. That left two possibilities: he was dead, or he'd been arrested, which amounted to the same thing. Hagath was lost, like so many of her brothers and sisters in faith. One more broken link in the faltering Communion.

She couldn't keep on like this. She couldn't stand idly by and watch the sacred places fall into ruin, her gods driven into myth. So she'd ask for guidance, the best way she knew how. She'd call on the spirits of this place, which had once been mighty, and see what wisdom they could offer.

The concoction seeped through her body, from her belly to her fingertips and teeth, through muscle and nerve, loosening her wherever it went. There was an acrid taste of metal in her mouth and a burning in her gut as her senses sharpened. She smelled Ruck strongly, the musky aliveness of her. Her sleeping sighs were loud in Vika's ears. From the lake came the odour of weedy rot, and the dry-hot scent of burning wood drifted from the grumbling fire.

Soon she began to feel jittery, and her joints started to ache as the poisons in the drink made themselves felt. She opened her eyes, stood and looked up to the sky.

Above the hollow, Sabastra's Ribbon was a faint, curling cloud of red and yellow, the only colour in the blackness. She took a breath, sucking the darkness into her lungs like water, and wobbled as she lost her balance. The stars wheeled overhead, blurring as they spun. She threw out her arms to stabilise herself. The concoction was powerful stuff, powerful enough to kill someone who hadn't spent years developing their resistance to its toxins. Once steady, she looked up to the sky once more, trying to recapture her calm.

But the stars were not where they'd been.

She frowned. Sabastra's Ribbon had been overhead a moment ago, but now it was some way to the south. New constellations had moved into view; the Gull was all but gone and the Fox had taken its place on the eastern horizon. The Sisters had appeared at half-moon, Tantera cracked and massive, pale Lyssa peering out from behind her.

A moment ago, it had been summer. Now she stood beneath autumn stars.

So it had begun. The spirits were guiding her. But what did it mean?

Something moved at the edge of her vision, a curling wisp of light, as if a tongue of flame had escaped the fire and was being blown around the broken pillars. She turned, but it was lost among the tumbled stones and thick grass.

Intrigued, she set off to investigate. As she went, she passed before a fragment of a god's face, lying on its side. The shadows shifted in the pit of its sunken eye, as if it had moved to follow her, and she felt a faint tingle, the presence of a stirring spirit.

Show yourself.

The fallen pillars formed a maze of shattered blocks taller than she was. She hunted through the sedge and bracken between the Aspects. Again and again she glimpsed the light at the edge of her vision and allowed it to lead her on, but at last she lost sight of it and came to a stop. She searched the hollow uncertainly, afraid that she'd missed whatever message had been offered. Suddenly she heard something move.

Behind me.

She whirled with a gasp, the charms in her hair and clothes clacking together, and her face was lit up by the figure standing there. It was a tall being of flurrying brightness, sparkling and shifting like sunlight on disturbed water. In its hand was a sword which burned fierce enough to blind. She shaded her eyes.

'What message do you have for me?' she cried.

The figure didn't speak, or move, or acknowledge her, but it emanated strength, and she knew in the way of visions that it was an ally. A champion of the land.

'Are you come from the Aspects? Have they answered the prayers of their people at last?'

The champion gave her no reply, so she narrowed her eyes and peered closer. Beneath the glimmering, turning light she could see a hint of a face. If only she could make it out, she'd know the nature of this herald. Tentatively, she extended a hand as if to touch its cheek, to feel its features like a blind woman.

The instant her fingertips touched it, it vanished like a blown-out candle and something thumped to the earth at her feet.

She blinked, surprised. Her night vision was ruined, so she knelt down and patted in the dark grass until her hands closed around what had fallen. It was cool, smooth and sharp. The sword, surely.

Yet when she stood and lifted it from the grass, it was nothing more than a crooked branch.

She frowned at it in puzzlement. The bright figure was gone, and the hollow had become chilly, the starlight steely and cold. She chewed at her lower lip and scanned her surroundings, searching for another sign. What were the spirits trying to tell her?

She looked down again and found she was no longer holding a branch, but an oozing rod of bone and gristle, the long, scrawny forelimb of some creature she didn't recognise. With a cry of disgust, she cast it away, and as it fell it became a black snake that slithered off through the grass. She jumped back instinctively; her boots caught in the undergrowth and sent her staggering. Seeking balance, her hand touched the stone face of snarling Azra, which lay broken in half. Her palm came away red and wet. Blood was welling from the cracks and splits, spilling along the rough channels of his features.

She stared at her hand, horrified. This was no dream-vision of guidance. The spirits were angry; she felt the dark weight of it. Events were tipping out of her control.

Movement, between the stones. She spun and spotted a blurred black figure a moment before it slipped out of sight. With a pang of terror, she saw several similar figures surrounding her. They stood still, unmoving, and yet they slid out of view whenever she tried to get a good look at them, moving sideways as if pulled on tracks. Each time one of them disappeared, the next appeared closer.

She began to panic. She'd bridged the Divide and invited the spirits through, but only some came from the Shadowlands offering knowledge. Others meant to do her harm, eager to avenge their sacred place, to take out their fury on anyone they could find. She didn't know who these strangers were, but instinct told her she should fear them. All her charms and tricks fell from her mind, and she ran.

The glowering faces of defiled gods loomed in the moonlight

as she passed them, her patchwork cloak flapping around her. Her only chance was to get beyond the boundaries of the Dirracombe and hope they wouldn't pursue. But no matter how fast she ran, the figures were faster, and closing in.

One rose up from the darkness in front of her.

She stumbled to a halt, head buzzing, mouth dry. It was cloaked in black and wore strange armour made from material like a beetle's carapace. Its face was corpse-pale and it had no lips, only a grotesque rictus of exposed gums and fangs. Across its eyes was a band of black iron.

She spun, seeking escape, but she was surrounded. Six of them pressed close, each a fresh vision of dread. One wore a net of tiny chains across its gaunt face, hooks planted in its eyelids, stretching them wide to expose the black, glistening orbs beneath. Another's face had been skinned below the ridge of its cheekbones, the muscle and bone of its jaw opened out like mandibles. Yet another had forearms and fingers that had been split open and doubled in length by some diabolical surgery, which waved restlessly in the air before it. They were like the experiments of some ghoulish chimericist.

The one with the visor of black iron seized her and clamped a cold hand over her eyes. A scream tore from her as everything went dark.

Then it showed her what it had come here to show.

Dawn found her wrapped in her cloak, staring into the fire as she drank a bowl of soup. She hadn't slept; it would have been impossible even if she had tried. The horrors of what she had seen were too fresh. She didn't understand all that the spirit had imparted, but she knew it couldn't be ignored. She needed wise counsel, and there was only one person to go to for that.

By morning she was on her way again, the ruin of the Dirracombe behind her and Ruck trotting at her side. She had her pack on her back, her staff in her hand and, for the first time in many years, a clear purpose.

12

Aren's pickaxe struck sparks as he worked, brief splinters of light that scattered and died. He swung, drew back and swung again in a steady rhythm. Not so fast that he'd kill himself with exertion, not so slow that he'd feel the guard's club for it. The fog of exhaustion lay thick on him, dulling the edge of his senses; his back ached and his leaden arms throbbed at the joints. He kept on going regardless, driven by the knowledge that each blow brought him a few seconds closer to the next break, the next meal, the end of his shift. It was how the shapeless hours passed, deep in the black cold of the mountain.

There were two dozen of them on the detail, lined up against the wall of the tunnel, shackles around their ankles. Lanterns hung from mouldering beams, throwing fitful shadows as the men chipped away in the dark. The air was full of stone dust and the maddening echoes of metal against rock.

Cade was next to him in the line, working mechanically with that dead-eyed look Aren had come to know well. At first he'd complained bitterly about the aches and scabs and blisters, the tiredness, the near-constant hunger; but there was little sympathy for him here, and no relief. They were all in the same boat, and eventually even Aren had tired of listening to him. Cade had stopped complaining then, and spoke a little less, and kept his pain to himself. The other prisoners liked him better after that.

'Strike harder! Strike harder!' shouted the Krodan guard down the line. For some of the guards, that was all the Ossian they needed to know.

Nobody looked to see who it was directed at. All they knew was that someone was flagging. If they didn't pick up the pace they'd be beaten. Everybody got hit by the guards now and then, but it was worse when a prisoner was approaching the end of their strength. Aren had seen two men beaten into unconsciousness for the crime of being too weak to swing a pickaxe. A third had been killed where he lay when he couldn't get up.

Spurred by the warning, Aren increased his efforts. His pickaxe barely nicked the tunnel wall with each blow, but now and then a small chunk would break off, a tiny shard of progress. A thousand of those, a thousand thousand, and the Krodans would have enough ore to extract a few drops of elarite. A thousand times more, and they might be able to mix enough witch-iron for a breastplate, or some greaves, or an elaborate helmet. Eventually, at the cost of unimaginable effort and uncounted lives, they'd have enough for a suit of witch-iron armour, which offered the strength of steel at a fraction of the weight. One day that armour would be worn by some mighty Harrish knight, or bought by a rich erl, or gifted to foreign kings, none of whom would ever consider how it all started here, in a dark, cold tunnel in the earth, with a sliver of stone cut free.

This was Aren's life now. This was his purpose. His glorious contribution to the Krodan Empire.

He struck and struck again, and the sparks flared and reflected in his eyes.

I deserve this, he thought with each blow. *I deserve this. I deserve—*

Aren was on slop duty that day. While his detail rested, he fetched food from the mine entrance, a task which was both a curse and a blessing. On the one hand, he was denied a break between shifts; on the other, it gave him the rare opportunity to grab an extra helping of food.

He waited his turn at a blackened metal trough where gallons of thin vegetable gruel bubbled over a bed of coals. Lamps hung from poles, casting an uneasy light over the haggard faces of the shackled men in line. The chamber was a small, dim cavern at the junction of several tunnels, and it was busy with traffic. Shabby pit ponies hauled carts full of rocks from the depths of the mine. There were guards everywhere, too; not the stern, efficient Krodans who became soldiers, but low men, glorified turnkeys and angry bullies who took every chance to vent their spite on their charges. This was far from the world the Empire showed its loyal subjects. Only the fallen saw behind the scenes.

When his turn came, Aren stood by the trough and ate as a small handcart was filled from a chute. The fire was a comfort, and he sidled closer as he scooped gruel from his bowl with a crust of old bread. It was always cold in the mine. The dank stone leached the heat from the air and their clothes were pitifully thin. Not even the effort of mining kept them warm.

Once he'd wolfed down his meal, he held his bowl under the flow of gruel for a refill. The man at the lever didn't even look at him. As long as you finished eating before the flow was shut off, nobody cared if you took another bowlful. It was the only perk of slop duty.

He pulled his handcart aside to make way, then ate his second helping with his wooden spoon, washing it down with water from his tin flask. He ate slowly this time, savouring every bite, letting the heat of the fire soak into his bones. The food was bland and watery, but as Cade used to say, hunger was the best spice. His stomach grumbled and ached, unaccustomed to being filled, but when he was done he felt as close to satisfied as he ever got these days.

He hung a bag of loaves off the side of the cart and trudged away. Some prisoners on slop duty would take another chunk of bread and a bowl from the tub on their way back to their detail, but Aren had never done that. There was never enough to go around anyway, so the other prisoners took a keen interest if the tub wasn't full when it arrived. Aren told himself his sense of honour stopped him from giving in to temptation, but it was just as much his fear of retribution.

As he left the chamber, pulling the tub behind him, he passed a wooden birdcage containing a pair of grey cavepipers. Once, the sight of them had given him a thrill of dread, but now he ignored them. It was only if they started to sing that he needed to worry. Elarite seams bled an explosive oil under pressure, which was bad enough, but in concentrated quantities the oil gave off an invisible, odourless and flammable miasma called fire-fume. It gathered in pockets, trapped beneath the earth until freed by a miner's pickaxe, when it would seep out into the tunnels until it became dense enough to ignite. The cavepipers were the only warning the miners would get. Somehow they could sense the miasma and would shriek an alarm. It gave the men some chance to escape, but not much.

Well, if disaster came, it came. Aren tried to live each day without thinking further than his bed. That was how he'd endure, until death took him, or until he and Cade were freed. It was that or give up, the way he'd seen others do. Despair gnawed a man down, first his body, then his soul, until he lost the will to live. And this was a place of despair.

But that wouldn't be Aren's fate. He was determined. He'd survive this day, and the next, and he'd ensure Cade did, too. There was no other option.

He made his way along badly lit routes where prisoners sat murmuring quietly or eating. He recognised some from the camp, but no one acknowledged him. No one had the energy.

The handcart was heavy and Aren had to rest on the way back, so he pulled the cart into a darkened side-corridor where no one would see it and be tempted to steal a meal. He thought he was alone until he heard a wet clicking sound and saw there were two men already here, sitting on opposite sides of the narrow tunnel. One was glaring at him with fierce eyes, mouth working restlessly as he sucked his teeth and smacked his lips. He was all skin and bone, hair in patches, features sunken. A ragweed addict.

Aren almost backed out then and there – it was best to steer clear of ragweed addicts, who could be unpredictable and violent – but something about the other man in the corridor caught his attention. He sat with his head back against the stone, eyes closed and very still. Aren stepped away from his cart and approached him cautiously, trying to make him out in the gloom.

It was nobody he recognised, but a suspicion had taken root in his mind and he had to resolve it. He reached out slowly and placed his palm against the side of the man's face. The man's head lolled sideways, eyes open but seeing nothing. He'd died where he sat, and recently.

Aren rested on his haunches and considered the body before him. A season ago, he'd never seen a corpse. Now the dead had lost the power to shock. They'd become part of the background of his world.

He glanced about and saw nobody except the addict, who seemed disinclined to do anything but glare. Aren shrugged at him and began to search the dead man's pockets. After all, if he didn't do it, somebody else would.

The sinking sun was half-hidden by the mountains as they trudged from the mine in a double line, shackles keeping their strides short, heads lowered against a bitter wind that blew flurries of icy rain down from the peaks. The summer had been punishingly hot, but the weather had turned of late, a warning of the deadly cold to come. Winter would reap them; they all knew it. The weak wouldn't see the spring.

Aren walked alongside Cade, too weary to make conversation. Guards rode with them, herding them down the trail. They carried swords and bows, alert for anyone foolish enough to run. The pine forest to their left offered the promise of sanctuary, enough to tempt the desperate. Nobody was desperate enough today.

My father is dead because of me. The thought ambushed him. Randill's death was a wolf in the hollows of his mind, stalking him, savaging him with grief and loss when it could. The Iron Hand would have seized the family lands by now. Randill would be remembered as a traitor, when he'd been nothing but loyal to the Empire. All because Aren had to be with Sora. All because he hadn't listened to Harald's warning.

He'd thought their wild love could overcome any obstacle, but reality had proved him wrong, and grief had doused his passion faster than he could have imagined. It was only a season since he'd seen her – a season of hard labour and sorrow, true, but a mere season all the same – yet her memory no longer stirred him. This wasn't the storybook love he'd imagined, which conquered time and death and the meddling of the gods. He'd believed he would wither and die without her, when in truth he hardly thought of her at all.

It had been a dream of love, and nothing more. The stupid delusion of a callow boy. All that loss and ruin for nothing. In his darker moments, it made him want to scream.

He glanced at Cade. His friend looked worn. The flesh had fallen off him, his boyish pudge long gone. Though he'd always been the stronger of them, the work seemed to tax him harder than Aren. Each day he lost a little more energy, joked less, spoke more quietly. His suffering was as much Aren's fault as his father's death was. But with Cade, at least, there was some chance to atone.

'Brother Cade,' growled a rum-roughened voice, and Cade stumbled as he was shoved hard from behind. Aren saw fleeting anger cross his face, but when he turned, his mask was in place and he was smiling.

'Have you been sharpening your elbows, Rapha? You near put that one through my ribs.'

Rapha gave him a tobacco-stained grin. He was a burly Carthanian pirate with a tangled black beard, his skin browned and weathered as gnarled oak. 'Do your impression of Hassan!' he said. 'Show my friend here!' The pockmarked man next to him leered encouragement.

Cade checked that no guards were nearby. Then he swept back his shoulders, firmed his chin and puffed out his chest. No longer was he a shuffling prisoner, but a figure of pompous cruelty.

'You!' he cried, his voice comically high as he pointed at Rapha's friend. 'Did you splash my cloak? Then where did this mud come from, hmm? To the dogs with you! To the dogs with *everyone*!'

Rapha and his friend cackled at Cade's parody of the guard captain, and a few others nearby managed a chuckle or a grin. They all knew Hassan's obsession with cleanliness and his fondness for feeding prisoners to the dogs. Even gallows humour was welcome here, where laughter was hard to find.

Aren didn't join in. They liked Cade when he was funny, but Aren knew how he cried to himself in his bunk every night. He performed for them because that was his nature, but it was only an act, and it drained him sorely.

'Now do Overseer Krent!' urged another prisoner.

Aren turned sharply, wearing a scowl. 'He's tired,' he snapped. 'We're all tired. Leave him alone.'

Rapha slapped him round the back of the head, hard. 'No one asked you,' he said, with enough casual menace to shut Aren up.

'Easy there, you southern lunk!' Cade said, his voice now genial and friendly, hands resting on an imaginary belly and a smug smile on his face. 'No need for that! We're not on the high seas now!'

Rapha's friend roared with laughter as he recognised the overseer. It was loud enough to attract the attention of a nearby guard, who yelled at them in broken Ossian to be quiet. Rapha and his friend subsided, still smirking.

Cade gave Aren an angry look. *Why did you get involved?* Aren had meant to defend his friend, but he'd been the one who needed defending in the end, and defending Aren was what had landed Cade here in the first place. Aren wished he'd kept his silence.

The pain of Rapha's blow quickly faded into the haze of other hurts. His feet were blistered from rubbing inside his boots. Every muscle ached from the day's labours, and being on slop duty meant he'd got no rest. But he had a full belly, at least, and something else, too. Six fat cheroots, taken from the dead man and now stashed inside his thin, ragged coat. Aren had no idea how the prisoner had got them, but they were no use to him any more, and a lot of use to Aren. Smokes were good currency in the camp.

They followed the trail downwards, with the forest to their left and high cliffs to their right. The journey from the mine wasn't a long one. Soon they heard the river over the blowing wind and rounded a shoulder of the mountain to see their destination ahead.

They called it a work camp, but it was a prison all the same. It stood on the north side of the river, sandwiched between the water and a sheer cliff face. A rough stockade surrounded it, a high wall of thick wooden stakes running out from the cliff, along the riverbank and back. Within, another stockade divided the camp into two sections. The smaller contained the barracks, stables, posthouse and the overseer's mansion. The larger was for the prisoners. On the far side of a dirt yard were the longhouses where they slept, arranged in uneven rows against the curve of the stockade. There was a graveyard near the cliffs, and clustered round the south gate were the buildings where luckier prisoners worked: the cookhouse, workshop, laundry, latrines and infirmary.

On the other side of the river was the village of Suller's Bluff, reached from the south gate by a stone bridge. It sat close against the forest, a drowsy settlement that now existed to serve the camp and accommodate the soldiers' families. The villagers were lighting fires against the chill of the coming night; white smoke drifted from the chimneys, whipped away by the switching wind. They'd be settling down to good meals of warm bread and meat, with ale and wine to wash it down. The prisoners gazed longingly across the river, envying their food and warmth. The village was no more than a hundred paces from their prison, yet it may as well have been in another land.

The trail took them via the east gate, trudging through the guards' section, past the mansion where the overseer entertained his guests in his dining hall. It had been built in the strict Krodan style on the spot where the mayor's house had once stood, over-looking the river. A daily reminder to the Ossian prisoners of who held power in their land now.

Aren glowered at it as he passed, and cursed the ill luck that had him born Ossian. If he and his father had been Krodan, none of this would have happened.

A movement in one of the upper windows caught his eye. Someone was standing there in the last light of the dimming sun, looking down on the procession. With a jolt, Aren recognised that bespectacled face.

Klyssen!

Their eyes met for an instant, then the overwatchman turned away and was gone.

Klyssen, thought Aren as he huddled by the back door of the cookhouse. *Was that really him?*

It was raining in earnest, drumming on the roofs of the long-houses and turning the ground to mud. He was free of his shackles for the night – the guards removed them once everyone was safely in the yard – but his boots let in water through the soles and his feet were cold and soaked, which made the rubbing of his blisters worse. If only the dead man had been wearing good boots.

Hugging himself for warmth, he stared through grey, wavering curtains of rain at the fence before him. It ran around the prisoners' compound, forming an inner ring of protection before the stockade itself. It was seven feet high, easy to climb if you had the will to do it. Few did. Between the fence and the stockade lived a pack of Krodan skulldogs, vicious killers who'd tear you limb from limb. Aren could hear one now, growling and grizzling nearby. Even if you could get past them, there was a walkway on the stockade wall patrolled by archers waiting to shoot anyone who tried to escape. Climbing that fence would be suicide. Escape was a fantasy.

His thoughts circled back to Klyssen again. That glimpse of him in the window had been so brief that he was tempted to doubt it. Maybe it had been a stranger who looked like him. After all, his presence made no sense. An overwatchman was the highest rank of inquisitor, second only to the Commander, head of all Iron Hand operations in Ossia. What would he be doing in a work camp in the mountains, thirty leagues from anywhere?

Has he brought a reprieve? The thought flashed into his mind. Had Klyssen come to right the injustice done to Aren and Cade? After all, their crimes were paltry. Neither of them belonged here with the dissidents and rebels, the thieves and murderers.

He snorted. An overwatchman riding all the way out here to pardon two insignificant Ossian boys? It was ridiculous. More likely he was here on some other business that had nothing to do with Aren. That, or he'd never been there at all. Exhaustion did strange things to the mind.

Best to focus on what was in front of him. Do what had to be done. Survive.

The cookhouse door squealed open and the cook's assistant, Tag, popped his freckled, horsey face out. He checked the coast was clear, then passed Aren a small cloth bag.

It was suspiciously light so Aren opened it and saw three cheese rolls inside. They were mean fare, a bit of old cheddar mashed into a ball of rough bread, but under the circumstances it was a feast.

'You said four,' he told Tag.

'Three was all I could get,' said Tag, looking affronted. 'And it's my neck on the block here. Take it or sod off.'

Aren had the suspicion he was being cheated, but he was in no position to bargain. With a scowl, he drew out two cheroots from his inner pocket. Tag snatched them off him.

'Pleasure doing business,' he said and nipped back inside.

Aren stashed one of the rolls in his pocket and put the bag under his shirt. Then he scampered to the side of the cookhouse and peered round the corner. The foul weather kept most of the guards inside, but he still needed to be careful. If he was caught with contraband he'd suffer for it.

He saw nobody but other prisoners, so he crossed the road that led from the yard to the south gate and slipped away between the buildings.

He caught up with Jan as he was leaving the laundry. Jan had a lazy eye and a ready smile, and whether by luck or by craft, he'd got himself on laundry duty five days a week, cleaning clothes for the guards. He was pushing a wooden trolley full of sacks and covered with an oilcloth, the end of which he'd pulled over his head to keep dry. He stopped pushing as he saw Aren come hurrying up.

'Got something for me?' he asked.

Aren held out the bag. 'Two cheese rolls, fresh as they come.'

Jan took the bag, rummaged under the oilcloth and pulled out a rolled-up pair of socks. They were made of thick wool and, as far as Aren could see, hardly worn.

'Fresh as they come,' Jan said with a wink.

A bell clanged somewhere in the gloom: the last bell before curfew.

'Better get on,' said Jan. Aren gave him a nod and they went their separate ways, Jan pushing his trolley, Aren towards the long-houses.

He felt his heart lighten a little as he hurried through the splattering rain. Fortune had smiled on him. He might be wet and cold and tired, but he had four cheroots, a cheese roll and a pair of good socks. Days rarely came better than this, in the camp at Suller's Bluff.

The longhouse was rank with stale sweat. The scent had seeped into the ratty blankets and permeated the thin plank walls, and no amount of airing would remove it. Prisoners shuffled between the narrow-packed bunks by the light of a single lantern, faces hollowed by shadow. Many had gone straight to sleep after returning from the mine. One man near the door had the kind of cough that wouldn't shift, and the sound of it quietened those around him. They recognised the herald of death, and it sobered them.

Aren, sodden with rain, sidled down the aisle, past loitering prisoners who hadn't yet gone to their bunks. He was headed for the far end where the glow of the lantern barely reached. When he got there, he found Cade already in bed, lying fully clothed on top of his blankets and staring vacantly at the underside of Aren's bunk.

He squatted down beside him. The men nearby were asleep, sighing and snoring, so Aren said his name quietly. Cade kept staring blankly upwards until Aren shook his shoulder, and he jerked as if shocked from a daze. When he saw Aren, he looked vaguely disappointed.

'I brought you a cheese roll,' said Aren, 'and some good thick socks.' He slipped them under the corner of Cade's pillow, making sure no one else saw. 'Days are getting colder. You'll need them.'

'Thanks,' muttered Cade, but there was no gratitude in it. It was just a word, without emotion.

Aren tried not to be irritated by that. He'd expected at least a little warmth as acknowledgement of his efforts. He could have kept the socks for himself. 'Put the socks on after lights-out or someone will take them. And eat that roll tonight: you need it.'

'Aye, I'll do that,' Cade said absently, and went back to staring at the underside of Aren's bunk.

His manner was beginning to make Aren concerned. He laid a hand on his friend's shoulder. 'What is it?'

Cade snorted. 'I don't know, Aren. What could it possibly be?' he asked sarcastically, waving to indicate their surroundings.

'I know it's bad right now,' said Aren, 'but I'll look out for you. We just have to hang on.'

'Hang on for what?'

'Till they let us out.'

Cade turned his head slowly towards Aren, face slack with disbelief. 'Is that what you think? They'll let us out?'

Aren was taken aback by his reaction. 'Well, yes. Once they realise my father was no traitor. Sora's father and the governor set him up, you know that as well as I do. Krodan justice is renowned for its rigour and fairness. It's not like the old, corrupt Ossian courts. The truth will come to light, Cade. I'm sure of it.'

Cade raised himself up on his elbows. 'You know Bard, right? The lad who works on the graves? Been here eleven years. You know what he did? Bad-mouthed the Empress when he was drunk. That's all. Gavan, the quartermaster's assistant? He was the son of a lord. They put him in here for owning a banned book. Six years now! Jottrey, on our detail, he don't even *know* what he did! They just took him away!' He was hissing with anger now. Aren had never seen him like that before. 'So let me ask you again: what are we *hanging on* for?'

'Because ...' Aren fought for an answer. 'Because it's not over. Because we're still alive.' He grew stern. 'Don't give up on me, Cade.'

Cade's face tightened with scorn. 'You still reckon everything's gonna be alright, don't you? Still believe in their system. Keep playing the game, keep pretending to be Krodan, and all this'll come undone.' He looked Aren square in the eye. 'It ain't gonna happen. They'll never let us out of here. And your da will always be dead.'

Aren was stunned by the unexpected cruelty of that.

'My da was right about you,' Cade snarled. 'You're a lost cause. They took everything you had and you're *still* a gods-damned Krodan-lover.'

He rolled over, showing his back to Aren, and after that there was nothing more to say.

13

I hate him.

Cade tried on the idea for size, wasn't sure it sat right. Da always said a bad workman blamed his tools. Take responsibility for yourself, that was what he meant. Aren never asked for his help. No one made him stand in that Krodan soldier's way.

But Nine, how he wished he hadn't.

It was a bleak morning on the yard, but they were all out in it, bellies rumbling and scalps itchy with lice and grime. A line of guards stood in front of them, swords drawn and eager for trouble. The archers on the walkway that ringed the compound had arrows nocked and ready to pull. On the far side of the yard was a tall wooden post stained with old blood and deep scratches. Deggan was tied there, Deggan with the missing front teeth he'd sold to a dollmaker for gambling money. He was lisping his way through a frantic prayer to Sarla, the Red-Eyed Child, Lady of Worms. Cade reckoned he'd be better served directing his prayers to Ogg, Aspect of Beasts. Maybe Ogg could do something about those two slavering skulldogs straining at their leashes, desperate to get at him.

Captain Hassan walked up and down before the ranked guards, addressing the prisoners. He was a big man with thick, dark brows and eyes set too close together, making him look simple. His voice was reedy and cut to the nerve, just as shrill as Cade's had been when he parodied him yesterday. Small wonder he was angry all the time, with a voice like that.

'Rules!' he cried as he stalked back and forth. 'We have rules here, and they are very clear! Rules are all that separate you from the animals.'

His Ossian was good, even if his accent wasn't. He still made that guttural back-of-the-throat sound which Krodans scattered throughout their speech. Cade had never understood Aren's love for their language. Ossian sentences glided like birds. The Krodan tongue sounded harsh and ugly to his ears, like being hit with a mailed fist.

'But rules mean nothing if they are not enforced!' Hassan went on. 'And this man broke the rules. Bribed a villager to help smuggle him out! Bad luck for him that this villager was a loyal servant of the Empire.'

A collaborator, then, thought Cade with distaste. They'd sold out a fellow Ossian for fear of being implicated in a crime. Da used to say the Iron Hand sometimes set people up that way, using Ossians to catch out their countryfolk. Tempt them into doing something illegal, then swoop. You never knew who to trust these days. That was how the squareheads liked it.

He stopped listening as Hassan ranted on. He'd heard it all before. How could Ossians be trusted if they couldn't follow the rules? If punishment was all they understood, then punishment they'd have. Like he was talking to naughty children. Like he was so damned superior.

Cade was done with all that.

I hate him.

But he didn't. He couldn't. Aren had been his friend for years. They'd had their arguments, even brawled a few times, but in the way of boys it was always forgotten in the morning, with no need for apologies. Aren had been as loyal and unfaltering as anyone could wish for. Cade just needed someone else to blame for all this misery, because the alternative was to blame himself.

What madness had made him stand up to a Krodan soldier like that? What had he hoped to achieve?

He'd thought on that question a lot in those first terrible days, but he'd arrived at no answer in the end. Perhaps he'd taken leave of his senses. Perhaps he was sick of the Krodans looming over his world, sick of submitting, the way he'd been forced to submit all his life. Or perhaps it was the thought of losing Aren, the one thing in his small-town life that wasn't mundane, the only other person who dreamed of adventure and excitement beyond Shoal Point.

Or maybe it was just because Aren was his friend, and Cade stood up for his friends, even if it wasn't always the brightest thing to do.

And look where that got you.

Overseer Krent stood at a safe distance from the dogs, his belly stretching his dark uniform jacket and a bearskin cloak across his shoulders. He looked permanently pleased with himself, a half-smile on his lips like a man well sated after a feast. The face he wore to an execution was the same face he wore when he led prayers to the Primus on Festenday, or when he assembled the prisoners to announce some new triumph in the Empire.

'There is no escape from this camp!' Hassan was saying. 'Beyond these walls, you would find cold welcome. The villagers will not help you. The road is constantly patrolled. Mountain and forest surround us, and if our dogs do not kill you, the weather or starvation surely will!'

He swept out a hand to indicate the skulldogs, as if everybody hadn't already noticed them. Two burly handlers held them back as they snapped and snarled. The dogs were thickly built, their blunt muzzles packed with fangs. They had short, black fur on their bodies and round their eyes, but white fur on their heads, giving them the skull-like mask they were named for. Krodan skulldogs were manhunters, bred for the kill. It was said they could smell Ossian blood and hungered for it, but Cade doubted that. Ossia and Kroda had been neighbours for centuries and they'd mixed together plenty. Despite the gulf of language and belief, the only real difference between Ossian and Krodan stock was that Ossians tended to darker hair and brown or green eyes, while Krodans tended to blond and blue. Even then, it was hard to tell them apart if you took away the clothes and the language and the mannerisms. Aren was dark-haired but could have passed as Krodan, he knew their ways so well. Cade was blond but as Ossian as they came. The Krodans acted like they were a separate species, but underneath they were just the same. It was more likely the dogs were trained to attack anyone in prisoners' clothes.

Deggan whimpered and prayed louder, barely able to get the words out through his fear. Cade watched without emotion. Who cared if he died? Cade had his own problems. He'd never see his parents again, and he missed his ma something fierce. His friends would have forgotten him already. Once, he'd lamented a life trapped in Shoal Point, damned to his father's workshop. What he'd give to have that back now.

Every morning, when he woke, there was a moment of disorientation before he remembered where he was. In that moment, he could briefly believe he was back in his bed at home, with the smell of breakfast wafting up from downstairs and the coastal sun shining through the curtains. Then reality would hit him, and he knew the mine awaited, and he wanted to die. Sometimes he thought he could extinguish himself by sheer force of will, but no matter how hard he tried, he just kept on living. There was only this misery of toil, and no end to it.

'Sarla, Lady of Worms, have mercy on me!'

Deggan pleaded with the Aspects, but not with his captors. He knew better than that. Hassan professed false remorse, telling him he'd brought his fate upon himself. Krent showed genial indifference, as if this were an after-dinner speech and not the prelude to the agonising murder of a human being. Cade wasn't sure which was worse.

Here's Krodan justice. Are you watching, Aren?

Of course he was. And he probably had some mud-mouthed excuse for the slaughter to come, something about how Ossians needed discipline and examples had to be made. Cade had been able to turn a deaf ear to that talk when they were back home, but he wouldn't suffer it now. Maybe Aren couldn't bring himself to blame the squareheads for what happened, but Cade could, for all the good it did him.

'*I'll look out for you,*' Aren had said; but Cade didn't *want* looking out for. Didn't need it. He was tired of Aren's relentless encouragement, angry at the mulish way he plodded into the future, dragging Cade with him. Every gift he gave Cade was a small atonement, another pebble tossed into the bottomless pit of his guilt. Each one a reminder that they were no longer the inseparable friends who'd run riot through the stone lanes of Shoal Point, who'd fought draccens and ogren, stormed imaginary castles and flirted with the local girls.

In some vague way that he couldn't articulate, he sensed he'd become Aren's redemption. Aren wanted to save him. But there was no getting out of this place, and Cade knew it.

Deggan's prayers became screams as Hassan gave the signal and the dogs were released. Cade watched them do their work, but it all seemed like it was happening at some far distance to a stranger, and he didn't feel a thing.

14

After the execution came breakfast. Even after what they'd just seen, none of the prisoners was inclined to turn it down.

They formed four lines across the yard and filed towards the cookhouse, where tureens of soup and baskets of bread had been laid out on a long table. When either time or food ran out, they'd be off to the mine. The execution had put everything behind schedule and Krodans were fastidious timekeepers, so the prisoners jostled and urged those ahead of them to be quick. When the next bell rang, those who hadn't been served would go hungry. It always paid to be near the front of the line at breakfast time.

Aren's stomach churned, and not only from hunger. He seethed with fury. He'd hardly slept last night, despite the tiredness weighing down his bones. He was too angry. He wanted to lash out but had nowhere to strike, so the rage stayed trapped inside him, heating his thoughts to violence.

Cade had wounded him. He hadn't thought a simple insult could ever cut so deep. They'd traded hard words before, but these had poison in them, and they festered. They felt like a betrayal.

His father was dead, his love for Sora proven false. The last true thing he had was Cade, a friend so stout and brave he'd stood up to the Iron Hand to defend him. It was the kind of selfless loyalty that Aren dreamed of possessing, the kind of sacrifice that made stories. It was the most heroic thing he'd ever seen. He'd hoped to repay Cade somehow, to support him through this terrible time, to be his strength when he needed it. But Cade had thrown it back in his face.

When Aren reached the front of the queue, he found Tag serving him. Tag gave him a wry smile, a generous helping of soup and one of the bigger pieces of bread. He'd enjoyed his cheroots, then. Perhaps this was his thank-you, or a form of apology for shorting him on the cheese rolls.

The man behind was hurrying him on, so he took his bowl and bread and scuttled quickly out of the yard. It wasn't wise to eat breakfast in the open, where bigger men might take it from him, and he had more than his hunger to attend to this morning. The remaining cheroots were still in his ragged coat. There had been no time to hide them last night, and only fools kept their stash in the longhouses, which were searched by guards and light-fingered prisoners alike. Carrying them around was dangerous, for if he was caught with them he'd be beaten hard. That meant he had to put them somewhere safe, and quick.

He had a likely spot in mind, a hollowed-out space behind a loose brick in the foundations of the workshop. He'd found it by accident several days ago, full of spiders and long abandoned. Whoever made it had probably died. He'd intended to take the cheroots straight there before breakfast, but Deggan's execution put paid to that.

The south gate had been opened and several horse-drawn carts were making their way across the bridge and into the camp, accompanied by a few dozen Ossian villagers on foot. There were cleaners and servants and messengers with post, carpenters for repairs and butchers bringing meat, all of them heading for the guards' section of the camp where the Krodans lived in relative comfort. On their way, they passed the bloody mass of torn flesh that had once been Deggan, still tied to the pole. Those that looked at all couldn't look upon him for long.

As he left the yard, Aren spotted Rapha standing near the gate, where the carts were being searched. The pirate didn't trouble to queue for breakfast; he had other sources and access to better food. Aren watched closely as a cart approached the gates, and a look passed between Rapha and the Krodan guard on duty. The guard gave the cart a cursory once-over and waved it through.

The driver, clearly in on the game, rolled by without so much as a glance at the guard or the pirate.

Rumour had it that Rapha had plenty of coin on the outside from his raiding days, having once captured a galleon sailing under the colours of the Baric League, loaded to the gunwales with enough gold to make a hundred men rich. Enough that his cohorts could grease a few palms, anyway. Enough that he could smuggle in luxuries and put a few guards in his pocket. If a prisoner wanted something that couldn't be got, Rapha could help. For a price.

Aren scowled at the thought of the scene he'd just witnessed. It was supposed to be Ossians who were weak-willed by nature, given to corruption, unfit for positions of responsibility. Krodans kept strict records, punished underhand behaviour and employed checks and balances to ensure their officials stayed honest. And yet here were Krodan guards turning a blind eye to a smuggler in return for coin, and barely bothering to hide it. Perhaps their system wasn't so flawless after all.

He shied away from that idea. It felt like blasphemy. The actions of a few low men didn't define an empire. Such thoughts were the work of the Nemesis, enemy of the Primus, bringer of chaos.

'*They took everything you had, and you're still a gods-damned Krodan-lover.*'

He saw Cade's face again as he said it, hateful in the gloom of his bunk. *Krodan-lover*. It was an easy insult for an Ossian to throw. Krodan-lover. Yes, he admired them; of course he did. He couldn't so easily undo his understanding of the world. He'd grown up surrounded by them, speaking their language, learning their lore. Some, like Nanny Alsa and Sora, had been dear to him. They lived in an occupied land; that was the reality. He'd rather deal with that than stay tangled in the past, mooning over forgotten ruins and hanging on to old traditions and out-of-date ideas. Ossia was no longer as it had been in their grandparents' day. The Aspects had waned and order had replaced chaos. He didn't understand why anyone would reject diligence, discipline and learning just because it came from a foreign source. It was the knee-jerk reaction of the ignorant when threatened with change.

Cade said the Krodans had killed Randill, and that should be reason enough for Aren to hate them. But he couldn't swallow that. A Krodan had killed him, yes, but his hand had been forced. After all, Randill had killed several soldiers first.

Why did you fight back, Father? Why didn't you just surrender? A judge would have found you innocent. None of this need ever have happened.

No. And none of it would have if he'd listened to Harald's warning and stayed away from Sora.

He shook himself from his reverie. This wasn't the time. If he was quick, he could stash the cheroots and still manage to eat his breakfast before the bell summoned the prisoners to be shackled and marched to the mine. Holding his bowl of cooling soup in one hand and his bread in the other, he hurried towards the workshop. Tag's generous portion had almost filled the bowl to the brim and Aren had to concentrate to avoid spilling it. He was so focused on his task that he didn't see the man step out from behind a longhouse into his path. A thump of colliding bodies, a momentary tangle of limbs, and Aren found himself flat on his back, his bowl overturned and his bread in the mud beside him. The prisoner he'd walked into had barely been rocked by the impact. Aren's heart sank as he saw who it was.

'Grub been looking for you,' he said.

He was squat, broad and ugly, with a wide, squashed nose, a heavy brow and the sly, surly face of a thug. Tattoos crawled all over one side of his face, across his shaven skull, down his throat to his chest. They covered his left arm to the fingertips, and Aren could only guess how much more of him was inked. It was the work of a master, a thorny mesh of foreign hieroglyphs and stylised pictures rendered in exquisite detail, ebbing and flowing across the skin. The only blot was the crescent of pure black arcing from cheek to cheek, across his eyelids and the bridge of his nose. That was clumsy and slapdash, marring the art on the left side of his face, as if added in by another hand without regard for what had been there before.

He was a Skarl, from the frozen lands to the north-east of

Embria, across the Baric Sea. He was also a bully and a brute, and he'd been Aren's enemy from the day he arrived.

'I see man from cookhouse smoking cheroots,' said Grub in clunking Ossian. 'Grub likes cheroots. Cookhouse man say they come from you. Where you get cheroots, little Mudslug?'

Suddenly Tag's unexpected generosity made sense. It had been an apology. Much good it did Aren, with his breakfast drooling away into the dirt. 'I found them,' he said, raising himself up on his elbows.

'You found them. Where they now?'

'I traded them.' Aren began to get up, but Grub put a boot on his chest and shoved him back down. Furiously, Aren tried to surge to his feet, but Grub kicked away his supporting hand and he crashed back to the mud. Aren glared at him, red-faced, breathing hard, enraged but unable to do anything about it.

Grub pulled up his sleeve, pointed to his tattooed forearm with one thick finger. 'See this? It say Grub killed fifteen men in one battle. Saved his wounded companion.' His finger moved to another cluster of pictograms. 'See this? This say Grub was attacked by ice bear on glacier. Ice bear end up pretty sorry when Grub turn him into tasty steaks.'

Aren seethed with frustration. He wanted to get up, to throw a punch, but Grub would just knock him down again. He was heavy with brawn where Aren was scrawny. Grub worked on the graves, so he always had dead men's clothes to trade for food. He laboured little and ate well.

'You not keep things from Grub, eh? Grub great warrior. Grub wiped better than you off his arse.'

Aren felt a sneer of defiance spread across his face. 'Picking on someone half your weight for some tired old cheroots? You *must* be a great warri—'

Grub kicked him across the face. Aren turned away at the last moment, so it was a glancing blow, but it still near broke his cheekbone and set stars exploding behind his eyes.

'Your mouth smarter than your head,' Grub told him darkly.

Aren spat blood into the dirt. 'I don't have any cheroots,' he mumbled.

'That true,' said Grub, holding up a handful of them. 'You don't.'

Aren stared. His hand went to his coat pocket. The cheroots were gone.

The Skarl showed him a mouthful of crooked teeth and brandished his prizes. 'See these?' he said. 'They say Grub damned good pickpocket.' He booted Aren hard in the gut, knocking the wind from him. 'That for holding out on me, Mudslug. I see you soon.'

Aren was still wretched and gasping in the dirt when a distant bell called him to another day of pointless, gruelling toil. Aching, battered, he picked himself up, inch by painful inch, until he was back on his feet again. The side of his face felt enormous, his head was light, one eye was swelling shut and his back was cold and soaked with mud. He clutched his ribs and shuffled off towards the yard.

Survive today. That was all he had to do. Survive.

15

'Strike harder! Strike harder!'

Aren attacked the tunnel wall with his pickaxe. His sore ribs stabbed him with every swing, his arms and back ached, his skin shone with sweat in the lantern light. The left side of his face had swollen up and was patched with ugly blues and purples, painful in parts, thick and numbed in others.

The guard had noticed his bruises and was looking for signs that he was slacking. Aren gave him nothing. He swung at the rock like it was Grub before him, as if he was burying the point of the pickaxe in the tattooed Skarl's forehead. Finally, the guard grunted, finding no fault to punish, and moved on down the line, his wooden club dangling loosely in his hand.

Cade was somewhere near the other end. They were working apart for the first time since they'd arrived. It was impossible to avoid each other entirely since Aren's bunk was above his, but they hadn't spoken since last night. Cade had seen Aren's injuries when he reached the yard for shackling, but he'd made no comment. Aren, for his part, was determined not to break the silence. Cade had wronged him, not the other way around; it was up to Cade to offer the hand of reconciliation.

The guard had gone by now, but Aren didn't let up. He swung again and again, putting all his frustration and anger into each blow.

'Ease up,' whispered the prisoner next to him in line. His name was Hendry, a gaunt, malnourished man with unshaven cheeks, much like a hundred others here. 'You'll not last the day.'

Aren ignored him. He knew overexertion was foolish. He hadn't eaten any breakfast, and if he fainted he'd be beaten or killed. It didn't matter. He couldn't stop. All the grief and rage and pain had to go somewhere. It was too much to contain.

Strike harder. So he struck, teeth gritted and eyes afire. Again, again, *again!*

With a crunch and a jolt, the stone split beneath his pick. A sliver of black rock the length of his forearm fell away and thudded to the ground. Aren stopped swinging, chest heaving, and stared at what he'd done. Elarite hid inside the hardest rock; they'd battered this wall for a season, making progress in chips and pebbles. The chunk Aren had knocked free would have taken weeks to dig out.

The men to either side gathered in and gazed at the wound Aren had made in a wall that had previously seemed invulnerable. Dusted across the black rock, faintly lustrous in the lantern light, were fat grey flecks of elarite. More than they'd ever seen in their lives.

Aren's detail were moved out of the tunnel while the engineers were called in to investigate. If a new seam of elarite had been found, plans had to be drawn up to exploit it, and they needed to assess the danger of elarite oil seeping out and flammable vapours building up. Aren and the others were dumped in a side-tunnel pending reassignment, with nothing to do but sit and rest for the remainder of the day under the watch of a bored guard. For the prisoners, it was as good as a holiday, and spirits were high.

Some of the prisoners clapped Aren on the shoulder, praising him for their good fortune. Hendry told everyone how Aren had attacked the wall like a demon, how he was stronger than he looked. Cade stayed sullen and avoided his eye. He seemed even angrier than before, as if Aren had purposely made himself the hero of the hour just to spite him.

Aren accepted the thanks of his grinning workmates and forced himself to be merry and join in with their talk. A grim face would win him no friends, no matter what he felt inside. But in those moments when he found himself alone, his thoughts turned to darker things, and his fingers strayed to his bruised face as he began to plot his revenge.

An autumn fog had settled by the time their shift ended, and they were led back to the camp through a dank, grey haze, a line of shadows filing through the murk. There were mutterings about making a break for the forest – the weather was perfect for it – but Aren heard no cry of alarm, and when they were counted and unshackled in the yard, nobody was missing.

It was Chainday, and that meant the bathhouse. They were sent there by detail, then made to strip and climb into a communal bath of freezing water piped from the river. Aren's detail was early so the water was still relatively clear; later, it would be brown and scummed with filth. He scrubbed himself and shivered, the caustic soap burning his eyes and stinging in every cut and scrape, his injuries throbbing in the cold. All around him were pale, naked men made pitiful by starvation and overwork. Three months and more had taken some of the meat from Aren and Cade, but those who'd been here longer seemed only held together by their skin.

They could feed us properly, if they wanted, said a treacherous voice in his mind. *But they know there will be more coming. Cheaper to use us up. We are called prisoners, but this is no sentence. This is a long, slow execution.*

Even that morning such thoughts would have made him afraid, as if the Primus or the Iron Hand might hear and visit greater punishment upon him. Normally he'd have argued with that voice, fought back with the wisdom of his tutors or his father, quoted from the Acts of Tomas and Toven. But anger had made him sullen and defiant, and he dared to listen to it now.

After the bath, they collected their clothes and hurried back to their longhouse to wrap themselves in blankets and warm up. Aren didn't go with them. He took station round the corner, within sight of the entrance, and waited with his arms about himself and his teeth chattering.

The fog helped to hide him as the other details came and went, cursing and beating themselves against the chill. From beyond the fence he could hear the muted barks of the skulldogs that patrolled the border of the prisoner's compound. They were silenced by an eerie wail from the peaks, the cry of something forlorn that made

Aren's skin creep. He was reminded of Cade's stories, of things that haunted forgotten places where the Divide was not so wide and the Shadowlands drew near. But he had no faith in stories today. It was probably just a wild animal.

Three details passed through the bathhouse door before Aren saw the man he was looking for. He'd grown skilled at spotting Grub after so long attempting to avoid him, and knew him in the fog by his bald head, squat body and lumbering gait. Once he'd seen Grub go in, he drew back and waited for him to emerge again, teeth clenched to still his juddering jaw. He knew he risked catching a chill, and a chill could kill you in this place, but it was a risk he'd take. Cold as he was, he was warmed by the fires of fury.

He meant to reclaim what was his, and more besides.

Grub worked on the graves. Aren knew that much about him. It was someone's idea of a joke, perhaps: Skarls were a people obsessed with death, who lived among the towering tombs of their ancestors in frosty necropolises and worshipped a deity they called the Bone God. Grave-work was highly sought after in the camp, for whenever there was burying to be done the gravediggers were excused the mine, and they had the pick of whatever the dead were carrying. Boots and clothes wore out fast and corpses had no use for them, so gravediggers always had something to trade.

With Deggan's execution that morning, the gravediggers had stayed in the camp to work while the others went to the mine. Grub would have had plenty of time to stash the cheroots he took from Aren, but little opportunity to smoke them; not unless he wanted to share them or risk the attention of the guards. No, a smart man would keep them safe until the hour before lights-out and then sneak away to enjoy them alone, somewhere deserted where nobody would be drawn by the smell of tobacco.

Grub's coat was thick enough that he'd have no need to scurry back to his bunk to warm up after his bath – besides, he'd boasted that Ossian cold was a summer's day to a Skarl – so unless Aren missed his guess, Grub would head straight for his stash. Every prisoner had a secret place where they kept everything they didn't want stolen, and Aren was betting Grub's was bulging with goods he'd taken from the dead.

Aren would follow him right to it and rob him of everything he had.

Grub was one of the first out of the bathhouse. Aren detached himself from his hiding place and slipped in among the others, keeping his eyes on his quarry. If anyone in the group noticed an unfamiliar face in the fog, they were too keen on getting back to their longhouse to care. Aren stayed with them as they hustled through muddy alleys, the fog turning the camp into a dreamlike netherworld of smeared lights and flurrying shades. The men around him clapped their hands and hugged themselves, huffing clouds of steamy breath.

After a time, Grub stepped away from the group, so quickly and smoothly that Aren almost missed him leaving. Aren felt a small triumph at predicting his opponent. *'You must think three moves ahead,'* he heard Master Fassen say. *'Know your intention before you act.'* He gave Grub a moment's head start, then followed him through the clutter of longhouses where lanterns glowed dim and blurred from square windows. They passed furtive prisoners taking advantage of the weather to carry out secret business, but Aren paid them no mind. The Skarl was a barely visible silhouette ahead of him, fading in and out of his vision. It was hard to keep him in sight, but Aren dared not get too close in case he was spotted. If Grub caught him, he'd put him in the infirmary, or worse.

They reached the northern end of the longhouses, where a strip of bare, stony ground and a drifting wall of grey awaited them. Grub headed into it without hesitation and Aren went after him.

It was only a few dozen paces from the edge of the longhouses to the graveyard, but once out of sight of the buildings the distance seemed to expand, and Aren suddenly became afraid. With no walls to define his position, the emptiness became oppressive and endless. He felt vulnerable, exposed and adrift. It was only a matter of moments, but it was enough to set Aren's heart racing, for panic to tighten his chest. Then, to his relief, crooked lines darkened ahead of him and he saw a low, rickety fence: the border of the graveyard.

He reached the fence, clutched it with both hands as if anchoring himself, and took a few deep breaths. *What was that?* he thought. *What just happened?* The nameless fear had taken him by surprise. Was it exhaustion? Lack of food? Or something deeper?

He realised with a jolt that Grub was nowhere in sight. He could see nothing beyond the fence but the leaning shadows of grave markers.

I've lost him!

He forced himself to be calm. Shivering, heart drumming against his ribs, he listened. A soft rustle came from somewhere ahead, so quiet that it could have been his imagination. He climbed the low fence and went in search of the sound. Any direction was better than none.

Small, knotty shrubs and twisted trees grew in the hollows, giant hags' claws reaching from the gloom. He knew the graveyard was little more than an enclosure at the foot of the cliffs, but it was large, and the ground was bumpy and treacherous, swollen with the remains of the dead. Grave markers surrounded him. Some were simple planks jammed in the earth with a name carved into them; others were crude cairns of piled stones. The dead who got markers were the lucky ones, those with friends who cared enough to leave something. Most went unremembered.

Something flew at his face. Instinctively he threw up his hands, and he tripped backwards and crashed to the earth as a thrashing, flurrying shape burst through the air above him. Then it was gone into the fog, flapping and croaking, and he knew it for what it was: a startled crow, nothing more.

He picked himself up, muttering in anger and clutching his ribs which hurt anew from the fall. He wiped a hand across his swollen lip – it had been dribbling all day – and looked about. He wasn't sure which direction the crow had come from, or which direction he was now facing. A glimpse of the cliff and he could have orientated himself, but the clutching fog thwarted him.

Grub was long gone. If he found his quarry now it would be pure luck, and it was just as likely the Skarl would find Aren instead, and that wouldn't end well. He was freezing and injured, and all sense told him to give up. But Aren wasn't easily dissuaded, no matter how sensible the argument, so he struck out blindly across the graveyard. If luck was all he had, then he might as well trust himself to it.

He jogged as fast as he dared between the grave markers, wary of turning an ankle on the uneven ground. The fog muffled sound and foiled echoes but he heard the rustle of crows nearby, the tap of stone on stone as a cairn settled, the hissing of the breeze off the river. A bell tolled: the last before lights-out. Aren fixed the direction in his mind as best he could. That way lay the longhouses, and he could navigate from that. He turned to head for the graveyard's centre, but suddenly his foot went from under him and he skidded down to one knee as the earth gave way and almost sent him toppling into an empty grave.

He pulled his leg out, shuffled a few yards on his arse and leaned against a pile of displaced earth. *Think*, he told himself sternly as he caught his breath. *Don't just run about. Think.*

As he was racking his brain, he saw a quick movement in the fog. A crow had hopped up onto a nearby grave marker. It strutted along the top of the plank, head jerking this way and that, one beady eye on Aren as it searched for worms.

Plenty of worms here, Aren thought bitterly.

And then it came to him. The cheroot! If Grub was coming here to smoke, then Aren would be able to smell it. It was just a matter of finding his scent. Inspired, he was about to get to his feet when there was a muted thump, and the crow disappeared.

Aren froze. A few feathers see-sawed to the ground in the spot where the bird had stood.

He rose slowly into a crouch. The fog felt heavy with threat as he crept towards a tall cairn and peered around it. The crow lay motionless on the ground in a tangle of wings.

He was about to move closer when he heard something that filled him with dread. Out in the fog, he could hear singing.

The voice was high and thin and quiet, and the words were in no language he knew, a sibilant, trilling tongue that drifted half-whispered from the white void. It sounded like a lullaby or a children's rhyme, but here among the dead it became the sinister lure of some catcher-spirit, a shade that had crossed the Divide to hunt the living. Cade's stories flooded into his head, of will-o'-the-wisps and trickster phantoms that drew lonely travellers to a dire fate. He dared not run for fear of attracting it, so he stayed where he was, hunkered behind the cairn, and prayed the owner of that voice wouldn't find him.

Something scurried between the graves. A jumble of limbs, partly seen, a creature like a spider but almost as big as he was. An instant later, it was lost in the fog again, but still the song went on, a haunting melody at the limit of his hearing, now hummed, now keened, now hissed on a breath.

Primus keep me, he begged silently, helpless before the terror of the supernatural. *Primus protect me.*

It scuttled from the fog, running low, and it was no longer a spider but something that wore the shape of a boy, a puny, tattered boy of twelve or thirteen. He had long, shaggy hair and wore a motley of ragged coats that disguised his shape. He carried a leather thong in one hand, trailing on the ground behind him: a sling. He'd taken down the crow with a stone.

A boy, then, not a monster. And yet his presence here was so bizarre that Aren couldn't bring himself to believe it. Spirits took the skins of children; Sarla herself was said to appear as a hairless girl with bright red irises, wearing a black cowled robe. So he stayed where he was and made no sound.

The boy crouched next to the crow, picked it up with both hands, and as his song came to an end, he sank his teeth into its breast.

Aren gasped, too loud. The boy looked up, directly at him, blood and feathers stuck to his chin. Aren's heart almost stopped as he was fixed with a pair of shockingly green eyes.

He bolted, running as fast and as hard as he could. He flew through the graveyard, driven by horror, expecting to be seized by some unknown force at any moment and snatched away. Vaulting the fence around the graveyard, he sprinted for his longhouse. It was only once he lay panting in his bunk that he began to believe the wild creature hadn't pursued him, and that he was, for the moment, safe.

16

Cade wasn't in his bunk to see Aren return from the graveyard. He was standing outside the door of a different longhouse, hovering uneasily in the fog, half ready to enter and half ready to walk away. Three times his courage had swelled; three times it had failed him before his hand touched the wood. He shuffled his feet and cursed, but didn't go in.

A figure emerged from the murk, a pinch-faced prisoner called Jeb. Cade was caught standing before the door, dithering like a fool. Jeb walked past him and pushed the door open with a scowl as Cade, flustered and embarrassed, turned to leave.

'You coming, then?' Jeb asked. He was holding the door open. 'Get a move on, I'm letting the fog in.'

There was nothing Cade could do but go inside.

It was a longhouse much like his own, inadequately lit and crammed with rows of bunks. But here there were strangers lying in the bunks, playing cards and idling in the aisles, and he was an intruder. Their gazes felt unfriendly as he made his way between the beds. He waited to be challenged, for some brawny arm to bar his way and prisoners to close in around him.

No challenge came. A few watched him with bored curiosity, then went back to what they were doing. None of them cared who he was, or what he was doing there. For once, Cade was glad nobody paid him any attention.

At the end of the longhouse, the bunks had been rearranged to form a den, some pushed to the walls and others turned sideways as a barrier. Several men lounged at the entrance, blocking the aisle. They were better fed than the other prisoners, bigger and stronger, and they had the surly alertness of hired muscle. One of them was the man he'd performed for yesterday, when he'd made fun of Hassan and Krent. A grin split his pockmarked face, and he leaned back and called into the den.

'Rapha! It's the funny lad!' He turned eager-eyed to Cade. 'Do Hassan again! *To the dogs with everyone!*' he screeched in a poor attempt to copy Cade's impression. Then he cackled. 'Deggan would've loved that.'

'Let him by, brother,' came the pirate's growling voice from the gloom of the den. 'He's here for business, not to dance for you.'

The man stood aside, still grinning, and Cade slid past.

Inside, the den was only a few paces wide. Three men sat on the bunks that formed the walls. One was up on the top bunk, leaning forward with his legs dangling and his face in shadow, a dark watchman overseeing those below. Rapha sat in a battered armchair, leafing through letters. Here, where Cade had thought no such luxuries existed, it might as well have been a throne.

'You read, brother?' Rapha asked, without looking up.

'Slowly,' Cade said.

Rapha sighed and squinted at the letter in his hand. 'Me, too. Between my slow readin' and their bad writin', seems I spend half my day at this.'

They? Who were *they*?

'Don't speak Carthanian, either, I take it? Any Shangi? Caraguan?'

Cade shook his head. They were far-off countries he'd only heard of in stories; the very sound of them impressed him. Rapha put the letters down and waved at a bunk, and Cade settled himself uneasily next to one of the thugs.

'So what can this humble pirate do for you?'

Cade swallowed, and asked what he'd come to ask. 'I have to get out of the mine.'

Rapha considered Cade, eyes shrewd in his weathered face, one hand absently tugging his knotty black beard. 'That's quite an ask, brother. Lot of people want to get out of the mine.'

You don't, though, Cade thought. Rapha took whatever duty he felt like, but even with all the easy jobs on offer, he sometimes chose the mine. Rumour had it he just did it for the exercise. There were lots of rumours about Rapha, and if even half were true then he was mad enough for Cade to believe it.

'I'm thinking you could put me in the workshop,' Cade said, his voice small. 'I'm a carpenter's son; I've got some skill with wood.' *Not much, but some.* 'I'd do a good job,' he added lamely.

The man next to him chuckled. 'Brother,' said Rapha, 'it's not about how good you are. You could be Athras the Carver himself and it wouldn't be a corn husk in a wheatpile to me. Question is, what can you do for me in return?'

Cade's palms were sweating and his throat was dry. 'I could make you things. Stuff you could use. Reckon I could be your eyes on the inside, tell you what's going on in there.' He saw from the look on Rapha's face that he was cutting no ice, and he began to feel desperate. He'd hoped merit alone might win him a place, but he hadn't thought what to say if it didn't. Plans were never his strong suit. It was always Aren who led the way. 'What do you want?' he blurted at last. 'I'll do whatever you need.'

'I'm hard pressed thinkin' what you *can* do,' said Rapha, with an apologetic tilt of the shoulder. 'I'm not wantin' for much within these walls. So if you can't do me no good in here, what can you do on the outside?'

Cade floundered. 'I ... I ain't sure what you mean.'

'Any rich relatives who'll pay on your behalf? Failin' that, I'll take a favour. Someone in a position of influence, someone who knows somethin' juicy, someone who can get my people on the outside somewhere they couldn't get otherwise.' He clasped his calloused hands together. 'Someone I can *use.*'

Cade struggled to think of anyone who had money, influence or any kind of special access to anywhere. But that wasn't his world.

'I'm a carpenter's son,' he said again, helplessly.

'What about your friend?' asked Rapha. 'He's no carpenter's son, that's plain. Maybe *he* knows someone who'll pay.'

Cade felt the last of his hope sink away. It always came back to Aren. Aren, who made the decisions. Aren, who had the money and the privilege and who'd ruined it all for some Krodan girl

Cade had secretly thought little of. Cade had never even been given the chance to make that mistake. He was born poor and would stay poor. His destiny was directed by others; only by clinging to Aren could he hope to change it. Cade had no value without him.

He couldn't stand alone, and that knowledge emptied him.

But he wouldn't ask Aren for help. It would be the final act of wretchedness to slink back to him that way. All that was left was the mine, the tiredness and the pain, the black horror that faced him every morning. That was all, for ever.

Rapha sat back and spread his hands. 'You're not makin' it easy for me to help you.'

Cade felt tears stealing into his eyes, his throat clamping up, and was too miserable to be ashamed of it. 'I have to get out of the mine,' he pleaded, as if the raw need in his voice might sway matters. The man next to him snickered and Rapha shot him a sharp look.

The pirate dug in his pocket, leaned forward and held up a small cylinder of waxed paper. 'Take this,' he said. 'Chew on it when you work. It'll make you feel good, feel strong, make the day pass like a dream. That'll last you the week. Come back after, and we'll talk.'

Cade knew what it was. Ragweed. He opened his mouth to say he didn't want it, because the very thought of it scared him; but he didn't know how to reject a gift from a man like Rapha.

'I know why you're here, brother,' the pirate said. 'Threw yourself in the path of the Iron Hand for your friend. Wouldn't be the first time a commoner paid the price for the doin's of the highborn.' He took Cade's hand and put the packet of ragweed into his open palm. 'There's no nobles in Rapha's kingdom, but even the lowliest man gets to feel like a lord. You don't have to suffer any more.'

The unexpected sympathy made Cade's eyes well up again, and he lowered his head to hide it. Rapha folded his fingers closed over the ragweed plug, then sat back in his chair.

'Thank you,' Cade whispered.

17

The next day dawned bright and clear, and though the air was cold, the sun warmed the prisoners' faces as they made their way up the mountain to the mine. Aren had passed a restless night, haunted by dreams in which a tattered boy with bright green eyes watched him malevolently from the rafters. But in the safety of the light, his fears faded, and he confided what had happened to Jan, who was on mining detail that day.

'You saw Rags?' Jan exclaimed, loud enough for others to overhear.

Hendry, Aren's dishevelled workmate, leaned in. 'You saw the dead boy?'

'Other people have seen him, then?' asked Aren, wiping his nose with the back of his hand. He'd caught a cold from his escapades last night and it had given him a foggy head.

'They'll *tell* you they did,' Hendry said, with a pointed look at Jan.

Jan gave Hendry a hurt look, or possibly Aren; his lazy eye made it hard to tell. 'I saw him, right enough. Coming from behind the cookhouse. It was after curfew, but we'd had a fever through the camp and had to boil all the sheets. Hassan gave us passes so we could get them done that night. I was pushing a load to the laundry and he came darting out like a rat!'

'That, or the lye fumes went to your head,' Hendry scoffed.

Jan gave a sullen glare to Hendry, probably. 'Scared me rigid, he did. And I ain't the only one who's seen him, either!'

'So who is he?' Aren asked.

'He's the shade of a Sard boy,' Jan said. 'It's the eyes, see? All Sards got that colour eyes. Unsettling folk, they are, at the best of times; twice as much when they're dead.'

The eyes. Aren should have made the connection himself. A family of Sards used to pass through Shoal Point with pedlars' stalls now and then, and sometimes a group of caravans would appear on the common for a few months, much to the annoyance of the locals. They were called thieves and tricksters, dirty folk without morals, but the more daring and rebellious townsfolk would associate with them, drawn by their mysterious nature. There was talk of wild nights of music and dancing in their camp, and those who visited came back with strange and unlikely tales of sorceries and bewitchments. Then one day the Sards would be gone without warning, leaving nothing but rumours behind. Aren remembered their visits from his childhood, but they'd stopped coming in recent years and Aren hadn't thought of them for a long time.

'Why would the ghost of a Sard be here?' Aren asked. 'No Sards in this camp.'

'Ah, but there used to be!' Jan said. 'It's not just Ossians buried in that dirt!' He tugged the arm of a prisoner walking ahead of them, a weary-looking grey-bearded man who might have been in his forties or his sixties. 'Farrel, tell him!'

'Don't drag me into this,' Farrel said over his shoulder. Aren knew him by reputation. He was a political prisoner, a scholar who'd spoken out against the Krodan regime. 'Ghosts and shades and such. There are enough terrible things in this world without making up imaginary ones.'

'Tell him about the *Sards*!' Jan urged, undeterred.

Farrel sighed heavily. It was best to give in to Jan's pestering early. Whether you resisted or not, the result was the same. 'It's true. There were Sards in this camp once. The Krodans kept them in a separate compound, over by the latrines. They weren't ever let out, not to work in the mine, nor to mix with the other prisoners. At first there were fifty or sixty, women and children, too. Then more started coming, a *lot* more, brought in on wagons, until they were crammed in that compound like chickens in a coop.'

'Why were they arrested?' Aren asked. 'What did they do?'

'What did any of us do?' said Farrel, gazing at the thick, dark forest, streaked with hazy sunlight as the morning mist lifted. 'What did *you* do? Does it matter?'

Aren thought it did, since he was innocent and had little sympathy for the criminals and traitors incarcerated here; but he kept his silence.

'You'd see them at the fence begging for food,' said Farrel, his tone turning darker. 'The new arrivals, anyway. The rest had given up trying. There wasn't any spare food to be had, and if there was, you could bet it wouldn't go to a Sard. Most of them just sat there, like they were waiting for something. The children cried but there was nothing to be done for them. No one knew why they were there, since they weren't being put to work.'

Farrel's eyes had become unfocused, and Aren knew he was seeing those scenes again. 'Two years ago – maybe three – we woke up to find the villagers taking the fence down around the Sard compound. They'd all been moved on in the night. No word of where they went, and not many missed them. Ossian prisoners were moved into the Sard longhouses, and that was the end of it.' He shrugged and turned away.

'And that's when Rags appeared!' Jan jumped in. 'He's the shade of some Sard boy buried in the graveyard, and his ma got taken away. So now he wanders the camp at night, searching for her. And he kills crows, 'cause everyone knows the crows work for Sarla. He don't want them telling the Lady of Worms where he is, in case she calls him away before he's found what he's looking for.'

Hendry gave a snort that showed what he thought of that.

'He's no shade,' said Farrel. 'Plenty say they've seen him. Must be blessed with the Mummer's own luck to have made it this long in the camp, though.'

Jan blew out his lips derisively. 'One Sard boy surviving this whole time on his own? I'd believe anything over that.' He looked around. 'Where's Cade? He'd know what manner of shade Rags is.'

Aren felt a knot grow in his stomach. 'He's about somewhere,' he said, and said no more.

★

Aren's detail were told on arrival that they'd been reassigned to a new location. The route there was different, but little else was. It was another dank, tight, gloomy tunnel held up by splintered beams, from which hung lanterns low enough for a man to hit his head on. A pair of cavepipers fluttered in a rusty cage. Yesterday they'd won a victory over their unyielding enemy, the mountain. Today brought a new wall, and it was as if they'd gained no ground at all.

They set to work again, and Aren swung his pickaxe steadily, not too fast and not too slow. He had no desire to repeat his feat of yesterday. His anger had burned off overnight and he no longer sought to punish himself. The cheroots were a lost cause and his business with Grub was unfinished, but that could wait. There was a more important matter. Cade.

He looked down the line and saw Cade hard at it, swinging with rare enthusiasm. Usually he was dull-eyed with misery as he laboured, but today his gaze was bright and fierce. Aren wondered if it was a change for the better, or for the worse. Either way, he intended to find out.

The sting of Cade's words had faded with time; the beating he'd taken from Grub and the encounter in the graveyard had put things into perspective. He and Cade had to stick together if they hoped to survive in this place. A friendship of half a lifetime shouldn't be broken by a few harsh words. He was determined to reconcile them, and if Cade wouldn't ask forgiveness, then Aren would be the bigger man and forgive.

Yet what was so simple and clear in his mind was muddy and frightening in real life, and he felt sick at the thought of it. To speak from the heart required more bravery than any physical risk. To heal a wound was so much harder than to cause one. But he'd do it, because it had to be done. He wanted his friend back.

His opportunity came when they took their break. A prisoner was picked for slop duty, and the others rested against the tunnel walls while they waited for their meagre lunch. Their guard was talking with another guard, barely paying attention to his charges.

Cade sat on his own, forearms resting on his knees, head hanging, nodding as though to some rhythm in his mind. Perhaps one of the Ossian folk songs he'd been fond of blaring drunkenly in the Cross Keys during better times. Aren slipped up the tunnel and dropped down next to him. 'We ought to talk,' he said.

Cade tilted his head to the side, enough to show one hostile eye. Then he looked back at the ground between his feet, toes tapping restlessly, hands twitching in time.

So Cade would give no ground. Well, Aren would say his piece anyway. 'Listen to me,' he said. 'I know it's my fault that you're here, and—'

'It ain't,' Cade muttered.

Aren frowned. 'Sorry?'

'Ain't your fault. I did it. It was *my* choice.'

'Uh...' Aren's planned apology had already fallen apart. 'You're right, of course it was your choice. I just meant... because of me and Sora...'

'You really think the moons and the stars revolve around you,' Cade hissed, raising his head. His face was shadowed and scornful in the weak light. 'Like your life is a bard's tale with you at the centre. What if it ain't, though? What if all this had nothing to do with you?'

Aren couldn't understand where this was coming from, or indeed what he was talking about. It was so far from sense that he didn't know where to begin.

'You think the Krodans have it right, ain't that true?' Cade went on. 'Think they've got the measure of the world, better than us Ossians ever did. You trust in their justice.'

'I mean...' Aren was struggling. 'I never said it was a perfect system, but it's the best we ha—'

'So what if they knew what they were doing when they came to your house, eh?' Cade snapped, talking over him. 'What if justice was done? What if your da *was* a traitor?'

Aren went cold, and his voice became flinty and sharp with threat. 'My father was a good man.'

'You can be a good man and a traitor both,' said Cade. ''Specially if you're ruled by a bunch of squarehead scum who murdered your queen, stole the Ember Blade and put your people under the boot.'

Aren had never witnessed such bald sedition. It shocked and

frightened him to hear it from his friend. 'Take that back!' he cried; but he wasn't sure if he meant the accusation against his father, or against the Krodans.

But Cade wouldn't be stopped. He was in full flow now, his voice rising, and he was *grinning*. 'Think about it, Aren! Your da was away all the time. He could have been doing anything! And didn't you say he was up near Salt Fork when the rebels took that town? He was, wasn't he?'

Their argument had drawn the attention of the nearby prisoners, and even the guard glanced over and scowled. But Aren couldn't quiet himself. He'd believed he could suffer any abuse, absorb any blow to win his friend back, but he was wrong. All his good intentions were pushed aside as rage swelled uncontrollably. He wanted to drive a fist into the face of the stranger before him. This leering, cruel impostor wasn't the friend he knew.

'My father was loyal! He raised me like a Krodan!'

'Aye, just what I'd do if I wanted to keep my son in the dark.'

'You're lying!' He wouldn't listen, wouldn't let it be true. And yet there was a horrifying kind of sense to it, if he dared to admit the possibility. Could it be that his rendezvous with Sora had never been discovered, that her father had said nothing to the governor? His father had seemed hunted the night of the ghost tide, and that was *before* Aren met with Sora. Had he read something in those letters Aren hadn't dared ask about? Had he known what was coming?

What if justice had been done, and a traitor had been executed?

Cade pushed the knife in. 'For all your money and education, you're as helpless as I am.' He was gloating, actually *gloating*. 'Know why? Because you're an Ossian. They'll let you dream of being like them, but all it takes is a wave of their hand and it's all gone. I reckon your da knew that. Reckon he was a better man than I gave him credit for. At least he fought back.'

Aren lunged at him, seizing him by the throat and driving him up against the tunnel wall. He drew back his fist to silence Cade, but the blow never fell because Cade was giggling now, a high, manic giggle tinged with madness. Aren saw his tongue move as he shifted something between his gum and lip, then began to chew.

The pieces fell into place. Cade had been behaving strangely all along, but Aren had been too wound up to see it.

'What have you done?' Aren breathed.

'You two! Settle down!' the guard shouted in Krodan from along the tunnel. It was plain he didn't want to leave his conversation to deal with them, but the disturbance had become too much to ignore.

Aren paid no attention. His fury had gone out like a candle, snuffed by anxious disbelief. 'You're using ragweed? Are you mad? Don't you know what that does to you?'

Cade stuck out his tongue to show Aren the soggy wad of black weed there. His smile said: *I don't care.*

'You won't last a year chewing that stuff!' Aren was pleading now. He could barely believe his friend had done this, that he'd surrender this way. 'You'll work yourself to death and you won't even know it!'

'We're already dead,' Cade said. 'Both of us. I'm just making it easy on myself.'

'We're *not* dead!' Aren shouted. 'I won't *let* us die!'

'You can't stop it,' said Cade bitterly. 'You can't do a thing.'

'Curse you, that's enough!' snapped the guard. He came storming up the tunnel, club in hand. The other prisoners shrank back against the wall.

Cade and Aren hardly noticed. 'You keep waiting, if you like,' Cade sneered. 'Keep waiting for Krodan justice to set you free. I'm done.'

Aren grabbed the front of Cade's shirt, stared hard into his eyes. 'You're not giving up, Cade,' he said. 'You're not.'

Cade laughed hysterically in his face.

'I warned you, you eel-eating sons of dogs!' the guard shouted as he closed on them. He raised his club, ready to bring it down on Aren's head. Aren threw up an arm in instinctive defence, but it was too late to escape the blow. He braced himself for the impact—

And the guard froze as a twittering, urgent melody danced through the air. Slowly he turned his head towards the cage where the cavepipers were kept, hanging from a hook driven into one of the beams.

The cavepiper sang again. It fluffed its breast feathers in agitation and its companion sang back. Two dozen terrified men watched their every move.

Together, they burst into a frenzy, flapping against the bars of the cage, shrilling the alarm that all elarite miners dreaded to hear.

It was the trigger for chaos. The prisoners surged to their feet, shouting in alarm, some pushing down others in their haste. The guard forgot about Aren and Cade and ran for his life in the direction of the mine entrance. His colleague, who'd been guarding a detail in the next tunnel, tried to follow but ran into the crush of prisoners and was felled by an elbow. There was no fear of Krodans now. Sarla herself stood among them.

Aren hauled Cade up with him. Even now, Cade struggled to throw him off, resenting his touch; but Aren held on until Cade was upright. The cavepipers were silenced as their cage was knocked from its hook and crushed underfoot. Someone screamed to put out the lantern, douse the flames. A panicked prisoner smashed it where it hung, but instead of bringing darkness, flaming streaks of oil lashed through the air, splattering skin, setting sleeves and trousers afire.

The tunnel turned hellish, echoing with screams and lit by the flailing shapes of burning men. A jumbled tide of limbs and shoulders swept Aren and Cade along. People tried to run, but the shackles round their ankles were too short and they tripped. A prisoner fell against Aren and he staggered and went to his knees, the man's weight across his back. He fought to rise, thrashing with frantic strength, knowing that to go under would mean never coming back up. The prisoner slid off his back and was lost beneath the boots of the stampede. Aren surged to his feet and plunged onwards as the people behind him tumbled over the fallen man and were trodden down in their turn.

Frightened, desperate faces lurched around him. He searched for Cade's, but in the jostle he'd lost him. Ahead was a dim light, the mouth of a larger chamber where the walls widened, promising relief from the deadly crush. He was carried into it and immediately moved to the side, where he stood, panting, scanning the crowd as they passed, looking for his friend.

The chamber was at the junction of several tunnels, one with the entrance painted yellow, indicating the way out. The prisoners hurried for it as fast as their shackles would allow, falling and getting up again, desperation pushing them onwards. But Aren wouldn't leave until he was sure his friend was safe. All the hard words they'd traded were irrelevant, now the cavepipers had sung.

Where is he?

He felt a sudden pressure inside his ears; his hearing went dull; the skin of his cheeks crawled as he sensed disaster. Then there was a sound from deep in the mine like the footfall of a god, and the mountain shook hard enough to make Aren stagger. A plume of black dust and smoke, shot through with licks of fire, blasted out of the tunnel into the chamber, knocking prisoners flat. Behind it came a crunching, tumbling thunder, as if Meshuk herself, Aspect of Earth and the fires within, was grinding her stone teeth. It tailed away gradually until, at last, a kind of silence returned. By then, the only ones left in the chamber were the fallen and the injured, moaning and sobbing as they tried to pick themselves up again. The fallen, the injured, and Aren.

He coughed as he drew in a lungful of dust. The mountain groaned and cracked uneasily, and every instinct screamed at him to run towards the light. There could be another explosion at any time. The ceiling might collapse and crush him. A rockfall could block the way out, entombing him in a black void beyond imagining.

Yet still his feet took him back towards the entrance to the tunnel, because he hadn't seen Cade escape, and so he couldn't be sure.

The tunnel was dark, but lit in patches by flickering spots of flame where oil still burned. Smoke and glowing particles swirled in the air. He heard moaning from within, the sound of trapped and wounded men scraping and scratching as they tried to claw themselves free. One wall had collapsed inwards, obstructing the tunnel but not blocking it entirely.

It stank of charred pork in there. Hungry as he was, his stomach turned. That wasn't pig cooking.

He hesitated at the threshold. Going on was idiocy. Cade was probably halfway to the outside by now; there was no reason to think otherwise. Yet there was something stronger than fear driving him. For all that he dreaded dying down here in the dark, the thought of abandoning Cade was worse. If there was even a chance that he was in there, Aren couldn't turn away. Though all sense railed against it, he stepped into the tunnel.

The dead lay about his feet, scorched and torn. He made himself look at them. Blank eyes stared from bloody and blackened faces. Some he recognised. One of them was Hendry.

A prisoner waved the stump of an arm. He sounded like he was trying to call out, but he could only manage strangled gasps. *Help him*, said the sly voice of cowardice. *You can't leave him like that. Help him to the entrance and the light. Then you can see if Cade is outside.*

Afterwards, he told himself. After he'd made sure. He steeled his will and went on.

The timbers of the beams overhead creaked ominously as he eased around the fallen wall. Beyond, the tunnel continued for a short way before ending in a mass of tumbled stone. The beams had split beneath the sagging ceiling and the poles that supported them were splintered and broken, unable to bear the terrible weight of the mountain.

'Just to the end,' he said to himself. If Cade wasn't there, then he could do no more.

The air reeked of burning fat. A corpse, face down, still flickered with flame and shadows jumped back and forth, setting the scene in queasy motion. He made his way deeper into the tunnel, searching the faces of the dead, hoping with all his heart that he wouldn't see Cade among them.

He heard men groaning, saw some of them stir. A prisoner he didn't know lurched out of the gloom and staggered past him as if he wasn't there. Horror pressed in on all sides, shortening his breath, forcing itself upon his senses. He flinched away as a tongue of flame ignited in the air above a burning spot of lamp oil. There was still fire-fume in the tunnel, and it could be building back up to explosive levels already.

'Just to the end,' he whispered again.

He found a Krodan guard trampled to death beside a half-starved Ossian who'd died the same way. It was said that death made all men equal, but their condition and their clothing told a different story. Only one of them wore shackles.

Aren stared at those shackles. He wondered how many more would have escaped if they'd been able to run. Instead they died down here, chained like animals, far from the touch of the sun. Whatever crimes they'd committed, nobody deserved such a fate. Krodans would never treat their own people so harshly, but they thought it acceptable for Ossians. Something in his gut curdled and turned bitter at that. How could their masters condone something so barbaric?

A wounded guard further down the corridor saw him and began begging for help. Aren turned towards him, but his heart jumped as he spotted Cade instead, lying motionless on his side, one arm flung across his face. Aren hurried over, shackles clanking, the guard's cries ignored.

'Cade! Cade, I'm here!' He dropped to his knees next to his friend. A grin of relief broke across his face as he saw Cade's chest rise. He patted Cade's cheek, felt the ragweed plug behind his lower lip. On a reflex, he dug out the soggy wad and flung it away in disgust. 'Cade!' he said again, and patted him harder. Cade's head lolled to the side and Aren saw blood in his blond hair. Relief faded into dread.

There was a long, loud creak above them. Aren looked up at the bowing beams that held up the tunnel and knew their time was short. He had to get Cade out of there. Now.

His bruised ribs blazed with agony as he hauled Cade from the ground, and he gritted his teeth to hold back a cry of pain. He shifted Cade's weight onto his back, draping his arms over his shoulders, and stood with a grunt of effort. Cade didn't weigh what he once had, but Aren wasn't as strong, either. It was sheer determination that powered him back down the tunnel, step by shuffling step.

The ceiling cracked as the beams split further. The guard began screaming as he saw Aren leaving him, but Aren had no help to give. He stumbled between the dead and the mutilated, murmuring a prayer to the Primus that the rock would hold long enough for him to get out. But the sound of Krodan prayer in his ears rang horribly false today, and he found he couldn't continue. His words petered out and he fell silent.

He wouldn't ask for help from the Primus. There was no point.

In that moment, something changed within him, deep down in his soul. He'd prayed to the Primus all his life, and all the more fervently after he arrived here, begging for some intervention to save them. No answer had come, no hope was offered, but he prayed anyway, because that was all he had. Now, for the first time in his life, his prayers felt empty, just words thrown against the dark. The Primus was a Krodan god, and the Krodans put those shackles on Aren's legs. The Krodans were responsible for what had happened to Cade.

The Primus didn't care about Ossians. Not even those who tried their hardest to be Krodan. And if the Primus didn't care about him, then he was no god of Aren's. Instead, in his desperation, he directed his appeal to Meshuk, in whose domain he found himself. At least she was a goddess of his own people.

Stone Mother, save us. I've never worshipped you, but the one I carry does. Let us out of here, and I swear I'll never scorn you again.

He dragged Cade past the collapsed wall and saw the entrance to the chamber ahead, and safety. Inspired by the sight, he hurried on, but was tugged back and almost fell as his shackles snagged on a dead man's boot. He kicked frantically and freed himself, but then he heard a low groan above him and knew the ceiling was about to give. With ferocious effort he surged onwards, an animal cry escaping him as he staggered past his dead countrymen, Cade on his back. Hampered by the shackles, his balance escaped him and he began to tip forwards, but by some unknown grace his feet stayed under him for the distance, and when he toppled, he fell out of the tunnel mouth and into the chamber beyond.

The pain of the impact was drowned out by the terrifying roar from behind him as the tunnel finally caved in. Dust and rock shards billowed all around him, stones crashed and tumbled, and all Aren could do was fling his hands over Cade's head and tuck his own in, his thoughts lost in the white light of fear.

But when it was done, and the last of the rocks had stopped rolling, he was still alive.

Aching, panting, he raised his head and looked over his shoulder. Where there had once been a tunnel was only piled rubble. Cade was by his side, still unconscious but whole.

Slowly, painfully, he got to his feet, staring at the tunnel in disbelief. Mere instants had separated them from death; it didn't seem possible that they'd come so close and survived. Then Cade coughed weakly, and Aren was pulled back to the moment. Cade was still injured, perhaps badly, and there was yet work to do. He hauled his friend up once more and began the long, slow journey to the light.

18

It had begun to rain by the time the prisoners returned to the camp. A fine drizzle misted the grim, unshaven faces of the men filing through the east gate. They trudged across the guards' section beneath the gaze of Overseer Krent, who watched from his mansion with that omnipresent smile of self-congratulation on his lips, as if this were a day like any other.

Once in the yard, with the gate to the guards' section securely locked behind them, they hugged themselves and stamped their feet for warmth while they waited to be unshackled. As they were released, Captain Hassan ordered them back to their longhouses until dinner, and most were happy to oblige; they were worn out and weighed down by tragedy, and they wanted the sanctuary of their bunks. When it came to Aren's turn, he made his way obediently out of the yard, but as soon as he could, he darted off into the alleys and headed for the infirmary instead.

His boots splashed through shallow puddles as he hurried through the back ways of the camp, blistered feet rubbing inside wet socks. Every part of him ached. Those muscles that weren't already bruised had been strained by carrying Cade out of the mine. He longed for his bed like the others, but rest was out of the question until he knew his friend was alright.

That afternoon had been the longest of his life. In the chaos that followed the explosion, the Krodans had been too busy keeping the prisoners under control to tend to casualties. Only when the rest of the guards from the camp arrived, and the Ossians were safely corralled outside the entrance to the mine, did they begin to load the wounded onto carts. Aren saw Cade, still unconscious, bundled in among men with broken limbs and deep gashes and taken away down the mountain. Those beyond help were hauled aside and abandoned, screaming, until Hassan ordered a guard to put them out of their misery. They were slain within sight of their countrymen, each despatched with a short, efficient sword-thrust between the collarbones, into the heart. The men that were last begged for mercy, but their executioner went on with his work until there was silence. He returned grey-faced, and his hand shook as he cleaned and sheathed his sword.

There was little talk among the prisoners after that. They were left under guard outside the mine while other matters were attended to. Hours dragged by. Clouds slid in from the west and Aren was left with nothing to do but dwell on Cade's condition. When they were finally collected by a double-strength escort for the trip back to the camp, Aren couldn't get to his feet fast enough.

The infirmary was a simple, flimsy wooden building standing near the south gate. The road from the gate to the yard was cluttered with carts, busy with villagers from across the bridge and prisoners who hadn't been in the mine. Men hurried from the laundry with bundles of sheets to use as bandages, under the watchful eyes of the archers on the stockade walkway. The camp was in a state of emergency, and in the confusion nobody saw Aren make his way to the infirmary and thump on the door.

It was opened almost immediately by a plump-cheeked Ossian girl with her hair bundled up under a cloth cap and bloody handprints smeared on her smock.

'I need to see my friend,' Aren said.

'We're too busy for visitors.' She began to close the door, but Aren grabbed it.

'Please,' he begged. 'I just need to know if he's well. He's about our age, thickset, dark blond hair … He was unconscious, with a head wound. His name is Cade of Shoal Point.'

She looked him over uncertainly. 'And you are?'

'Aren,' he said. 'Of Shoal Point.'

Understanding dawned in her eyes. She looked over her

shoulder, into the infirmary, then back at Aren. 'Can you make yourself useful?'

'Yes!' he said, relief making him eager. 'I'll help any way I can.'

She sighed, as if exasperated by her own kindness. 'Come on, then,' she said. 'We could do with another pair of hands.'

The infirmary was laid out much like a longhouse, but twice as wide. Rows of bunks were filled with groaning casualties, and the air was pungent with blood and the sharp stink of poultices and medicines. Villagers and prisoners alike hurried between the beds, carrying buckets and bandages, pausing here and there to offer the touch of a hand or a word of comfort. As Aren entered, he passed a small room where a lanky, balding apothecary was taking down a phial from shelves that were almost empty.

'You know anything about the healing arts? Not shy of blood, are you?'

'I learned how to clean and staunch a wound as part of my sword training,' Aren said. 'And we studied a little from Harvik's *Anatomy*.' Not that he remembered any of it.

She gave him a look that was both surprised and impressed. 'Maybe we *can* use you. We're short-handed and short-stocked. Only me and the doctor know how to set a bone or stitch, and I'm only an apprentice yet.'

She indicated a short elderly man with spectacles and a long white beard, dressed in a frayed jacket and trousers that were too short for him. He was leaning over a patient and muttering to himself. Doctor Baden was feared – as all doctors were feared by Ossians, who had little grasp of Krodan methods of healing – but those he'd treated said he was gentle and wise.

'You're studying Krodan physic?' asked Aren, surprised and impressed in his turn.

'Aye. Beats the herbcraft the old mothers teach.'

'But you're … er …'

'A woman? Well spotted. The doctor doesn't hold with the Krodan idea that women are only good for staying at home and raising children. I'll never go to the Glass University, and I'll never hold a title, but at least when the doctor's gone there'll be someone in Suller's Bluff who can do more than crush up a few foul-smelling roots, pray to the Aspects and call it a remedy. Speaking of which, there's a druid about. Did you know?'

Aren, distracted by searching for Cade among the bunks, was taken off-guard by the question. 'Uh, no. Between the imprisonment and the relentless toil, we don't get much news,' he said absently.

She laughed loudly, making him jump. It seemed jarringly out of place amid all this suffering, and yet it was pleasing to hear, a welcome antidote to the sounds of pain.

'You should keep your ear to the ground,' she advised, an amused gleam in her eye. 'All kinds of thrilling things you might miss.'

Aren couldn't help a faint smile. He liked her. She moved quickly and talked quickly and her face was lively and mobile. It had been a long time since Aren encountered anyone with vigour to spare.

She carried on talking as she dodged between the bunks, leading him further in. 'I've lived in Suller's Bluff since I was a cribling, but I've never seen a druid. Thought they'd all died out, to be honest. But now Red Mabel says she's seen the signs in the forest, and Brak Steeltooth swears he laid eyes on one, though he's half-blind these days, so it's just as likely it was a bear. Still' – she scratched under her cap – 'there's *something* out there. The animals have been acting spooked ever since the season turned, and you hear cries off the peaks at night that don't come from any wolf or beast I know.'

'I see them!' A shriek lifted above the moans and the pleas of dying men calling for their mothers. 'I see them!'

'There's your friend now,' she said, 'making his racket.' A moment later, Aren saw him, lying on a low bunk in the corner of the room. His head was bandaged and he was awake, but his eyes were wide and he was staring at something no one else could see.

'They stalk the shifting lands around me!' he shouted, and thrust out a finger to point at nothing. 'Skin thin as tissue, eyes dead as stone!' His voice dropped to a conspirator's whisper. 'They can't see me. Not unless I show myself. But I never will!'

Aren hurried to him, alarmed. 'What's wrong with him?' he asked as he knelt down by Cade's side.

'We don't know. He took a bad knock but he's not carrying a fever, and there's no other injury we can find. Best we can guess is that his wits have been addled by the blow to the head.'

'Will it pass?' Aren asked, distraught.

'Maybe,' she said, with optimism. Then her face fell a little and she said: 'Maybe not.'

'Kel!' A young Krodan boy came hurrying up. 'The doctor needs you. Amputation.'

Kel became brusque and businesslike. 'Keep him quiet as best you can. Talk to him, let him hear the voice of someone he knows. It might bring him back to sense.'

'Doctor Baden says to see the apothecary on the way,' the boy told her in Krodan as they hustled off.

'Draccen tears?'

'Yes.'

Aren was left gazing helplessly at Cade as he rolled his eyes and raved.

'I've walked the streets of Carradis, jewel of the Second Empire, where the blood of the Sorcerer Kings flows in the gutters,' Cade said. 'I've seen the undercities of the urds where my ancestors were enslaved, and walked in the shadow of Ashgrak's mountain where his body smoulders still! But this is no place for the living; only ghosts tread these lands!'

Aren seized his friend's hand, clasped it in both of his. The sight of Cade in such a state frightened him. It would be too much to bear if Aren had rescued him from death, only to condemn him to madness.

Talk to him, Kel had said. And say what? His mind was a blank.

'Cade!' he said. 'Cade, do you hear me? Do you know where you are?'

'The Shadowlands! Where castles melt like wax and oceans turn to steam.'

'No, no! You're in the infirmary, Cade. And I'm right here.'

'I feel them, stirring in their prison!' He sat up suddenly, clasped Aren's forearm and stared hard into his eyes, features slack with fear. 'The Outsiders!' he shrieked. Then he flung himself down on his yellowed pillow and began to mumble gibberish.

'You're dreaming,' Aren said, his voice weak and pleading.

And yet he wondered if that were true. Was it not said that the mad were shade-touched, that their souls had strayed across the Divide into the Shadowlands where the spirits dwelled? Once, he'd have dismissed such thoughts as legends and superstitions, fragments of a fallen empire. Ossian fancies that didn't belong in the new order of things. But he wasn't so sure of himself any more.

He clasped Cade's hand harder, willing him back from the brink. There was a time when life hadn't been a bleak, grinding procession of days, when they'd run free with the sun on their faces and the breath of the sea in their ears. Aren wanted to be back there now, more than anything, and it was that yearning which finally loosened his tongue.

'You're not in the Shadowlands,' he said. 'You're not in the infirmary, either. I'll tell you where you are. Remember the shipwreck, Cade? That old elaru galleon on the beach at Shoal Point? That's where we are. Both of us. And I'm hiding, I'm hiding from Darra and Ged and Ham. You remember that day? I bet you do. That was the day we met...'

The ship's name was *Wave Dancer*, or so old Mattoc the Learned told the town before he died, and it was said he could read the tongue of the elaru. It was also said that it had been on the beach since the days of Kala the Dawnwarden, who kept watch from the tower on the cliffs, and that it was a remnant of the invasion force she helped repel. That was less probable, for even elaru galleons would rot and break after so many centuries. More likely it had been driven onto the coast by a storm, but that didn't make for such an exciting tale, so most of the townsfolk preferred the other explanation.

There were other tales about the *Wave Dancer*, too. Dark tales that crowded the mind of the eight-year-old boy racing towards it.

That boy was Aren, all limbs and angles, his arms pumping as his sandals pounded the hot sand. To his left were the cliffs, patched with hardy salt-loving shrubs, where petrels fussed about their nests. To his right was the sea, bright beneath the burning blue sky of a summer afternoon. Behind him were three boys with sticks in their hands, baying for his hide.

Ged, Ham and Darra had chased him all the way from the town and down the switchback wooden stairs from the cliffs. An hour ago they'd been playing seek-and-tap through the winding stone alleys of Shoal Point, darting like cats among the bun-sellers. It had been Aren's idea to play and they'd followed his lead, as they usually did. But then the day had turned, and they'd turned on him, and now Aren was on the run. He'd get more than a tap if they caught him.

The galleon loomed before him. It had foundered on the rocks not far from the shore and listed to starboard with its prow tilted upwards. The impact had toppled the masts, and the stern had broken free and lay half-submerged nearby. Barnacles encrusted its hull below the tidemark; droppings splattered its decks; sea air and sun had bleached and chewed its planks and gunwales. Yet it was still elegant in its ruin, a sleek silver vessel built by strange crafts unknown to men.

Looters had long since taken anything of value from inside, but the carcass had remained largely undisturbed. Elaru whitewood defeated all but the hardest saws, harder than anyone in Shoal Point possessed, and it was thought to bring ill fortune to those who took it into their homes. Stories were told of an elaru captain who'd been pierced through the heart by a broken spar when his ship ran aground, whose shade walked the decks with a witch-iron sabre, ready to slay any humans foolish enough to find themselves aboard when night fell.

Beyond the shipwreck, the beach tapered into the sea and the cliffs reached out to cut off the sand. There was nowhere for Aren to run, nowhere to hide from the beating that was coming.

Nowhere but the galleon.

The tide was out and the rocks that had smashed the hull were exposed, a jagged ridge that humped out of the sea onto the beach like the spine of some buried leviathan. Chest heaving beneath his sweat-damp shirt, Aren climbed the ridge and scrambled out towards the decayed and brooding hulk.

'Where are you going, Aren?' Ged cried as they reached the feet of the rocks. 'Come back and get what's owed you!'

'Watch out for the captain's shade!' Darra called gleefully.

'Don't be stupid! It's dangerous in there!' pleaded Ham, who was kind-hearted and quite fond of Aren, despite temporarily planning to beat him up.

Aren didn't listen. He didn't care what they said, as long as they didn't follow; and they didn't sound eager to do that. The waves pushed up against the ridge below him as he hurried on, clambering hand and foot along the sun-dried stone. When he reached the hole in the galleon's flank, he stopped and looked back. The boys were watching him uncertainly, hoping he'd change his mind. Chasing him across a beach was one thing; braving the galleon was something else entirely.

'You can't hide in there! We're not scared of any elaru!' Ged called. But he made no move to climb the rocks.

'Leave me alone!' Aren yelled. With no other options left, he climbed through the gap in the hull.

Inside was a jumble of splintered planks that shifted and creaked with the movement of the sea. Below he could see salt waves lapping around the smashed lower decks, jagged edges ready to impale him if he fell. He picked his way gingerly through the mess, testing each spot before moving ahead. The boards squeaked alarmingly beneath his weight, but they didn't give way. He climbed through a narrow doorway into a cramped chamber and leaned up against the wall, relieved to have solid wood beneath his feet.

Once he'd caught his breath, the distress of pursuit faded away to be replaced with a more subtle form of terror. A child's fear of the monster in the dark, of dead things in dead places. But though he dreaded to go further in, he couldn't stay where he was. The others might still decide to follow, and if Aren was to escape a thrashing, he needed to keep moving.

The interior of the galleon was claustrophobic and stuffy with heat. Slices of white sunlight cut through gaps in the boards overhead, illuminating strange, sad corridors warped and scabbed with the passing of empty years. Everywhere he saw touches of elaru craft, wood made to flow like water. The cornices over the doorways were works of art; the walls were chased with carven motifs of leaf and vine. This galleon had been a thing of beauty once, before it fell to must and mould.

Rats scattered ahead of him as he trod along sloping floors. Timbers moaned as the galleon rocked with the waves sloshing in its belly. Had he gone far enough? Maybe they hadn't followed him after all. Perhaps he should go back and check.

A long, low creak cut through the quiet: the unmistakable sound of a sneaking foot pressing on a floorboard.

Aren whirled, heart thumping hard. He was standing in the middle of a tight corridor with several doorways. Further along, a narrow stairway led to the deck.

He saw no one. But somebody was here.

An image flurried into his mind, a vision of the elaru captain cobbled together from stories and a painting he'd once seen. He was tall, pale and sharp as an icicle, with hair the colour of new snow. His features were haughty and beautiful, his mouth thin and cruel, his ears without lobes. He'd come striding from the dark, a shade striped in sunlight, the tattered tails of his fish-eaten jacket flapping behind him and a long, narrow sabre of grey witch-iron in his hand. Aren could hope for no mercy from him, for his kind had none.

Panic bubbled up in his gut as he realised what an awful miscalculation he'd made. He should never have come here, never have risked this. But Ged and the others still waited for him outside, and he was afraid of the beating he'd get if they caught him. Paralysed by indecision, he dithered in the corridor, searching for danger but doing nothing to escape it.

'*Yah!*'

Aren screamed and flailed his arms in front of his face as his attacker leaped out from a doorway. So violent and surprising was his reaction that his attacker screamed as well. After a few moments, when Aren appeared not to be dead, he dared to lower his arms. Standing uncertainly before him was a pudgy boy he vaguely recognised from town. He was wearing a woollen blanket round his neck as a cape, and holding a carved wooden shortsword.

Remembering himself, the boy squared his shoulders and levelled the makeshift weapon.

'Surrender!' he demanded.

'Who are you?' Aren asked, bewildered.

'I'm King Haften Urdsbane!' the boy declared. He brandished his sword. 'And this is the Ember Blade of old!'

'Who are you *really*, though?'

'Oh.' He deflated, disappointed that Aren wasn't playing along. 'I'm Cade. You're Aren, ain't you? I've seen you about.' He stuck his sword awkwardly in his belt. 'What are you doing?'

'I'm hiding.'

'You ain't doing the best job of it,' Cade observed.

'Well, I haven't found a hiding place yet,' Aren said testily.

'Who are you hiding from?'

Aren shrugged, as if it was no big thing. 'Ged, Ham and Darra. They want to beat me up.'

'Why?'

'I hit Ged.'

'Why?'

Because he'd said some things about Aren's father and the elegant, pretty women who sometimes came to dinner at the house, and who were often there at breakfast, too. Sometimes they were Krodan, sometimes Ossian. Some he only saw once; others would visit frequently. Aren thought them fascinating, especially those that spoke sweetly to him and gave him toys, but they made him feel odd as well, like something was happening that he didn't understand. Every so often, Randill would sit him down and tell him very seriously that nobody would ever replace his mother, and not to be worried, even though Aren had been thinking nothing of the sort. Then there'd be no women for a while; but eventually a new one would appear.

He didn't really know what Ged had been implying when he said what he said about Randill. He didn't even really remember the words. But it had the tone of an insult, and it touched a nerve, and since he didn't know how to respond with his tongue, he'd used his fists instead.

But Aren couldn't explain all that to Cade; he could barely

explain it to himself. All he knew was that he didn't want to talk about his father any more, so he turned the question back on Cade. 'Why are *you* here?' he asked, making it an accusation.

'I'm pretending,' Cade said. He tugged at the end of his cape to show Aren.

'On your own?'

'Nobody else wanted to.'

'Aren't you scared of the elaru captain?'

'I've been here loads of times and never seen him.'

'What if the tide comes in?'

'I'll swim?' Cade said, as if it was obvious.

Aren smiled. Having some company pulled the sting from his fear, and Cade was reassuringly blithe about the danger. The galleon felt a lot less scary with him here.

Cade saw his smile and smiled back eagerly. 'You want to play pretend with me?' he offered.

A plan hatched in Aren's mind and his smile became a grin. 'Yes,' he said. 'Let's play pretend.'

While Aren had been inside the galleon, Ged, Darra and Ham had been squabbling on the beach. They argued and cajoled, whined and threatened, changed their minds and changed them again. Finally Ham went home, walking at first, until Ged threw a rock at him and he took to his heels. Then Ged and Darra picked up their sticks and climbed onto the ridge where the hulk of the *Wave Dancer* lay.

'We're coming for you, Aren!' Ged shouted.

Cade turned away from the gap in the planking through which he'd been watching. 'They're coming for you!' he said excitedly.

'I heard,' Aren told him dryly. He pushed a strand of kelp away from his face. 'How do I look?'

Cade gave him a double thumbs-up. Aren wasn't sure his disguise was as convincing as the other boy made out, but his enthusiasm was heartening. He was wearing a ratty rug they'd found near a bulkhead with some empty bottles of wine. His shoulders and head were draped with straggling water-weeds and black, leathery chains of snapfish eggs. Cade's cloak had been tied around his head in a bundle to secure the cap of oozing kelp in place, giving the impression of long, green hair hanging over his eyes and down to his waist. The costume of an elaru captain was beyond them, but the shambling shade of a drowned boy would do well enough in a pinch. At least, Aren hoped so.

'You'll be waiting where we said?'

Cade hefted a rusty chain onto his shoulder, which they'd dug out of the water on the lower decks. 'Oh, aye,' he said, hardly able to contain his glee. 'Reckon I know what to do.'

They headed off through the galleon to their appointed spots. The day had turned again, and this time in Aren's favour. Meeting Cade had changed everything. No longer alone, he'd found his courage, and with a willing accomplice at his side anything felt possible.

Cade had suggested the best spot for an ambush, a dark chamber which Ged and Darra would have to pass through on their way in. It had been a cabin once, but the roof was rotted through, the mattress had dissolved to rags and the bed frame had collapsed. At one end was a shadowed compartment that had once been a wardrobe or a storage cupboard, now empty but for rats' droppings. Aren made some last-minute adjustments to his costume, which kept wanting to slip off, and then hunkered down in the wardrobe to wait.

He didn't have to wait long. They came whispering and hissing to one another, creeping on wary feet with their sticks ready to defend themselves.

'I bet the captain's already got him,' Darra said. 'We ought to go.'

'Shut your mouth,' said Ged. 'He's in here somewhere.'

'I think I hear the tide coming in.'

'I said clam it, scab-wit!'

Aren tensed as they reached the doorway. Now it came to it, he felt his bravery ebbing. Maybe he could let them pass by and sneak out when they were gone. Wasn't that a better plan than confronting them? He watched from his hiding place as they crept into the room and wondered if he'd be able to move at all when the time came.

The crash of chains from overhead killed his qualms. The game was on, and there was no going back.

'What was that?' Darra gasped as the two boys turned their eyes to the ceiling.

He was answered by a shriek of such blood-curdling horror that they physically cringed from it. Suddenly the chamber was full of noise: crashing, howling, stamping. Dust sifted down from the rotted boards overhead as they were pounded from above.

'It's the captain!' Darra squeaked.

But of course it was Cade, who'd watched the boys enter through the holes in the ceiling and was now doing a thoroughly convincing job of playing the spectre. He was throwing himself about and screaming his throat raw. Aren was so impressed that he almost forgot to do his part; but inspired by his accomplice's performance, he surged out into the chamber.

Arms raised, moaning like the dead, he stumbled towards Ged and Darra, a mass of weed and rags that was transformed in their minds into a dreadful apparition. They screamed at the sight of him – everyone was screaming now – and stumbled back in abject panic, dropping their sticks. Then there was a loud crack from above and Cade plummeted through the ceiling with a crash of chains and falling timber. Ged and Darra ran, shrieking at the tops of their lungs, back the way they came. They were still shrieking when they reached the beach.

Cade groaned, sloughing off broken planks as Aren helped him to his feet. He dusted himself down, wincing as new bruises made themselves known, then caught Aren's eye and began to chuckle.

'Did you hear 'em?' he said. 'We got 'em, didn't we?'

'We got them,' Aren agreed. He was giddy with victory. Then, on impulse, he said: 'Do you want to be friends?'

'Alright,' said Cade.

And so it was.

'We let Ged and Darra tell everyone how they'd seen the captain and lived, then we let on what we'd done,' Aren said. He'd lost himself in memories, but now the sounds and smells of the infirmary intruded again, and he was reminded of the hunger in his belly and the pain in his muscles. A loud scream came from the surgery as the amputation began. He ignored it and tried to smile. 'They never lived it down. I swear that was half the reason Ged apprenticed as a navigator, just to get out of Shoal Point.'

Cade had fallen quiet, and now he turned restlessly in his bunk, eyes roving. Aren gripped his hand and attempted to catch his gaze. His story had done some good, it seemed. He dared to believe his friend had calmed at the sound of a familiar voice.

'Cade? Can you hear me?'

'Icky-picky spit–spat–spot,' Cade whispered urgently. It was a snatch of a children's rhyme they used to sing in the plazas. Now the whole thing tumbled from his lips.

Spit–spat–spot, better poxy than not,
The old man's hot to keep safe from the rot.
Hide in the stables till the bolt gets shot.
Icky-picky spit–spat–spot.

The hope in Aren flickered and died. Was this all that was left of his best friend? A witless buffoon, swinging between hysteria and delirium? Had the Krodans taken the last person he loved?

He shied from that thought, overcome with guilt and the fear of some unknown punishment. But the sight of his friend muttering and babbling made him angry. *Say it*, he told himself. *Say it out loud.*

'Krodans did this,' he said. 'Krodans put us here. Krodans hurt you.'

Cade rolled to his side, clutching his sheets, mumbling nonsense. Aren checked if anyone had heard him, but all the patients nearby were asleep or unconscious. To say it was blasphemy. He'd never thought of the Krodan people as enemies before, never dared to. The Primus would hear; the Iron Hand would know. And yet, seeing Cade condemned to idiocy set something boiling inside him, bubbling up till he could taste rancid hate on the back of his tongue. For the first time, he no longer cared what retribution might come. If Cade didn't recover, he'd never forgive them. He swore it.

The patient in the surgery was still screaming. He heard Kel shouting from the back of the infirmary: 'Draccen tears! We need more draccen tears for the pain!' Other patients groaned for aid as helpers busied themselves among the beds. Aren ignored it all. The world had shrunk to the width of Cade's bunk.

'I'll look after you,' he said quietly, and those words pushed tears to his eyes. 'I won't let them give up on you.'

He searched Cade's face for any sign that he'd been heard, but found none. He hung his head, and slowly let go of his friend's hand. An immense sadness welled up in him, an ocean of sorrow so deep and wide that he knew there'd be no limit to it.

Meshuk, Stone Mother. I called on you to save him. I even thought you might have answered me. But you're just a fiction, like all the other Aspects. Like the Primus, like love, like my father ... like every other thing I believed in.

'Aren?'

His head shot up at the sound of Cade's voice. Cade was staring blindly upwards, pawing at the air above his bunk.

'Aren, is that you?'

'Yes!' he cried, and he grabbed Cade's hand again. 'Yes, I'm here!'

'I was far away ...' Cade said dreamily. 'Then I heard your voice ...'

'Yes! Yes, I was talking to you! Can you see me?' He was desperate, eyes glittering, overwhelmed with emotion and exhaustion.

'You're so dim ... like a shade ...' He coughed weakly. 'Aren ...'

'Yes?'

'There's something I need to ask you ...'

'Yes?'

'I just need to know ...'

'*Yes?*'

Cade's eyes focused on him and he raised an eyebrow. 'When did you become such a blubbering sap?'

Aren gaped. Cade grinned.

Then Aren said, very slowly and very clearly, 'You absolute bastard.'

Cade whooped with laughter as Aren pounced on him, fending

away Aren's half-serious attempts to beat and strangle him. 'You can't hit me! I'm crazy!' he protested.

'I believed you, you maggot-sack!'

'Sssh!' Cade motioned for him to keep it down. 'I *am* mad. And I'm gonna *stay* mad as long as they'll keep me here.'

Aren stopped assaulting him and sat back on his haunches. He was so relieved that his urge to murder Cade was temporarily forgotten. 'You want to *stay* here?'

'Three square meals and I get to lie in bed all day?' Cade replied. 'Ain't in a hurry to give that up.'

'You could have let on earlier!'

'But you were being so nice to me.'

Cade was making fun of him, but Aren didn't mind a bit. If Cade was joking again, then his friend was back, and everything that had divided them had been pushed aside.

'Listen,' said Aren, leaning closer. 'I understand now. You were right.'

''Course I was,' said Cade confidently. 'Er ... about what?'

'We can't just *survive* in this place. We can't just wait it out. No one's coming to save us. No one's going to set us free.'

'Well,' said Cade, his voice heavy with sarcasm, 'you know how to cheer a feller up, I'll give you that.'

'That's why we have to escape.'

Cade's face became grave. Suddenly it was no longer a joke. 'You mean it?' he said.

'I promise you,' said Aren. The moment he said it, he was certain. 'We'll break out or we'll die trying, but I'll be gods-damned if I'll let us fade away here.'

'You got a plan?' Cade asked eagerly.

He was about to say no, but before he could, the plan came to him, springing whole and clear into his mind. With a shock, he realised he must have been thinking about it all along, storing away details and information ever since they'd arrived. He just hadn't allowed himself to entertain the idea of escape until now; it was an inconceivable act of rebellion for someone who had such complete faith in the Krodan way.

That faith lay in shreds now. He was taking matters into his own hands.

'I've got a plan,' he said. 'And I need you to do something for me.'

'Do I have to get out of bed?'

'Luckily, you don't. You need to stay right here. Do you still have your water flask?'

Cade shook his head. 'I lost it in the explosion.'

'Take mine.' Aren pulled the tin flask from his belt, slugged the last of the water and handed it over. 'You can hide it somewhere, but they won't even look inside if they find it. It's just a water flask; everyone's got one.'

Cade studied it, puzzled. 'So what exactly do I have to do?'

'You have to pretend,' said Aren. 'You can do that, can't you?'

'Oh, yeah,' said Cade, a wicked smile spreading across his face. 'I can do that.'

19

In the shadow of the Ostenberg Mountains lay the Auldwood, spreading thick and dark across the land from horizon to horizon. Its edges were dotted with small settlements and mazed with forester's trails, but few ventured deeper than that. Among the dense tangles at its heart lay places that hadn't known the tread of human feet for centuries.

Wild tales were told of what lay within: beasts of enormous size; shade-touched creatures that spoke as men; malevolent trees that would strangle the unwary or crush them with a falling branch. At the centre, overseeing all, waited something as old as time, vast and unknowable, which jealously guarded its lands from invaders.

Vika didn't know the truth of that, but she knew better than to dismiss such tales as nonsense. The Auldwood was enormous and strange, and though she'd walked deeper than most dared, much of it was still a mystery to her. Even for a druidess, who knew the ways of the land, there were dangers.

Ruck padded by her side as she followed a sunken path between the trees, hollowed out by a long-vanished stream. Knuckled roots poked from the earthen walls and ancient trees creaked and groaned as she passed. It was evening, and the sun was still up, but beneath the canopy it was chilly and sombre.

She'd travelled far since the Dirracombe, and her journey had done nothing to cheer her. Everywhere the old ways were being forgotten, the signs of the Nine quietly erased. Shedding her druidic trappings, she'd ventured into a town to gather supplies and learn what she could. There she found a temple to the Primus, newly built on a hill overlooking the streets, a magnificent beacon of red and beige stone. There were no such monuments to the Nine, only neglected shrines and a temple falling into ruin.

Small wonder they were losing the people. The young saw little evidence of the old gods of Ossia, and nothing of the druids who spread their wisdom. The Nine were part of their parents' world, but not of theirs. The only voice they heard was that of the Sanctorum at Festenday convocation, which taught that the Aspects were primitive gods and denied them.

She thought of the champion, the bright figure with the sword of light, and then of the nightmarish creatures that had come after, and the vision they'd shown her. Something terrible was approaching. She only hoped she might make sense of what she saw, while there was yet time to avert it.

The crack of a twig made her stop and raise her head. One hand on her staff, she listened. Something had been tracking them for a while now, something large that kept its distance. Ruck growled low in her throat.

'Be calm, my friend,' said Vika, rubbing the scruff of Ruck's neck. 'We are no enemies of this forest.'

And yet she wasn't so sure that mattered these days. The spirits were not welcoming of late. They'd grown resentful and restless, less inclined to differentiate between the druids who sought to protect them and the Krodans who cut down their trees for lumber and farmland.

Another crack, louder and closer, and now she was concerned. She heard a whuff of animal breath. Birds scattered explosively as a brake of ferns thrashed with the movement of some ungainly beast.

From the undergrowth at the edge of the sunken path, the brown muzzle of a bear poked out.

Vika stepped back in alarm as it ambled into the open and down to the stream bed, blocking her path. It snuffled at the air, turned its head towards her and fixed her with a beady gaze.

'Peace,' she said, raising one hand. 'We have no quarrel with you.'

The bear was in no mood to be pacified. It reared up on its hind legs, towering over them, and its lips peeled back from its fangs as it roared a challenge.

'These woods are not safe, traveller. Haven't you heard?'

Vika whirled at the voice. The woman had appeared silently behind her. She wore a thick, tattered cloak stitched with faded red and brown patterns. A voluminous hood shadowed her face, and she carried an elaborately carved oak staff split into a fork at the tip, with the skull of a young goat fixed between the tines.

'I dreamed your coming, Vika-Walks-The-Barrows,' the woman said in a low, slow voice. 'You are expected.'

She raised her staff towards the bear and spoke words in an elder tongue. The bear gave a yawning cry, thumped down heavily onto its forepaws, then turned and plodded away up the path.

The woman lowered her staff and pulled back her hood, revealing a head of short-cropped silver hair and a face smeared with two vertical streaks of red paint. Her lips spread into a smile. 'Ten years it has been, my erstwhile acolyte, and now you return an equal.'

'Agalie-Sings-The-Dark,' said Vika, spreading her arms. 'I've searched long to find you.'

'You are welcome,' said the older woman, and the two druidesses embraced in a warm clutch of furs and bodies.

Agalie's camp was in a glade by a narrow stream, roofed with tangled branches. A tent of sticks and hide stood to one side of the glade, a fire at the other, ringed by stones. The night insects were loud and glowflies danced above the water.

Vika and Agalie sat together on a tuffet, eating seared doe-meat off the spit and mushrooms and potatoes fried in fat, which they ate from the pan. A skin of sloe liquor lay between them. Ruck gnawed a bone, lazy in the warmth of the flames.

'And what did you see, after the spirit uncovered your eyes?' Agalie asked.

Vika stared into the fire, a frown settling on her face as the memories flooded back. 'The dark figures were gone,' she said. 'I was still in the hollow, but it was withered and dead now, and the sky was strange. I went to the edge of the Dirracombe, where it was open to the hills, and saw ...' Her breath shuddered as the sight hit her anew. Ruck looked up from her bone and whined. 'It was madness, Agalie. An ever-changing wasteland, where the wretched remnants of humanity were prey to monsters from beyond the Divide. I saw an armless creature with a white face like a mask, chained like a beast of burden to a spiked cart overflowing with body parts. Twisted, fanged things lunged and snapped at a ragged woman as she fled across a cracked plain. There was something chitinous and gigantic with a shape part spider and part flea which stalked along the horizon, while behind it a black sun rose vast and close.'

She swallowed, and her gaze was distant, blurred by tears of horror. 'Beyond the wasteland there was a city, a sprawling vileness upon the parched earth, with avenues of sinew and towers of bone and knuckle. The stretched and screaming faces of those who'd died to build it still yawned on the walls of its cathedral. Rivers of blood and body fluids spilled in falls from aqueducts of gristle. It steamed in the heat of the rising sun, and cackling things ran in the streets, imps of the Abyss and worse, and worse, and *worse*.'

She came to a stop; she could say no more. She wiped tears away, irritated at herself for letting them fall, and waited for Agalie to speak.

'You were right to come,' said Agalie at length. 'Matters are grave, if what you have seen is to be trusted.'

'*If*,' said Vika. 'The spirits deceive, and never more so than now.'

'Perhaps,' said Agalie. 'But I, too, have seen omens. I walked beneath a storm and watched lightning carve the sign of Azra into the sky. I dreamed I heard pounding beneath the earth, as if some great creature fought to be free of its prison, and when I awoke, the pounding still shook the forest. Nor am I blind to what is happening in our land. And now you bring me this news.'

She handed the skin of liquor to Vika, who swigged from it. Heat bloomed pleasantly in her chest and she recovered a little.

'Then give me wisdom, Agalie. If it's news, I don't understand it.'

The flames made shadows in the lines of Agalie's face. 'The dark figures you saw, the mutilated horrors with flayed skin – you were visited by the Torments.'

'The Torments do not cross the Shadowlands.'

'Not for many years. But that is how the Lorekeepers described the Torments to me; though I remember little else they said about them.' She shrugged. 'It was a long time ago. If my mind made perfect records, I would be a Lorekeeper myself.'

Vika took another swig of liquor to stave off the cold thought that she'd seen the keepers of Kar Vishnakh, the citadel on the far side of the Shadowlands that guarded the way to the Abyss. Kar Vishnakh, which hung suspended on chains over an immense and bottomless pit where the Outsiders languished, imprisoned for eternity.

'These are black days, when the Torments themselves leave the Citadel of Chains to bring us warning,' she muttered.

'The Outsiders stir in the Abyss and Azra the Despoiler strains at his bonds. All that lies ahead is death and war and destruction,' Agalie said despondently. 'These are black days indeed.'

'What I saw … the ruin of the land … they were showing me the future?'

'*A* future, perhaps,' Agalie threw another stick of wood on the fire. 'Once, there was only chaos upon the face of the world. The living and the dead shared the same earth, and nothing was certain.' Her eyes became distant and her voice took on the tone of a recitation. It was a story well known to them both. 'It was the Age of Chaos, when the Outsiders ran amok and brought corruption and disorder to all the Creator had intended. Joha saw that nothing good could thrive there, so he drew the Divide across the world, the great chasm separating the living and the dead.'

'To the living, the world beneath the sun,' Vika murmured. 'To the dead, the Shadowlands.'

'But the Outsiders resisted, so Joha led the Aspects in war against them. For a thousand years they fought, till at last the Outsiders fell. For their actions, Joha condemned them to the Abyss and set the Torments to watch over them.' Agalie plucked a steaming potato from the pan and bit into it. 'But they have never stopped coveting the light. Always they are seeking their freedom, and vengeance upon those that took it from them. If they are ever released, all you have seen will come to pass.'

'Something has changed, then,' said Vika, frowning. 'It has been a century since last they threatened the world of the living, and we've heard nothing of them since. What new danger brings their wardens to warn us?'

'That is what we must discover,' said Agalie. 'Perhaps the champion you saw can provide the answers.'

'I did not see their face, Agalie. How am I supposed to find them?'

'The Aspects will give you guidance.'

Vika shook her head sadly. 'It has been long since I heard their voices.' She watched Ruck worrying at her bone in the firelight. Here in the forest, with strong drink in her belly and Agalie next to her, she felt a soft, sad yearning for a simpler life. No more wandering, no more hiding from Krodan druid-hunters. All she wanted was fire, food and good company, with Ruck at her feet. It wasn't much to ask. Better that than all this doubt, all this supplication, with only silence as an answer. Better than bearing the burden of faith.

'I think the gods have left this land, Agalie,' she said. It was the first time she'd spoken it aloud, and it was like a stone laid on her heart. She looked over at her mentor, the woman who'd trained her in the ways of the druids. Tears came to her eyes, loosened by liquor. 'I'm not sure they were ever here at all.'

'They are here,' said Agalie, with that calm certainty Vika had always envied. 'Do not despair. This is their land. In Ossia they first made themselves known, and from here they spread throughout the world. They are in the very earth beneath your feet and the air you breathe. If the Aspects are silent, it is because we have forgotten how to listen.'

'But I heard them *before!*' Vika cried, surging to her feet. Ruck raised her head, startled, as she stalked away from the fire in agitation. 'I heard them clear as a bell! They appeared before me, as real as you are now!'

'I know,' said Agalie. 'I remember the day I found you. A child whom half the village thought touched by the gods, and the other half thought possessed. They didn't know whether to worship you or drown you.'

'And you took me, and taught me, and sent me out to teach those who would hear what wisdom we had.' She came back to the fire, snatched up the liquor and took an angry swig. 'And my reward? The Aspects stopped speaking to me. I dedicated *my life* to them, and now they lie supine while some foreigners' god sweeps through the land, razing all our faith has built.' She threw out an arm, as if to take in the whole of the night. 'So tell me, Agalie: those visions I saw in my youth – were they just some hysteria of the mind? All these portents and omens, is it the gods and spirits that grant them, or the poison herbs we drink? Are we all mad? Did the Apostates have the right of it?'

'Do not speak such foolishness!' Agalie snapped, rising to her feet and snatching up her staff, eyes hard with fury in the firelight. With her red-streaked face and the goat skull suspended in the dark beside her, she was suddenly fierce. 'Doubt the Aspects if you will, but do not invoke the Apostates! They have corrupted and perverted everything we stand for, and I will not hear it from one whom I thought wiser!'

Ruck was on her feet, barking now. Vika held Agalie's gaze in defiance for a moment, and then looked away, ashamed.

'Forgive me,' she said quietly. 'You are right. I spoke in haste.'

She walked to the edge of the stream and stared across it to the far bank, where the trees gathered close and the glowflies blinked in the darkness.

'A month before you found me,' she said, 'I met Hallen in the fields and walked with him. He told me it would be a good harvest, and that the blight would end that year, and so it did.' She looked over her shoulder sadly at her mentor. 'I know I saw him, Agalie. He was *there*. Tall and blond, with a crown of wheat and barley, a cup in one hand and a sickle in the other. Just to be near him was a comfort and happiness so profound I will never again experience the like. I knew the Aspects existed then, as sure as I knew there was ground beneath my feet.'

She felt a wet nose as her hand, then a warm tongue. Absently, she scratched the top of Ruck's head.

'Five times I was visited by the gods. Five times, and then no more. Can you imagine that? To be so blessed and then ... not to be?'

'I have never seen them,' said Agalie. 'Only their signs and agents.

Be grateful for what grace was given you. We are each tested in our own way.'

Vika looked into the babbling water. She was no longer angry, but sad instead. Her moods had always surged and faded suddenly. Emotions crashed upon her like stormy waves on the rocks, and it was hard to know how much of it was her and how much a result of the potions she'd been taking most of her life. You didn't get to walk in the Shadowlands without paying a price.

'I believed you had been sent by the Aspects that day,' she said to Agalie. 'I think, if you had not come, my neighbours would have killed me.' She gave a faint smile. 'Now I think of it, you did not look much younger then than you are now. Twenty-five years, it has been, but you've hardly aged a day in my mind.'

Agalie laughed. 'You're no Lorekeeper, either,' she said. 'Your memory plays tricks on you, I think.' But Vika heard mischief in her voice, and she wasn't so sure.

She put a hand on Vika's shoulder. 'Doubt is healthy, but do not give up hope,' she said gently. 'The Creator did not put us here to solve our problems for us. The giants cursed the Long Ice, I suspect, yet from that disaster came the Six Races. Once, we were all enslaved by the urds, and then came Jessa Wolf's-Heart and soon we had built an empire. Each setback makes us stronger.' She squeezed Vika's shoulder in encouragement. 'The Torments are the servants of the Aspects. It matters not that the gods did not show themselves in person. You were chosen as the bearer of great tidings; do you not see that?'

Vika nodded. She felt churlish now. For all her complaining about the Aspects' silence, she'd seen them five times more than most. Others with stronger faith had never been shown such proof.

'Why do they not call a Conclave?' Vika asked helplessly.

'We will know when they do. Perhaps your news will inspire them. I will spread the word, as should you.'

'It will be too late by then,' said Vika. She tipped her head back, her hair falling away from her face. Few stars were visible through the knotted canopy, but Vika didn't need to see the sky to know the night. 'The Communion is breaking. It took me longer than I expected to find your druidsign and track you. The stars in my vision were those of an autumn night not long from now. Whatever is coming will happen then.'

'Then you must go at first light,' said Agalie. 'Go out into the land and let your feet lead you where they may. The Aspects will guide your steps. Your fate will not find you in the deeps of the Auldwood.'

Onward, ever onward. Vika felt the stone on her heart grow heavier. 'And what will I do, Agalie? Out there, in the land?'

Agalie smiled. 'You will find our champion.'

20

The next day was Festenday, and morning found the prisoners lined up in the yard for convocation. Festenday prayers to the Primus were obligatory for all subjects of the Empire, and most forms of work were forbidden. Despite the tragedy that had befallen them, some of the prisoners still grumbled at their luck that the mine was closed on a day which they were due to have off anyway; but they were cheered by the rumour that mining wouldn't resume for at least a week while the engineers made it safe again. They sang to the Primus with gusto after that, though the Krodan hymns they'd been forced to learn by heart meant nothing to most of them.

Aren stood among them beneath a bright, cold sky, listening to the priest give his sermon. To outside eyes he was anonymous in the crowd, another pale figure in ill-fitting grey clothes, shivering and underfed; but today he felt transformed, steely with purpose.

'Do not grieve,' the priest was saying, 'for your brothers have joined the Primus in His light. And was it not said by Tomas that if a man toil for the glory of Kroda, whether he a farmer or warrior be, let all men call him noble?'

Aren stared at him with loathing. He was a soft, portly man with the milky look of someone who'd been roundly bullied as a boy. He wore beige and red robes, beige for parchment and red for blood, stitched with Krodan rays across the shoulders and chest. The blade and open book of the Sanctorum hung round his neck, wrought in gold.

Shut your mouth, he thought fiercely, heated by defiance. *All your talk. What does it mean? They didn't believe in the Primus, those men who died. You put them there, you and your people. You killed them. And you nearly killed Cade, too.*

'Their toil is ended, their earthly sufferings over,' the priest continued. 'They are beyond the reach of the Nemesis now, and the crimes that brought them here have been burned away in the radiance of the one true god. Let those of us who remain honour their memory with the strength of our backs, and redouble our labours in service of the Empire, that their sacrifice will not be in vain.'

Overseer Krent lowered his head in pious agreement. Captain Hassan swept the assembly with a keen gaze, alert for signs of dissent. The guards surrounding the yard fidgeted and looked bored, while the archers up on the wall kept an eye on those below. Nearby stood the scratched and bloodstained pole where uncounted prisoners had been eaten alive, clawed to pieces by Krodan skulldogs.

Aren stopped listening and turned his mind to his plan.

There were two gates out of the prisoners' compound, one to the east that let into the guards' section and one to the south that opened onto the bridge over the river and the village beyond. Both were heavily guarded and securely locked when not in use. Carts were searched going in and out. He'd briefly wondered if they might smuggle themselves to freedom that way, but it would require Rapha's cooperation, and he'd have nothing to do with that pirate. He was still angry at him for giving ragweed to Cade. Besides, he had nothing to offer in exchange, and the risk was too great that Rapha might betray them.

No, they were going over the wall.

Sneaking out after curfew would be easy; the camp was dark at night and the patrolling guards were simple to avoid. Getting past the vicious skulldogs was the challenge. The area they patrolled was divided up into fenced sections, with three dogs in each to ensure they were evenly spread around the perimeter; but three skulldogs were still three too many, and all they had to do was bark to raise the alarm.

Still, if they *could* get past the dogs, it wouldn't be hard to clamber up the wooden scaffold to the archers' walkway on the inside edge of the stockade wall. During the day, the archers were alert and watchful, but at night, when their commanding officers were abed, they drifted about idly and chatted. With luck and guile, they might slip past them in the dark, but he had to reckon on facing at least one, and they were all big, well fed and carrying shortswords. Perhaps he and Cade could overpower a man like that with surprise on their side, but he wasn't at all sure of it.

Once past the archers, they'd have to get down the outside of the stockade without breaking a leg. That required rope, and time enough to tie it. Then all that was left was the escape through the mountains, with guards and skulldogs tracking them, and winter closing in. They'd need food, warm clothing, weapons and supplies, and even then the chances of survival were slim.

But it could be done.

'The Primus loves not the laggard!' said the priest. 'He grants no favour to the prostrate man who pleads. But he who has the will and strength of character to strive, on him does the light of the Primus shine!'

I'll strive, alright, Aren thought, addressing the Primus. *I'm going to strive right out of this hell you put me in, and I'm taking my friend with me. Stop me if you can.*

It felt good to shake his fist in the face of a god. He'd always been afraid to before, scared that some misfortune would befall him if he questioned what he'd been taught. But misfortune had befallen him anyway. What good was piety, then, if it won you no favour?

He brought his mind back to the matter at hand. Scorning the Primus and his servants got him no closer to his goal. There were things to attend to before he could put his plan into action, and the first of them was Grub.

He found the Skarl in the crowd, and felt hate and fear stir in him. The marks of their last encounter were still bright on Aren's body. Stealing his cheroots had only been the latest in a long line of abuses and humiliations. Aren never knew when Grub would turn up next, to take his food, to rob him or beat him. Maybe next time he'd take something really vital, or put Aren in the infirmary.

Grub had come to the camp soon after Aren, and as near as Aren could make out he had no friends here. He did, however, have plenty of victims. Aren was only spared worse bullying because Grub picked on weaker prisoners more often. He chose the young, the feeble and the unpopular. Cade had been overlooked because he made other men laugh and they might decide to defend him; Aren had no such protection. He'd mostly kept himself to himself, because he believed the other prisoners were traitors and criminals who likely deserved to be here. Because he believed Krodan justice didn't make mistakes. Unwittingly, he'd made himself an easy target.

If his plan were to even get off the ground, that ended today.

The prisoners dispersed once convocation was over. Without work, most of them would be gambling for contraband, cutting deals, hustling for survival. Others would talk, pray to the Aspects or tell tales. The little things that kept them human, in this inhuman place.

Aren watched Grub as the crowd broke up into groups, and when the Skarl headed into the alleyways between the longhouses, he followed.

'*To overcome your enemy, you must first understand him.*' Master Orik's favourite maxim. It was time to put his teachings into effect.

Aren knew little about Grub, but he knew something of Skarls. They came from Skara Thun, to the north-east of Embria, a hostile white wilderness of giant sabre-toothed beasts and blood-drinking witches. Their tribes had existed in a state of permanent conflict over their limited natural resources until one visionary leader, Tharl Iqqba, began the tradition of the Scattering. From that day on, the firstborn of each family were cast from their tribes when they reached adulthood and sent across the seas to other lands. While the rest defended and cared for their homeland, the firstborns won glory for themselves and their people, so that one day they might return heroes. Feats of arms, mercantile brilliance, labyrinthine cons, acts of soaring romance: the object was to make a story of themselves and have it scribed on their skins, that the Bone God might read it when they died. In the process they'd win renown for their people and, ideally, return with great gifts and wealth for their tribe. The greatest among them were honoured with towering sarcophagi, their legends inscribed on the sides, and placed among their ancestors in snowbound necropolises that sprawled across the frozen plains.

Aren knew he had a shallow understanding at best, but it was all he had, and any advantage was better than none.

Milling knots of prisoners, relieved to be released from convocation, clogged the routes out of the yard. Aren dodged through them, keeping Grub in sight. He had compact, thick legs and a lumbering gait, but he moved fast for all that, and Aren struggled to keep up. Once, he thought he'd lost him, but then the back of that bald head bobbed into view again, half-covered in those black, crawling tattoos that chronicled the deeds of his life.

As they made their way further from the yard, the crowd thinned and soon the way between them was clear. Grub appeared to be heading for the graveyard, but Aren wouldn't let him get there. It was time to make his move.

The Skarl was walking with his head down, apparently deep in thought. Aren quickened his step to catch up. As expected, Grub turned behind a longhouse in the direction of the cliffs. Aren rounded the same corner and found to his surprise that he had vanished.

He halted, staring at the empty space between the longhouses, a simple muddy path walled on either side with flaking planks. There was no cover here, nowhere to hide, nowhere to go. The apparent impossibility of Grub's disappearance blanked Aren's mind, and he stood there gaping.

Then he heard the scrape of a boot from above, and looked up just in time to see Grub dropping down on him from the longhouse roof.

He reacted fast enough that the Skarl's first blow didn't land true. Instead he was smacked across the shoulder, shoved hard by his attacker's weight so that he slammed palms-first against the side of the longhouse opposite. Before he could turn, an arm wrapped around his throat from behind. He struggled, but the Skarl was stronger and it was like pushing against an oak. Panic sparked as his throat was crushed in the crook of Grub's arm.

'Think Grub doesn't know what Mudslug is up to?' Grub snarled in his ear. 'Think Grub doesn't see Mudslug follow him? Mudslug looking for Grub's stash, yes? Very brave or very stupid. Grub thinks he knows which.'

'No ...' Aren gasped, his eyes bulging. 'Talk ... came to ... talk ...'

'Grub believes you. That sound very likely to Grub.'

Aren fought unconsciousness, his head going light for lack of blood. He was hit by the chilling realisation that Grub might not let up. He could die right now, and he was helpless to prevent it.

'Stop ...' He could only grab snatches of air. 'Want to ... trade ...'

'Trade? You trade with Grub? Grub *takes*!'

Then the arm was gone from his throat, and Grub turned him round and shoved him back against the longhouse wall. Aren sagged, dizzy with relief, hauling in air as Grub patted him down and rifled his pockets.

'What Mudslug got? It better be good, or Grub break something Mudslug not want broken.'

Aren laboured to get the words out. 'Not ... in my pockets. Going to give you ... new tattoo.'

Grub stopped searching, his eyes narrow within the ugly black crescent that crossed his face. 'Mudslug better make sense quick,' he warned.

Aren put a hand to his aching throat. 'Your tattoos,' he said. 'Each one tells a tale of your mighty deeds.'

'Mighty deeds!' Grub roared in agreement. He jabbed a finger at a line of hieroglyphs running along his collarbone. 'This one say how Grub climb down cliffs with his men to surprise camp full of Boskan smugglers. Then when their ship turn up, Grub surprise them, too! Get plenty rich!'

'You've done great things,' said Aren. 'You'll be a hero when you return to your people, I bet. And you'll make fine reading for the Bone God when your time comes.'

Aren saw something flicker across Grub's face, a fleeting expression that might have been uncertainty or fear. Whatever it was, it was gone as quickly as it came, and as Grub's features darkened to a scowl, Aren sensed he'd made a mistake. He plunged on before the Skarl could hit him.

'What I mean to say is ... are you finished?'

'Uh? Finished?'

'Well, your whole right arm isn't filled in yet. Half your face, too. Seems like there's still space for great deeds, but I can't see much opportunity for heroism here. So is that it? Are you done?'

'Grub is not done!' Grub snapped. 'Grub not dying in here! Grub will make such a story that the Bone God marvels at his deeds!'

'You want to do something your bards will sing of?'

'Yes!'

Aren leaned forward. 'Then this is my trade. Help me, and I'll cut you in on my escape.'

Grub stared at him long and hard, suspicion and threat in his gaze. Then he took a step back and dusted Aren's shoulder with the back of his hand.

'Alright,' he said. 'Now Grub is listening.'

21

The autumn fogs came often in the high passes of the Ostenbergs. The next time they did, Aren was waiting.

It was an hour past curfew. The light had left the sky and the camp was muffled and stilled. Gauzy murk stirred in the spaces between the darkened longhouses and most of the prisoners were abed, snoring and sighing in their bunks. But for Aren, there'd be no rest tonight.

He sat on the edge of Cade's empty bunk while he laced his boots, his breath steaming. Four days had passed since the explosion in the mine, four days of healing, resting and planning. His bruises were mostly faded now, the swelling in his face gone down. He felt stronger than he had for a long while, both in body and mind.

Cade was getting better, too, not that you would know it by the way he screamed down the infirmary several times a day. His madness had mysteriously passed, but in its place he suffered inexplicable and agonising pains throughout his body. Doctor Baden was at a loss as to the cause. The only thing that helped was a spoonful of draccen tears to sedate him and ease his pain. Kel fretted about giving him too much – draccen tears were a powerful drug, and lethal in excessive doses – but nothing else worked.

She need not have worried. As soon as she left his bedside, Cade spat the draccen tears into Aren's water flask. It was already half-full; a little more and they could put their plan into action.

Aren had been assisting with the wounded when he could, both out of a genuine desire to help and to keep in touch with his friend. In the quiet moments, they had the opportunity to talk.

Outwardly, he was the Cade of old, quick to joke and to mock himself, friendly and easy in his manner. But Aren sensed he was in fragile spirits under the mask. All his hopes depended on Aren, and thoughts of escape were his only refuge from despair. Aren felt the weight of that responsibility, but knowing that Cade trusted him gave him courage.

He moved between the bunks, feeling his way to the door. His fellow prisoners were blue shadows against the shuttered windows, made anonymous by the dark. Some raised their heads as he passed, but none spoke to him or tried to stop him. He'd be far from the first to steal out after curfew on some secret errand.

The longhouses were not locked. Instead of bolts and padlocks, Captain Hassan had a simple rule: anyone caught outside after curfew without a pass would be fed to the skulldogs the following morning. No excuses, no exceptions. For most, it was an effective incentive to stay inside.

Aren had heard tales of prisoners forging passes, but if they existed they were beyond his influence to obtain. He'd just have to be careful.

The fog wasn't as thick as it had been last time, but it was full dark and he could barely see anything. He slipped through the chilly murk with nervous speed, pressing close to the longhouses, heading for the graveyard. Tonight, he meant to have a reckoning with a spirit.

Not a spirit. The dead are the dead, and they don't come back. It was just a boy.

A boy who'd survived, alone, for two years or more within the walls of the prisoners' compound. It felt easier to believe Rags was a shade, but Aren refused to accept that. His faith in an ordered world had been shaken, but he wouldn't embrace the folk wisdom of his ancestors in its place.

He was still scared, regardless.

The shifting fog made his eyes unreliable, showing him movement where there was none. He calmed his breathing and listened instead. There was little to hear in the eerie quiet but the song of the blood in his ears.

A creak of leather broke the silence.

Aren peered around the corner of a longhouse, his heart thumping hard. The noise came again, closer, and then closer still. It was unmistakably moving towards him. He tried to fix the direction but the fog thwarted him. Suddenly there was a brightening of the murk and a shadow moved. A guard walked out from around the corner, carrying a lantern, and in fright Aren flattened himself against the wall and went still. The guard passed by within a few feet of him, oblivious to his presence in the fog, and Aren, to his amazement, remained unseen.

He didn't move until the creak of the guard's leather armour had faded into silence. Only then did he dare to detach himself from the safety of his hiding place and go on. He tried not to think of Deggan as he went, but he couldn't help recalling his screams as the skulldogs went at him, the way his flesh fell apart beneath the dogs' red claws and teeth.

They won't take me alive, he promised himself. *I'll throw myself on their swords first.* But the gap between intention and action was always wider than he thought, and he wondered if he'd be brave enough for that.

He reached the strip of open ground between the longhouses and the graveyard and struck out across it. This time, as the walls on all sides disappeared into nothingness, there was no sense of clutching dread, and he climbed over the graveyard fence with a small sense of satisfaction.

Once among the graves, he felt more confident. The guards didn't patrol the graveyard; it was easy to turn an ankle on the broken earth or fall into a hole in the fog, and even the relentlessly sensible Krodans were not immune to fear of the supernatural on a night like this.

He crept towards the cliffs at the back of the camp. Lifeless trees, twisted as in torment, were feathered with roosting crows. Cairns of piled stones and leaning planks commemorated the dead. He picked his way between humps of earth, listening hard, but nothing moved among the graves, and no spirits rose to attack him.

He stopped deep in the heart of the graveyard, judging this spot as good as any, and sat down, leaning his back against a tall cairn.

Well, he thought. *Here I am.*

Cade had told him a story once, about the bloodmare, a horse-spirit with fanged teeth and bladed hooves that could bewitch travellers with its prancing. The enchanted travellers would climb on the bloodmare's back, and it would take them on a wild ride through the forest, which would end when it bucked them off a cliff or plunged them into a river to drown. Then the unlucky traveller would be eaten. It was pure Ossian folklore, though Cade had dressed it up as Krodan, for Aren's sake.

In the story, a clever hunter learned that a bloodmare might be lured and pacified by the song of a virgin girl. He set his daughter to the task and hid nearby, hoping to slay the beast when it arrived. The bloodmare came as expected, but, unbeknownst to the hunter, his daughter wasn't quite as virginal as she'd claimed to be, and the tale didn't end well for either of them.

There were no such thing as bloodmares, Aren told himself, but Sards were real, and their love of music was well known. He remembered the unsettling tune Rags had been singing when they first met. Now it was his turn.

He took a breath, let it out. He was trembling, and only partly from the cold. Then, in a small, thin voice, he began to sing.

His nannies and tutors had taught him Krodan songs and hymns in praise of the Primus, but they wouldn't do here. The song that came to his lips instead was an Ossian one, sung in the gliding tongue of his homeland.

It was known as 'The Mourner's Elegy', a song of loss, a celebration of a life together and a chronicle of quiet intimacies shared. To the unknowing, the grieving singer might have been a farmer or a merchant or a lord, or anyone who'd ever loved another to the limit of their ability. But there were hints to the truth in the verses. The dead woman was Jessa Wolf's-Heart, the greatest leader and hero Ossia ever had, and the man singing was Morgen, her lover and companion. 'The Mourner's Elegy' was a personal portrait of a woman otherwise known only as a legend.

It had been long since Aren had sung anything at all, for he wasn't fond of the sound of his voice, and there had been little to sing about of late. It had been longer still since he sang in Ossian, and the first verses came out frail with fear. He risked being overheard by a guard, if one came near enough, and he still had doubts about trying to lure Rags this way. He couldn't quite forget the sight of the shaggy-haired Sard boy eating raw crow.

But there among the graves the song found him, and it sank into his chest and warmed him like whiskey. His voice strengthened, and he closed his eyes and abandoned himself to the music. If he was to be heard, let him be heard, by friend or foe alike. There could be no half measures. This song, this course he'd set himself on, was life and death. He wouldn't shrink from it.

Time slipped away from him. He didn't know if his voice carried in the fog-shrouded night, or if he was the only one hearing it. Only when the song had finished did he come back to himself, and his voice quivered into silence.

He opened his eyes and his heart bucked against his ribs. There, crouching in the dark, was Rags. He was half-hidden behind a plank, his green gaze piercing in the gloom.

Aren's mouth went dry as each watched the other, and neither moved.

'No ghost you are,' the boy said at last, in heavily accented Ossian.

'Neither are you,' said Aren, and saying it broke the spell. It was only a boy, after all, and his fear left him.

A twig cracked somewhere in the fog. A muffled Krodan curse. The boy twisted in alarm, then turned back to Aren.

'You come,' he said urgently.

Aren needed no second invitation. There were Krodan guards in the graveyard. They'd heard the song. He scrambled to his feet, and together they hurried into the fog.

22

The boy led Aren through the graves to the foot of the cliffs, where a tangle of evergreens and shaggy vines grew close against the stone. There, he pulled aside a low branch and wriggled through the narrow space. Aren followed with considerably more difficulty.

He emerged, arms scratched and clothes torn, in a tiny hollow between the trees and the cliffs. Crammed in with the boy, he could smell the stink of him, old sweat and mould.

'Safe,' said the boy. 'Come.' There was a rustle of movement, and he was gone.

His disappearance startled Aren, who could see no way out of the hollow beyond the way they'd come in. He found himself alone in a distressingly tight space, with cold rock at his back and trees pushing in on him. He began to paw about, carefully at first but then with increasing panic as claustrophobia took hold. Cade's tales of trickster spirits came to him again, and he imagined himself caged here till he starved, lured to his doom by a shade in the shape of a boy.

Then, movement again, and the boy was back, seizing his wrist in a warm grip. 'Come!' he said impatiently, and tugged Aren. He felt about and found a corner, a fissure in the cliff that he'd somehow missed in this tiny space. The boy backed into the crack like a spider, still tugging at him, and Aren crushed himself down and followed. As he did so, he caught sight of something painted on the rock, a strange, twisting symbol of curves and slashes dense with meaning, stark and clear despite the darkness. After he went inside, it stayed floating before his eyes for a time, like an after-image of the sun.

'Come, come,' the boy said again. Aren felt along with his hands. Fabric brushed against his face, making him jump: a crude curtain, hanging in his way. The boy pushed it aside and guided him onwards.

'Come. Careful be.'

Can he see in here? Aren wondered. But that was ridiculous: the darkness was total. The boy simply knew the space like a blind man knew his home.

'Stay,' the boy said, and Aren did, surrounded by the void. The darkness and confinement should have frightened him, but he felt himself calming instead. He'd found the boy, and he was real. That was a victory.

A flint sparked. The wick of a rusty lamp caught and warmed into life, filling the space with a comforting glow. They were in a small cave, barely big enough to stand in, which was cluttered with junk and bric-a-brac and scattered with clothes. Piles of mildewed blankets were heaped untidily at one end like a nest, and there were bloody black feathers everywhere. In a crevice in the rock, arranged like ornaments on a mantelpiece, were the boy's treasures: coins, a ring, a handful of teeth, some damp cheroots. There was a pile of small round stones in a hollow off to one side: ammunition for his sling.

Aren looked about and marvelled. To find such a place here, hidden away in the joyless world of the camp, was like slipping through a portal into some shabby wonderland. Though it was freezing and dank and resembled the lair of a scavenging beast, it was a secret place, right under the noses of the Krodans. A place they had no power over. Its very existence was a rebellion.

The boy settled back on his haunches, scratched his dirty scalp and gave Aren a shy smile.

'Eifann,' he said, patting his chest.

'Aren,' said Aren, and did the same. 'How long have you been here?'

Eifann shrugged. 'When the others they are taking, me they are not seeing,' he said. He spoke in sing-song tones, the way all Sards did. 'I make it so.'

'You hid?'

Eifann shook his head, his filthy locks bobbing about his thin face. 'I *make* it so they are not seeing.' He patted his chest again. '*Ydraal. Ydraal.*'

Aren didn't know that word, and wasn't sure the boy had understood his question, so he let it go. 'I like your cave,' he said. Now he was here, he wasn't quite sure how to proceed, and it seemed best to be friendly.

Eifann grinned, showing brown teeth. 'Your song I like. In the past I hear.'

'You've heard it before?'

The boy nodded. 'I like.'

Aren studied him. He was a filthy scrag of a thing, with a thin face and dark brown hair, grinning at him in the lamplight. Belatedly it occurred to him that the light might be visible from outside, but when he looked over his shoulder, he saw a coat hanging across the entrance to the chamber and remembered the curtain that had brushed his face on the way in.

'Safe,' said Eifann, catching his thought. 'No Krodans.'

'How ...' Aren couldn't think of a delicate way to say it. 'How have you *survived* here?'

Eifann made a face that Aren couldn't read. A Sard expression, meaningless to him. 'Things I find. Things people leave. When I can, I steal.' He spun an imaginary sling and let fly. 'Crows.'

Aren looked at the items Eifann had collected and wondered if those cheroots had once belonged to him, and later to Grub. 'You steal from the prisoners' stashes?'

He nodded. 'Also from dead men I take. And the cookhouse. Risky, though.'

'And it's enough?'

'Sards tough. Hard to kill.'

They'd have to be, Aren thought. It seemed beyond the realms of possibility that a boy could survive undetected for so long, through the deadly winters and punishing summers, avoiding starvation and sickness and guards. 'Have you been alone this whole time?'

Eifann shook his head.

'There are others?'

'Them, you can't see.'

Aren frowned. Eifann's grasp of Ossian was shaky. Sards were insular folk by reputation, and many never learned to speak any language but their own. He was forcing Ossian words into the grammar of his mother tongue, which made him hard to follow at times.

'You mean you don't want to show me?'

Eifann giggled. 'You can't see! In the graves they are!' He patted his chest again. '*Ydraal.*'

'*Ydraal?*' Aren struggled to pronounce it. 'What does that mean?'

'Eifann is *ydraal*!' he said enthusiastically.

Aren was getting nowhere, and he was beginning to doubt the boy was entirely sane. Not surprising, given the circumstances. He decided to push on to the reason he'd come. 'Do you know a way out of here, Eifann?'

The boy looked uncertain. He shook his head.

Aren leaned forward. 'I do.'

Eifann made no reaction, just gazed at him with those bright green eyes.

'Do you want to come with me?' Aren said.

Eifann shook his head. Aren frowned in surprise. He hadn't been expecting a no. 'You don't?'

Eifann bit his lip. 'Out there is the not-knowing.'

'Isn't that better than staying here?'

Eifann shrugged and picked at a hole in the knee of his trousers. 'Here, I surviving. I eating. Out there, maybe not.'

'You eat crows! You shouldn't have to steal and hide and eat birds raw. That isn't living.'

Eifann didn't answer. He busied himself tidying his ammunition, patting the stones into a neat pile. Pretending Aren wasn't there.

Aren watched him incredulously. He'd expected the boy to jump at the chance to leave. Would he really rather live as he was, skulking and scavenging, hiding from the Krodans' notice? Who in their right mind wouldn't seize the chance to be free of that?

'You're scared,' he said. Scared of change, scared of leaving the world he knew. He saw it in the boy.

Eifann shook his head with the sulky defiance of someone who really meant yes.

'I'll look after you. I'll make sure you're safe, if you come with me.' Aren held out a hand. 'You just need to be brave.'

'Why?' Eifann snapped. His face was hard with suspicion now. 'You come to graveyard, you sing. Why?'

Aren let his hand drop; Eifann wasn't going to take it. 'I came to ask for your help,' he said. 'I hoped to offer you the chance of freedom in return.'

'Chance to die.' Eifann snorted. 'Better here.'

Aren sensed he'd lost the boy's goodwill by pushing him and cursed his own stupidity. He should have been gentler. 'I'm sorry. You're right. Better here. But not for me. I want to leave. Me and my friend.'

'Then go!' Eifann scrambled to the back of the cave and dug into the nest of blankets, pulling them over his head.

Aren stayed where he was, absently rubbing his arms for warmth, the acrid scent of burning oil wafting thinly around the cave. The sight of Eifann burying his head in his blankets moved him to pity. He was just a boy, and he'd been alone a long time. Aren suspected his imaginary 'friends' had made poor company. And yet he needed Eifann's help; it was essential to his plan. He softened his tone and tried again.

'Eifann.'

'Go!' Eifann demanded, his voice muffled.

'I can't, unless you help me.'

Eifann unleashed a string of curses in his mother tongue. The trilling, rolling language of the Sards was ill-suited to swearing. Even their anger sounded musical.

He's the shade of some Sard boy buried in the graveyard, and his ma got taken away. So now he wanders the camp at night, searching for her. Jan's words, spoken on the way to the mine the day after he first saw Eifann. They came to Aren now, and an idea came with them.

'If you don't want to leave, is there someone out there who might want to know where you are?'

Eifann shut up, and Aren knew he'd scored a hit.

'Help me now, and when I get out, I'll—'

'No!' Eifann snapped. Then he burst from his nest and scrambled over. 'Yes!' he cried eagerly. 'Yes! You get out, you help Sard! *Lled na saan*. What you giving me, give them.'

'I ... I'm not sure what you mean. Which Sard should I help?'

'All. Any. Find one. Offer you.'

'You want me to—?' Aren began, but suddenly Eifann seized his hand and pulled it towards him. He put the thumb of his other hand between his teeth and bit down on it, hard enough that blood squirted out in a thin jet between his lips. Before Aren could pull away, Eifann pressed his bloody thumb to the inside of Aren's wrist.

'Now,' he said with an air of angry finality. 'You find. Offer you.'

He took his hand away, leaving a red smear where his thumb had been. Aren fought down his repulsion. 'This is ... this is a promise?' he asked. 'Instead of helping you, I help another Sard? You're passing on my debt to someone who needs it?' he asked.

Eifann nodded. '*Lled na saan*. You find.'

Aren held up his wrist to show Eifann the mark. 'I promise, then,' he said solemnly. 'My debt to you will be repaid to another Sard. But first you must help me escape.'

Eifann sat in a pile of coats before him, breath steaming the air, green eyes sharp behind the matted ropes of his hair. 'What are you needing?'

Aren picked up a bloodstained wing bone from the floor near where he sat, and held it up. 'Crows,' he said. 'I need crows.'

23

Dull evening light seeped through the mud-flecked windows of the infirmary. Unlike the longhouses, which only had shutters, there was thick glass in the frames to keep in the heat from the stove at one end. It wasn't what Cade would call warm, but it was better than freezing in his old bunk. He pulled his blankets closer as he blearily roused from a dreamless sleep.

He'd become accustomed to napping through the afternoon to kill the time between lunch and dinner. They served decent food here, and while it still didn't have any meat in it – that was only for the guards – at least it came in quantity. Prisoners barely got enough to keep them alive and working, the result of some cold-blooded Krodan mathematics balancing the cost of food against the cost of replacing them. Casualties had a better time of it, as the doctor insisted his patients were well fed to aid their recovery, and he obviously had some clout.

Eight days had passed since the accident: three days short of a whole week. Eight days of nothing but eating, sleeping and lying about, and all for the price of feigning mysterious agonies now and then. The apothecary grumbled about the amount of draccen tears Cade was consuming, but he was so disruptive when he was screaming that Kel would do anything to quiet him. The apothecary would have grumbled a lot louder if he'd known that his precious draccen tears were all going into Aren's water flask. Soon it would be full and Cade would have to leave; but for now, just for now, he enjoyed the luxury of being idle.

The infirmary was quiet. The hectic activity after the explosion had long since died away and most of the casualties had recovered or perished. Only a few remained, men with infections or minor breaks, or malingerers like Cade. Those with no hope of recovery were taken from the infirmary. When Cade asked Kel where they'd gone, she evaded the question and looked distressed. That was all the answer he needed.

So much death. So much suffering. And yet…

He blinked. Something was different.

He felt alright.

Ever since he'd been brought to the camp at Suller's Bluff, he'd been greeted by despair each time he woke. Reality would sink slowly down upon him, a weight that pressed him into his bunk, weakened his muscles, turned his bones to rods of lead. His chest would become tight with cold panic, but before it could take him, there'd be a retreat into emptiness, as if all his emotion had been shorn to a stump. When he clambered reluctantly from his bunk to ready himself for the mine, he felt neither joy nor anger but indifference and endless weariness as he went about his day, and only by nightfall would he have gathered enough sorrow to let him cry a little.

That had been his life for more than three months now. But this evening, there was no sad, grey weight waiting to lay upon him.

He took a breath and let it out, testing this new sensation, as if by recognising it he might cause it to disappear. Despite everything, he felt like his old self again.

We're getting out of here, he thought.

He should have been terrified, but he was more excited than scared. He had hope for the first time since their arrest, since *before* their arrest. Beyond the stockade lay true freedom, and a future that didn't end in his father's workshop. They couldn't return to Shoal Point; they'd be recognised as fugitives and shopped to the Iron Hand within days. What adventures they might have instead, then! Perhaps they'd join an actors' troupe. Perhaps they'd find a ship that needed a good cook, and they could take to sea. He knew the risk they ran, the hardships that lay ahead and the very real possibility of death; but they were pale threats compared to the alternative. And Aren would have a plan. He always had a plan.

A smile broke out across Cade's face, unforced and real. It felt so good, he could have wept.

'Well!' said Kel as she made her way through the bunks towards him. 'Someone's in a good mood. Feeling better?'

'Aye,' said Cade. He sat up. 'Aye, I really am. Pain's been less of late. Might be I'll be good in a day or two.'

'Glad to hear it,' said Kel. 'The body's a marvel, ain't it? So much we don't know. But like as not, if you leave it long enough, it'll fix itself.'

Her smile eased him. She had a comforting face that spoke of scones by the hearth, warm snuggles under a blanket on a cold night, tousle-haired children clambering to their places at the kitchen table. He realised he was attracted to her, and it made him blush.

'Aw, you've got some colour in your cheeks, too!' Kel said. 'You really are on the mend. Lucky for you – the doctor was just reading his old books for remedies.'

'A hot herbal bath, a massage, that kind of thing?' Cade suggested hopefully.

Kel let out her big belly-laugh. 'Reckon he was thinking of something a little more stabby.'

Cade winced. 'Suddenly I feel completely recovered.'

'You stay right there for the moment. Let's not rush things, eh? Couple more days in bed won't hurt.' She winked at him. 'I'll hold off the doctor.'

Cade yawned. 'You know, after all that sleeping, I *could* do with a bit of a rest.'

'I bet you could.' She gave him a pat on the cheek, which Cade found both touchingly maternal and slightly arousing. 'I'll get you your dinner first, though.'

'I'll take the pheasant with plum sauce today, I reckon.'

'Ha! I think you might have to stay longer; you're obviously delirious. Oh! I nearly forgot! Tell Aren someone was asking for him in town.'

That brought Cade up short. 'Er ... someone was *asking* for him?'

'Aren of Shoal Point. Seems that a stranger paid Little Edd

the baker's lad to find out if he was in the camp. Reckon it was supposed to be done on the quiet, but they picked the wrong boy. Little Edd couldn't keep his pie-hole shut if the fate of the world depended on it.'

'But … who? Did the stranger give a name?' Cade had no clue what to make of this news, but he sensed it was important.

'No name. I thought you might have an idea. Exciting, though, eh? Sounds like someone's come to get him out. I could tell Aren was a highborn boy.' She saw the look on Cade's face and her own face fell. 'I thought you'd be pleased. You and him, from the same town … I just assumed you'd been put in here for the same thing. He goes free, you go free. Was I wrong?'

He didn't know. All he knew was that someone had turned up in the village asking for Aren. Just Aren. Cade had no connections, no money to grease the wheels. What if they were only interested in getting Aren out, and not him?

'Did Little Edd say what the stranger looked like?' Cade was desperate for any clue to make sense of it.

'Well, yes, he did,' said Kel dubiously. 'It just didn't sound very likely.'

'What does *that* mean?'

'Apparently he has a big scar from here to here.' She drew a finger across her neck. 'I mean, there's only one way you get a scar like that. And there's not many that keep walking after someone cuts their throat.'

Cade went cold. 'The Hollow Man does,' he said, his voice faint.

Kel only half-caught what he said. 'The who?'

Cade was already clambering out of bed.

'Hey, hey, no!' she cried. 'You're supposed to rest!'

'Ain't no need,' he said distractedly as he pulled on his boots. 'I'm feeling much better. You're a miracle worker, Kel.'

'But what about those pains you've been getting?'

He dug under his pillow, pulled out the water flask and stuck it in his pocket. 'Probably just trapped wind.'

'Trapped wind!' She was getting angry now. 'We had to keep you sedated for a week! It was more than trapped sodding wind!'

She looked around for someone to assist her, but there were no other staff nearby.

Cade got to his feet. His legs felt weak from lack of use and Kel caught him as he swayed. 'Look at you! You're in no state to go anywhere!'

Cade steadied himself, holding on to her arms. He became aware that they were in something like a clinch, looking into each other's eyes. His face heated.

'Thank you for all you've done,' he said earnestly. Then, on a wild whim, he added: 'You're really pretty.'

'Uh?' Kel was baffled by the sudden turn in the conversation.

Cade realised he'd miscalculated the moment somewhat. 'Never mind,' he said. He hurried away, spurred by the awkwardness he left behind. 'Trapped wind!' he called again over his shoulder, and he was out through the door.

24

It was the end of a dreary day, and the short dirt road to the south gate was busy as curfew approached. The prisoners who staffed the laundry, the workshop and the cookhouse were finishing up their duties and leaving. There was no holiday for them when the mine was closed, and they paid for their easier labour with longer hours. A few men and women from the village – nannies, servants, infirmary workers and the like – stayed overnight in the camp, but most left before darkness fell. A queue of carts had built up at the gate as they waited to be searched.

Aren and Grub loitered on a corner, watching the activity. The Skarl had a habit of standing closer than Aren was comfortable with – he had an unpleasantly musky smell about him, like a damp bear – but Aren was learning to tolerate it. Since their uneasy alliance had been forged, Grub had taken to hanging around him a lot. At first, Aren thought it was because Grub wanted to keep an eye on him, but he soon found the true reason. Nobody else would put up with Grub.

The smell of him was the least of it. He boasted constantly and at length of his great deeds. His sense of humour was unpleasantly cruel and revolved around vulgarity and belittling others. When he wasn't boasting or joking he was threatening Aren, and yet despite his apparent dislike of the younger man, he came trailing up like an errant puppy whenever he was at a loose end. Aren had suggested that such an important hero might have better things to do than hang about with an insignificant Ossian like himself, but Grub hadn't taken the hint. He was annoying to be around and impossible to shake off. Aren wondered if he'd been better as an enemy.

'There he is,' Aren said.

Across the road, Tag was emerging from the cookhouse. He was followed by Gren, the stout, waddling master of the kitchen, buttoning his coat as he came. Gren was an amiable Krodan with a shiny bald head and flowing black moustaches, who was always happy to ramble on about the merits of Krodan cooking to any prisoner who'd listen. Even in the days when Aren had envied all things Krodan, he'd have been hard pressed to agree that their bland, stodgy cuisine was superior to that of Ossia. Ossians knew how to eat and drink; nobody could deny that. Nobody but Gren, anyway, who possessed an evangelical spirit and sense of self-belief wildly out of proportion to his actual ability. Every day he took on the challenge of transforming the meanest and cheapest ingredients into something that would delight the palate, and every day he failed.

Diligence. Temperance. Dominance. The credo of the Sanctorum and the motto of Krodans everywhere. Evidently it didn't always work, since Gren could barely dominate a potato; but the prisoners appreciated his enthusiasm, at least.

They watched Tag lock up the cookhouse and hand the key to Gren, who popped it in the pocket of his pigskin overcoat. Unlike the prisoners, people from the village got to wear clothes appropriate to the weather.

'Right side pocket, same as always,' Aren said.

'Same pocket always, yes, yes. Grub not as stupid as you. Grub take key, no problem. Grub slip fake key in pocket. Fat man not know difference till morning.'

He brandished the fake key in front of Aren's face. It was a crude approximation they'd obtained from the workshop, cut from a splinter of metal by a prisoner Aren had bribed with new boots. Grub, like the others who worked on the graves, had more dead men's clothes than he knew what to do with since the explosion in the mine.

Aren eyed the key uncertainly. This was the part of the plan he wasn't sure of, mainly because it wasn't his idea. Grub had pointed out that Gren would notice the missing key first time he put his hand in his pocket. They needed to replace it with something.

'And you're sure you can do it? Take one key and slip in the other, without him noticing?'

Grub's hand twitched and the key disappeared before Aren's eyes, as if it had vanished into thin air. The Skarl gave him a flat stare.

'Grub could just pick the lock, but stealing key is easier. Cookhouse got the best lock in the camp. Take time. Grub not want to get caught. Then he have to kill many guards, things get messy.'

'You're a man of many talents,' said Aren. 'An excellent thief *and* a peerless warrior.'

'Grub impresses himself sometimes. Also, he can detect sarcasm. Watch your mouth, Mudslug.'

Aren couldn't help but be sceptical. He knew Skarl society forbade them to falsify their history; it was a severe crime to lie about their deeds, otherwise anyone could get themselves tattooed and call themselves a hero. There was even some kind of priesthood called the Black Triad that existed to verify their claims. But even though Grub came from a people for whom honesty was a religion, his stories of might and valour were hard to square with this noxious bully nobody liked.

'So, once you've switched the key, what then?' Aren prompted.

Grub rolled his eyes. 'Grub go to the graveyard, pick up the package.'

'Which will be buried where?'

'Behind big cairn in north-east corner. Grub still want to know who put package there and what's inside.'

'Grub doesn't need to know that.'

'Grub got two fists says he does.'

'Then Grub is going to spend what's left of his life in this prison, and he'll die with half his body clean as an idiot's conscience.'

The beatings Aren had taken at Grub's hands were fresh enough that he still had some fear of the man, but he was no longer the victim he once was. Grub's threats were empty, and he was desperate to escape. As long Aren refused to tell Grub the details of his plan, he had the upper hand.

174

Grub bared his teeth in a snarl, but he backed down and said nothing more about his two fists.

'What are Cade and I doing while you're at the graveyard?' Aren asked, as if nothing had happened.

'You hiding in the bathhouse, which Grub will get you into,' he said pointedly, sulking. 'Putting on warm coats and boots which Grub will give you. Meanwhile Grub will get package from graveyard because it less suspicious to see Grub digging there. Seems like Grub doing all the work.'

Aren ignored that. 'We'll make a blanket rope while you're gone, and after that—'

'Grub got you spare blankets as well. Cold in mountains. Thank you, Grub!'

Aren gave him an *are you finished?* look which he'd learned from Master Fassen. 'After that, it should be curfew. We'll sneak out to the cookhouse, take as much food as we can carry and escape.'

'Yes. Past the dogs, who will bark and then pull our guts out like shiny sausages. Unless someone has a plan ...?' Grub waited expectantly.

'Someone does.'

Grub muttered something unpleasant in Skarl.

'So we get past the dogs. Next are the guards on the walkway,' Aren continued. His eyes lifted to the archers watching the carts passing through the south gate below them. 'Ideally we'll slip past in the fog, but if someone should see us—'

'Someone will have to kill them. Who could it be?' Grub put a finger to his lower lip and looked upwards in a parody of deep thought, then gaped in mock surprise. 'Could it be ... Grub?'

'That's right,' said Aren patiently.

'Using the weapons that Mudslug still hasn't got.'

Aren didn't dignify that with an answer. The man in the workshop who'd made him the fake key had promised him three crude blades for the extortionate price of a new coat, trousers and socks, but it would be days before he could forge them. The wait made Aren uneasy. At least he'd managed to get them some makeshift hooks and line for fishing.

'Once we're beyond the camp, we can follow the river to Hailfell and then go our separate ways.'

He glanced at Grub, hoping the Skarl didn't have any ideas about tagging along, but Grub's attention was elsewhere. He was watching a crow that had perched on the ridge of the cookhouse roof. The crow was watching him back.

'We go soon, yes?' His voice was distant.

'The next fog,' Aren said. There wasn't much sign of it, though. The weather had turned towards rain of late and the mine would be open again in a few days. Right now they were less hungry than usual and well rested, but that would change if they had to wait too long. They'd be in no state to run all night through the mountains if they spent all day in the tunnels.

If only the mine would stay shut a while longer. If only the weapons would come quicker. If only the fog would return.

Grub nudged him roughly with his elbow. He suppressed a scowl. 'What is it?'

'That your friend?' Grub pointed, his brow creased in puzzlement. To Aren's surprise, he saw Cade hurrying up the road from the infirmary. It was clear something was wrong.

Aren hailed him, and Cade, wary of drawing attention, walked over as fast as he could without running.

'You're supposed to stay in the infirmary till the flask is full!' Aren said.

'There's a man in town asking for you!' Cade blurted. 'With a scar across his throat!' He noticed Grub, raised a hand in greeting. 'Cade. Pleasure. Heard a lot about you.'

Grub raised a hand in a grudging half-greeting.

Aren had gone cold with shock at the news. 'A scar on his throat?'

'Like it's been cut, Aren! Like someone cut it! The Hollow Man is here! We have to go!'

'Tell me exactly what you heard.' His face was grim, set hard to mask his real feelings. Instinct told him that to show fear and uncertainty in front of Grub was unwise at best, if not outright dangerous, but he could see Grub becoming narrow-eyed with suspicion as Cade finished his tale.

'Who this Hollow Man? What he want with you?'

He's come to kill me, thought Aren in terror.

His father had warned him about the Hollow Man all his life. What he'd thought was a tale to scare a child was no tale at all, but real, and just beyond those walls. Now all those nightmares came swarming out of the past.

'We're not waiting for the fogs,' he said. 'We're going tomorrow night, whatever the weather.'

Grub looked worried. 'Tomorrow night blood moon.'

'Exactly,' said Aren. He hadn't known that until Grub said it, but he adapted quickly. 'Lyssa won't be in the sky. By Tantera's light alone, it'll be hard to see. We can slip past the archers then.'

Grub crossed his arms stubbornly. 'Blood moon bring bad luck. Spirits come out to play, everyone know that! Only stupid men travel on blood moon. Grub think this is bad idea.' A long shriek echoed through the drab evening, coming from the peaks, mournful and unutterably sad. 'Even horrible thing in mountains think it bad idea,' Grub added.

'Am I hearing you right?' Aren asked. 'Aren't you Grub, the great warrior? Grub who slayed ten elaru single-handed? Grub who bedded a Harrish noblewoman and escaped a household of angry guards when her husband came home? Grub who took on an ice bear and won?'

'Yes!' Grub cried. 'Yes, that was Grub!'

'Didn't you slay a whole shipload of Boskan smugglers? Didn't you fight in the Sixth Purge against the urds and live to tell of it?'

'Yes! Grub did all those things!' He beat his chest with his fist.

'And is this mightiest of warriors scared of children's stories about ghosts and shades coming out on a blood moon?'

'Yes! Wait, no! Grub punch ghosts in the face!'

Aren slapped him on the shoulder with as much manful swagger as he could muster. 'That's what I wanted to hear! I'll see you on the morrow. Be ready!'

He strode away quickly, leaving Grub standing on the corner. By the time the Skarl realised that Aren had never answered his question about the Hollow Man, Aren had gone.

Cade caught him up a few dozen yards down the road. 'Was that the same feller who was pounding your chops in a week ago?' he asked in amazement.

'You just have to know how to talk to people,' Aren said. 'Have you got the flask?'

Cade patted his pocket. 'It's nearly full, though I'll own a fair bit of it is my slobber.'

'It'll serve,' said Aren. He was flint-eyed with purpose. They'd set their course now, and it had all become very real.

'Are we really going to do this?' Cade asked. 'Escape? I mean, if the Hollow Man's here for you, maybe you're safer inside.'

'Whoever the Hollow Man is, my father was scared to death of him,' Aren said. 'If he's found me, he can get to me.'

He didn't know how it would happen, but he knew with certainty that it would. A prisoner, bribed to poison him? An arrow from the trees as they marched to the mine? Or could the Hollow Man walk through walls as in Aren's nightmares, a shade not subject to the limitations of human flesh? Would Aren wake in the night to find his murderer standing by his bunk, a blade in his hand, the wound in his throat gaping?

If you ever see the Hollow Man, you run. You run and you don't stop.

His father knew of the Hollow Man. His advice was to run. Aren thought it good counsel.

'There's something I need to do before curfew,' said Aren, fear making him brusque. 'I'll see you back at the longhouse.'

'Aren.' Cade stopped him with a hand on his shoulder. Aren saw the look on his face and softened. Cade was as scared as he was.

'We're going to make it,' Aren assured him. 'When the sun rises the day after tomorrow, it'll find us free.'

'Aye,' said Cade. 'One way or another.'

Aren clasped his forearm, and Cade clasped his in return, and Aren pulled him into a fierce Ossian hug. It felt like what men did, and it made them feel like men. No words could do more.

Aren headed off, his mind awhirl. There was a bigger story here, he was certain of it. The Hollow Man, his father's secrets, that glimpse of Klyssen in the windows of the overseer's mansion. Unsettled animals in the village, sightings of a druid in the forest. Somehow it was all connected.

If he lived past tomorrow night, he'd find out how.

First, though, he was going to the graveyard, to leave a little crow-bone charm by a cairn, where Eifann had told him to place it.

The thought of the boy saddened him. Aren had no love for Sards, but still, it was hard to leave him in a place like this. The tragedy of it was that Eifann didn't *want* to leave, that he was too scared of what was beyond the limits of his tiny world to act.

Aren would have tried to persuade him again, but he'd seen nothing of him since that strange night in the fog. He'd gone back during the day but had been unable to find Eifann's cave. There were several places where trees grew thick against the cliffs, but none looked quite right, and he didn't want to endanger the boy by investigating too closely. Singing wouldn't work, either; Eifann would only be found if he wanted to be.

He rubbed his thumb against the mark on the inside of his wrist, the mark left by Eifann to seal the promise Aren had made. Blood against skin, that was all it was; and yet no matter how hard Aren wiped or rubbed it, it refused to come off.

25

Gren the cook was a man of impressive girth, and Grub had to crash into him with considerable force to knock him over.

'Oh! Grub very sorry!' he cried. He'd gone down with Gren and was now struggling to get to his feet while trying to pull Gren up at the same time. 'Grub not look where he going!'

'That's alright. Just an accident, no harm done,' said Gren with forced patience, trying to extricate himself from the tangle of Grub's arms. The road to the south gate was always busy near the end of the day, and some of the other prisoners were smirking at his misfortune.

'Cook-man not hurt?' Grub straightened the sleeves of his overcoat for him. 'Grub got mud on Cook-man's coat.'

'Don't concern yourself,' said Gren, stepping away. 'It'll wash out.' He smoothed his moustaches, raised his chin and put on a smile. 'Those are some magnificent tattoos!' he observed.

'They tell story of Grub's mighty deeds. This one mean—'

He was interrupted by a blow. 'Get out of here, you clumsy Skarl freak,' the guard said in Krodan. Grub glowered and slunk away, holding his ear.

'Was there any need for that?' Gren asked. 'It was an accident.'

'Do I tell you how to cook?' snapped the guard.

Aren, who'd been loitering nearby, detached himself from the wall of the laundry and slipped away from the road, into the alleys between the close-packed buildings. It was another grey day, and steely clouds hid the highest peaks of the mountains. Cade had told him that he'd been praying to Joha for fog to cover their escape, but if the Heron King heard him, he'd been ignored.

At least they had clouds to obscure the stars and mute the weak red glow of the cracked moon. It would be dark tonight. Very dark.

That would have to suffice.

He'd barely slept last night, kept awake by a cocktail of excitement and nerves. His mind raced with plans and it was a long time before he felt tired enough to close his eyes. When he did, he imagined the Hollow Man standing by his bed, and they flew open again. But dawn found him still alive, and he managed to doze for a while before first bell roused them for breakfast.

He found Grub among the longhouses, at the corner where they'd agreed to meet after his encounter with Gren. Cade was already there.

'Do you have it?' he asked Grub.

'Ha!' said Grub, producing the key. 'Easy. Fat man not notice anything.' He winced and rubbed the side of his head. 'Grub going to get that guard, though. Rip his throat out and stuff it up his nose.'

Aren wasn't certain that was even possible. 'It was well done, anyway.' He held out his hand for the key.

'Ah-ah! Grub thinks he'll hold on to this. Just in case.' The key disappeared back into his pocket.

Aren felt a flash of anger. 'You don't trust me?'

'No,' said Grub, with brutal honesty. 'And Mudslug doesn't trust Grub. That why Grub still doesn't know half the plan.'

'Reckon that's fair enough,' said Cade quickly, seeking to defuse the confrontation he saw coming. 'We're all in this together, ain't we? Let him keep the key.'

Cade was right. They'd never actually agreed that Aren would keep the key. Aren just didn't like Grub's defiance. He needed everyone to stick to the plan, and the Skarl's temperament made him a liability. But this was a battle he didn't need to fight, so he let it pass.

'Fine,' he said. 'Let's go. We have a lot to do.'

The bathhouse was tucked away in the south-west corner of the compound, where the river ran up close against the stockade. It was locked when not in use. Stone walls and a stout door secured by a padlock and chain kept prisoners out.

They stopped at the corner. Nobody was around, and the surrounding buildings obscured the archers' view. Grub slipped up to the door and pulled on the handle. It opened a short way before the chain stopped it, just enough for Aren and Cade to slip through.

'Padlock *look* sturdy,' Grub told them. 'Cheap, though. Grub know the kind. Pop open easy if you know how.' He'd been here earlier in the day, opened the padlock and moved it further down the chain. The bathhouse still looked secure, but the chain was now slack on the handles.

'Grub go to graveyard now, fetch package like good little errand boy,' he said, once Aren and Cade were inside. He glared at them suspiciously through the gap between door and jamb. 'It better be worth it.' He pulled the door shut and they were alone.

'That feller's actually pretty handy to have around,' Cade observed, once he'd gone.

'You haven't spent the last week trying to scrape him off,' Aren said. 'We'll dump him the moment we get to Hailfell.'

They were in a bare grey antechamber with wooden cubbyholes built along one side. Here the prisoners would strip and stash their clothes before heading to the bath beyond. Aren had never been in here when it was empty before, and he felt the thrill of trespassing.

'At the back, he said,' Cade reminded him, and walked into the bathing chamber. Aren followed warily, half suspecting an ambush.

The bathing chamber wasn't large; the smallest pool in the public baths in Shoal Point had been bigger. Tiled walls chilled air that was already cold, and high, narrow windows did little to lighten the gloom. Water dripped from the ceiling, stealthy wet plinks and taps echoing in the hollow space. In the centre was the rectangular bath, empty now. Sluices at either end were used to fill it from the river and drain it again. Many a bathing prisoner had wished they could exit as easily as the water did, but the sluices were covered with iron grilles and far too small to crawl through.

Cade skirted the pool to the far corner, where brooms and mops and pails leaned untidily. He dug among them and pulled out a hemp sack. Aren checked the back rooms to be satisfied nobody was hiding there, and returned to find Cade pawing through the contents of the sack.

'Looks like he was as good as his word,' Cade said, holding up a coat. He pulled out a pair of woollen gloves. 'Gloves! Nine, I didn't dare to *dream* of gloves!'

Here were the clothes Grub had promised, taken from the dead. The shirts and thin coats were a pitiful defence against the cold, but they were more effective when layered. Some were bloodstained and torn, and they reeked of old sweat, urine and something worse: the acrid taint of death, which Ossians called Sarla's perfume. But none of that was anything to Aren and Cade, who'd endured too much to wrinkle their noses at a few bad smells. They buttoned up coats on top of coats, pulled trousers over trousers excitedly.

'I think I'm warming up,' said Cade. 'I'd forgotten how that felt.'

'When we get to Hailfell, you'll forget what hungry feels like, too.' Aren was sitting on the floor, levering off his boots. 'First thing we'll do is find an inn and buy a dish of meat.'

'Oh, don't,' Cade begged. 'Delicious, delicious flesh. You know how long it's been since I ate something that had a heartbeat?'

'Proper bread, made from actual wheat and warm from the oven,' Aren said. 'Thick, dark ale. Whole trout as long as your arm, cooked in butter and herbs with golden potatoes.'

Cade groaned and shovelled imaginary food into his mouth with both hands.

'Wild boar in truffle sauce! Strake eggs and capers! Bacon!' Aren got his boot off at last and a hiss of pain escaped him, interrupting his culinary fantasies. The socks beneath were worn to a webbing, the skin of his foot raw with blisters, his little toe bruised blue. The smile fell from Cade's face, and Aren knew he was remembering that night when Aren had brought him a cheese roll and new thick socks for the winter, traded for cheroots he'd taken from a dead man.

'Aren...' he began.

'Doesn't feel as bad as it looks,' Aren lied. 'Don't worry about it.'

'No, I need to say it. I'm sorry. I'm really sorry about ... before.'

Aren waved it away. 'You were having a bad time.'

'No, that's ...' He struggled with what to say. Real apologies never came easily, especially among friends. 'That ain't an excuse. I shouldn't have said that stuff. You always had my back, and no one else ever did.'

'We've always had each other's,' said Aren. 'And we always will.'

'You could've left me behind in the mine. I didn't deserve what you did.'

'I'll never leave you behind, Cade,' said Aren. 'Never.'

Cade turned away and made out he had something in his eye. 'Well,' he said. 'Well.' But his voice wobbled and he went no further.

Aren picked out some new socks and eased them over his toes. 'You know, if you're ready, there are blankets in the sack that need knotting into a rope,' he said casually.

'Aye,' said Cade. 'Aye, I'll get right to it.' He set to work, glad of the distraction, and neither of them said anything else until they heard the chain clink on the bathhouse door and Grub stormed in.

'What is this?' he shouted, holding up a small, dirty sack. He tossed it to the ground and its contents tumbled out.

'Those,' said Aren, getting to his feet, 'are crows. Nice fresh ones, killed and plucked just last night.' He felt a flood of relief at the sight. Eifann had honoured his side of the deal.

'Mudslug not say package full of dead crows!'

'I didn't say it wasn't,' Aren pointed out. 'Why are you angry?'

'Crows are eyes of Urgotha! Bone God! Not supposed to kill crows!'

'I didn't know that,' said Aren as he came walking over with Cade. 'Ossians have a similar legend about Sarla. You think they work for *both* gods, or do some work for one, and some the other?'

'You not take Bone God lightly! Mudslug not worth the ink on Grub's arse!' he raged. 'Why you need dead crows? Better be good reason, or Grub kill you!'

'I'll show you.' Aren knelt down and picked up a crow. Eifann had done a rough job of plucking them and feathers still clung to their bloody stippled skin. 'They don't stock meat in the cook-house, since prisoners aren't allowed any. It's all kept in the guards' section. So this is the best we could do.' He drew out his tin water flask from his pocket with his other hand. 'Draccen tears.

A spoonful of this will knock a grown man out. Much more will kill him.'

He popped the cap off the flask with his thumb and poured some of the mixture into the crow's open beak. Then he pinched the beak shut. 'Now it's a tasty snack for a skulldog. Cade, could you?'

He handed it to Cade, who was waiting with a twist of string to tie the crow's beak closed.

'Dog eat crow, dog fall asleep!' said Grub, his face clearing as it dawned on him.

'Or it dies,' said Cade. 'Whichever is fine.'

A broad smile split Grub's tattooed face. 'Dogs sleep, we creep past, climb up to walkway and sneak over!' He appeared to have forgotten his earlier reservations about dead crows. 'You smarter than you look!'

'If that ain't faint praise, I don't know what is,' said Cade wryly.

Then the sound of slow clapping stilled them all.

26

'Brothers!' said Rapha as he walked into the bathing chamber, followed by half a dozen brutes with long knives. 'Look at you! A merrier band of rogues I've not seen in longaday.' His arms were open wide in a friendly gesture that wasn't fooling anyone.

Aren gave Grub an accusing glare. His first thought was that the Skarl had betrayed them.

'Ah, don't put the blame on him, now,' said Rapha. 'You ought to be smarter about who you go askin' for weapons, highborn. Word gets around. People start to pay attention.'

His cronies spread out, circling both sides of the bath. Aren felt bitter anger in his gut. One little mistake, when everything had been going so well. Failing now would be too cruel to bear.

He raised his palms. 'We don't want trouble, Rapha. Do you want in? Is that why you've come?'

Rapha let out a low chuckle. 'Brother, I could leave this prison tonight if I had the mind. Half the guards in Suller's Bluff take my coin, and the other half know what'll happen to their families if they cross me.' He looked at Cade. 'Didn't you tell him? This is *my* kingdom.'

'It's your kingdom,' Aren agreed. 'We just want to leave.'

'Ah, but if things were that simple, what an easy life we'd all have, eh?' said Rapha, in a tone of insincere regret. 'But bein' a king carries certain responsibilities. Keepin' order, that's one. So when I hear a man wants to get his hands on some blades, I get to askin' what for? Might be they're plannin' to even a score with another prisoner. Might be they got designs on killin' a guard or two. Maybe the overseer himself, given the chance.'

He strolled around the edge of the pool to Grub. The Skarl shrank back against the wall, baring his teeth like a cornered cur, showing no sign of the great warrior he professed to be.

'The key,' said Rapha.

Grub handed over the cookhouse key without protest, and Aren's heart sank further as Rapha pocketed it.

'Gren's a good man,' said Rapha. 'Heart's in the right place, Krodan or not. What do you think'll happen to him when they find the cookhouse robbed and his key gone? Who'll feed his family when he loses his job? Who'll feed your fellow prisoners? You think the food's bad now, but that's 'cause you weren't here before Gren turned up. The man's a sorcerer in the kitchen considerin' what he has to work with. Consequences, brothers. Any of you think of that?'

Aren hadn't, and on another day he might have felt a pang of guilt. Under the circumstances, however, Gren's plight didn't concern him in the least.

Rapha walked over to him, tugging his beard absently. 'When order in the kingdom breaks down, people start to ask if the king knows what he's doin'. If he's really up to scratch, so to speak. Maybe he has to pay out a whole pile o' guilders to make it right. Maybe he has to make promises he don't want to. And maybe the *next* king starts to think he's a soft touch, and gets to sharpenin' his blade. All 'cause a few little rats bit the hand that feeds them.'

'We didn't mea—' Cade began.

'You shut up!' Rapha snapped, turning from genial to terrifying in an instant. 'I was there when you needed help, and this is how you repay me?'

Cade clammed up, shocked into silence, and Rapha turned back to Aren.

'You're highborn, but you're Ossian even so,' he said. 'You know how it is. You need a permit from your masters just to leave the town where you live. Used to be that way where I came from, too. Peasant wanted to up and move, he had to ask permission from his lord.'

'And you're the king in here,' Aren said, keeping his voice steady. Though his heart was hammering, he met the pirate's gaze steadily. Even more than with Grub, he knew weakness would prove fatal.

'I'm the king,' Rapha agreed. 'And you didn't ask my permission.'

'We didn't know.' No chance that excuse would wash, but he tried anyway.

'Too late for that. Might be I'd have given you my blessin', had you asked, but that time's past. So this can go two ways. Either my boys take two fingers from each o' you, make the next fool with an idea think twice before they step outside the chain o' command.' He leaned closer and his voice was a low snarl. 'Or you offer me somethin' precious enough to salve my hurt feelin's and let you carry on with this little endeavour o' yours.'

There it was. For all his talk, the pirate just wanted his price. Only Aren had nothing to give him.

When Cade had met him in his den, Rapha had been looking for something that might be of advantage to his contacts on the outside, someone he could leverage or extract a bribe from. But Aren's father had been disgraced and executed, his lands and goods seized. Aren's very name was poisoned. He had no money, no possessions and nobody of influence would be unwise enough to associate with him any more.

Still, he could lie. He could lie, and pretend his father was still alive and rich, and promise Rapha anything under the sun. But it was a desperate gamble, for he wasn't sure how much Rapha knew; and he couldn't make himself do it anyway. It would be giving too much of himself away. Even if it meant their escape, he wouldn't be a craven deceiver.

His hesitation lasted too long and Rapha stepped back, fleeting disappointment on his face. 'Shame. It was a good plan. Thought you had potential.' He motioned at Cade without looking. 'Him first.'

'No!' Aren cried. Two of Rapha's men seized Cade while two others menaced Grub with their knives. He stayed against the wall, disinclined to interfere. Cade struggled and cried out as they pulled the glove from his left hand, forced it open and put the edge of a blade to it. His horrified gaze met Aren's. *Don't let them do this!*

'I have nothing you want!' Aren protested to Rapha.

'That's probably true,' said Rapha, implacable. 'But there needs to be a price.'

'A king can show mercy!'

'Mercy's cheap coin if it's given too freely.' He thought a moment. 'But you've got a point.' He looked over at his men. 'Take the little fingers. That way he can still hold a pickaxe.' He turned back to Aren. 'There's mercy. Seems I'm a soft touch after all.'

Aren sought desperately for a way to avoid what was coming. Two fingers or all of them, the end would be the same for Cade. His courage hung by a thread. If he didn't escape tonight, his will would be broken for good. A month, maybe a year, and he'd be dead. Aren didn't even think of his own fingers, only of his friend's. If he was maimed, all was lost.

'Think fast, little rabbit,' Rapha said, with something wicked in his eye. This was a game to him, Aren realised. He just wanted to see if Aren could think his way out of it. He won respect in the eyes of his men either way.

Rage heated his thoughts. He wanted to spring at Rapha, steal his blade, turn the tables. But such heroics were the stuff of Cade's fictions.

To overcome your enemy, you must first understand him.

Rapha was more than just a pirate. He chose to stay in a Krodan work camp rather than walk free. He'd sailed the seas as a reaver and made a great fortune, but now he hid behind a stockade like some reclusive mastermind, running his schemes in the world outside but never seeing the results. He sometimes worked in the mine just for the exercise – or possibly the risk. He'd given ragweed to Cade, perhaps out of misplaced kindness, perhaps to see him hooked.

Why was he hiding? Were Baric League assassins really hunting him in revenge for plundering their galleon, as rumour had it? Was he hiding at all, or was there some other reason for his staying here? What did it mean? Who *was* he?

In that moment, something happened to Aren. He felt it like a revelation. The scraps of information he'd gathered about Rapha were like swiped brushstrokes on a canvas. By themselves, they signified nothing; but step back, see how they joined, and a picture emerged that was truer than the sum of its parts. Aren saw that picture now, and he saw Rapha, too, and knew him. Cade's distress gave him the courage to speak.

'I'll tell you what I'll give you, Rapha,' he said. Something in his tone impressed the pirate, for he held up his hand to halt his cronies just as they were preparing to make the first cut. 'I'll give you *me*. One service, whatever you want, for you to claim any day from this until my last. One task, one deed, one favour, no matter what the cost to myself, no matter how despicable I might find it. If you let us go.'

A slow sneer of disdain spread across Rapha's face. 'Is that all? What worth are you to me?'

'Now? None. But I will be more than this. I can't say what fortune holds for me, but in ten years I'll not be a cooper or a cart-driver, I'll tell you that. And wherever I am, whatever I become, I'll remember my vow. When you call, I'll answer. Who can say what worth I'll prove to you then?'

Rapha looked amazed. 'You'd have me give you your freedom on the strength of a promise? You're saying that, should you end up as more than wolf dung in the forest, you *might* one day be of use? Forgive me, brother, I vastly underestimated the size of your balls.'

But Aren was deadly serious. 'I think you know the value of what I'm offering,' he said. 'You trade in favours, you gamble and you look to the future. You're not planning to stay in this hole. One day, all those friends of yours on the outside will have dealt with whatever keeps you here, and you'll be back on the seas where your heart is. You don't want our fingers; what use are they to you? The potential for value is better than the guarantee of none.'

He could have stopped there, but he didn't. He was driven on by his own momentum, intoxicated by how sure of himself he was.

'You know what else? I think you *want* us to escape. You're bored cutting deals with Krodan lowlifes when you used to take down galleons. You're dying for a little chaos. And you'd like to see

Krent's fat face sweating when he explains to his superiors how he's lost three prisoners. You want to know if we can do it, and deep down, you want to see us try.

'So take the offer, Rapha. Let us go. And I promise you, when the time comes, I'll be your man.'

His last words rang from the tiles into silence. They were all staring at him. He felt elated, breathless, a little mad. Then, as the silence dragged on, his certainty began to crumble like a sandcastle before the tide. His face drooped as he realised that maybe, just maybe, he'd been drastically mistaken.

But Rapha threw back his head and roared with laughter, loud enough that his men cringed for fear the guards would hear. He slapped a beefy hand down on Aren's shoulder and suddenly he was all smiles. 'Might be you'll be worth something after all!' he said. 'You've got a tongue on you, I'll give you that. But don't think this is a debt you can forget once you're away, brother. Should I want you found, you'll be found. And you'll lose more than a couple of fingers if you refuse my call.'

'I know what a promise means,' Aren said. He'd made three now: one to Cade, one to Eifann and one to Rapha, the latter two given to fulfil the first. Trading away pieces of his future so they might have a future at all.

There is no victory without sacrifice. He'd said that to Master Fassen once, before he really knew what sacrifice was. Perhaps he still didn't, not really. But one day he was certain he would.

Rapha seemed satisfied. 'Well enough, then. I accept your offer.' He motioned to the men who were holding Cade and they let him go. He scrambled away, holding his hand protectively to his chest. He was bleeding where the blade had bitten the skin, but no worse than that.

'And the cookhouse key?' Aren asked.

'Don't push your luck, brother.'

'We'll be dead out there without food.'

'Plenty in those mountains to feed a man, if he's got wits,' said Rapha. 'Otherwise, you can starve a few days, I'm sure. But I'll not see Gren disgraced. He'll get the key back before mornin', and he'll owe me a favour.'

Aren opened his mouth to argue. Rapha's look told him not to.

'But a king can show mercy,' Rapha said, once he was content that Aren wouldn't challenge him further. He snapped his fingers at his men and pointed to three of them. 'You, you, you – hand over your blades.'

They looked at each other in confusion. 'To *them*?' one asked at last.

'Do it,' said Rapha. 'It'll give them a chance, at least.'

Rapha's men parted with their knives unhappily.

'You read me right,' said Rapha to Aren, with a nasty grin. 'I'd like to see a little chaos. And if you kill a guard or two on the way out, I won't salt the earth with my tears any.'

He walked away and his men followed. Aren heard the rattle of the chain on the door as they left and then the three of them were alone in the gloom, gazing at the knives they'd just gained.

'Grub don't know how you did that,' said the Skarl with reverent awe.

'Me, either,' said Cade. 'You should have that tattooed somewhere.'

'We lost the food,' Aren said grimly. 'We won't get far without it.' It was a bitter blow to their chances, and even if they survived the mountains, he dreaded to think what might one day come of the promise he'd made.

'Aren,' said Cade. He wiggled his fingers in front of Aren's face. 'Let's take the positives, eh?'

A bell rang in the dark outside and Aren raised his head. 'Last bell before curfew. Anyone wants to reconsider, now's the time.'

Nobody said a word.

'Thought not,' said Aren. 'Get some rest. It's going to be a big night.'

27

They sat against the cold tile walls of the bathhouse, faces dour in the faint red light. It was an hour past curfew and as dark as it would ever get. Out there, above the roof of cloud, Tantera loomed over the world, a charred orb riven with fiery cracks, the herald of misfortune.

It was an inauspicious night to attempt an escape, but the Hollow Man was on Aren's heels, and he had no more time to wait.

Nobody had spoken for a long time, each occupied with their own thoughts. Grub worried at a fingernail with his teeth. Cade hung his head, elbows on his knees and hands in his hair. Aren examined his knife, lost in memories of his father.

Randill had once told him that grief was as individual as love, and each felt their losses in their own way. Aren's grief for his father was muddled and incomplete. The man was still a mystery to him, and it was hard to lay him to rest with so many questions left unanswered. Had Cade been right when he said this whole tragedy had nothing to do with his dalliance with Sora? Maybe his father had been a traitor after all, then.

His grip tightened on the hilt of the knife. *Stop*, he told himself. *Stop shifting the blame.* Whatever his father had or hadn't done, all Aren's misfortune could be laid at the same door. Krodans killed his father. Krodans threw them into this gods-forsaken prison to die. And they did it because they were Ossians, second-class citizens in their own land, without rights or recourse to the law. Slaves, tricked by the trappings of freedom.

No country that called itself civilised should incarcerate a boy for courting the wrong girl, nor should sons be punished for the crimes of their fathers. Whether Randill was traitor or not, the Krodans were wrong. He turned the blade in his hand, fury smouldering in his breast. He wanted to use it on someone.

Cade lifted his head. 'You want to hear a story?' he said. 'I've got a good one. It's about how Hallec Stormfist escaped the dungeons of the Revenant King.' He smiled weakly. 'Might be we'll pick up a few tips.'

But Aren had been inspired by fictions too long. 'I'd rather hear the tale of Cade, Aren and Grub,' he said. 'How they broke out of a Krodan work camp like shades in the night. It'll be the first tale you tell of us, but it won't be the last; and I'll hear it in an inn, far from here, over meat and mead. How's that?'

'Aye,' said Cade, his voice quiet. 'That sounds fine.'

Raindrops tapped against the roof, soft and tentative at first, then louder and faster until the bathhouse rang with impacts and a fierce hiss swelled beyond the walls. They lifted their eyes to the windows, where the glass ran with water. A smile grew on Cade's face.

Heavy rain. If they couldn't have fog, this was the next best thing.

'Looks like Joha was listening after all,' Aren said to Cade, and he got to his feet. 'It's time.'

He went to the bathhouse door and cracked it open. Muddy puddles jumped and seethed in the downpour, their water stained red with moonglow. A guard splashed away between the buildings, a lantern in one hand and a cloak over his head, seeking shelter.

Aren checked for archers on the walkway that ringed the inner side of the stockade. The rain made it hard to see anything at a distance, but at last he spotted one beside a struggling pitch-soaked torch, shoulders hunched, too wet to pay attention to anything but his own misery.

There'd be no better opportunity. He pushed the bathhouse door open to the limit of the chain and slipped out, the others close behind.

They were soaked in moments, but that was a small price to

pay for the cover as they darted through the alleys, watchful for guards. Cade carried the bag of crows, the blanket rope tied around his waist and shoulders in ungainly loops, ready for their climb down the outside of the stockade. The rest of the blankets they wore knotted round their necks like capes, to protect them from the elements once they were free.

Aren had chosen a spot in the north-west corner for their escape, as close to the cliffs as they could get while staying concealed among the longhouses. The torches there were widely spaced, leaving darkness between, and there was nothing beyond but bare grass and riverbank, and the edge of the forest some way distant.

They huddled up under the eaves of a longhouse, within sight of the skulldog pens. Cade held out the bag of crows. Grub sketched a sign in the air; a gesture of protection, perhaps, or an apology to the Bone God.

'Stay here,' Aren said. He took the bag, glanced once more at the walkway, then darted to a gap in the fence that he could peer through.

The pen was a stretch of sodden ground with cross-fences dividing it from its neighbours. Three skulldogs sheltered beneath the wooden scaffolding under the walkway. They shifted and prowled between the poles and struts, moving with predators' grace, hulking killers in the dark. Aren saw Deggan's execution in his mind again and remembered how these creatures had reduced a man to a jumble of parts while he screamed and ran red into the earth.

Courage, Aren, he told himself. He looked back at where Cade and Grub were waiting, watching him expectantly. *They're relying on you.*

He pulled out a crow and lobbed it over the fence. A quick glance through the gap showed him that it had landed in a puddle near the foot of the scaffold. He threw two more. One fell short; the other bounced off a beam and almost hit one of the skulldogs.

Now they were roused, and they came sniffing. The crows were unfamiliar meat and they were cautious, but skulldogs were not known for their patience. The biggest of them shouldered the others aside and crunched a crow down, bones and all.

Aren threw another, aiming for the far side. Eifann had brought him six crows in all, and each dog had to eat at least one. Two went for the same crow and began to tussle over it, snarling and growling. When one of them won the battle and tore the crow away, the other barked angrily in protest.

Aren panicked; he hadn't planned on the dogs making such a racket. He flung the last two crows over the fence, careless of where they went, and hurried back to the others. The skulldogs, driven to excitement, snapped and barked as they fought over the unexpected morsels.

'Dogs bring everyone!' Grub hissed furiously as Aren slid in under the eaves. As if to prove his point, a thickset guard came into sight along the walkway, one side of a grizzled face outlined in the torchlight. He leaned down and peered into the pen, sheltering his eyes from the rain with one hand.

'Shut up!' he yelled in Krodan. 'Mangy bloody mongrels.'

Aren and Cade exchanged a glance. In the shadows of the eaves they couldn't be seen, but the noise might bring other guards.

'Let's get out of here,' said Aren. 'We'll come back when it's all died down.'

Cade nodded. Aren turned to say the same to Grub, but the Skarl had vanished.

'Where'd he go?' Cade asked, alarmed.

Aren cursed under his breath. He should have known Grub would be trouble. 'Come on,' he said darkly.

They slipped along the wall of the longhouse, away from the fence. The rain hissed and splattered around them, sluicing off the sloped roofs. Aren was jumpy, feeling hunted. First Rapha, now this. He thought he'd considered every angle, but the plan was coming apart. Where had that gods-damned Skarl got to? Had he taken fright and run out on them? Or had he something more sinister in mind?

'Who goes?'

Aren froze and Cade bumped into the back of him.

'Who goes?' came the voice again. A guard was approaching from a side-alley, sword in hand, a slender shadow in the night.

He carried a lantern, but it was dark, perhaps leaky and doused by the rain.

Cade made a sudden motion, as if to run, but Aren grabbed his arm. 'We have permits from Captain Hassan!' Aren said.

As the guard approached, they saw that he wasn't much older than they were, barely old enough to shave. He had bulbous eyes and a nervous look about him. Aren stood in front of Cade to block him from view. It was strange enough that they were wearing blankets as capes; if the guard saw the blanket rope tied round Cade's body, they'd be finished.

'Why are you out at this hour?' the guard snapped.

'Blocked latrine,' said Aren, over the din of the rain. 'Captain told us to stay until we'd cleared it. We were just heading back.'

The guard was suspicious, but too green to risk calling for help and looking like a fool. He wanted to deal with this himself, if he could.

'Show me your permits,' he said.

'Here,' said Aren, closing the distance between them as he reached towards his pocket, *past* it, his fingers closing round the hilt of the knife in the waistband of his trousers.

His heart began to pound, his mouth went dry and everything felt suddenly remote. He was going to kill a man. It seemed impossible, and yet it was happening now. It was the only thing that *could* happen.

Him or us. Him or us. Him or us.

There was a flurry of movement in the dark. The guard half-turned, but too slow. Grub crashed into him, bearing him roughly across the alleyway and into the wall of a longhouse. Before he could cry out, the Skarl stabbed him, quick and hard, over and over. There was something appallingly intimate about it, the way Grub hugged him close, crushed against the wall, as his blade plunged in and out. The guard whimpered and jerked, but made no more noise than that. When Grub finally let him go, he slid to the ground, folding up like a dropped puppet.

Grub turned towards Aren, breathing hard, savagery in his eyes and blood on his coat. Aren stared at him in shock. He'd been a fool to ever take this man lightly. Grub was far more dangerous than Aren had given him credit for.

'Fargan? Is that you down there?'

At the guard's voice, all three hid under the eaves. It was the archer on the walkway, the one who'd yelled at the dogs. They saw him by the light of a torch, squinting into the alley below.

'Fargan? Did you call, boy?'

Fargan lay on the floor like an accusation, his eyes half-open and blank. Aren felt panic rising again. Everything was slipping out of his control. The alarm would surely be raised now. There'd be no escape; instead they'd be caught and fed to the—

'All's well!' Cade called out in Krodan. His voice was higher than usual, his vowels harsher, coming from the back of his throat. It was a near-perfect imitation of Fargan. 'A mistake! All's well!'

The archer kept on squinting into the dark, seeking the source of the voice. He sensed something amiss but couldn't find the cause. Aren willed him to move on, as if he could command him by the desperate force of his thoughts.

'Fargan?' the archer said again.

'All's well, I said!' Cade called, adding a note of irritation.

The archer grunted and wandered away. Aren let out a long, slow breath of relief and nodded gratefully at Cade.

'I knew those Krodan lessons I gave you would come in handy one day,' Aren said.

'Aye,' said Cade. 'Lucky he backed off, though. I'd about reached the limit of my vocabulary.'

'Grub say we better move this body,' Grub put in.

They dragged Fargan into the side-alley he'd emerged from, where any other guards were unlikely to see him. Once, touching a corpse might have disturbed Aren, but life in the work camp had hardened him, and they divided up Fargan's gear and disposed of the body matter-of-factly. He had good boots, thick socks and a proper cloak. Cade suggested that Aren take his armour as a disguise, but Aren wasn't used to wearing armour, and anyway, they'd have to travel light if they hoped to outrun the pursuit once they escaped. In the end, Aren took his sword, belt and scabbard. Grub didn't protest; he didn't seem to want them.

'I'll check on the dogs,' Aren said.

'More careful this time, yes?' Grub said unhelpfully.

Once again, it was hard to find the dogs in the dark. They were all beneath the scaffolding, having retreated from the rain. One had lolled on its side and was obviously unconscious. Another was curled up nose to tail, asleep. The third was still on its feet, but barely. It wobbled here and there until its legs gave way, after which it twitched on the ground a few times and lay still.

Aren licked his lips, which were dry with nerves. The draccen tears had done their job. The dogs were drugged. But were they drugged *enough*?

He dared not hesitate, or his courage would falter. He jumped up, grabbed the top of the fence poles and pulled himself over.

The skulldogs didn't react. He crept closer, ready to run if they stirred. His senses blared an alarm; instinct told him this was suicide. Each step took him further into danger. He ignored it and pushed on, willing himself forward.

Beneath the walkway and out of the rain, he could hear the heavy sighing of the skulldogs and smell their warm animal dampness. They looked even larger up close, piles of muscle and fang that might spring into life at any moment and savage him. He kept his stolen sword ready, but even with a blade, he wouldn't stand much of a chance. The thought made him sick with fear. He was keenly aware that he'd bet his life on a drug he knew almost nothing about.

Did you all get your fill?

One of the skulldogs jerked. Aren's heart lurched and he jumped back, blade raised high. Then it gave a long sigh and settled back into unconsciousness.

Hearing no screams or barks, Grub and Cade came over the fence and hurried across the pen. Grub, his knife between his teeth, started to climb the scaffold, moving smoothly between the criss-crossing poles.

Cade followed him. 'Reckon it's a sight safer up there than it is down here,' he said, eyeing the skulldogs.

Aren agreed.

The scaffold was an easy climb even when wet, and they soon

caught up with Grub, who was balanced on a crossbeam just below the walkway, knife back in his hand. The Skarl jabbed upwards, where the wood was creaking beneath the tread of an approaching guard.

'We wait for him to pass,' Aren whispered. 'Then we go.'

Grub gave him a steady look. 'You think like child. Sneak past impossible.'

Aren opened his mouth to argue, then didn't. In his heart, he knew the Skarl was right. Slipping over the stockade behind the guard was the stuff of stories. He tasted bile in his throat, swallowed it. 'I'll follow you up.'

Grub put his knife back between his teeth. Footsteps passed overhead again, the dejected tread of a drenched man grudgingly doing his duty. Aren felt a moment of pity. Krodan or no, he had a life, and perhaps a family. Maybe he was a good man, a decent man. But right now he stood between Aren and freedom, and that meant he had to be dealt with.

Grub went up and over the edge of the walkway with a grace belied by his bulk. Aren heard quick, running footsteps, and when he pulled himself up he found the two men struggling in silence. Grub's knife went in and out; the guard stiffened and sagged. Once he'd stopped moving, Grub pushed his limp body over the stockade wall.

Aren felt a moment of crawling horror at the sight. A man's life, extinguished with such frightening ease. It didn't sit right. But then he remembered all the other lives, all the *Ossian* lives, that had ended here. It didn't seem so much like murder after that. More like retribution.

Aren crouched next to Cade and unravelled the sodden rope of blankets while his friend tied one end around a stockade spike. Even in the dark between the torches, concealed by the driving rain, they felt exposed; Grub looked up and down the walkway for signs of other guards, taut with nervous energy. Haste made Cade clumsy and the rope slipped off the wet, pointed tip of the spike. He tried again, and failed again. Aren resisted the urge to scream at him to get on with it. The third time, Cade made the blankets fast.

An arrow smacked into the inside of the stockade wall, inches from his face.

'Prisoners escaping!' came a shout from the dark.

Grub reacted first. He shoved past Cade, grabbed the rope and flung it over the wall, sending it uncoiling into the night. Then he went over himself, clambering down hand over hand.

'Go!' Aren said to Cade, searching for the archer who'd fired on them. A guard, alerted by the cry, was running towards them, drawing his sword as he came.

Cade hesitated, reluctant to leave Aren behind, but Aren shouted, 'Go!' again, more forcefully. This time he did as he was told, seizing the blanket with both hands and scrambling over the top of the stockade.

Aren ducked as another arrow flew out of the rain. It nicked his shoulder, cutting through several layers of fabric but missing the meat by a hair's width. Now he saw the archer, up on the walkway near the cliffs, nocking another arrow. Only the darkness and rain had ruined his aim thus far, but Aren didn't want to try his luck a third time.

There was a short, sharp tearing of fabric, a cry and the thump of a body hitting the ground. Aren, heart in his mouth, rushed to look out over the edge of the stockade and saw the tattered edge of the blanket rope flapping loose beneath him. The knots may have held, but the cheap material had torn beneath the weight of Grub and Cade. He searched for signs of his friend, but his night vision had been destroyed by the nearby torches and he could see nothing down there.

'Jump, Aren!' Cade called from the dark. 'I ain't hurt! Jump!'

The guard with the sword had almost reached him. The archer was drawing his bow. Aren couldn't see the ground, but he knew from memory that the stockade was high, the fall enough to break a limb or worse.

He jumped anyway.

Air roared in his ears. His clothes flapped against him as he plunged through infinite dark. Then his feet hit the earth and his knees buckled hard, slamming him onto his side, his head whiplashing down after. It was an impact that would have killed him, if not for the rain. Soil had turned to spongy mud in the downpour, and though the impact almost knocked his wits out of him, it wasn't hard enough to prove fatal.

Cade dragged him up, frantic in the bloody half-light. 'Come on! Move!' Grub was already sprinting for the trees further along the riverbank. An arrow whipped through the air and hit the earth with a wet thump. 'Aren, run!'

The urgency in his voice cut through Aren's daze. Despite the pounding in his head, he was whole. He was alive. And he could run.

He forced his muscles into motion, and with Cade's arm round him, he found his feet. Stumbling at first, then faster and surer, the fugitives fled into the rain, the sound of alarm bells clanging in their ears.

28

The mountains lit up from horizon to horizon as lightning cracked the sky and thunder tumbled away across the peaks. The wind whistled and howled, flinging rain where it went, and the clouds raced overhead. What had started as a downpour had become a storm of rare fury.

'I might have prayed a bit too hard for bad weather,' Cade muttered as he clung to the slippery rock face with freezing fingers and tried not to think about falling. Above him, Aren was grimly focused on the next handhold, the next ledge, while Grub was almost at the top already; that ugly bastard climbed like a spider. Cade, stronger than Aren but never as nimble, came slowly and steadily behind, choosing his way with care.

He found a position to rest in for a few moments and looked over his shoulder at what they'd left behind. Between the folds in the mountainside, he could see all the way back to the camp, where torches marked the perimeter. Beyond it, across the black absence of the river, lights glowed in the village. It was still dishearteningly close. They'd run for what felt like for ever, but they hadn't come half so far as he'd imagined.

Between them and the camp was a pine forest covering the slopes, a sea of branches thrashing in the wind. Lanterns moved among the trees, carried by the guards that chased them. The barking of skulldogs drifted up into the reddened night.

'Cade!'

He looked up to see Aren frowning at him.

'Alright?' Aren asked.

Cade wiped rain from his face. 'Aye,' he said. 'I'm alright.' And he reached up and found his next grip, and then the next.

When he got to the top, Aren helped him over, and the three of them crouched together in a brake of ferns at the base of some shivering pines. Cade breathed into his hands to warm them and put his gloves on. Cold as he was, climbing in gloves was a recipe for disaster.

'Grub see hundreds down there,' said Grub. The tattoos round one side of his mouth curved as his lips twisted into a smile. 'But they not catch Grub!'

Cade figured that a wild exaggeration; there were dozens of lanterns at best. He wondered what else Grub had exaggerated. Despite Aren's insistence that Skarls weren't allowed to lie, Cade had doubted Grub's boasting from the start. Could be that ice bear he'd slain was more like an ice squirrel.

'We keep heading up, straight as we can,' Aren said. He was all stern efficiency, the way he got when he had a plan. 'The storm's on our side; it'll put the dogs off our scent.' He sniffed, wiped his nose with the back of his hand. 'The further we get, the better our chances. They'll call off the search eventually. We just have to outlast them.'

Cade took heart in that. No one did dogged persistence quite like Aren. When he set his mind to something, he was unstoppable. They'd outlasted prison; they could outlast this pursuit as well.

They set off again beneath the dripping trees, following Aren's lead. The branches moved restlessly. Shadows wavered and darted. They saw phantoms all around them, their minds conjuring soldiers from the rain. Cade fixed his eyes on Aren's back and forged ahead.

At last, they came to a wide trail cutting across their path. Aren waved them back and they hunkered down among the foliage as two mounted soldiers galloped past them. Once they were gone, Cade stuck his head out and peered up the trail, which climbed steadily towards a narrow defile, a pass between the cliffs. Four men waited there, blocking the way.

'They're ahead of us,' Aren said. 'Trying to cut us off.' On the other side of the trail, the slope was thickly forested, rising towards a bare peak. 'Keep going. We'll find a way up. Climb if we have to.'

'Grub say only idiots follow trails anyway,' the Skarl sneered.

To their left, they could see lanterns approaching, and they heard the barking of dogs.

'Huntsmen. Best be elsewhere before they get here,' said Cade. He thumbed at Grub. 'Don't need to be a dog to smell this feller.'

'Grub hope your razor wit come in very handy when skulldog eating your face.'

'Shut up and move,' Aren snapped.

An ill-timed bolt of lightning lit them up as they scampered across the trail. They crowded breathlessly into the foliage on the other side, listening to the thunder as it rumbled away into the distance.

'Nine, I thought the storm was on *our* side,' Cade complained. 'You reckon those huntsmen saw us?'

'Grub think they didn't,' the Skarl opined.

The lowing of a horn came to their ears, carried on the wind.

'Aren think they did,' said Aren. 'Go!'

They fled through the trees, half-blind in the dark, their feet finding the ground more by instinct than sight. Twigs grabbed at their clothes as they slipped and stumbled on wet roots and muddy rocks. Behind them, they heard shouts from the huntsmen. The horn sounded again and the skulldogs barked eagerly, sensing prey.

The slope steepened and they began to struggle. None of them was at their strongest, and Cade had spent a week idle in the infirmary, hardly moving. The sounds of pursuit drove them all on. The pain in Cade's chest and limbs would be nothing to the pain if they were caught.

Soon they heard running water over the rain and came to a narrow, rocky channel, a trench in the mountainside that crossed their path. There was a shallow stream at the bottom, shin-deep and several paces wide. Aren was climbing down into the channel and was about to cross when Cade, stumbling after, grabbed his arm.

'Upstream,' said Cade, pointing. 'It'll help throw off the dogs.'

Aren saw the sense in it. 'Upstream,' he agreed, and he stepped into the water and splashed up the channel. Cade and Grub followed, slipping and sliding on the loose rocks underfoot. It was hard going, and Cade went over on his hands and knees more than once; but the next time the horn blew, it sounded further behind them.

The stream ended at a sheer cliff. A thin waterfall spewed down from high above. There was no hope of scaling it, so they started to make their way along the foot of the cliff.

Cade was shivering despite the exertion, his waterlogged clothes weighing him down and his feet squishing in his boots. A stitch was growing in his side and he could still hear the dogs, too close for his liking. Staggering, nearing exhaustion, he blundered through the branches, following glimpses of Aren and Grub as they moved in the shadows.

Those guards ain't much fitter than we are. And they're weighed down by armour. We just need to outlast them.

Then suddenly the trees ended, and they came out into the open with stone beneath their feet. Lightning flashed the scene and showed them the bare lip of a gorge, a ragged slash in the land with steep sides and a river at the bottom: the same river that flowed past Suller's Bluff. They could see the lights of the camp downstream. Somehow they'd got turned around, come back on themselves. Beyond the gorge, the mountains rose crooked and wild, a savage, empty land under the storm. Savage, empty and utterly beyond their reach.

Aren swore, looking about like a hunted animal. Cliffs rose to their left, barring progress along the gorge. The only choice was to go back, or to follow the gorge downslope – back towards Suller's Bluff and the camp again.

'Which way, Mudslug?' Grub demanded.

Aren didn't have an answer for him. He was still trying to find one when his eyes fixed on something over Cade's shoulder. Cade turned, heart sinking, knowing what he'd see when he did.

Men were moving through the trees. Soldiers with bows and swords, huntsmen with skulldogs straining at their leashes. There was a shout as they spotted the fugitives.

Cade's guts turned to water. He backed towards Aren, and the lip of the gorge. There was nowhere to run now. They were trapped.

Grub bared his teeth and pulled his knife as the guards reached the edge of the trees. There were six of them, and two dogs. The archers covered them with their bows; the swordsmen drew their blades.

Cade looked to Aren, hoping for signs of a plan, but there was only devastation in his friend's eyes. It was a look Cade had seen once before, when Aren was being dragged from his house with his dead father lying in the dining room. Here was defeat, and it was final. He hadn't even drawn his stolen sword.

'I won't go to the dogs,' said Aren, and he looked over his shoulder into the depths of the gorge.

Cade felt sick with terror as he realised what Aren was saying. But there was death coming either way, quick or slow, and he found it hard to argue with Aren's line of thought. He remembered Deggan's fate and feared to share it.

'There's a river. Maybe we'll live,' he heard himself say.

'Maybe,' said Aren with a wan smile, but there was a farewell in his voice.

'Not Grub!' Grub cried. 'Grub not ready to go to the Bone God yet!' He raised his knife in the bloody light, and at the top of his lungs he roared a challenge in Skarl. '*Aqqad Urgotha jegg kaumm!*' Then he ran at the guards, screaming like a mad thing.

The guards let slip their leashes and the skulldogs burst from the undergrowth, racing across open ground to meet Grub's charge. Lightning flashed and they were frozen in tableau: the tattooed Skarl, veins bulging at his neck and insanity in his eye, his pitiful blade held aloft; the skulldogs wearing masks of death, saliva spooling from their fangs.

Bowstrings thrummed and the dogs folded mid-stride, crashing to the ground. They threw up fins of rainwater as they rolled and skidded to a halt in two heaps, one with an arrow in the back of its head, the other pierced through the ribs.

Grub stumbled to a stop as he saw movement in the trees behind the guards. A sword swung out of the shadows and cleft an archer from collarbone to pelvis. Bowstrings snapped again and blades met flesh. Half the guards were dead before they knew they were under attack; the others had a heartbeat to make peace with the Primus before they followed their companions.

In moments, it was over. Grub stood bewildered in the storm, staring at the skulldogs as if uncertain whether their deaths had been his doing. Aren and Cade shivered by the lip of the gorge, their backs to the abyss as they waited to know the nature of these strangers.

Four figures stepped from the trees. Two held bows: a well-dressed, handsome young man with a neat moustache and a stern young woman with ginger hair tied back from her face. The other two carried swords and had the bulk and the walk of warriors. One wore his hair in a strip along the centre of his skull, falling to one side of his face in the manner of the whalers of the Bitterbracks. His companion had a thick black beard and wore an expression darker than the thunderheads piled at his back.

'That him?' asked the Bitterbracker, pointing his sword at Aren.

They walked past Grub, ignoring him, and stood before Aren and Cade. The bearded man looked hard at Aren.

'It's him,' he said at last, with something like disgust in his voice. 'He's got the look of his father.'

Lightning flickered and revealed a wide, puckered scar that ran across his throat, where no hair grew and which his beard couldn't quite hide.

'Aren of Shoal Point,' the Hollow Man said. 'I've been looking for you.'

29

The wind skirled up from the gorge at Aren's back, flapping his wet clothes against him. His limbs had no strength in them. Shock had stolen it away. He stared at the face of the Hollow Man and was frozen in place by the sight of a childhood nightmare come to life.

'Going to jump, eh?' said the Bitterbracker in Ossian. He peered over the edge. 'Wouldn't recommend it.'

'You know who I am, boy?' the bearded man growled. His voice was deep and damaged, gargly with phlegm.

'You're the Hollow Man,' Aren whispered.

The Bitterbracker gave a surprised bark of a laugh while his companion's expression became darker still.

'Is that what your father called me? Well, it's as good a name as any, and I've gone by a lot. But you'll call me Garric. This is Keel.'

Aren belatedly remembered the sword at his belt. His hand moved towards it, but his fingers had barely closed on the hilt before Keel's blade was at his throat.

'Wouldn't recommend that, either,' said Keel.

Aren's eyes roved frantically, looking for escape. More strangers had moved up on Grub while their companions covered him with bows: a tall, black-haired woman carrying a shield and broadsword; a whip-thin young man wielding a slender blade. Hanging back was a small, studious-looking youth in spectacles, clutching a wet pack to his chest.

Sense overcame his panic. They were outnumbered and fighting was hopeless. He took his hand slowly from the sword hilt.

'Have you come to kill me?' he asked, his voice as firm as he could make it.

Garric glowered at him with enough hate that Aren could guess the answer.

'Had I the choice, perhaps I would,' said Garric. 'But I don't.'

Before Aren could puzzle that out, a horn blew in the forest, near at hand. 'Garric ...' warned the last of the strangers, a squat, thickset old warrior with a bushy brown beard and an axe in each hand.

'If you want to keep drawing breath, come with me now!' Garric snapped at Aren. He glanced at Cade, then back at Grub. 'Those two can go their own way.'

Cade stepped forward in alarm. 'Hoy, no! Wait!'

'Cade comes with me,' Aren said, grabbing Cade's arm.

'We don't need the baggage,' Garric said impatiently, and seized Aren to drag him away; but Aren twisted and tore free from his grip, violently enough that he almost went over the edge of the gorge. Keel grabbed him with his free hand and pulled him back.

'You *do* have a death wish,' Keel said in amazement.

Aren shook him off and glared defiantly at Garric. 'Cade comes, or I don't.'

'Garric ...' said the axe-wielding man, with less patience than before.

'Alright, Tarvi,' said Keel, waving a hand at him. 'It's not worth the argument, Garric. Let's go.'

Aren looked past the two men to Grub, crouched at bay in the rain and red darkness, looking like a beast surrounded by hunters. He met Aren's eye across the distance and his lips pulled back in a slight snarl. Aren remembered the feel of his fists, the anger and humiliation, the insults, the petty viciousness. Grub was a vile bully, a fool and a liability.

'Him, too,' said Aren, motioning with his hand. Cade stared at him in surprise.

'Garric!' Tarvi snapped.

Garric turned away with a curse and stalked towards the others, jamming his sword back in its sheath. Keel frowned slightly at

Aren, as if trying to work him out; then he took him by the shoulder and pushed him after Garric.

'Varla! Otten! Dox! Let him be!' Keel called to the men and women watching Grub. 'We're leaving. Fen?'

The slender red-headed girl pointed off into the trees.

'Good. You're in the lead. Osman, bring up the rear.'

'Understood,' said the other archer, the handsome man with the moustache.

Aren went ahead of Keel through the rain, the Bitterbracker staying close at his shoulder. Was he a prisoner again, or had he been freed? It had all happened too fast to be sure. At least Cade was still with him; he felt his friend clutch his arm, though whether he was offering reassurance or seeking it, Aren didn't know.

The others had left Grub alone and melted back into the treeline. The Skarl watched them go, likely calculating whether he'd be better off on his own or sticking with this well-armed group of strangers. At least he had that choice now, Aren thought. Wretch though he was, he deserved more than to be abandoned to the Krodan dogs.

As Aren passed him, Grub blew a plug of snot from his nose, squared his shoulders and followed, away from the gorge and into the trees.

Thunder grumbled distantly as they hustled through shadowed ways beneath the pines. The worst of the storm was over but rain still splashed and trickled about their feet, pooling in the imprints of their boots. Aren was surrounded by strangers, their faces flashing in and out of the darkness, caught in moonlit moments and gone again. Some were grim with purpose, like the swordswoman Varla. Others looked as nervous as Aren was, and almost as young: the spectacled youth, and the thin one with the coif covering his head. Otten and Dox, but he didn't know which was which.

What does the Hollow Man want with me? He dreaded to guess. The only comfort was that these people were Ossian, and therefore better than the alternative.

A horn blew again, just ahead of them, then came the ring of steel on steel. The sound of combat tumbled towards him like a wave and suddenly the forest was full of enemies, men and women fighting everywhere.

Many times Aren had dreamed of facing real combat, but in his mind it was never like this, this wet confusion of huffing breath, thrashing branches, fearful glimpses of metal. The fight swallowed him so fast that he stumbled to a halt and looked about dazedly, trying to locate the threat, to make some sense of the chaos around him.

Keel was clashing with a Krodan guard nearby. As Aren stared, the Bitterbracker warrior made three swift parries and took the guard's arm off at the elbow. The guard was still staring at the stump when Keel's next blow took his head off.

Grub rushed past, keeping his head down, Osman behind him. The archer halted when he saw Aren and Cade, wide-eyed like frightened rabbits in the rainy dark.

'Come on, friends! Now's not the time to hang around.' His accent was highborn, nasal, from the Rainlands in the south. He raised his bow and fired into the trees. 'Is that a sword at your hip, Aren? Can you use it?'

Cursing himself for a mudwit, Aren drew the sword he'd taken from the dead guard. Master Orik had trained him for this ever since he was old enough to hold a practice blade. He'd hoped one day to fight in a noble war against the urds or the godless Durnish. Now they were under attack, the least he could do was raise his gods-damned weapon.

'That way!' Osman said, pushing them ahead of him. They hurried off through the trees, Aren holding his sword tight, Osman slipping watchfully along in their wake. Cade gripped his knife in his fist, eyes skittish in the dim red light.

The ground beneath their feet sloped sharply and they skidded down through mud. Aren almost tripped over the body of a dead man lying agape among the roots and rocks. Distant lightning flashed and he caught sight of Fen, crouching on a boulder ahead of them, loosing a shot into the darkness. The crack of thunder didn't quite cover the scream of the man she killed.

A bush thrashed to his left, loud and sudden. Aren whirled in surprise as a Krodan guard came stumbling through, half-falling in his haste. Aren raised his sword instinctively and braced himself as the guard, unable to check his momentum, plunged forward onto its point. He felt the guard's leather armour give way, then the awful slithering resistance of muscles and organs as the blade pushed into his chest. His eyes bulged; his cheeks puffed; air hissed through lips pressed tight together. He began to tip sideways, and Aren stepped back and pulled his blade free before it could be yanked from his hand, just as he'd been taught. The Krodan slumped hard to the earth.

'Nine!' said Cade in amazement. 'You killed him!'

Aren wasn't sure if that even counted. It felt more like the Krodan had used Aren to inadvertently kill himself.

'Move, Mudslug!' Grub snarled at Aren, emerging from the trees ahead of them. 'Don't die yet. Grub still needs Mudslug's friends.' He spotted the dead man, grinned nastily as he realised what had happened. 'Heh,' he said. 'Mudslug a warrior now.' He slapped Aren on the shoulder, then shoved him into motion again.

The sounds of fighting diminished as they crashed onwards through the branches. Varla appeared, having run out of Krodans to fight; then came bushy-bearded Tarvi with his axes. They reached a shallow hollow where the trees were sparse and the grassy earth was patched with new rain pools, and found Fen waiting there with Otten and Dox.

'Garric and Keel?' Varla asked.

'Mopping up,' said Fen.

Keel pushed through the undergrowth, Garric with him.

'We get them all?' Keel asked.

'Think so,' said Varla. She gave the bespectacled youth a worried look; he was wheezing. 'Alright, Dox?'

'He'll be fine,' said Otten, rubbing Dox's back. 'His lungs, you know.'

'Everyone here?' Garric asked, scanning the group, black hair plastered to his brow. His gaze lingered balefully on Aren.

He hates me, Aren thought. *And I don't know why.*

Garric's eyes flicked to Fen. 'You have a way out?'

Fen pointed with one slender finger. 'There's an old rope bridge, crosses the gorge. We can cut it free behind us and the Krodans will be stuck on this side. If it's still there.'

'Well, I, for one, am keen to find out,' said Tarvi. 'So what are we—'

He was cut short as Garric raised his hand for silence. They tensed, weapons ready.

'You hear?' he whispered.

'I hear nothing,' said Keel.

'Exactly.'

And now Aren understood. The rain splattered and slapped, distant thunder rang across the peaks, but no insect called, no animal stirred, no night-bird squawked at the storm. All the small sounds, so faint and frequent that they usually went unnoticed, had stopped. Aren felt something cold crawl up his spine.

A sharp hiss to his right. The whip of leaves, a blur of movement and a dull thump. All eyes went to Otten, who staggered back from Dox, looking down in puzzlement at the thick arrow with ragged black fletching sticking out of his chest. Then his eyes rolled up in his head and he crumpled to the ground.

'*Dreadknights!*' Garric roared. 'To the bridge!'

They took to their heels. Keel seized Aren and shoved him after Fen. As he stumbled into a run, he glanced back to check on Cade and saw Varla dragging Dox away, the younger man still gasping for breath, eyes wide with panic behind his spectacles. He was trying to say Otten's name, but he couldn't get it out.

There was a crash of branches and an enormous warrior burst from the trees. He was a giant of a man, clad head to toe in tarnished black iron armour. Aren had never seen the like; it was all hard edges and straight lines, brutality without elegance. A heavy helm covered his head, with horizontal slits concealing his eyes and circular breathing grilles. He held a massive hammer, and as he emerged, he swung it in a great lateral arc.

Varla yelled and threw herself aside. Dox wasn't so quick and was swept up by the blow, flung bodily away to slam into a tree with a horrific cracking of bones. Varla was back on her feet in a moment, sprinting towards the others with abject terror written on her face. The giant swung his great head to track her and lumbered after.

'Dreadknights! Joha's mercy, what are *dreadknights* doing here?' Osman demanded, his voice high with desperation as they scrambled and slid through the tight-packed trees.

Aren wiped sodden hair from his face, panting with fright and tiredness, his heart battering at his ribs. Krodan soldiers and skulldogs were one thing, but this was another level of horror. The sight of the dreadknight inspired some primal reaction in him, his ancestors' fear of the dark beyond the campfire and the nameless toothed terrors that shunned the sun.

Keel ran at their side, the brawny Bitterbracker searching the trees as he went. Aren saw glimpses of the others up ahead, shadows among shadows, frantic movement in the glistening rain. An arrow slashed through the air, making him duck, and buried itself quivering in a tree. He looked back as he heard a rustle of branches, but it was only Varla catching them up, having outpaced her huge opponent.

Then the lightning stuttered again and a cloaked figure moved through the trees beside her, flowing like liquid night. Beneath the black cowl, he saw a metal face frozen by the flash, wearing an expression of anguish, like a mummer's mask of tragedy. Two thin blades in two gloved hands, one long and one short, glinted cruelly in the red glow of the blood moon.

His mouth opened to cry out a warning, but the cowled figure lunged and Varla disappeared beneath his flowing cloak. The flash of lightning faded, leaving her lost in the dark behind them.

'Keep going! She's gone!' cried Keel over the rumble of thunder that followed, and they ran recklessly onwards, branches lashing their faces, death at their heels.

Two shoulders of rock loomed ahead, slick and wet with rain. Angling between them was a narrow stony path, down which Osman and Grub sprinted. Aren, Cade and Keel plunged out of the forest and raced after them, single file along the path, until they were spat out onto a small ledge with sheer walls of rock to either side and the whistling expanse of the gorge before them.

The gorge, and a bridge to cross it.

It was fashioned from ropes and planks, tattered with age, and it swayed perilously in the wind. None of that had deterred Grub, who'd somehow managed to be first across and had almost reached the other side. Osman followed him, less surefooted, while Garric and Tarvi stood arguing to one side, and Fen eyed the bridge uncertainly.

'Don't be a fool!' Garric said to Tarvi. 'Are you that eager to throw your life away?'

'You're the fool if you think they won't catch us before we cut that rope,' Tarvi said. 'Our mission is more important than me. More important than all of us. They'll butcher us in the open, but I can hold them on that path, where they can only come at me one by one. Go! I'll buy you what time I can. Fen, get your arse on that bridge!'

Fen jumped at the sound of his voice and did as she was told. Tarvi hefted his axes and headed back the way they came as Keel herded Cade after Fen. At the entrance to the defile, Tarvi stopped and looked back at Garric. His mouth was a grim line, and his gaze held the sorrowful determination of a man going willingly to his end.

'Make this worth something,' he said, and turned away. Aren saw a look of grief pass over Garric's face.

'Get moving!' Keel urged. Aren sheathed his sword and went teetering out over the gorge, both hands on the ropes to steady himself. The drop yawned beneath him, the river at the bottom a dim sparkle, and the wind shoved and pulled, seeking to tip him over. Chilled and soaked and terrified, he could do nothing but forge forwards through the tempest, his eyes fixed to his feet as he went from plank to plank as fast as his nerve allowed.

Keel was close behind him, Cade ahead. To either side was the gorge, which felt vaster than it ever had when he was on solid ground. The planks creaked beneath his weight, but even though the bridge shivered and swung, it held firm. Osman was waiting at the other end to haul Cade in, and was just reaching out for Aren when they heard a thin cry from the far side of the gorge, carried on the wind. Tarvi's cry, a sound of pain and terror, for even warriors' courage faltered when faced with the uncertainty of the end.

Osman's lips were pressed tight as he pulled Aren past him, and his eyes were distant with anger and sorrow.

Keel and Garric were the last to cross. On the far side, where the defile widened to a ledge, a scrawny figure emerged. He was tall and skeletal, wrapped in a close-fitting garb fixed with many belts and straps, and carried an enormous black bow almost as tall as he was. As he pulled an arrow from the quiver at his back, he raised his head. There was something wrong with his features, something off-kilter, but the rain blew between them and Aren couldn't see clearly.

'Cut the ropes!' Garric was yelling as Keel reached the end of the bridge. 'Be ready!'

Osman threw down his bow and drew his blade as the dreadknight nocked the arrow and sighted.

'Look out!' Aren shouted, pointing.

A bowstring thrummed next to him and an arrow shot past, close enough to make him jump. It was Fen. Her arrow flew out across the gorge, wobbled in the wind and struck the ground inches from the dreadknight. A moment later, the dreadknight let fly, aiming for Garric; but whether it was the wind or the distraction of Fen's arrow, the shot missed its mark and thwacked heavily into a support pole on Aren's side of the gorge.

'Cut 'em!' Garric cried as he reached the end of the bridge. Osman swung his blade, and Keel, too. In three or four hacks, the ropes were severed. The bridge slumped and fell free, drifting down into the gorge to slap uselessly against the other side.

When Aren looked up next, there were three of them on the far ledge: the monstrous armoured man with the hammer, the skeletal archer with the deadly bow, and the metal-masked man with the cowled cloak and paired blades. Three dreadknights, heavy with threat, like predators thwarted of their prey. The gorge lay between them now and the fugitives were hidden by the sheltering dark of the trees, but there was something in the way they stood that said this wasn't over yet.

Eight men and women had rescued Aren, Cade and Grub from

the Krodans; only half of them remained. Aren felt himself seized by the front of his coat and was pulled face to face with Garric, whose eyes were dark with hatred.

'This is on you, boy!' he snarled. 'All of their deaths are on you!'

He shoved Aren away and raised his head to address the others. 'We don't stop till dawn! You can be sure those accursed bastards will be following after us.'

They obeyed without word or argument, moving off into the undergrowth. Aren felt Cade's hand on his shoulder.

'He's wrong,' said Cade. 'Ain't none of this is your fault.'

Aren looked away, full of shock and hurt and anger. *Damn you, Garric the Hollow Man. Damn you, whoever you are.*

But the others were leaving now, and for all the loathing and resentment that welled up inside him, there was nothing he could do but follow.

30

One foot, then the other. Ain't no more to it than that.

Cade stumbled towards the dawn on leaden feet. His eyelids drifted closed, jerked open, slowly closed again. He was drenched and cold and impossibly weary, yet still he drove himself on. He'd hoped to leave this kind of misery back in the mine, but here he was again, half-alive and dreaming of a respite that felt like it would never come.

One foot, then the other. But it wasn't that easy. He wasn't like Aren, who could trudge like a mule until he dropped dead. He didn't have that kind of determination. He couldn't go another step.

And yet somehow it happened anyway.

The storm had blown itself out, but it had rained throughout the night and a chill wind blew in the mountains. There was no forest to shelter them now; they'd reached the high passes, where icy streams splashed between slopes of dank grass and black flint. Cade had no idea where they were headed, only that they were going there at a punishing pace.

Dreadknights, he thought. They were only whispered of in Shoal Point. Da said they were just a Krodan lie to keep people in line, and even his ma had thought them myths. But Cade knew the truth of it now. He wondered what else the world had to teach him, and if he'd like any of it better than the lesson he'd just learned.

Aren coughed at his side. He'd been coughing for hours. At first he tried to suppress it, but soon it slipped from his control and wracked him, leaving him doubled over, wheezing and breathless.

The sound worried Cade. He'd heard coughs like that in the longhouse at night, coughs that rattled in the lungs like dice. The kind of cough that killed you.

'Easy now,' said Osman, a hand on Aren's back. 'Here's Fen. Let's see what she's found.'

Fen was picking her way towards them along the bank of a rain-swollen stream. She was clad in a drab green hooded cloak, her ginger hair the only bright colour in a grey and grim world.

The faces that surrounded him were grim, too. Barely a word had been spoken since they left the gorge. Garric was a mass of bunched rage, his shoulders tight; Keel was dour and lost in thought; and Osman sorrowed. Grub was silent, too, for once, though his expression was sly and restless. Like Cade, he was wary of this rescue and looked ready to bolt if he had to.

'What news?' Keel asked as Fen reached them.

'There's a place up ahead,' she said. 'It'll do.'

'Hear that?' Osman said to Aren. 'Not far now. Then we can rest.'

Aren gave him a grateful glance and a nod. Cade was grateful, too. Of all of them, only the highborn man had showed kindness. Fen was aloof and uncaring, Garric puzzlingly and frighteningly hostile. And Cade couldn't make Keel out at all.

'One foot, then the other,' Cade murmured.

'That's right,' said Osman. 'Good man.'

At the top of the slope, the land flattened into a high, narrow valley dotted with dead trees. Fen led them to a hollow in a cliff face where the stream ran close. There, beneath an overhang, was a patch of earth and smooth stone that had remained relatively dry during the downpour. Cade bundled into shelter with the others, shivering with cold, his legs trembling. Unable to stand any longer, he threw himself down with an arm for a pillow and was mugged by sleep the moment he closed his eyes.

The pain of a dead leg hauled him halfway back to consciousness. He'd fallen asleep on his side and the hard ground had cut off his circulation. There was a blanket covering him. He didn't know who'd put it there.

He rolled over to ease the discomfort in his thigh. Daylight narrowed his eyes, and he heard the splashing of the stream nearby. The rain had stopped, and a fire burned in the hollow directly in front of him. The heat had dried his wet hair, and now his clothes were merely damp and stiff rather than entirely soaked. Lulled, he sank back towards sleep.

'And then?' said a voice. Keel, the Bitterbracker. He was standing with Garric, their backs to the hollow, looking down the valley.

'And then what?' grunted Garric in his phlegmy bass.

'Once we're done with all this business with the boy. What comes after?'

'We go on as planned,' said Garric.

Keel spat on the ground. 'We were scraping the barrel before we started. Otten and Dox were barely old enough to shave. Even with Varla and Tarvi, this was a skeleton crew. Now they're gone, too.' He scraped at the spot of bubbled saliva with the toe of his boot. 'It's time to go home.'

Cade was desperate for oblivion, but something hooked him and kept him listening. Distantly, he sensed this was important.

'We go on,' said Garric. 'To the last man, if we have to.'

'They had three dreadknights watching him, Garric! This isn't a game!'

'It never was. There's still Yarin and Mara. We'll find others.'

'Haven't there been enough? How many more need to die?'

'As many as it takes,' said Garric, and he walked away. Keel threw up a hand in angry exasperation and went the other way.

Soothed by the fire's warmth, smothered by exhaustion, Cade gave up the struggle to stay awake, and his memory of the conversation was lost in a jumble of dreams.

'Come on, you. Have some of this.'

Osman roused Cade with a cup of hot, salty soup. The day was bright and clear and the sun was high. Cade sat up stiffly, took the cup and sipped at it while he came to terms with consciousness again.

Fen was hunkered down on one knee, scattering the wet ashes of their fire with a stick. Her face was long and narrow, like the rest of her. She was so thickly freckled that they'd joined together in a cluster that covered her cheeks and forehead. Sensing his gaze, she glanced up at him without interest, then back at the fire again.

'Well,' said Aren. 'We escaped.'

Aren was sitting wrapped in a blanket, wearing a weak smile and shivering. He was white and there were dark hollows around his eyes. Underfed and tired, soaked and chilled, the cold had got into his bones. He didn't have Cade's constitution: the carpenter's boy almost never got ill.

'You ain't looking too good,' Cade croaked.

'I'm not the one with my own knuckles imprinted on my face.'

Cade felt his cheek, sore from where he'd lain on his fist. He managed a smile at that.

'You both look ugly to Grub,' Grub offered helpfully. He stretched his arms and yawned, as if he'd just woken from a refreshing nap. 'Skarls tougher than Ossians. Grub walk twenty leagues a day, easy.'

Cade was too tired to even hate him this morning.

'Well, you three are resourceful sorts, I'll give you that,' said Osman, doling out strips of dried fish which they chewed with their soup. It was tough and near tasteless, but compared to prison fare it was fine cuisine. 'Broke out of the camp before we could spring you ourselves. You're lucky we found you at all, out there in the forest. If the Krodans hadn't been so keen on blowing their horns whenever they saw you, we probably wouldn't have.'

'Right,' said Keel. He looked pointedly at Garric, who was standing nearby. 'Imagine what'd have happened if they *hadn't* escaped before we sprung them.'

Garric scowled and turned away. Cade sensed there was something in that comment that he'd missed, but he was too tired to chase it and disinclined to talk to their rescuers for fear of drawing their wrath.

'Well, at least we ain't going to starve now,' Cade said with forced optimism. 'We planned to grab food before we left, but we hit a snag.'

'Hallen provides,' said Osman cheerily.

'That's not all he provides,' said Keel, coming over with a pile of clothes in each arm. He dumped one on the floor before Aren, the other between Cade and Grub. 'These ought to serve you better than those rags you're wearing on the road ahead. We brought gear for Aren, though we had to guess at his size. The rest I've cobbled together from spares. I doubt they'll fit well, but they'll do for now.'

'Thank you,' said Aren warily. They still weren't sure if they'd been rescued or kidnapped.

Osman helped Cade to his feet. Everything ached, but somehow his legs still supported him. 'You look like a stout one, friend. I'll bet there's some distance in you yet. A little further, then we can get some proper rest. I'll wager the squareheads will have a hard time tracking us through these mountains with the lead we've got.'

'It's not the squareheads I'm worried about,' muttered Keel.

'Get dressed and get moving!' Garric snapped.

'There,' said Fen.

Cade peered over the edge of the ridge and tried to find what she was pointing at. All he saw was the bleak saddle of the pass, scattered with boulders and scoured by a rising wind.

'I see nothing,' said Garric, who was lying on his belly to Cade's right.

'Look further,' said Fen, a hint of impatience in her voice. 'Among the rocks.'

Cade squinted and redoubled his efforts. When Fen had called Garric and Osman over, Cade had tagged along. Nobody bothered to stop him. He wasn't sure why he wanted to be here himself. Perhaps he was just tired of not knowing what was going on.

'Ah,' said Osman. He nudged Cade and directed his gaze with a finger. 'Beyond the pass, where the mountains meet.'

Now Cade saw it. A movement glimpsed among the stones. At first, he thought it was a warg or a bear, but a moment later, he saw his mistake and his belly tightened in fear.

It was a dreadknight.

He came slinking out into the open, crouched low to the ground, cloaked and hooded. It was the one with the metal mask, the one who slid like a shadow. At this distance he was only a black blot, but Cade knew his shape, and knew what he was doing. Hunting them.

'They've gained on us,' said Fen.

'How?' Osman exclaimed. 'We put the gorge between us!'

'And they went round it.'

'Godspit! Don't they rest?' Garric snarled.

Cade was transfixed by the sight of them. Behind the hooded dreadknight came his companions: the scrawny, ragged one with the bow, wary and watchful; the lumbering giant encased in black armour. Faceless, relentless, they didn't seem like people at all, but mindless forces set upon their trail, implacable as fate.

What had they done to bring down such terror on their heads? They were just two boys from the coast. They'd thought themselves beneath the notice of the Krodan Empire; they'd thought they could slip away from Suller's Bluff and be forgotten. And yet the Krodans had sent these *things* to bring them back.

They had three dreadknights watching him, Garric. He remembered hearing that somewhere; or had he dreamed it? He wasn't sure. Still, he thought sourly, it would make sense if it was only Aren they were chasing. Keel had said *him*, not *them*. Of the two of them, Cade had always been the unimportant one.

'What are they?' Cade asked, for now he wasn't sure how much of the stories he was supposed to believe.

'The Iron Hand's elite,' said Osman. 'Nobody's certain how many there are. Maybe a dozen in Ossia, perhaps more elsewhere.'

'Are they men, or … I've heard tales …'

'Don't let them frighten you. That's what the Krodans want. Beneath that fearful show, they're men like us. Deadly warriors, but men for all that.'

'Are you sure?' said Garric, his eyes dull and flat as he watched them. 'I'm not.'

Osman gave him a look. 'Whatever they are,' he said, 'when the Emperor needs something done, something vital, he sends the dreadknights.'

'So they're like the Krodan version of the Dawnwardens, then?'

Garric pushed away from the ridge with a snort. 'They're nothing like the Dawnwardens. Move. We're wasting time.'

They joined the others at the base of a pebbly slope. Aren was sitting bundled up, glistening with feverish sweat; they heard him coughing before they saw him. Keel stood guard nearby. Grub sat a way off, picking at his nails with his knife.

'By the looks on your faces, I don't want to hear what you found,' Keel said as they approached.

'They're on to us,' said Garric. 'Fen, can we shake them off?'

She thought a moment. 'We can change direction. Take the higher, harder route. Maybe they'll miss us.'

'The *harder* route?' Cade said. 'Aren's sick. Ain't you noticed?'

'We noticed,' said Garric. He turned to Fen. 'Lead the way.'

'Hoy!' Cade said to their backs, but neither of them paid him any mind. 'Hoy! I said he's sick!'

'It's alright,' said Aren as Osman helped him to his feet. 'I'm not done yet.'

No, you ain't, thought Cade, his brow furrowed with worry. *But it won't be much longer till you are.*

They struck away from the passes after that, spurning well-trodden trails for scrambling climbs, narrow fissures and half-visible paths that clung to the mountainsides. More than once, they were forced to backtrack when their route became impassable. At times, it felt like they were making no progress at all, but when Cade suggested taking an easier way, he was told to be silent.

'They'll run us down sure as the tide if they've got our trail,' said Keel. ''Specially with your friend slowing us up. Our best chance is to lose them. Fen knows her craft.'

The temperature dropped as they ascended and the wind came sharp and fast, whistling down from the peaks. Aren staggered against it, a blanket thrown over his shoulders and Cade's arm thrown over that. Tired as Cade was, fear put steel in his legs. He was used to looking to Aren for strength, but Aren had turned feeble and frail overnight. The effort of keeping them alive for so many months in the camp had used him up. He had nothing left for this new trial.

It was Cade's turn to be leaned on, then. He didn't have Aren's force of will, but he had the broad back and strong arms of a carpenter's son. So he bore his friend onwards, the way Aren had borne him in the past.

The ways became steeper and harder, and there was no end in sight. They ate while walking, chewing on dried meat, hardapple and biscuit, but it wasn't enough to satisfy them. Wane of day found them labouring along a trail that snaked up a steep slope of shale and scree. One wrong step would mean a deadly tumble, and the wind was doing its best to push them into the ravine. Cade's cheeks were numb and his legs quivered. He walked hunched over, with one hand as a shield ahead of him, the other holding Aren up. All the energy from their brief rest was long since spent. Even Garric and Keel, hardy men both, were visibly tiring. Only the need to support Aren kept Cade from sinking to his knees and giving up.

One foot, then the other.

Aren's breathing was wheezy and he stumbled like a drunkard, tripping over his feet. His eyes were half-open and ringed with shadow, and his curly hair straggled across his forehead.

'Just a little further,' Cade said, but he was so exhausted that it came out a slurred mumble. 'Just a little more.'

Aren went boneless and his legs buckled. Cade tried to catch him as he fell, but the shift in weight pulled him down, too, and they collapsed onto the trail together, perilously close to the drop.

Osman, who was bringing up the rear, called out to Garric as he hurried to their side. The others stopped, grateful for the halt.

'Get them up,' Garric said dispassionately.

'He can't go any further!' Cade said angrily as Osman helped him back to his feet.

'Look at the boy, Garric!' Osman said. 'We'll kill him if we keep on this way.'

Garric did, his face like stone. Aren's eyelids fluttered, but he stared blindly into the distance. Garric's gaze flicked to Grub.

'Carry him,' he told Grub. 'That, or get gone. He's the only reason you're here, after all.'

Grub's lip twitched in the hint of a snarl.

'You have a problem taking orders, Skarl?' Garric said.

Cade wondered if Grub might lunge at him; the look on his

face said he might. Keel had the same thought, and moved closer with his palm on the hilt of his sword.

Then Grub raised a hand and slowly pressed a finger to his neck, where tattoos crawled from the collar of his coat.

'See this? It say Grub carried his friend thirty leagues to safety after fight with urds in Sixth Purge. Friend was a fat bastard, too. Grub never saw him without a chicken wing in his mouth.' He lowered his hand and shrugged. 'Mudslug skinny. Grub carry, easy.' He picked Aren up and slung him across his shoulders like a slain deer. 'So? We go, then?'

'Down!' Fen snapped suddenly. They dropped into crouches, making themselves as small as they could on the exposed mountainside. Breath quick and short, Cade searched for the source of the danger. Then Fen pointed, and he saw.

Three dark figures moved below them in the gathering gloom. Cade's heart sank. The dreadknights still had their trail. Slowly, relentlessly, they were closing the distance.

Osman breathed a curse. He looked over at Garric, but the Hollow Man's mouth was a hard line.

'There's a wayfarers' hut not far from here,' Fen said. 'Warmth. Shelter. Four walls to defend.' She never took her eyes from the dreadknights below. 'It's something.'

She's talking about making a stand! thought Cade, wild with fear. *She's saying we can't outrun them!*

He looked at the others and saw that they, too, understood her. Their gambit had failed. The dreadknights would catch them by dawn.

'Lead the way,' Garric said.

Night had fallen by the time they found the hut, standing stark and exposed on a slope of shattered slate. The ground crunched underfoot as they approached, heads down, forcing their way through the wind. The Sisters hung at half-moon among the stars to the north, pale Lyssa peeking out from behind her cracked and glowering sibling. Even obscured, she was far the brighter, and the spectral light she cast was only a little bloodied by Tantera's presence.

The hut was mean and low, walled and roofed with the same slate that surrounded it, and they bundled inside, grateful for sanctuary. There was a single room within, cold and long unoccupied, holding a few pallets for sleeping, a stove and a cupboard. Hide coats with furred hoods hung on hooks, and there were packs and blankets and stout travel clothes bundled up in one corner. Fen went to the stove and found a fire already laid within. She set to work with a tinderbox and flint while Grub dropped Aren on a pallet and Cade covered him with a blanket, grim with concern. In the moonlight that spilled through the door, Aren muttered and turned, caught in the grip of a fever dream.

'Thank you,' Cade murmured.

'Mudslug can't hear you, stupid,' Grub said.

'I was talking to you.'

'Huh,' said Grub. He snorted back some snot, then snatched one of the warm coats from its hook and began to pull it on in place of his own.

Cade bowed his head over his friend's chest. When Grub had boasted about Skarl endurance, he hadn't exaggerated. A life in the far north had made his people tough. He'd carried Aren as if he was no weight at all, and even now showed no sign of fatigue.

The rest of them had gone as far as they could go. There was no more strength in them, and any hope that the dreadknights had lost them in the dark felt slim indeed.

Fen's sparks caught on the tinder and she pushed it into the fire. Flames gathered and light grew in the room until Cade could see into the corners. Keel was ransacking a cupboard which held biscuits, jars of preserves and a wheel of cheese sealed in wax.

'Who lives here?' Cade asked, unable to understand why anyone would leave such bounty in such a desolate place.

'It's a wayfarers' hut,' said Osman. 'A shelter for travellers in winter, lost in the mountain snows. A remnant of the old times, before the Krodans, when hospitality was a tradition.' He looked about approvingly. 'Someone still keeps it.'

'At least we'll die with our bellies full, eh?' said Keel. Then he paused, struck by the weight of his own words, and Cade saw his bravado falter. 'Damn it to the depths. Mariella. Tad ...'

Garric laid a hand on his shoulder. 'Your brother will provide for them.'

'He will,' Keel said bitterly. 'But that task should have been mine.'

Cade was surprised to hear affection in Garric's gruff voice. The others were comrades-in-arms, but these two were friends. True friends, of the kind that were more like brothers. He hadn't seen it till now.

'Stand guard with me outside,' said Garric. 'They'll not catch us unawares, and we have little need to warm our bones.'

'That's so,' said Keel. 'We've weathered worse storms together, you and I, when the seas tossed and the whales were breaching and harpoons were in our hands.'

Together they stepped outside and closed the door behind them. Whatever talk they'd have, they'd have it in private; their conversation would be between them and the night.

The heat from the fire built quickly in the small hut and Cade's fingers prickled as they thawed inside his gloves, but all his attention was on Aren, muttering incoherently beneath his blankets. Fen busied herself stoking the fire, caught up in her own thoughts. Grub, clad in his new coat, had stripped the cheese and was devouring it, apparently intent on leaving none for the others. Osman hovered anxiously at Cade's shoulder, watching Aren with a worried expression on his face.

'Can't we do something?' Cade said at last.

'Would that I could,' said Osman. 'I don't have the craft.'

'So we're just going to wait here for them to catch us up?'

'It's that or have them come upon us in a pass, when we're too tired to raise our blades,' said Osman. 'At least this way we'll give them a fight.'

'Not Grub,' said Grub, with his mouth full. 'Grub not staying here. Grub take his chances with the mountain. Right after he's done with this cheese.'

'You'll be missed,' Fen said sarcastically, not looking up from the fire.

'You'll be dead,' he replied, dipping a wedge of cheese into a pot of gooseberry jam.

Cade's teeth were gritted hard enough to make his jaw ache. Anger pushed exhaustion aside and he wanted to lash out at something. Aren was fading before his eyes and a doom bore down on them in the dark that couldn't be escaped or overcome. He'd die as he'd lived: without control of his own destiny, dragged along by events beyond his knowledge. He'd been a fool to dream he could change that.

A howl cut through the night, mournful and eerie. Grub jerked his head up, listening, jam on his face and a piece of cheese sticking out of his mouth. A moment later, Garric burst in, sword in hand.

'Outside!' he barked.

'They've caught up already?' Osman said.

'Should have eaten faster, Skarl.' Fen snatched up her bow and hurried out. Grub looked this way and that, eyes wide with alarm, as Osman grabbed his own bow and followed.

'Take Aren's sword, Cade,' he advised. 'Make such an end as you can.'

Cade looked down at Aren, at the waxy white effigy he'd become. There was no time for regrets now, only time to do what had to be done. He dug under the blankets and pulled Aren's sword from its scabbard.

'Got any tattoos for killing dreadknights?' he asked Grub. Grub shook his head. 'Aye, that's what I thought.'

He stepped out into the dark, guts churning, the blade a clumsy weight in his hand. A hard wind and a lifeless, moonlit landscape of cold stone greeted him. The others stood ready around the perimeter of the hut, searching for the enemy. As he emerged, another thin howl drifted down the mountainside.

'I don't see them,' Keel said. The strip of lank hair atop his head blew about his face. 'Where are they?'

Grub pushed out of the hut, knife in hand. He had the same frightened, feral look in his eyes that Cade had seen last night, when they were backed against a gorge with the Krodans closing in. Only Cade was close enough to hear what he was murmuring to himself. 'Grub not supposed to die here. Not yet. Not yet.'

Cade had never really thought he was supposed to die anywhere, but he felt Sarla standing close now, and it turned his knees to water. He could barely hold his sword.

'Courage, lad,' said Osman, fingers on the string of his bow, eyes roaming the night.

'There!' said Keel, pointing.

A cowled figure rose into sight at the top of the slope, ghostly in the moonlight. Cade's blood ran cold as it came towards them with slow, fearful purpose.

'Where are the others?' Osman demanded, casting about desperately.

'What does it matter? Shoot him!' Keel snapped.

Fen and Osman drew together; but Garric threw out a hand and cried 'Hold!'

They held, bowstrings quivering at full draw as Garric peered closer at their target.

'No dreadknight I know of walks with a staff,' he said slowly. 'Nor do dogs suffer their company.'

Now that the figure had cleared the rise, Cade saw that Garric was right. They carried a jagged staff with a splintered tip, and at their side was a lean, shaggy hound. Cloak and cowl were a patchwork of furs that blew and flapped about them as they approached. It was a stranger, but not one of those they'd feared.

The stranger stopped, seeing the raised bows. At their feet, the dog crouched down, flattened its ears and let out another sorrowful howl.

'Who goes?' Garric demanded.

They pushed back their cowl. Long black hair curled and whipped around a black and white striped face.

'I am Vika-Walks-The-Barrows,' she called. 'I saw your light, and I would share your shelter.'

31

Strange is the speech of spirits. They will send you by crooked paths.

Vika had learned that lesson well studying under Agalie-Sings-The-Dark, and during the years of wandering that followed. Everything was changeable in the Shadowlands, truth most of all. Messages from there were unclear, subject to many interpretations, and they only revealed themselves by degrees. Many times Vika had conversed with the spirits, many times they'd shown her signs and portents, but rare indeed was the vision that meant what it first appeared to. Seeking one answer, she'd often find a different one, or discover that the question itself had changed. The Shadowlands were a place of chaos and its denizens were all in some way mad.

Yet here, on a bare mountainside on this night of all nights, she'd found these travellers. It was hard not to find meaning in that.

'Is that a druidess?' she heard one of them say. He was young, with a sturdy body, a broad face and incongruously delicate features. The wonder in his voice saddened her. He'd never seen one of her kind.

The man who looked to be their leader had the archers lower their bows. 'You walk a lonely way,' he said, his voice thick with suspicion. 'What brings you to this bleak place?'

'It is in my nature to wander,' Vika replied. She put a hand on Ruck's back. 'And as you see, I am not lonely.'

It wasn't an honest answer and he knew it, but how could she explain in a way he'd understand? She'd followed signs since leaving the Auldwood, subtle nudges from the spirits, beneath the notice of the untrained. The flocking of starlings had sent her in one direction; a grey fox had sent her in another. She'd seen black clouds over the mountains that looked like an open hand, fingers spread like a puppeteer's. She'd bled herself into a bowl and cast the bones into it, seeking wisdom, and they'd sent her into the storm.

At last, abandoning herself to fate, she'd walked up into the Ostenbergs, though all sense told her it was pointless. The champion she'd been shown was unlikely to be in these barren heights. She'd have a better chance staying in the Auldwood.

As the night fell and the moons rose, a fear had begun to grow in her, for the stars and the Sisters above her now matched her vision at the Dirracombe. This was the appointed time, then; but she'd found no one, and the stain of doubt spread across her heart. Had she been a fool? Were the signs merely the addled dreams of a poisoned mind? Ruck, sensing her mistress's mood, had become distressed and set up a plaintive howl.

Then she'd seen the glow of a fire through the shuttered windows of a wayfarers' hut, a beacon in the blowing dark, and she doubted no longer.

She approached carefully, descending the slope of broken slate towards the strangers clustered around the hut. Six of them, wary as wounded wolves. She sensed the danger that clung to them.

'I am Garric,' said the black-bearded one, whose throat had been cut long ago. 'It gladdens me to see a keeper of the faith, but you'll find small shelter here. Dreadknights are abroad tonight and they hunt for us. You'd do well to keep walking.'

Dreadknights. The word struck her like a blow. No wonder the night felt so ominous; no wonder Ruck had howled.

Keep walking, Garric advised. Keep walking, as she ever had, always on the move. Dreadknights would have no mercy for a druidess.

But what then? She knew what waited if she didn't find the champion. She'd seen it at the Dirracombe.

'My friend is sick!' the boy blurted out. 'Badly sick. Can you help him?'

That made her mind up for her. She had to at least take a look. 'Aye, I'll help.' She turned her gaze on Garric. 'If you'll let me in?'

Garric gave the boy a dangerous glare, but he stepped aside. 'Your choice, druidess.'

They watched her uncertainly as she entered the hut. The warmth of the stove was blessed relief from the clawing wind, and there was the sick boy, lying on a pallet beside it. She crouched by his side and examined him, and it only took a moment to see it was serious.

'What's your name?' she asked the other boy, who'd crowded in alongside her. Ruck bustled restlessly about the hut, sniffing her new surroundings.

'Cade of Shoal Point.'

'Heat some water for me, Cade.' She pointed to a battered pan that hung on the wall and he set to it, pouring water from one of the travellers' skins. Vika exposed the sick boy's scrawny chest and put her ear to his ribcage. He'd been halfway to starving even before he fell ill. These boys made odd companions to the others, who had the air of capable warriors.

'Tell me,' she said. 'Why do the dreadknights hunt you?'

'We escaped from the camp at Suller's Bluff!' Cade said. Even with all that was happening, she heard pride in his voice at that. 'Aren and me and the Skarl. The others are helping us.' He frowned. 'I think.'

'Grub,' said Grub as he came back inside. 'Not "the Skarl". Plenty Skarls, only one Grub.'

'I thought you were leaving,' said Cade spitefully. 'Now's your chance.'

'Grub leave when he wants,' he said. 'Not done with the cheese yet.' He picked up the wheel of cheese and took a bite, his eyes on Vika.

'If the dreadknights seek you, you must be someone of note,' Vika suggested as she raised Aren's eyelids and looked at the whites beneath. 'Dreadknights do not waste their time on runaway boys and foreigners.'

'They're of no note,' said Garric as he came through the doorway. The hut was small and cramped, and he seemed to take up more than his share of space. 'Nor are any of us.' His tone ended that line of enquiry.

'There's three of them!' Cade said. 'One with a hammer, one with a bow and one—'

'Who carries two blades,' Vika finished for him. 'I've seen them.'

'You have?'

'We crossed paths near Salt Fork.' Vika was grave. It couldn't be coincidence that she'd encountered those dreadknights hunting fugitives before. Now, leagues and months away, here they were again.

'Who are they?' Cade asked her.

'Their names are Ruin, Plague and Sorrow,' said Garric. 'I saw them at Salt Fork, too. And I know that together, they're beyond us.'

Vika turned her head to him. 'You were at Salt Fork?'

Garric's face showed nothing, his eyes shadowed in the shifting light from the stove. 'You're wasting your time with the boy. He'll be dead by sunrise if the dreadknights find us, and we have neither the strength to outrun them nor the craft to evade them. If you have some way to help, speak now, for I'd rather not die here. If not, save your herbs and your neck, and go while you can.'

'I am not yours to command, Garric, and I do what I will,' she replied. She plucked a pouch of dried elmenthorn from inside her cloak and passed it to Cade. 'Empty that into the water and give it a stir. Don't let it boil.'

'As you wish,' said Garric. 'I've warned you twice. Let's hope the Aspects are kinder to you than they were to the faithful at Salt Fork.' He moved to leave, but Vika stopped him.

'Your sword,' she said. 'Will you show it to me?'

Garric frowned but did as he was asked. It was old and finely crafted, nicked with the memories of many battles and speckled with flecks of dried blood.

'Has it a name?' she asked, thinking of the bright sword that had burned like the sun in her vision.

'Names are for noble blades, earned through great deeds,' said Garric. 'Ossia is no land for heroes now; not since we sold ourselves to Kroda. This sword is only a sword.'

Vika heard bitterness and disappointment in his voice, and felt an answering anger. He was in his fifties, perhaps. Old enough to have been an adult when the Krodans came. Old enough to be cheated of all the hopes and dreams that had formed him, to stand witness as his gods and values were eroded. Maybe he wasn't the champion she sought, but he'd been at Salt Fork, and she recognised that tone of weary resistance. Whoever this man was, he'd fought back. And that was more than she'd ever done.

We are each tested in our own way.

She reached inside her cloak, deft fingers plucking out a clay phial that she knew by the imprint on its wax seal. She handed it to Garric.

'Have everyone take a sip of this. The barest sip, I warn you! More than that and you may not survive.' She looked back at the boy on the pallet. 'I will see to him now, but someone must carry him onwards.'

'Grub will carry him,' said the Skarl. Cade gave him a surprised look. 'Grub has a lot of skin to cover yet,' he said, and then he grinned. 'Painted Lady has an idea.'

'What is this?' Garric asked, eyeing the phial doubtfully.

'It will put strength in your limbs. Tell the others to take what clothes and food they can from this place. I see you are wearied, but we must travel hard and fast now.'

'Travel where?'

Vika felt her stomach turn over at the thought of what she intended. 'To a place even dreadknights might not follow. If I can find it at all.'

Garric's frown loosened as he understood. 'You speak of Skavengard.'

'Aye. And perhaps there we will meet worse horrors than those who follow. But any chance is better than none.'

It was a wild notion to take them to Skavengard, but if her faith had ever meant anything, if her whole life and all she believed was not a lie, then it was the only thing she could do. If she left them now, she might as well give up being a druidess. She buried her fingers in the warm fur of Ruck's ruff, and there found the steadiness she needed.

'Why would you join us, knowing what hunts us?' The sullen

suspicion had vanished from Garric's tone as he realised she was genuine. Now he sounded amazed.

'If the Aspects are silent, it is because we have forgotten how to listen,' Vika said. Agalie's words, spoken at their last meeting. She got to her feet and faced him, firm with purpose. 'I'm listening now.'

32

The wind flayed them as they struggled along in single file, insects against the bleak flank of the mountain. They walked a ledge little wider than a man's outstretched arms, with a killing drop to cold grey rock on one side. The sun wasn't yet above the peaks, but the sky was a serene blue threaded with twists of cloud. To the east, the slopes were edged in bright fire.

Let each dawn find you different. Agalie used to say that, back when Vika was just an acolyte. Every day, a person should learn something, experience something, do something that left them changed, even in a small way.

Agalie would be proud of her today.

Vika's patchwork cowl flapped about her face as she planted her staff before her, leading the line up the narrow path. Her eyes roamed the landscape, searching for indications that she was still on the right track. They'd rounded the broken peak, found the leaning stone and the waterfall. But where was the cock's-comb ridge or the cleft that led to the valley? Where was the tree and the stair and the door? It had been hours since the waterfall, and she worried she'd led them astray.

Years had passed since Hagath had told her the way to Skaven-gard, and even that information was second-hand. It was Polla-Calls-The-Waters who'd actually travelled there and returned with tales fit to still the blood in her veins. Had Hagath missed a step in his explanation, or had Vika's memory failed? It had never been entirely trustworthy, mixed up as it was with potions and dream-visions until fact and fiction blurred together.

But she'd found the broken peak, the leaning stone and the waterfall. By the grace of the Communion, the shared lore of the druids, she had a chance to save these people's lives. She had to believe she was on the right path.

Have faith, Vika-Walks-The-Barrows. You always were too quick to doubt.

She looked back along the line. Ruck was close at her heels, head down, tongue lolling. Behind her walked Cade, and behind him the Skarl they called Grub, who carried the sick boy on his shoulders. The others came after, faces flinty as the mountain. They'd walked through a night and a day and another night since their escape, with only a few hours of rest, yet there was still vigour in them. Vika's potion had put it there. They wouldn't feel the fatigue until later, but when it came, it would be crushing.

'Is Aren going to live?' Cade asked her, catching her eye.

'With rest, he will recover,' Vika told him. 'But we must reach shelter soon. He will not survive the elements much longer.'

'Are we close?'

'I think so,' Vika said, with a smile she hoped was reassuring. She was used to solitude and the niceties of society didn't come naturally to her. She headed onwards, but Cade spoke to her back.

'You're afraid of Skavengard, ain't you?'

'As should you be.'

'My ma told me tales of that place, but I thought they were just stories. She said it was home to one of the Sorcerer Kings.'

'Azh Mat Jaal,' Vika said absently, scanning the riven landscape. 'The Sorcerer Kings and Queens of Old Ossia wielded great power, but for all that, they were men and women like you and I. Some were noble and just; some decadent and cruel. Towards the end, there was more cruelty than justice. But even among such infamous company, the name of Azh Mat Jaal rings loud across the ages.'

She felt a hand run up her back and stiffened. No, not *her* back: Ruck's. Cade was stroking the hound as he walked. She felt a warm wash of pleasure from her companion, and it warmed her to the boy in turn.

'I know not what cataclysm befell the Second Empire, nor

239

what became of the Sorcerer Kings of old. But terrible things were done in Skavengard and the memory lingers in those silent halls and empty cloisters.' Her painted face darkened. 'Something walks there, it's said. Something that does not love the living.' Then suddenly she raised her staff. 'Ah! That is our path!'

Ahead, a deep, narrow cleft split the rock. It was just as Hagath had promised. Somehow she'd missed the cock's-comb ridge, but her instincts had steered her right.

The cleft took them out of the wind, leading them up a sheltered incline. The stone beneath their feet was uneven and sharp, gullied by old waters. They struggled upwards with single-minded purpose, grunting with effort. All their focus was on their destination; they didn't think beyond that. These were men and women who hadn't expected to see the dawn, and they dared not hope too far.

They emerged from the fissure into a small rocky valley, a wound in the mountains with steep sides that stood high and close. Alone amid the lifeless stone was a tree, black and warped with age, a mass of knots and boils without a single leaf on it.

The tree, thought Vika. *Joha be praised.*

But after the tree there was supposed to be a stair, and after that, the doors to Skavengard. Yet though the valley was small enough to see to its end, there was no stair here.

'Where now, druidess?' Garric rumbled at her shoulder.

'Give me a moment,' said Vika. 'The path to Skavengard is not easily found.'

'If it exists at all,' muttered Fen. It was pitched for Keel's ears, but Vika's hearing was sharper than most. She felt a surge of annoyance at the ingratitude. Fen had been as keen as anyone to follow her, back at the hut.

She walked away from them, her boots crunching on the stones, Ruck panting at her side. There was something wrong about this. There was no stair, and no break in the valley walls that might lead elsewhere. Yet she'd followed Hagath's instructions to the letter, and there was the black tree he'd promised.

Had she been misled? Had Polla-Calls-The-Waters really been to Skavengard at all?

Go back, she thought. *This is not the way.*

'It's a dead end!' Keel said.

'We should backtrack while we still can,' Fen told her. 'Skavengard is a fireside tale. We've walked all night and I barely feel it. With your potions we'll outlast the dreadknights. Let me guide us out of these mountains.'

They're right, Vika thought. *Go back. Go back quickly, before the dreadknights catch us all.*

Something tickled at the edge of her senses. Something she couldn't quite place.

'Come, then,' said Garric, making the decision for the group. 'There's no time to waste. Let's—'

'Hold!' Vika cried, lifting one hand in the air. She looked over her shoulder at the travellers, who were already heading back towards the entrance to the valley. 'You are all suddenly very eager to leave.'

'Because there's nothing here!' Keel told her. 'Any mudwit can see that.'

'You've trusted me this far,' said Vika. 'Trust me now. Besides, you'll not outrun anyone without me.'

They cursed and grumbled, but they stayed where they were as she turned her attention to the tree. She didn't blame them for their mistrust. She, too, wanted to leave. It was like a physical pull. Her thoughts flowed towards escape like rivers to the sea, and no matter how she tried to divert them, they still reached the same end.

She was always too quick to doubt. But not this quick. Something was pushing them away.

She reached into her cloak and ran her fingers over the phials there. Each was sealed with a stopper carved with a symbol in Stonespeak, the secret tongue of druids. She found the right one, drew it out and took a swallow.

'Now,' she said to herself. 'What is here?'

The potion crackled through her body like flashfire, spreading from her nape over her skull, racing along her limbs. Her pupils grew wide, irises thinning to almost nothing, and her breath surged in and out like a tide. She felt as if she was falling gently backwards, sinking into another state of being.

Alderbright and haglock, a potion for clarity, to slow the mind and senses. Life was a flurry, seen through a tunnel, always rushing from task to task. It was easy to miss what was right in front of you.

Everything expanded around her. The barren valley became vast, teeming with the ticks and taps of insect life. Every edge turned sharp, cutting the shadows like blades. She smelled the sickness in Aren, heard the wet chill that lay on his lungs. Fen and Keel were murmuring about her behind her back, casting doubts where they thought she couldn't hear, but beneath the words she sensed things they didn't mean to say: how distrust came so naturally to Fen that she knew no other way; how Keel had a hole in him he could never fill; and how both had enough belief and affection for the old faith that the presence of a druidess gave them hope.

She wouldn't let them down.

She approached the tree. It looked huge now, swollen with the centuries and scarred with age. She placed her hands on the bark, closed her eyes and let her fingers roam the cracks and ridges. Immediately, she felt it: a scar that had been placed there with intent. She found another, a line that was too neat and straight, and a knothole, round and perfect. She stepped back and opened her eyes, and what she hadn't seen before was now clear. A symbol had been crafted onto the tree, a ward of some kind, hidden in the bark. The very sight of it repelled her.

Go back, it said.

'It's here!' she called, grinning with relief. 'The stair is here!' For how could it be otherwise, when someone had gone to such lengths to turn seekers away? She stepped back from the tree and swept the valley with her newfound sight. A jagged line in the stone, which she'd taken to be handspan wide, stretched apart beneath her gaze. She saw a perilous set of steps, concealed by folds in the rock, zigzagging upwards.

'There!' She threw out a hand and pointed with a wild laugh.

'She's shade-touched! There's no stair!' Osman said to the others, but Vika hurried towards it, stumbling as the potion dizzied her.

'It's here!' she said again as she reached the foot of it, with Ruck barking excitedly and running around her. Only when she was close enough to touch it did it seem real. Cut into the stone at the base of the stair was another symbol, an arrangement of whorls and curves that branded itself on her mind.

A ward to deter the curious; a ward to hide the stair. Small wonder few ever found this place. I'd wager even the Delvers do not know Skavengard.

They came reluctantly, still half ready to turn back. Only when they were by her side did their faces clear.

'How did we not see it before?' Osman wondered.

'Someone did not want you to,' said Vika.

She turned to the Skarl carrying the sick boy, and just for an instant she saw something in the tattoos on his face, found sense in a language she didn't understand. Impressions leaped into her mind, made possible by her state of heightened consciousness. Pictures of heroism, strength of arms, the bloody brotherhood that existed between warriors, and all of it marred and made rotten by the ugly black swipe across his eyes.

Grub saw something in her reaction, and his gaze became dark and hot with danger. She switched her attention to Aren before he could read her. 'The way is hard. We will need to lash the boy to you. Can you bear him?'

'Grub can carry Mudslug,' he said. She could tell by his voice that he suspected something.

'Then we climb!' said Garric, with new fervour. Their doubts had fallen away now the power of the wards had been overcome; there was no more griping and grizzling at her lead. Vika took some satisfaction from that.

The stair was steep, sometimes so steep they had to climb it like a ladder, and Ruck had to be hauled up. The steps were worn, made smooth and slippery by centuries of rain, and they went with care: a tumble might take them all down. Vika worried about Grub, who was carrying Aren piggyback, but soon she saw that he was the most surefooted of them all. Though he looked lumbering and clumsy, his sense of balance was superb.

The stair switched back on itself over and over, and they followed each twist, hugging tight to the stone. The wind began to pick up again as they made their way up the valley wall, carrying to Vika a whiff of terror-sweat and the sound of a hammering heartbeat. The way was precarious and there was fear in all of them, but one more so than the others. Looking back down the line she saw Fen, her freckled face half-covered by a hood, eyes fixed firmly on the next step. She gave no outward sign of it, but inside, she was terrified.

She's afraid of heights, Vika thought. *And determined none should know.*

Who were these people she'd tied her fate to? Who were these strangers the Krodans had sent their most deadly agents to catch? Was one of them really the champion she sought?

Her thoughts scattered in alarm as Cade stumbled, his foot slipping out from under him; but Keel was close behind, and he grabbed the boy so that he only fell to his hands and knees, and no worse.

Vika breathed again. Her craft would only sustain them so far, and fatigue was setting in as the potion wore off. She dared not give them another dose – the withdrawal from such a powerful drug might kill them. She could only hope they'd last until Skavengard.

'Thanks,' said Cade sheepishly as Keel picked him up. He peered over the edge of the stair and the colour drained from his face.

'Long way down, eh?' said Keel.

'No,' said Cade, and pointed. 'Look.'

A cold wash of fear ran through Vika. Three figures were entering the valley, sliding out of the fissure like cockroaches from a crack. They were made small by distance, but it didn't diminish their presence. She sensed them as much as saw them, and with her expanded awareness they possessed a strange density, as if they were more real than the rock that surrounded them. They were like black holes punched in the fabric of the world, sucking in light and life, windows to elsewhere.

These were the enemy she'd pitted herself against. For the first time, she understood the scale of what she'd taken on.

'Make haste!' she hissed. 'The gate cannot be far!'

They began to climb the stair at reckless speed. Vika led the way, heedless of the drop, her lichwood and lightning-glass staff gripped tight in her hand. Cade slipped again – his prisoner's boots were not well suited to climbing – but Keel was ready to catch him once more.

As they went, Vika cast glances down below. The dreadknights had stopped at the mouth of the valley as the same arts that had repelled Vika made them doubt themselves. The cowled one, Sorrow, came creeping forward, crouched low to the ground, searching the earth for signs.

Turn back, she thought at them, adding her will to the power that guarded the valley. *Turn back. There's nothing here.*

Then Sorrow straightened and lifted his face to reveal a metal mask of howling grief. Though she couldn't see his eyes, Vika felt his gaze meet hers. The world slowed around her, and just for a moment there was only him and her in it.

She knew one thing with certainty then. She'd been marked, and there was no hiding any more. Wherever she went, Sorrow would find her.

'I see it! The top of the stair!'

Osman's voice jerked her back to the moment. Now she saw it, too: the end of the climb, where a hidden shelf, invisible from ground level, cut into the side of the valley.

'Courage!' she cried, more for her own sake than the others'. 'We will outrun them yet!'

Sorrow lifted his swords, and at his signal the dreadknights rushed into the valley, making for the foot of the stair. But Vika felt Skavengard within her reach now, close enough to grasp. She surged forward, and the others followed her headlong into the unknown.

33

They clambered up the last of the steps and onto the ledge, their legs weakening with every step. There they paused, panting before a dark, gaping portal with pillars to either side, worn down to mere bulges in the rock. If there'd been a gate here once, it was long gone, leaving only the faintest signs that this entrance was the work of human hands.

'Lantern!' Garric called as soon as he saw it. Osman unhitched one from the side of his pack, and he and Fen set about lighting it with flint and oil. Cade drifted to the portal and peered inside while Vika looked back into the valley. The dreadknights were already at the foot of the stair.

She drew out another phial and unstoppered it. A warning buzz at the back of her skull told her she already had a dangerous amount of poison in her veins, but this was only a mild concoction and she was afraid enough to risk it. She tipped it into her mouth, tasting bitter herbs on her tongue, then turned away from the edge and strode towards the portal, Ruck at her heels.

'Catch up with me,' she said. 'I will see the way is clear.'

'It's pitch dark in there!' Osman said.

'There is light enough for me,' she replied as she swept past him.

The corridor beyond was a smashed echo of grandeur. Flagstones were broken and tilted. The vaults overhead had cracked and dropped huge chunks of masonry on the floor. Crumbling pillars marked the way, with tall, shadowy figures between them, mutilated by the ages.

Yet despite lying in ruin, the work of her ancestors struck Vika with awe, and she felt small as she hastened inside. She saw its ancient greatness in hints and patterns: a sculpted edge here, the remains of a mural there. Entering this place stirred some primal, collective pride deep inside her.

Her potion was making her head throb, but it lent her owl's eyes, and the light from the portal showed the corridor in shades of grey. Ruck followed her, sharing her vision, past dripping stalactites and fallen rubble. To either side were statues of men and women in strange robes and towering elaborate headpieces. They'd been carved from some black, glistening stone that hadn't held detail well, and their faces were smooth, impassive and alien.

The corridor turned at the end, sending her down ancient steps overlooked by a guardian demon in the shape of a mantis. She was approaching the limit of the light now – even owls couldn't see in total darkness – but she didn't want to wait for the lantern. Every moment counted, and if they were to stay ahead of the pursuit, she had to find their path.

She rounded another corner and, with a small gasp of relief, she saw new light. The thinnest sliver, but light nonetheless, creeping beneath the doors at the end of the corridor.

These were the doors Hagath spoke of. If Polla's story was true, Skavengard lay beyond.

She hastened towards them. Twice her height and cut from metal, they had survived the centuries better than the blank, mouldering statues standing to either side. They were still dense with detail, a swarming tangle of curves and angles that flowed and eddied without symmetry. She searched for a handle or lever and, finding none, she pushed against the metal. When that failed, she found holds with her fingertips and pulled. The doors remained shut.

She stepped back, frustrated. Hagath had made no mention of how to get through the doors once she found them. She searched them again, more carefully this time, and found two hidden key grips recessed in the metal. She tried to turn them, but they wouldn't move.

I would be fortunate indeed, if it was that easy.

She began to feel around the door, exploring the crevices and edges of its complex surface. Something gave beneath her finger-tips with a click. A button! She tried the keys again, to no avail.

There had to be more. The Old Ossians loved their puzzle boxes and finger traps. There was a trick to this. She just had to find it.

Ruck bustled about her feet, snorting with growing agitation as she located another button, and another, and another yet. Soon she'd found buttons hidden all over the door. When some were pressed in, others popped back out.

A combination. But how to guess it?

She heard footsteps behind her, and light grew there.

'They are coming!' Osman called as he hurried round the corner, lantern held high. The others came clattering after him.

'Why doors not open? Open doors!' Grub cried, Aren still jogging and jerking against his back.

'They're locked?' Cade said, panic in his voice.

'Put your shoulders to them!' Keel barked. 'We'll break them down!'

'Silence!' Vika shouted and rapped her staff against the floor. 'Brute strength will not help us here. Let me think!'

'Think fast, then,' rumbled Garric. 'They're not far behind us.' He began snapping orders to the others, arranging them along the corridor in defensive positions.

Vika set herself to the task again. Her eyes flickered over the maze of shapes and patterns, searching for meaning, finding none. A dark pressure grew at the back of her mind, growing greater with each passing moment. It was the dreadknights, bearing down on them, their presence weighty as the mountain.

Prinn, Ragged Mummer, Aspect of Deceit and Trickery, help me now. Give me the wisdom to solve this.

Ruck barked at her side, calling for her attention. Vika ignored her at first, so intent was she on the puzzle of the doors, but Ruck barked again, and this time Vika sensed her insistence. The wolfhound was sniffing at the foot of one of the statues. Vika caught the faintest of scents, so weak as to be almost a memory. A human scent. Female.

She crouched next to Ruck, her arm over the dog's back, and

peered at the base of the statue. Scratched in the stone were three spidery symbols, with a smaller one beneath them as a signature.

Polla-Calls-The-Waters had left druidsign.

Excited, she bent closer. The symbols were messily carved and hard to read, but she made sense of them at last. When she did, her eyes widened.

Enter by Shadowlands.

Quickly she stood, fumbling inside her cloak for another phial. She was already close to the limit of her tolerance; another potion, especially one as strong as this, might do her untold damage. But all their lives were in her hands and she dared not hesitate. She drew out the phial, broke the seal and tipped it down her throat.

'I hear them!' Fen called down the corridor.

'Druidess!' Garric cried. 'Whatever arts you have, use them now! Open these doors!'

The potion crashed through her brain like a wave, sweeping her thoughts before it. She staggered and leaned on her staff. It felt as if her head was expanding, ready to split and burst. This was the kind of brew that demanded preparation, meditation and prayer before it was consumed. Swilled down like this, it sent her mind reeling. She hadn't tried to bridge the Divide to the Shadowlands since that terrible night at the Dirracombe. Now she flung herself across recklessly, and madness swarmed around her.

Find the way. Everything crawled with movement, glimpses of that other realm that lay beneath the surface of the visible world, a dark mirror to the land of the living. She saw strange and twisted reflections wavering just beyond reality. This ancient corridor existed there, as did those statues, this mountain. Those doors.

The doors. Focus on the doors.

She furrowed her brow and marshalled her splintered mind. Some power had been laid over this entrance, a taut membrane seething with dangerous energies. She brushed against it tentatively, ready to recoil, but it didn't harm her. Whatever sorcery this might be, it wasn't meant to stop her.

Polla had passed this way and survived. So, then, would she.

Feel it. Feel the answer.

She sensed a shape there, invisible to the casual explorer but not to one trained to see beyond. It was written plainly on the doors, but only in the Shadowlands, as if drawn by a finger on a fogged mirror. She concentrated, and all at once it came to her. A pattern in the buttons, as clear as if she'd been given a diagram.

With a cry of triumph she surged forward, fingers finding the buttons. Now *this* one, now *this* one, now *that*! Something clanked behind the door. She seized both key grips together and twisted. They turned inwards with a crunch and she pushed hard. There was a moment of resistance as the membrane of the invisible barrier stretched and snapped, then a line of white daylight split the doors as the way to Skavengard opened.

'Help her!' someone shouted as the light swelled and filled her vision, and the grinding of the ancient hinges drowned out all else. Like a drunkard, she tottered through the doorway and came to a halt, amazed.

She stood on a broad balcony set into the side of a valley enclosed by snow-tipped peaks. A delicate balustrade ran around the edge of the balcony, and at each corner was a pedestal on which stood broken stumps that might once have been guardian beasts. To her right, a stairway led down, but she ignored it, captivated by the sight before her: the magnificent and sombre stronghold of Azh Mat Jaal.

The sun was directly ahead, moments from rising over the eastern slopes. Warm light was creeping down towards three rocky islands in the still, weedy lake which covered the valley floor. One island was massive, dominating the valley. The others were small by comparison, lumpen outcrops hugging close to their larger brother. Skavengard covered all three, clinging to their sides, perching on their tips, sprawling where there was space to sprawl. Narrow bridges linked the islands. She saw skeletal spires, mournful towers, colonnaded walkways brooding in dusty silence. It was a castle, perhaps, or a palace, or a manse; a folly of a fallen empire, the size of a town. In the last of the morning's shadow, it was sad and hollow, crumbling beneath the weight of its emptiness.

'Close the doors!'

Garric's shout jerked her from her daze. She looked back to see Fen, the last of them, sprinting through the doors onto the balcony.

'They're right behind me!' she yelled.

Garric and Keel had each taken a door and were shoving against them. Grub dumped Aren on the ground and ran to help. Cade went with him while Fen and Osman readied their bows. The heavy doors began to close, screeching on their thousand-year-old hinges. Vika stared into the dark between them, and horror grew in her heart as she heard the thumping of heavy feet and saw an armoured giant come charging out of the gloom.

'Brace yourselves!' she cried. Before the doors could close, Ruin crashed into them from the other side, throwing them back enough for his huge hands to grip their edges. He loomed into the gap, holding them apart.

'Push!' bellowed Garric, and they dug their toes in and re-doubled their efforts. Yet even with four of them against him, the dreadknight forced the doors wider with irresistible strength.

Vika, her mind still scrambled from the overdose, gazed at Ruin in terror. In that moment, she saw beneath that tarnished armour and found only emptiness beyond, a void so vast and profound that she shrank from it.

Osman and Fen let fly with their bows. Osman's arrow caromed off Ruin's armour, but Fen found a gap in the plates at his thigh and her arrow struck flesh. Ruin gave a roar of pain and stumbled back, his grip loosening. The doors began to grind closed, but Ruin gathered himself and seized them again, arresting their progress.

A whisper of premonition warned Vika of danger and she pulled her head aside as an arrow shot past Ruin and sailed over the balcony towards Skavengard. It had been aimed at her. Her blood began to boil with poison and rage, and she felt her fear turn to loathing. She'd run from these creatures long enough. There was something in the dreadknights' very existence that was in opposition to her nature, something that repulsed her. Whatever they were, these agents of the Krodan Empire, their presence could not be borne.

Unnatural. Hateful. Enemy.

Osman dropped his bow, drew his sword and ran to attack Ruin, seeking to drive him back from the doors. His blade was caught by another before it could find its target. Sorrow darted under Ruin's arm, his shortsword thrusting for Osman's belly, but Osman leaped back before it could find its mark.

Like a snake, the dreadknight slipped through onto the balcony, his fangs the points of his blades. Osman retreated hastily before him. Leaving Grub to hold one door, Garric lunged at Sorrow from the side, sword in hand, and then all three of them were thrusting and dodging in a deadly dance of steel with Sorrow at the centre. Yet even two against one, Garric and Osman were overmatched, barely able to keep up with their opponent's speed. It was as much as they could do to defend themselves.

Fen nocked, drew on Ruin and released. Sorrow's shortblade swept out, faster than the eye could follow, and batted the shaft from the air without missing a beat in his battle with Osman and Garric. It was done with such casual ease that it was almost an insult.

Seeing his friend in difficulty, Keel drew his blade and threw himself into the fray with a yell. The three of them together managed to check Sorrow's advance, but that left only Cade and Grub holding the doors, and they were no match for the armoured giant beyond. Steadily the doors were forced back. Once Ruin got through the gap, Plague would follow, and it would all be over then.

As if moved by some will that wasn't her own, Vika stepped forwards and raised her staff. The chaos of the Shadowlands surged and roiled about her, churning beneath the skin of the world, half-visible to her potion-clouded eyes. She felt something well up within her, some blazing force undammed by the fury and terror the dreadknights inspired.

'Back, you demons! In Joha's name, you shall not enter here!'

At that moment, the sun rose above the peaks behind her and cast its light full upon the balcony. Within that light, she fancied she saw a greater light, which blazed out from her staff to dazzle her. It burned in the eyes of the dreadknights and they cringed from it.

'By the Nine, I forbid you!' she shouted, thrusting her staff towards them. Ruin staggered back from the doors, his arms before his visored face, and Sorrow disappeared through the gap, flowing out of sight like quicksilver.

'Now!' yelled Garric, and they put their shoulders to the metal and heaved.

Vika kept her staff held out as the doors screeched together. Light filled her and surrounded her, scorching through her veins, consuming her in agonising ecstasy. Only when the doors to Skavengard finally crashed shut did the light snuff out like a candle, and she collapsed into darkness.

34

The boom of the closing doors echoed around the valley like thunder. Cade kept his weight against the metal, panting, waiting for an impact from the other side. None came. Whatever Vika had done, it had discouraged them for now. Eventually, half-disbelieving, they all stepped away from the doors. Cade caught Keel's eye, and the Bitterbracker grinned.

'Reckon that'll hold 'em,' he said.

Cade slumped against the door and grinned back, warmed by the unexpected camaraderie. Now he was no longer in fear for his life, an immense tiredness stole into his limbs. They'd climbed and run and fought past the limits of their endurance, and there was a toll to pay.

Aren lay unconscious where Grub had dumped him, ropes still tangled round his body. He was frighteningly pale and his breath fluttered past dry, cracked lips. Cade stumbled over and knelt by his side.

'Hoy,' he said quietly. He put his hand on Aren's shoulder and shook him, but there was no response. 'Hoy. We made it.'

'Did you see?' Osman said. He was staring at the druidess, who'd fallen in a heap of stitched hides and straggly black hair, her lightning-glass staff lying beside her. 'Did you see what she did?'

'We saw,' said Garric. He surveyed the balcony, his eyes lingering on the strange castle on the lake. 'We can't stay here in the open.'

Cade lifted his head in despair. The idea of getting up again was almost inconceivable.

'Skarl. Pick up the boy,' said Garric. He looked down at Vika, and when he spoke again, Cade heard new respect in his voice. 'I'll carry the druidess.'

Ruck, who'd been circling her mistress anxiously, growled low in her throat as Garric approached. He stooped and held out a hand to the hound.

'Peace,' he said. 'She will not be harmed.'

Ruck sniffed at him and appeared satisfied with that. Garric picked her up carefully and Osman took her staff.

'On your feet, eh?' Keel said to Cade. His tone was rough but not unkind, and when Cade pulled himself upright, Keel clapped him on the shoulder.

Grub sloped over and hefted Aren onto his back again. 'Come on, Mudslug,' he said with weary cheer. 'Grub think you not dead yet.'

A wide stairway with a crumbling balustrade meandered down the cliffside, broken up by landings cut from the same white stone as the balcony. They followed it to a boathouse of some kind nestled beside the lake, with delicately moulded cornices and a domed roof as smooth and rounded as an egg. Entering through a doorway on the upper floor, they found themselves in a large room, empty and dusted with rubble from cracks in the roof. Arched windows gave a view of the lake.

Garric looked it over critically. 'Fen, Osman, find something to make a fire. Everyone else, get some rest. No one sets foot on Skavengard till we're recovered.'

Cade was pathetically relieved to hear it. Grub put Aren down and Cade wrapped him in blankets, then lay by his side. Briefly, he entertained the thought of trying to stay awake, as if that could prevent Aren from being taken by the illness that wracked him. But his eyes were already drooping, and sleep wouldn't be fought off. The last thing he saw was Aren's face, white as a corpse.

Don't leave me here, Aren. Don't leave me here alone.

When he woke, it was night. A low fire smouldered in the centre of the room with humped bodies lying round it, wrapped in blankets. Ruck was curled up at Vika's feet, her muzzle hidden beneath her tail.

Cade listened to the sound of sleeping sighs, the murmur of

the fire, the lapping of the lake outside. It was quiet here, and the fire was warm, and he felt at peace. Then, with a jolt of alarm, he remembered Aren and lurched upright.

Aren had turned onto his side, facing Cade, his eyes still closed. Cade's panic eased a little as he saw Aren was still breathing. More, his breath was deep and steady, and there was colour in his cheeks again. Cade brushed lank strands of curly hair back from Aren's forehead and checked his temperature. He was no expert, but he felt no fever-heat there.

His face brightened with hope. Had the druidess's brew worked? Was Aren over the worst of it?

He watched his friend for a while, but it soon became clear he'd get no further signs of recovery, and he could do nothing but leave him to sleep. He lay back and worried, staring at the ceiling, but that did no good either. Sleep was beyond him. Though his body was tired, his mind was wide awake and his stomach was growling.

He got up quietly and looked around. Everyone was sound asleep, but Osman's pack lay open by the fire. Digging into it, he found dried meat and hardapple. Mean fare, but he wolfed it down all the same, glancing about to make sure no one was watching. He took some more and stuffed it in his pockets for Aren when he woke, then he took even more, because the lessons learned in the work camp were still fresh in his memory. He wasn't sure if it counted as stealing or not since they'd been sharing their food anyway, but the small rebellion of taking without permission made him feel better.

That's for calling me baggage, he thought at the sleeping bodies surrounding the fire.

Then he remembered that Osman, of all of them, had been the friendliest, and he felt a little guilty. Not guilty enough to put the food back, though.

There was a small stack of broken planks nearby, so he fed a few to the fire to keep Aren warm. That done, he decided to stretch his stiff and aching legs. He left the fire behind and found a narrow stairway that took him to the lower floor of the boathouse.

Downstairs was another room like the one above, with one side open to the lake via a row of pillared arches. Beyond, a small stone wharf pushed out into the dark water, where a few rotten rowing boats bobbed at their moorings, capsized and half-sunken. One had been dragged out and smashed. Cade guessed that was where Fen and Osman had found the fuel for the fire.

There was another boat, too, larger and finer than the rest, braced in a wooden cradle to one side of the room. Cade wandered over and examined it. It looked relatively intact, even after all this time. He could still make out the swirling details of whales and waves along the gunwale and prow. He found himself thinking of the elaru galleon that had foundered off Shoal Point, how its whitewood hull had resisted the ravages of time. Maybe this boat was made of something similar. He ran his hand along it, and it was as smooth and hard as ivory.

A soft noise made him raise his head: the sound of some small movement amplified by the eerie silence of the valley. Warily, he crossed the room to the pillared arches. A low stone wall ran around the edge of the wharf, and sitting on it, one leg dangling, was Fen. She was looking out over the water, where the islands of Skavengard rose silver in the night. The Sisters were caught in a net of stars overhead, on opposite sides of the sky.

Cade studied her profile by their light, her long face and heavy-lidded eyes. She'd thrown back her hood and her red hair was gathered in a loose ponytail that hung over one shoulder. They'd all been running since the moment they met, and Cade had found her chilly and terse until now. But in the moonlight his imagination recast her, making her thoughtful, aloof and mysterious.

As if she could hear his thoughts, she turned her head and saw him, hiding in the shadows of the pillars. He jumped, caught staring, then raised a hand in greeting to cover his embarrassment. She held his gaze for a few moments, then turned away with crushing disinterest.

Crushing disinterest was no deterrent to Cade, however. He was used to it from the girls back home, and Fen wasn't much older than they were. He walked out onto the wharf, climbed atop the wall next to her and let his legs dangle over the water.

'My ma loves the night sky,' he said, gazing upwards. 'We'd go up on the roof of the workshop with mugs of cocoa and she'd tell me how the constellations got their names, and point out the planets. You know the story of Sabastra's Ribbon?'

He pointed one stubby finger at the east end of the valley, where a cloudy swirl of red and yellow hung faint in the dark.

'Well, one day, Sabastra, Aspect of Love and Beauty, was dancing in a forest, and Ogg – he's the Aspect of Beasts and Nature—'

'I know who Ogg is,' said Fen, annoyed.

'So Ogg, he's on a hunt and he comes across Sabastra dancing alone in the night. And Ogg, being a lusty sort, he thinks he's got to have her. So he creeps close and lunges for her!' He lunged to show her and came dangerously close to overbalancing and falling into the lake. 'But Sabastra's too quick. She dances away, and all Ogg gets is a single ribbon torn from her dress. He's so mad, he flings it away, and it floats off into the sky. It's still there now.'

Fen made no reply and showed no further interest in talking. Cade blew his cheeks out and tapped his heels against the wall. She was a tough audience.

'But it wasn't only Ogg chasing Sabastra,' he said, brightening as he remembered another story. 'Joha was, too. That's how the moons came to be. See, Joha is the Heron King, Aspect of Sea and Sky—'

'I *know*.' Cade suspected by her tone that her teeth were gritted. That was alright by him. At least she was paying attention, and Cade had always believed that any attention was better than none at all.

'One day,' he went on, 'a fish told Joha that Sabastra desired his company for the night, and he was to meet her in a secret grotto. Except the fish was no fish at all, but Vaspis the Malcontent, up to his mischief. So Joha went to the grotto, and there he found a potion and a note from Sabastra telling him to drink it and wait for her.

'Eager with lust, Joha did as he was told. But the potion had been put there by Vaspis, and it was a love potion. Whoever drank it would fall for the first person they saw. Then who should turn up, guided there by Vaspis's trickery? Meshuk! Meshuk the Stone Mother, fat old Meshuk, with skin of rock, and lava in her belly, and great big boobs right out to here—'

He was still miming their enormous size when he became aware that Fen was looking at him with the kind of mild disgust gener-ally reserved for garden vermin. He coughed and scratched his jaw.

'Anyway, Joha fell for her on the spot, and they went at it. Meshuk got with child, and when the time came she had two of them. One was pale and fair; the other was like her ma, cold outside and fiery inside, full of rage. Well, Joha, he loved the first but not the second, and Meshuk's a cruel, hard mother who don't care much for her children. Joha tried to convince fair Lyssa to live with him by Joha's River – that's that big, bright smear up there near the Hangman – but Lyssa wouldn't abandon her sister, and she said no. See, nobody could take care of Tantera but her. Nobody else could keep her sister's fury in check.

'Joha was impressed by his daughter's kindness, so he set them both in the sky together, between the stars and the earth. And every night, Lyssa goes chasing after Tantera, who's always trying to slip her sister's watch. On the nights Tantera escapes, when Lyssa's not around, that's when it's a blood moon night. Then Tantera gets up to her mischief, and the spirits come out to play, and it's ill fortune all around.'

'Certainly turned out to be ill fortune for Varla,' said Fen. 'And Tarvi. And Otten and Dox.'

Cade sobered as he remembered Fen's dead companions, and the terror of the dreadknights' first assault. 'Reckon it did at that,' he said. He glanced at her but she didn't seem sad, only indifferent.

'Anyway,' he went on, seeking to lighten the conversation, 'even if Joha only loved one and not the other, the sea knows his daughters. That's why it strains towards the moons whenever they pass over. And ... er ... that's the story of the Sisters,' he finished, somewhat lamely.

There was silence between them for a time, before Fen said, 'Joha's a real bastard sometimes, isn't he? Turning his back on his daughter like that.'

Cade had never really thought about it, but she had a point. 'Reckon you're right. Gods don't make the greatest role models.'

They went quiet again, but Cade fancied the silence was more companionable than before. The lake water sloshed against the wall beneath their feet while he studied the piled walkways and wings of Skavengard, its bridges and spires, the outbuildings that clung like limpets to the vertical rock. After a time, he became uncomfortable and looked away. He had a growing sense that Skavengard was watching him, rather than the other way around.

'Were *you* at Salt Fork?' he asked.

Fen stirred next to him, as if she'd forgotten he was there. 'We all were.'

'What happened?'

Fen considered her answer for a long time. 'We tried to make a difference,' she said. 'We failed.'

Cade frowned. 'Not much of a storyteller, are you?'

'Never had much opportunity to practise.'

'Well, you start by adding in a few details. Was there a battle? Treachery and betrayal? That sort of thing.'

'Fifty of us went to Salt Fork to start something. Eight of us got out. Now there's four. What else is there to say?'

Cade was disappointed. She wasn't a very forthcoming sort. He supposed that was one of the downsides of being mysterious.

'But you *are* with the Greycloaks?'

'There's no such thing as the Greycloaks,' she said, bitterly.

'Course there is! Not everyone's willing to put up with things the way they are. Who's fighting back against the Krodans, if not the Greycloaks?'

'Scattered groups like us. Too small to do much good. Some of them claim they're with the Greycloaks, but they're just using the name. If there was any great resistance movement, we'd know by now. But this secret underground network you've heard of, these freedom fighters battling the Krodans on your behalf? They don't exist. The Greycloaks are a folktale.'

'Can't you all team up or something?'

She gave him a tired look. 'People have tried. Sooner or later, someone sells them out. The Iron Hand had Ossians betraying their own kind right from the start.' Faint anger flickered across her face. 'The more people you trust, the more you're asking to let you down.'

The idea shocked and saddened Cade. 'The squareheads have a saying: "Tie two Ossians to a cart and they'll pull in different directions." Never believed it before now.'

'Time to start,' Fen said.

He examined his reflection in the water. 'Is Garric going to kill us?'

She snorted. 'You think he'd go to all this trouble to rescue you if he was?'

'*Did* you rescue us? Or did you capture us? 'Cause I gotta say, it ain't exactly clear.'

'Well, seeing as you were about to die at the hands of the Krodans, I'd say you were rescued,' she said. 'We came for Aren. Garric wanted to get him out of the camp and take him somewhere safe. Apparently that's the limit of his obligation, though, so the first town we find, you're on your own. Assuming your friend makes it that far.'

'But Garric acts like he hates us! Aren especially.'

'Maybe he does.'

'So why rescue him?'

'I don't know. You'll have to ask Garric.'

Cade made a strangled noise of frustration. 'You came all the way to the middle of nowhere to pull Aren out of a Krodan camp, and you don't know *why?*'

'We regrouped after Salt Fork, made plans for what to do next. Then Garric got some news and the plans changed. He said there was a boy called Aren of Shoal Point in a camp at Suller's Bluff, and we had to make a detour to break him out. We asked why – of course we did.'

'And?'

'He said it was a debt of honour. Wouldn't say who he owed it to. Wouldn't say why. Said he'd do it alone if he had to. I guess Garric's not much of a storyteller, either.'

'A debt to Aren's father?' Cade guessed. 'But Randill said the Hollow M— Garric would kill him!'

'I don't know anything about that. But we all owe Garric enough that there wasn't much question of saying no. Once we were sure Aren was in there, we made a plan to strike from the forest while the guards were marching you up to the mine. They weren't real soldiers; they would've run, first sign of trouble. The prisoners would likely make a break for it, and the Krodans would've been too busy hunting all those runaway Ossians to notice one missing.'

'But we got wind the Hollow Man was looking for us, and we broke out first,' said Cade, as it started to make sense in his head. He harrumphed. 'Reckon we needn't have bothered, since you were going to break us out anyway.'

'No, it was lucky you did,' said Fen. 'We had no idea there were dreadknights around. If you hadn't slipped their notice and got away, they'd have been on us much faster, and it would have been eight of us dead instead of four.' She raised her eyes to his briefly. 'Don't listen to Garric. Wasn't your friend's fault Varla and the others died. If anything, it's down to you that we survived.'

Cade glowed at that. Even if he didn't fully understand the situation, it definitely sounded like a compliment. 'So what's the plan now?'

'What plan?'

'You said you made a new plan after Salt Fork. We were just a detour. Where were you going originally?' He jabbed a finger at her. 'And don't say you don't know.'

'I know,' she said. 'I'm just not going to tell you.'

Cade threw up his hands and swore. 'Why not?'

'If I told you the plan and Garric found out, he might change his mind about leaving you safe in a town, and leave you dead in a ditch instead. What you don't know, you can't tell the Krodans.'

'I'd never tell the Krodans!' Cade protested.

'That's what they all say, until they do.'

'But you *are* on a mission, though?' Cade asked slyly. The thought excited him. 'Something secret? Something important?'

'We were,' she said. 'That was before. Now, I'm not sure.'

Another half-answer. 'I'm sick of being left in the dark,' he complained.

'We're all in the dark,' she said. 'Get used to it.'

Cade tried a new tack. 'Tell me about yourself, then,' he said brightly, and slapped his knees. 'Where are you from?'

'Does it matter?' she asked. Then she swung her leg over the wall and walked away towards the boathouse without so much as a goodbye.

He studied the water, disappointed. He'd been ripped from his home town, worked near to death, rescued by strangers and pursued with inexplicable determination by Krodan dreadknights. All his life he'd been tossed on the tides of fate, letting others make his choices for him. That was the way things were, it had seemed. Foolish for a carpenter's son to expect anything more from life.

But everything was different now. That carpenter's son from Shoal Point had seen things, *survived* things. In breaking out of that prison, he'd climbed walls in his mind that he hadn't known were there. It had always been Aren who called the shots, Aren who looked out for him. Rich, educated Aren, the highborn boy. But it was Aren who needed looking out for now, and there was no one but Cade to do it.

He needed to know what they were mixed up in. And if Fen wouldn't tell him, well, he'd have to find out for himself.

Dawn was just touching the sky when he climbed down off the wall and headed back towards the fire. It was a new day, and with it Cade felt an unfamiliar sense of purpose. The future was full of wild possibilities for the first time in his life. As he climbed the stairs to the chamber where the others slept, he felt happier than he'd been in months.

He entered the room, and his heart froze in his chest.

The others were awake and gathered round Aren's still form, wearing grave expressions. The druidess had her ear pressed to his naked chest, her face-paint smeared with sleep and her eyes closed in concentration, while her hound sniffed at him cautiously.

He let out a cry and ran over to them. 'What's happened?' Suddenly his momentary happiness felt selfish and disloyal. How could he think of the future while his friend was still in mortal danger?

'Easy, lad,' said Osman, reaching out to calm him; but he knocked the hand away angrily.

'Is he alright?' Cade demanded of the druidess. She didn't reply, just stayed there with her eyes closed and her head against Aren's ribs. '*Is he alright?*' he shouted.

She opened her eyes slowly, sat back on her haunches and looked up at him, serene. Then she smiled, and Ruck barked happily. 'The worst has passed,' she said. 'Do not fear for your friend. He will live.'

Relief flooded through Cade, a rush so strong that it made his knees weak. 'You're sure?'

'I am. Another day of rest will see him back on his feet.' She tried to stand, and needed Keel's help to do it.

An unstoppable, silly grin spread across Cade's face. He looked around for someone to share the joy that threatened to burst out of him, found only Osman and hugged him impulsively. Osman chuckled and hugged him back.

'Sorry about the, er, your hand,' said Cade afterwards, miming a swipe.

Osman waved his apology off. 'I'm just glad the lad will make it.'

'Lucky for you that he will,' said Garric, glaring at Cade and Grub.

'Grub was born lucky,' said Grub, which Cade thought unlikely, considering his face.

'My thanks, druidess,' Garric said. 'I owe you a greater debt than you know.'

'If you want to thank me, you can start calling me by my name,' she snapped. Keel handed Vika her staff and she limped tiredly back to her blankets. Cade noticed she was dragging one foot, and one arm hung loosely at her side. 'And get more wood for this fire.'

'Vika, then,' said Garric, with a nod. 'If it's wood you want, I'll fetch it myself.'

'Is she alright? What's up with her leg?' Cade asked Keel.

'Joha only knows,' said Keel, frowning. 'She's been half-lame since she woke up. Doesn't seem much surprised by it, though.' He shrugged. 'She's a druidess,' he said, as if that explained it.

Cade gave up trying to understand and plonked himself down next to Aren, where Ruck had also settled herself, as if watching over him. He scratched her under the chin, his eyes on his friend. Aren's pallor had all but faded, and there was blood in his cheeks again. '*I'll never leave you behind*,' he'd said to Cade once; and he was true to that, as he was true to all his promises. He was going to live. He was going to stay.

'Never doubted you for a minute,' he told Aren.

Ruck barked at him disapprovingly. She knew a lie when she heard one.

35

After the sun was up, the Hollow Man decided to scout the valley. No sense going through Skavengard if they could go around. Grub volunteered to row the boat, which surprised everybody.

'Grub strong!' he said, with a grin that was meant to be ingratiating but ended up horrific. 'Grub make himself useful!'

The Hollow Man gave Grub a look that oozed suspicion and distaste, but Grub kept grinning until he waved his assent. 'Fen, Keel, you come, too. Osman, keep an eye on the boy.'

'You mean Aren?' Moustache said pointedly. 'He has a name.' Grub was pleased with that. Even Hollow Man's own people didn't like the way he treated Mudslug.

'You know who I mean,' replied the Hollow Man dangerously.

Painted Lady was mixing up a paste to smear on Mudslug's chest and back to warm him. She was making a messy job of it – it wasn't easy with one working hand – but she'd refused any help. She reminded Grub of the blood-witches back home, who filed their teeth to sharp points and huddled by the fireside in their furs, casting the bones of babies that had died in the womb. She was strange, and not a little frightening, but even Hollow Man respected her after what she did at the gate.

Mudslug was still asleep, but he was in good hands, and Grub was glad of that. He wouldn't want to see Mudslug die. Not yet, anyway. He might still be useful.

They took the stairs down to the lake. The Bitterbracker examined the boat that rested in the cradle there, and seemed impressed,

265

so they lifted it and carried it to the water, where it bobbed among the remains of other, inferior boats.

'Doesn't even leak, after all this time,' said the Bitterbracker. 'What we'd have given for a craft like this in our seafaring days, eh, Garric?'

Grub made a show of examining it, too, humming and haahing his agreement, but in truth he saw nothing to get excited about. It was just a boat.

Once they were on the water, the eerie quiet closed in. The only sound was the splashing of Grub's oars, the squeak of the rowlocks and the lapping of water against wood.

The lake was a murky green. Great patches of weed floated on the surface and it smelled faintly of rot. The islands of Skavengard reared above them, cliffs of grey stone which were eventually consumed by the lower reaches of the castle. The valley walls to either side were bleak and lifeless, rising to jagged snowy peaks with tatters of cloud clinging to them like wind-blown rags caught on a fence.

'The spine of the Ostenbergs,' said Freckles, looking up at them. 'This valley cuts through the worst of it.'

'Can they cross it?' asked the Hollow Man. 'Will they be waiting for us on the other side?'

'I wouldn't like to guess what a dreadknight can do. But the passes will be snowed under by now, and it will take them several days at least. If the way out of Skavengard is as well hidden as the way in, I don't give much for their chances of finding it. I think they're behind us for now.'

'Mountains in Skara Thun higher than this,' Grub put in. 'Skarls cross them all the time.'

'Is that so?' sneered the Hollow Man. 'Seems every Skarl I ever knew spent half their time boasting about their homeland. Shame so few of you stay there.'

'Skarls free spirits!' Grub said with forced good humour.

'Aye,' said the Hollow Man. 'And I never met one wouldn't stab you in the back, soon as it afforded them advantage.'

'Oh, Grub not that way!' he protested. 'Grub want to *help* excessively angry man.'

The Bitterbracker coughed back a chuckle and the Hollow Man scowled. 'Just row,' he said.

Grub's smile faded as soon as no one was looking, and the loathing in his heart bled out onto his face. Let them treat him like a cur; it was no more than he was used to. The only account of him that mattered was the one made when he died, when the Bone God spread out his skin and read upon it the deeds of his life. Then all these humiliations would be as nothing.

But Grub had half a body to cover before he dared let the Bone God lay eyes on him; and for that, he needed these people, whether they liked him or not.

Half a body, to atone for the other half.

He tipped his head back to look up at Skavengard, its doleful spires reaching towards the sky. He sensed fear and wariness in the others, and that excited him. There were stories within, dangers to face, deeds to be done. That was good. He needed more tales of valour and craft, more victories to bring back to the Sombre Men, so that the skin-scribes might mark them on his body. Breaking out of the camp at Suller's Bluff had been a good start; escaping the dreadknights had been better. But he had a long, long way to go yet.

'There's a wharf,' said Freckles. At the foot of the nearest and smallest island was an inlet where a stone landing had been built, studded with mooring posts. 'A door, too.' She narrowed her eyes and peered closer. 'I think it's ajar.'

'If we put in there we'll have to make our way through the whole length of the castle,' said Garric. 'Keep looking.'

Grub rowed them further out into the lake until the huge central island loomed above them. A thousand dark windows looked down on them from the clutter of buildings and walkways and domes. Strange skeletal structures like scaffolds of bone bulged from its sides. In all the immensity of Skavengard, nothing moved.

There was no further landing spot, and the sheer cliffs made for an impossible climb for anyone but Grub, so he rowed on. No one spoke, as if reluctant to disturb the uncanny peace. Soon the rhythm of the oars lulled him and he began to daydream of better times. The cold, crisp air and snow-capped mountains brought to mind summer in Skara Thun, and those brief, precious months when he hadn't been a cur, when no one had thought him wretched. He had a different name then, and the skalds had sung of his deeds, and all of Skara Thun had lifted their drinking-tusks in his honour. As they toasted him, Grub had allowed himself to believe that no one would ever sneer at him again, or despise him, or kick him like a dog.

In that, he'd been sorely mistaken.

He came from the slums of Karaqqa, somewhere amid the maze of crumbling tunnels and chambers that surrounded the greatest necropolis of the north. There he was conceived in a dirty wrestle in the corner of a crowded sleeping hall, between a man he'd never know and a mother he could scarcely remember. All his recollections of her were yearning and desperate. He was forever pawing at her leg, clamouring for her breast, cowering from her. He couldn't see her face in his mind; she was a shadow to him, ever looming in fury or turning away in disgust.

Sometimes, when he was very young, he'd find her in a stupor, and he'd cry and push at her, afraid she'd never wake. Sometimes he had to pretend to be asleep, shivering in the chill while she grunted and hunched beneath a blanket and a strange man. Other times she disappeared for days on end, and he was forced to forage for food among the sleeping families, or wander the tunnels looking for her.

The last time she disappeared, she never came back. Strangers came instead, and took him away to a grim dwelling in the city. His mother had struck and killed a man while drunk, they told him. She'd been hanged for it.

He was six years old.

Things scarcely improved after that. His mother's tribe saw that he had a place to sleep and enough food to survive, but that was as far as their obligation went. Life in the orphanage was brutal, and neither the master nor the other children had any mercy for the newcomer. There was something in his manner that set people against him, and he suffered for it.

The city was his saviour. Now that he was out of the slums, he had access to the boulevards and tunnels of the necropolis proper. He haunted the undermarkets where the furriers hawked their wares and the air was thick with the smell of fried spiced blubber. He went to the pens, where the hardy nomads of the ice plains traded livestock with the city folk while enormous shaggy varanth shook their great horned heads and snorted steam into the air. He sneaked into the longhalls, where men and women feasted by the firepits, swigging brown ale from drinking-tusks while dogs ran about their feet. He begged food when he could, stole it when he dared, but mostly he just stood about and warmed himself, and listened to the skalds sing tales of heroes. Sometimes those very heroes were present to hear them. They sat at the best tables, their bodies dense with tattoos, and drank together while young Skarls edged close, hoping one day to be as glorious.

When the weather wasn't too cold, he went up to the surface, where the tombs of his ancestors reared high above him, carved from black stone. In the distance, made blurred and dark by frost-haze, a colossal statue of Balik the Sunderer stood astride a splintered peak, holding aloft the god-axe Magoth with which he'd made the mountains and the seas. Grub would walk the snowy streets and read deeds of legend carved on the tombs by the stonesingers, and he'd dream.

In time, he made a friend, a boy who'd noticed him often at the undermarket and who spotted him taking fruit from a stall. That boy brought him back to a chamber where he lived among a dozen other boys, beneath the watchful eye of a crook-backed old man called Nuk. Grub was welcomed and treated as a brother. He never returned to the orphanage after that.

Nuk recognised Grub's talent for theft and nurtured it. He was particularly skilled at climbing, despite his clumsy appearance. No wall or gate seemed beyond him. Though he was still beaten from time to time, as all children were, he was eager to please, and he pleased his new master well.

But theft was a dangerous game in Karaqqa. The narrow tunnels and underground chambers left few places to run and hide, and thieves were especially reviled among Skarls. Ever since Tharl Iqqba united the tribes, it had been all Skarls together against the world, for they were a people small in number and living in a hostile land. Foreigners could be swindled or killed without conscience, but to harm or betray a fellow Skarl, even to lie to them, was a terrible crime, and punishment was swift and pitiless.

One by one, Grub's brothers were caught and hanged. Soon enough, his master Nuk was hanged, too. Grub fled the city, knowing the Grave-guards would be coming for him next. He made his way to the harbour where the grey sea lapped against the shore. It was early autumn, but the waters hadn't yet iced over. With no other choice, he approached a captain and claimed his right of passage as a firstborn embarking on the Scattering. The captain couldn't refuse him.

He sailed away from his homeland that day, a young man with his body hardly marked but for a few identifying details inked on his left cheek in the geometric runes of Tombtongue. He returned fifteen years later with half his body covered. How things were different then. How they celebrated their returning hero. How the women wanted him. He sat at the best tables in the longhalls, and nobody dared to beat him, despise him, dismiss him any more.

For a few months, he was loved. And then it was over.

'Hold here,' said the Hollow Man. Grub stopped rowing and let the boat drift.

'There's our way out,' said the Bitterbracker, pointing. Ahead, a bridge supported by slender white arches reached across the lake high above them. It extended from a towering building on the edge of the third island and ended at a gatehouse in the valley wall.

'Aye,' said Garric. 'But I've yet to see any place to land except that one wharf. Nowhere to climb, either.'

'Maybe on the other side?' the Bitterbracker suggested.

'Maybe,' said the Hollow Man, but he didn't sound hopeful.

While they talked, Grub leaned over the side of the boat and looked into the water. Reflected back at him was a face he'd known all his life: broad, squashed and toadlike, his shaved head turning dark with stubble. But the black band across his eyes hadn't always been there, that swiped crescent running from cheek to cheek, drawn in a burning arc by the palm of a skin-scribe while he screamed and begged for mercy.

The sign of his disgrace. The mark of the outcast, hated by his people, spurned by the Bone God himself.

He looked away, up to the spires of Skavengard. It was a hard journey to forgiveness. He didn't know if it would ever be possible. But he'd started, and there was some victory in that.

'Take us round the island,' the Hollow Man said. Grub laid his hands on the oars and put his back into it.

36

Cade watched from an upper window as the boat returned, studying its occupants closely, as if careful observation might answer the question that now obsessed him.

Who are you people?

His conversation with Fen had changed his rescuers in his eyes. No longer were he and Aren in the company of dangerous rogues who might harm them. They were rebels, and that excited him. Even surly and hateful Garric was somewhat redeemed by it. He was their leader, after all, and one held in great respect, even if Cade couldn't forgive him for the way he treated Aren.

After the others had gone scouting, Cade quizzed Osman, hoping to prise some information from him. But he wasn't as clever with people as Aren, and Osman proved even less forthcoming than Fen, if considerably more polite.

'I'm afraid our business is our own,' he said. 'If you want to know more, it's Garric you should ask.'

Cade snorted. 'He's more likely to give me the back of his fist than an answer.'

'Then I would keep my peace, if I were you.'

He returned to Aren, who lay sleeping next to Ruck. It was cold enough that they needed a fire even in daylight. Vika sat a short distance away, staring into the flames while she reapplied the paint on her face.

'Is he—' Cade began.

'He is well,' she said. 'As he was the last five times you asked. Do not fret, Cade. He will wake when he's ready.'

It was kindly spoken, but Cade felt foolish anyway. The Red-Eyed Child had walked close alongside them these last two nights, but she'd walked closest of all to Aren. He was only just getting used to the thought that she was going to spare him.

'What news?' Osman asked as the scouts made their way back to the fire.

'There's no way around,' said Fen. 'We found a few wharves on the north side, but one's buried under rubble and the other is shut fast. The nearest entrance is open, though.'

'We still have plenty of daylight,' Garric said. 'Eat, all of you. Then we'll go over there and take a look around inside. Vika, will you stay with the boy?'

'I will.'

'Good. Osman, you're coming, too.'

'And me!' said Cade, thrusting a hand in the air. Garric turned a stony glare on him and his arm wilted uncertainly.

'I'll watch out for him,' said Osman. Cade gave his best grin, showing all his teeth, which had the unintended effect of making him seem harmlessly moronic.

'So be it,' said Garric. 'It's your neck. Make ready, then.'

Cade scampered over to Aren. Ruck stirred briefly, opened an eye, then closed it again.

'I'll be back before you know it,' Cade said. Then he leaned closer and dropped his voice so only Aren could hear. 'I'm going to find out who we're dealing with. Leave it to me.'

Ruck twitched an ear and Vika, still applying the finishing touches to her face, smiled to herself.

They sat round the fire to eat. They'd topped up their packs from the wayfarers' hut and taken extra packs for Aren, Cade and Grub, but even so Fen insisted they ration carefully.

'There's nothing to hunt here, not even birds,' she said. 'And we can't resupply till we've crossed the mountains.'

'If my belt gets any tighter, it'll cut me in half,' Keel complained.

'Oh, stop it,' said Osman. 'It's not three days since we were eating rabbit outside Suller's Bluff.'

'Really?' Keel chewed a piece of dried meat thoughtfully. 'Feels longer.'

'One time, Grub walk for three days without food.'

'Didn't you eat a whole wheel of cheese back at the hut?' Fen said acidly.

'Ha! One time Grub ate *five* cheeses! He only stop when cheese ooze from his ears!'

Cade spluttered. 'I thought Skarls weren't allowed to lie?'

Garric gave a derisive laugh. 'Who told you that?'

'Aren did,' he said uncertainly. 'He learned it in school.'

'Always said school was a waste of time,' Keel replied, biting off a piece of bread.

'Skarls aren't allowed to lie *to each other*,' Osman explained. 'It doesn't apply to foreigners. In fact, there's a saying—'

'"When you speak with a Skarl, don't forget your shovel",' Keel quoted happily, still chewing.

'What for?' Cade asked, mystified.

'To clear away the dung that comes out of their mouths!' Keel said, and he and Garric roared with laughter, until Keel began to choke on his bread.

Cade's eyes went wide with understanding. 'You know, that explains a *lot.*'

'Hello! Grub sitting right here!'

It was late morning when they rowed across to Skavengard, leaving Aren, Vika and Ruck behind. The druidess warned them to be back before sunset.

'Polla spoke of a terror that came with the night,' she said.

'Seems empty enough,' said Keel.

'So it does,' Vika replied. 'But I do not trust that place, even in daylight. Keep your wits about you.'

Grub rowed them to the stone landing where Keel moored the boat with a seafarer's knot. There was another boat moored alongside, smaller and lighter. It had capsized but was still afloat and looked intact.

'Polla's?' Fen suggested.

'Maybe,' said Garric.

Before them was a copper door, green with verdigris and stud-ded with black metal nails. It hung invitingly ajar. The stonework round the outside crawled with carved beasts and figures eroded into smooth lumps by the rain. Cade eyed them uncertainly and put his hand on the hilt of the sword he'd borrowed from Aren. He thought about drawing it, but nobody else had drawn theirs, so he left it where it was.

'No sense pulling steel unless you mean to use it,' said Keel, who'd noticed his indecision. 'Swords get damned heavy after a while.'

Cade nodded in a stout fashion, as if from one warrior to another. Keel looked away, suppressing a smile.

'Do not fear,' said Osman. 'I've heard many tales of haunted places, but superstition is all they are. I've still to see anything with my own eyes that I couldn't explain.'

'Aye, well. You're young yet,' said Garric, and pushed the door.

It swung open lightly and without a sound at his touch, as if partly propelled by its own will. Like it was eager to let them inside. Dust stirred in the displaced air, blowing across flagstone floors.

They stepped into a high-ceilinged chamber lit by a narrow window above the entrance that cast a blade of daylight into the room. There was no furniture, no tapestries, nothing but blank walls and emptiness. Silence settled around them like a damp fog, and with it a vague and sourceless unease.

It's just an old, abandoned place, Cade told himself. *Just stone and dust and stories, nothing more.*

But he couldn't quite make himself believe it.

They passed through a small antechamber before coming to the foot of a spiral staircase with light spilling down through its hollow centre. At the top of the stairs, they emerged into a long corridor, ribbed and spined like the fossilised insides of some great serpent. A dozen or more doors could be seen along its length and other corridors led off it, deeper into the island's interior. They listened, and heard nothing but the scrape of their own boots, the chink of buckles and the creak of their leather armour as they shifted about.

'Pair up and take a look around,' said Garric. 'Don't go too far, and be back here by midday. If you find anything odd, call out. Joha knows, we'll have no trouble hearing you.'

'You're with me, Cade,' said Osman. Cade opened his mouth and shut it again, disappointed. He'd hoped Garric would pick him, frightening as that thought was; he wanted to get him alone, to winkle out whatever secrets he had. But Garric and Keel, by unspoken assumption, were going together.

'Grub go with Freckles!' Grub announced happily.

'*What* did you call me?' Fen said, in a tone that could have iced the lake. Keel burst out laughing, but the sound echoed strangely in the silence and he abruptly stopped.

'Should have left him behind when we had the chance,' Fen muttered as she walked away.

'Take care!' Keel called after her; then, under his breath, 'Freckles.'

Fen's anatomically improbable reply was graphic enough to make Cade blush, but it just made Keel grin all the wider.

Grub trotted after Fen, humming discordantly to himself. Garric and Keel went the other way. Osman headed through an open doorway opposite the stairwell, leaving Cade casting regretful glances in Fen's direction. After their encounter on the wharf, he found himself picturing her face whenever his thoughts were idle and had developed a puppyish urge to please her. If he couldn't pair up with Garric, he might at least have gone with her; but he was denied even that. With a sigh, he followed Osman.

The ceiling here was lower than the corridor, held up by a dozen narrow pillars in a double row, each one carved with intricate script. Several large windows looked out onto the valley. At either end, the room was divided by a partition wall and a scalloped doorway. There was no clue as to what the room was used for, but Cade imagined robed figures drifting about it, doing whatever courtly things Old Ossians did.

'You're highborn, aren't you?' he asked Osman.

'I am,' said Osman. 'Whatever that means in this day and age. A highborn Ossian is still lower than the meanest Krodan peasant, when it comes to it.'

'Is that why you joined Garric?'

'I wasn't yet born when the Krodans came,' he said. 'My grandfather was the head of the family and he, like many others, submitted to save his own. But my father was a man of fierce conviction, and he held to the old ways. He never forgave my grandfather, not even on his deathbed.'

As he talked, he headed across the chamber to investigate one of the doorways. He peered inside, then went through.

'When my father inherited our lands, he already had a reputation for criticising the Empire,' Osman went on, studying whatever he saw beyond the partition wall. 'My brothers had taken to Krodan ways and begged him to keep his opinions to himself for the good of us all. But my father was proud. He hated what had become of Ossia, and was full of anger at what we had lost.'

His voice became sorrowful.

'The Iron Hand heard of his sedition and took our lands away. My grandfather had powerful friends, but not even they could save my father from the gallows. My brothers disowned him in exchange for modest lives as clerks and scribes, and we do not speak any more.' He sighed. 'As to me, I left the day my father died. He had friends, too, of a more rebellious mind, and they had connections. I went to them and told them I wanted to join the fight against the Krodans. Once they were convinced, they set me on my path to Garric, and Salt Fork, and so to here.'

As he emerged from the doorway, he was shaking his head, and he gave a little laugh. 'But perhaps that is a longer answer than you hoped for. We all have our stories, I suppose, and—'

He stopped as he realised he was talking to an empty room.

'Cade?'

Cade heard his name being called, but he was already well away, having nipped out into the corridor the moment Osman's back was turned. Now he followed the echo of voices through empty rooms, on the trail of Garric and Keel.

'...place is a maze!' It was Keel, in the room ahead. Cade crept closer. 'You saw it from the lake. Buildings piled on buildings, hanging over cliffs; pillared courtyards open to the drop. It must have been dreamed up by a madman, eh?'

'We'll keep the lake in sight and stay on the south side. Wouldn't take us half a day in a straight line.'

'If we can *find* a straight line,' Keel said. 'Still, if it's all as lonely as this, we'll have nothing to fear but hunger.'

'Let us hope,' said Garric.

Cade peeped round the corner just in time to see Garric and Keel disappear through a doorway on the left side of the room. He looked over his shoulder, but there was no sign of Osman. Encouraged, he slipped across to the doorway, nervous and determined in equal measure. It was important that he brought something back for Aren, some news that would prove his worth: *I did this, without you.*

Garric and Keel stood in the ruins of an enormous indoor garden beneath a great dome as white and smooth as ivory. It was cut with dozens of massive windows, row upon row of them set close in a semicircle. The garden spread over many platforms and tiers, with paths winding among them. Stone channels and miniature aqueducts had once carried water between three elaborate fountains. Statues of beasts both mythical and otherwise waited to surprise the unwary: glaring birds of prey, sinuous draccens, roaring bears.

In days gone by, it must have been green and pleasant here, and exotic flowers had bloomed in the soil. Nothing grew now. The stones were cracked, the statues broken, the dome ruined where pieces between the windows had fallen away. Water still trickled from some unknown source, but the channels had cracked and leaked puddles onto the pathway. In the crisp, bright light of the mountains, it was a pale and mournful place. Cade was both awed by it and saddened.

'Have you ever seen anything like this?' Keel asked, amazed.

'I've seen its like,' said Garric. 'In Carradis.'

'You said you didn't go closer than the outskirts.'

'Nor would you, if you'd seen what I saw. But the outskirts were enough. The old capital ... There are strange forces at work there. Time doesn't flow as it should. A man can't trust his own mind. But I saw Old Ossian buildings, and gardens even finer than these.'

Keel tilted his head back, his eyes roaming the windows. 'All they had, all they made ... How did it end in barbarity and chaos?'

'Empires fall,' said Garric. 'The urds had their turn, and so did we. The Krodans style themselves as the Third Empire, but their time will come, just as it did for all the others.'

'Shades, don't you think of anything else?'

'Not since I lost my country.'

They wandered further into the gardens, searching for an exit. Cade stayed where he was, pressed against the stone jamb. It was easy to hear their conversation in the quiet open space.

'You need to go easy on Aren,' Keel said. 'Osman doesn't like it. Fen either. They don't understand.'

'They don't need to.'

'They do, Garric. You asked them to help you save him, and they did, and it cost us Otten and Dox and Tarvi and Varla. It's sore hard on 'em to see how you hate that boy when their friends gave their lives to rescue him.'

Cade waited for Garric's reply, heart bumping with the thrill of eavesdropping.

'When I look at that boy, I see his father's face,' he said at length, and the words were so bitter he spat them. 'And all I can think of is how I missed my chance to put a blade in that bastard's heart.'

Cade went cold. *If you ever see the Hollow Man, you run. You run and you don't stop. For he's come to kill you.*

'Then tell them, eh?' said Keel. 'Tell them why you risked their lives to save the son of a man you hate.'

'And then what? I tell them that, I'll have to tell them all of it. And I won't do that. My shame is mine to keep.'

'Strikes me you've been letting shame set your path long enough.'

Garric rounded on him, eyes blazing, fists clenched. 'Be damned,' he snarled. 'You've no right to say that to me.'

The Bitterbracker was uncowed. 'Who does, if not me? You need to hear it from someone.'

'If you want to go home to your family, just say so,' Garric snapped.

'I don't,' said Keel. 'I mean to say, I *do*, but—'

'Aye, you never could quite decide, could you?' Garric said spitefully.

Cade saw the Bitterbracker control himself with some effort. He

279

put up his hands as if to simmer Garric down, but it was himself he was calming. 'All I'm saying is, there's only four of us left, and we need every one. Even then it won't be enough. We need to join up with another rebel group, bring them in on the plan. If anyone can convince them, it's you.'

'There's no *time!*' Garric snarled in exasperation. 'Everything is in motion. You think the royal wedding will wait for us? Ottico will marry in a matter of weeks! We have to be at Hammerholt by then.'

Cade listened in bewilderment. The wedding? Hammerholt? What did that have to do with anything?

'Can't be done, Garric,' said Keel. 'Not with who we've got left.'

'It *can*,' Garric said through gritted teeth. 'This is our only chance, our *last* chance! You want another Salt Fork? And another after that? You saw how fast those spineless bastards turned on us. We'll never be free if our own people won't stand up to the Krodans. They don't believe, Keel. But we'll *make* them believe!'

'Godspit, Garric! You're talking about breaking into the most impenetrable fortress in Ossia and snatching the Ember Blade from under the nose of the crown prince!'

'It *can* be done,' said Garric, with steel in his voice. 'It *will* be.' He stalked away, leaving Keel cursing behind him.

Cade pulled back from the doorway, his mind reeling. The Ember Blade? They were planning to steal the *Ember Blade*?

He remembered how Shoal Point had been abuzz with talk of the marriage of Prince Ottico to Princess Sorrel of Harrow, just before he and Aren had been arrested. As part of the celebrations, Prince Ottico would become Lord Protector of Ossia and receive the Ember Blade as a symbol of his right to rule. Da had raged at the mere thought of a Krodan holding the Ember Blade until Ma told him to still his flapping lips before the Iron Hand heard.

But Garric wanted to take it back. Take it back for the Ossians. A disbelieving smile spread across Cade's face. Wouldn't stealing it be a poke in the eye for the Krodans! Wouldn't that show everyone the Ossians still had some fight in them!

Garric and Keel had gone by now, but Cade didn't follow. He'd pushed his luck enough for one day. If they caught him, they might wonder what he'd heard, and now he understood Fen's warning. Garric might take drastic action if he thought they knew too much.

He was practically hopping with excitement as he retraced his steps. With luck, Osman would just think he'd wandered off, too curious for his own good. But what a story he'd have to tell Aren when he awoke!

He slowed and came to a stop, a frown settling on his brow. This chamber didn't look familiar. He went back a room and picked another direction, but he didn't recognise that room, either. Concern became alarm as he tried room after room and recognised none of them.

He hadn't strayed far from the corridor in his pursuit of Garric and Keel, and the route had been straightforward enough. He should have been able to find his way back with ease. Yet, somehow, Cade had become completely and hopelessly lost.

37

Nine, what have you got yourself into now?

Cade peered down another corridor, as grand as the last and just as deserted. He thought he'd been here before but couldn't be sure. He took it anyway. It felt like the right direction to get him back to the boat, and he judged it better to go forward than to endlessly retrace his steps.

As he went, he looked this way and that, searching for anything he recognised. It was no good. He might have walked this corridor twice already and he wouldn't know it. There was something about these chill stone walls and alien curves that foiled the mind's grip. Remembering a route in Skavengard was like climbing ice.

He stopped at a junction, drumming his fingers against his thigh in agitation. He remembered that room, didn't he? That frieze of symbols which ran around the walls? Maybe. Or perhaps it was another frieze in another room.

His stomach rumbled. How long had he been walking now? He had a vision of wandering till he starved to death, to be found as a skeleton by the next group of travellers to brave this place. They'd imagine he met some heroic end, never suspecting he'd died of plain stupidity.

Can't you do anything right?

It was his da's voice, that tone of angry exasperation he used when Cade's ineptitude in the workshop became too much. Today, he deserved it. He was furious with himself for getting lost. And if he didn't find his way out before sunset, starving might be the least of his concerns.

'Polla spoke of a terror that came with the night,' Vika had said. Whether rumour or fact, he didn't much want to find out.

He decided to find an outside window. If he kept the lake to his left then he'd reach the boat eventually. It was just so hard to find a straight way through. Every time he made progress, he was turned aside, led up this stair or down that passage until he found himself travelling in a completely different direction.

I should start shouting, he thought. *That's what Garric said to do. The whole valley would hear me if I just shouted.*

But he refused to spoil his achievement by calling for help. He was proud of himself for discovering what their rescuers were really up to. Usually Aren thought up the plans, but this time it was Cade's plan, Cade's triumph, and he'd spin a great story from it one day. Unless, of course, it ended with him bleating like a lamb for rescue, because he was too mud-headed to find his way back to the others.

Besides, there was something in the silence that discouraged loud noises, something that made him want to remain unnoticed. And he wasn't looking forward to facing Garric if he learned Cade had gone missing.

It couldn't be midday yet. He still had time to get back and give some excuse to Osman.

He made his way through several chambers into a room that had been designed like a rock garden, where dripping, rusted spouts hung over upright stone tubs half-full of green water. This had been a place for bathing once. Now it was just a dead end.

He went to the windows, which looked over the valley. At least he could see the lake from here. He put his hands on a sill and leaned out, the cold breeze blowing against his face. Skavengard stretched dizzyingly away above and below, bulging with turrets and overhanging balconies, tumbling down the cliffs to the water. He was higher up and further from the wharf than he'd thought. If he craned his head, he could see the edge of Skavengard's main island to his left, hulking into the sky.

Then he noticed the shadows in the folds of the castle, longer and deeper than they should be. With a thrill of alarm, he saw that it was past midday already, *long* past midday. The sun was dipping in the west. Somehow, time had run away from him. He could have sworn he'd been wandering for less than an hour, yet evening was creeping up fast. Suddenly the distant threat of sunset felt very close indeed.

Call for help. They'll come. Call before it's too late.

No. He was still determined to do this one thing on his own. He wanted to enjoy Aren's amazement at the news that they were not among villains but revolutionaries, and Garric planned to steal the Ember Blade itself! Maybe, if he and Aren played their cards right, he'd even let them join him.

Spurred by that thought, he headed back to the corridor. He had his bearings now. This time he wouldn't go astray. *This* time, he was on the right track.

His optimism was misplaced. Before long, he was forced out of sight of the water, and the only light came from cleverly angled shafts and windows too high to see through. He managed to descend a few levels, which was good, but worry still gnawed at him. Was the light dimming already, or was it just his imagination? He found himself wishing for the sight of another living thing, even a spider or a mouse, but there was nothing: not a web nor a dropping, no bones or nests, no indication that anything had ever been here except the building itself. This place wasn't just dead, for death was rancid and messy. It was the eradication of life.

And then, in the midst of that colossal, echoing emptiness, he heard a woman's laughter.

The sound brought him to a dead stop. It had been brief, and faint enough that he suspected his mind was playing tricks on him. A high, delicate sound, there and then gone. Which way had it come from? He looked through a doorway. Down there, he thought, if he'd heard it at all.

A murmur of conversation blew past him, carried on a breeze from outside. Muttered speech, like two people talking on the edge of a busy room. Common sense urged caution, but anything was better than wandering this forlorn, deserted place alone. Ignoring the voices didn't seem like an option.

He hurried through pillared chambers, down narrow passage-ways in the walls that must have been used by servants. He caught a whiff of perfume, a heady contrast to the faint scent of decay that rose from the lake and hung stagnant in Skavengard's halls. Ahead of him there was a hubbub, the clink of goblets, laughter and talk. There was even music, though it was unlike anything he'd heard before. A stringed instrument plucked tinny notes, accompanied by a strange atonal jangling and tinkling bells.

It's a party, he thought, perplexed. But not like any party he'd ever been to. His imagination filled in the scene. He pictured a glittering ballroom, highborns drifting here and there in bizarre finery, sipping exquisite wines and plotting one another's downfall beneath a bladed veil of politeness.

The servants' passage dead-ended at a small door of beaten metal. Cade pressed his ear to it. The party was on the other side. A woman laughed suddenly, so close to the door that he jerked back.

He hovered uncertainly in the gloomy confines of the passage. Should he make himself known? They didn't sound threatening, but it was hard to tell.

At last he could stand it no longer. Cade had always preferred action over excessive thought, so he cracked open the door.

There was nobody beyond.

Puzzled, he pushed the door open all the way and stepped into the hall. It was as empty as the rest of the castle. Crumbling galleries ran around the room and sunlight slanted in from a row of windows high on one wall, shining in his eyes. Dusty mosaics sprawled across a cracked stone floor. There wasn't a soul to be seen.

But he could still hear them.

The sounds were all around him now. Laughter, conversation, music. They spoke in a lilting tongue like running water, frightening and wonderful. The language of Old Ossia; it had to be. He closed his eyes, and it was like he was among them. Voices become louder and faded as their owners walked past him. He could smell them, their perfumes and oils, and hear the crinkle of their fabrics, the soft step of their shoes. He felt a touch on the back of his hand, a trailing finger brushing past, and his eyes jerked open again.

They're still here, he thought. *This place remembers them.*

Movement caught his eye and he looked over his shoulder. With a chill of wonder, he saw the occupants of the room at last.

They were cast against the wall by the light from the windows, shadows on stone. There were dozens of them, some with fantastical hairstyles or towering headdresses, others wearing large rigid hoods and robes with wide shoulders. Some drank from slender glasses and gossiped, while others moved to the music in a slow formal dance, appearing and disappearing as they stepped in and out of the sunlit patches on the wall. The musicians themselves could be partially seen in the corner, a black tangle of limbs and long-necked instruments.

Cade stared. He'd never believed in ghosts, even when he was young. They were just stories, like all the others his ma told. He was a boy who only dealt with what was in front of him, like a chisel that wouldn't do what he wanted, or his father's glowering disappointment. Ghosts were too fanciful to be part of that life.

As he watched the shadow-party in awe, his own shadow standing among them, he knew he'd crossed some threshold, stepped all the way into one of Ma's tales. His life as a carpenter's boy was behind him. No longer was he a prisoner, condemned to drudgery and toil. At last he was out in the world, and it was stranger and scarier and more exciting than he'd dared to dream.

Were they really there, he wondered, or was this just a scene from the past, played out a thousand years ago? Before he'd really considered the wisdom of it, he opened his mouth and said:

'Hello?'

The music clattered into silence. All conversation ceased instantly. His greeting echoed around the hall, throbbed away down the empty corridors beyond.

Then, slowly, every shadow turned its head towards him.

'Er,' said Cade. He had the creeping suspicion that he'd just made a terrible mistake.

And now the voices began again, this time a sinister susurrus, a vicious, hungry whispering like the sea rushing in over a pebble beach. Though he couldn't understand the words, Cade knew they were talking about him. His skin crawled and he took a nervous step back. The air in the room, already cold, became sharp enough for frost.

The ghosts glided aside, leaving Cade's shadow standing alone where it was thrown against the wall. From the far side of the room, a new silhouette entered the hall, this one taller and somehow darker than the others. Cade felt his knees go weak as it moved from the light of one window to another, growing taller as it came towards him: a slender robed figure, as elongated as a shadow at sunset, wearing a twisted crown with seven prongs. Dread emanated from it in freezing waves, making Cade's mouth dry up and his breath grow short. He wanted to run, but he was rooted to the spot.

Azh Mat Jaal, he thought. *The Sorcerer King.*

The figure, so tall now that it had to stoop, reached out towards Cade's shadow. Sharp-nailed fingers slid from voluminous sleeves, stretching across the wall, lengthening impossibly until they were almost touching his silhouette ... almost ...

A hard, hooked nail scraped Cade's shoulder, dragging at the fabric of his coat.

The touch broke his paralysis, and he screamed and bolted. He flew out of the hall, arms flailing, moving almost too fast for his feet to keep up. Stumbling and skidding, he ran headlong through the corridors and chambers of Skavengard. As he fled, he glimpsed the crowned figure again and again. There, rising in a patch of sunlight on the wall! There, sliding out of a dark corner, those terrible hands always reaching for his shadow!

He sprinted round a corner, crashed into someone and was roughly seized. Screaming and thrashing, he kicked out, and there was a grunt as his boot connected with a shin. He was grabbed and thrown violently away. His face struck a doorframe and he went down, boneless and stunned, all the panic knocked out of him.

'Cade! Cade, it's us!'

It was Osman, crouching next to him. Keel hopped on one foot nearby, cursing elaborately. Garric pushed Osman aside and hauled Cade up by the front of his coat. It was he who had pulled

Cade off Keel and thrown him against the door; Osman would have been gentler.

'You damned little fool!' he growled, his jaw clenched. 'Do you know how long we've been looking for you?'

'And we've found him!' Osman interposed himself quickly, for Garric looked angry enough to strike him. 'Let's be thankful for that, eh?'

'Aye,' said Garric sarcastically. 'Whatever would we do if he'd been lost?' He let Cade go, turned away and spat on the ground. 'Children!'

Cade looked frantically around the room, and only began to relax when he was sure there were no shadows but their own. 'I saw him,' he gasped. 'Azh Mat Jaal! I saw him!'

'This place is deserted, friend. It was your own fears you saw,' said Osman in calming tones. 'That, and nothing more.'

'Get him moving, Osman,' Garric snapped. 'He was supposed to be your charge. Perhaps you'll do a better job shepherding him this time. Damned if I'll go chasing after some idiot boy again.'

Cade was shamefaced. Far from returning as a hero, he'd only embarrassed himself. Fen looked at him with disdain, Osman with disappointment; even Grub was amused at his expense. But he'd take all of that happily, just to be back in their company. He never again wanted to be alone in this place.

Cade felt a bruise already forming on his cheek where he'd hit the doorframe. 'I *did* see him,' he muttered sulkily to Garric's back.

'Now who the big liar?' Grub said, and walked away cackling.

38

The first things Aren became aware of were the crackle of the fire, the heat on his face and a deep ache in his bones. His mouth was dry, his thoughts fuzzy and his eyelids too heavy to open. He rolled onto his side and let out a groan.

Something hot and wet slithered across his cheek and the smell of rank, meaty breath filled his nostrils. He startled awake, eyes flying open. Inches from his face was a black wet nose and the shaggy grey muzzle of a dog. She licked him again, right on the lips this time, and he pushed her away with a cry of disgust.

'Peace,' said a low, weary voice to his right. 'Ruck will not hurt you.'

A woman sat there, buried beneath a cloak of stitched furs, her face swiped with black and white paints. She was dipping a bowl into a pot that rested on a tripod over the fire.

'Welcome back, Aren.'

Aren looked about dazedly. He didn't recognise his surroundings at all. It was evening, and he was in a wide, empty room, packs and blankets scattered everywhere. The air was chilly and sharp and carried a faint scent of rot. Beyond the arched windows, the lower reaches of a strange island castle could be seen. He stared at its jumble of walls and angles and fought to remember how he'd come to be here.

'Who are you?' he asked, raising himself up on his elbows. The effort dizzied him and he swallowed down the urge to be sick. 'Where's Cade?'

'I am Vika. Ruck, you have already met.' Ruck barked happily

289

at her name, sending another wave of reeking breath into Aren's face. Vika pointed to the castle. 'Your friend is yonder, and will be back before long, I hope.' He heard concern in her voice. 'It is getting late.'

'He left me?' Aren was surprised to find he was hurt by that.

'He left you in my care, which is the best place you can be,' said Vika. Despite her odd appearance, she wore a smile and her eyes were kind. 'Had you been in any danger he wouldn't have done so. As it was, I believe he had some pressing purpose. No doubt he will tell you himself when he returns.'

Aren was a little reassured by that, but he still felt an uneasy sense of abandonment, left helpless and vulnerable in the company of a stranger. Ruck lurched forward and slurped his cheek again, and he fought her off.

'Ruck!' At her name, the hound retreated and sat on her haunches, panting. 'She likes you,' Vika informed him. 'You should be pleased. Ruck has good instincts.'

Aren wiped his face with his sleeve. 'You're a druidess.' It was a statement, not a question; he'd heard enough about them to recognise her attire.

'I am. Vika-Walks-The-Barrows.'

'That's a strange name.'

She blew on the soup. 'It is my taken name. Once I was Vika of Tanner's Fell, but no longer. When we become acolytes, we give up the names that connected us to our birthplaces, for we belong to all of Ossia. We seek our new names in visions. It is one of the first steps to becoming a druid.'

Aren winced as his head began to pound. 'And what was your vision?'

'I saw myself striding over grassy hillocks under a blood moon. Beneath my feet were the graves of kings and queens of old, and I felt them stir and mutter in their eternal sleep as I passed over them. At length, I came to a portal: an open doorway to an empty burial chamber, a barrow that was as yet unoccupied. From within, I heard a terrible voice, as of something ancient and foul. *Bring me another*, it said. I did not want to do what it said, but I knew, in the end, I would have no choice.' Her gaze, which had become distant, sharpened again as she reached the end of her tale. 'That is how I took my name.'

Aren was about to ask what it meant, but a sudden memory jerked him upright. 'The dreadknights!'

'They are kept out by whatever lost sorcery guards the gates. We are safe, for the moment. Now you should eat.' She began to get to her feet, to carry him the bowl of soup, but she stopped halfway with a hiss of pain. Aren watched as the spasm passed, and she drew herself upright and limped over to him, balancing the bowl carefully.

Aren took it and thanked her. It had only spilled a little. 'Are you hurt?' he asked.

She lowered herself down next to him with a rueful smile. 'Merely reckless. But pain is good. I have hardly been able to feel my left arm and leg since I awoke, but I certainly feel them now.' She lifted her hand and tried to flex her fingers. The tips twitched feebly. 'It seems I will recover.'

She gave him a quick smile, but Aren saw the flash of fear beneath. *Unless you won't*, he thought.

'Will you tell me what happened?' he asked.

'Eat your soup.'

Aren looked about himself. 'I don't have a—'

'Spoon, yes, a spoon!' said Vika. 'My apologies. I am still not … quite right. Ruck?'

Ruck scampered over to her blankets, picked up a wooden spoon in her mouth and presented it eagerly to Aren. Aren hesitated for a moment, then decided this wasn't the time for squeamishness – or, evidently, hygiene – and took it.

The soup was herby and rich, floating with bits of dried meat and shredded leaves. After the first spoonful, his hunger overcame his distaste for dog slobber and he dived in. His headache began to fade, and as he ate, Vika recounted their flight to Skavengard and the battle at the gates.

'You fought them? How did you beat them?'

An odd look passed over Vika's face, an expression of almost childlike wonder. 'I don't know,' she said. 'I knew only that suddenly, I had to oppose them. As if I was a vessel for some other will. There was light ... at least, I *think* there was light ...' She trailed away. 'I have met the Aspects five times, but never since I was seventeen. For the first time in many years ... it felt like ...'

She ran out of words; her voice faded to a whisper and then silence. Aren wasn't sure if it was passion or madness he saw in her eyes.

'I ...' he began, stopped, and then made himself go on. 'I don't know your gods. I was raised by the light of the Primus. But of late, I've wondered if he casts his light for Krodans alone.'

It felt somehow dangerous to say it. He'd been taught that it was arrogant to question the teachings of Tomas and Toven and, in some unspecified way, he'd believed he or those close to him would suffer if he dared. But he'd defied the Primus in the mine at Suller's Bluff and he was still here. So maybe that threat had been a lie, like so much else.

'The Aspects are your gods, too,' said Vika, 'whether you worship them or not. The Aspects are Ossia. It was in Ossia that they first made themselves known. It was the Ossians they first freed from slavery and from here they raised the greatest empire in the world. They are all around you, in the very bones of the land. You belong to them, as they do to you.'

Aren found that unsatisfyingly vague. 'I suppose ... I don't mean to insult you, but they always seemed so ... *primitive*.'

Vika smiled. 'I would say *old*. The Krodans fashioned a new god to suit them, a cold god of industry and rules, who demands you show yourself at temple on a certain day and mouth the same words over and over. But the Aspects are wild. They may heed your prayers, but they do not need your worship. Nor do they need ranks of priests and clerics to tally donations and preach to the people.' She became grim then. 'Perhaps that is why they are so easily forgotten. The Primus, at least, will not suffer himself to be ignored.'

Aren didn't want to be drawn on the subject, but he felt compelled to argue. 'Aren't druids priests of a sort?'

'Not in the Krodan way. We do not instruct or threaten. We are caretakers of the land. In freer times we would visit temples when we passed, and people would gather to hear such wisdom as we had gained on our wanderings. Bards listened to what we had learned and took our tales with them. We would heal and advise as we could. Once, kings and queens and Dawnwardens consulted with the best of us.' Her face darkened a little. 'But we have been aloof too long, I think, and ten years have passed since the last Conclave. I fear there are few of us left.'

Aren nodded to be polite, but the conversation was making him feel awkward. His belief in the Primus had been a house built of straw which had fallen at the first push. But the Aspects didn't inspire him, either, and the stories of the Ossian gods sounded no different to the fables of dancing fish or shapechanging maidens that Cade was so good at telling. Vika fascinated him, for he'd never met a druidess before, but she spoke with too much certainty; he found it overbearing.

Fortunately, Vika changed the subject. 'What is that mark on your wrist?'

Aren turned the spoon in his hand and looked, and a frown of puzzlement and alarm creased his brow. The bloody thumbprint left by Eifann had mostly flaked away during his convalescence, but there was something visible beneath. He rubbed the last of the crusted blood off to reveal a tiny red symbol hidden on the inside of his wrist. It had straight lines and regular curves, neat as a scribe's hand. He stared, amazed and not a little worried.

'A Sard put it there ...' he said, weakly. 'But ... I'm not sure *how ...*'

'*Ydraal! Eifann is ydraal!*' A memory of the ragged boy sprang to mind, biting his thumb and pressing it fiercely to Aren's wrist. '*Lled na saan.*'

'I made three promises in that camp,' said Aren. 'One to Cade; one to a pirate; and one to that Sard boy. I have to help another of his kind, to repay my debt to him. But who or how, he didn't say. It's some custom of their people, I think.'

Vika studied the mark dubiously, then took the empty bowl from him with her good hand. He was beginning to feel invigorated, as if raw, glowing health was flowing into his muscles from his stomach. 'What was in that?' he asked.

'A few herbs, a few prayers,' she said. Then, with a twinkle of mischief in her eye, 'A touch of the Aspects' favour, perhaps.'

'Who'd have thought the gods' favour would taste so much like soup?'

'Ha! Let that settle, and then you can have more. You'll be up and about soon enough. In the meantime I would hear your story, if you'll tell me.'

Aren was feeling considerably better already, and he found he wanted to talk. He'd hardly had a real conversation with anyone but Cade for months, having kept his distance from his fellow prisoners because he believed he and Cade were the only ones wrongfully incarcerated. He was ashamed of how naïve he'd been.

Vika listened as he began to tell his tale. He spoke of Sora and the ghost tide and how he'd ignored her brothers' warning to stay away; of his father and his talk of the Hollow Man; of that day when Randill had been arrested by Overwatchman Klyssen of the Iron Hand, and died on the blade of a man named Harte.

There he faltered, and his throat became thick and his eyes stung. Vika said nothing, merely waited until he had himself under control again; but Ruck laid her head in his lap, and he put his hand on her head.

'I don't know why my father was killed,' he said finally. 'Was he a rebel? A collaborator? Or did he die because I was a stupid boy in love with the wrong girl?' Aren felt tears rising again and gave up trying to hold them back. 'He was afraid of Garric, deadly afraid, but that man came to Suller's Bluff to rescue me. And Klyssen was there at the camp, I saw him, and he must have sent those dreadknights after us when we escaped. It all has something to do with me but I don't know what, I don't know *what*! I don't know if my father was a hero or a coward and now I'll never be able to ask him … I'll never …'

The reality of his father's absence crushed him like an avalanche and he wept uncontrollably, his nose streaming and his shoulders shaking, gasping and snorting, a torrent of ugly, unrestrained grief.

'You poor child,' said Vika, and put her arms around him. He buried his head in her breast, in the furs and the softness there, the smell of old sweat and dog and earth. He clung to her as he cried for the father he'd lost and the mother he never got to hold like this, and for the rage and injustice of a lifetime deceived.

Everything that he'd held back in the camp, dammed up by the need to be strong for Cade, burst out of him in one scalding flood. He cried and cried until it felt like he'd never stop.

But stop he did, in the end, when he could dredge up no more sorrow. Vika kissed the top of his head, then stood and limped away to fetch wood, leaving Aren staring into the flames, drying his sore eyes. He felt washed out and empty, and for a time he just sat there, his gaze vacant. At last he sniffed, straightened and wiped his nose with the back of his hand.

'Enough,' he said quietly.

When Vika returned, she found him stone-faced and thoughtful. She sat on her blanket and looked towards Skavengard, scratching Ruck's scalp. Presently they heard the creak of oars as the others returned from the lake. Running footsteps clattered up the stairs, and then:

'*Aren!*'

Cade raced across the room, dropped to his knees and hugged him so hard it drove the breath from his lungs.

'You're back! You're back!' Cade cried.

'Steady, you ox!' Aren laughed. 'I'm still brittle.'

'Nine, you gave me such a scare! I reckoned you gone back there, I really did. I really ...' His eyes glistened with tears. 'I reckoned you gone.'

'Cade?'

'Aye?'

'I just need to know one thing.'

'Aye?'

Aren grinned. 'When did you become such a blubbering sap?'

Cade gaped, then burst out laughing as he recognised Aren's revenge for his trick in the infirmary. He aimed a mock-serious blow at Aren's head, but Aren threw up his hands and cried, 'You can't hit me! I'm sick!' Then he saw the bruise on the side of Cade's face and all the laughter drained out of him. 'Who did that?'

'I did,' said Garric as he walked into the room, followed by the others. He glared at Cade. 'And if I ever have to go looking for you again, I'll do worse.'

'Wasn't nothing, really,' Cade said to Aren, with a sheepish shrug. 'My own fault. Hit my head on the doorway.'

But Aren wasn't listening. He was staring over Cade's shoulder at Garric, a knotted ball of anger gathering in his gut. Cade's attempts to dismiss it cut no ice with him; Aren knew the truth. It was Garric who'd hurt him. He'd admitted it. Was *proud* of it. Not content with heaping accusations and derision on Aren, now he'd brutalised his best friend, and he'd done it while Aren wasn't there to protect him. If Aren could, he'd have killed him right then.

Coward. Bully. Bastard.

His gaze was too obvious a challenge to ignore. 'Something to say to me, boy?' Garric snapped.

'Garric ...' Keel warned, but Garric ignored him.

'Well? Speak up!'

Blood rushed to Aren's face and his heart hammered. He couldn't fight this man, but nor would he look away. Let him know how much he was hated. Let him feel it.

But he didn't dare say it. Not yet.

He heard movement behind him. It was Ruck, who padded round to stand by his side. She squared herself, bared her teeth and growled at Garric.

'It is brave work, to menace a sick boy,' said Vika, her voice low and stern. 'But he is under my care, and if you touch him you will answer to me.'

Garric held his gaze a moment more and Aren saw fury burning there. Then he looked away with a grimace.

'The whelp's not worth the beating,' he said. 'And that ruin is dead as the men that built it. Take what rest you can. Sick or not, at first light we go to Skavengard. And this time we're not coming back.'

He walked from the room, past Fen and Osman, who stood aside and watched him pass with uncertainty plain on their faces. Keel shook his head and raised his eyes to the ceiling.

'Are you cracked?' Cade said to Aren, once he'd gone. 'Picking a fight in your condition? He's half your size again!'

Yes, he is, Aren thought in bitter triumph. *But still he looked away first.*

39

The next day, they were up with the dawn and ferried across the lake to Skavengard. It took them two journeys, for the boat was not large. Aren and Cade were in the second boat, with Grub rowing and Osman there to keep an eye on all three.

Cade looked back at the boathouse as they left, trepidation on his face. Aren knew his mind. It had been a bleak sanctuary, but he feared to leave it after what he'd seen in Skavengard. Aren suspected the shadow people had been his imagination playing tricks on him – it was not so long ago that he'd turned a glimpse of a wild pig into a giant she-warg – but Cade clearly believed in them.

Aren sat wrapped in a blanket as they glided across the weedy lake. Though weak, he was capable of travelling again; Vika's brews had restored him with miraculous speed. His nose ran uncontrollably and he had a persistent cough, but he felt much better, though he was still dogged by a vague sense of shame. He'd been a burden these past days, and he'd let Cade down by not being there to protect him. The bruise on his friend's face was a reminder of that. He'd faltered once; he wouldn't falter again.

They reached the wharf where the others waited and made their way through the chilly, quiet chambers of Skavengard, grey in the flat light of early morning. This time, they all travelled together, and Aren was glad of it. He understood now why Cade had been spooked. There was an eerie feel to the silence, as if the castle itself was holding its breath.

Soon Cade began to talk, rabbiting on about nothing in

particular to hide his nerves. While he spoke, his gaze flitted about, watching for shadows. At first, nobody wanted to engage him, as if loth to disturb the silence further; but he carried on regardless, and soon they relaxed. When Cade started doing caricatures of the people of Shoal Point, some of them even began to chuckle. He mimicked grouchy old Nab, the innkeeper of the Cross Keys; fat Rollo, the baker's lad, who believed himself a stud bull but was more of a prize hog; crazy Mairie and her obsession with whelks. Aren began to feel homesick listening to it.

Before long, Cade was cracking jokes, with himself as the butt more often than not. As they laughed, any ill feeling for the trouble he'd caused yesterday was forgotten; by all but Garric, anyway, who remained grim.

Aren knew what Cade was up to. He always had the enviable skill of making people like him; everyone loved a clown. Now he was ingratiating himself with the group, and Aren wasn't sure he liked that. Cade told him last night how he'd overheard Garric and Keel talking about the Ember Blade, and he'd been shiny-eyed with admiration as he did so, caught up in the romance of their quest. He clearly wanted to join them, though he'd stopped short of saying it outright. It was as if he'd forgotten the bruise on his cheek, or the plain and obvious hate that Garric bore for Aren.

Aren didn't know why Garric had an obligation to see him safe. But he was his father's enemy and plainly no friend to Aren. If Cade thought they were staying with these people a minute longer than they had to, he was mistaken. He was sure Garric felt the same.

Don't get close to them, Cade, he thought. *It'll only hurt the worse when we leave them behind.*

'So how'd you escape the camp, Cade?' asked Keel.

'Mostly it was Grub's doing,' Grub said modestly.

Cade gave him a sidelong look. 'Well, before I tell you how we escaped, you'd better understand what we were escaping *from*. I ain't soon going to forget that first day, when they threw open the doors of the prison cart and we saw what it was lay before us ...'

And so, as they walked, Cade told the story of their imprisonment. He made them laugh with his imitations of Overseer Krent and Captain Hassan, and they laughed harder when he imitated Grub. Grub laughed, too, but it was the cold-eyed laugh of someone pretending to be a good sport. Then Cade took them to darker places: his despair, how he'd turned to ragweed for solace, and the events that led to the explosion in the mine.

'Fire, blowing through the air?' Keel asked.

'Aye. Like thunder and lightning, and a force such as you've never felt, like being swatted by Meshuk herself. I was lifted up, and I knew nothing else, until—'

'What *made* the thunder and lightning?' Garric said. It was the first he'd spoken in a long time.

'Elarite oil,' said Aren sullenly. He didn't even want to speak to Garric after what he'd done to Cade, but he couldn't resist the chance to show he knew more than that bitter old bastard. 'Elarite rocks bleed oil which pools in the hollows of the mountain. The oil breathes out an invisible miasma called fire-fume. When it touches flame, it ignites the oil and—'

'*Boom!*' Cade shouted.

Garric gave Aren a cold stare and looked away, losing interest again.

'Amazing!' Osman exclaimed. 'I'd heard rumours of a weapon that turns the air to fire, some terrible device cooked up by Xulan chimericists. I hadn't thought it possible, but now I'm not so sure. And to think you faced such peril and survived!'

'I almost didn't. It's only thanks to Aren that I got out alive at all.'

Now Cade told the story of how Aren had saved him by carrying him out of the mine, and how he'd planned their escape and inspired them all to freedom. He told them of Aren's encounters with Eifann, and Grub was finally enlightened as to how he found himself carrying a sack full of dead crows. Grub made a sign of protection and complained bitterly about being left in the dark. Then Cade recounted their confrontation with Rapha the Carthanian pirate and how Aren had faced him down.

Aren was uncertain they should be sharing their story so openly with people he didn't trust; but Cade did such a good job of it, and he cast Aren in such flattering light that Aren didn't want to stop him. By the end, they were all looking at Aren with admiration, and Cade's face was flushed with the triumph of a tale well told.

'And here I thought we were just in the company of two unfortunate boys fallen foul of Krodan injustice!' Osman laughed. 'But that's a story worthy of a bard's song. Dead crows filled with draccen tears! Ingenious! And you're quite a surprise, too, friend Grub. Though I'll watch my valuables closely from now on, such as they are.'

'Grub not a thief. He just good at finding things. Besides,' said Grub, with a winningly hideous smile, 'Grub not steal from his *friends*.'

'Now, where'd I leave that shovel of mine?' Keel pondered aloud, and Garric cackled nastily.

'Hoy!' said Aren. 'Weren't you listening? We'd never have made it out at all if not for him. He deserves more than mockery.'

Grub gave him a look of bare surprise, shocked to find Aren defending him. He wasn't used to being defended by anyone, Aren guessed. But although Aren disliked him, he wouldn't see him ganged up on by the others. It offended his sense of fairness.

Keel raised his hands and grinned. 'Just a joke, eh?'

They walked through the first half of the morning. Their pace was kept slow by Vika – her leg was improving but she still limped – and by Aren, who tired quickly and had to be carried on Grub's back for stretches. The place was as mournful and still as Cade had described it, but there were no ghosts that Aren could see, and though it was indeed a maze, it wasn't so hard to navigate. They were helped by Vika, who spotted marks here and there that they'd have otherwise missed: druidsign left by Polla.

By mid-morning they reached a bridge of milky stone which spanned the gap to the central island. Windows along its length, carved to resemble open fans, gave them a view of the water below, a narrow channel sandwiched between the cliffs.

The sun was bright and warm, and they rested in its light with their breath steaming the air and their spirits high. Ruck stood up with her paws on a sill, tongue lolling as she surveyed the world from her vantage point.

'What did I say?' Garric called triumphantly to Keel, who was handing out hardapples. 'We'll be out of here by nightfall, if we make haste.'

'Then perhaps we should do so,' said Vika, and they all knew what she was thinking. They were soon on the move again.

After that, it wasn't so easy.

The main island of Skavengard was a different experience. The ways became winding where before they'd been straightforward. Vika lost track of Polla's druidsign and couldn't locate it again. They found themselves forced from their path again and again, and were reduced to wandering helplessly through rubble-strewn halls and up long, echoing staircases. Sometimes they were diverted into gloomy corridors that ran into the heart of the island rock, sometimes illuminated by crafty lightwells, and sometimes not at all. Then they had to proceed using lanterns and the castle took on a newly sinister air in their flickering glow. They were always relieved to emerge from the dark, but whenever they did, they found it was later than they thought and they were heading in the wrong direction.

'See?' said Cade. 'It ain't that simple finding your way about in here!'

'Indeed,' said Vika suspiciously. 'And yet it was very simple until now.'

'What's your meaning?' Keel asked her.

'Merely thinking aloud,' she said, but she was grim and wary after that, and even Cade lapsed into silence.

Despite its frustrations and the persistent sense of unease, there was much that Aren marvelled at in Skavengard. There were halls built on a scale that seemed unachievable today. They found walkways wide as streets, rows of strange statues standing between broken columns, soaring aqueducts fashioned with spidery grace. They climbed a double spiral staircase, the two halves winding round each other like snakes, a column of light at its centre. For all the orderly magnificence of the Krodan temple at Shoal Point, and the paintings he'd seen of the Emperor's palace at Falconsreach, none of it matched up to this. He felt an absurd sense of ownership at that thought. This was the work of his ancestors. What did the Krodans have to compare?

They rested and ate lunch beneath a vast orrery in an enormous domed chamber, brightly lit where the sun shone through a ragged hole in the roof. Above them hung representations of three planets and their satellites. Calva, the giant; their own planet Thea with its two moons Lyssa and Tantera; striped Valta beyond them. A fourth planet, Elve, lay dented on the floor among slabs of broken stone, its supporting arm twisted and bent by falling rubble. Aren had heard of orreries like this in foreign lands, but never of one so large. Once, the whole thing would have turned, moving the planets around the sun. Aren wished he could have seen it.

'Why are there only four?' Cade wondered at his side.

'They didn't discover the other two till long after the Second Empire fell,' Aren said absently. 'Not till after they'd built the observatory at the Glass University.'

'They thought there were only four planets?' Cade scoffed. 'Can't have been *that* smart, then.'

'Skarls say there *seventh* planet, out there in the big dark,' Grub put in.

'Aye, well, you would, wouldn't you?' said Cade dryly.

'You have something on your mind, Vika,' Garric said as he sat against the orrery and chewed his meagre lunch. 'Will you speak?'

'I fear this place,' she said at last. 'I fear it is trying to keep us here.'

'Walls are walls,' Osman said. 'They cannot move to block us.'

'No, indeed,' said Vika. 'And yet we cannot find our way past them.'

'Is there aught you can do?' Garric asked.

'I dare not, unless the need is dire. Our flight from the dreadknights has taxed me sorely. But we will not leave this place before night comes. I know that now.'

'Let it come, then, and we will see what comes with it,' said Garric. 'I will not fear a rumour.'

Vika said nothing to that.

★

They moved onwards, and it seemed that the way straightened before them and they made good speed for a time. Vika's leg was improving by the hour, and she flexed her left hand often and was pleased and relieved by its responsiveness. Aren, too, was feeling stronger; after lunch, he walked on his own again. The rest of the day passed so swiftly that evening's arrival was a surprise. It became clear they wouldn't even reach the third island tonight, let alone find the way out. The insidious sense of unease grew steadily more intense, and Cade's tale of shadow figures didn't sound so fanciful then.

Presently they found themselves at the bottom of a set of ancient steps, standing before wrought-metal doors, their surfaces crawling with tangled symbols. Guardian demons writhed across them, reaching from the doors with palms out: *Halt!* The pillars to either side were wrapped in carvings of feathered, snake-headed men holding spears towards them to keep them at bay.

'Reckon someone doesn't like visitors,' Cade remarked.

'Aye, well, it's in our way,' said Garric. He reached for the door, but Vika laid a hand on his arm to stay him.

'Wait. There is sorcery here.' Ruck growled low in her throat, hackles raised. 'Let me.'

She approached the door, looked it over and then touched it lightly with her fingertips. When nothing happened, she passed her staff to Keel and laid both hands upon it, and finally her cheek. She closed her eyes as if listening for a heartbeat.

'I do not have the strength right now to divine its nature,' she said, 'but I do not think it will harm us. Like the power laid upon the gate, it is meant to guard against something else.'

She pushed the door firmly. It was unlocked and swung open without a sound.

Aren sensed the change in atmosphere as soon as they crossed the threshold. It was as if they'd walked through an invisible curtain. The corridors of Skavengard ached with emptiness, and the cold air felt thin and brittle like new frost; but here, the air was thick and oppressive. Aren felt unwelcome, and the shadows were murky and oily. The others felt it, too. Ruck flattened her ears and whined, and even Garric hunched his shoulders and lowered his head as he entered.

The chamber had nine sides; one for each Aspect, Aren presumed. High overhead, the walls gathered into a conical spire studded with small oval windows. Aren reckoned it to be an occult sanctum of some kind, or an alchemist's laboratory, or some combination of the two. His eyes were drawn first to the circle on the floor, a ring of silver wards and signs set into the flagstones. They pulled his gaze with a force that was hard to resist, but soon he felt a headache building and he had to look away.

The rest of the room was cluttered with bizarre apparatus. Some were familiar from his studies, like the broken alembic and crucible lying among a heap of copper distiller's pipes. Others were harder to guess at. There was a rectangular screen criss-crossed with web-like filaments that glittered in the gloom. Next to it was a crumpled suit of rotted hemp attached to an iron helmet fashioned in the shape of a screaming harpy, her long fingers meshed together to cover the wearer's eyes.

Then there were the instruments of death and torture. There was no mistaking those. He saw a surgeon's table, rusted blades, hooks for rending and embalming jars to store organs in. Standing against one wall was a fearsome sarcophagus made of metal, ivory and obsidian. It had the shape of a fanged and many-eyed spider whose legs curled around to hold whomever was put within. Aren peered inside and saw long, needle-like blades in various states of retraction.

'Terrible things happened here,' Vika said gravely as she surveyed the scene. Aren didn't doubt her.

'We shouldn't linger,' said Garric. 'This place is a dead end.'

They left in haste and retraced their steps until they found another way onwards. But even after it was behind them, Aren felt befouled, as if some of the atmosphere of that place still clung to him. His admiration for the wonders of Skavengard was tainted now. He didn't want to think what his magnificent ancestors had done in that room.

They hadn't travelled much further before Garric called a halt. 'We won't escape Skavengard tonight, and I won't waste oil travelling in the dark. Let's camp here. At least we'll have the moonlight.'

The spot he'd chosen was a long hall set over two levels connected by a wide staircase. A gallery attached to the higher level overlooked the lower, and narrow floor-to-ceiling windows ran along one side. There was a gaping hole where some of the wall had fallen in, revealing a colonnaded walkway that was open to the air, and a long-dead garden beyond it.

'It will be cold without fire,' Fen said, eyeing the windows.

'If you can find anything to burn in here, be my guest,' said Garric.

'What happened to all the furniture?' Keel wondered. 'Didn't they sit down in Old Ossia? Didn't they sleep?'

'Time would have turned most to dust, I imagine,' Osman said. 'Once, perhaps, there were tapestries and carpets.'

'The boats survived,' Aren pointed out, 'even if most were rotted through. And there was furniture in the sanctum.'

'Aye,' said Vika. 'The place feels ... emptied. As if what was here simply vanished. Perhaps the boats survived because they were outside.'

'And the sanctum?' Aren prompted.

Vika didn't answer him, merely looked thoughtful.

They laid down their packs and huddled together to eat in the cheerless hall, drawing their coats close. The temperature dropped as the sun dipped behind the mountains. Fen muttered about rationing and made sure nobody got quite enough.

'All the stories I've heard about heroes and quests and adventures,' said Cade, 'none of them made mention of how much time you spend being cold and hungry and miserable.'

'And bored,' Keel added. 'Still, there's worse fates. Waking every morning to the same view, the same labour, the same faces day after day. I'll take a hard life in the wild wide world over a soft one in a hutch.'

'You're not wrong there,' said Cade. Then he frowned. 'Don't you have a family, though?'

'I do,' said Keel. 'A wife fair as the sun after a storm, and a young boy, too. I miss 'em sore when I'm away.' He grinned. 'Not so much when I'm at home.'

'How long since you last saw them?'

'When was it, Garric? Midspring?'

'Gallian's Day, I think.'

'Thereabouts, anyway. Not long enough for the echoes of her parting words to fade.' He chuckled. 'By Joha, I love her something fierce but we can't be around each other for long. And that damned town! Wracken Bay is the end of all hope.' He shrugged. 'She knew I was a wanderer when she picked me. Never could stay still for long. I send them what money I can, but noble causes don't pay much, and dragging about after this ugly fool is a full-time occupation.' He thumbed at Garric and gave Cade a wink.

'Hearth and home and the love of a good woman sound fine to me,' said Osman, 'but not in a land ruled by Krodans. There's much to be done before I'll settle down.'

'I'd just take a hearth right now,' said Cade. 'And maybe an ale with it.'

The room dimmed as the last of the light bled from the sky. They heard a low rumble and a tremor ran through the hall, as if the castle itself had shivered. Dust sifted down from the ceiling.

Cade patted his stomach. 'Reckon I'm hungrier than I thought.'

No one laughed. They froze like statues, listening. When no further sound came, Keel let out a breath, and at last they relaxed.

'Nine, this place gives me the jitters,' he said. 'If only—'

He was cut short by a thunderous gurgling bellow that echoed down the valley, the sound of something not quite animal and definitely not human. Aren's blood ran cold as the cry pulsed through the empty corridors and halls, reverberating around Skavengard until finally it chased itself into silence.

'The terror that comes with the night,' Vika whispered.

From somewhere in the heights of Skavengard there was a dull, heavy boom, as of some great gate thrown open. They heard the bellow again, and then quiet.

'Did your fellow druidess speak of the nature of this ... terror?' Garric asked.

'Polla never saw it. Perhaps she slipped beneath its notice.'

'Perhaps we should do the same,' Fen murmured.

The unseen thing gave another cry, somewhere between a squeal and a roar. Or perhaps it was many, not just one: a dozen sounds overlapping. They heard a pounding noise, as if something massive was battering at the walls and doors of the castle. It was closer now, moving along a corridor somewhere above them. Aren took a step back, instinctively wanting to run.

'It's hunting,' said Vika.

'You don't know that!' Osman sounded edgy. His confident denial of the supernatural was being tested hard.

'No,' said Vika, her eyes on the ceiling. 'But I feel it.' Suddenly her head snapped around and she fixed her gaze on Garric. 'The sanctum!'

'What? That butcher's den?'

'It is protected,' Vika said. 'And it may be our only chance.' She raised her voice. 'Run, all of you! Run!'

They needed no second invitation. Snatching up their packs, they fled back the way they'd come, leaving the debris of their meal behind them.

Fen took the lead and they moved as fast as Vika's limp would allow, down dusk-dark corridors and narrow stairs. When Aren began to flag, Grub scooped him up onto his back and the tireless Skarl bore him onwards. From above and behind them came that thunderous booming again, and a sound like grinding teeth. A wind sprang up, blowing down the corridors and rustling their clothes. It was hot and foetid, and smelled of rank meat, greasy metal and death.

'Are you sure it's this way?' Keel asked urgently as Fen took them down another side-corridor.

'I'm sure,' she replied.

'I remember it was further—'

'I'm *sure*, Keel.'

Aren jolted against Grub's back, his sword – reclaimed from Cade – bouncing on his thigh. From the corner of his eye he saw their hurrying shadows against a wall. Just for a moment, he thought he saw other shadows there, too: men and women in flowing robes and elaborate headpieces, also fleeing from the beast. They were gone again in an instant.

'Sounds further behind us now,' Cade said breathlessly.

Fen slowed and cocked an ear. 'You may be right.'

They listened. The sound *was* fainter now. Soon it fell quiet, and for a while they heard nothing more. The wind dropped until they only caught faint whiffs of that rotten breeze. Their pace began to slow as fatigue dragged on them, and hope grew that their pursuer had given up the chase.

'Not far now,' said Fen, her chest heaving. 'We're close.'

'Keep going,' Vika urged, her staff clicking on the stone floor as she lumbered onwards through corridors turned grey with Lyssa's light.

Suddenly, from behind them they heard a ferocious, bubbling roar of outrage and hate, a snarl and a scream all together. It was followed by a hurricane-force wind which blasted through the corridors, strong enough to push Vika to her knees. She struggled to rise again, leaning on her staff as the wind swirled around her. A furious pounding shook the walls.

It was coming closer. *Fast.*

'It must have found our camp,' Vika said. 'It has our trail now! Flee, if you value your lives!'

Flee they did, dashing in a panic for the dubious safety of the sanctum. The wind howled after them, and Aren thought it carried faint screams from far away, the sound of people in suffering.

'Which way?' Garric demanded of Fen, who'd stopped at a junction.

'I don't remember this—'

'Pick one!'

'I don't …' She trailed off. Then her expression firmed, and she knew. 'That way!'

They ran through a pillared chamber and around the upper gallery of a hall where the floor had collapsed. Aren knew they were on the right track then, for he remembered this place. They fought through the battering wind to a flight of stairs, and below them were the sanctum doors, crawling with wrought-metal demons.

A shriek of unearthly fury came from the chamber behind them, loud enough that they felt the force of it against their ears. As they raced towards the sanctum, thumping down the steps, the air darkened and congealed around them, cloying in their throats. The taste of it was so vile, it made Aren retch. He heard slopping and slithering and the sound of many mouths, mewling and chomping hungrily.

Eager to be first inside, Grub sprang recklessly past the others, carrying Aren through the open doorway on his back. In his haste he lost his grip on his passenger, who tipped sideways, and the shift in weight sent them both tumbling to the floor. Fen vaulted over them, with Keel behind her, and the two of them took hold of the doors and began shoving them closed as the rest came through. Fen had her shoulder to the metal, but Keel was looking through the gap as he pushed; his eyes widened and his face went white as he saw what was coming down the stairs behind his companions.

'Do not look upon it!' Vika cried, but it was too late.

Keel screamed and fell back into the room, his hands over his eyes. Osman rushed to take his place; he and Fen slammed the doors and flung the two heavy levers across, engaging the lock an instant before something crashed against them with a bellow.

Aren scrambled to his feet, backing away into the room as the doors were pounded again, again, *again*, the blows so strong they bowed the doors inwards. Cade scurried to his side and they stood there together, paralysed with fright as the creature slithered and gnashed just outside the sanctum. Garric, Fen and Osman had their weapons drawn, holding them uncertainly. All they could do was wait, and hope the doors didn't give way.

Then, as suddenly as it had attacked, it retreated again. There was a flurry from without, a diminishing scream, and the thing fled up the stairs and away. They heard it pounding off in another direction, its squeals echoing through the halls. Finally it faded to silence, and there was only the sound of their panting breaths in the moonlit gloom of the sanctum.

Garric ran over to Keel, who was kneeling and rocking with his hands over his eyes. 'Are you hurt, Keel? Show me!'

Vika joined him, and gently pulled Keel's hands away. The Bitterbracker's palms were red, as were the whites of his eyes. Tears of watery blood trickled down his cheeks.

'I saw it,' he whispered, and Garric held him tight as his friend trembled and shuddered like a frightened child.

40

When dawn's light crept through the windows they emerged from the sanctum, hollow-eyed and wary. Aren had slept in snatches when tiredness overwhelmed him; most of the others hadn't slept at all. Keel had to be led out by Garric, blinking, his eyes so bloodshot and swollen that he saw only smears of colour. He wouldn't speak a word of what he'd seen.

The sanctum doors were dented and buckled, but though they screeched on their hinges now, they'd held firm against the creature. Aren eyed the damage and wondered if they could have stood much more.

They set out with all speed, hoping to make as much progress as they could while the morning held. They'd made it almost halfway across Skavengard on their first day, despite getting lost in the afternoon. They might make the rest of the way before sunset.

Aren felt stronger despite his tiredness, as if he'd fought off the last of his sickness in the night. Vika, too, seemed much recovered. She could make a fist easily with her left hand now, and her limp was so slight it hardly hampered her at all. Fen left marks behind her as they went, scored in the stone with her knife. 'In case we have to make our way back,' she said. It was a precaution they hoped they wouldn't need. None of them wanted to be here when the night found them again.

They retraced their steps to the hall where they'd rested the night before. The debris of their camp was gone, the room as clean and empty as all the others, and they pressed on quickly. If they could make it to the third island by the afternoon, they might yet make camp in the Ostenbergs tonight. Even those bleak stony passes felt welcome now, compared to the alternative.

'You know what it is, don't you?' Aren asked Vika quietly as they walked together. 'You know what seeks us.'

'You're an observant one. What makes you so certain?'

'I'm not sure. I just... I see it in you.'

'I have a suspicion,' she admitted.

'Will you tell me?'

She sized him up, deciding if knowledge or ignorance would serve him best. Aren felt a touch of anger at that.

'To overcome your enemy, you must first understand him,' he said, before she could make up her mind.

'This is not an enemy you can overcome,' she said.

'I don't believe that. Nothing is without weakness.'

He wasn't sure whether she was amused or impressed by that, but either way, it convinced her to speak. 'Let me tell you something of the nature of sorcery, then,' she said, 'for I have read a little of the elder arts. When Joha drew the Divide between the living and the dead, he also separated order from chaos, because his people could not thrive in a land where nothing was permanent. And so we, the living, have rules: up is up, down is down, stone is hard and water is wet.

'The Shadowlands are different, fluid and ever-changing. There, a thought might conjure a castle or collapse it. If we wish to change something of permanence in our world, we need a little of that chaos; a pinch of disorder, and the will to enforce the outcome.' She held up her arm. 'You see the sleeve of my coat. Is it possible it will burst into flame, right now?'

Aren sensed a trap, but said no anyway.

'Wrong. Nothing is impossible. It is merely fantastically unlikely. But if a sorcerer chose to bridge the Divide with their arts, so that a little of the essence of the Shadowlands leaked in, then they could will the most unlikely of outcomes into existence. The more unlikely it is, the more chaos is needed, and the greater the force of will required. My sleeve is made of cloth; it would be relatively easy to make it burn. To make your sword burst into flames would be another feat altogether, for metal is not given to burning.'

She peered through a doorway as they passed it. Beyond was a chamber that might have been a temple to the Nine, except there was only a single statue there. Old as it was, Aren recognised the hooded figure that loomed over the altar. Vaspis the Malcontent, Aspect of Vengeance and Treachery, patron of outcasts and underdogs. Ruck stopped and took a look, ears raised, while Vika walked on.

'It is said that in the Age of Legends, even the meanest sorcerer could achieve astonishing things,' said Vika. 'Other histories of the Second Empire speak of the great and strange powers of the Sorcerer Kings and Queens. But if such accounts are true, those arts are long forgotten. Those who call themselves sorcerers today are mere tricksters by comparison.'

'Are you a sorceress?' Aren asked.

'I am a druidess. I speak to the spirits. And perhaps there is a touch of chaos in my potions.' She gave him a sly glance. 'But I am no sorcerer. I could no more make your sword burst into flames than I could fly.'

They turned into a new corridor. Bright sunlight slanted in through the windows but did little to alleviate the pervasive sense of threat. Ahead of them, Garric was leading Keel, who held himself like a frail old man, diminished by the terror he'd witnessed. Garric's expression was grim. Aren hadn't seen him exhibit much concern for any of his other companions, including those that had fallen to the dreadknights, but his worry for his friend was obvious.

So there's more than just anger and hate in you, he thought.

'There is another kind of sorcery, though,' said Vika. 'An altogether more abhorrent kind of magic. A century ago, there was war in the Communion. Druid fought druid. Our order was brought to the brink of extinction, and though it has recovered since, we were weakened for ever after. A group formed under the leadership of Carlac-Parts-The-Flames. They called themselves Apostates, and declared the Aspects dead, and sought their gods in the Shadowlands instead. The other druids thought them harmless and let them be, not knowing that Carlac had unearthed forbidden knowledge and was making dark pacts with entities across the

Divide. By the time we learned of it, it was almost too late to stop them.'

Aren thought of the tools in the sanctum, and understood. 'Blood sacrifice.'

'Aye. Sacrifice, and torture, and worse.' Her face hardened. 'There is potency in blood, but we use only animal blood, or that which is given willingly. To take a human life is to deny all possibilities from that day to the day of their natural death. The Apostates discovered how to harness that, and it made them terrible. It is only by Joha's grace that we found them out while they were still few, but our order has borne their taint ever since.'

'You think this creature comes from the Shadowlands?'

'This is no mere shade. It may even come from some place beyond,' she said. 'I believe it is a servant of the Outsiders.'

Aren felt dread touch him. He had no more reason to believe in the Outsiders than in the Aspects that had imprisoned them in the Abyss, yet it was easier to fear the unknown than to love it.

'All this is the work of the Sorcerer King Azh Mat Jaal, I suspect,' Vika said. 'He meddled with forces best left alone. Whatever happened here, he brought it upon them.'

'And yet whatever force protects the sanctum remains undisturbed.'

'It may not be the only sanctum in Skavengard. It may not even have been Azh Mat Jaal's. The Second Empire was a time of sorcery and many practised it. There are tales of the rulers of the great city-states waging magical battles with usurpers, sometimes their own children.'

'Maybe we'll find another sanctuary further on,' said Aren.

'Maybe,' she replied.

But they didn't. Instead, the way began to twist again, and as before, they found themselves going in circles. After the gains they'd made in the early morning, it was doubly frustrating to find their path blocked again and again. Once, when they tried to retrace their steps, Fen found she'd inexplicably forgotten to mark the corners, and they wasted an hour searching out their path again.

They paused to eat in an oval room with smooth sides like an egg. A slice of its narrow end was open to the air, as if the wall had simply parted there, and beyond it they could see the rocky slopes of the valley and the sharp blue sky above. Set around the room were a dozen bronze stelae taller than a man, vaguely oblong but tapering towards the top. On the south side of each, facing the open wall, were complex rows of hieroglyphs, broken up by larger pictures depicting scenes in bas-relief.

While Vika and Garric, Keel and Fen discussed the next step in grave tones and Grub stuffed his face industriously, Osman pulled Aren and Cade from stele to stele.

'They're histories, do you see?' he said, excited. 'That's Sarla bringing the plague to the urds; and there's Jessa Wolf's-Heart and Morgen, leading our people from slavery!'

Aren studied the strange flattened figures on the stele. They were angular and disproportionate and curiously posed, but he saw Osman was right. A hooded child stood with the dead lying round her. Elsewhere, urds fled before a man and woman bearing swords. The urds were squat, slope-browed and lantern-jawed, grotesque in their fear.

'Ugly things, ain't they?' said Cade, through a mouthful of stale bread. He pointed. 'That one looks like Grub.'

Aren had never seen an urd except in a painting once, howling beneath Toven's armoured boot as the great Krodan swordsman drove his blade into his enemy's breast. That had been enough to haunt his dreams when he was young. Later, his father's bodyguard Kuhn had told him tales of his time in the Sixth Purge, when he fought alongside the Knights Vigilant in another ultimately unsuccessful attempt to eradicate the urdish tribes from the face of the world. He spoke of the hordes that attacked in the night from hidden tunnels that mazed the lowlands, and of a great underground city that no one had ever found. For centuries, the Barrier Nations had stood as a bulwark against the vengeance of the First Empire. If occupation by Kroda was bad, occupation by the urds would be infinitely worse.

'Aren! Come here!' Osman's enthusiasm was infectious. He'd forgotten the danger in the thrill of discovery.

He was pointing to a strange chart, a tangled family tree running down the face of one of the stelae. At the top was a single mighty figure, drawn in an attitude of pride and strength. Six lines spread downwards, crossing and overlapping, passing through various scenes in which people sailed in ships, or hid from the sun in caves, or warred. Scene by scene, the people changed gradually, becoming shorter or thinner or more brutish, until at the bottom there were six figures standing side by side.

'What's it mean?' asked Cade, looking over his shoulder.

'It's how the Six Races came to be,' said Aren, and Osman grinned. Aren traced with his finger. 'There are the giants at the top, along with the draccens and monsters that ruled the lands after the Age of Chaos came to an end.'

'Then here, the Long Ice,' Osman said, 'and the Breaking of the People. The giants scattered, fleeing the ice. Some to the caves, some to other lands. Some became cannibals, some herders.'

'Wait, I see it now!' said Cade. He was recalling his ma's stories. 'There are the elaru, leaving for the west, and the drudge-men they enslaved. And that's when the gnawls betrayed the urds and ogren in the Reclamation and came over to our side!' He dropped to one knee and counted along the bottom. 'Elaru, human, dwarrow, urd, ogren, gnawl!' he finished triumphantly.

'The dwarrow are lost to us now,' said Osman, 'and the ogren in thrall to the elaru. Time marches past us, the years in their thousands, and the fortunes of uncounted souls ebb and flow with the centuries. Against such a measure, thirty years under a Krodan boot is a mere moment in history. Yet still it feels eternal.'

'But you were surely born after the occupation?' said Aren, guessing at his age. 'How can you miss something you've never known?'

'How do the birds know where to fly, when they go south for the winter? The heart knows,' said Osman. 'Doesn't yours?'

Aren didn't know how to answer that, but he was saved from the need by Garric, who walked over to them with Vika at his side and Ruck loping behind.

'Pick up your gear,' he said. 'We're going.'

'You have a way onward?' Osman asked.

Garric glanced at Vika and looked like he wanted to spit. 'We're going *back*.'

'Back where?' Cade asked.

'Back to the sanctum,' said Vika. 'We will not escape Skavengard today, or any day, unless something is done. This place will not let us leave. It merely seeks to lure us far enough from safety that we will have nowhere to hide when night falls. We have almost lost the way back once. The next time, we may not find it again.'

'And what then?' Osman asked, aghast. 'Another night in that vile place? How will tomorrow be different?'

'When dawn comes, I intend to have a way out. But I need time to prepare. And we need to get ourselves to safety.'

'What do you mean to do?' Aren asked her.

She turned a flat gaze on him, and he saw the fear that lurked behind the façade of stern determination.

'The beast will come again tonight,' she said. 'I mean to speak with it.'

41

Aren sat with Cade against one of the sanctum's nine walls, watching the light fade through the windows of the spire high above them. Dusk was falling after long hours of dreadful anticipation. They'd passed the time staring uneasily at the sarcophagus full of needles, the cutting table, the screen of sharp filaments. The air was heavy with remembered murder. There had been little conversation to speed the waiting, each of them lost to their own dark thoughts.

Only Vika had been busy. She'd ordered Garric and Osman to break up a table for firewood and lit it with a roll of parchment covered with arcane notes. Osman protested: what wisdom might be set upon those pages, he argued, if they could get it to the scholars at the Glass University? But Vika treated them with disgust.

'The secrets this place contains are what destroyed it. I will not have the curious tempted to repeat the same mistakes. Take nothing from here.'

'Do as she says,' said Garric, who hadn't much cared for Osman's idea anyway. 'If we survive, we have more urgent business ahead than delivering sorcerers' scrawls to Estria.'

Vika fashioned a brew with a pot and tripod from her pack, adding herbs from her many pockets and dashes of liquid from clay phials. She murmured over it in Stonespeak and passed her hand around it in a circle many times. Later, she cut her forearm with her knife, adding another scar to the dozens already there, and let a little of her blood roll over her skin to drip into the pot.

When satisfied, she took herself to the circle in the middle of the sanctum and settled cross-legged inside the silver ring of wards with the brew cooling before her.

'No matter what you see or hear, do not try to help me,' she said. 'And do not – do *not* – step inside this circle, on your life and the lives of everyone here.'

She closed her eyes and began to whisper a chant to herself, while Ruck prowled the perimeter of the ring. After more than an hour, it had become an unsettling background susurrus to the tides of Aren's mind.

Cade was as restless as Aren. He tapped his toes against the floor, drummed his fingers and fidgeted. Grub picked his nails with the point of his knife. Osman investigated the sanctum, turning everything over in his hands, studying books written in a language he couldn't read. Keel sat with Garric, shoulders bunched, a tight ball of tension. His eyes, though still sore, had recovered; but the easy humour had gone out of him. Garric glared at the flagstones and occasionally threw a dark look towards Aren.

Fen had sat alone all evening and spoken to nobody; but just as the last light was seeping from the sky, she got to her feet and walked across the room to Aren and Cade. Aren looked up at her quizzically as she stood over them. For a moment, she seemed lost for words. Then:

'I'm from the Auldwood,' she said to Cade, in the tone of an angry retort.

'Uh ... what?' Cade said stupidly.

'Back in the boathouse, you asked me where I was from,' she told him. 'The Auldwood. That's where.'

'Did I? Oh.'

Fen stood there awkwardly.

'We're from Shoal Point,' Aren offered.

'I know.'

A few moments passed in which no one knew what to say. Then Fen coloured, tutted loudly in disgust and stalked back to her place, looking furious.

Aren and Cade stared at each other in bewilderment. Then Cade grinned and nudged him.

'I think she likes me,' he said.

Aren looked over at Fen, who was glowering at the floor. *No, that's not it*, he thought. *She's scared. She needs company, but she doesn't know how to ask for it.*

That spurred him to his feet. She'd reached out to them, however clumsily. He couldn't ignore that.

'Where are you going?' Cade asked in surprise, but Aren was already on his way across the sanctum. Fen saw him coming and stiffened, looking half ready to run and half to fight. He sat down before she could do either.

'Where in the Auldwood?' he asked. 'It's a big place.'

She eyed him warily. In the gloom, she seemed slight and delicate. Given the company she travelled with and how capable she was, it was easy to forget she wasn't much older than him.

'Deep in,' she said. 'Nowhere near anywhere. Buckscuttle was the nearest settlement, but that was a day away. We lived out on our own.'

'Who's we?'

'Me and my da.'

Aren took a calculated risk. 'What about your ma?'

'She died when I was ten.' She said it casually, like it meant nothing at all, which meant exactly the opposite.

'I lost mine, too,' he said. 'Not like yours, though. I was too young to remember her. Her name was Lyssa, like the moon.'

'Cade told me a story about the moons.'

'He'll tell you a story about anything, given half a chance.'

The ghost of a smile passed over her lips at that. There was silence between them for a few moments.

'I lost my father, too,' said Aren. He felt his throat thicken as he said it, but he went on regardless, talking past the pain. 'The Iron Hand murdered him.'

She didn't reply to that, but her posture softened a little.

'So why did you leave?' Aren asked, in an attempt to keep the conversation going.

'Krodans drove me away,' she said. 'Trappers and hunters moved into the area, dozens of them, all working for some company in Gallowcroft. Soon there was nothing to eat, and soon after, a cleric turned up at my door with two soldiers. He told me I was evicted, and when I refused to leave, they started to smash things.'

'They threw you out?'

She snorted. 'Not exactly. Krodan women aren't allowed to do much but bake cakes and raise children, so they didn't expect me to have a bow. They definitely didn't expect me to use it.' She gave him a quick glance, and he saw a flicker of savage triumph in it. 'But I knew there'd be more coming, and in greater numbers than I could handle, so I packed up and left.'

And your da? Where was he? Aren wondered, but he kept the thought to himself. Too many questions would drive her back into her shell.

'There are spirits in the Auldwood,' Fen said at length. Her gaze had drifted to the sanctum doors, and he knew she was thinking of the beast. 'Where I'm from, any fool knows that. You have to be a stranger to the wild places to think as Osman does. He's a good man, but he's lived in a Krodan's world his whole life. The real Ossia still exists, but you won't find it in the towns or along the roadside.'

'I grew up in the same world,' said Aren. 'But I'm learning.'

He looked over at Cade, who was watching them closely with a sour expression on his face.

'Did you ever meet any?' he asked. 'Spirits, I mean.'

'I think so,' said Fen. 'In a way. I got lost while hunting once, far from home. Night was falling, so I looked for shelter. I found a glade ... it was so beautiful, I've never seen its like since. I knew it was a place where spirits lived. But it felt like a kind place, and I was frightened, so I slept there.' She shifted, watching him for signs of mockery. 'I had strange dreams that night, and when morning came, I found myself elsewhere. Not more than a league from home.' She shrugged one shoulder. 'Perhaps the spirits carried me. It's hard to say. I was eleven. My imagination was more vivid in those days.'

And why were you hunting far from home at eleven? Aren thought, but again he didn't say it.

'So the spirits can be friendly as well as fearsome?' he said.

320

'They can. Though I don't expect much friendship from the one that chased us yesterday.'

'We know that Polla-Calls-The-Waters passed through here and survived. We will, too. We just have to endure one more night.'

'Yes,' said Fen, and she gave him a real smile then, the first he'd had from her. 'One more night. We can endure that.'

Aren sensed his moment to leave, before he outstayed his welcome. He got up and went back to Cade.

'Have a nice talk?' Cade asked with sullen envy.

Before Aren could reply, a shudder ran through the stones of Skavengard and a shriek rose up in the gathered dark. Keel jerked as if stung and looked towards the doors as if to assure himself they were locked. Osman lit a lantern to stave off the shadows. Vika, her eyes still closed, picked up her brew and drank it. She retched twice, but kept swallowing till it was all gone.

A gate crashed open somewhere in the heights and the beast came tumbling along the corridors, screaming and roaring. It knew its course this time. Last night it had searched all over the island. Tonight it moved with purpose, charging from its lair and heading straight for them.

Ruck curled her lip and snarled. Keel and Garric drew their swords and stood by the circle, facing the door in case anything should come through. None of them believed blades would do any good, but it shored up their courage.

A wind gathered and blew against the door. Vika twitched violently where she sat and made a long gagging sound like she was choking; but they'd been instructed not to interfere, so they stood by helplessly until the spasm passed.

Screaming, the beast bore down on them. The wind became a hurricane, and the walls shivered with a pounding that got louder, and louder, and louder still. They heard it rushing down the stairs, slithering and howling and grinding its teeth.

Aren and Cade huddled together instinctively. Keel and Garric raised their blades and set themselves. Osman lurched to his feet and joined them, his own sword ringing as he pulled it free. Grub had retreated to a far corner of the room and was now half-hidden behind a bookcase. Fen sat where she was, pulled her hood over her head and waited.

Just as the beast reached the doors, silence fell, sudden and complete. Aren listened to his own racing heartbeat. He sensed it out there, slick and piled and massive, a thing of madness, appetite and rage. Waiting.

Vika let out a low mewl, a deranged animal sound, and arched her back. Her eyelids fluttered and her eyes rolled up in her head.

The beast crashed against the doors; Cade jumped out of his skin. Shrieking and snarling in a cacophony of many mouths, it assaulted the barrier over and over. Each time, it recoiled with a howl of pain as if burned; each time it attacked with greater fury. The doors screeched and stone puffed around their hinges with each blow. Cade covered his ears against the relentless din, the hellish cries of the beast, the wind laced with human screams.

Vika jerked with every impact. She was still gasping words in Stonespeak, but her spine had arched so severely that she was bent back with the top of her head almost touching the floor. Her hands were claws, clutched to her chest; her face was flecked with spittle and her eyes rolled. The sight of her contortions was almost as alarming as the sound of the creature outside, and Aren fought the urge to rush into the circle and help her. Whatever she'd intended when she drank that potion, it appeared to have gone badly wrong.

'The door won't hold!' Keel cried, and there was an edge of hysteria in his voice.

'It'll hold,' said Garric grimly.

'Use your eyes! It's giving way!'

Aren, Fen and Cade all scrambled to their feet then and seized what weapons they had. Keel was right. The doors were buckling and the hinges coming away. Despite the pain it was suffering as it threw itself against the doors, the beast wasn't going to stop.

Aren trembled as he held his sword, ready in the stance Master Orik had taught him. It was a pitiful needle against the thing that raged outside. What would it feel like, when the beast crashed through in a slimy flood of teeth? What would it feel like, to be crushed by it, drowned in it, *devoured*?

Vika screamed, a high, raw sound, ending in a series of convulsive gulps. The next attack was half-hearted in comparison to the others, and after that there was quiet. They stood rigid with tension, awaiting a final, mighty blow to smash the doors wide. But nothing came, and gradually they dared to believe the assault had stopped.

Vika, still cross-legged and bent double, dragged a dry, rasping breath into her lungs. Slowly she pulled herself upright, her vertebrae creaking and popping. Her head lolled forward, sweat-damp hair stuck across her brow and cheeks. She wobbled, swaying like a drunk. Then her lips drew back to expose teeth washed red with blood and a low murmur came from her: a growling, hoarse voice they'd never heard before.

'...*gristly little meatbags oozing dripping taste your bright bright souls*...'

Her eyes snapped open, and they were black and empty. A horrible smile spread across her face.

'I see you,' she crooned.

Ruck snarled, baring her teeth; but then Vika turned her gaze upon her and she fled to a corner, whimpering.

Osman took a wary step closer, his blade held ready by his side. 'Vika?'

'The druidess is in here with me,' said the thing that wore her skin. Her voice was hoarse and gasping, broken by snatched breaths, as if she were not accustomed to using lungs to speak. 'She writhes and turns like a fish on a spike. So weak, your bodies are. So frail. Bones and tubes, a rack to hang your souls upon.'

She chuckled, then cocked her head as if listening. 'Do you seek to bargain with me, druidess?' she said. 'You have no power here. Your faith is a glass castle; no god can help you now.'

Her black eyes widened as she listened again, and she looked at the horrified assembly that surrounded her. 'Who among you is her champion?' she demanded. She pointed at Garric. 'You,' she said. 'She has chosen you.'

Garric exchanged an uncertain glance with Keel. Then his face hardened. 'Aye, I'll be her champion.'

'Then face me, champion!' Vika cried. 'Unbolt the door! Defeat me and save her!'

'Try harder, demon. I am no fool.'

'No fool, but a coward!'

'That is a pale insult coming from a ghost that hides in a woman's body.'

There was a bellow from outside and the beast slammed against the sanctum doors. Vika and the beast screamed together in pain.

'It hurts, doesn't it?' Garric said. Aren was amazed at his steely calm. 'Why don't you stop?'

Vika bared her teeth at him. 'You are brave, champion, but only because you cannot conceive of the suffering I will visit upon you. You will be devoured a thousand times! You will ... you will ... *aaaaaaah!*'

The beast's threats dissolved into a strangled scream and Vika pitched forward onto her hands and knees, then fell on her side, arching and contorting. 'Help me!' she cried, and it was Vika's voice again. Her eyes were no longer black, but desperate and terrified. She reached out weakly towards Garric. 'I have driven the beast back, but only for a moment! Pull me from the circle!'

Garric stood there, impassive, watching her beg.

'Help her!' Aren demanded, appalled. He took a step towards her, to take her hand himself, but the flat of Garric's blade slapped across his chest, barring his progress.

'I think not,' said Garric, not even looking at him.

Vika's attention switched to Aren and she strained to reach him, tears filling her eyes. 'Aren! Please!'

Aren trembled with hate. He wanted to swat Garric's sword aside, bury his blade in the Hollow Man's throat, finish up the job that someone else had failed to do. Vika was in agony and Garric was doing nothing, and worse was the way he just overruled Aren like he was some callow child not worth listening to.

Cade grabbed his shoulder before any furious impulse could overwhelm him. 'She said not to break the circle!' Cade told him. 'Remember? Remember she said that?'

Aren looked down at the floor, at the silver ring of wards that surrounded Vika. Of course he remembered what she'd said, but it wasn't easy to stand there and watch her suffer. The impulse to save her was almost overwhelming.

'Aren!' Vika pleaded. 'I did not know what I was dealing with! Help me!'

It was Vika there, behind those eyes. It *had* to be! She was hurting, she needed his help, and yet...

'You said not to break the circle,' Aren told her, his jaw tight as he glared at Garric. 'Under any circumstances.'

Vika crumpled with a howl of despair, throwing herself down on her face. Then, slowly, her howl became a malicious croon, and then broke into cackles. Ruck barked at her from the corner where she hid.

Garric turned his head and gave Aren a cool stare down the length of his sword. Aren stepped back, his cheeks flushing, and allowed Cade to draw him away. He was horrified by how close he'd come to being duped, and he loathed Garric for being right.

Vika threw her head back and leered, blood and spittle drooling from her lower lip. 'You have chosen your champion well!' she said, addressing the voice they couldn't hear. 'I accept your bargain, druidess! In exchange for one of you, I will let the others go free.' She thrust out a finger. 'Him!'

'Grub?' asked Grub, pointing towards himself. He was still half-hidden behind the bookcase.

'Give him to me, and the rest of you will leave Skavengard alive.'

Garric turned that passionless, calculating gaze onto Grub. Aren opened his mouth to protest on the Skarl's behalf, but shame kept him silent. He'd humiliated himself once already. He'd see what Garric said first. Let the Hollow Man throw Grub to the wolf, let the others see what kind of man he was. Only then would he step in and stop it, if he could.

Grub drew his knife, his teeth bared. 'Try it. Grub not planning to see the Bone God yet,' he said.

'Garric...' Osman said, a warning in his voice.

Garric held up a hand to silence him. 'Vika offered you that bargain?' he asked the beast in the circle.

'Yes! The life of a worthless criminal in exchange for safe passage! Either he dies, or you all do.'

Garric thought that over for a few moments longer, but when he spoke, it sounded like his decision had never been in doubt. 'You lie, demon. She'd never make such a bargain.'

'Who are you to speak for her?' she cried. 'What do you know?'

'I am her champion,' said Garric. 'And I know enough not to trust you.'

Her face twisted angrily. 'Skarls have no love for anyone but their own kind! *He'd* betray *you* in a heartbeat!'

'Aye, perhaps,' said Garric. 'But there's been too much betrayal in this land already. I won't add to it.'

Aren stared at Garric in surprise. It was no bluff; Aren would have seen through that. He was entirely unintimidated. He was speaking with a creature of the Abyss and he wasn't afraid. It was a kind of bravery he'd never witnessed before.

'Now I have a deal for *you*, demon,' said Garric. 'Take your parlour tricks and sorry deceptions, and fly back to whatever hole you lurk in. You will have *none* of us, this night or any other.'

Vika snarled; the beast roared and crashed against the doors. Together, they screamed as it was thrown back.

'You're a prisoner here!' Garric barked. 'Trapped inside these walls, hiding from the sun. Caught by man's magic! Why should I fear you?'

Aren jumped in alarm as the doors were pounded again, screeching as their hinges bent. Vika shrieked, clawing at her cheeks with her nails, hard enough to draw bloody scratches. *What's he doing? Does he want that thing to break in?*

'We are leaving Skavengard!' Now Garric's voice had risen to a shout. 'And you cannot stop us! You will remain here alone, and forlorn, bubbling in your own damned misery until the end of time!'

The beast roared again, a howl of anger and anguish loud enough to make them cringe. It smashed against the doors with such force that they almost fell inwards. Vika lunged at Garric with a scream, her painted face a rictus of hate, nails clawing at his eyes.

As she crossed the circle of wards, there was a sound like the cracking of bones, and Aren felt a blow that seemed to come from inside his skull. The others felt it, too, flinching and staggering from the invisible force. Vika went instantly limp and collapsed against Garric; he stumbled backwards and barely held her. Then they heard a squeal from beyond the doors, the thrashing, slopping sound of the beast flailing away up the stairs, and it was gone.

Aren blinked, his head throbbing. Vika stirred in Garric's arms and opened her eyes. He steadied her while she found her balance. Her eyes were clear, and somehow Aren knew she was herself again.

He beat it, thought Aren, awed. *He faced it down and beat it. I've never seen anything like it.*

'Is it gone?' Garric asked Vika.

'For tonight,' said Vika. She spat to clear her mouth. 'But it will be back.'

'Those doors will not withstand another assault,' said Keel.

'Then all is lost,' said Osman. 'We are no closer to escape than we were yesterday.'

'No,' said Vika. 'For as the beast saw into my mind, so I saw into the beast's. And it showed me more than it wanted to.' She took her staff from Garric and drew herself up to her full height with a red grin. 'I know the way out.'

42

The hour before dawn found Aren huddled in his blanket, his eyes shadowed in the moonlight. Despite the horror they'd witnessed, exhaustion had taken the others, who hadn't slept the previous night. They lay bundled in their cloaks, silver in the gloom. Cade snored next to him. Keel cried out softly and pawed at some unseen thing in front of his face. Vika lay on her front, one hand twitching and blood still on her lips, looking like the fallen wounded.

Garric slept on his side with his cloak over his head. Aren watched his shoulder rise and fall with each breath and wondered who he really was, this grizzled old warrior his father called the Hollow Man. Worn out and scared, his feelings had become confused. Garric was his father's enemy, that much was true; but Aren admired him, damn it, he *admired* him for how he'd dealt with the beast. He was grim and sullen and foul-tempered, but he'd rescued Aren at terrible cost to fulfil a promise made to someone he loathed. Other men might have ducked that obligation, but not him. That spoke of honour, more honour than most had. Not only that, but he'd fought at Salt Fork, and he planned to steal the Ember Blade from the Krodans.

Garric was brave, then. Toweringly, fiercely brave. A man that could goad a servant of the Outsiders into attacking him across a circle of wards in order to drive it out of Vika's body. It was harder to hate him, knowing that.

But then he remembered the bruise on Cade's face, the scornful dismissal in his eyes after Aren was almost tricked into breaking the circle. He remembered how Garric had laid the blame for his companions' deaths at his feet, the disgust and scorn he'd greeted Aren with at every turn, and his admiration turned to anger and humiliation again. Why would he care for the approval of such a man?

And still I don't know who my father really was. Or who Garric was to him.

Well, Aren was sick and weak no longer, and he wasn't afraid of Garric any more. If Garric planned to offload him at the first town they came to, then that was fine with Aren. But before that day came, he'd have his answers. He swore it to himself. As soon as they were out of Skavengard, he'd demand them.

His eyes skipped to Fen, who lay with her face half-concealed by her hood. They lingered on her mouth, her lips slightly parted, her breath sighing between. The sight of her asleep made him feel protective, though she was obviously better able to take care of herself than he was. The contradiction didn't bother him. It made him feel good to imagine she needed him.

Don't get close to them, he reminded himself. *It'll only hurt the worse when you leave them behind.*

And yet he watched her sleep anyway, for a long time there in the twilight.

Ruck stirred as morning was approaching and barked to wake her mistress. Vika struggled to her feet and then flopped down on her arse, looking bewildered. She moved her jaw from side to side, snorted and began to mumble gibberish to herself.

While the others roused themselves, Vika went between them, offering each a sip from a phial. She walked in an ungainly lope and chewed the inside of her cheek. Her gaze skated about like a woman deranged.

'Just a sip. Keep you walking, hah! We won't stop. Won't rest. Eat on the move.' One side of her face twitched. 'Leave Skavengard by sunset, or we'll all be dead.'

The others exchanged doubtful glances. This new behaviour unsettled them. Tangling with the beast had bruised her sanity and battered her body, though how badly and how deep remained to be seen.

'Well, how long can it take, now that Vika knows the route?' Aren said. The concoction had energised him; he felt a surge of irrepressible optimism. 'Skavengard is not so large that it can't be crossed in a day, and we're halfway there already.' He met Vika's gaze firmly. 'This place will *not* be our end.'

Osman let out a laugh. 'Ha! Friend, you have a lion's heart!'

'Grub wrestled a lion once,' said Grub, but was generally ignored.

'Let's all take a little of this lad's courage,' Osman carried on, as if Grub hadn't spoken. 'Vika has given us a chance! Onward, then!'

They set off at a jog as soon as dawn broke. The druidess led them, shambling rapidly ahead, her staff clicking on the flagstones. There was something wild and disordered in the way she moved, all rolling hips and jutting elbows, like an ineptly handled marionette. Her chin scabbed with dried blood and her hair a greasy tangle, she gabbled and cackled quietly in Stonespeak, in conversation with herself. Occasionally she stopped at a junction while the two voices debated, back and forth. Ruck ran tight circles around her, or gnawed restlessly at a spot on her leg which was becoming raw and bloody.

They didn't retrace their steps but struck out on a new path. Aren felt a strong and immediate sense that this was a bad decision, that they were heading the wrong way, perhaps even back towards the first island. When he mentioned it to Cade, Cade said he thought exactly the same. In fact, he was sure of it.

'Ain't that strange? I don't even know which way is up in this place, but I'm certain this direction's wrong.'

'It *is* strange,' Aren said. 'Why do we both feel that?'

Because someone or something wants us to feel that way.

Cade had the same idea at the same time. They exchanged a look, then Cade glanced at Vika, up ahead.

'Might be she knows what she's doing after all,' he said.

They couldn't suppress the feeling of wrongness, but they could stop themselves acting on it. They shut their mouths and hurried on.

'The beast knows these halls well,' Vika told them. 'For a thousand years it has roamed here, hah! From its memory, I took a map!' She tapped the side of her head with one crooked finger.

330

'Now it's in here.' She sucked her teeth and looked uncertain. 'Mostly, anyway … Sometimes …'

She trailed off and her eyes went distant.

'So you have a route out?' Osman prompted.

'Aye,' she said. 'To the last bridge, anyway. The beast's never been beyond that. Something there stops it, something bright as the sun.' She squinted as if dazzled, then dashed away the memory. 'Fah! This way!'

Later, they passed through a room with an enormous circular pit in the centre. Stairs spiralled down the edge of the pit, leading to a flooded cave far below. Here Vika stopped and drew her knife.

'I need a volunteer,' she announced.

'Reckon you can count me out already,' said Cade, eyeing the blade in her hand.

'Perhaps if you told us what we'd be volunteering *for*?' Osman suggested.

'Ah. Hmm.' She chewed her cheek again. 'To bleed you, that's what I want. Can't use mine. Too fouled with poison. That's why it didn't look too hard for Polla, mmm? Smelled her, didn't like the smell. Even servants of the Abyss can be choosy!' She cackled. 'It's our blood it smells,' she said, suddenly weary, like a schoolmistress teaching dunces.

'And you want to give our blood to it?' Osman was as worried as he was confused.

'Splash some here, splash splash. Leave it in a bowl like milk for the cat. Smells stronger on the outside, eh? Beast will come find it first.' Her eye twitched in what might have been a wink. 'We go different way. Slow it down a bit. Elsewise, beast come straight for us at sunset … *snap*!' She lunged towards Garric, fingers and thumb making a crocodile mouth, and snapped it shut in front of his face. He didn't flinch.

'Take some of mine,' he pulled back his sleeve.

'Just a splash!' Vika chuckled, raising her knife.

It soon became clear that Vika's route wasn't as direct as they'd imagined, nor was her memory as sound as they'd hoped. They diverted and detoured. Occasionally Vika threw up her hands and

331

admitted she'd led them astray, and they were forced to backtrack. The first time, it was an easily forgivable error. By the third, doubts were creeping back in, and Aren saw the others exchanging glances. Were they being played for fools by a demon and a madwoman? Was that why this path felt so wrong?

Aren began to fear they'd lose their faith in the druidess entirely and take the direction they felt was right. It would seem sensible, but it would doom them all. It was Skavengard's will that swayed them – and that was his proof they were on the right path.

He hurried up alongside Vika. 'Can you make a small detour?'

'Hmm?'

'Take us outside. Just for a few moments.'

Vika squinted at him strangely.

'We can lay some more blood there,' Aren suggested. 'Another trick to throw the beast off our trail.'

She consulted with herself in Stonespeak, then abruptly switched direction.

They were not far from the outer walls, and soon they emerged through a doorway onto the upper tier of a semicircular amphitheatre. Stone benches surrounded a stage which projected out high over the lake. The sky was grey with cloud rolling in from the west and the valley walls were close and forbidding, but from here it was possible to see the edge of the third island, bulging to their left. After spending most of the morning in the bewildering thoroughfares of the interior, it was a surprise to get a sense of where they were again.

'We're most of the way across the island already!' Aren said, almost as soon as they emerged. 'Skavengard can try to stop us, but it can't stop Vika!'

Osman was cheered by that. 'He's right! At this rate, we'll soon be there!' Grub grinned, and Fen stood up a little straighter. Only Garric gazed at him narrowly.

He knows what I'm doing, Aren thought. *They're loyal to him, they admire his strength. But he doesn't know a thing about people. People need to believe.*

He looked up at the bright smear of cloud-hidden sun and fear touched his heart. Despite his words of encouragement, it was later than he'd imagined.

Vika ambled up to him and held out her knife. 'Did what you said,' she muttered. 'Blood, please.'

The rain began soon after, and it came down hard. The empty quiet of Skavengard was filled with a steady hiss and the corridors became dim as twilight. Water dripped through cracks, spattered down stone gutters and blew in through windows to speckle the sills and floors.

Midday came and went, and they didn't stop. Vika's brew kept fatigue at bay, though they'd travelled for many hours. Fen doled out their rations and said they'd go hungry if they dallied here much longer. There were grim smiles at that. If they had to spend another night in Skavengard, hunger would be the least of their worries.

Keel didn't smile with the others. His eyes were nearly healed now, but his face was drawn and haunted, and he said little.

Presently they came upon a chamber where the roof had collapsed and smashed through the floor, so that the doorway opened to a sheer drop through the cavernous hall below onto a bed of rubble and timber. The outer wall had fallen away and grey sheets of rain blew in, setting the stone glistening.

'Well,' said Cade, surveying the hole, 'we ain't getting past that.'

Grub leaned out, hawked and spat. A blob of phlegm pendulumed from his lip, stretched and snapped. He watched it fall with close interest, then straightened up and sniffed, as if he'd proved something to himself and was well satisfied.

'What? What exactly did you learn just then?' Cade asked, irritated by his theatrics.

Grub didn't deign to answer, but swept off up the corridor instead.

'Not supposed to be like this,' Vika mumbled to herself. 'Must've happened recently, yes. Hmm. That's why the beast doesn't know it.'

'Let's go around, then,' said Garric. When Vika made no reply, he said: 'You know the way around, don't you?'

Vika frowned. 'Some of it ... Hazy ... Fading like a dream, I think ...'

'I'd take that as a no,' Cade advised morosely.

'I have rope,' Osman suggested. 'We could lower ourselves down to the rubble? The exits may be blocked but we could climb up the other side?'

'There's an overhanging ledge on the far side,' Fen pointed out. 'Nobody could get up that.'

'Then let's backtrack.' Osman was fighting to stay optimistic.

'We'll get lost!' snapped Keel. 'This accursed place will turn us about till we don't know where we are!' He rounded angrily on Vika. 'You said you knew the way!'

'I do,' said Vika. She pointed across the chasm. 'It's that way.'

'Grub has an idea.' The Skarl was leaning out of an arched window at the end of the corridor. He looked over his shoulder and grinned at them. 'Who likes to climb?'

43

Grub's idea was for them to take a precarious route along the outer wall of Skavengard, where dozens of dwellings and galleries blistered out over the lake. He led them down a weathered stone gutter pipe to the flat roof of a jutting building, then over a jumble of other roofs, some sloped and treacherous, some busy with statuary. To their right, far below, waited the weed-patched waters, restless with raindrops.

At first, the way was easy enough. Going from roof to roof carried little threat of falling, except where they were slanted and slippery, and the gaps between them were close enough to step across. But soon the roofs came to an end, with no windows to let them back inside, and the only buildings were far above. Before them was a bare expanse of brick, with nothing beneath but the cliffs and a long drop to the lake.

Grub and Garric went to the lip of the rooftop to examine the way ahead. 'I suppose we go back, then,' said Fen, before they'd even got there. Aren wondered at the nervous haste in her voice.

Grub ignored her. 'Grub can see a window. Take us back inside, past room with broken floor.' He pointed one thick finger downwards. 'Look. Ledge there, follows wall, passes below window. Grub can climb up to window, drop rope. You all climb after.'

Fen and Aren came up alongside and looked over. 'That's not a ledge!' Fen cried. 'It's barely big enough to stand on!'

That was an exaggeration. It was an ornamental shelf, still marked with fragments of scrollwork along its edge, and it would have been wide enough to walk along comfortably if it had been lying on the ground. But this high up, it seemed awfully narrow.

Keel joined Garric as he studied the ledge. 'I'll not go back, Garric,' he muttered. 'I'll take my chances with the water. And I know you were never one for turning back, either.'

'No,' said Garric. 'No, I never was.' He straightened. 'The Skarl is right. We'll climb.'

Aren watched Fen's face turn ashen. He looked away before she could notice him.

The ledge was only a dozen feet below the level of the roof and could be reached by climbing down the guttering. Grub went first, a rope coiled over his shoulder. He stepped onto the ledge and loped along it, heedless of the drop. When he got to the spot beneath the window, he climbed up again, scaling the wall with steady confidence until he disappeared through the window.

'By the depths, do all Skarls climb so well?' Keel asked.

Garric was watching the window, his face thoughtful. 'Aye, he made that look easy, didn't he?'

'Bet you're glad you didn't leave us behind after all,' Cade piped up. 'Not so much baggage now, are we?'

'Shut your mouth, boy.'

A rope sailed through the window, uncurling in the air to slap against the ledge. A moment later, Grub's head poked out and he beckoned to them.

'Come on, then!'

One by one they followed him onto the ledge. Vika went first, and Ruck was handed down to her. At the other side, the hound was tied into a blanket sling and hauled up with some difficulty, and a lot of snarling and bumping. Keel went after, then Osman. They moved nervously, pressing close to the wall, rain-soaked and awkward with their packs and weapons hampering them. Aren watched as they inched along, fearing to see them fall at any moment. But they didn't fall, and when they reached the rope they climbed it with ease, their muscles lent strength by Vika's empowering brew.

'I'll go next,' said Cade. 'Waiting's worse.'

Aren was twice as tense watching Cade go, even though they'd climbed rocks and cliffs all their lives. Cade took a moment to steady himself on the ledge, then side-footed carefully along until he reached the rope.

'Ain't as bad as it looks!' he called back to Aren. He took hold of the rope and climbed up to the others.

Garric went next, and he showed no fear; but when he was halfway along, a small section of the ledge broke off beneath his boot. Fen gasped as he threw his weight forwards and crashed up against the wall, gripping it tight. His dangling foot found a place on the ledge again and he continued on, slower than before. It was only when he reached the rope that Aren let out the breath he'd been holding.

'Have a care! The ledge is weak!' Garric shouted back to them. Then he climbed up in his turn.

Fen blanched even whiter at that and looked like she was going to be ill. 'You go,' she told Aren.

'No, you go next,' he told her. For he saw her fear, and he knew she might not set foot on that ledge at all if there was no one there to make her.

'I'll come after you,' she said, too casual.

'No, you won't,' he said. 'You'll go back and try to find another way round. You'll get lost, and the sun will go down, and you'll die.'

She looked like a trapped animal. If she could have, she might have run. He'd stayed till last to make sure she didn't.

'I'll be right behind you,' he told her, and his tone left no room for argument. Either she had to admit she was frightened out of her wits, or take the plunge. In the end, the ledge was the least terrible option.

Aren offered a hand. 'I'll lower you down to the ledge.'

'You will *not*,' she snapped, giving him a hot glare. 'I'll climb down on my own.'

Aren stepped back, raising his hands. 'Whatever you want.'

She looked over the side of the roof, her breathing fast. She swallowed to wet a dry throat.

'You won't fall,' he said, his voice calm. 'The ledge is wide enough, and it's only water at the bottom.'

'I don't need your help,' she said through gritted teeth. 'Stop talking.'

She climbed gingerly over the side, and Aren went to the lip of the roof to watch her descend. It was slow going, even for such a short way. Every new handhold and foothold took a gathering of courage, a jerky lunge, a few moments of recovery. But she got one foot on the ledge, then the other, and clung to the wall as if magnetised.

'Freckles! What taking so long? You be here by sunset?' Grub called from the window.

Aren closed his eyes in exasperation and Fen muttered something foul, but her anger got her moving again. Inch by agonising inch, she shuffled out along the rainswept ledge, her cheek to the stone.

Now it was Aren's turn, and when it came to it, he felt little of the calm he'd shown to Fen. As he climbed out over the edge, his mind was filled with visions of a fall: the slip, the tumble, the wind rushing past his ears as he screamed. *It's only water at the bottom*, he'd told her; but it was far enough that the impact might break an arm or a rib, leaving him unable to swim, flailing helplessly as he was dragged under by his sodden clothes. Or perhaps he'd survive and swim away uninjured, with a choice between taking on Skavengard again – alone – or returning to the gate to face the dreadknights. And if they weren't waiting there to kill him, then the mountains were: he'd likely freeze or starve before he found help.

So don't fall, he told himself. *Just don't fall.*

He stepped onto the ledge and shuffled along after Fen. His hands were wet and cold from the rain and the wind pulled at his pack, trying to turn him away from the wall. The stone felt unsteady beneath his boots, as if trying to break beneath his weight. He told himself it was his imagination.

If he took tiny steps, he wouldn't trip. And if he didn't trip, he wouldn't tumble. The ledge was *wide*, he told himself. Wide enough.

If it held.

Ahead of him, Fen had stopped moving. She'd reached the point where the ledge had broken under Garric. It was a gap scarcely wider than Aren's forearm was long, but it brought her to a halt. He shuffled up alongside and found her panting with fright.

'You just have to step over it, Fen,' he said gently. 'It's not far.'

She shook her head mutely.

'You can do it,' he told her. 'And since you can't stay here, you really have to.' Then a thought occurred to him. 'Remember the night we met? You ran across a rope bridge then. A rickety old rope bridge, across a chasm, in a storm.'

'There were dreadknights behind us then,' she said. 'It was different. Ropes to hold on to.'

'It *wasn't* different,' he said. 'You could do it then, you can do it now. You need me to put on a scary helmet and wave a sword to get you on your way?'

She snorted half a laugh, surprised by the joke. Then a gust of wind threw rain against them, and she closed her eyes and whimpered and pressed herself closer to the wall.

'Fen,' said Aren. 'Look at me.'

She met his eyes, and for the first time Aren noticed hers were green.

'I'm going to take hold of your pack,' he said. 'I'll make sure you don't tip back. You step over the gap.'

'No!' she said, as if the very idea alarmed her. Then she relaxed a fraction. 'No, I'll do it myself. Just … stay there.'

Aren nodded. She steeled herself and stepped over the gap so hastily and clumsily that she almost overbalanced and had to grab on to the wall again.

'That's it,' said Aren. 'Worst is over.'

She shuffled on, towards the rope. Aren stepped over the gap with care. As he did, he caught a glimpse of the drop to the water below and his stomach turned.

'Come on, Aren!' Cade called down from the window. 'This ain't nothing to Shuck's Cliff over the Wreake!'

The memory brought a little smile to Aren's face. A sunny day, two boys daring each other to foolish risks. A terrifying climb and the triumph at the top. To fall from Shuck's Cliff would have been lethal, but they were boys, and death happened to other people. It didn't happen then. It wouldn't happen now.

He took a breath, flexed his freezing hands and got moving again.

A slow agony of time went by, marked by the sound of thumping hearts and scraping boots. Fen reached the rope first, but when Aren arrived alongside her, she was still looking up at the window where Garric and Keel waited.

'Go on,' said Aren. 'Nearly there.'

Fen ran her hands over the wall in front of her, tested it with her fingertips. The years had roughened it till there were deep trenches in the mortar. 'Think I'll climb,' she said.

'Take the rope,' said Aren. 'It's easier.'

She gave a small shake of her head. 'Grub climbed the wall,' she said.

'Of course he climbed it: he's half spider. But it's simpler to take the—'

'I want to climb!' she snapped. She found a handhold, dug the toe of her boot in a crack between the stones and lifted herself off the ledge and up.

'What are you doing, Fen? Take the rope!' Garric called. She ignored him, as she ignored the rope dangling next to her.

Aren followed her progress upwards, perplexed. He'd thought she was simply terrified of heights, but it was something more complicated than that. She was afraid to fall, but more afraid to take the rope she could climb to safety.

What happened to you? he thought.

There was a loud crack, a jolt through his legs, and the ledge broke off beneath his feet. He fell backwards with a cry, the void yawning to receive him, iron-hard water waiting below.

Instinct took over. His flailing hand found the rope and clamped on.

He swung out along the wall, tipping and turning wildly, hanging on with all his strength. Only his desperate grip kept him from the fall. He banged against the stone but hardly felt the pain; it gave him the chance to slap his other hand onto the rope. He held tight as he was dragged along the wall on the backswing, tearing his coat at shoulder and elbow, until he finally scraped to a stop.

'Aren!'

It was Garric, his voice deep, damaged, commanding. The sound of it brought him back from panic. It might have been the first time the Hollow Man had called him by name since the moment they met. Above him and to the right, Fen still clung to the wall; above her, Garric and Cade stared down at him from the window, Cade afraid, Garric stony.

'Aren,' Garric said again, now he had his attention. 'I've not brought you this far to see you die now. Climb the bloody rope.'

Aren let out a shuddering breath, dug his toes into the wall and stabilised himself. He still felt strong, thanks to Vika's brew. There was no danger of his muscles betraying him. He had the rope. He wouldn't fall.

But there was Fen, flat against the wall, her ponytail a wet draggle. The rope hung near her shoulder, within easy reach, but she was paralysed. And though he wanted a solid floor under his feet more than anything in the world right now, he wouldn't climb past and leave her there.

'Fen!' he called.

She didn't reply.

'Fen, you have to take the rope.'

Her throat moved as she swallowed. The slightest shift in her gaze showed she'd heard him.

'Fen. Think of all that's ahead of you. Think of all the things you'll do. On the other side of this, there's a lifetime waiting. You just have to beat this moment. A little bit more, that's all. It'll be over before you know it. Take the rope.'

A flicker of her eyelids. Slowly, she moved her arm. Took another handhold on the wall. Pulled herself up. Found another, and another. She climbed, spurning the rope, spurning Garric's hand reaching down from the window. She climbed to the sill, and they stood back as she pulled herself over and disappeared inside.

Cade stuck his head out again. 'Joha's sake, Aren! Are *you* gonna climb the damned rope?'

Aren climbed to the window, where Garric and Cade helped him in. Standing there dripping among them, he could have cried with relief. Instead his eyes found Fen, who was adjusting her bow and her pack.

'I knew you could do it,' he said.

She gave him a look of pure hate and spat on the floor.

'There's gratitude!' said Cade, baffled. Aren was stung, but did his best not to show it.

'Grub think *he* deserve a little gratitude, too,' Grub said sulkily.

'Well, you have mine,' said Osman. He put a hand on Grub's shoulder – Grub jumped at his touch – and addressed the others. 'Skarl or not, this man's shown his worth, I say. We would have been lost without Grub.'

'That's so,' said Keel. 'You have my thanks, too.'

'Aye, and mine,' said Garric, grudgingly.

Grub beamed, eager as a praised puppy. 'No need for thanks! Grub happy to help!'

'We should go,' said Vika. 'The days burn fast in Skavengard.' She pointed confidently with the tip of her staff. 'That way.'

44

By late afternoon they'd reached the bridge between the second island and the third. They barely slowed as they crossed it, but Cade gave a whoop of joy as they stepped off the other side, and a ripple of relieved laughter passed through the group. It began to feel as though they'd broken the back of Skavengard. However it tried to turn them, Vika was equal to it. All they had to do was have faith.

They began to talk of cool, clear mountain streams and making camp beneath the stars, as if the Ostenbergs were a gentle meadow instead of a barren and treacherous wasteland. Even Keel cracked a joke or two, and that lifted them all. He'd been a different person since he laid eyes on the beast, and this was the first sign of the man they knew before. His recovery, small as it was, diminished the threat of sunset.

But though they went swift and sure across the third island, darkness was catching them fast; and Skavengard wasn't done with them yet.

'We are close,' said Vika as she led them through an abandoned shrine. Faded murals depicted Azra the Despoiler, Vaspis the Malcontent and Prinn the Ragged Mummer. They represented strength, cunning, art, but also war, discontent and deceit. Aren wondered which the worshippers had prayed for.

'Not close enough yet,' said Garric.

'We have been delayed and the hour has run away from us,' Vika said, 'but we will be there before nightfall if the way holds true.'

'Then let us hope it does,' said Osman, glancing out of a window.

The rain had stopped, leaving the castle dank and dripping. The sun glared red between the ceiling of cloud and the mountain tops, bathing them in eerie light. It would be a near thing, to reach the bridge in time, but they were already going as fast as Vika could manage, and they could hardly leave her behind.

They emerged from the shrine into a tall, narrow chamber with three galleries running round its walls, decorated with grotesques. It might once have been a magnificent library, but there were no shelves now, nor books, only cool white walls and echoes. As they entered, a whisper of displaced air made Aren look up, and to his surprise he saw something falling. Falling fast towards him.

Suddenly he was shoved aside, and he went skidding and rolling along the flagstones as something smashed on the spot where he'd been standing. He raised himself on his elbows, shocked, and the shattered snarling face of a gargoyle glared at him. It had toppled from the gallery overhead.

It was Garric that had pushed him. Garric who'd saved his life again.

Garric drew his blade, eyes searching the galleries as he backed into the room to get a better view. The others took their cue from him, pulling out blades and bows.

'That was no accident,' he growled. 'Show yourself!'

Aren let Cade pull him to his feet, scanning the gloomy heights of the chamber as he rose. Were there people moving about up there? It was hard to tell.

The doors at either end of the chamber slammed shut.

'Who's there?' Garric demanded.

Grub tugged on the door they'd just come through, to no avail. 'Grub doesn't see a lock,' he said. 'But door stay shut.'

Now there was definite movement in the galleries overhead, but somehow whoever was up there remained elusive in the dim light. Cade tugged hard at Aren's sleeve.

'What is it?' he hissed in irritation, still trying to catch sight of the figures in the galleries. Then he saw the look on Cade's face and realised it was serious.

Cade pointed to one side of the library, where sunlight slanted through a row of tall, narrow arches to fall against the wall. Their shadows were cast there in stark black against the smooth white stone. Their shadows, and other shadows besides.

'They're here,' said Cade in a terrified whisper.

Aren was sorry he'd ever doubted his friend now. The shadows were just as he'd described, slender courtly people in strange robes. But these people were not dancing or gossiping or sipping drinks. They rose into sight at either end of the hall as if they'd been crouched in wait just below the range of the light. They had long, thin knives in their hands, and as they flowed silently towards the intruders' silhouettes, there was murder in their movements.

'The ghosts of Skavengard,' Vika said. 'Those who died here when the beast was unleashed. They would see us stay here with them for ever.'

'They're shadows!' Garric snarled. 'What can shadows do?'

'We must leave this place!' the druidess cried. 'Break the door down!'

They ran through the library towards the door on the far side. A section of stone banister tumbled down and smashed to powder nearby. Aren was halfway across the room when he felt a stinging blaze of pain on his cheek. He put his hand there and his palm came away damp and red. He stared at his blood in bewilderment, then at the wall where the shadows moved.

As Keel's running silhouette passed by, one of the ghosts struck at it, quick as a snake. Aren saw a shallow slash appear on the Bitterbracker's pack, parting the canvas there even though nothing had touched him. A moment later, Fen cried out, and as she raised her arm, they saw a long cut had been scored through her coat, from her wrist to her elbow.

'That's impossible!' Osman gasped.

They had no time for his denials. Garric and Keel came up against the door on the far side of the hall and put their shoulders to it. It gave a little, but then it was shoved closed again.

'The bastards are *holding* it!' Keel said, and they slammed against it again, with no better result.

Cade yelled and clutched his thigh as he was struck, too. The shadows circled like predators, darting in and out. Though their blows were glancing, they cut deep enough to bleed, and deep enough to pierce a vein or an eye if they found the right spot. Aren and Fen staggered this way and that, holding up their arms to defend themselves from their invisible opponents. Another piece of masonry crashed down, and this one nearly struck Grub on the head. Ruck dashed about wildly, barking, snapping at the air.

'We must fight shadow with shadow!' Vika said. 'Use your silhouettes, hmm? Fight back!'

'What madness is this now?' Osman demanded. 'Shadow with shadow?'

But Aren saw her meaning and, caught up in a wild moment, he cried: 'I'll show you!' Then, with his eyes on the wall, he raised his sword and swung it at the air. His silhouette copied him and the shadows darted back from it, retreating beyond his reach.

Now Fen, who saw what he'd done, raised her bow and drew the arrow she had nocked and ready. 'Dodge this!' she spat, and let fly down the length of the library. Her arrow was aimed at nothing, but its shadow streaked along the wall, flitting between the pillars of the tall window-arches. The ghosts ducked out of the way, but one was too slow and the arrow's shadow buried itself in his forehead. The real arrow lost all momentum and clattered shadowless to the floor as the ghost crumpled, dissolving with a distant shriek.

'So the dead can be killed again!' Garric cried in triumph. 'Spread out! Send them back to the Shadowlands!'

They slashed here and there, and their shadows did the same, but it was clumsy and dangerous work. Their eyes were on the wall and not on each other, and more than once a sweeping blade almost hit one of their companions. The ghosts, for their part, were nimble. They hovered at bay, darting in when they could. Occasionally one was struck and dissolved like the first, but more appeared, rising up from the darkness.

Aren took another cut, this one across the back of his upper arm. He saw Grub stabbing at the air, blood running into his eyes from a wound on his shaven scalp. Garric and Keel, fighting back to back, flinched and swore as they were cut and cut again.

Soon they were all bleeding from shallow wounds, and still the ghosts came on. They might not have the force to strike a deadly blow across the Divide, but enough small ones would end in the same result. Cade slashed here and there with his knife, panting in panic. Aren spared a moment to check his friend was holding up and almost tripped over Ruck, who was whirling around their feet.

It was then that he realised Ruck was entirely unhurt. There wasn't a scratch on her. Why had they not struck her, even once?

He raised his head and looked over at the wall. She was low enough that her body didn't block the light from the windows. She cast no shadow among the ghosts. And if there was no shadow to strike ...

'Get down on the floor!' he shouted. 'Get below the light!'

He threw himself down and his shadow disappeared from the wall an instant before one of the ghosts lunged at him with a dagger. The others stared at him as if he was insane, but Garric bellowed 'Do as he says!' They flung themselves to the floor, and as their shadows sank out of sight, an angry hiss rose up from the ghosts.

Aren went scrambling across the flagstones towards Fen. 'Oil and tinder! Quick!'

Fen shucked off her pack and dug through it. The shadows on the wall prowled, hunting anxiously, but no one was within their reach.

Garric crawled over, his collar wet with blood. 'What's your thinking, boy?'

'Ever seen what happens to your shadow in firelight?' he said as he took a clay flask of oil from Fen. He pulled off the stopper, tore a rag from his shredded coat and stuffed it in. It was a trick he'd learned from Kuhn, his father's bodyguard, and it had led to a particularly shameful adventure when he'd accidentally burned down a barn and never admitted it. 'Light it,' he told Fen, holding it out to her.

Fen was already striking sparks into her tinderbox, trying to ignite the small wad of kindling there.

'The doors are held fast! Do you want to burn us alive?' Keel said as he saw what they were doing.

Garric held his hand up to his friend. He studied Aren closely, and there was something new in his gaze, something that wasn't loathing or disgust. Something that gave Aren a surprising and unwanted flush of pleasure, even in this most dire situation. Something like respect.

'Let him try,' Garric said.

'Oh, Nine, hurry up!' Cade wailed. 'He's here! Azh Mat Jaal!'

A wave of cold washed over Aren as the Sorcerer King slunk into the library. He was taller and thinner than the others, hunched and robed, a seven-pointed crown upon his brow. The other ghosts drew back, retreating to the corners as he loomed larger, growing in size as he approached. Fen chipped frantically with her flint and steel, striking sparks, and the tinder caught at last. She blew on it to give it life as Aren put the end of the rag into the smouldering kindling.

Azh Mat Jaal searched the room slowly, as if he knew they were hiding but not where. He lifted one hand, clawlike fingers cupped as if cradling a globe. Then he began to squeeze.

A crushing force began to build around Aren's jaw and head, vicelike, inexorable. At first it was uncomfortable, then painful, then excruciating. The pressure increased until his cheekbones felt they must shatter, his jaw break, his skull crack like an egg. The others were afflicted by the same force, holding their heads, suppressing screams.

Finally, the rag caught fire. With the last sensible thought in his mind, Aren threw the flask of oil. It shattered on the floor and burst into flame, and suddenly, between the ghosts and the intruders, there was an inferno.

A loud screech echoed through the chamber and the pressure on their heads was released. Azh Mat Jaal retreated from the flames, his hands before his face, his shadow thrown this way and that by the restless, changing light. The other ghosts fled in panic to the edges of the library. The flickering, jumping fire tore at them as they passed, flinging their shapes back and forth, making them wail and howl and paw at themselves.

'The door!' Vika cried. 'Now, while they are weakened!'

Keel shoulder-charged the door with reckless force and it flew open, sending him sprawling into the room beyond. The others followed his lead, scrambling through the heat and poisonous

348

smoke, out of the library and off through the cold and darkening halls. But however fast they went, wherever there was light the ghosts gathered, pooling like ink in their wake.

'Which way, Vika?' Garric demanded, over and over. 'Which way?'

But Vika didn't know. In the confusion of their escape, she'd become lost. She led them onwards anyway, jerking and twitching and mumbling to herself, and with no better option, they followed.

We are close, she'd said. Close to the bridge, close to freedom, and yet it felt so far away now.

Vika staggered to a halt and Garric's face became taut with anger. As Aren caught them up, he saw why.

That scalloped ceiling. That mural.

'We've gone in a circle,' Osman said.

As they stood there panting, the shadows began to swarm in. They rose from the floor, deathly memories of the living, with their tall headdresses and elaborate robes and their knives. Foremost among them was their king, dark and terrible as he drew himself up to his full height.

Aren felt his stomach sink. There was no outrunning them. Azh Mat Jaal raised a hand, fingers curled, and as he began to squeeze them together, Aren felt a familiar, dreadful pressure building behind his eyes ...

The last light of the sun flared and died on the peaks, and the room dimmed sharply. From the heights of Skavengard, a great shriek heralded the waking of the beast. The ghosts cringed and fled at the sound, until only the shadow of the Sorcerer King remained, tall against the stone, emanating hatred. For a long moment he stood there, clawed hand squeezing tighter, loth to release his prey. Then he swept his cloak around himself and stepped from the light into nothingness, leaving Aren panting in relief as the pressure on his skull receded.

His relief did not last long. There was a distant boom as the gate to the beast's lair was thrown open. They'd outlasted the ghosts of Skavengard, but it was a poor reprieve, for something far worse was coming.

Vika's eyes were closed in deep concentration. She leaned on her staff as if she'd fall without it, sorting through the fragments of her addled mind. They heard the beast begin its rampage and knew their only hope of escape lay in their guide remembering the way out before the doom of Skavengard found them. It was a slender thread to hang their lives upon.

'Vika!' It was Fen, crouching by a doorway on the far side of the hall.

'Leave her be!' Osman was uncharacteristically sharp. 'She needs to think!'

Fen ignored him. 'Vika. I think this is one of the marks you've been following.'

Vika's head snapped around, her eyes flying open. She shambled quickly over to Fen, who was pointing at a small symbol etched in the stone, invisible to all but the keenest eyes. Fen's eyes, it seemed, were keen indeed.

'Polla's druidsign,' said Vika, and suddenly she cackled. 'Fortune smiles on us yet! We have the path! This way!'

One last push. One last effort. Powered by the potion coursing through their veins, they hurried on. Doorways flitted past to their left and right in the grim twilight. Narrow corridors twisted and turned as they headed down back ways. Vika led with confidence again, following the druidsigns, crying out 'There!' and 'There!' as she spotted them. It was slower than before, for at every junction they had to search for the marks, but any progress was better than none.

They were running through a pillared atrium, open to the sky and dripping with the recent rains, when they heard a titanic shriek of outrage echoing across the valley.

'Reckon it just found out we ain't where it thought we were,' Cade said.

'It's found the sanctum, and found it empty,' said Vika. 'Now it will follow the scent of our blood.'

They fled from the pounding that followed, out of the atrium and down a set of spiral stairs. The beast boomed and raged behind them, closer and closer.

It wouldn't catch them, though. Believing that was the only thing that kept the strength in Aren's legs. When they escaped Skavengard there'd be no pursuit, no more enemies on their tail, only a straight shot to safety and liberation. Then he and Cade could make their own choices, beholden to nobody.

I'll have that freedom, he swore to himself. *No one will control me again. Not through false promises and lies, nor chains, nor force of arms. When I die, I'll die free. That's more than my father could say.*

Another distant scream of outrage sent shivers up his back.

'Found the blood we left at the pit, hasn't it?' panted Vika.

And it knows it's been tricked, Aren thought.

Running, gasping, the clatter of scabbards and the rustle of cloaks. The dark closed in on Skavengard. They heard another scream in the distance, and Aren knew it had found *his* blood, left at the amphitheatre on the south side of the central island. This time the chill he felt was deeper, more profound, as if something unutterably cold and endless as the void had brushed past him. It was enough to make him stumble and clutch at his chest, and though it passed a moment later, Aren knew the beast had tasted him, and now he was marked.

The druidess had been wise; the beast had been deceived by false trails, sent zigzagging around the island. But now there were no more diversions to delay it. The sound of its pounding increased in volume and a foul breeze began to blow.

'It's reached the third island!' Keel said.

'Take heart! It has yet to find us!' Osman said.

'Grub don't know about you,' said the Skarl, raising an arm slashed by shadow-daggers, 'but he leaving pretty good blood trail.'

They rounded a corner and found themselves at the bottom of a long, wide stairway, stretching many storeys upwards. There were landings flanked by doors on either side, with time-smoothed statues of black stone standing between them. Visible at the top was a pinched arch, and Vika's face lit up at the sight of it.

'The bridge!' she called.

As if in answer, the beast screamed, an overlapping howl from a legion of mouths; and they knew they had no time left.

They surged up the steps, thighs burning, for even Vika's art had its limits. The wind gathered around them, growing in force as the air thickened and became resistant, and the choking stench of the beast forced its way into their nostrils and down their throats.

It slammed and crashed and raged its way towards them, tearing through Skavengard in search of its victims. White-faced in the moonlight, eyes fixed on the arch, they climbed and climbed as the wind became a hurricane.

Grub led the pack up the stairs; he had no interest in waiting for Vika any more. Keel was hard on his heels, driven by fear, and Aren and Cade came after. They laboured up the last steps and saw the bridge before them. It was a long, wide tunnel through the air, with curving walls and teardrop-shaped windows along its length. Midway across was a huge circular gateway, its surface inlaid with stark silver runes that troubled the eye.

The beast howled, so close now that they heard the cracking of jaws and clashing of teeth, and they put their heads down and sprinted as the bridge started to shake around them. The runes began to glow, their light growing fiercer with every moment. Grub raced through without hesitation, Keel close behind him. Cade's arms pumped and his cheeks puffed, his gaze fixed on his goal, and he and Aren ran through it, too.

Safe! Safe, surely! These symbols must keep the beast at bay, like the circle in the sanctum.

Instinct told Aren he should keep running, but it felt like cowardice, so he slowed and glanced back to check on his companions. He saw Fen, Garric right behind her and Osman following. Vika had fallen behind. She staggered and stumbled frantically, jerking and lunging as she fought to keep up.

She couldn't. Her disordered body betrayed her, her staff slipped on the flagstones and she tumbled in a heap.

'Vika!' Aren yelled. The hurricane stole his voice but Osman saw his face. He turned his head and saw Vika lying there, Ruck barking frantically at her side. Without a moment's hesitation, he went back for her.

The screams of the creature reached deafening pitch as Fen and Garric raced through the ring of wards. Now they were so bright they hurt, and Aren had to cover his eyes with an arm.

'Move, boy!' Garric shouted as he approached, but Aren just pointed over his shoulder. When Garric saw Vika had fallen, he blanched.

Osman had pulled her to her feet by now and shoved her back into motion. Fighting against the wind, they hurried for the gateway, where the glare was so intense that it was like looking into the sun, and they were reduced to black shadows limned in burning light. Ruck rushed through and whirled, barking madly at the beast they could hear crashing up the stairs.

'*Run!*' Aren screamed over the wind. '*Ruuuuuun!*'

The beast reared up at the top of the stairs. Aren saw nothing more than a hint of its form in the blinding glare, but it was enough to root him in place. He glimpsed a flailing monstrosity, yawning with mouths and mouths within mouths, propelled by massive tentacles that coiled slimily around it like a thrashing nest of eels.

It boiled into the corridor and shrieked as it was struck by the glow from the wards; but though it burned and wailed in agony, still it tried to fight its way onwards. Aren was transfixed, his tearing eyes locked on the dread shadow battling against the light, as the rotten wind blew against him and made him want to gag.

Osman and Vika struggled through the hurricane, Osman with his arm round the druidess, propelling her forward. They stumbled out of the blaze of light, gaining form and features as they neared, and Aren heard himself screaming at them again to run, run, *run*!

A barbed tentacle came snaking from the whiteness. It wrapped round Osman's body, once, twice, and then buried its daggerlike tip into his shoulder. He was pulled suddenly to a halt, mere feet from the ring of runes. Vika staggered onwards, carried past Garric and Aren by her own momentum.

Osman's eyes met Aren's, and Aren saw pleading there, as if someone, *anyone* could avert his fate now. Aren and Garric lunged towards him, reaching out to pull him through.

Then he was wrenched away like a rag doll, yanked back down the corridor towards the terrible shadow at the top of the stairs. The beast screamed and plunged out of sight, and Osman was gone.

Garric and Aren stumbled to a halt, numb, staring along the bridge as the light dimmed and the beast's cries fell to silence.

In exchange for one of you, I will let the others go free.

Skavengard was behind them. But the beast had exacted its price after all.

45

On the far side of the bridge there were pillared corridors, and steps, and smooth-faced statues in the lanternlight. Aren barely saw them. They passed through the dark of the mountain without a word, their hearts heavy as lead, and before long they came to a gate wrought with surpassing craftsmanship that guarded the way to the outside. There they paused, waiting for Vika to deal with whatever sorceries were laid upon it, but she simply motioned at them to go on. They turned the handle and pulled it open.

'Easier from the inside, hmm?' she mumbled as she shuffled through.

They emerged into a glassy night, the stars sharp as crystal, the Sisters crescents in the sky. A winding path took them through a narrow channel in the rock onto a pebbly slope. The folded mountains rose around them, snow-capped and silent; a natural silence at last, not the oppressive hush of Skavengard.

They saw nothing ahead to cheer them, and when they looked back, they could no longer find the path through the rock that had brought them here. There was no sign of the dreadknights, or any other pursuit. An immense weariness was settling into their bones as Vika's brew wore off, but they all wanted to put some distance between themselves and that accursed castle. By unspoken consent they trudged on, breath steaming the air, black thoughts swarming in their minds.

The shock of Osman's death was beginning to fade, and with it the protective numbness that had kept Aren going. He brushed against the fringes of the grief that lurked in wait. The others, who'd died at the hands of the dreadknights, had been strangers. Osman was different. He'd been a man of kindness and compassion, who'd treated Aren and Cade with respect and friendship from the start. Aren had only known him a short while, but that was enough to feel his loss.

'Chalk another one up to you, boy,' Garric snarled as he passed Aren on the slope.

Aren came to a halt, his boots scuffing the gravel. He stared at Garric's back as he made his way downhill. The casual cruelty of that comment stunned him.

'Ignore him,' said Cade.

But he couldn't. Something fractured inside and set him to boiling, turned his grief to scalding heat.

'Garric!' he shouted.

Garric heard the challenge in his voice. He stopped, turned his head slowly. The others slowed to a halt around them, sensing the confrontation to come.

'Aren, what are you doing?' Cade murmured, shuffling his feet nervously.

But Aren was past warning now. Osman's death was the tipping point and he'd be gods-damned if he'd suffer any more of Garric's scorn. Not after what they'd all just been through.

'Tarvi,' he said, the name an accusation. 'Varla. Otten. Dox. Osman.' He swallowed against the pain of the memory. 'Not my fault. *Yours.*'

Garric turned to face him, fury and death in his eyes. Aren knew he was close to the edge, that they were all ready to break. He shouldn't push any further. It was dangerous to push this man.

But he *wanted* to push.

'I didn't ask you to come for me,' he said. 'I don't even know who you *are*! But Osman was a better man than you'll ever be, I know that much. And now he's dead.'

Garric was turning back up the slope towards him now. Cade shrank from his side and Aren saw what was coming, but he refused to run from it.

'I asked nothing of him, and I asked nothing of you!' Aren spat.

'His death is not on my shoulders. He died following you! A *lot* of people die following y—'

Stars exploded across his eyes as Garric's fist slammed into his jaw. The force of it made him reel and he fell to one knee. He blinked, gasped, let his head clear. Then he got back to his feet.

Garric hulked before him, face red, eyes bulging with rage. But Aren was beyond fear now. The blow hadn't broken him, but hardened him instead. 'That's the best you can do, you coward bastard?' he sneered.

Garric punched him again, and then again, and then he gave up all pretence of restraint and began raining blows down. Lights detonated in Aren's head. His ears rang and thought evaporated in a dizzy whirl as he was struck over and over. Instinctively he tried to protect himself with his arms, but he could only flail clumsily. At last, his balance failed him and he stumbled to his knees, but Garric seized him by the front of his coat and hauled him back up again.

'*Garric!*'

It was Keel's voice, snapping through the chaos. Sharp enough to stop the assault, but not enough for Garric to let him go. When Aren's swaying vision settled down again, he found himself face to grizzled face with the old warrior, close enough to smell his sweat and breath. He looked ready to burst with hate.

Aren's cheek and ear and eye stung with pain. His lip was thickening and his jaw felt like it had been knocked loose from his skull. He gathered his scattered thoughts, moved his tongue about his mouth experimentally.

'You think hitting me makes it otherwise?' he croaked. 'You're their leader. Take some responsibility.'

Garric threw him to the ground in disgust. Aren went to his knees, skinning his hands on the pebbly slope. He heard Garric's boots crunching as he stamped away down the hill.

He could have let him go. He didn't want more punishment. But it wasn't finished, and he wouldn't end this on his knees.

'Garric!' he shouted, through lips drooling with bloody spittle. He hauled himself to his feet and stood there, swaying. 'I'm not done with you yet!'

Garric swung about with a ring of steel and his blade was in his hand, the final argument of his anger. Ruck barked in agitation. Then another blade sang out and Keel stepped in front of Aren, his sword raised to Garric.

'Joha's sake, have you lost your senses? He's just a boy!'

Garric was trembling with rage, facing his friend with the others frozen in horrified tableau around them. His every muscle was taut. Temper and violence had robbed him of reason, and he looked like he might actually attack. For a dozen heartbeats they hovered on the edge of battle, but then the madness passed from Garric's face and sense returned. He sheathed his sword with one dismissive thrust. Keel stepped aside and sheathed his own warily.

'You talk of responsibility,' Garric said to Aren. 'I'll tell you something of that. There's no man, living or dead, I wish I could have killed more than your father. But we were close as brothers once. In that time I swore an oath, that if ever he or his were in peril, I would do all in my power to see them safe. And though I came to loathe him, I have honoured that oath. Would that it had cost my life, and not the five that have fallen.'

'Who was my father to you?' Aren demanded. His eye was swelling shut and his puffy lips made the words indistinct and weak, but he didn't care.

'That I won't say, and you should be glad of it. Keep your illusions. You'll be happier.'

'I don't *want* illusions! I want the truth! Why did he die? Why was I imprisoned? Why are there dreadknights after me?'

Immediately he knew he'd said something wrong. It was on Garric's face: the flicker of surprise, a moment of recalculation behind his eyes. Fen and Keel exchanged a glance, so they knew as well. And suddenly Aren did, too, and the realisation doused the heat in him.

'They were never after me at all, were they?' he said to Garric. 'They were after *you*.'

Garric's expression softened in sorrow, and he sagged. 'Aye,' he said. 'Now you see.' He was about to say something else, but it became a sigh of resignation. He had no words that would do

357

anything but make it worse, so he turned and walked away down the moonlit slope.

Aren, mind spinning with the implications, set off after him. Keel put out a hand to stop him.

'Leave him be. He's grieving, too. Walk with me, and I'll give you what answers I can.'

Aren wavered, but Keel was firm and calm, and in the end Aren went with him. The sting had been pulled from the confrontation. He didn't feel like chasing Garric down, and doubted he'd get any response if he did.

'Come on,' said Keel, putting a hand on Aren's back. 'The rest of you, keep going. Fen'll find us a place to rest. We'll need time to recover from Vika's brew, if it's aught like the last time.'

Cade looked reluctant to walk on with his friend in such a state, but Vika led him away, Ruck at their heels. Fen and Grub followed, leaving Keel and Aren alone on the bleak slope.

Aren looked up at Lyssa, her soft light pinched by his steadily closing eye. His face burned like fire and his neck seemed half broken, yet he felt more of a man now than he had an hour ago. He'd stood up for himself, taken a beating and got back on his feet again. The boy who'd been pushed around by Sora's brothers in the Shoal Point alleys was buried today. It was Garric who'd lost here, not him. The pain was nothing compared to that.

'Anything broken?' Keel asked.

Aren wiped blood from his upper lip, sniffed back more and shook his head.

'He's got his reasons for how he treats you. Doesn't excuse him, but still.'

Aren said nothing to that.

The others were out of earshot, so they began to follow them down the hill towards a crease in the land that would take them eastwards. Aren wondered about the dreadknights. Had they given up, or were they hunting the Ostenbergs for signs of their quarry even now?

Their *true* quarry. Garric.

You really think the moons and the stars revolve around you. Cade's words, spoken back in the mine. *Like your life is a bard's tale with you at the centre. What if it ain't, though? What if all this had nothing to do with you?*

'Salt Fork was the start of it,' Keel said. 'Course, it goes further back to when me and Garric met, and further still beyond; but a story's got to start somewhere, eh? We'd just taken the garrison. Spilled a little blood, but the rest surrendered once they saw the game was up. The town was on our side, revolution in the air. Not many victories to cheer about these days, but that felt like one of them.

'Garric and me and a few others opened a cask in the officers' quarters, and we drank. Probably shouldn't have, but we knew it'd be days before the squareheads could react, and we deserved it, besides. We were well into our cups when I made a slip. Called Garric by his real name.'

Aren spat ropey red phlegm to clear his mouth. Some of his teeth felt loose. 'His name's not Garric? Then what is it?'

'Likely it'd mean nothing if I told you, but still, it's not my place to do it.'

'Naturally,' said Aren, his tone dripping with scorn. *More secrets.*

Keel let that pass with a warning glance. 'A man like him has many names. He wasn't Garric till recently. Laine of Heath Edge, that was how they knew him at Salt Fork. He had other names before that, but I know the one he was born with, and was loose-tongued enough to say it. I passed off my mistake as the drink talking, but one of them recognised the name. Highborn feller called Edric. He waited till the others had gone, then he confronted us.'

Aren rolled his jaw tenderly. 'What did Garric do?'

'Nine, it was like a relief to him. A chance to confess. No one else knew but me. He told the lad everything: who he was, who your father was, and a lot else besides. When he was done, he swore Edric to secrecy, and that was that.'

Who your father was. 'Only it wasn't,' Aren guessed.

'No. 'Cause the people of Salt Fork turned on us, and we scattered, and we never saw Edric again. Thought he'd died with the others, but apparently he didn't. He was caught, and he talked.'

'How do you know?'

'Because if he hadn't, you and Cade would still be at home, climbing trees or chasing skirt or whatever it is boys your age do in Shoal Point.' He saddened, and gave Aren a sympathetic look. 'I'm sorry, eh? Whatever it is they said your father did or didn't do, whatever you think he died for … Truth is, they killed him to get to Garric. No other reason than that.'

Aren was numbed by the casual simplicity of it. 'Edric told them about the promise Garric made to my father.'

'He did. So they murdered your father, sent you to Suller's Bluff and spread the news in whispers, till your father's name – his *true* name – came to Garric's ears.'

'His name was Randill,' Aren said weakly, but already he knew that it wasn't.

'He left his real name behind. Had he not, Garric would have found him long ago.'

A memory came to Aren then, sharp and clear. His father in his study, lost in thought with letters open on the table, before lunging at him with a knife, the madness of a cornered rat in his eye.

'He said he was up near Salt Fork when it all happened …' Aren said. 'He told me he was delayed.'

'Might be coincidence. Doubt he'd have dared go anywhere near Garric.'

But Aren felt the pieces fall into place then. The revolt. The delay. The letters, and his reaction to them. 'No,' he said faintly. 'He was making enquiries. He heard about Salt Fork. He must have guessed Garric was involved and went looking for news.'

Randill had hoped for word of Garric's death. What he got was the opposite. No wonder he looked so hunted. His nemesis had escaped again.

If you ever see the Hollow Man, you run. You run and you don't stop. For he's come to kill you.

'He said Garric would kill me if he ever found me,' Aren said.

'Then I reckon he didn't know Garric as well as he thought. That man's got more honour than sense.'

Their boots crunched on the stones underfoot. A chill wind blew around them. 'Will you tell me my father's real name, at least?'

'Were it up to me, I would. But it's not my story to tell. And five people are dead because I spilled the truth at Salt Fork.'

'It's my *father*!' Aren cried in frustration.

'And was he a good one? A good man to you?'

'Yes!'

'Then that's to his credit. Let him remain so.'

Aren felt bile rising. So close to an answer, and yet it was withheld again, because of a man who'd just brutally beaten him, a man he despised with all his heart. He couldn't believe that he'd almost started to admire him after that night in the sanctum. Now he'd be happy if they never spoke again. And yet to shun him would be to give up any chance of finding out who his father really was.

Visions of Klyssen and Harte sprang to mind, one mole-like and bespectacled, the other tall and haughty and handsome. Harte sliding the knife into his father's neck. A glimpse of Klyssen in the window of Overseer Krent's mansion, back at Suller's Bluff.

'They used me as bait,' he said. 'That's all I was. Bait for Garric.'

'They knew honour would force him to come for you, once he heard. They had dreadknights waiting. Fact is, they'd have slain us all with ease if we'd tried to rescue you. It was only because you slipped their notice and escaped that we were spared that end. But the cost was high anyway.'

'And that's it, then?' Aren said. His bitterness was turning to anger again; he couldn't stop it. 'My father killed for no crime, Cade and I thrown into the mine, all so they could get their hands on *him*?' He threw a gesture towards Garric, who was walking alone ahead of them.

'There's Krodan justice,' said Keel in commiseration.

Krodan justice, Aren thought. Yes, one day there'd be justice for this. For Harte. For Klyssen. And for one other.

He stared at Garric's back. All his heartache and strife, the ruination of his childhood, his father's death and Osman's, too – all of it could be laid at the Hollow Man's door. However it came about, it came about because of Garric.

He died because of you, Aren thought. *One day you'll answer for that.*

46

Fen woke shivering in the brittle hour before the dawn. She sat up with a groan, muscles aching from sleeping on the hard ground. Grimacing at the foul taste in her mouth, she pulled her blanket tight around her shoulders.

Their fourth night since escaping Skavengard had been as miserable and uncomfortable as the three preceding it. Everyone was strung out and tired, worn down by the mountains. The clear autumn nights brought a cold that sank into their bones, and they were hungry, having found nothing to hunt. Their shelter was a patch of stony ground between two projecting outcrops, offering scant protection from the elements. There had been no fire, for trees were sparse on the eastern side of the Ostenbergs. Those they found were hard and gnarled, too much effort to break up and carry.

The others grumbled, but Fen was no stranger to discomfort and it hardly bothered her. Her da had been taking her out into the forest since she was eight, and even the most skilled hunter sometimes came up empty-handed, or got caught in a storm. Hunger and cold were rites of passage to her. They made her different from the soft town folk, who panicked if they missed their dinner and thought a night without a blanket would kill them. Most people stuck to their roads and streets, never daring to stray a hundred paces from safety. To free yourself from that was to unlock the world.

Pain passed. Hunger passed. Everything passed in time.

She surveyed the campsite with bleak disinterest. The others were still huddled inside their blankets, curled up for warmth. Ruck slept in the hollow of Vika's belly. Only Garric was awake, sitting watch with his back against one of the outcrops. Their eyes met in grudging salute to the morning, then he looked away again.

She studied him in the gathering light. He didn't waste words, that was for sure. She'd liked that about him, at first. Less so, these days. Once she'd been happy for him to keep his secrets, but now they were chewing away at her confidence in his leadership.

When she'd met him, he'd called himself Laine of Heath Edge, and the fire of revolution burned in his eyes. He gave her direction, a way to strike at the enemy that had driven her from her home. Now he had another name, and he was a different person: angry, bitter, driven and sometimes cruel. Someone the Iron Hand wanted badly enough to send dreadknights after him. Someone she didn't know.

Nothing had gone well since Salt Fork. His detour to Suller's Bluff had proved disastrous. His plan to seize the Ember Blade, audacious and reckless with eight of them, looked like fool's thinking with three. Yet still he wouldn't be swayed from his path. Even if Yarin came through with the information they needed, even if Mara was the genius he said she was, they were a pitifully small force. What had been admirable conviction now looked like idiocy.

Her gaze found Aren amid a bundle of blankets. His face was still puffy and discoloured, but his bruises were fading already thanks to a salve provided by Vika. Bruises Garric had given him.

Her da had been right. Never rely on anyone. They'd only let you down.

She got to her feet, shucking off the blanket, and found her bow and pack. No sense sitting still; she'd warm up faster on the move. 'Going to scout ahead,' she told Garric as she passed him.

Garric grunted in acknowledgement, and said no more than that. He'd spoken little since the incident and wouldn't meet Aren's eye. Reading people wasn't her strong suit, but she guessed he knew he'd gone too far. There was angry shame in the set of his shoulders. Even Keel looked at him differently.

She suspected he was just biding his time till they reached a safe place and he could offload his charge, his mysterious oath satisfied. Then Aren would leave, and Cade and Grub with him, and probably the druidess, too. After that they'd be back to three.

It wasn't enough.

She set her course towards a ridge to the east, where the sunlight was turning the grey sky blue. With luck, it would give her a view of the way ahead, and at least she could watch the dawn from there. Her da used to call it 'the daily miracle', back when there was joy on his lips. In that, at least, she understood him. Nature was where she found her wonders, and dawn was her time for stillness and contemplation, when she was brought face to face with the scale of creation and her insignificant place within it. It made her feel small and alone and perfectly contained. In that moment, there was nothing in the world but herself and the sun, and that suited her fine.

She should have left them all behind after Salt Fork. She should have gone her own way long before now. It was just that the world was so vast, the people so numerous. She knew nobody, and had no idea how she might come to know them. The only home she'd ever had was lost to her. She could survive well enough in the wide world, but she was ill equipped for living in it.

The idea gnawed at her as she laboured up the channels between the rocks. She was almost at the top now and the way had steepened. The camp was out of sight somewhere below, and the breeze off the warming earth ran fingers along her cloak.

Garric, Keel and her. Three of them, to take on the near-impossible task of stealing the Ember Blade. How long before they all ended up like Osman?

She shut her eyes, seeing him snatched away by that foul tentacle, lost to the burning light.

Strike east, she thought. *Strike east, and keep going. Forget them. Elsewise when they fall, you'll fall with them.*

But she wasn't sure she had the courage.

She gained the crest of the ridge and crept to the edge on her belly. Only fools and heroes stood on clifftops where they could be seen for leagues, and she was acutely aware that the dreadknights might still be hunting them.

The land fell away in layers before her, mountains tumbling into hills and onwards to a flat horizon. Rivers snaked in the distance, burnished gold by the rising sun. Peaks and ridges carved up the light, and a morning mist softened the hard edges of the world with a serene amber haze.

Her heart lifted as sunlight fell on her face. A new dawn, a new start, and new hope. The daily miracle.

She saw a winding road among the shadows of the hills and traced it with her gaze. Not far to the north was a building: a large inn, its windows lit and smoke rising in wisps from the chimneys.

Hot food and a hot bath, strong ale and a warm bed. The very thought made her light-headed. They could be there by late afternoon if they set off soon. By tonight, all their hardships would be forgotten, and they could drink to their fallen in the Ossian way. Perhaps she'd leave Garric and Keel and set off on her own afterwards, but that was a decision for another day.

Companions passed. Grief passed. Everything passed in time.

Her belly growling in anticipation, she scrambled off the ridge and hurried down to tell the others the good news.

47

They reached the inn as afternoon was turning to evening, and a golden light lay on the mountains at their backs. Lattice windows reflected the sun from diamond-shaped panes. It was a rambling two-storey building of stone and wood, weatherworn and somewhat ramshackle, with a sign creaking in the cold breeze by the roadside: The Reaver's Rest. Above the name, crossed swords were carved in relief, and a skull with two faces.

'Well, that's vaguely sinister,' said Cade as they trudged up the road, footsore and tired.

'Grub say it could be called "The Certain Death", still wouldn't stop him going inside,' the Skarl declared thirstily.

'No need to fear, eh?' said Keel. 'All the reavers are long gone now. It's named for the Battle of the Red Hills, which went on hereabouts.'

The name tickled a memory in Cade's mind, but for once he didn't have a story to put to it. 'I don't know that one.'

The prospect of staying at an inn had put Keel in good spirits and he was happy to tell a tale. 'It was back in the time of the Fall, after the Second Empire crumbled and barbarians ran wild. Madrach Stonetooth was the warlord of a Brunlander clan that used to raid eastern Ossia. One of these raids went badly wrong and two of Madrach's sons were killed. He swore he'd take his whole clan and reave his way to the coast and back in vengeance.'

They'd reached the turn-off from the road and headed up a stony drive that led through an archway into a galleried stable yard. Fen eyed the place suspiciously as they approached.

'Thing is,' Keel went on, 'there were a lot of warlords about in those days, and in Ossia the most feared was Baggat the Crude. His lands were right in Madrach's path, so when Baggat heard about this oath, he gathered *his* clan, and they marched to meet Madrach's forces. No one knows who won, just that it was a bloody day all round, and neither Madrach nor Baggat was ever heard of again. They wiped each other out, or near enough so it made no difference.' He waved a hand to indicate their surroundings. 'Lot of bodies in the ground hereabouts.'

'The Reaver's Rest,' said Cade. It made sense now. He was already composing a more lurid version of the story to tell later.

'I did not reckon you a Lorekeeper, Keel,' Vika said. 'How do you know all that?'

'Been here before,' said Keel. 'The innkeeper told me.'

Vika laughed. She was much recovered from her encounter with the beast of Skavengard. Her coordination had improved day by day, and she no longer mumbled to herself. Hearing word of the inn that morning, she'd washed off her paint in a stream, removed her druidic charms and trinkets and wrapped her staff in rags. With her sturdy boots and patchwork cloak of pelts, she looked more like a wayfarer than a druid now, a ranger of the wilds.

They entered the cobbled stable yard. Horses snorted in their stalls and the scent of hay and dung was in the air. A group of stable boys were hitching a cart to a grey mare while a few travellers leaned on the gallery banister, idly watching the activity below.

A thickset young man with a face made for scowling came over, wiping his hands on his trousers. Garric drew out a gold half-falcon from a pouch. 'We want rooms and hot bath for us all, and a meal fit for seven starving souls.'

Ruck barked, annoyed.

'*Eight* starving souls,' Garric amended. 'What's left over, you can keep for your trouble.'

The stable boy brightened. 'Aye, Master. We have Krodan or Ossian baths—'

'Ossian,' said Garric. 'It's our country, isn't it?'

That was dangerously close to sedition and it made the stable boy nervous. He glanced about as if the Iron Hand might spring out of nowhere. 'I'll see to it, Masters,' he said, and hurried off.

Keel raised an eyebrow at Garric's generosity.

'It's been a difficult path we've travelled,' he said. 'Tonight we feast for the dead.'

Aren groaned with joy as he sank into the bath, letting the warmth seep into his knotted and abused muscles. No pleasure had ever been so hard won; no kiss from Sora as sweet.

'Nine, that's good,' Keel declared, lowering himself into the enormous wooden tub they all shared. 'I thought I'd never be clean again.'

Aren watched the Bitterbracker through the rising steam as he settled himself. A black kraken tattoo snaked its tentacles up the side of his taut and hairless torso. Garric, Cade and Grub were soaking nearby, sitting on the underwater bench that ran round the edge of the tub. He'd seen Cade naked a hundred times, but he was different now from the boy who'd hunted she-wargs with Aren in the early days of summer. His puppy fat had melted in the Krodan camp, though he'd always be broad in the shoulder. Garric, under his armour, was thickly furred and scarred with a dozen wounds, but none were as ugly as the puckered slash across his throat. Grub was squat and stocky with a hard, round belly, and the full extent of his tattoos was now revealed. He was a canvas, his body neatly divided into light and dark, the artistry marred only by the black swipe that had been drawn across his eyes.

Krodans were prudish and bathed in private, but Ossians did most things in groups and were unashamed about their bodies. Nudity was unremarkable to them, and they found it strange that their neighbours worried about it so much. They bathed together as families, and communal bathhouses could be found in every Ossian town; indeed, older Ossians sometimes refused to do business anywhere else. They had a proverb: 'You don't know a person's heart till you've seen their skin.' Stripped of finery, everyone was equal there, and it was one of the diminishing number of places where you were unlikely ever to see a Krodan.

The men occupied one side of the tub while Vika sat on the

other, with Ruck curled up on the floor nearby. Baths were mixed more often than not, with a rope dividing the genders or – as here – a polite gap.

Aren had been taught to think of the Ossian way of bathing as uncouth. In Kroda, only prostitutes and low women showed a lot of flesh. But as much as he'd admired Krodan ways, he always found bathing by himself lonely and boring, and it was hard to avoid communal bathing and swimming when most of your friends were Ossian and you lived by the sea. Now, as he soaked in water hot enough to boil an eel, sweat trickling across his scalp, he wondered why anyone would want to do it any other way. They'd won this respite together; it was only right they should enjoy it together, too.

This is the first hour of the rest of my life, he thought.

His face still hurt from the beating Garric had given him, but not enough to ruin his mood. He'd fulfilled his promise to Cade, seen him through horror and hardship to safety. The world had done its worst and he'd overcome it. He felt a deep calm, a new confidence in himself.

There was a splash from behind him; Fen washing herself down. Bathers were expected to clean themselves before soaking in the tub, and for that purpose there was a sunken stone trench and a well, where buckets of mountain water from an underground stream had been drawn up ready. Aren averted his gaze as she padded over to the tub, but he was surprised by how readily his imagination filled in for his eyes. The girls he was drawn to had always been joyful, teasing and curvy, and Fen was the opposite; yet even though he mastered the urge to look at her, it took an effort of will to do it.

He turned to Cade, seeking something to distract himself. 'I think I might never get out of this bath,' he said.

'Uh?' said Cade. He was mesmerised, his face slack, gawping at Fen as she slipped into the bath next to Vika.

Aren shoved him on the shoulder. Cade jerked out of his trance, saw Aren grinning at him and blushed.

'Lost you there for a minute,' Aren said, then lowered his voice to a whisper. 'Anyone ever told you it's bad manners to stare in a bathhouse?'

Cade scowled and huffed. 'I was thinking, that's all.'

'I bet you were. What happened to Astra, then? Remember her?'

'What happened to Sora?' Cade countered acidly. 'Remember her? Squarehead pain in the arse who had you under her thumb, and nobody knew what you saw in her?'

Aren laughed. 'Fair enough. I suppose they're both in the past now. Shoal Point's in the past. The future's what we've got to look forward to, and it's as changeable as steam.' He waved a hand in the air to illustrate his point, setting the haze over the water to billowing, but Cade's attention had already drifted back to Fen.

Aren gave up. He recognised the signs of infatuation. Cade was lost.

Fen noticed Cade staring and met his gaze coolly. He responded with one of his extra-wide smiles he reserved for girls he'd set his heart on. It was a grin of such gormless width and surpassing idiocy that Aren feared the top of his head would fall off. Fen looked faintly startled by it.

Keel, who was sitting with his elbows on the edge of the tub, threw back his head and began to sing. His voice was deep and surprisingly mellifluous, and it rang from the damp walls.

Borek, he were a whalin' sort,
Sing hey-o! Hey-o!
A lusty lad with an appetite
And a keen shot with a harpoon.

It was a shanty Aren was vaguely familiar with, having heard it drunkenly bellowed from the fishermen's inns in Shoal Point more than once. Cade nudged him excitedly; being a dockside boy, he recognised it, too.

A tale I'll tell of a whale he sought,
Sing hey-o! Hey-o!
A tale of revenge and rage and spite
And the journey that brung him to doom.

Unexpectedly, Garric joined in then, his rough, phlegmy voice a salty accompaniment to Keel's smooth bass.

Hey-o! Hey-o! Stay abed, Borek.
Hey-o! Hey-o! The seas are cold alright.
Hey-o! Hey-o! Your maiden's arms will warm you.
Hey-o! Hey-o! Don't you sail tonight.

Cade began singing along uncertainly as they swung into the next verse, dredging the words up from his memory.

Well, Borek he hunted a dreadful whale,
Sing hey-o! Hey-o!
A monstrous beast of terrible size
And he swore to bring it to land.

'Twas ninety feet from nose to tail,
Sing hey-o! Hey-o!
Out of the water it did rise
And its teeth went snap on his hand.

Now Cade joined in, too, and Vika and Grub sang along to the 'Hey-o!'s even though they didn't know the rest of the words. The rhythm, the joyous pull of the song, was infectious. Aren found himself wanting to sing, though he'd never been able to hold a tune.

Hey-o! Hey-o! Stay abed, Borek.
Hey-o! Hey-o! The seas are cold alright.
Hey-o! Hey-o! Your maiden's arms will warm you.
Hey-o! Hey-o! Don't you sail tonight.

Half a man he returned to port,
Sing hey-o! Hey-o!
He raised a toast to his missing paw
And his mates drank a jar to his wound.

371

'I'll rest no more till that whale is caught.'
Sing hey-o! Hey-o!
His wife begged him to sail no more
But he launched by the light of the moons.

As the third chorus approached, Aren could hold back no longer. Even Fen got swept up in it. 'Hey-o!' they hollered and sang in raucous discord, with grins on their faces. Grub splashed the water with his hand and Garric thumped on the side of the tub with his fist. Ruck, who'd woken up, ran in circles and barked.

A dreadful storm blew up that night,
Sing hey-o! Hey-o!
The wind did blow and the waves did crash
And the whale, it breached to his aft.

'Twixt man and beast was a deadly fight,
Sing hey-o! Hey-o!
Then the whale flicked his tail with a mighty splash
And Borek went down with his craft.

'Hey-o!' they roared again. Steam billowed and water slopped over the side. Aren sang at the top of his lungs, not caring who heard him or what they thought. A giddy sense of release swept over them: they were here, now, *alive* against all the odds. Naked, unguarded, they sang together, and Aren felt the barriers collapse between them. In that moment they were his companions, his *friends*, and they were all in it together.

This tale I tell to caution ye,
Sing hey-o! Hey-o!
A vengin' heart will see you dead
And set your wife to weep.

A foolish man to fight the sea,
Sing hey-o! Hey-o!
Now Borek's found another bed
Down in the watery deep.

Hey-o! Hey-o! Stay abed, Borek.
Hey-o! Hey-o! The seas are cold alright.
Hey-o! Hey-o! Your maiden's arms will warm you.
Hey-o! Hey-o! Don't you sail tonight!

The last chorus was the loudest of all and ended with a cheer and laughter. Ruck barked at them, and even Garric was smiling.

You don't know a person's heart till you've seen their skin, Aren thought; and for this brief time at least, all their hearts were happy.

48

'So the king summoned Josper to his castle and met him in his throne room, with all the nobles of the land assembled.'

Cade took a bite from the chicken leg in his hand, swaying slightly as he surveyed his audience. Mouth still full, he raised his voice theatrically as he took on the role of the king.

'"You've slain the draccen that has plagued my lands, restored my fortune and rid me of my treacherous half-brother! Ask, and I will grant you any boon! Titles! A castle! A chest of gold!"'

Aren wiped his mouth on his sleeve, for lack of a napkin. His belly was full to bursting, he was nicely drunk and he was enjoying the show. The table before him was crowded with platters that had once held roasted birds, crackly bacon, fluffy potatoes with crunchy skins, warm bread and dripping, cheese and apples and pickles. There was little left of it now. The others lounged in their chairs, sated, jolly with ale and ready to be entertained with a story of Josper the Accidental Dawnwarden. Only Grub was distracted; he was devouring a marmalade-encrusted ham hock with terrifying industry.

'"My liege!" Cade cried. His imitation of Josper's boozy slurring was all the more convincing because it was only half faked. '"All these things I have done, I admit, but they were not my intention. A giant raven stole my steak pie while it cooled on the sill, you see. All that followed was in service of one goal alone: to get my delicious pie back from that thieving bag of feathers! So if you would grant me one boon, let it be this: lend me a hundred men, and I will find that raven, put paid to his evil ways and get back the pie that has so long eluded my jaws!"'

Keel cackled to himself at that, and Vika chuckled, but Aren knew the real punchline was still to come.

'At this, the king was bewildered,' Cade went on. '"But it has been a year and a day since your quest began!" he said. "That pie is surely eaten, and even if it is not, its crust must be so hard that the Stone Mother herself would chip her teeth on it. If you will give up your quest, I will give you my youngest daughter Alessa's hand in marriage. Her beauty is renowned throughout Embria, her wit will delight you, and her grace shames the stars, it is said."

'"My liege," said Josper. "That's all well and good ... but can she *cook*?"'

The others roared with laughter and Keel pounded the table. Grub looked up from his ham hock, startled, worried that he'd missed something important while he'd been concentrating on his dinner. They applauded as Cade gave a little bow, then he sat back down next to Aren and reclaimed his ale.

'I swear you told me that story once,' Aren murmured to him. 'But as I recall, the hero was called Goyle the Unfortunate, and everyone in it was Krodan.'

Cade shrugged and grinned into his flagon. 'Reckon I know my audience.'

Aren threw an arm round his shoulders. 'You're a good friend. Did I ever tell you that?'

'Aye, but I can always hear it again,' said Cade, and reached for a hunk of bread and some cheese.

Aren sat back, stuffed and pleasantly hazy. Beyond the latticed windows the hills were dark. Lamps had been lit and fires burned brightly in two hearths. There was a bar at one end, behind which stood the lanky Xulan who owned the place, his skin black and shiny as obsidian. Serving girls scurried briskly around him.

There were other travellers here, perhaps two dozen in all. They clustered round the fires, huddled in shadowy booths or loafed at the bar. A pair of drunks in tatty cloth coifs and fingerless gloves shared a flask of plum liquor. Three Boskan merchants murmured together, their strange clothes making them look like hunched desert beetles. Their faces were hidden by domed hoods of stiff-ened hide so that only their noses and beards showed in the dim light, and pungent smoke rose from the exotic cigars they smoked. In a corner, a Krodan family and their Brunlander bodyguard ate quietly. At the back of the room, a Sard lutist was tuning up while an armoured Harrish man who shared her table surveyed the room with a stern gaze.

I've never seen so many different peoples in one place, thought Aren. The world he'd known growing up in Shoal Point felt small and far away now.

Of them all, it was the Sard his eye was drawn to. She was beautiful, with a drowsy elegance about her, and she wore complex layers of lace and patterned cloth. Tiny silver ornaments were sewn into her sleeves, and little chains of them hung round her wrists and ankles. Her ears were pierced many times with studs and rings. Black hair tumbled down her back, held there by combs and pins of chalcedony and amber. Her skin was a shade darker than the Ossian norm – Sards always looked tanned, as if from an outdoor life – but her eyes gave away her origins. Her irises were so green they almost glowed: the unmistakable mark of her kind.

She began to play, plucking delicate arpeggios while her fingers spidered and slid across the fretboard. A few of the patrons looked up from their drinks, mildly interested. It was only when she sang that people really started to pay attention. Her voice was husky and warm and smooth, too exceptional to ignore. As Aren watched her, his thumb absently rubbed the mark on his wrist.

The song was a rolling, swooping folk tune from the misty forests of Trine, far to the north-east. It was the story of two brothers competing for the love of their cold-hearted father by goading each other to ever-greater acts of valour until, inevitably, tragedy occurred. Trinish history was littered with such tales. They were a warrior people, argumentative and violent by nature, which was why there was rarely peace and stability in their land. Even now they were locked in a civil war to settle their succession, while trying to fight off the encroaching elaru in Peth and squabbling with the Quins for the best fishing spots in the White Sea.

Just like us, he thought, *always pulling in different directions*. Just like at Salt Fork, or during the centuries of disorder before the Krodans came. The Ossians weren't warlike, as the Trinish were, but they were fiercely opinionated and didn't take orders well – at least, not until the Krodans forced them to. They prized their families, good food and loud conversation over discipline and obedience. Getting Ossians to do anything en masse was akin to herding cats.

But we weren't always like that. We fought our way out of slavery and built the greatest empire the East has ever seen. Why couldn't we do it again?

He caught himself before he could follow that line of thought to its end. Just the idea made his chest swell with an unfamiliar pride, and that scared him. Now wasn't the time for heroic dreams, when they'd only just escaped the clutches of the Krodans. Garric's plan, whatever its details, was doomed to fail. Why hitch themselves to a burning cart?

They weren't going to fight the Krodans. You *couldn't* fight the Krodans. They weren't Greycloaks, just a couple of boys looking to keep their heads down and start again.

He glanced at Cade. At least, he hoped that was the case.

'Ah! Here's the sweetwine!' Keel said as a serving girl approached their table with a tray. 'Make some space!'

They cleared a spot on the table and the girl set down a stone jar with seven stone cups; stone was traditional when toasting those who'd returned to the earth. Garric poured for them all and stood to pass out the cups. Grub tried to neck his immediately, but Vika slapped a hand on his wrist to stop him.

When they all had a cup, Garric raised his, and the others did the same. Grub copied them resentfully.

'Tarvi. Varla. Otten. Dox. Osman.' Garric said each of their names slowly, his expression grim and his eyes faraway. 'Good people, all. People who believed in something, who thought to make things better than they are. I knew none of them as well as I'd have liked to, but for a time they were brothers and sisters of mine.'

He moved his cup towards his lips, and they were all about to drink when he held up a hand. He wasn't finished. For a few moments, he struggled with what he had to say.

'Their dying is on me,' he said at last, his voice hard as he forced out the words. 'They followed me, though they didn't know the reason why, and did it willingly. But it was my oath, my responsibility. I should have shouldered it alone, and they're dead because I didn't.' His eyes flickered to Aren, then away again. 'That's all I want to say. Sarla's grace be on them.' He swallowed his drink and sat down.

'Sarla's grace be on them,' echoed the others, all except Grub, who was just happy to be allowed to drink at last. Aren watched Garric over the rim of his cup as he finished his sweetwine.

Did he just admit he was wrong? That none of this was my fault?

There was a sombre pause as they thought of the men and women they'd lost. Then Keel clapped his hands.

'Who's for another round? It ain't Amberlyne, but it'll do.'

'Grub is!' Grub cried, but Keel was already pouring.

'They reckon Prince Ottico won't have any sweetwine but Amberlyne at his table,' Cade told them knowledgeably.

Keel and Garric exchanged a quick look at the mention of the prince. 'Is that so?' said Keel. 'I didn't know that.'

'Nor I,' said Garric, studying Cade thoughtfully.

Aren turned his cup around in his hand, a wistful look in his eye. 'My father used to like Amberlyne,' he said. Then he saw Garric's expression and realised what he'd said. Merely mentioning his father was enough to raise Garric's hackles.

Well, damn him. He'd speak of his father if he wanted. In fact, he'd do more than that.

'I never drank to him,' Aren said suddenly. 'Never had the chance to, till now.' He got to his feet, hot with defiance, and raised his cup. 'My father. Fallen to a Krodan blade. It may be I never knew who he really was, but he was a good man to me, and I loved him.'

The table was silent; they sensed the tension there. Aren held the older man's gaze as he said 'Sarla's grace be on him,' and drank.

'Sarla's grace be on him,' echoed Vika, and she drank, too.

Cade was wary of Garric's wrath, but his hesitation lasted only an instant. 'Sarla's grace be on him.' He downed his cup quickly, before he could have second thoughts.

Fen went next, and then Grub. This time, he said the words along with the others.

Only Keel and Garric were left. Keel gave his friend a long look. *Let it go*, he was saying. *It doesn't matter.* Garric was impassive.

Do as you will. So Keel shrugged and drank. 'Sarla's grace be on him.'

Garric slowly pushed the full cup away from him and got to his feet. He didn't look angry, but weary instead. 'Ought to see about fixing us some transport,' he rumbled.

'Yes!' Grub said. 'Grub want to know what adventures he's getting into next! Grub still got a lot of skin to cover!'

Garric said nothing to that; he only walked away. The others said nothing, either. The Skarl clearly didn't understand. Garric didn't want him as a companion. Nor did Aren, in truth. Just because they'd shared the road for some way, it didn't make them friends.

They all fell into their own private conversations after that. Cade leaned close to Aren and opened his mouth to speak, but Aren intercepted him.

'I know what you're going to say. You don't want to leave, do you?'

'Why should we?' Cade said. 'They're an alright bunch, aren't they?' He saw Aren's expression and quickly backtracked. 'I mean, aside from Garric punching your face in that time. But he's sorry! Look at him! He's just too gruff and beardy to say it.'

'Beardy?'

'Well, he is.'

'Cade . . .' Aren fought to put his feelings into words straightforward enough for his friend to understand. 'I *hate* him, don't you see that? Everything that's happened to us has been down to him.'

'Ain't true,' said Cade, raising a finger. 'Who killed your da? Krodans. Who sent us to rot in a work camp? Krodans. You always were slow to blame the squareheads for what they're rightfully responsible. Now, if you ask me who saved us when we had the choice of getting torn up by skulldogs or stepping off a cliff—'

'Yes, you've made your point,' Aren said waspishly. He knew it was true, but knowing that didn't change a thing. It was so much easier to hate Garric – who was surly and violent and hated him back – than it was to hate a whole nation whose beliefs he'd been taught to admire and share.

'We had a plan, remember?' he said. 'Get to safety, then see where the wind takes us. All of Ossia awaits us. I thought you wanted to be an actor?'

'Aye, but that was before,' said Cade. 'They're doing something *noble*. Something *right*. They're fighting for our country, and they need our help.'

'Help?' Aren scoffed. 'You can't even swing a sword, and I'm no warrior. How can we help?'

'Dunno,' said Cade, pushing a pickle around his plate. 'But I know my da would be right proud if he heard I'd joined the rebels.'

Aren sobered at that. Sometimes he forgot Cade still had a stake in Shoal Point. Aren's bridges had all burned when his father died, but Cade still had family there. What agonies his parents must have suffered, not knowing the fate of their only son.

'Do you miss them?' Aren asked.

Cade shrugged. 'Da, not really. Ma ... I missed her sore when we were in the camp, but since then, not so much. Feels good to be on the move, you know? Any direction, as long as it's away from there.' He frowned slightly as a thought occurred to him. 'Been meaning to write them a letter, though, when we get ourselves sorted. Reckon you could help me with that?'

'Of course. What do you think you'll say?'

'Oh, I dunno. That everything's alright and I'm making my way in the world. And I'll tell Da where he can stick his gods-damned chisels and saws.' He grinned.

Aren's gaze found Garric over at the bar, deep in conversation with the innkeeper. The Xulan was perhaps in his forties, perhaps his sixties; it was hard to tell. He wore a purple waistcoat too fine for working in, and there was something courtly about the way he stood and the gestures he made. Likely he'd come from wealthy stock: Xulan highborns were notorious fops. Aren wondered how he ended up managing a remote inn in occupied Ossia.

'Listen,' said Aren, 'I know you like the idea of what Garric stands for, but he's a hunted man. Hunted by *dreadknights*. We've no worth to the Krodans, we were just bait. Nobody's after us now. We can do anything, *be* anything. Isn't that what you always wanted?'

'I suppose,' said Cade gloomily. His eyes were on Fen, smiling and relaxed as she talked with Keel, made loose by food and drink. When Cade fell for a girl, he fell fast and hard. It wouldn't be easy to make him leave her.

'It's not our decision, anyway,' Aren said. 'He doesn't want us.'

'You could change his mind,' Cade said optimistically. 'You always know how to persuade people.'

Aren began to despair of letting his friend down lightly. Blinded as he was by his new infatuation, he didn't see that this wouldn't work, *couldn't* work.

'Besides,' said Cade, as a new point occurred to him, 'don't you want to know who your father really was? The only one who can tell you is Garric.'

'And for that I should lash myself to him, until he decides I'm allowed to know?' Aren said, more sharply than he'd intended. Cade looked hurt; Aren softened. 'Sorry,' he said. 'Something prevents him from telling me, I don't know what. And even if I could make him, I doubt I'd like what he has to say. But I'll think on it.'

He waved his hand then, dashing the subject away. 'Ah, begone with all these decisions,' he said, louder now there was no need for secrecy. 'Here's ale and sweetwine, good food and good company. Let tonight be tonight, and tomorrow be tomorrow.'

Cade gave him a mischievous smile. 'Time was, you thought Ossian sayings like that were just for us bumpkins.'

'Well, then call me a bumpk—'

'*Bumpkin!*' Grub yelled in a wave of beery breath. He cackled and took a swig from his flagon, well pleased with himself.

The lutist had finished her song to scattered applause and taken her seat to retune. Aren saw his opportunity and got to his feet.

'Where are you off to?' Cade asked, but Aren was already heading across the common room.

When Keel saw his direction, he yelled 'You don't think you've got a chance with *her*, do you?' loud enough for everyone to hear. Aren blushed to the roots of his hair and walked faster.

The lutist's companion stood as Aren approached, placing himself between them. He was very tall, clad in a fine splint-mail shirt that was probably expensive, and polished greaves and bracers.

A longsword hung at his hip, and his hand stayed near it. But though his size was intimidating, his features were not. His head seemed too small for his body, he had hardly a chin to speak of and his mouth was small and puckered. His dark brown hair was bowl-cut above his ears, and his expression was fixed in an attitude of haughty blandness.

'Halt!' he said. 'Approach no further!'

His voice was high and fluting. If Aren hadn't already guessed he was from Harrow by his hair and his ramrod-straight stance, his crisp accent and superior tone would have given it away.

'Be calm,' said the lutist. Her speaking voice was silken and low, with the sing-song lilt of her people. 'You are too protective.'

His expression changed not one bit. After an uncomfortable pause, he stepped aside; but he kept his hand near his sword.

'Sit, please,' she said to Aren. 'I am Orica, and this is Harod.'

'Aren,' he said, before he could consider the wisdom of providing his real name. He cursed himself for his lack of wit, but her beauty had flustered him. He remembered the tales of illusions and bewitchments that the young men and women of Shoal Point brought back from their visits to Sard campsites, and resolved to be more careful.

He pulled out a stool, scraping it awkwardly along the floor, and sat. Harod loomed at his shoulder, silently threatening. Aren was suddenly conscious of the fading bruises that still discoloured his face. He looked rough and unkempt in his battered travel clothes, even after his bath. Small wonder Harod was cautious.

'I ... er ... I very much enjoyed your music,' he said politely.

'Thank you,' she said with a tilt of her head. 'I'm surprised you could hear it over your companions.'

Aren looked sheepish. 'Were we that loud?'

'I am teasing. No music is finer than the sound of people enjoying themselves. Life is laughter, yes?'

'I like that idea,' said Aren. 'There's been little enough laughter of late.'

'All the more reason to treasure it.'

He glanced nervously at Harod. 'Have you journeyed far?'

She finished tuning her lute and turned her sleepy green gaze upon him. 'I have been away a long time,' she said. 'Five years as an apprentice to a master bard, travelling Embria and gathering songs as we went. Two years playing for the High Houses of Harrow. That's where I met Harod.' She smiled up at him. 'He is my most faithful friend, and my guardian in these troubled times.'

'Speak your business, boy!' Harod demanded.

'He also has a marked lack of patience with strangers,' she said pointedly, giving him a harder look. The slightest bobbing of his throat was the only outward sign that he was chastened.

'I won't keep you from your performance,' said Aren quickly. 'I just have one question. Er ... Do you need any help?'

She laughed in surprise. 'Do I look like I do?'

'It's just that, well, I met a Sard and ...' He drew back his sleeve to show her the tiny red symbol there. 'He gave me this mark.'

Orica's eyes widened. 'Where did you meet him?' she asked sharply.

This time, Aren thought it best to be cautious. Admitting that he was an escaped prisoner wouldn't be a smart thing to do. 'I can't tell you. He wanted to stay hidden, and I must honour that wish.'

Orica seemed to grudgingly approve of that. She took his hand, turning it left and right, studying the mark.

'He helped me. When I offered to help him in return, he told me to help another Sard instead.'

Orica nodded thoughtfully. '*Lled na saan.*'

'Yes, he kept saying that.'

'It means to pass one's fortune forward. To give it to another. We do not like to let anything go to waste, whether food or favours. If we cannot make use of something, we make sure it goes to someone who can. But this is strange ink. Did he tattoo it on your skin?'

'He bit his thumb and pressed it to my wrist. When the blood flaked off, this mark was left behind.' He remembered something. 'He called himself *ydraal*.'

Orica looked stricken. '*Ydraal?*' It was only by contrast that Aren realised how badly he'd mispronounced it. 'You met an *ydraal?*'

'What *is* an yd ... one of those?'

'Have a care, milady,' Harod intoned, leaning down to glare at

383

Aren face to face. 'He seeks to trick you! That mark could be faked to win your confidence!'

'*Tsss*. It would take a spy of great craft to know this sign and *ydraal* both, and I am but a bard, not worth the effort.' She let his hand drop.

'Will you tell me about this mark?' Aren asked. 'And the nature of the boy who gave it to me?'

Orica's eyes were guarded. 'I will, because if you are false then you know the answers anyway, and if you are not then you deserve to have them. That is the sign of a Sardfriend: one who is not of our blood, but who is willing to aid us. Without such a mark, many of my people would likely not talk to you at all, much less accept help from you. We have become suspicious of late, and with good reason.'

Aren stared at his wrist, perturbed by this new information. 'Um ... And how do I get it off?'

'You do not want to be a Sardfriend?' Her voice had taken on an edge.

'No, of course I *do*, it's just ...' He flailed. 'Well, after I've done what I promised ... I mean, I didn't *ask* to be marked like this.'

'I understand,' she said flatly. 'Do not fear, young Ossian. None but Sards will recognise it.'

Aren was ashamed at the disgust in her voice. She'd read him right. He didn't really want to be a Sardfriend, and he certainly didn't want to declare himself one in public. It was too much of a risk. At best, he'd look untrustworthy and suspicious; at worst, he'd draw the attention of the Krodans. Such arguments seemed reasonable in his head, but they withered in the face of Orica's disdain.

She sighed and looked back to her lute. 'I do not know how you would remove that mark. It was put there by an *ydraal*: one of the true blood. They are our seers and mystics, and their powers are strange. When your task is done, perhaps he will remove it himself. Perhaps it will disappear on its own. But I do not need your help, so it must remain there yet. Now, please excuse me, I have neglected my duty tonight.' She slipped the lute strap over her head. 'Goodbye, *Sardfriend*,' she said, disappointed.

'You are no longer wanted here,' Harod told him firmly.

Aren didn't need telling. He went back to his table, mortified and humbled by the scorn in the bard's words. It didn't seem fair that he'd been made to feel so small. After all, when he'd implied he didn't want to be a friend to the Sards, he hadn't meant *her*. She was beautiful and looked kind. He'd only meant... well, the *other* Sards. The deceitful ones. The swindlers and the liars.

Just thinking it made him realise how pathetic that sounded. No wonder she'd been disgusted at him; he was disgusted at himself. Shaking his head, he took a bitter swallow of ale as Orica struck up a new tune.

'No luck, eh?' said Keel jovially. But he didn't press the issue, because Garric returned then.

'You and old Rapapet had a lot to say to each other,' Keel observed as Garric sat down.

'He misses his home. We were discussing the wonders of Xulan military technology, among other things.' He leaned forward over the table and dropped his voice so only those around it could hear. 'Our plans have changed,' he said. 'Dreadknights have been seen on the south road.'

It was like having cold water thrown over them. 'The same three that followed us to Skavengard?' Keel asked.

'I don't know. But that road is too dangerous now. It would be a risk to travel so close to Salt Fork anyway; the countryside is still crawling with Krodans. We will take a different route.'

He turned to Aren. 'I've arranged transport for you and Cade to Greenrock. A caravan of merchants is leaving at dawn. I'll pay the Skarl's passage, too; he's earned that much. After that, your paths are your own.'

Cade looked at Fen, upset. He hadn't expected the decision to be made for him so soon, nor so firmly.

Grub was even more distressed. 'But Grub wants to go with you to do dangerous deeds!' he cried.

Garric ignored that. 'Whither you, Vika?'

'I will go with you,' she said. 'If you'll have me.'

'You do not know what you ask. There will be great risk.'

Grub groaned in exasperation and threw up a dismissive hand.

'I was guided to you, and I cannot ignore that,' said Vika. 'There are greater forces at play here, and I am set upon a purpose I do not yet understand. My way lies with yours, for now.'

'Then you are most welcome,' said Garric.

'Why Grub not most welcome when Painted Lady is?' Grub protested, but was ignored again.

Garric tossed a small pouch onto the table. It landed with a chink of coins. 'Ten guilders for the merchants. Don't let them charge you more,' he said to Aren. 'The rest is for you, to keep or divide as you wish. It'll get you started, wherever you go.'

Aren nodded gravely in thanks. Whatever he felt for this man, it was right to be gracious. 'You may have been my father's enemy, but you saved my life more than once and held to your oath when many would not have. Whatever else you are, you're a man of honour.'

Garric grunted, taken aback by the unexpected praise. 'We are none of us responsible for the sins of our fathers. I shouldn't have held yours against you.' He got to his feet. 'Be in the stable yard at sunrise. Speak to Tarpin. I'll say farewell now, for I won't see you again.'

He departed without ceremony, leaving the others with the remains of their meal. They looked at one another uncertainly. The atmosphere had turned morose. Aren realised that neither Keel nor Fen nor Vika would be happy to see the back of them. Perhaps they'd half-hoped they'd all continue on together. Apparently it wasn't to be.

'Let's not get maudlin, eh?' said Keel, and he took up his flagon. 'Hallen gave us the perfect remedy for a heavy heart. The night's young, and if it's to be our last all together, let's not waste it on sadness.'

Fen picked up her own flagon. So did Cade and Vika. Grub reached surreptitiously across the table for the bag of coins, but Aren put his hand on it first.

'Why don't I keep hold of this?' he said.

49

The sun was cresting the hills to the east as Garric watched the merchant caravan crawl up the road. The room he shared with Keel faced full into the morning and the upper panes of the latticed window had turned to dazzling fire. He squinted against the glare, seeking Aren among the pack, but the men and horses were only silhouettes and he couldn't find him. He was likely inside one of the covered carts in any case.

That's the end of it, then, he thought, and he felt a stone shift and tumble away from the cairn piled over his heart. His duty had been discharged. Aren was safe, and he could move on.

But Nine, the cost. The bloody cost of it.

He wouldn't dwell on it. If he started counting his losses, he'd never stop. There was only onward, onward, onward. Keep going. Never quit.

Never again.

The latch rattled and Keel came in.

'You saw them down to the stable yard?' Garric asked.

'I did,' said Keel. 'Didn't stay, though. I'm not much for farewells.'

He joined Garric at the window. The caravan was growing smaller in the distance now.

'Was it worth it?' Keel asked.

'You ask as if I had a choice.'

'Other men might say you did.'

'Other men place little value on their honour.'

Keel sat down on the edge of his bed and massaged the back of his neck. He looked none the worse for the night's revels, but then, he always could drink like a horse. 'Well, they're on their way, for better or worse. What of our path? You've not changed your mind?'

'About the Ember Blade?'

Keel gave a derisive snort. *Small chance of that.* 'About Wracken Bay.'

'I said we're going, and we are. As soon as we can find someone willing to take us north.'

Keel blew out his breath, though whether in relief or trepidation Garric couldn't tell. 'I'm going home!' he said, as if in amazement.

Had he secretly hoped otherwise? Garric wasn't sure. Returning home was never simple for Keel. He loved his wife and boy as fierce as a man could love, but there were other things waiting for him in Wracken Bay. Things he'd taken to the road to avoid, because he couldn't bear them any longer. Responsibility. Judgement. Limits.

Every time Keel went back to Wracken Bay, Garric feared he'd never leave again, that the pull of family would prove stronger than his need for freedom. Keel was the only man he counted a true friend, and losing him to Mariella would be a blow hard to take. But there was no choice this time. Garric had business in Wracken Bay, business that he couldn't share with anyone. Not even Keel.

'Yes. To Wracken Bay we go,' he said. 'We'll take a ship from there, round the west coast and up the Redwater to Morgenholme, where we'll meet Mara and Yarin. We'll lose some time, but it's the safer route.'

'Better than running into those dreadknights again,' Keel agreed.

'Aye,' said Garric faintly. The dreadknights. He wondered where they *really* were, as despite what he'd told his companions, they weren't on the south road.

Secrets. Lies. It didn't sit well with him, to deceive his friend so. But he'd understand. They'd all understand, in the end.

They headed to the common room, knocking at Fen and Vika's room on the way.

'They'll be at breakfast already, no doubt,' said Keel. 'Did you see the druidess last night? She can eat, I'll say that for her. I like that in a woman, eh?'

Garric gave him a sidelong look.

'What?' Keel protested. 'I'm just saying I like a woman who can eat!'

'All women can eat, Keel. They'd be dead if they couldn't.'

'You know what I mean.'

There were scattered groups around the common room when they arrived, breaking their fast with new-baked bread, bacon and fresh eggs. Garric saw the Krodan family that had been there last night: a pale, meek couple and their children dwarfed by their hairy Brunlander bodyguard. He searched for Fen and Vika and found them tucked into a booth in the far corner. They were eating as Keel had predicted, but not alone.

Garric felt a knot pull tight under his breastbone and heat rise up in his throat. Aren was there, with Cade and Grub.

The Bitterbracker saw them, too, and held up his hands in innocence. 'I watched them get on the cart, Garric.'

'Looks like they got off again,' he growled. Anger drove him forward as he stamped across the room.

Vika jumped to her feet as she saw him approach and spoke before he could. 'Is it true?' she asked urgently. 'Is it true what Aren says?'

Garric turned his gaze onto Aren. Aren was looking back with that impertinent, arrogant calm he'd taken on of late. This new fearlessness infuriated him.

'What does Aren say?' he snapped.

'That you seek to claim the Ember Blade!'

Keel spat an oath. 'Will you keep your voice down?' He looked around in case anyone had overheard, but this booth had been chosen for privacy. By Aren, no doubt.

You insidious little bastard.

'The champion with the burning blade ...' Vika breathed. 'The blade that shines like sunlight. It is you!'

Garric didn't know what she was talking about, and he was too incensed to care. 'Who told you?' he demanded of Aren, looking at the others to find his betrayer.

'I didn't say a word,' said Keel.

Fen shook her head.

'How we know isn't important,' said Aren. 'We know, that's all.

And now Vika and Grub do, too. I thought a little openness would make a refreshing change.'

'You're a fool, boy. A fool who can't keep his mouth shut. So you've endangered us all, put the whole plan in jeopardy. Is that your hope, to ruin us? I shouldn't be surprised. It's in your blood to sell out your own.'

The insult had no effect. Aren looked at him coolly. It was absurd that one so young should be so controlled, so in command.

'You're short on bodies,' Aren told him. 'I'd say you could use all the help you can get.'

His meaning dawned on Garric then. 'You're *volunteering*?' he asked in disbelief.

'I'm sure you wouldn't want the three of us running round Greenrock, knowing what we do. Krodans might catch us, and who knows what they'd make us say?'

'Grub rubbish at keeping secrets!' the Skarl added enthusiastically. 'One time, his friend love another man's woman in secret. Grub tell whole town, friend kill himself! Throw himself off cliff, *splat*! True story.'

'As you see,' Aren said, 'better if we stick together, so you can keep an eye on us.'

'Ha!' said Keel. Garric glowered at him, but he just shrugged. 'We *are* thin on numbers. The Skarl's got his uses and the boys have brains and guts. They broke out of a Krodan work camp on their own, didn't they?'

'You must take them!' said Vika. 'Can't you see? As I was guided to you, so they were, too. If you are the champion in my vision, then all this was meant to be.'

Garric had great respect for the druids, but that kind of talk sounded like zealotry. 'If this was *meant to be*, Vika, then the Krodans were also meant to crush us thirty years ago, and Osman was destined to die. Nobody decides my fate, neither god nor man.'

And yet, despite his protests, it was being decided without him. Ever since he'd heard the name of Aren of Shoal Point, his influence over his companions had been slipping. Fen was on the edge of leaving already. Even Keel was beginning to doubt him, and there was a real danger he might choose to stay in Wracken Bay.

He'd never really believed they could fulfil their mission after they lost Tarvi and Varla and the others. Rejecting Aren now could be the final straw for him. And no matter how determined Garric was, he couldn't do it all alone.

Aren was still watching him, waiting for a decision. Nine, how he reminded Garric of his father then. Crafty enough to out-manoeuvre him, brave enough to face him down. As much as Garric had hated that man, he'd loved him as a brother once. Maybe the boy did deserve the chance to stand on his own merit.

We are none of us responsible for the sins of our fathers.

He wondered if he really believed that.

Handbells clanged outside and they heard the clopping of hooves on the flagstones. 'Hear this, in the name of the Emperor!' called a voice in Krodan. 'Stay where you are and prepare your passes for inspection!'

Keel raised his head in alarm. 'Road patrol!'

'But we don't have passes!' Cade said.

Garric grabbed Grub by the arm and pulled him from the booth. 'Hide,' he said. 'Don't leave the building. The place is already surrounded and they'll be looking for runners.'

'Grub good at hiding,' Grub told him. 'One time, Grub hid from—'

'Just go!' Garric shoved him towards the door. Another man got up and ran after him; he obviously had no pass, either. It wasn't uncommon to risk a journey without the proper authorisation and most considered it a very minor crime, but the punishment if caught was still harsh.

The other travellers watched them leave. Garric scanned the room for anyone who might report them. The Ossians and foreigners would likely keep their peace, unless pressed by the inspectors; it was the Krodan family that worried him. The father looked at Garric, sensing his attention. He'd seen Grub in their group, and seen him run. All of them looked guilty now.

'What about us?' Cade asked, afraid. 'We didn't exactly have the chance to pick up paperwork while running for our lives from the dreadknights!'

'I carry no pass, either,' said Vika. 'I do not need Krodan permission to walk in my own land.'

'Today you do,' said Garric, digging into a pouch at his belt. He handed her a folded and battered document. 'Your name is Lana of Houndbridge.' To Aren and Cade, he gave two more passes. 'Barrin of Oxfell. Dredge of Hog's Wallow.'

'Dredge of Hog's Wallow?' Cade whined.

'Shut your mouth, boy. I'm trying to save your life.' He handed passes to Fen and Keel and took out his own.

'Why do you have so many spare?' Aren asked.

'They were not spare when we met at Suller's Bluff,' said Garric. He nodded at Vika. 'That one was Varla's. I have none that would work for the Skarl; his tattoos give him away.'

'You will present your passes!' said the inspector as he strode into the common room, accompanied by four armoured soldiers in black and white livery. Footsteps sounded in the corridor as soldiers fanned out through the inn. Two soldiers took station by the entrance; the others stayed close to the inspector as he moved from group to group, studying passes as they were presented, snapping out questions. Soon he came to Garric.

'Passes,' he said, holding out a gloved hand. He was a long-faced man, blond hair combed unconvincingly across a balding scalp. A monocle was sandwiched between eyebrow and cheek.

Rot in the Abyss, you filthy squarehead dog, Garric thought as he handed over his pass. The inspector unfolded it and examined the spiky calligraphy, the forged governor's signature, the faked official seal.

'Your business?'

'I'm a guard. We're transporting goods from Bannerport to Morgenholme.'

'These passes are almost expired. You'll not make Morgenholme in two days.'

'A broken axle delayed us. We will stop at Arkencross tomorrow to apply for an extension from the governor.'

'See that you do,' he said. He folded up the pass, handed it back and motioned to the others with the peremptory arrogance of the officious. 'Now the rest.'

They produced their passes. 'That's quite a wound you have on your neck,' he observed as he shuffled disinterestedly through them. 'How did you get it?'

'Low men waylaid me in my younger days. Cut my throat and left me for dead. The land was lawless before the Emperor came.'

The inspector looked up sharply, alert for signs of sarcasm or mockery. Garric gave him none.

'Indeed it was,' the inspector agreed. 'Hail to the Emperor.'

'Hail to the Emperor,' Garric said as the inspector returned their passes.

Now the inspector walked over to the Krodan family. 'Good morning, young fellow!' he said as he ruffled the boy's blond hair. Then, to his father: 'May I see your identity documents, and a pass for the Brunlander?'

'Nine, he's got a better attitude when he's dealing with Krodans,' Keel muttered.

Garric wasn't listening. He was staring at the father, who was casting uneasy looks in their direction as he showed his documents.

Say nothing, Garric thought at him. *He hasn't asked. Don't tell.*

'Everything appears to be in order,' said the inspector, barely glancing at the paperwork before he handed it back. The father took them with a weak smile, then drew a quick breath: a decision made, he was about to speak.

Here it comes, thought Garric, and his hand moved towards his sword.

The father saw it. His gaze flicked to his son and daughter, sitting opposite. He swallowed the words down again.

'Thank you, Inspector,' he said, looking faintly ill.

That's right, keep your mouth shut, Garric thought. *You don't want a swordfight in here.*

A soldier hurried into the room. 'Inspector! We found a Sard in the stable yard, trying to leave. Her companion is giving us trouble.'

'Stay in your seats, all of you!' the inspector barked at the room, and he left with the soldiers following him.

Once he was gone, the travellers in the common room began to mutter between themselves again. Keel relaxed and let out a low whistle of relief. 'Thought for a moment there he wouldn't believe us.'

Aren surged up from the table. 'They're going to arrest her!' he blurted.

'So what?' asked Cade.

'They'll take her away, like they did to those Sards at the camp!'

'That's what happens when they arrest people, Aren. We should know, it happened to us.'

Aren clenched and unclenched his fists, looking towards the door in evident agitation. 'She needs our help,' he said, and then he was past Garric and running towards the exit.

'Hoy! The inspector said to stay here!' Cade called.

'He'll get us all caught!' said Keel.

'Still glad he didn't leave with the merchants?' Garric growled, and they set off after him.

50

'I am a knight of Harrow and a scion of High House Anselm!' Harod's voice rang out across the yard. 'And this lady is under my protection!'

A small crowd had gathered around the cobbled yard. Others watched the commotion from the gallery. In the gate of an empty stall, Harod had taken up a combat stance that looked at best theatrical, at worst ridiculous. Five Krodan soldiers stood before him; Orica sheltered nervously behind. Nearby, a cart had been hitched up to two horses that were now being held by stable boys. Garric presumed they'd been caught trying to leave.

'Get up on the balcony,' he told Fen. 'We may need your bow. The rest of you, stick close.'

They pushed their way to the front of the crowd, where Garric seized Aren by the arm.

'What's in your head, boy? This isn't our fight!'

Aren pulled away from him with the sullen fury of the young. Garric let him go; a struggle here would attract attention.

'When *will* it be our fight?' Aren demanded.

'When the time is right! Pick your battles. There are more important things at stake here than some Sard, no matter how pretty you think her.'

Aren gave him a look of disgust, but though he was desperate to do something, there was nothing to be done.

'Let's just shoot the fool!' said a crossbowman to Garric's right, his weapon aimed and ready.

'Hold,' said the soldier next to him. 'He says he's a Harrish noble.

You don't want to upset the apple cart right before the prince's wedding, not with the Emperor trying to make an alliance.'

The crossbowman spat in the dirt. 'He's on Krodan soil now,' he said, but he didn't fire.

The inspector walked out into the yard and put his fist across his chest in salute. 'Hail to the Emperor!' he declared loudly, addressing Harod. 'If you are indeed who you say you are, then you're a civilised man. Put up your sword. There is no need for violence.'

'You shall not have her,' said Harod, his eyes never leaving the men arrayed against him.

'If she has the correct paperwork, she will be allowed to continue on her way. If not, she will be detained. There is nothing to fear if you've done nothing wrong.'

'In this land, that has not been true for a long time.'

The inspector stiffened. He glanced around at the waiting crowd. His air of authority was slipping, and his temper with it.

'This land is part of the Krodan Empire!' he said, a note of indignity creeping into his voice. 'And we follow the rule of law here! I say again: put up your sword. We will show you no mercy if you do not! Neither you nor the Sard you protect.'

Garric didn't miss the distaste in the inspector's voice. *Sard*. Harod didn't miss it, either.

'Tell me, Inspector,' Harod said, with that unwavering, haughty calm, 'what law protects the Sards? We have been to Addisport, Tatterfane, Maresmouth. Once, there were hundreds of Sards in those towns. Now there are none. Disappeared, almost overnight, and taken east in secret. Where do you send them? To the ghetto in Morgenholme? Is that where you will send milady?'

The inspector's nostrils flared. That was too much defiance to be borne in public. 'You have refused to obey a representative of the Emperor before all these good citizens. Your noble birth does not entitle you to act like a criminal here. One last time: put up your sword, or I will have you both executed!'

'Harod!' said Orica. 'Do as he says. You can't fight them all.'

'And surrender milady to whatever fate they have in store? I think not.' He raised his voice. 'Come at me, then, if you must; but you will pay a heavy price for it.'

'As you wish,' said the inspector. 'Kill him!'

The soldiers edged closer, keeping him at sword's length. The crossbowman to Garric's right sighted but didn't fire.

'They're in the way,' he muttered.

'There's five of them,' said his companion. 'He won't last long.'

One of the soldiers lunged. Harod tapped his blade aside, ran him neatly through and reverted to the same awkward, constipated fighting stance as before.

'Four now,' said Garric, unable to resist.

'*Kill him!*' the inspector yelled, his face reddening. Soldiers ran in from the crowd to join their fellows, including the crossbowman's companion. Garric saw a second crossbowman nearby, circling for a shot.

Now they all set upon Harod together. He'd chosen his spot well, for with the wooden walls of the stall to either side they could only approach two at a time. His sword flicked this way and that, his movements coiled, economical and disciplined. The Harrish fighting style was designed to frustrate, a patiently defensive art aimed at luring the enemy into overextending themselves. When they did, they died. It was quickly plain that he was an expert at it.

Another Krodan soldier dropped at Harod's feet. His companion, angered by the sight, pressed harder and got a blade in the belly for his trouble. But now there were a dozen soldiers moving in on him, and he couldn't win against those odds. He'd be killed soon enough, though Garric couldn't help admiring him for putting up such a fight.

'We have to do something,' Aren said.

'It's not our business,' said Garric.

Aren was rubbing at an odd mark on his wrist. 'A Sard helped me escape that camp. I'd never have got out if not for him.'

'Dying's a poor way to honour his efforts,' said Garric. 'World's a bad place, and sometimes you have to turn away. You can't stop this.'

'I owe him a debt.'

'Boy, you know nothing of debts.'

'I know what lengths you went to in order to pay yours.'

Garric let that pass. The fight around the stable stall had become a bloody farce for the Krodans. Two men were dead and another was screaming and holding in his guts as blood spurted across the cobbles. Those behind him were trying to step over their fallen, while Harod fended away any who came near.

The inspector's fury grew as he saw some Ossians in the crowd daring to smirk. 'Make space, you moonwits!' he shouted at his men. 'Crossbows, take aim!'

Aren's hand was clasped around the hilt of his sword, his pulse jumping at his neck. 'Turn away,' Garric warned.

'I can't,' said Aren, and he surged forward with a cry, drawing his sword.

'Aren, don't!' Cade cried from behind him.

'I knew he had a death wish,' Keel muttered, and he muscled out of the crowd, pulling his own blade as he ran after Aren.

So be it, thought Garric, and a flare of eager violence lit in his breast. He barged sideways, knocking into the crossbowman on his right. The trigger clicked, the bowstring thumped and the quarrel meant for Harod buried itself in the meat of a soldier's arm instead.

The second crossbowman, who also had Harod in his sights, hesitated as he heard the soldier scream. Fen shot him through the neck from above and he fell gargling, his crossbow firing harmlessly into the cobbles.

Garric wrapped his arm around the first crossbowman's throat and pulled him roughly onto his waiting dagger. He plunged it in three times, then let the man drop and drew his sword, his blood igniting in his veins. 'For Ossia!' he roared, his blade held high; then he charged.

The inspector scrambled back into the crowd as Aren, Keel and Garric laid into the soldiers from the rear. Aren reached them first and caught his target by surprise. The soldier was still turning when Aren plunged a sword through his ribs. Boy and man stood shocked and still, one realising what he'd done, the other what had been done to him. Then the soldier toppled, pulling the sword from Aren's numb hands.

Aren stumbled back, dazed and appalled. The boy was no killer; he wasn't used to death up close, or the look in a man's eyes as he died.

A Krodan soldier bore down on him, his blade raised. Garric moved to intercept, but before he could, an arrow punched through the soldier's cheeks. It was Fen, still shooting from above. The soldier dropped his sword and staggered back, pawing at his face, blood spilling over his lips. Garric decapitated him while he was defenceless.

The crowd scattered, screaming and shouting, running for the safety of the inn. Stable boys fled this way and that. Garric pulled Aren behind him.

'Stay back, boy. You've done enough.'

He ran to join Keel and together they laid into the soldiers, while Harod pressed the advantage from the other side. The Krodans panicked as they found themselves surrounded, their discipline crumbling, and after that they were mere meat for the cutting. Garric hacked and stabbed, hot blood spattering his cheek as his blade bit bone. He gave a cry of exultation and hate, swept up in the joyous throes of killing. He was unleashed now, and Nine, how he wished he could slaughter them all this way, how he wished every Krodan could die at his hand!

But the fight was all too brief, and as suddenly as it had begun, it was over. Garric stood panting among the corpses. The stable yard had emptied, the surviving soldiers put to flight. The man with the belly wound was still groaning weakly on the ground. Garric put a sword in him with less thought than he'd give to slaying a chicken.

He straightened and glanced over at Aren. The boy looked sick. 'Pick up your sword,' Garric told him. 'You killed a man, that's all. You'll do worse than that if you mean to follow me.'

Aren wavered for an instant, then his face firmed. He stooped, pulled his sword out of the dead soldier and sheathed it again.

'Thank you for your aid,' said Harod formally, 'but it was not required. I had the matter in hand.'

Keel laughed in disbelief. 'You'd have had a crossbow bolt in each eye, Harrow man!'

'I beg to differ.'

'He begs to differ,' said Keel flatly, looking at Garric.

'Beg all you like, and save your thanks,' Garric told Harod.

'Those Krodans will be back with reinforcements. We'd best not be here when they do.' He eyed the cart, hitched and idle at the edge of the yard, the horses stamping nervously at the smell of blood. 'That's yours?'

'Out of the question!' Harod said. 'We travel alo—'

'What Harod means to say,' said Orica, emerging from the stall behind him, 'is that we are deeply grateful for your help, and it would be our honour to have you travel with us to Morgenholme, in return for your protection on the journey. Isn't that right, Harod?'

'Milady!' Harod protested. 'I am quite capable of defending you myself!'

She laid a hand on his arm. 'I know you are,' she said gently. 'But there's no harm in a little help, yes? And these people are no friends of the Krodans.' Her green eyes found Aren.

Garric caught her look and wondered what had passed between them last night in the common room. But now wasn't the time to ask. The battle-fury was leaking away, leaving him trembling, and they needed to go.

'Fortune smiles on us,' he said. 'The capital is our destination, too. But the way south is too dangerous now. We plan a safer route, first north and then by sea.'

Orica inclined her head. 'That is wise,' she said. 'We will go that way.'

Harod said nothing. The slightest tic of his right eye was the only sign of his anger. Garric cared nothing for his feelings, as long as he didn't oppose them.

'Well and good, then,' said Garric. 'Now where's that cursed Skarl got to?'

A door at the edge of the stable yard was booted open and Grub emerged, dragging the corpse of the inspector by the arm. He dumped the body on the cobbles and dusted off his hands.

'What did you kill him for?' Cade asked. 'He was running away.'

'Grub didn't like his face,' he said. Then he popped the inspector's monocle over one eye and grinned a crooked grin.

'One less Krodan to burden the world,' said Garric. 'But enough escaped that could recognise us. Get your packs, all of you. We're leaving.'

He set off across the yard. Aren stared at him hollowly as he approached.

'I had to do it,' Aren said, as if Garric had asked for an explanation. 'You think I'm a fool, but you'd have turned away. You'd have left them to die.'

'Aye, I would. But you didn't,' he said as he walked past. 'That's why there's still hope for you.'

We are none of us responsible for the sins of our fathers, he thought as he went inside. When he was sure nobody could see him, he let a grudging smile cross his lips. *And perhaps we're not doomed to repeat them, either.*

51

There's nothing so fleet as news, thought Overwatchman Klyssen as he watched the hills roll by beyond the carriage window. It was a popular saying among the Ossians, who liked talk for talk's sake and were never averse to stating the obvious. *And nothing so slow as justice.*

News of the incident at the Reaver's Rest had been fleet indeed. By now, every settlement within twenty leagues had heard how a road patrol was humiliated and slaughtered there. How the malcontents would be rubbing their hands with glee.

Well, let them savour this small act of resistance. Let them gloat at how their masters were given a bloody nose in some backwater den. If the deaths of a dozen soldiers excited them so much, it was only a measure of how powerless they were, how rare their victories. Klyssen had other things to worry about.

The man once known as Laine of Heath Edge was still alive. Against all odds, he'd evaded the dreadknights and crossed the mountains. As the saying went, justice moved slowly, and it was long overdue for the ringleader of the Salt Fork rebellion. But it was coming, and he was bringing it.

Klyssen shifted on the bench to ease the pain in his tailbone. He'd been sitting still too long. Across from him, Harte gazed mildly out of the window into the clouded day, his face in three-quarter profile. A handsome face, a good Krodan face, orderly and firm of features. Klyssen loathed the sight of it.

Did Commander Gossen send you? he asked silently, for the thousandth time. *Who do you work for?*

Harte noticed his gaze and held it arrogantly. There was no deference there. Anyone would think he was Klyssen's superior, rather than the other way around. Perhaps he thought he deserved to be.

Your time will come, Klyssen thought.

'The trail is three days cold,' said Harte. 'We will be fortunate to find them now.'

Klyssen studied him owlishly through his spectacles. 'What would you suggest, Watchman Harte?' He never missed an opportunity to use Harte's title when he could. He needed reminding that he was a mere watchman, and a watchman second class at that. Not an overwatchman like Klyssen. And certainly not an overwatchman in line to be Commander.

'They'll have gone to ground by now,' Harte said. 'Inform our spies. Cast the net wide. Better than chasing them all over the country.'

'You don't think our quarry is worth the effort?'

'There are other ways to hunt him. How many weeks did we waste at Suller's Bluff, waiting to spring your trap?'

The trap that didn't catch him. That's what you want to say, isn't it?

'I just think we could be doing something more productive for the Empire than this,' Harte went on. 'This land is riddled with sedition, and there are better uses for three dreadknights and two watchmen of the Iron Hand than—'

'One of us is an *over*watchman,' Klyssen said prissily.

'Of course,' said Harte. His defiance was so bald, he didn't even blush. 'But perhaps, *Over*watchman Klyssen, we wouldn't be chasing our quarry with quite such vigour if you hadn't rashly staked your career on it in front of Chancellor Draxis himself?'

Harte wanted a reaction; Klyssen gave him none. It was only a rash move if he failed, and he didn't plan on failing. Salt Fork had made the Chancellor nervous, with the wedding – and a critical alliance with Harrow – so close at hand. By pledging to bring the leader of the rebels to justice, Klyssen had publicly thrown his hat in the ring to be the next Commander of Ossia, a position that everyone had assumed would go to Gossen's sycophantic second, Oskar Bettren. If Klyssen could get his man, the Chancellor would be grateful indeed, and Gossen's job would surely be his once the old slug was pensioned off to the motherland.

'You need not worry about my career, Watchman Harte.' Klyssen fussed with a button on his sleeve which kept slipping loose. He'd have to see a tailor about that. 'For myself, I thank the Primus the trail is *only* three days cold. What good fortune we were so close, otherwise we would have no chance of catching them at all.'

The rest didn't need to be said. If they'd heeded Harte's advice and left the fugitives to perish in the mountains, they'd still be west of the Ostenbergs and the news wouldn't yet have reached them. Despite Harte's protests, Klyssen had insisted they travel to Crowbridge, on the east side of the range. In case the fugitives survived the mountains, Klyssen wanted to be there waiting for them. And so he was.

Harte hadn't missed his meaning. He sniffed and looked out of the window again, trying and failing to hide his frustration.

There, thought Klyssen. *Back in your place, for now.*

He'd wanted Vecken as his partner on this task. Vecken was a good watchman, and not half so ambitious. But Vecken had been conveniently unavailable, so they'd assigned him Harte instead, who'd been a thorn in his side ever since.

Was he Gossen's man, or not? Klyssen couldn't prove it, but it was always better to err on the side of caution. Long experience had taught him that it paid to be paranoid.

Watch me, then, if you must, he thought. *Maybe you'll learn something.*

They rolled into the stable yard of the Reaver's Rest in the early afternoon and found soldiers already there. The bodies had been removed and rain had washed the blood from the cobbles. When the driver opened the door, Harte began to get out, but Klyssen leaned across and ensured that he was the first to step down.

Small details mattered with Harte. Every day was a battle to keep him from getting above his station.

The arrival of a black carriage bearing the double-barred cross inspired a skittish uncertainty in the soldiers, guests and stable boys alike. They began to wonder if they'd done anything wrong, examining themselves for sedition. *Just as it should be*, thought Klyssen, sweeping the stable yard with a narrow gaze. He wanted to stretch, to relieve his aching muscles after the journey, but he resisted the urge. He was the authority here, and authority didn't ache, or tire, or become irritated or impatient. Authority was inhuman and perfect.

Captain Dressle, the most senior Iron Guardsman to travel with them, presented himself.

'Show me the bodies,' Klyssen said. 'Then organise my lunch and send in witnesses. Stable hands, then servants. I'll see the innkeeper last.'

'Yes, Overwatchman.' Dressle saluted smartly, fist across his chest, and headed off to obey.

Dealing with Dressle was a pleasure in comparison to Harte. He was respectful, trustworthy, capable and prided himself on doing a good job. Would that there were more like him.

'Why not start with the innkeeper?' Harte said. Ever questioning, ever contrary. 'If anyone will know about the guests, it's him. I thought speed was of the essence?'

'If he's seen me talk to everyone else first, he'll wonder what they've said, and he won't be tempted to lie or leave anything out in case he contradicts them. You know how people are in Ossia. Misplaced loyalties to the old ways tend to make them less than forthcoming.'

'He's Xulan, not Ossian,' Harte pointed out. They'd learned as much before they set off.

'His clientele are mostly Ossian, and Ossians don't like informers. He won't be eager to help us. So let's make it easy for him to do the right thing.'

The bodies of the dead had been wrapped in hessian and laid out in a barn, away from the inn and guests. Klyssen's men uncovered them and a cleric noted their names while a group of men waited to load them onto a gravedigger's cart. The air was thick with a musty smell, but it had been cool these last few days and the stench wasn't yet overpowering. Though Klyssen had a delicate stomach for food, bad smells and gore didn't bother him. He'd seen enough corpses that they all looked like mannequins now.

Some were pierced, some slashed. One unfortunate had been decapitated and had an arrow through his cheeks. So many ways to die, but all the same result in the end. Klyssen wasn't sure what clue the bodies might reveal, but he was ever thorough and liked to leave no stone unturned. He inspected each of the fallen, noting how they'd died, which had been neatly stabbed, which hacked and which shot. One among their opponents was clearly an expert swordsman. He killed so tidily that his victims were scarcely marked at all.

When he was done, he waved at the men to take them away. 'That was a waste of time,' Harte commented as they went back to the inn.

'Time is never wasted in service of the Empire,' Klyssen said, imagining Harte's corpse being loaded onto the cart with the others.

Dressle had set up a booth for him in the common room, and he was brought a meal by a timid servant girl. It was good Krodan fare: lamb shanks in rich gravy, stewed greens, nutty yellow potatoes. None of that fussy, over-spiced Ossian cooking, or those vile eels they so enjoyed. Once he was ready, he sent Dressle to round up the witnesses in the corridor outside and had Harte bring them to him one by one. It was a particularly pleasing arrangement because it kept Harte on his feet and prevented him from eating. Instead, he was forced to stand by the booth, able to smell the food while Klyssen conducted his interrogations. Klyssen took no small satisfaction in hearing his stomach gurgle. He hadn't forgotten how Harte had executed the prisoner at Shoal Point without Klyssen's permission, claiming the credit for himself.

It didn't take long to build up a picture of events in the court-yard. Of the eight fugitives that had escaped his dreadknights, seven had survived. The Skarl was still with them, and so was the traitor's boy and his haybrained friend. The druidess, too, though no one recognised her as such. And now they were travelling with a Sard and a Harrish noble. Likely he was the swordsman who'd so precisely impaled those men in the barn. But what was their connection to the others?

The fugitives could have kept their heads down and passed

unnoticed. Instead they'd got into a fight in front of dozens of witnesses, ensuring they'd all be remembered. They might as well have blown a horn to announce their presence.

Klyssen sensed weakness. First, his quarry had fallen for the trap at Suller's Bluff. Only the incompetence of the camp's guards and an unfortunately timed breakout saved his life. Now he'd slipped up again. He was like a wounded animal, harried and exhausted. It was only a matter of time.

Finally, his meal long finished and washed down with a glass of strong Krodan red, he called for the innkeeper.

His name was Rapapet. He had a long, sensuous face and delicate hands, a fluting voice and a cat's grace. Klyssen distrusted him instantly. The Xulans were godless, worshipping only their own bodies. Their shameless, overt sexuality and raw narcissism disgusted him. They'd rejected their deities for a doctrine of self-love and a cultish belief that they could perfect themselves without the need for higher powers.

In practice, of course, it was only the nobility who had enough idle time to explore their own orifices with such mystical fervour. The lower castes starved and slaved as they did in all lesser societies. The Xulans thought themselves sophisticates, but the way they neglected their own poor was barbarous.

Those who do not stand united will fall apart. That was a Krodan saying. The Ossians, predictably, had nothing similar in their language, and Klyssen suspected the Xulans didn't, either.

'This is a strange place to find a Xulan,' he observed. 'Deep in the heart of Ossia, far from anywhere.'

Rapapet spread his hands. Elegant lace ruffs surrounded narrow wrists. 'Fate is strange, Overwatchman. I came here as a young man seeking adventure and fell in love with the woman who owned this inn. We had twelve happy years together, before Sarla took her. Now I own it.'

'Sarla?' Klyssen raised an eyebrow.

Rapapet smiled. 'Forgive me. My wife's gods became mine, and I keep them to honour her. Of course, I would also attend convocation to praise the Primus if I could, but the nearest temple is far from here.'

I bet you would, thought Klyssen. He adjusted his spectacles. 'I'll be blunt. My interest is in a man with a large scar across his throat. Do you know him?'

A hesitation. Deciding whether to lie. It was answer enough for Klyssen, but he waited for a reply nonetheless.

'I know him a little,' said Rapapet. 'He was here a few days ago. He calls himself Garric now, though he used a different name before that.'

Right answer, thought Klyssen. 'And you spoke to him?'

Another flicker of uncertainty. Calculating what he could safely say.

'It's a simple question,' Klyssen said, sharp and quick, before he could formulate a response. *Stop thinking. Tell me the truth.*

'Forgive me,' said Rapapet, getting a little flustered now. 'Yes, I did. We spoke in the common room, the night before the road patrol came.'

'What did you speak of?'

'He needed transportation for his companions. The two boys and the Skarl. Any city or town would do, he said. I knew of some merchants who would take them to Greenrock and he seemed happy with that.'

Interesting. 'But they did not leave.'

'No. I don't know why.'

Klyssen believed that. Xulans were hard to read, especially the highborn ones; their faces revealed only what they wanted them to. But his instincts told him that this, at least, was true.

'And Garric?' he asked. 'Surely he needed transport, too?'

'He sought passage to Morgenholme.'

The slightest change of tone in his voice, the uncertain way he ended the sentence, told Klyssen there was more to say. He held the Xulan's gaze. Specks of sweat were beginning to glisten on his shiny black scalp. 'And?'

Rapapet looked down at the table, discomfited. 'Then we talked of other things,' he admitted. 'He was interested in the siege engines of my homeland.'

'Siege engines?' This was a curious turn, and too bizarre to be false. People lied in a straight line; they thought they had to construct a narrative to be believable. But the truth usually came jumbled, and from all directions at once.

'Yes. He had heard of the *xattax* – I think the translation is "fire-flinger" in Krodan. I am no student of history, but I told him what I knew. It was a ... ballista of sorts that would throw great ceramic balls coated with pitch and set alight. The balls were hollow and held some alchemy that few understood. They destroyed their targets with great force, thunder and fire; but they often proved more dangerous to their users than their targets, and many were destroyed when the substance ignited prematurely.' He made a dainty motion in the air, some Xulan gesture Klyssen didn't recognise. 'That is all I can say of them.'

'An unusual thing to ask about.'

'Yes. He was very interested. And after that, he changed his mind about Morgenholme. He asked if I knew anyone going north.'

'And did he say where he was heading?'

That hesitation again. Klyssen decided it was time to push. 'I have travelled far to get here, Xulan, and I don't have time to waste,' he said. Cool, controlled, detached. 'You will not wait to be asked the correct question. You will tell me everything you know, and leave out nothing, or you will be arrested as a collaborator and I will have you hanged from the sign of your own inn.'

'Wracken Bay!' said Rapapet, almost before Klyssen had finished. 'He was going to Wracken Bay.'

'Why?'

Rapapet was frightened now. 'I do not know! He asked me if I knew of a reliable Xulan merchant. I know of only one: my cousin Atatep. He's a sailor who trades along the coast and often visits Wracken Bay to restock. But Atatep is a lawful man, I swear! I did not know that this Garric was wanted by the Iron Hand!'

You did not want to involve your cousin. Now I see why you were reluctant to talk.

'If what you say is true, he will not be harmed. It is Garric I'm after. Did he say what he wanted from your cousin?'

'I asked, Overwatchman, but he would not say!'

Rapapet was desperate for Klyssen to believe him. Klyssen gazed into his eyes until he was sure that he did.

'You may go,' he said. Rapapet sagged like a fish taken down from a hook. He hurried clumsily from the booth, all grace lost in his haste.

Harte sniffed. 'I still say you could have started with him and saved us an afternoon.'

Klyssen ignored him. 'Captain Dressle!' he called, getting to his feet. Dressle walked over and saluted smartly. 'Gather your men and send to the dreadknights. We leave for Wracken Bay immediately.'

'What about *my* lunch?' Harte cried indignantly.

'You can eat on the road,' said Klyssen, sweeping past him. He treasured the sound of Harte's outraged curses all the way back to the carriage.

52

The morning was chill and damp, and the wind carried the threat of winter. Keel stood at the crest of a gentle rise, with the wide water of the Cut at his back and bracken rustling all around him. At the end of the trail was a small cottage of stone and thatch with a thriving vegetable patch to one side. Smoke unwound slowly from the chimney.

He'd been standing there for some time now, watching the cottage. Caught between the desire to run to the door, and the desire to turn around and leave unobserved. A tight band squeezed his chest and he felt lightheaded with nerves born of equal parts excitement and dread.

What are you afraid of? It's your family!

But he *was* afraid. Afraid that things had changed. Afraid of the reckoning he faced each time he returned. Afraid this cottage would become his hutch.

He took a bag of coins from his pouch, weighed it in his hand. Krodan money from the Salt Fork coffers. It was more than he usually came back with, but it never felt adequate. Half of what he took had been spent on the way. Money always had a way of slipping through his fingers. Perhaps he just didn't care about it enough. It was deeds, not coin, that brought him to life.

But his tales of adventure would get no welcome here. It was coin that counted, and in that he was always destined to disappoint her.

'Keel, you're a fool!' he said aloud, to shame himself into action.

'All this way, and you think of turning back? Stop wasting time out here, when your wife waits inside!'

Heartened, he replaced the bag of coins and set off down the trail, putting a swing in his stride. Yes, they'd fight. Didn't they always? But there'd be love, too, as there always was. And how he'd missed her eyes, her smile, the soft, warm touch of her body. Roamer though he was, he'd lain with no other since they were married, and his step quickened at the thought of what the night might bring.

He thought of Tad, too. Strange, quiet Tad, distant and beautiful, the fey changeling they'd brought into the world together. He didn't smile often, but when he did it was like the sun breaking over the sea. Keel ached to see that smile again. His son was a puzzle he'd never solve, but those occasional moments of connection, those small victories when his face cleared and there was laughter in his eyes, made all the struggle worthwhile.

Joy welled up within him and his doubts dissolved as he reached the door and threw it open. 'Wife! To me!' he roared. 'I'm back!'

Two startled faces turned towards him. Their owners were halfway through a breakfast of fish broth and bread, sitting at a small table that stood against the wall of the stone-floored kitchen. One was Mariella, fairer to his eyes in real life than in his most rose-tinted memories. The other was his brother Fluke.

'What's this?' he said, his face falling a little.

'Keel!' Mariella cried, knocking back her stool as she surged to her feet. She flung her arms round his neck and kissed him, hard and hungrily. He forgot everything in the white heat of her. It was all so right: the smell of her skin and hair, the way she fitted in his arms, the way she wanted him. Past and future faded away, and there was only sensation, and nothing else.

The sound of a stool scraping along the floor jerked him from bliss. He opened his eyes and there was Fluke, dark and sour, wearing that half-scowl of disapproval Keel knew so well. His younger brother was stockier than he, broader of face. Once he'd styled himself whaler-fashion, as Keel did, with a strip of long hair down the centre of his skull and shaved elsewhere; but he'd been a landsman for many years now and his black curly hair had grown out thick all over.

'Brother,' he said in greeting.

Keel let go of his wife and embraced him without enthusiasm, because form demanded it.

'It's good you're back,' said Fluke.

'It's good to *be* back,' said Keel. Neither of them sounded quite sure if they meant it.

Fluke grunted, as if the business of his brother's sudden appearance had now been concluded and there was nothing more to be said on it. 'I'll let you catch up, then,' he told them. 'Reckon I'll head back to the farm.' He patted Keel on the shoulder, as if in consolation. 'Come see me after, eh?'

'I'll do that,' said Keel.

Fluke gave Mariella a meaningful look, which Keel didn't much like, and sloped off.

Keel rounded on his wife. 'Well, this is some homecoming.' He didn't want to get angry but it was happening anyway. Fluke's presence had spoiled his grand entrance and he felt foolish.

'Don't,' said Mariella. 'He comes over for breakfast after he's fed the animals and I like the company in the morning. Makes the place feel a little less empty.'

He heard the resentment in that. Things were already sharpening between them. He knew where that would lead, and it wasn't anywhere he was keen to go. With some effort, he reined himself in and tried to dismiss the spectre of his younger brother.

'Forgive me,' he said, laying his hand on her arm. 'It was just a surprise.'

'Did you expect me to be here on my own, staring at the door like a good wife, waiting for the day you choose to return?' She didn't respond to his touch. The passion of a few moments ago had gone; she'd remembered her grievances.

'Of course not. Forget all that. I'm back.'

Still she didn't melt. 'And how long are you back for?'

He felt his heart sink a little. She had to ask *that*, didn't she?

'I don't know,' he said, removing his hand.

She said nothing in reply. There was frost in the set of her shoulders. Joha, he'd only just walked in after months away! Couldn't they go back to the kissing? Couldn't she be happy to see him *now*, without complicating it with talk of the future?

He stepped away, feeling unwanted, out of place in his own house. Things had been moved and changed in his absence. Mariella had a new tablecloth; there was a new pot on the sill. Someone had repaired that broken chair; Fluke, no doubt. The thought irked him. Likely his brother's coin had paid for the tablecloth and pot, too. Every time he returned, this seemed less like his home.

He dug into his pouch and dropped the bag of coins on the table. There! Let her see that *he* could provide, too.

Mariella looked down at it. No gratitude there, of course. He shouldn't have expected any.

'It's not much, but it'll see you through the winter,' he said, his voice tight as he fought the unmanly urge to sulk.

She raised her eyes to his, and there was a bleak sadness there that sent tendrils of dread wrapping round his heart. He thought of Fluke's meaningful look as he left, and suddenly he knew its cause.

'Where's Tad?' he asked.

Tad's room was dim with the curtains drawn. A floorboard creaked beneath Keel's boot as he came in and he cursed softly. He always forgot about that floorboard.

He remembered the smell of this room more than the sight of it: the clean, healthy scent of boyhood. But the air was musty now and reeked of convalescence. In the bed, tucked up to his neck in blankets, was Tad; or, at least, a sallow approximation of him. His eyes were closed, the sockets dark, and his breath bubbled as he pulled it in and out.

The sight of him was a shock. It was hard to see him so changed. Keel looked away, needing a moment to gather himself.

Mariella had come in behind him. She slipped her hand into his.

'It's his lungs,' she said. 'He's got the grip.'

The grip. Keel had known from the moment he stepped into the room, but the confirmation sent a wave of weakness through him nonetheless.

'How?' was the first thing he could think of to say.

'Off the boats? Some merchant from the Rainlands? What does it matter?' She sounded washed out, resigned. He wasn't used to that tone from her. 'He's had it since Aspects' Day, or thereabouts.'

'He's been like this since Latespring?' Keel hissed, appalled.

The accusation in his voice awoke her temper. 'What should I have done?' she hissed back, snatching her hand away. 'Should I have had old Ganny write you a letter? And what would he use as an address?'

Keel bit back a reply. *You could have tried. You could have found me.* But she couldn't. He wasn't anywhere to be found. He was furious at himself, not her.

He stared at his boy, listening to the moist wheeze that came with every breath, the tide of his life, in and out. It didn't feel real.

'What does Podrey say?' he asked.

'Little of worth,' she replied. He knew what she thought of the town herbalist. Everyone thought the same. 'He prescribed some weeds which did nothing. I went to another herbalist, and another after that, and each gave me something different and all of it was useless. In the end, Fluke sent for the Krodan doctor from Harlsbeach.'

Keel felt something curdle in his gut at that. It was *his* job to provide for his family. Who gave Fluke the right to bring in the squareheads? Wasn't the Ossian way good enough?

Once again, he stopped himself before he could say something he'd regret. Seemed like he was always doing that round Mariella. Just being near her turned him into a stroppy boy.

If he was honest with himself, in Fluke's shoes he'd have done the same. Difference was, he wouldn't have had the money. His family couldn't live on what he brought back, and if it weren't for Fluke's charity, they'd starve. The only way he'd have been able to afford a Krodan doctor was by begging his younger brother for help. Every moment he spent in Wracken Bay, he was reminded of that.

'Don't you want to know what he said?' Mariella said, when he didn't ask.

'Yes,' he said. *No. I don't want to hear it.*

'He said we need to take him somewhere the air is drier. Away from the coast. He needs the care of a proper doctor, a *Krodan* doctor, not some quack who'll serve him root stew and call it medicine. And he needs some kind of device … It's like a helmet that he puts on, like a mask … There's a contraption that makes vapours from herbs and he breathes them …' She tailed off. 'I don't understand it all. Fluke can explain it better than I.'

Keel's heart sank further. He didn't need to hear Fluke explain it. They'd never have that kind of money, and moving away would be nigh on impossible. Even buying the permits was beyond their means. Just one visit from the doctor would have cost Fluke more than he could spare; regular care was out of the question for all but the richest Ossians. Krodans had access to doctors for free, paid for by the Empire, but that courtesy didn't extend to their subjects.

A drier climate. Doctors. A vapour mask. Might as well try to pull the moons down from the sky.

'What happens if we can't?' he asked grimly.

'You know what happens,' she whispered, and her eyes glittered with tears. 'Within a year, the doctor said. If he was strong, he'd last longer. But he's never been strong.'

Tad's breathing changed then, and he snorted and stirred.

'I'll get him some broth,' said Mariella.

Keel almost reached out to stop her, but she was gone too suddenly. What would he say, anyway? *Don't leave me alone in here!* How could he? She'd never understood that part of him, the way he feared himself and dreaded solitude. He needed the company of others to stop his thoughts turning inwards, devouring themselves and him with them. As a young man, he'd stared into that abyss more than once, that terrible place where joy and ambition became pointless and he was surrounded by the cold profundity of death. Time and toil brought him out of it, but the experience had left its mark and he never wanted to go back. Better to distract himself; better not to dwell on things.

He'd found that distraction in the camaraderie of sailors, in Mariella's love, in a friendship with Garric that was more like brotherhood. And given the choice between following Garric or staying in Wracken Bay with his family, it was the lure of the road that decided it. Routine led back to the darkness. He needed to make the world new every day.

He stood awkwardly by the door, watching Tad struggle up from sleep as the void billowed in his mind. He tried to push it back, but he didn't know how, and

eyes tendrils mouths with teeth like hooks and the smell of it was like

He crushed his eyes shut, mashed them with the heels of his hands as if he could press out the memory of the beast of Skavengard. The others had glimpsed it in silhouette, protected from its horror by blinding light. But he'd looked into its ungodly eye and seen the foul intelligence there. He'd been scorched by the force of its mind. He hadn't slept since without seeing it, and it ambushed him during his waking hours as well.

Skavengard had marked them all, but none so deeply as he. He'd glimpsed the nature of the things that lurked beyond the Shadowlands, the vast and hungry entities that stirred in their prison beneath Kar Vishnakh, the Citadel of Chains. How could anything be the same after that?

'Da?'

He took his hands away from his face. Tad's eyes were open, his head turned to one side on the pillow. His gaze was clear and steady, and he had that half-puzzled, half-curious expression on his face.

The sight of his son shredded the darkness in his mind. He was a father; he wouldn't greet his son with weakness.

'My boy!' he said, and a smile came easily to his face. He opened his arms wide. 'I'm back!'

There was no smile from Tad, no happiness at his father's return. Keel's arms wilted under that calm regard; his enthusiastic greeting felt forced and theatrical now. Keel had always wanted a son he could knock about with, one who'd be pleased with the rough, bluff parenting he'd learned from his own da. But Tad hated romping, and found manly humour bewildering. Not for the first time, Keel wondered how he and Mariella had managed to create a child that was nothing like either of them.

He sat down on a stool next to the bed and pushed Tad's hair back from his forehead. 'Your ma tells me you're not feeling well,' he said.

'Sorry, Da.'

'Nothing to be sorry about. Even the strongest man can be felled by illness. Evric the Red spent half his youth abed, but he went on to unify Ossia after the Fall, conquered the barbarian warlords and began the Age of Kings. He was the first to wield the Ember Blade in four hundred years, after everyone thought it was lost. The Dawnwardens had been keeping it secretly all that time, waiting for someone like him. How about that? Not bad for a feeble boy.'

Tad just looked up at him. Keel stroked his head gently and felt himself pierced by a cold shard of grief. His helplessness frightened him. He didn't know what to say or do. How was it possible to love somebody so, and yet be strangers?

'Have you had adventures?' Tad asked.

'I have. All over the country. We faced many perils, me and your Uncle Laine. High seas, Krodan soldiers ...'

Monsters, he thought, and it flashed through his mind again, black tentacles squirming down the corridors, a dozen mouths gnashing behind them.

'Ma says you're fighting to save Ossia. That's why you're always away.'

Something twisted in his chest at that. Yes, that was the story he told. Sometimes he even believed it himself.

He heard Mariella on the stairs. 'Here's your ma now,' he said, relieved.

She came in with a bowl of fish broth and a brave smile for them both. Tad struggled to sit up against the headboard, so Keel helped him. Even that small movement appeared to exhaust him, and he slumped there limply, wheezing.

'Can I?' he asked Mariella, holding out his hand for the broth.

'He can feed himself,' Mariella said. 'Just give him a moment to rest.'

'I want to,' said Keel, quietly insistent.

Mariella handed over the bowl. He filled a spoon, blew on it, held it up for his son. 'Some of your ma's broth,' he said. 'Make you strong again, eh?'

Tad opened his mouth and accepted it like a baby. Keel filled the spoon again. He felt Mariella's eyes on him, but he wouldn't look up at her. He was afraid she'd see the pain in him, the feeling in his chest as if he was splitting open from the inside.

'I'm here now,' he murmured as he fed another spoonful of broth to his son. 'I'm back.'

Later, when Tad was asleep again, they made love in a hot tangle of blankets and limbs. The first time, it was desperate, savage, driven by their need to be together after so long apart. The second time, they were gentler, lingering as they rediscovered each other's bodies, finding old flaws and new scars.

Afterwards, they lay together, her head on his chest while his gaze roamed the ceiling, tracing familiar whorls and cracks in the beams. They, at least, were the same as they'd ever been. With Mariella in the circle of his arm and the sweat cooling on their skin, he didn't need to think further than the walls of their bedroom, and everything was perfect.

It didn't last, of course. Soon she began to talk, to tell him of what had passed in Wracken Bay while he'd been away. Grievances between neighbours; Abna's boy running wild; bad fishing due to summer storms. Little Espy had got herself with child and wouldn't say who the father was. Keel listened and nodded and tried to ignore the feeling that his soul was shrivelling with every new tale. The same names he'd known all his life, the same petty gossip, none of it worth a whale's fart to anyone outside their little town. While he'd been trying to start a revolution, she'd struck a deal with a fisherman to shave a few bits off the price of her weekly shop.

He wanted to care, because she cared, but the best he could do was pretend. Even together, they were so far apart, and the distance was only increasing.

'Jadrell's worse than ever,' she was saying. 'He styles himself a lord, as if that has meaning any more, and he treats us like we're serfs of old. Everyone knows how *he* keeps his title! His father did well out of the invasion, but Jadrell's done better still. Seems like every month another building or farm falls into his hands. He owns half the town now.'

'Collaborator,' Keel muttered angrily. Lord Jadrell was news he could care about. He'd love to put a sword through that treacherous snake. He and his father had been brazen in their support for the new regime, and plenty of Ossians in Wracken Bay had gone to the camps and gallows because Jadrell had whispered in a Krodan ear. The only crime most of them were guilty of was owning something Jadrell wanted.

'He's got his eye on this place, too,' Mariella warned. 'And your brother's farm.'

Keel saw through that one. Jadrell didn't care about some insignificant cottage or one barely prosperous farm. He felt the last of his inner peace fade away as he prepared for the inevitable argument to come.

'Where's Laine, anyway?' she asked, circling towards her point. 'Or Garric, now, is it? Why'd he change his name?'

'Because Laine's a dangerous name to bear these days. He's down in the town, seeing to business.'

'Securing your escape, no doubt,' she muttered.

He sighed. *Must we do this again?*

Mariella was determined they must. 'Haven't you done enough for him?' she asked. 'Aren't you tired of following him about? Let him fight this crusade on his own.'

'I don't do it for him. I do it because it needs doing. So people like Lord Jadrell can't take our house from us just because he knows which Krodan arse to kiss.'

'That's not why you do it,' she said, and rolled off him.

He turned onto his side, too, facing the other way, and pillowed his head with his arm. It was a grey day outside and the bracken was stirring on the hill.

'You need to stay,' she said quietly.

'We need money,' he said. 'A lot of it. I can't make that kind of money in Wracken Bay.'

'No!' She rolled back again with a rustle of blankets and sat up, her fingers clutching his shoulder. 'No, don't go again! Tad needs you. Fluke will give you a job on the farm, he's said he will all along.'

'Ha! And suffer his judgement every day of my life? I'm gods-damned if I'll be employed by my little brother. If I stayed, I'd go back to the boats.'

'And then you'd only be away a month at a time, instead of whole seasons. Quite an improvement that'll be,' she said sarcast-ically. 'I want you *here*, Keel. I want to wake up with you, I want you to be there for our son.'

'I have to *do* something!' he cried, flinging off the covers and sitting up. 'I won't stand by and watch him die!'

'No. You'll turn your back so you don't have to.'

The defeat in her voice was the worst of it. He wanted her to scream and shout, to pound him with her fists. Not to give up like that. He couldn't go on if she gave up on him.

'We have a druidess with us,' he said. 'Maybe she can do better than Podrey.'

She was hardly listening. She knew the Krodan cure was beyond them and in her heart she'd accepted that Tad would die. She wouldn't dare admit hope.

'I love you, Keel,' she said. 'I wish to Joha I didn't. Every day, I wake up alone. All this time ... at least I had Tad. But now ...' She couldn't finish. 'Stay with me.'

He kissed her, because he knew she needed it, and because it was better than an answer. His hand found her breast and he pushed her back onto the bed. She was just as eager as he to forget the world. For a time, they almost managed it.

If only there weren't any words, he thought. If only they could just be together.

If only.

53

The docks were busy beneath the steel-grey roof of the morning. Merchant vessels rocked at anchor while burly stevedores of many nations loaded them with produce. Krodan customs men roamed about, nosing into this and that, quills waggling as they scribbled down their observations. Fishing boats crept back with the morning's catch while gulls wheeled and called overhead, and the air smelled of salt and wet wood.

Garric leaned against a warped fence, shucking an oyster with his knife. He cracked open the shell with a twist, ran the blade expertly round the inside and tipped the oyster into his mouth.

Fresh Wracken Bay oysters. Nothing tasted quite like them. If there was any place he might have called home these last thirty years, this was it. He'd never loved the town, but there was comfort in familiarity and it eased his heart to be back.

A light fog lay on the water. The north bank of the Cut was lost to sight, but the crooked silhouette of the Ghoulfort was still visible in the murk. Half-ruined, it brooded out in the channel on a lonely island of rock, a hulking pile of spikes and angles patrolled by crows. Folk called it the Ghoulfort because in high winds it howled like the undead still walked there, and they steered well clear of it. But Garric knew it by another name. *Annach-na-Zuul*, it was called in the harsh tongue of the urds.

It had been built in the days of the First Empire, when men were slaves and the urds ruled Embria from coast to coast. Their strongholds had mostly been destroyed during the Reclamation, torn down for materials, taking the bad memories of former masters with them. But it had been the wish of Jessa Wolf's-Heart, left to posterity by her lover Morgen, that some strongholds should remain, abandoned. They were to be a warning from history, a plea to never relax their vigilance lest evil creep back in.

Would that we had taken more heed, Garric thought. Instead, they'd become soft and divided, squabbling among themselves while their neighbours in Kroda were reforged by the Word and the Sword. They'd become appeasers, denying the threat from the east till it was too late.

When Kroda invaded Brunland and Ozak seventy years ago, reclaiming their old territories, Ossia didn't react. When the Krodans took Estria and the Glass University thirty-five years later, Ossia should have begun making ready for war, but the nobility were too busy with their own small struggles. All that warning, and it was still a surprise when Kroda attacked. Ossia crumbled, Queen Alissandra Even-Tongue was executed, and the Ember Blade was seized by a crafty young Krodan general called Dakken, which effectively ended the resistance.

But what would have happened if it *hadn't* been seized?

The question had obsessed Garric for thirty years now. He'd turned it over and over and never found an answer he could believe with any certainty. If the Krodans hadn't taken the Ember Blade so early in the invasion, the Ossians could have rallied. Queen or no queen, the Ember Blade might have been enough to unite the nobility. Wars had been won from worse positions.

Or perhaps he was deluding himself and it would only have extended the slaughter. The Krodans were tactically superior, better armed, more disciplined and, most importantly, they fought together for a common goal. To battle on would have cost tens of thousands more lives, and when the surrender came, they'd have been crushed into near-slavery for their efforts. Just like the brave men and women of Brunland, who refused to give up and paid the price.

Aren's father had believed it was better to submit, to exchange a hopeless war for a merciful peace. Garric's opinion was different.

He pulled another oyster from the string bag, stuck in the knife, twisted till its shell cracked.

Damned be all the peacemakers, he thought. *Cowards by another name.*

'Laine of Heath Edge,' said a voice at his shoulder. 'As I live an' breathe!'

'Surprised to see you living and breathing at all, Ambrey,' said Garric with half a smile.

Ambrey cackled. He was a scrawny man, muscles slack with age, his sagging face haggard with white stubble. Almost seventy years lay on his bones, and a life at sea had rubbed him ragged. He walked with a crutch under one arm, and his trousers were tied below the stump of his right leg, where a crude peg took the place of his foot.

'Whale get you at last?' Garric asked.

'Ha! *Hey-o! Hey-o! Stay abed, Borek!*' he sang, and gave Garric a rotted grin. 'They won't write a song about me, though. Rusty nail did for me foot. It started goin' black, so off it came!'

'You always swore you'd die at sea.'

'Life has its turns, don't it? Nine, the peg rubs something awful, though. What I'd give for one of them nice Malliard Limbs.'

He leaned up next to Garric and laid his crutch against the barrier, looking out across the dock.

'Back for long?' he asked.

'Just passing through.'

'Ah, probably wise. The hunt's not what it was. Carthanians catch most of 'em these days, the bloody thieves. All the old hands are dyin' off or turn to drink when they're too feeble to sail. Their sons run the boats now, and bein' young, they got to do everythin' their own way – which, needless to say, ain't so good as ours.'

Garric snorted his agreement and offered Ambrey an oyster. Ambrey thanked him and he shucked another for himself. The old man was easy company, a friend from his whaling days, though they'd never been close. They listened to the gulls with the salty, meaty taste of Wracken Bay oysters on their tongues.

'There's our lord and master,' said Ambrey, tilting his chin out towards the water.

A boat was coming down the coast, painted in the colours of Jadrell's house. It was his personal launch, which he used to visit other towns on the far bank of the Cut: an open boat with raised and covered decks at both ends, big enough for the Lord of Wracken Bay and a few guests to travel in comfort with a skeleton crew. Oars sculled the water to either side, for the winds and tides in the channel were too unreliable for a small craft to travel by sail alone.

'I see he still prospers,' Garric said scathingly.

'He does. Primus be thanked for his wise stewardship in these troubled times.' Ambrey's tone was so dry, his words could have been used for kindling. 'Most times we don't even see him, except at a distance. Spends all his time with the squareheads.'

'You should be more careful,' said Garric, wryly. 'I could be an informer.'

'You could,' Ambrey agreed. 'Give my regards to our geometric- ally perfect overlords when you see 'em.'

Garric barked with laughter. It had the sound of a quip heard elsewhere and oft repeated – Ambrey didn't have the vocabulary to come up with that himself – but it was a good one nonetheless.

They shared the rest of the oysters while they watched Jadrell's boat approach. As Ambrey had said, it didn't come into the harbour but docked further up the coast, pulling in to a private jetty at the foot of a steep slope. Three men disembarked, all wearing stiff jackets, straight trousers and boots: Krodan dress. One of them was likely Jadrell, but at this distance he was indistinguishable from his guests.

'Our lord's more Krodan than the Krodans these days,' said Ambrey, catching his thought. 'Funny thing is, the young square- heads get more Ossian every year. To annoy their folks, I reckon.' He chuckled. 'Kids are kids wherever they're from.'

Jadrell and his companions climbed a set of stairs up the slope towards the base of a cliff, topped by an imposing mansion which overlooked the water. The crew busied themselves with attaching thick ropes and hooks to the boat's hull and manoeuvring it round to a wooden slipway running down the length of the slope.

'Are they going to winch that thing in?' Garric asked in surprise.

'Never were much of a sailor, were you? Storms come on quick this time of year. That jetty's no shelter, and a boat like that's too fine to smash up. There's a boathouse at the top of the slope, see?'

Garric saw it now, a large shed below the mansion. The crew shouted up to the boathouse and Jadrell's craft was slowly pulled from the water, sliding up the slipway until it disappeared inside.

'Easier to put in at the harbour, surely,' Garric said. There was a breakwater out there, a kinked bank of piled stones reaching out into the Cut which protected the boats moored at the docks.

'Lords and fishermen, side by side. That's the tradition, since anyone can remember. Ain't like that now, though. Been longaday since *Lord* Jadrell put in at the harbour. Too good for us.'

'Times change,' said Garric.

'They do,' said Ambrey. 'And they'll change again.' He offered Garric a plug of tobacco, and when Garric refused, he popped one in his mouth and chewed. 'Young 'uns now, they don't know what freedom is. But we remember, don't we? All them nobles who bent over for the Krodans, they're on top now; but they'll get theirs when the Dawnwardens come back.'

Garric gave him a look of vague incredulity. 'The Dawnwardens are gone,' he said. 'They've been gone two hundred years or more, since they collaborated in the overthrow of King Danna the Moon-Touched.'

'Pfft. You believe that?'

'He wielded the Ember Blade, and they betrayed him.'

'For good reason! He was a halfwit in thrall to his cousin in Harrow. He'd have signed over everything north of the Cut to those stuck-up bastards, and the rest of Ossia would've gone after. We'd be bowing to the Harrish now instead of Krodans, only we'd have had two centuries more to get used to it.'

'That's true,' Garric agreed bitterly. 'And if not the Krodans, it'd be the elaru, or the Durnish, or someone else. Some days I think we were born to be slaves.'

'Pah! You sound like you used to in the Bellied Sail. Always were a maudlin drunk,' Ambrey complained. 'A Dawnwarden's loyalty was to the Ember Blade, not the one who wielded it. To Ossia, not its rulers. They done right by their oath, and by the land.'

'The king they put on the throne didn't see it that way.'

426

'He loved the Dawnwardens well enough till his own right to rule got called into question. Reckon he was afraid they might play kingmaker again, so he got rid of 'em. They've guarded this land since the first days of the Second Empire, since Rannis the Librarian put 'em together. Think a coward like Garam Hawkeye could tear 'em apart?' He waved a gnarled hand and spat brown juice over the barrier. 'They disappeared for centuries after the empire fell, but they came back when we needed 'em, and brung the Ember Blade with 'em. That's what they do. Mark me, they're out there somewhere, waitin' for their chance. And now the Ember Blade returns to Ossia. If that ain't a sign, I don't know what is.'

Garric felt his mood blackening and the oysters turned sour in his mouth. 'Maybe that's our problem,' he said. 'Too long we've waited for heroes to come and save us, instead of saving ourselves.'

Ambrey took up his crutch and straightened. He pointed across the Cut to where the Ghoulfort lurked in jagged silhouette.

'There were a sight more of us than the urds. We could've risen up against 'em any time, but we didn't. We was slaves 'cause they took away our hope. Took a plague to show us they could be toppled, and even then we needed Jessa Wolf's-Heart to get us off our knees.' He chewed on his tobacco plug with a wet smacking sound. 'Folk won't fight 'less they believe they can win. She made us believe. An' the Dawnwardens'll make us believe, too.'

He eyed Garric closely. 'Think I don't know what you an' Keel have been up to? I heard you talk when you was in your cups. I know why you left. You with the Greycloaks now?'

'There's no such thing as the Greycloaks,' Garric said.

'That's what I'd say if I was in the Greycloaks.' Ambrey cackled. 'This land ain't done yet. The blood o' the wolf still runs in Ossian veins, same blood that built the Second Empire. You can't cage a wolf.'

'You can,' said Garric. 'We call them dogs.'

Ambrey snorted. 'Between waitin' for a hero and listenin' to a cynic, I know which I'd choose. Today's empires are tomorrow's ashes. No one knows that like we Ossians.'

'I never reckoned you an optimist.'

'Gettin' your foot sawn off gives you some perspective, I reckon.'

427

Garric smiled grimly at that and patted him on the shoulder. 'It was good to see you again, Ambrey.'

'Likewise.'

Garric walked off along the dock. When he looked back, the old man was staring across the foggy water, his eyes faraway as he gazed into white emptiness.

54

'There.'

Aren scanned the woods. Bracken and thorn grew thick between the trees, and leaves rustled in a cool wind that smelled of salt and rain.

Fen pointed. In the distance, grazing between the trees, was a doe. She flashed him a hunter's sign he didn't recognise, but he got the gist. They began to sneak closer to the doe, Fen leading, Aren close behind.

A loud snap sounded beneath his boot, and they froze as the doe tensed and lifted its head. Its hindquarters trembled as it hovered on the edge of bolting, but they were some distance away and it didn't see them. Warily it returned to grazing.

Fen looked over her shoulder with a scowl. Her voice was a harsh whisper. 'Feet! What did I tell you?'

He made an apologetic face. 'It's my first time,' he offered as an excuse.

She sucked her forefinger and held it in the air. 'The wind's still with us. Can you feel the direction it's coming from?'

Aren copied her. If he was honest, all it did was make his finger cold. He decided not to be honest.

'I feel it!' he said with a dawning amazement on his face that was entirely fake.

It seemed to please her, anyway, for she softened. 'Always come at them from downwind. If they smell you, they'll run. Hunting is all about patience.'

They crept closer to the doe. Aren tried to concentrate on

his feet, but he found himself sneaking glances at Fen instead. At first, he worried she'd notice him, but her eyes were fixed on her quarry and soon he was studying her openly.

He wanted to be able to *see* her, to understand her the way he'd done with Rapha back at Suller's Bluff. But she was closed to him, a puzzle still. She'd offered no thanks for his help in Skavengard, nor any apology for being cold and rude afterwards. In fact, she'd been angry with him for the last few days. And yet this morning she asked him if he knew how to hunt, and when he said no, she offered to teach him.

He knew Cade would sulk when he found out. He told himself he was doing it because hunting was a useful skill to have when you were out in the world on your own. But in truth, his decision had nothing to do with that.

It wasn't even that he thought her pretty, it was just that her features were so *fascinating*. Her freckles were so densely packed they'd merged into a kind of mask; he'd never seen anyone with so many freckles. The delicate curve of her jawbone held an inexplicable interest for him, as did the way her nose wrinkled when she laughed, when she *really* laughed. It wasn't often she laughed like that, but Cade had the knack of making her, and Aren was surprised to find he was a little jealous about that. He took a certain childish pride in the fact she'd asked him to hunt with her, and not Cade.

Where's the harm, anyway? Cade wanted us to stay, didn't he? He's not the only one who can make friends.

Distracted, his foot caught a stone and he stumbled against a bush with a loud rustle. Fen grabbed his arm and yanked him down into the bracken as the startled doe's head shot up again. They crouched there, pressed close. Aren became uncomfortably, thrillingly aware of the contact between them as the doe stood trembling, ears twitching, deciding whether or not to flee. Aren knew how it felt.

Neither Fen nor Aren moved a muscle until the doe trotted a short way off and began to graze again. When she at last shifted away from him, he was both relieved and disappointed.

'Reckon I'll get no closer with you in tow, bumblefoot,' said

Fen. She slipped her bow from her back. 'We'll kill it from here. You know how to shoot?'

'A little. Most of my lessons were in the sword.'

'Want to try?' she said, holding it out to him.

He gave her a rueful smile. 'That's got to be sixty yards through the trees. I'm not that good. We'd lose the kill and waste an arrow.'

The look she gave him was uncertain, as if she thought she'd done something wrong by offering. Then she shrugged to show she didn't care, and slipped off through the bracken to the cover of a nearby tree. She stood slowly, nocked, drew and aimed. The doe raised its head, perhaps warned by some instinct.

Shoot! Aren urged her silently. *Before it runs!*

But she didn't. She waited, the muscles in her arms beginning to tremble, till the doe relaxed and lowered its head once more. Only then did she let fly.

The arrow whisked through the leaves. The doe shied and bolted. Fen bolted with it.

Aren, surprised, was slow to follow. He hadn't expected her to run. Had she hit it? He wasn't sure; it had all been too quick to see. By the time he was on his feet, she was almost out of sight, chasing her target through the undergrowth. He blundered after her, but she was nimble and he couldn't keep up. He tripped over a stone and fell, and when he picked himself up, she was gone.

Cursing his clumsiness, he forged onwards, following the sound of breaking branches until at last he stumbled across them again.

The doe had fallen at the edge of a clearing and was lying limp on its side, its fur stained with blood and Fen's arrow buried in its flank. She was kneeling next to it, one hand on its ribs next to the wound. Her head was bowed, her eyes closed and her mouth moving in prayer.

Aren approached as quietly as he could, loth to disturb her. There was something intimate about the scene, a connection between hunter and hunted, the living and the dying. As he came closer, he heard some of what Fen was saying. She was offering thanks to the doe for the gift of its life, and to Ogg, Aspect of Beasts, for a successful hunt. When she was done, she raised her head and began to stroke the doe's neck, murmuring softly.

'There, you. It'll be over soon. Rest now. Rest.'

The deer breathed its last, and its eye went glassy and blank. Fen stood to find Aren staring at her in wonder. He'd never imagined death could be so tender. In that moment, he was seized by the urge to kiss her, but he thought it would be unwelcome and he didn't dare.

If she had any idea what was in his head, she gave no sign. 'We'll start you on something easier next time,' she said. 'Since you're here, you can carry it.'

Fen was irritable and tense as they made their way back to the camp. Having Aren near put her on edge. When he spoke, she had to fight the urge to snap at him. When he didn't, she felt like *she* was supposed to speak. She fancied she could sense his expectant gaze boring into her back. He demanded her attention just by being there.

He'd hardly said a word since she'd slain the deer, and the silence was agonising as he trekked along in her wake with the dead animal slung across his shoulders. She wanted to leave him to make his own way back, but he'd be lost within minutes and the deer with him.

Why did you invite him along?

She had no good answer. Was it thanks for what he did in Skavengard? She'd never have gone out on that ledge if not for him, and she did feel a little bad about the way she treated him afterwards. It was just that she'd been so angry; angry at herself for being weak, angry at him for seeing it. Angry because he'd made her climb, when he didn't understand what it meant to fall, to have the world disappear from beneath your feet.

And yet, as much as he annoyed her, there was something re-assuring about him. He was content just to be there, and that made her feel content. He didn't ask anything of her, or pester her with questions. It was certainly easier to be alone, but there was a strange sort of pleasure in sharing the day with another. And mostly it wasn't that hard, except that sometimes he looked at her in a way that triggered a vague sense of alarm deep inside her. She wasn't sure if she liked that feeling or not.

Was this how people became friends? Nine, why did anyone put themselves through it?

'So, how did your mother die?' she asked, as lightly as she could manage.

Aren stopped and stared at her. Fen felt herself curl up inside and burn like a leaf on a fire.

'I'm not good at small talk,' she said sullenly, as if it was his fault.

He shook off his surprise, raised a hand in apology. 'That's alright. It was just a bit... abrupt. Er... She was ill. I don't know exactly what she died of. Nobody ever told me, and I suppose I never asked. Isn't that funny?'

'Funny,' Fen agreed, though she didn't really see why it was.

'What about yours?'

Fen felt a wave of panic. She hadn't meant to open up the subject to include herself. But of course, that was how it went, wasn't it? Get something, give something. Even if you didn't want to.

'She cut her hand. It went bad.' The words came out dull and terse. She didn't want to elaborate.

Aren got the hint. 'I'm sorry.'

'Sorry for what? *You* didn't cut her hand.'

'Just... you know.'

She didn't. The conversation faltered again.

'What was it like growing up in the Auldwood?' he asked, in an attempt to spur it back to life.

Fen wasn't sure how to answer that. What remained of those days were fragments of memory. Da's palm on her back to feel the pace of her breathing as she took aim at a stag. Climbing trees near the cabin while Ma sat out front, singing and whittling in the sun. The doll Ma carved for her; the scent of apple-sweet griddle cakes; her parents holding hands beneath the table. Her early life was so filled with happiness and love that she found it hard to believe it wasn't some hazy dream.

'Good enough,' she said. 'Till Ma died. Da was different after that.' She fought for some words that wouldn't sound false or stupid, but found none. He sensed her awkwardness and mercifully changed the subject.

'Do you know what Garric has in mind for us?' he asked.

'What do you mean?'

'We're heading for Hammerholt, right? It's the most formidable fortress in Ossia, and it'll be swarming with guards for the royal wedding. How are we actually going to get the Ember Blade?'

'He'll tell us when we reach Morgenholme.'

Aren snorted. 'He likes his secrets, doesn't he?'

'It makes sense. What if one of us were captured and inter-rogated? The Iron Hand would know everything then. This way's safer.'

'I say he's paranoid.'

'If you're not paranoid by now, you just haven't been paying attention. I'm sure it's in hand.'

'Are you?'

'You didn't know him before Salt Fork,' she said. 'Back then, we'd have followed him anywhere. I have my doubts about his temperament now, but I don't doubt his heart. I'll hear him out, and if I don't like his plan then I'll leave.'

'Where will you go?'

She thought for a moment. 'Elsewhere.'

Aren nodded. She supposed he understood. His home was as lost to him as hers was, and he knew as little of the world. But he, at least, knew how to connect with people, and he had Cade. He'd do well enough. She wasn't so sure about herself.

'You could have left us back at the Reaver's Rest,' she said. 'Why didn't you?'

'Cade didn't want to.'

She gave him a sceptical look. *You can do better.*

'*I* didn't want to,' he admitted at last. 'I never knew my mother. My father was everything to me. I remember how it used to feel, when he'd come home after one of his trips away...The happiness, the *relief* at having him back... He was warm and strong and kind, he was everything I wanted to be as a man.' His face twisted into a scowl. 'I didn't even know his *name.*'

Fen lowered her gaze. The bitterness in his voice made her uncomfortable.

'I need to find out who my father was,' he said at last. 'Only Garric can tell me that.'

'And the Ember Blade? Doesn't that mean anything?'

'The Ember Blade...' His eyes went distant. 'Do you think Ossia really could rise again, if we took the Ember Blade back?'

'I don't know,' she said. 'I don't know how people think.'

They walked on a short way.

'If I knew who your father was, Aren, I'd tell you. Whatever Garric said.'

Aren was taken aback by that. 'Thank you,' he said, and he gave her a look of such gratitude and affection that she blushed angrily and turned away.

'We're wasting time,' she snapped. 'Let's get moving.'

She didn't say another word the whole way back to the camp.

55

The trading houses were set back from the waterfront, hidden among the cobbled lanes far from the noise of the warehouses and the smell of fish and boiling blubber. Garric walked down familiar streets, between grey stone houses streaked with black lichen. Wracken Bay was a tangle of alleys with dwellings built higgledy-piggledy wherever they'd fit. Shopfronts appeared from nowhere; sullen plazas lurked in ambush around blind corners; windows were scattered without symmetry.

On an overcast day like this, the town was cheerless and cold and damp, but anticipation kept Garric warm, and he walked with purpose. If he could conclude the day's business to his satisfaction, it would be a good day indeed.

He knew the Xulan trading house, though he'd never visited it before. Foreigners were common in Wracken Bay and most nationalities had a trading house somewhere in the town. The ships that docked here were crewed by elegant Xulans, swaggering Carthanians, secretive Boskans, tattooed Skarls and slow-talking Quins. Once in a while, a Caraguan vessel would arrive from the distant west, disgorging missionaries to spread word of the Incarna, or a boatload of squabbling Lunish would turn up, unable to pass a single night without starting a fight. In the main, these visitors were met with mistrust, and few settled here. Wracken Bay liked their coin and trade, but not their strange customs. Ossians were a welcoming and tolerant people by and large, but the Bitterbracks were peopled with harder folk, close-mouthed, stubborn and resistant to change.

The trading house was unremarkable from the outside, a building of weathered stone with small windows, nestling on a corner. Only its sign was unusual. It was written in the beautiful and mysterious ideograms of the Xulan alphabet, and meant nothing to an Ossian. Above it was a painting of a robed man sitting cross-legged with his arms splayed. He was lean and bald, his head dipped so that only the top was visible. Half his skull was white, the other half black.

Garric recognised him, at least. The Pradap Tet, spiritual shepherd of the Xulans, whose teachings they worshipped in lieu of any god.

He pushed open the door and a tiny bell rang, high and pure. Stepping inside was like stepping into another land. There was nothing of Ossian decor here, none of the exuberant colours, mismatched fabrics, old wood or scuffed stone. Instead, the room was practically bare, and everything was spotless and neatly arranged. A polished bronze ball sat on a black shelf. A framed expanse of parchment was marked with a few strokes of paint, suggesting a shape beyond Garric's ability to interpret. A low table of rare elaru whitewood, shaped like a teardrop, sat off-centre in the room, with an obsidian beaker and two glass-and-silver cups placed upon it.

The sound of the bell faded, leaving an eerie silence behind. A young Xulan glided in from the back, his slippers whispering on the floor. He was fine-boned and shaven-headed with a neat black beard, and he moved with the same silken poise as his countryman from the Reaver's Rest.

'Welcome,' he said in lightly accented Krodan.

'Greetings to you,' Garric replied in Ossian. 'I am looking for a man named Atatep. His cousin told me he often visits here.'

'Alas,' said the merchant, switching smoothly to Garric's mother tongue, 'Atatep departed several days ago with a cargo for my homeland. What unfortunate timing.' He made an airy gesture, waving one hand limply before him.

Garric wasn't sure whether to believe that, and the Xulan's face and tone gave him no clue. It was said that in Xulan society their faces were their weapons. Every conversation was a deadly dance, and they were trained from birth to master their expressions in order to convey exactly what they wanted to.

'A shame,' he said. 'I'm in need of something... unusual. The kind of thing only a Xulan might know how to get. I need it found and delivered fast and safely, and I was assured he was reliable.'

'Perhaps I can help? Our reputation and services are second to none.'

'Perhaps you can,' said Garric.

The Xulan made a florid gesture of invitation towards the table. Garric, who knew enough of Xulan customs to expect no chair, seated himself as comfortably as he could on the floor. Habit made him reach for his sword to adjust it as he sat, but he'd left it back at the camp. Ossians were forbidden swords within town limits, and he didn't have a permit for Wracken Bay.

'My name is Katat-az,' said the Xulan, seating himself gracefully. 'My brother and I oversee all Xulan trade in Wracken Bay. May I have your name?'

'Danic of Hearthfall,' Garric lied. He'd lived under so many aliases these past thirty years that new names sprang quickly to his tongue.

'Honoured.' Katat-az poured two glasses of water. He smelled of perfume, something musky softened with a hint of jasmine. 'And this item you need?'

Garric pushed a folded piece of paper across the table. 'My requirements,' he said.

Katat-az unfolded it, glanced at it, put it down again. 'Four barrels of Amberlyne we can, of course, provide. But this other... this is dangerous cargo.'

'Can you get it for me?'

'I can. We sell it in our homeland, and sometimes to the Glass University for their experiments.' One eyebrow arched and he pursed his lips. 'You are no chimericist, nor are you a scholar. What is your interest?'

'That's my business.'

'I see. You understand that if anyone comes asking about it, I will co-operate with the authorities in all matters?'

'You needn't fear. It's not contraband, and I'm no Krodan informer.'

Katat-az gave him a knowing smile. 'Of course you're not,' he said.

Garric didn't argue further. Mistrust of foreigners ran both ways. He took a sip of water; it was flavoured with something sweet, and a touch of mint.

'I need it delivered to Morgenholme in seven days,' he said.

'Impossible,' said Katat-az, and raised a hand to forestall Garric's argument. 'Impossible!' he said again, firmly. 'The cargo is not in Wracken Bay and it will require a considerable diversion to collect it. Fifteen days. It cannot be done faster.'

The wedding was on the last day of Copperleaf. Garric did some calculations in his head. If the cargo arrived on time, it would come eight days before the wedding. That was time enough. 'Very well.'

'It will be expensive,' Katat-az warned.

Garric tossed a bag of coins onto the table. Katat-az didn't even look at it.

'More expensive than that,' he said.

'That's a deposit. I'll pay twenty falcons more on delivery to Morgenholme.'

Other men might have shown surprise or suspicion at such a ridiculously generous offer. Katat-az showed nothing. 'And this money is where?'

'In a bank in Morgenholme,' said Garric. *Though not in any account of mine.*

'I am sure you have further conditions,' Katat-az said, and sipped his water.

'I have three,' Garric said. 'One: it must be on time. If it's late, it's useless to me and you'll get nothing.'

Katat-az dipped his head and fluttered his lashes in acceptance. 'It will not be late.'

'Two: you'll tell nobody of this transaction. Especially not your brother.'

'I will keep it confidential. But as I have already said, if the authorities ask—'

439

'Which brings me to three: you will oversee the shipment personally. You'll leave on the ship tonight, and you'll be there when I meet it at Morgenholme.'

Katat-az studied him carefully. Garric held his gaze.

'It's that, or no deal,' he said.

Garric saw that the Xulan understood. He wouldn't compromise himself by withholding any information from the Krodans, but by insisting he was on the ship, Garric had ensured he wouldn't be around to ask.

Katat-az sighed and steepled his fingers in front of his mouth. 'You realise this is a considerable inconvenience?' he said. 'However, I do have interests in Morgenholme, and business I can conduct in the ports along the way. My brother can oversee things here in my absence.' He spread his hands and smiled. 'Very well. I will do it ... for thirty falcons.' His gaze went cold and his smile took on a sharper edge. 'It's that, or no deal.'

It was robbery, an absurd amount of gold for the undertaking. Garric agreed without hesitation. Negotiation was a waste of time. The only thing that mattered was that he got what he needed.

'I will draw up the paperwork, to ensure there is no misunderstanding about the price when I arrive,' said Katat-az.

'Nothing that your brother can find. Nothing in your records,' Garric warned.

'I will carry it with me,' the merchant assured him, 'and enter it into our records on my return.'

Garric grunted and scratched at the edge of his scar.

'It occurs to me that you will need transport to Morgenholme yourself,' said Katat-az. 'Perhaps I can help there also?'

'I need passage for nine, and a dog. But we need to be there long before that shipment arrives, to prepare.'

'There is a fast ship departing at dawn the day after tomorrow, direct to Morgenholme. You will be there by Draccensday.'

Garric nodded. Though he'd have liked to leave sooner, it would have to do. The Krodans would follow their trail to Wracken Bay eventually, after the mess they'd left at the inn, but he doubted they'd be quick enough to catch them. As far as anyone at the Reaver's Rest was concerned, Garric and his companions were nothing more than Ossian rogues who'd killed a road patrol. Only the dreadknights and the overwatchman who held their leash would have any chance of running them down, and they were probably still on the other side of the mountains, yet to hear the news.

'I will book you passage,' said Katat-az. He flowed to his feet and collected the forms to be signed and stamped, along with the details of the ships. When they were done, Garric eased himself up stiffly and they clasped each other's forearms, Ossian style.

As Garric made to leave, the Xulan lifted a finger thoughtfully to his lips. 'Forgive me, but I must say something. When a man bargains as you do, he is either rich, desperate or no longer cares what happens to him.' He looked Garric up and down. 'I do not think you are rich or desperate.'

Garric gave him a level stare. 'Fifteen days,' he said.

Katat-az waved a slender hand. 'It shall be done.'

A short walk east of the harbour was an inn called the Bellied Sail, a dour flint building perched just off the coastal path, hunkered down as if in anticipation of rain.

Garric pushed the door open and stepped into a flood of memories. This place was the closest thing to home he'd found, these past thirty years. The gloom and the familiar warmth of the fires comforted him. He breathed in the smell of old smoke and ale and roast beef from the kitchen. Low, heavy beams, notched by a hundred knives, had dented the heads of generations of drunkards. He walked the narrow way between the cramped wooden booths to the bar, and a feeling of welcome and warning stirred in his heart. The Bellied Sail had borne witness to some of his best times, and some of his worst. As much as he loved this inn, he feared it a little, too.

His eyes tightened, a fractional wince of shame as he remembered his hopeless years of drunken drifting, seeking death at the bottom of a bottle or anywhere else he could find it. Eight years ago, he'd washed up here with nothing left to live for, after two decades of failure had brought him to despair. Two decades of resistance against the Krodans, of plotting uprisings and fomenting discontent, of disruption and sabotage, assassination and blackmail. Two decades of doing terrible things in the name of freedom, and all of it worth naught in the end. His allies had died or given up the fight. His countrymen's desire for revolt had diminished as they came to accept the new way of things. In the end, the disappointment had broken him.

It was a stranger who put him back together. In his darkest hour, he'd confessed the shame that lay at his core, told his true name to a man he'd met over a bottle of black rum. Keel took him in, invited him onto his boat and into his crew, showed him the fury of the sea. In pain and toil, Garric found new purpose, in the red-raw joy of rope-flayed hands and the icy slap of sea spray on his face. He witnessed the wild terror of nature, and was made puny by the waves and the slick humped backs of breaching monsters.

It took years, but as they rode the waves and slew the monsters, Garric had become himself again. Eventually, his spirit renewed, he turned his back on the sea and set about his task once more. When he left, Keel left with him, desperate to escape Wracken Bay and a life that was strangling him.

In such a way, they'd saved each other.

It was early yet and only a few patrons had taken their stations. Most of them drank alone, gazing out at the half-empty room with blearily placid expressions. Garric used to wonder what drunks thought about all day as they nursed their mugs of ale and spoke to no one. Then he became one, and he realised they weren't thinking about anything, and that was the point.

Morvil the landlord was behind the bar, a scrawny, lanky man with a bulbous nose and a little pot belly. He was fascinatingly ugly, as if some clumsy deity had assembled him from the parts of various other men and none of them quite matched. Right now he was half-heartedly wiping the counter with a rag, perhaps because he knew the stains wouldn't be shifted by anything short of burning the inn down.

He looked up as Garric approached. 'Laine,' he said, as if it had been only yesterday since he'd last seen him. Nothing was remarkable to Morvil; nothing excited him. He was a man without judgement or opinion. Keel had once joked that if he ever had an emotion, it would be swiftly followed by a massive stroke.

'Morvil,' Garric said, equally gruff. 'Give me a mug of ale and a hot eel pie, and I'll need paper and something to write with.'

'Gonna be three decims for the paper and ink. Eight and three bits in all. Call it eight even.'

Garric took out a guilder, got two decims back, then headed to his favourite nook. After a time, Morvil brought over his drink and his meal, and a quill and ink and paper. He put them down and left without a word.

Garric ate slowly, washing it down with the hoppy brown ale of the Bitterbracks. When he was done, he ordered another pint and set himself to writing.

He'd learned his letters as a boy, but he was no scholar and had fallen out of practice since. It took concentration and care to set the words down, more so because he knew the recipient would notice every mistake. Mara *was* a scholar, and a pedant, too. He detailed exactly what he needed her to do, then read it over half a dozen times to ensure he hadn't missed anything. This letter was too important to be misunderstood. When he was finally satisfied, he folded it up, wrote the address and called for some wax to fix the letter shut. He put no seal into it. He had no crest or mark he could claim as his own any more.

He handed the letter to Morvil with a coin. 'First and fastest post you can.'

'I'll send a boy down to the town,' Morvil grunted.

Garric sat back and finished his ale. Gradually he relaxed, tension leaking out of him. The endgame had been set in motion, then. He was committed, and he found great relief in that.

Once he'd fallen to despair; he wouldn't do it twice. If the people of Ossia needed something to get them off their knees, as they had in the days of Jessa Wolf's-Heart, then he'd give it to them.

Hold the course. That was all he had to do now. Hold the course, to the bloody end.

56

The day had grown late and the shadows in the woods were beginning to merge, but a merry fire burned in the camp. Orica's covered cart stood on the edge of the clearing, busy with bright fabrics and trinkets; her horses were tethered nearby, cropping grass. The others sat around the fire, on blankets or fallen logs or, in Grub's case, a large flat stone. The doe was suspended over the flames on a metal spit, filling the air with the delicious smell of cooking meat. They ate with their fingers from tin plates, accompanied by boiled potatoes from Orica's supply, wild mushrooms Vika had gathered, and coarse bread. Aren devoured his food, leaving nothing. He'd been hungry for months before their feast at the Reaver's Rest, and he no longer took meals for granted.

Cade chewed in silence across the fire from him, lost in an ecstatic daze. If hunger had been hard on Aren, it had been worse for Cade, who found eating a form of meditation. Aren hoped the meal would improve his mood a little. He'd been pouting ever since Aren and Fen returned with the kill, pretending there was nothing wrong when there obviously was.

Orica wiped her hands and took up her lute. It was a Sard instrument, with a long, thick neck and a bewildering array of tuning pegs for its thirteen strings. After a few runs up and down the fretboard to stretch her fingers, she strummed a sequence of chords that Aren had come to recognise.

'What *is* that song?' he asked. 'I've heard you play it over and over. I feel I've known it all my life, but I can't place it.'

Orica gave him one of her languid smiles. 'I would be surprised if you could. It is a song of my own devising. One I've been working on all my life, I think; but only now am I beginning to hear it true.'

'Will you play it for us?'

'It is far from finished,' she said. 'But I will play you what I have.'

She began, and Aren was struck again by how familiar it sounded, how it recalled other melodies from his childhood without imitating them. He heard old Ossian folk tunes in there; stout, grave battle songs harking from the days of the Fall; even a touch of 'The Mourner's Elegy', which he'd first heard as a child, sung by a woman as she hung out her washing. It rang with echoes of his ancestors, and hearing it stirred something in Aren's breast, the same dangerous sense of pride he felt when he thought of the Ember Blade.

The others felt it, too. Vika straightened, and Ruck raised her head and sat up. Fen, who was whittling a short way back from the fire, stilled her knife and listened. Harod, poised stiffly by Orica's side, closed his eyes in mute appreciation. Only Grub seemed unaffected. He sliced another piece of venison off the doe and set to it noisily, grease dribbling down his tattooed chin.

Then Orica began to sing, her husky voice rising into the quiet of the woods, and Aren felt himself swept away.

The king stood at his window in his castle on the shore.
His family were sleeping, his foes were no more.
As he looked o'er the sea, he heard knuckles on the door.
'Twas his seer, white as a ghost.

'Sire, please beware, for a storm does draw near
That will tear down your walls and take all you hold dear.'
But the king laughed and knew he had nothing to fear
And he turned his old eyes to the coast.

He said, 'I see no clouds, and the waves are not high.
Your omens mislead you, your bones fall awry.'
But the seer said, 'Sire, not all storms come from the sky.
There are depths to which you cannot see.'

445

She let the final chord fade away, and for a few heartbeats her audience sat in silence, expecting another verse. Then Grub thumped his chest and let out a thunderous belch, loud and sudden enough to startle a nearby fox from hiding. Harod gave him a glare of furious disapproval, but Grub didn't notice, occupied as he was with stuffing more venison into the space vacated by the burp.

'There is more,' said Orica, 'but it is not ready yet.'

'I love it!' said Cade. 'Especially the diddly-daddly bit at the start.'

Aren winced on his behalf. Cade's talent for musical critique was almost equal to his skill at flirting. 'The tale feels familiar, somehow,' he said.

Cade frowned a moment, then clicked his fingers. 'King Cavil the Lionhand!' When Aren looked at him in puzzlement, he explained. 'Cavil was a king in the Age of Legends. His father usurped the throne from the Bastard Lord and Cavil went on to conquer half of Embria, driving out the urds and almost pushing the elaru back into the sea. If he hadn't died, the urds probably would never have conquered us at all, and the First Empire would have looked a lot different. But he got a bit, er, full of himself in the end.'

'Grub want to hear what happened!' thundered the Skarl, who was a lot more interested in Cade's story than Orica's song.

'His seer dreamed an army of the dead marching from the sea, made up of all the urds he'd slaughtered, and he warned the king to stay away from his castle on the coast,' said Cade. 'But Cavil did the opposite and went there straight away. He wanted to show everyone that he wasn't afraid of ghosts, that the Lionhand was too mighty to pay heed to omens. Many of his followers went with him in support, the best of his army, his right-hand men and women. Not long after, the omens proved true. A great wave came from the sea and washed the castle away, and in the struggle for the throne that followed, the urds invaded and conquered us.'

Grub bellowed with laughter, spraying flecks of meat. 'Ha! Stupid king not listen to omens! No wonder urds squashed you!'

'Is that what it's about?' Aren asked Orica.

'Perhaps,' said Orica slyly. 'And perhaps not. It is ... it *will* be a lament for our land, a song for what was lost and what will be again.'

Aren opened his mouth to speak, decided against it, and was grateful when Cade said what he'd been thinking.

'But you're a Sard!' Cade said. 'I thought you…You know…' He coloured and fell silent.

'Yes, I am a Sard,' she said. 'One of the Landless, the Chosen Folk, forever exiles. But I am Ossian, too. I grew up in this land, ate the fruits of its soil, danced under the same skies as you. My people keep no histories, but there are more of us here than anywhere else, and that must mean something. We are all children of the wolf.'

'Not Grub! Grub has bear blood, like all his people. Urds never conquered Skarl lands.'

'Small wonder,' said Cade. He was eager to take out his pique on someone, and Grub was a safe target. 'Frozen wastes, howling winds and beasts with teeth as long as your arm. Who'd want it?'

'Grub does! Grub will go back one day, when his body is covered in glorious deeds.'

'No one's stopping you,' said Cade, glancing at Fen to see if she approved of his retort; but she was back to whittling and wasn't listening.

Grub shook his head. 'Not yet. Grub has much to do still. Escaping camp not enough. Outwitting dreadknights not enough. Even when Grub defeated Beast of Skavengard, it not enou—'

'Hang on, you never defeated the Beast of—'

'Grub must do deed so great his people stand in awe!' he cried, thrusting one stubby finger into the air. 'Only then can he return in triumph!' He picked up the meat on his plate and muttered bitterly. 'Grub show *them*.'

Aren wasn't sure if Grub knew he'd spoken that thought aloud. He changed the subject before Cade could pounce. 'Harod, back at the inn you said you'd visited several towns, and the Sards had been moved on from all of them.'

'That's so,' said Harod, but didn't elaborate.

'That is why we came back to Ossia,' said Orica, her mouth in a grim line. 'I am searching for my family.'

447

'What happened?' Aren asked.

She gave him that look again, appraising him, judging whether he could be trusted. Though she always seemed relaxed, she was permanently on her guard. Aren was beginning to see why the Sards had a reputation for secrecy.

'There were rumours in Harrow,' she said. 'Sard caravans disappearing. My people quietly moved out of settlements along the coast. We made for my home town, but we were too late. The Sards had gone, and no one knew where. It was the same in other towns. Asking questions was dangerous. Twice I would have been arrested, if not for Harod.' She laid a hand on his forearm in gratitude.

'It was no more than my duty,' he said solemnly; but Aren saw a tiny flare of triumph in that impassive face.

'Morgenholme has the largest concentration of Sards in Ossia,' Orica said. 'Not all of us wander. Some choose to live in cities, though it is not a life I would choose, penned like cattle as they are. The Krodans have been moving my people east, so it is likely they are heading to the capital. That is why we must go there, too.'

'But why are the Krodans taking them there?' Cade asked.

'That is the question,' said Orica darkly. 'I believe they want to keep us all in one place, the better to control us. We have always been free, answering to no masters, and that unsettles them. Maybe they want to stop our wandering for good. We shall see.'

Aren felt a chill. It was hard not to see the parallels. The Krodans had confined his people, too, with permits and passes. Would the Ossians be moved on one day, to make space for more Krodans?

He rubbed the mark on his wrist with his thumb, as had become his habit. His promise to Eifann had been fulfilled, at least to his mind, but the mark remained. Would it fade, in time? He wasn't sure he wanted it to, now. Standing up for Orica had been one of the proudest moments of his life.

You made another promise, too, he reminded himself. A promise to a pirate to complete one task for him, without condition, no matter how abhorrent he might find it. He wondered if Rapha would ever claim that debt, and what its nature would be. He doubted he would be quite so proud to fulfil it.

'And how did a noble from Harrow become involved in all of this?' asked Vika from across the fire. She was scratching Ruck's neck. The wolfhound closed her eyes and flexed her claws in rapture.

Harod stiffened at the question. Aren suspected that the druidess discomfited him, with her painted face and unwashed hair, her motley of trinkets and hides. She wasn't like the women of Harrow, who were said to be beautiful and cold, their behaviour and dress dictated by strict codes of etiquette.

'I … was compelled,' he said at length.

Orica favoured him with a smile. 'He followed my song,' she said fondly. 'I played at his father's house, and afterwards he swore himself to my service, and told me he would ever after be my guardian. He is my knight, and my dear, dear friend.'

Harod looked like he was about to choke with embarrassment, or joy, or both. Aren couldn't help marvelling that two people with such opposite personalities had come to travel together.

'Bowlhead followed a *song*?' Grub spluttered. He cackled and rolled his eyes.

'I wouldn't expect you to understand.' Harod sniffed. 'The height of Skarl musical accomplishment is knocking a bone against your ancestors' skulls.'

'Ha! Grub think you need to pull that bone out of your arse. Hey, Grub got a song! Listen!' He began to blare tunelessly:

Once there was man with no chin
He had a stupid haircut
He heard song and went 'Duh-duh-duh.
Bowlhead better go that way!'

The Skarl chuckled at his own wit, ignoring the appalled stares of his companions, and clambered to his feet. 'Ah, Grub done here. Grub going to take enormous brown dump in woods. You should come, Tonsils. They tell tales of this one for centuries!'

'T-Tonsils?' Harod squeaked in horrified disbelief.

'That is a kind offer,' said Orica to Grub, unfazed. 'But if it is as you say, I would likely not survive being close enough to witness it.'

'Your loss,' Grub said with a shrug.

He waddled away from the fire, leaving Harod wobbling like a kettle on the boil with the effort of suppressing his indignance. Red splotches crept up his neck and one eye twitched furiously.

'Sorry about him,' said Aren. 'He takes a bit of getting used to.'

'Think I'll go for a walk, too. Stretch my legs,' said Cade. He watched Fen hopefully in case she wanted to go with him, but she showed no interest. Crestfallen, he threw a sullen glance Aren's way and headed off into the gloom beyond the clearing.

Harod made his excuses and retreated to the covered wagon, where he could nurse his battered pride in private. Orica set to work on her song, trying new variations, stopping and starting again. Every so often, she put her lute aside and scribbled some marks on a roll of parchment. Aren knew it was musical notation, but the signs were a mystery to him. He'd seen Krodan sheet music on Nanny Alsa's harpsichord, but he'd never been interested in learning and his father thought music a waste of time.

He roused himself, walked round the fire and settled next to Ruck and Vika. Ruck licked his hand and he stroked her back absently.

'Did you really see Garric in a vision?' he asked. It was a question he'd wanted to ask since the Reaver's Rest. He was reluctant to engage her in talk of the Aspects – they didn't see eye to eye on matters of faith – but he couldn't bear wondering any longer.

She'd been staring into the fire, lost in thought – she had the habit of going blank now and then – but she stirred at his words.

'I saw a bright warrior, though I could not see their face,' she said. 'They carried a blade that shone like the sun, and I knew them for a champion who would stand against the evil that is coming.'

'The Krodans?'

'The Krodans are not evil, Aren. They just see the world differently from us. I speak of forces more dreadful than any empire Embria has ever known. You have glimpsed them yourself, in Skavengard.'

450

Aren felt icy fingers creep up his back. 'And you think this champion is Garric?'

'The stars were right on the day I met him. He faced the beast of Skavengard and overcame it. Now I learn he seeks the Ember Blade: a beacon of hope if ever there was one. I have had many visions, walked the Shadowlands a hundred times, and rarely have the signs been so clear.'

Aren frowned, frustrated. The idea that Garric was chosen by the gods didn't sit easily with him. 'I know little of visions, but if you didn't see his face—'

'I know it is hard for you,' Vika said. 'You do not know whether to hate or admire him. But a person can be many things. There is good in the worst of us, and bad in the best. Garric has treated you despicably and he is your father's sworn enemy, yet he may be the man we need to lead us against what is to come.'

'He's no champion,' Aren said angrily.

'Are you sure?'

'Are *you*?'

Vika tilted her head in acknowledgement of his point. Ruck snuffed and got up to pad away from the fire. Aren picked at the crusted dirt on the toe of his boot.

'The world's changed,' Aren said. 'Seems only yesterday I was certain of everything. Now it feels like there's nothing I can trust. Only Cade, and even he ...' He faltered, unsure whether to go on; but there was something about Vika that comforted him, a kindness that made him want to confide. 'If I left now, I'm not sure he'd come with me.'

Vika's eyes went to Fen. 'Aye, I've seen how he looks at her. And how you do.'

Aren didn't bother to deny it. He didn't know what he felt for Fen, but after today, he was sure he felt something.

'May I offer you counsel?' Vika said.

'Nine, I'd welcome some.'

'Have patience,' she said. 'Answers will come in their own time, and when they do, you may wish you'd never asked. The young are always in a rush to know everything, but knowledge only brings more questions. Forget the destination, Aren; enjoy the journey.

You are free now in a way you have never been, and the choices you make now will determine who you are to become.'

It did little to satisfy him, but he sensed wisdom in her words. He wished he were strong enough to beat the truth from Garric, or brave enough to hold a knife to his neck, but they were fantasies born of adolescent anger. If he wanted Garric to give up his secrets, he'd have to be cleverer than that, and wait till the moment was right.

One way or another, he'd learn the truth about Garric and his father. And only then, when all the cards were on the table, would he decide the matter of vengeance.

57

Keel pushed open the door to his son's bedroom as if he were afraid of what might be on the other side. When he poked his head around, he found Tad sitting up against the headboard gazing back at him, like he'd been waiting there all morning. Maybe he had; his patience and stillness were almost eerie at times. At other times, he was anything but patient and still.

'I thought you might be asleep,' Keel said awkwardly. The grim daylight leached all comfort from the room. Tad's sickness hung in the air like a spectre.

Tad just kept on staring. Keel cleared his throat, pushed the door open and entered. Vika came in behind him, Ruck loping at her heels. Tad stiffened at the sight of the druidess, bolt upright against the headboard, eyes wide in alarm.

'Peace! Peace!' Keel said, holding out his hands. 'She's a friend.'

Tad looked from his father to Vika and back again, betrayal in his eyes, as if Keel had tricked him by bringing her here. Suddenly he was a cornered animal, hair wild with sleep, skinny limbs tensed as if to flee.

'He doesn't like strangers,' Keel told Vika. There was an apology in his voice, and a tinge of embarrassment, the vague shame he'd carried ever since he realised his son would never be the strapping young man he'd dreamed of. No matter how much Mariella said otherwise, his son's strangeness reflected on him. Tad's nature, his weak body and now his illness all felt like Keel's failing. His fault.

'Hello, Tad,' Vika said gently. 'I suppose I must look quite unusual to you. I expect you're wondering why my face is painted this way. It's because I'm a druidess. Do you know what that is?'

Tad was breathing rapidly now. This was how it started, panic building on panic until he became hysterical and shrieked and thrashed. When it was particularly bad, his eyes would roll back in his head and he'd shake and judder and foam at the mouth.

Keel felt panic rising in his own breast. Why hadn't he thought to ask Vika to wash the paint off? Why wasn't Mariella here to handle this?

'Tad! Tad, I'm here! All's well, I'm here!' he cried, but his voice was anything but calm and it only made things worse.

'Druids help people, Tad,' said Vika, as if gentling an animal. 'I've come to help you get better. Would you like that? I'm Vika, and this is Ruck.'

Tad's gaze fixed on the wolfhound and he held his breath. In that fragile balance, Keel saw curiosity warring with fear in his son's eyes.

'Let him pet the dog,' Keel said.

Without word or sign from Vika, Ruck padded over and laid her head in Tad's lap. Uncanny how it knew what to do. Sometimes it was as if the dog could understand them.

Tad, his attention captured by Ruck, put out a tentative hand, drew it back, reached out again. Finally he plucked up the courage to run a hand down her neck. Keel gave Vika a relieved glance as Tad's breathing returned to normal and a faint smile touched the corners of his mouth.

'Talk to him. Keep him calm,' said Vika. She drew a phial from her cloak, unstoppered it and touched it to her lips. 'Think of something nice,' she advised, and took a sip.

Keel struggled to find a suitable topic. Mariella was always better at that kind of thing, but she was in the kitchen with Fluke. Wouldn't have any part of this. They'd rowed bitterly about it, but nothing would change her mind.

'You think you can turn up out of the blue and fix this, Keel? Another quack herbalist peddling wishful-thinking remedies? He needs *real* treatment, not more Ossian tinctures and potions! I'm done with looking for miracles!'

Well, damn her scorn. He had faith in Vika, even if Mariella didn't. He *would* fix this. Somehow, he would.

Think of something nice. It came to him at last. He sat on the bed and held Tad's hand.

'You remember when I took you to the fair? The painted men, the mummers in their make-up and masks? You liked them, didn't you?'

Tad dragged his gaze away from Ruck, looked at Vika, then back to Ruck: a safer place to leave them.

'That's right,' said Keel. 'She's like the painted men. You'll like her. You like her dog, don't you?'

Tad nodded.

'What else did you see at the fair?' Vika asked, moving slowly closer.

When Tad didn't answer, Keel answered for him. 'That was some day we had, wasn't it? I remember how the sun sparkled on the Cut as we set out westwards in my boat. There must have been a hundred craft on the water, barges flying pennants and little rowing-boats, all of them heading to Marisport for the fair.'

'I liked the boats,' Tad said quietly. Then he began to cough, his thin body wracked with spasms, shoulders bumping against the headboard. Keel thumped him on the back. It was all he could think to do.

Vika had slipped up to the bedside now and was watching Tad owlishly, pupils huge amid the black-and-white smears on her face. Keel was reminded suddenly of Skavengard, of how her eyes had looked when the beast was in her, and terror ambushed him.

the teeth the mouths it'll never stop devouring me forever

'I'm going to put my hand on your back, Tad,' Vika warned. 'It will help me tell what is wrong with you.'

Tad was too busy coughing to protest, and Vika didn't give him time to. She slid her hand down the neck of his shift, then drew it out and put it on his chest.

'Stop trying to suck in your breath,' she told him firmly. 'Breathe out for as long as you can.'

To Keel's surprise, Tad did as she said. The coughing petered out immediately.

'Now don't pull the air in. Your lungs will fill on their own. Let them.'

Tad's chest rose again. He let out another sigh. No coughing.

'There,' said Vika, satisfied. 'Well done. Now, about this fair ...'

Keel stared at her, amazed by her effortless competence. Then he remembered what he was supposed to be doing and took up the story again.

'Ah ... yes. You remember all the things we saw, eh, Tad? Nine, they didn't sell us short! There were magicians from Caragua who made a bear disappear, and red men from Helica who performed a spear-dance, and three acrobats from Kedda with wooden masks and clothes of leaf and bark. While they were tumbling, they told us how they do everything in threes in their homeland. They rule in threes, fight in threes, they even get married in threes! You laughed at them and clapped like you would never stop.'

As he spoke, Vika moved her hands over Tad's body, now holding his wrist, now pushing her fingers under his jaw. He submitted to it all, watching her with nervous trust, one hand still mechanically scratching Ruck's neck. Keel wasn't sure if Tad was listening to him, but he didn't want to stop. The memories were as much for him as his son.

'There were dog-warriors from Zotha, you remember? Men with dark skin who scarred their faces. And such fierce dogs! You've never seen dogs so big! They bond with their dogs as puppies, and they can live thirty years or more, and when the dog dies in battle or of old age, they retire as warriors.'

'It sounds like you had a wonderful time together,' Vika said. She bent over and put her ear to Tad's chest. 'Now pull in a breath, big as you can, and hold it. Good.'

It *had* been wonderful. A rare and perfect day, without tantrum or distress. Tad had just turned five and Keel would leave Wracken Bay soon afterwards, but on that day, there was no thought of it in his mind. It was only later that he realised the sights he saw at the fair had inspired him, set him dreaming of places far away from this small, small-minded town.

As soon as Vika let him release his breath, Tad began to babble excitedly. 'There were Xulan chimericists, too! They showed us scaly monkeys, and a fish that had legs, and a concoction that made rusted armour shiny just by dipping it in!'

'No!' Vika said in mock surprise.

'We saw it, didn't we, Da?' His face was alight, his eyes dancing and a true smile on his lips. At last, he was connecting with them. Keel's heart hurt for the love of him. If only it could always have been like this.

'We did,' he said, patting his son's hand. 'We did. And you'll see such wonders again, one day. By Joha and Hallen and all the Aspects, I promise you.'

'Really?' Tad was agape. 'You mean it?'

'I promise,' Keel said again.

Vika gave him a look, and said nothing.

Vika's visit exhausted Tad and he fell asleep again soon after. Ruck led the way out onto the narrow wooden landing between the upstairs bedrooms and Vika closed the door behind them. No sooner had the latch dropped shut than Keel's face crumpled and he wept.

'It's not fair,' he whispered through his tears. 'Damn it to the depths, it's not right. What kind of gods would allow this?'

Vika embraced him and said nothing, for which he was grateful. He had to fight to keep his sobs quiet enough that his wife and brother wouldn't hear them downstairs.

When he got himself under control again, he felt a little better. He'd drained off the bare minimum of his grief, but it still lurked just below the surface. He needed to be alone, where no one could see him and he could let himself go without shame. But being alone now seemed like the worst thing in the world.

'Dry your eyes,' Vika told him, not without kindness. 'Your wife needs your strength now. She has been bearing this burden for a long time.' They spoke a little further on what might be done for Tad, and then went downstairs.

Mariella and Fluke were at the table in the kitchen, drinking nettle tea. They looked up as Keel and Vika entered, their faces closed and suspicious. Keel had the feeling they'd stopped talking just a moment ago.

'He's asleep again,' said Keel.

'Good,' said Mariella.

Vika took the temperature in the room. 'I'll see you back at the camp,' she told Keel. 'Farewell to you all.'

Mariella watched her go with evident resentment on her face. Fluke did the same; he supported Mariella, as he always did. Keel seated himself at the table, feeling more like an intruder than ever.

'Well?' Mariella asked.

'I thought you didn't care?'

'Just tell me what she said.'

Sulky, churlish, obtuse. They were not like this with anyone else, only each other. If they were supposed to be in love, why did they act like enemies?

'She can make him a potion that will ease the coughing and stop the grip getting any worse. He could live a long time that way. But a druid or druidess will have to prepare it once a month, and it isn't a cure. He needs long-term care to get better.'

'So it's no solution at all, then.'

'It's *something*,' Keel snapped.

'It's nothing!' she cried. 'More false promises, more false hope!'

'I told you, she's a druidess, not some washed-up herbalist! I've seen her *do* things! She can help him!'

Mariella's mouth screwed up in disbelief. She didn't want to believe that. Didn't want to give any ground at all, to hope even a little, in case all her defences should collapse. 'And what would it give him? Another month confined in bed? Another year?'

'Isn't that worth it? Isn't even another *day* worth it?'

'Maybe it is, but what's that to you if you're not here to see it? If you have such faith in her remedies, stay and administer them yourself!'

'Godspit, Mariella, it's our child's *life* we're talking about! One of us has to earn money, and I won't get it fumbling with cows on a farm!'

'*You'll never come back!*' she screamed, surging to her feet. 'Don't you think I know what all this is about? You don't want me, and you don't want *us*!' She swept her mug of nettle tea to the floor, where it smashed into steaming shards. Her voice became low and hard. 'If you walk away, you're my husband no longer,' she said. 'I swear it, Keel. You'll find no welcome here again.'

Keel stared at her, shocked. Before he could say anything else, she stormed out of the cottage. He heard her stamping up the path, sobbing with rage. He stood to follow, but Fluke grabbed his arm. Keel almost punched him for that, but Fluke's steady gaze took the heat out of him.

'You'll do no good when she's that upset,' Fluke said. 'Why don't you and I take a walk up to the farm? We ought to talk.'

Keel shook him off angrily. He nearly went after her anyway, but sense triumphed. Fluke was right. Better to let her cool. Better to let *himself* cool.

She'd never made a threat like that before. Never.

'Alright, then,' he said. 'Let's talk.'

58

'You don't know what it was like,' said Keel as they walked across the damp fields. 'The first three years, he just screamed. Nothing helped. Screamed till he was exhausted enough to sleep a few hours, and we could, too.'

The hillside was divided by fences, ditches and hedgerows. Shaggy sheep cropped grass beneath a grey sky. Distant thunderheads were piling up on the horizon.

'Just before his fourth birthday, he went quiet.' Keel snapped his fingers. 'Like that. Overnight. That was worse. Nine, at least we knew what we had before. Mariella didn't trust him any more. She talked about changelings and I think she meant it, too, for a time. We'd try anything to get a response out of him, a *good* response, you know? A smile, a laugh. The things we tried...'

He felt a drop of rain on his cheek, tipped his face up to meet it. No more fell. It was only a promise of what was to come.

'I hated this town long before he was born. Afterwards, the only peace I got was out on the boats. More than once, I took a launch with naught but a harpoon against a breacher that should've swatted me flat, and when that whale was bubbling in the try-pots and my crewmates were calling me a fool and a hero, I'd be sorry. I wanted that whale to kill me, not the other way around. But somehow I could never quite let it happen.'

He spat into the grass. Fluke offered no comment.

'Setting foot on shore again, it was like the world closing in on me. Like a cold iron mask fixed around my skull. I'd go to the

Bellied Sail and drink till word reached Mariella I was back, and she'd send you to drag me home.'

'I remember,' said Fluke. 'Da always used to say he never felt alive unless he was out in the tempest with a harpoon in his hand. Used to hate him for that, for telling us he'd rather be elsewhere. Saying it to his own sons.'

'Never thought of it like that,' said Keel.

'Well, you always were his boy.'

They turned onto a muddy track that ran along the edge of a bramble-choked ditch. A horseman was just cresting the rise at the top of the hill, coming their way at a canter.

'Heard about Salt Fork,' said Fluke. 'Any of you in that?'

Keel didn't reply.

'Iron Hand executed a lot of people afterwards.'

'Gutless turncoats should've stood and fought, then,' Keel said bitterly. It sounded like something Garric would have said.

Fluke grunted, somehow conveying his silent judgement as clearly as if he'd accused his brother aloud. He was a master of leaving things unsaid. At least Mariella yelled at him so he could yell back. Fluke's method was slow poison.

'You ought to be careful,' Fluke advised. 'Word's already out that Laine's back so you can be sure Jadrell's already heard. Everyone knows you two come as a pair, and there's rumours about what you get up to out there. Some say you went to join the Greycloaks. Well, those who don't say the other thing, anyway.'

Keel didn't rise to the implication. He knew well what the *other thing* was. Typical Bitterbracker thinking, when two men couldn't share a close friendship without raising eyebrows. He loathed this town, the mean-mindedness of its people, the walls they built around themselves. He pitied his brother, and he suspected Fluke knew it. It was one of the many reasons they didn't get on.

'Rumour's not worth a shark's piss in this place,' said Keel. 'I'm just one of a hundred whalers who left town one day and is back for a visit. Jadrell's hardly going to hunt me down 'less he gets the say-so from his Krodan masters, and whatever I did or didn't do out there, my name's not on any of it.'

461

'I suppose it matters naught, in the end,' said Fluke. 'You'll be gone again before long.'

'Who said I'm going anywhere?'

Fluke smirked humourlessly.

Keel watched the rider coming closer. He was dressed Krodan-style, but it was no soldier's outfit, nor the uniform of an official. Keel's hand hung a little closer to the sword at his hip just in case. It was only a matter of time before they stopped Ossians carrying weapons outside the town boundaries as well as within, and if a few more locals got killed by bears and wolves and bandits, then so be it. But that wasn't the law yet.

'You know him?' he asked Fluke.

'My neighbour Endrik. He took over the farm from Starren.'

'What happened to Starren?'

'Turned out he didn't legally own the land. Some mistake in the paperwork half a century back.'

'And Lord Jadrell righted that injustice?'

'Course he did. Been righting all manner of injustices lately.'

'Hail to the Emperor,' said Endrik as he neared, arm across his chest in salute. He was a robust and vigorous-looking man whose fine features were not best served by an unnaturally rectangular moustache and a rigid military haircut.

'Hail to the Emperor,' Fluke replied. Keel saluted after a suitably defiant interval.

'Who is your companion?' Endrik asked Fluke.

'My brother Keel. Keel, this is Endrik.'

Keel nodded with the sullen chill of a Bitterbracker.

'Now I see the resemblance,' said Endrik. 'Family is so import-ant. The very foundation of the Empire, as Tomas says in the Acts. Your brother is staying with you, I take it?'

'He has lodgings elsewhere. I'm just showing him my farm.'

Endrik's smile didn't reach his eyes. 'Excellent, excellent,' he said. Then, when it became clear he'd get no more conversation from them, he straightened in his saddle. 'Well, I mustn't keep you.' He shook the reins and his horse walked on.

Keel waited till he was out of earshot. 'Friend of yours?'

'One of Jadrell's informers. The farm was his reward for it. If Jadrell didn't know where you were before, he will now.'

'You could have told him I was someone else. He didn't know my face.'

Fluke snorted. 'And when he learns I lied? I'm not keen to attract any more suspicion than you've already brought me. I'd find my farm next on Jadrell's list of injustices.'

He set off again and Keel walked with him. Presently, they rounded a hedgerow and saw a farm down the hill, a scattering of outbuildings surrounding a low stone house, with a handful of animals out to pasture nearby. Fluke came to a halt and they gazed upon the deep green land of their birth, the swooping slopes, the dramatic, cloud-wracked skies. Keel saw only mud, thorns and gloom.

'Mariella says you'd have me work with you,' Keel said.

'The offer's there,' said Fluke. 'Don't reckon you'll ever accept it, though.'

Keel dug at the turf with the toe of his boot. 'She really wants me to stay this time.'

'She wants that every time. Hasn't stopped you before.'

'Things are different now. There's Tad.'

Fluke grunted.

'He's my son,' Keel said, as if by speaking the words aloud he was explaining something to himself.

'He is,' Fluke agreed. 'So what are you going to do about that?'

Keel wished he had an answer, but every path forward seemed impossible. He couldn't stay and he couldn't go. He had to help Tad somehow, and he couldn't do that while scratching a living in Wracken Bay. Yet if he left to seek a solution, he'd lose Mariella. Hard as it was to be with her, it would be harder without. He needed to know he was loved, even if it came from afar. She was his anchor to the world while he went roaming. Without her, the black pit inside would surely consume him.

'Do you reckon she meant it? About leaving me?' He resented having to ask, but his brother knew her better than he did these days.

'She meant it,' said Fluke. 'Whether she could do it, that's another question.'

They stood there for a time, contemplating the farm below.

'Didn't you ever want to get away from this town?' Keel asked.

'No,' said Fluke. 'I have all I need right here.'

'Da always dreamed we'd stay on the boat, working together, after he died.' He waved a hand at the scene below. 'He'd have hated all this.'

'The old bastard hated a lot of things. I hated the sea, but that didn't count for naught with him; I had to be a whaler all the same. Now my farm feeds your family.'

'I know it,' said Keel, then forced himself to add, 'I'm grateful.'

'Don't be. I don't do it for you.'

Fluke showed no sign of moving. Keel realised he was building up to something.

'Say your piece, Fluke. You brought me out here for a reason, and I reckon it wasn't to admire your farm.'

'Right you are,' said Fluke, casting him a sour glance from beneath his dark fringe. He sniffed. 'I reckon you ought to go.'

Keel raised his eyebrows. He'd been expecting the usual lecture on responsibility.

'Go and don't come back,' Fluke said. 'Ever.'

Keel gave a bitter laugh of surprise. 'If you want to tell me how you feel, I'll settle for a brotherly embrace,' he said sarcastically.

Fluke ignored that, as he did all humour. 'You're killing her, Keel.'

Keel sobered at that. The tone of his voice, the way he said it, it didn't sound like an exaggeration.

'Every time you go, you leave her waiting,' Fluke went on. 'That's her life. She gets through the day, and she waits. For you.' His voice went dark with anger. 'Then back you come, for a day, a week. Just long enough that she thinks you might stay this time. But you don't. You never will. And each time you break her bloody heart a bit worse than before.'

'She knew my nature when she married me,' said Keel. Angry resentment swelled beneath his words. 'She's the fool if she thought she could change me.'

'She's the fool,' Fluke agreed. 'And she's paid for it, and paid again. She thought a child might keep you by her side, and that was foolishness, too.' He balled up a fist, rubbed the side of his neck with his knuckles, the way he did when he was tense. 'You need to let her go, Keel. She's trapped, and she always will be while she's hoping you'll come back. Tell her you're not, and don't.'

Keel had to fight down the urge to strike him. 'You've got a lot to say about my family these days, brother. Any advice about my *dying son*?' Speaking the words almost pushed him over the edge into tears.

'Tad's in the hands of the Aspects now,' said Fluke, rolling on with his argument, his opinions slow and heavy as stone. 'Best your druidess friend can do is stave off the inevitable. You'll never get the money to cure him, and you know it.'

'And what will you do when I'm gone?' Keel sneered. 'You'll look after them in my stead, then?'

'In your *stead*? I've been looking after them for four years already, excepting a few donations when the mood strikes you. Can't see that changing anytime soon.'

That was too much to bear. Keel seized him by the coat, pulled his brother around to face him, so furious he couldn't speak. Fluke gazed at him, unafraid, possessed of that same dull determination with which he ploughed through the seasons.

'You're bad for her,' Fluke told him. 'Do what's right and go.'

The only choice then was between driving a fist into Fluke's impassive, bovine face, or flinging him away. Keel shoved him hard before the temptation to punch overwhelmed him. Fluke staggered a few steps down the trail, righted himself and looked back at Keel, unruffled.

'She doesn't love you,' Keel flung at him. 'She'll never love you, no matter how many times you pick up the pieces. She doesn't love you, Fluke. She's *mine!*'

He saw the flicker in his brother's eyes as his words struck home, and took vicious satisfaction in it. *Where's your sanctimony now? Where's your superiority? Where's your advice?*

Fluke dropped his gaze, then looked off across the hills to where the black clouds were heaping. 'The rest of your lot are nearby?'

'We made camp in the woods,' said Keel. Their confrontation was over, as suddenly as that. They both sounded weary and deflated.

'Tell them to come for dinner,' said Fluke, jacking a thumb towards the farm. 'They can stay in the barn.'

'You sure?'

'This is still Ossia, last I looked,' said Fluke. Still Ossia, where strangers were offered hospitality, where a table was for sharing and generosity was the measure of a man.

There was no bitterness about it, even after their angry words. Fluke never could hold a grudge. 'I'll tell them,' Keel said.

Fluke hooked his thumbs in his trousers and squinted at the sky. 'Make it quick. Storm's coming,' he said, and walked away down the track.

59

Thunder snarled and a curtain of rain came out of the night. The woods, dark and quiet a moment ago, turned riotous as the secret rustle of animals was drowned out by the hiss and splatter of the storm. Leaves bowed and nodded; trails turned to muddy pools; a family of boars ran snorting for shelter.

Vika hurried through the doorway of the derelict cottage, carrying a dead rabbit by the ears. Ruck had gone ahead, not minded to wait for her slower companion, and was shaking herself off in the gloom. Inside, it was dank with rot and mould, and the rain dribbled through the roof in half a dozen places, making puddles among the decayed rushes strewn across the floor. There was a crude table, a few stools, a bed with a hand-stitched mattress. A tin plate and mug lay on the floor near the table.

A mean and meagre dwelling, then, but it was drier than outside, and Vika thanked the Aspects for that. She dropped the rabbit on the floor and raised a warning finger at Ruck as the hound came over to investigate. Then she took off her hide cloak, which had saved her from the worst of the deluge, and wrung out her hair where it had got loose from her hood.

She poked around the cottage a little. It didn't take long. There was a pantry, a tiny area for storage and the main room. Given the state of the place and the way it had been left, she guessed that the owner had intended to return and never did. Likely they were killed by something in the forest, a wild animal or perhaps a fatal fall. She said a prayer to the Red-Eyed Child for the previous owner and then set about smashing up furniture for the fireplace.

She'd left the others back in Fluke's barn. Keel's brother hadn't been a particularly sociable or talkative host, but he was willing to extend the hand of friendship to strangers, and to give generously of what little he had. Vika respected him for that. It heartened her to know that the old ways hadn't been entirely forgotten under the Krodan yoke.

Keel hadn't dined with them, but gone back to his cottage. He had bridges to repair, and wanted to spend what time he could with his family. The ship to Morgenholme was leaving at dawn on the morrow, and he'd yet to decide if he would stay or go. The uncertainty was hard on Garric, who feared to lose his oldest friend, but he kept his silence on the matter.

When she had a decent pile of stool legs, planks and wool in the hearth, she sprinkled it with firedust and dug through her wet cloak till she found the phial she needed. She dripped its contents onto the firedust and it began to fizz and sparkle, burning furious white, spreading outwards until the whole hearth was filled with blinding glare. Gradually it faded, white to yellow and orange, leaving fire licking and crackling the wood.

'I know, I know,' she said to Ruck. 'Wasteful. But it's so much easier than flint and tinder.'

If Ruck disapproved, it wasn't enough to stop her enjoying the flames. She slunk closer to warm herself. Vika gave her a rough pat and got to her feet.

'Now then. Let's set to it.'

She hung her cloak to dry by the fire and pulled out some cooking implements from her sodden pack. Then she found her foraging bag and counted her gains from the night. Herbs, mushrooms, roots and flowers. Most had been readily given by the forest, but the catfoot briar had proved troublesome to find, and it had delayed her long enough for the storm to catch up. She'd hoped to be back in the barn before it broke, but she had no choice but to persevere. She needed to make Tad's potion tonight.

The fire held off the night and warmed the dank corners of the cottage while the storm boomed and rolled outside. Vika and Ruck dried as she worked, peeling twigs with her knife, baking leaves till they were crisp, chewing roots to pulp and spitting them

468

out again. She collected rainwater through the leaking roof, filling two pots: one small, the other smaller. These she set to boil, and when they were bubbling, she began to throw the ingredients in. The air filled with earthy scents. Ruck, recognising the process, laid her head on her paws and watched with anticipation.

When the basics of both concoctions were in place, she took up the dead rabbit, cut off its head and drained its blood into the smallest pot, saying a prayer of thanks as she did so. She tossed the carcass to Ruck, who fell on it eagerly, her patience rewarded at last. While the wolfhound crunched and chewed beside her, Vika drew a shallow cut on her forearm and added a few drops of her own blood to the mix. That done, she set the smallest pot aside to cool.

Rabbit blood was weak sauce for the brew, but her own contribution would add potency. Blood was the power, blood the fuel, blood the catalyst. It was said that the blood of elder druids, steeped in the essence of the Shadowlands and distilled through a lifetime of potion-taking, could make concoctions more powerful than Vika could dream of. An elder druid might have been able to cure Tad's condition rather than merely delaying its progress, but Vika didn't have craft enough for that.

There were other ways to increase the potency of a potion, of course. Ways she could outstrip even the elders, were she tempted to take them. But those were forbidden paths, and not for her.

She drank from the bloodied pot and let the brew seep into her. Tendrils of acid heat spread from her belly to her groin, up her neck, wrapping round her skull. Her mind opened outwards, an unfurling flower of consciousness, and her senses sharpened till she could hear the tick of insects in the boles of the trees, and smell the spoor of mice and deer, wildcat and fox. Air sighed in and out of her, drawn into her lungs and expelled back into the world, altered. She was no longer a separate thing, one and alone, but a part of her surroundings, a channel through which the flow of existence moved, out of the past and into the future.

She closed her eyes and saw Agalie-Sings-The-Dark, her friend and mentor, sitting by the light of another fire as Vika complained of being abandoned by the gods. It had sounded churlish then, and more so now. Her last doubts had been swept away at the entrance to Skavengard, as she held the gates against the dreadknights with sacred light. What else could that have been but the Aspects working through her? Her task had been set by the gods themselves, to walk at Garric's side and protect him from the servants of the void, for that was surely what the dreadknights were. She'd sensed its taint on them, and they'd been kept out of Skavengard by the same sorcery that kept the beast in.

But how did it all connect? What did Garric's plan to steal the Ember Blade have to do with the hellish future the Torments had revealed? Why were the Krodans consorting with dreadknights, and whatever dark force lay behind them?

Time would tell. Until then, she had work to do.

Her trance had deepened enough that she was everywhere and nowhere, hyper-aware of her surroundings and no longer aware of herself. She sensed the borders of the Shadowlands on the fringes of her consciousness and made a channel to it, in the same instinctive way as she might move her fingers or clench a muscle. She willed it, and it was so.

She siphoned off a mote of chaos – a firefly glimmer, a spark – and sent it into the bubbling pot on the hearth before her. In that moment, the contents of the pot were no longer rainwater and herbs, but something else: a tumble of possibilities all existing at once, waiting for her to choose one. Given more power, more chaos, it could become blood, or oil, or wine; but the bigger the channel she opened to the Shadowlands, the more likely something unwelcome would find its way through. All she needed was to make a small adjustment to the essence of the concoction, turning it into something potent, imbuing it with the power to bring change of its own.

Quick as a blink, it was done. The mote of chaos winked out, randomness became order and there was a new reality inside the pot. She drew her mind back from the Shadowlands and relaxed. Moving as if in a dream, she picked up a rag and used it to take the pot off the heat. Then she let herself rest, and stared into the fire while her mind roamed in strange places and molten ribbons writhed like worms across her vision.

Some time later, she stirred, aware of herself again. She took the pot and poured its contents into a boiled leather flask, which she sealed with pitch and put in her pack. It was still raining, and the lightning-lit woods hissed and seethed. The puddles on the floor had spread and were creeping towards where Ruck dozed. She put her cloak on again, now dry and warm from the heat of the fire.

The assault came without warning, an ambush from her subconscious that staggered her with its force. Her eyes went dark and her mind was plunged into greasy blackness. Something cold, cloying and rancid was against her skin, pressing at her face, forcing itself down her throat. She flailed against the slithering movement, choking on foulness.

The beast!

The blackness around her became a yawning maw, stuffed with concentric rows of teeth, a slimy gullet into the Abyss. Vika screamed—

—and found herself on her hands and knees on the floor of the cottage, retching, Ruck barking frantically at her. She gasped, disorientated, the taste of it still in her mouth.

'Peace, Ruck,' she said, reaching for the water skin from her pack. She took a swig, spat it out and drank the next. 'Peace.'

She felt anything but peaceful. Swimming through the beast's alien thoughts had sent her dangerously close to madness. It had taken her days to heal her bruised psyche and take control again, but still the remnants lingered. Maybe she'd purge herself in time; maybe she never would. That was the price of dealing with servants of the Outsiders.

She feared more for Keel than herself. She had plenty of experience with madness and knew how to handle it. Keel didn't, and he'd stared into the eye of that foul thing. She feared he'd carry the scars for ever.

Something passed by the doorway in the rainy dark outside and she whirled, all senses alert. The potion in her blood had faded somewhat, but her hearing was still keen as a fox's. She'd heard nothing. But she'd *seen* ...

Or had she? Nine, it was so hard to know. So hard to pick out what was real, and what was a trick of the brain.

Ruck had no such doubts. She was stanced ready for attack, snarling at the doorway. Lightning flickered, showing waving branches and thrashing bushes. Thunder barrelled away into the distance. There was a familiar sense of otherness in the air: the taint of the Shadowlands.

A slow dread soaked into her. *What did I bring through?*

She swept up her pack and staff. This place felt suddenly dangerous; no shelter, but a trap. If there were enemies abroad, they could see in, but she couldn't see out.

A dark figure slid past the window behind her. She half-saw, half-sensed it, but by the time she turned, it was gone. Ruck barked furiously at the spot where it had been.

'We will not cower in here,' she said to her hound. 'Let us see who has come calling.'

She pulled up her hood and stepped out into the storm. The rain blew against her face and her cloak flapped about her. Keen-eyed, she scanned the trees. The woods were bright to her under the influence of the potion, the colour of steel and silver.

'Show yourself!' she cried. Ruck padded up alongside her, grey fur plastered to her lean body and her bearded muzzle dripping. 'Show yourself, shade!'

There was no response.

Vika walked into the trees, wary for signs of movement. Anger made her brave. If this was a shade, she'd know its purpose. She was anointed of the Aspects; she'd faced down the beast of Skavengard. She didn't fear the pale tricks of ghosts.

That, at least, was what she told herself. Agalie would have counselled caution. Of late, the spirits had become unpredictable, harder to treat with, while reaching the Shadowlands had become easier by the year. Neither change boded well. Some said the Divide was narrowing, bringing the worlds of the living and the dead closer together. Soon it wouldn't only be the wild and ancient places where the shades came creeping through.

But that was still rumour as yet. It would take a Conclave to determine the truth of it. If another Conclave was ever called.

Her senses strained. She could smell and hear nothing but the woods and the rain. Only her prickling instincts and the buzz in her head told her there was something else present.

'Show yourself!' she cried again, and this time it did.

It slid out sideways from behind a tree and Vika's breath froze in her chest. The Torment towered over her, terrifyingly close, its eyes empty pits ringed with tendrils of gangrene, its mouth a toothless puckered O in a white, shrivelled face. The sides of its throat had been slit lengthways, the skin held open in wet red diamonds by a structure of hair-thin metal, exposing the glistening muscle and twitching arteries beneath.

Ruck flattened herself to the ground, whining like a cur. Vika was paralysed, locked in place as she stared into the void of its eyes, which swelled in her vision as if she was tipping into them—

—*a hulking man clad in black metal, hammer in hand, riding a destrier through the rain—*

—*a ragged scarecrow with a longbow, his face a jigsaw of other people's skin, beetles and worms swarming from his footprints in the turf—*

—*a hooded shadow with a metal mask twisted in a grieving howl, hunched in his saddle, the glitter of swords like fangs beneath his cloak—*

—and she was cast back into herself, blinking and shaking. The Torment was gone, if it had been there at all. The storm growled and flashed, the rain drove down from the sky, but the night was only the night again.

Ruck whined deep in her throat as Vika realised what she'd seen.

The dreadknights, riding through a wood. *This* wood. And suddenly she understood the warning, as clear as if it had been spoken aloud.

'They're here,' she said, aghast. Then, breaking into a run, 'They're heading for the farm!'

60

Klyssen hunkered in his saddle and looked down the hill at Fluke's farm. The rain pounded out of the night, splattering off his wide-brimmed hat and the black overcoat that enshrouded him, and a distant flicker of lightning lit up his spectacles, two white circles in the shadow.

By the Primus, if I get through tonight without a chill, it'll be a miracle indeed.

'All's quiet,' said Harte, who sat astride a roan mare at his side, sheltered by an identical hat.

The redundancy of his comment irked Klyssen. 'It wouldn't be much of an ambush if it wasn't.'

Harte said nothing to that, just mopped his running nose with a handkerchief. His overcoat, like Klyssen's, was entirely ineffective against the downpour. He, too, was pretending to suffer no discomfort.

All of us, desperately keeping up appearances. How did we ever get like this? We're the greatest power in Embria and yet we're all scared of not measuring up to the next man in case our peers think less of us.

Sometimes he wondered if the Ossians had it right after all. They didn't spend their days fretting about how they might seem more loyal and efficient, or sizing up their rivals' backs for the best place to stick a knife.

'I always had my suspicions about that man Laine ... Garric, you say he goes by now?' It was Lord Jadrell who'd spoken, a short, pudgy man with a piping, nasal voice and a pencil-thin tracing of facial hair to furnish the illusion of a jawline. 'Given to seditious talk when drunk, as I recall.'

'Then you should have reported him when you had the chance,' said Klyssen.

Jadrell panicked and began to bluster. 'Would that I had been able to, Overwatchman! But the knowledge only reached my ears after he had left Wracken Bay. And Keel! Nobody expected such treasons from Yarren's boy. He was whaler stock through and through.'

Klyssen let silence be his reply. He'd despised Lord Jadrell on sight, and their brief acquaintance had only confirmed his opinion. There was nothing more embarrassing than an Ossian aping his betters. He talked enthusiastically about artists and composers he'd just discovered when most Krodans had long since tired of them, and made laboured references to fashions already ten years out of date. And the things he did to the Krodan tongue! The language of Tomas and Toven wasn't meant for Ossians, who rolled their r's like purring cats and threw their words together in a jumble.

But for all Jadrell's failings, it was Klyssen's job to suffer him. The Emperor had decreed that Ossian highborns should be encouraged to assimilate. They should be dazzled with Krodan learning and Krodan culture, steeped in the superiority of their new masters so that they'd aspire to be like them, and their children, too. Conquer them with peace; make them *want* to be ruled. The Emperor had learned in Brunland that brute force and bloody repression were not the most effective ways to subdue a country.

'The men are almost in place, Overwatchman Klyssen,' said Captain Dressle.

Stealthy figures, barely visible, moved through the muddy fields surrounding the farm. They went in threes, with disciplined efficiency. The fugitives had a master swordsman among them, but they wouldn't find the Iron Guard such easy prey as the road patrol they'd slaughtered.

'It is fortunate indeed that I could be of service,' Jadrell said, with forced jauntiness. The presence of the Iron Hand in his town had made him nervous. 'If I hadn't instructed my man to keep a close watch, he might never have seen the cart arrive!'

'If our man is inside, you will have done a great service to the Empire,' Klyssen assured him dryly. *And you'll be rewarded. That's what you're really asking, isn't it?*

'Then let us hope he is,' said Jadrell, 'for nothing would please me more!'

Yes, let us hope he is. And how dearly Klyssen looked forward to catching him, so that he could go back to Morgenholme, and Vanya, and his golden-haired daughters and his silly old cat. It would be a relief to surround himself with people he loved instead of those he loathed. He was so tired of sycophants and back-stabbers, wearied by the endless suspicion. Dressle was the only man in his present circle he didn't actively dislike.

'May I ask why this man is of such interest to the Iron Hand?' Jadrell enquired.

Because my promotion depends on him. Because I swore to Chancellor Draxis that I would bring him in. Because I'll be ruined and humiliated if I don't.

'The Iron Hand's business is its own,' said Harte sternly, and Jadrell shut up. Klyssen was vaguely annoyed that his subordinate had answered in his stead, but he had bigger matters on his mind right now.

Garric. Laine of Heath Edge. Whatever name you go by, I know who you really are, Cadrac of Darkwater. And soon you will know my name, too.

He raised a gloved hand. There was a creaking of harness from behind them and the dreadknights moved into view on his right, sitting astride their enormous black destriers. They halted in a line, waiting for his order.

Having them so close made his skin creep. His face and chest began to itch, as if there were tiny insects crawling all over him, and his horse pranced and sidestepped uneasily. Yet still he didn't drop his hand; still he held them back. Let them know, whatever they were, that they were servants of the Empire first and foremost. *His* servants, for as long as they were assigned to him. He trusted them less than he trusted Harte, and that was saying something. At least Harte was loyal to Kroda, if not to Klyssen. How could he say the same of the dreadknights, when he didn't know who they were or where they came from?

The moment stretched out. Plague turned his dead-flesh mask to Klyssen, making a low, quiet clicking sound, a rattle like bones in his throat.

'Go,' said Klyssen, and he dropped his hand.

They went like dogs after hares, racing downhill towards the farm. Harte looked from Klyssen to the dreadknights and back again, waiting for a signal of his own, but Klyssen gave him none. He was staying right here. Only fools put themselves in the way of swords.

He saw realisation dawn on Harte's face: they wouldn't be following the dreadknights into battle. The younger man struggled with the concept of obedience for a moment, then his expression hardened. He unsheathed his blade, wheeled his horse and plunged down the hill with a cry.

Klyssen bit back the urge to swear. Now Klyssen *had* to follow or look like a coward in front of Dressle and the Ossian prig by his side. With a reluctant kick to his horse's flanks, he went riding into the folly. So did Jadrell and Dressle, all driven onwards by the fear that they'd be deemed less loyal to the Empire than their brave and stupid fellow.

Falcons to ducklings. What have we become?

Down the slope they went, their horses' hooves churning up the dirt. Klyssen jounced and swung in his saddle, holding on for his life. Lightning flashed, showing Harte hunched over his horse up ahead. He was an expert rider, of course, trained in the saddle from a young age. Just one more advantage to add to all the others his appearance and upbringing afforded.

The animals went berserk as the dreadknights rode past the outbuildings. Pigs squealed and goats screamed, clamouring in their pens. It would give those within the barn some warning, but not much. It didn't matter, anyway. If they fled, they'd be met by the Iron Guard hidden among the hedgerows.

Ruin dragged his horse to a halt and dismounted as he reached the barn, landing on his feet with a crash of metal. Plague and Sorrow slid down to either side of him as Ruin hefted his hammer, swung it in a giant arc and smashed the barn doors open with one blow. His nimbler companions darted inside, and Ruin stamped after them.

Harte reached the flat ground between the outbuildings and charged onwards. Klyssen followed, his stomach rolling, with Dressle keeping pace to his right and Lord Jadrell whooping and squeaking behind him in polite distress. As they approached the barn, Harte began to slow, his sword lowering uncertainly, and by the time Klyssen saw the towering figure of Ruin emerging from the barn unbloodied, he knew what had happened.

'They're not there!' Harte cried as they came to a stop next to him. Klyssen was surprised to hear anger in his voice. The watchman turned an accusing gaze to Jadrell. '*Where are they?*'

Jadrell's eyes were wide, shocked and fearful as a child's. 'But Endrik saw them going into the barn. They dined here.'

'Their cart is here, but *they* are not!'

Klyssen, sweaty and sodden and short of breath, willed ice into his veins. It was time for clear thinking and command. 'Leave a perimeter and search the outbuildings,' he told Dressle. He pointed at the dreadknights, who'd all emerged from the barn. 'You three, search the farmhouse.'

'Every third man to me!' Dressle roared over the wind. 'The rest hold fast!'

His order was repeated in the distance, echoing out for the benefit of those who hadn't heard it. The dreadknights stalked into the farmhouse as soldiers of the Iron Guard melted out of the dark, gathering round Dressle. He led them towards the stable, leaving Klyssen alone with Harte and Jadrell.

Klyssen looked inside the barn. Bitter anger gathered in his belly. Their bedrolls had been left behind, as had their gaudy Sard cart and the horses that pulled it. He'd bet that if he peered inside that cart, he'd find it full of possessions.

Yet their weapons and packs were gone. The fugitives had left in a hurry, taking only the minimum with them.

'Somebody warned them,' Klyssen said.

'Does it please you, Ossian, to see the Iron Hand embarrassed?' Harte demanded of Jadrell.

Jadrell gaped like a fish, searching for any reply that wouldn't be considered impertinent. 'I ... I acted in good faith—'

'Yes, your kind always has an excuse, don't you? And yet you always manage to fall just short of being *actually helpful*. What do they call it, now? Passive resistance?'

'I am a loyal servant of the Emperor!' Jadrell protested.

'Yes, this country's full of loyal servants like y—'

'*Watchman Harte!*' Klyssen snapped. 'Control yourself. You are an officer of the Iron Hand.'

Harte glared at him hotly, then swept away towards the farmhouse, stung. Klyssen watched him, outwardly calm, inwardly calculating.

Commander Gossen's dearest wish was to see Klyssen fail in his mission to catch Garric, so he could install his lapdog Bettren as his replacement; but Harte was furious that Garric wasn't here. That didn't square with Klyssen's suspicions that he was spying for Gossen. Klyssen had assumed his general negativity about their mission was Harte being purposefully obstructive, but it was possible he'd been overly paranoid. Maybe Harte was just bored when he was idle. After all, he'd been enthusiastic enough when he killed the prisoner at Shoal Point. *Too* enthusiastic, in fact.

Interesting.

'My information was good, and given gladly,' Jadrell mewed. 'I swear by the Primus.'

Klyssen, whose back was to Jadrell, rolled his eyes. *And so it's left to me to smooth the ruffled feathers.* He turned and gave him an unctuous smile. 'Of course, Lord Jadrell. It's through the efforts of men like yourself that the will of the Emperor is done. Forgive my subordinate; he's just excessively disappointed he didn't get to serve the Empire tonight.'

'Well, I'm glad *you* understand, Overwatchman.'

'Klyssen!' Harte called from the farmhouse.

Klyssen clenched his teeth. How long before that insufferable bastard learned to address him by his title? He stored the insult away, adding it to the long list of grievances Harte would pay for when Klyssen was Commander of Ossia.

Harte was dragging a man dressed in long johns and a roughspun

479

bedshirt out of the farmhouse. Plague walked at his shoulder; the other two dreadknights headed off towards the other outbuildings. By the time the man was pushed to his knees in front of Klyssen, his clothes were soaked through and his dark brown hair hung in sodden curls over his eyes.

Klyssen peered down at him from beneath the dripping brim of his hat. 'You own this farm?'

Fluke glanced at the open door of the barn, then back at Klyssen. He had the sullen and defiant look of a Bitterbracker, but there was fear in his eyes all the same. 'I do.'

'Where did they go?' Klyssen asked.

'I don't know,' said Fluke.

Klyssen gave Plague a tiny nod, a silent instruction. 'Where do you *think* they've gone?' he asked.

'I don't know ...' he said again, but this time he tailed off uncertainly as his attention was caught by something else. He raised a trembling hand in front of his face, stared at it in growing horror.

'Guess,' said Klyssen.

Fluke pulled down the collar of his bedshirt and gazed uncomprehendingly at his chest with a low moan of fear. Lord Jadrell shifted uneasily, bewildered, but Klyssen merely waited and watched. He'd seen Plague at work many times. The disease and corruption spreading throughout Fluke's body were entirely in his mind, invisible to the others, but it was no less effective a torture for that. Right now he was watching his skin flake, crack and blister at an impossible rate. Usually Klyssen preferred the elegant art of interrogation, but he didn't have time to be subtle now.

'Joha!' Fluke cried out. 'What's happening?'

'Joha's not here,' said Klyssen. 'He's a figment of your imagination, like all your barbarian gods. But I'm here, and I can make it stop. Just tell me where they went.'

'I don't know!' Fluke said through gritted teeth. 'I put them up in my barn because it was the right thing to do. I didn't know they'd left. I only woke when I heard the animals.'

'But you have an idea, don't you?' Harte snarled. 'You Ossians stick together close as winter ravens. Tell us!'

'Step back, Watchman!' Klyssen told him sternly, incensed at the interruption.

Harte ignored him. 'Tell us, you damned oaf!' he shouted, and struck the kneeling man on the top of his head with the pommel of his sword. Fluke tumbled face-down into the mud.

'Harte!' Klyssen shouted in outrage and disbelief.

'He knows! You can see it!' Harte insisted, pulling Fluke up by his hair. Blood and rainwater ran in rivulets down his face. 'Where did they go? *Where?*'

Fluke managed to shake his head mutely before Harte smashed the pommel of his sword down on the bridge of his nose, splintering it to mush. 'Liar!' he roared.

'Don't know don't know don't—' Fluke mumbled, dazed with pain.

'Liar!' Harte hit him again. 'Filthy subhuman Ossian *liar!*'

Klyssen stared at Harte in shock. The situation was spiralling out of control. Harte had been recalcitrant before, but never outright disobedient. Now he was red-faced, grimacing, far past reason. Klyssen looked for support from Captain Dressle, but he was in one of the outbuildings. There was only Plague, and Klyssen wouldn't ask for help from him.

'Stop this now!' he said, conscious of Lord Jadrell cringing behind him.

His command fell on deaf ears. 'Tell us!' Harte screamed, pulling Fluke to his feet. 'Tell us where they've gone!'

But Fluke was beyond listening. Overwhelmed by horror, pain and the imaginary disease still eating at him, he staggered towards the farmhouse, gargling and pawing at his face.

'Where are you going, bumpkin?' Harte sneered. Then he grabbed Fluke's hair again and ran him through with his sword.

Fluke went stiff, his head tipped back in Harte's grip. He coughed once, blood flooding over his lips, then slid from the blade and fell to the ground in a heap.

Harte turned to Klyssen, panting, a savage, joyous challenge in his eyes. The same look he'd worn when he slew the prisoner back in Shoal Point. A look of triumph, as if to say: *That's how it's done.*

Klyssen stepped forward, pulled off a glove and delivered a

481

stinging slap across his face, hard enough to send his hat flying. Harte gaped at him, stunned.

'You are no watchman but a common butcher!' Klyssen barked. 'An embarrassment to our uniform! We are the Emperor's representatives in this land and if that man was a traitor, we would have shown it by procedure and due authority! Rest assured I will be reporting your *many* infractions in Morgenholme, and with the stain I will put on your record, you will be lucky if you ever make watchman first class, let alone overwatchman. Any further insubordination and I'll ensure you spend the rest of your days rotting at a desk in the most remote backwater of Ozak I can find. *Are we understood?*'

Klyssen was shaking by the time he finished. He couldn't remember ever being so angry before. He wouldn't have thought himself capable. But he saw now what Harte was: spy or no, he was a bully who enjoyed killing far too much.

Klyssen hated bullies. He'd had enough of that in his youth. And he wouldn't permit the reputation of the Iron Hand to be sullied by an overprivileged upstart who thought that pinning the double cross to his shoulder meant he could murder with impunity.

Captain Dressle was hurrying over now, having become aware of their confrontation. Klyssen held Harte's gaze long enough to see surprise turn to humiliation and outright loathing, then he turned to Dressle.

'Anyone else?' he asked, as if nothing had happened.

'Only farmhands,' said Dressle, eyeing the scene.

'Might I suggest something?' said Lord Jadrell meekly, raising a finger. He looked somewhat nauseous at the sight of Fluke. 'His brother Keel... His cottage is not far from here. Along that track to the west. Perhaps that is where they went?'

'Very well,' said Klyssen. 'Go back to the town with all haste and raise the garrison. The fugitives have no horses so they may try to escape by the docks. Harte, go with him. Dressle, gather the Iron Guard. We will head to the cottage.'

'Yes, Overwatchman,' said Dressle.

Klyssen clapped his hands at Jadrell. 'All haste, my lord. We are losing time.'

Jadrell jumped and scampered off towards his horse. Dressle began calling for his troops to form up. Before he walked away, Klyssen reserved a final glare of scorn for Harte, whose blond hair was plastered flat, face set in an expression of pure hate.

Back in your place, rat, Klyssen thought with righteous fury. *And this time, you'll stay there.*

61

Keel's eyes flew open at the sound of a fist pounding on the door of his cottage. He lurched out of bed, stumbled into his trousers while reaching for the sword propped up in the corner. Haste made him clumsy; his foot snagged, he hopped a step and then crashed to the floor.

'Who's there? Who's knocking at this hour?' Mariella was bolt upright in bed, her face a picture of fright as thunder tumbled overhead.

It's them, thought Keel. He'd been waiting for a knock at the door ever since he took up arms against the Krodans. Dying in combat had never scared him. What scared him was the quiet efficiency of men in dark coats, who turned up late at night and spirited their victims away to unguessable torments.

'Keel? Who is it?' Mariella cried again. He felt a flare of anger as he struggled to pull on the rest of his clothes. *Stop bothering me with stupid questions.* If he faced them, he'd face them dressed and armed and—

'Keel?'

'*I'm going to see!*' he shouted, fear making him furious. She cringed against the headboard, shocked. Keel instantly regretted his tone, hated himself for scaring her. 'I'm going, eh?' he said, more gently, and left before she could marshal her own anger and shout back.

He hurried past Tad's door – it was mercifully quiet inside – and down the stairs into the kitchen. As he neared, he heard a voice he knew on the other side and the tension in his belly loosened a little.

'Keel! Open up!'

Not the Iron Hand, but Garric. Keel pulled the latch and opened the door, sword in hand. Garric was grim-faced beneath his soaking hood, the others gathered in the dark beyond, hunched and nervous.

'They found us,' Keel said flatly.

'They found us,' Garric agreed. 'We have to go.'

'I can't.' The words came without thought. He wasn't ready. He was supposed to have one more night with his wife. He didn't have to decide until tomorrow.

Garric had no time to be gentle. 'What do you think they'll do if they catch you here? What'll they do to Mariella and Tad to make you talk? Best thing you can do for them is leave. They can't use them against you if they can't find you.'

Keel fought for an answer, unable to accept this moment had come. There had to be another way. He heard Mariella on the landing, drawn down the stairs by their voices, and felt trapped.

A flicker of lightning lit the sodden yard and bracken-thick hill beyond. He saw the Skarl; tall Harod standing protectively by Orica; the two boys; Fen and Vika and Ruck, too. But not his brother.

'Is Fluke with you?' he asked.

'He's still at the farm,' said Garric.

'You left him there?' Keel was aghast.

'Should I have told him we were escaping? We'd be dead if Vika hadn't warned us. For all I know, he was the one who sold us out.'

'He'd never do that!' cried Mariella as she reached the bottom of the stairs, hair in a tangle and her face screwed up in rage. 'Now you've brought the Krodans down on our heads? Get out of our lives!'

Garric gave her a look of disdain that made Keel angry on her behalf. They'd disliked each other from the start, which was why Keel endeavoured never to bring them together.

'You're only part of this if you make yourself part of it,' Garric told her. 'You don't want that. We'll lead them away. They likely won't come here at all if they can chase us.'

'We *are* part of this! He's my husband, and he's staying to look after our son!'

'I'll answer for myself, Mariella!' Keel snapped, moved to sharpness by stung pride. He wouldn't have the others think his decisions were made by his wife.

'I wish you would!' she snapped. 'Stay or go! Too long you've had the best of both!'

'We could find somewhere to hide,' Keel told Garric. 'My family and I. My uncle's house is half a day from here; we can stay with him till the Iron Hand leave Wracken Bay.'

'In this storm?' Mariella said. 'Tad can barely get out of bed! The journey would kill him!'

Garric ignored her. 'Everyone in Wracken Bay will know you're a wanted man after tonight. Even if you lay low, you'll be arrested the moment you emerge. What's done is done, and I'm sorry for it, but you can't stay here and you can't come back to Wracken Bay. *Ever.*'

Keel felt like the walls were closing in on him. Mariella was right: he'd procrastinated too long, unwilling to give up the freedom of the road but afraid to lose his family. Now the choice was out of his hands, and what he wanted didn't matter any more.

'This is my home …' he said weakly.

'Aye, but no longer,' said Garric. 'You don't like that? Fight with us! The only way you'll get it back is if the Krodans are driven from our land.' Garric saw him waver and pressed his argument. 'We need you, Keel! The boats are the only way out and none of us can steer a course through a storm such as this. None but you.'

Keel looked over his shoulder at his wife, who was still poised at the foot of the stairs.

'I meant what I said,' she told him. 'If you leave, you're dead to us.'

'Would you have me stay and die anyway?' he asked. 'Garric's right: they'll torture you just to punish me. They'll take this place from us.'

486

'You didn't do anything!' she argued. 'They can't do anything without proof.'

Garric snorted. 'They've never needed proof in the past—'

'*Get out of my house, you bastard!*' Mariella screamed. 'I rue the day you ever came to this town! Would that you'd drunk yourself to death like you wanted, instead of taking my husband from me!'

A rising wail sounded behind her, an insensible blare of distress coming from upstairs.

'Now see what you've done!' Mariella said, tears of frustration welling. 'Keel! Shut the door. I don't care if you're on this side of it or that, but make up your mind.'

Keel held her gaze, pleading, desperate. He couldn't find the words, but his eyes said it for him. Her face fell. Even at the last, she hadn't truly believed he'd leave. Now she knew better.

'Farewell then, husband,' she said, her voice cracking. Then she fled up the stairs.

He was still staring after her when Vika pushed past Garric and thrust a flask into his hand. 'A small amount of that in boiled water each day,' she told him. 'Have Tad breathe the vapours. Go and tell her.'

'Leave it on the table!' Garric snapped, a hand on his arm. 'You need to come with us *now*.'

His touch ignited something in Keel. A burning fury, lashing out in search of a target. It was Garric's fault it had come to this, Garric who'd led him astray! He pulled away violently; he wouldn't let it end like this. 'Mariella!' he cried and ran up the stairs, Garric shouting after him.

He caught her at the top of the stairs, on the narrow landing, with her hand on the door to Tad's room. Tad was screaming in there, upset by the raised voices. She turned to him with pathetic hope in her eyes.

'You'll stay?' she breathed.

The hope died as she saw the flask in his hand.

'A little in boiled water, once a day. He should breathe the steam,' he said.

'I told you, Keel,' she said. 'If you want him to take that quack medicine, stay here and deliver it yourself. Be a father.'

He fought for the right words. 'Don't let me go like this, Mariella. I'll be back. I'll find the money for Tad, I swear. But I need... I need to know you...'

'Love you?' Her face had gone hard. He'd caused her too much pain, too many times. There was no more kindness in her. 'No, Keel. You just want me to make you feel better about abandoning us. But I won't. I hope it kills you every day.'

Her cruelty shocked him, so much that he refused to believe she meant it. 'Go and see old Ganny. Get him to write to me.'

'I'm not going to see Gan—'

'Write to me! Send it to the Burned Bear in Morgenholme. Let me know you and Tad are well, that Fluke is well.'

Her face was immobile. Only the tears in her eyes showed her suffering. 'I won't,' she said. 'And I'll burn any letter from you before anyone can read it to me.'

That took his breath away, and he couldn't look at her after that. He reached for the door instead, to go past her into Tad's bedroom, desperate to hold him and stop the screaming if he could. She put her hand on his chest, without force, but stopping him as surely as any wall.

'How will you help? Will you tell him you're going away again?' she asked. Her voice was iron-calm now. 'You can't make it better. Let him forget you. Let *me*.'

She stepped inside the bedroom and shut the door behind her, leaving Keel on the landing alone, rejected, laid waste. He listened to Mariella soothing their son, and knew that he'd lost her at last, lost them both for ever. He was on one side of the door and his family were on the other, separated by a few inches of wood and an impassable gulf of hurt.

He put the flask on the floor and walked away.

62

The rain splattered and swirled along the gutters of Wracken Bay, crawling down walls, racing between cobblestones. The town had taken shelter, retreating inside, and the narrow grey lanes were ghostly with shifting light and wet whispers. Silent as ghosts themselves, hidden by heavy cloaks, the fugitives went unseen.

Aren checked over his shoulder for the dozenth time, afraid of what followed. Dreadknights, Vika said. He remembered how they'd killed four of Garric's band the first time they met, the horrific efficiency of that slaughter, like a grinder chewing meat. They were no mere men, but a force implacable as time. They could be delayed, but not stopped.

Cade hustled along at his side. He caught a glimpse of his friend's face, pallid with suppressed terror, and gave him a brave smile that convinced neither of them.

In a few hours they'd have been on a ship to Morgenholme, safe from pursuit. Surely not even dreadknights would be able to find them in the mazy capital. But the enemy had caught up with them faster than they'd believed possible, and though nobody said so, they all knew why.

If only they'd kept their heads down and stayed out of the fight at the Reavers' Rest, they'd have passed unnoticed. But Aren had got them involved, and now they might all end up paying for it.

Beyond the tall, tight-packed buildings of Wracken Bay was the harbour. Warehouses, jetties and a shipyard cluttered the shore. Boats at anchor rocked on the restless waves, protected from the worst of the storm by the breakwater. Further out, the Cut was churning, crashing up against the foot of the Ghoulfort.

Garric found shelter at the corner of a shuttered bakery and looked out towards the docks. Aren took station across the street. At first he saw only curtains of rain and flapping tarpaulin stirring on empty boats. Then lightning blasted the scene, showing him Krodan soldiers moving along the waterfront.

Garric swore. 'The squareheads second-guessed us.' He strained to see in the dark. 'Docks are sewn up tight. We won't get out that way.'

Thunder boomed overhead, crackling away into the distance.

'Head for the woods?' Aren suggested.

'Dreadknights don't tire. Even with Vika's aid, they'd run us down on foot.' Then his face cleared, and a decision was made. 'There's another way,' he said.

A shout of alarm made them whirl: a Krodan soldier, emerging from a street to their left. Fen put an arrow in his chest before he could draw breath again, but it was too late; already his fellows were running up behind him. Garric's sword sang free of its sheath and he sprang forward, Keel and Harod with him. They met the soldiers at the mouth of the street in a clatter of steel, water spraying from their blades as they darted and swung.

The soldiers were twice their number and more, but they found themselves matched by the three men that opposed them. Harod held the centre, stiff and disciplined, his blade flicking here and there while his body barely moved. To either side, Keel and Garric fought savagely. Keel was formidable, but Garric married brute force with technique and was by far the superior of the two.

Aren drew his own sword uncertainly, trying to gather enough courage to join them. Before he could, Cade drew his attention. Four more soldiers were approaching down the stepped, sloping alley behind them.

His guts pulled tight. Keel, Harod and Garric were occupied with the first patrol. There was no one to defend them from these newcomers.

Fen swung around and loosed a hasty shot which thudded into the pelvis of the foremost guard, sending him tumbling with a scream. The rest kept coming and Aren ran towards them, because it was that or wait to die. A soldier loomed before him; their swords crashed together. The other two rushed past to either side, seeking other targets.

Aren parried desperately, fending off the Krodan's hacking strokes. There was no stopping, and no surrender. He didn't really know how to fight, so he was going to die. The terrifying finality of that swamped him, and in a moment of panic he let his guard down.

The Krodan knocked his sword aside and plunged in for the killing thrust. Aren reacted on instinct and did what he'd done a thousand times before under Master Orik's tutelage: he stepped aside, knocked the blade down with his sword and swept it back up at his opponent's head.

He should have hit the soldier's throat, but he was clumsy and the tip of his sword caromed off the soldier's cheek-guard, hard enough to ring his head like a bell. The soldier staggered back. For a heartbeat, they stared at each other in surprise.

Realisation sunk in: he'd been trained for this. All those years of the sword with Master Orik, feinting and parrying and watching his footwork, had been for this moment. So that when it came to it, he could move faster than he could think, react without question.

I can fight, he told himself, and he did.

Their blades met again and again. Aren was no longer on the back foot, but he fought carefully and defensively. With every block, his confidence grew. Every time he pushed his enemy back, he felt stronger. Panting breath, clenched teeth, sword on sword. His arm was starting to ache but it didn't matter. They'd only fought for seconds but it seemed like an eternity.

Out of the corner of his eye, he saw one of the soldiers scream and arch his back as Grub drove a knife into his spine. He saw Orica hiding in a doorway, heard Fen's bow again. More soldiers were coming from somewhere. He couldn't see Cade and didn't have time to look for him.

To overcome your enemy, you must first understand him.

Master Orik's favourite maxim. It brought clarity out of chaos and sharpened his mind. For the first time, he saw beyond the armour to the man he was fighting, a young man hardly older than he was, with doubt in his eyes. Suddenly he *knew* this Krodan, this boy trying to be a man, an unwilling soldier pushed into the life of the sword. He knew as little of real combat as Aren did. Less, in fact: this was his first fight with death on the line. He'd never killed anyone. Uniform or no, Aren had been blooded where his opponent hadn't.

I'm better than him, Aren thought in amazement, and with that he attacked.

A quick feint. The soldier lurched to defend against it. Aren went the other way, under his guard, and struck a glancing blow to his ribs, cutting between the plates of his armour into the leather and flesh beneath. The soldier screamed in pain, his guard collapsing as he stumbled back. Aren swung hard and chopped through the forearm of his off-hand. His scream became a breathless wail as he dropped his sword and clutched the stump of his arm, then tumbled onto his arse on the rainy cobbles.

Run him through, said Master Orik in his head. But his opponent was out of the fight, white with shock, and Aren didn't have the stomach to slay a helpless man. He stepped back, chest heaving.

'Vika!'

It was Cade's voice. Aren whirled to see the druidess backing up as a burly soldier advanced on her. Harod had broken away from his fight and was standing with Orica; Cade had wisely stuck close to him, sheltering behind Harod's blade rather than Aren's. There were more soldiers lying dead, pierced by Fen's arrows, and Grub had a man on the ground with his head pulled back, sawing at his throat with goblin glee as blood gushed out onto the cobbles.

Aren ran to help Vika but Ruck got there first, racing out of the rain to sink her teeth into the soldier's calf. The soldier roared and tried to stab the hound; but Vika stepped forward then, dashing a handful of powder in his face. His roars became shrieks as he pawed at his eyes, Ruck still savaging his leg. By the time Aren reached him, his face was blistered and burned, tear-streaked and smoking in the rain.

Aren gritted his teeth and drove his sword through the man's belly, up into his heart. He gargled, shuddered and went slack.

After that, there was no one left to fight. Aren looked this way and that, and saw only dead and wounded Krodans. The soldier who'd lost an arm had fallen silent, lying on his side, the stump drawn up against his chest. He was probably going to bleed out and die. Aren found he didn't care. The brutality of battle had numbed him to sympathy and grief. Survival was the only goal.

Garric and Keel came striding over. Harod was breathlessly apologising to Orica for not being there earlier. Between them they'd killed nine.

'There's more coming up from the docks,' Garric told them. 'Keep moving.'

'Where to?' asked Aren.

'Jadrell's got a launch in his boathouse, small enough for us to sail.' He surveyed the junction, the dead there. Then he gave Aren a rough slap on the arm. 'You fought well,' he said.

Aren felt a flush of pride at his words, and a grateful smile jumped onto his face. Then he remembered who he was talking to and wiped it off, angry at himself.

You do not know whether to hate or admire him, Vika had said. But couldn't he do both?

Through thunder and storm they ran. A horn sounded behind them and they hid as a Krodan patrol hurried past in the next street. The whole garrison was on the alert now. They went up sloping lanes and stairs running with water as they climbed towards Lord Jadrell's mansion.

Soon they saw it, perched on a cliff overlooking the Cut. Next to it was the boathouse: a stout timber construction with a thick door that opened onto the street. The door was securely padlocked.

'Out of the way! Grub good with locks!'

The Skarl produced two thin slivers of metal, one with a hooked end, and got to work. The others took up positions watching the approaches. From where they stood, they had a good view of the way they'd come. The rainswept thoroughfare ran downhill towards the heart of the town, crossed by half a dozen others.

Some way down the hill, a patrol emerged onto the street. One of the men saw them and shouted. In moments, they were joined by a larger group, and twenty or thirty soldiers swarmed towards them.

'Skarl! Make it fast!' Garric said.

'Hollow Man not helping Grub's concentration,' Grub muttered.

This time, when Keel, Garric and Harod formed a defensive line, Aren went with them, his blade ready. The numbers against them were greater, the street wider, their chances slim. But Aren would fight nonetheless, without thought of retreat.

Let them come.

He saw a figure on horseback riding up behind the troops and a thrill of recognition ran through him. Though he was some way off, he knew the man by his dress and his posture. He didn't need to see beneath the broad-brimmed hat to identify the man who'd killed his father.

Harte.

A red rage swarmed behind his eyes and he was seized by the urge to charge, to hack through the enemy so he could wrap his hands around that throat. But this was no bard's tale, and he was no hero. If he was to take revenge on his father's murderer, it wouldn't be today, not with so many standing in his way.

There was a click from behind him, and a clanking of chain.

'Grub done it!'

Garric turned away from the oncoming troops, wrenched the heavy door open. 'In! In!' he shouted, ushering the others past him.

'Thank you, Grub! Good job, Grub!' the Skarl grumbled resentfully as he went inside; but Aren didn't move. He was still looking down the street. *Let him see me,* he thought. *Let him know I'm coming for him.*

As if he'd heard, Harte raised his head and their eyes met across the distance, Aren's hot hate against the watchman's cool arrogance.

'Aren!' Cade tugged at him, but Aren wouldn't break that gaze. Not until he heard hooves clattering and three terrible figures rode into view in front of the troops.

Dreadknights.

'Inside *now*!' Garric snarled, yanking him out of the rain and

494

into the boathouse, where Grub bolted and padlocked the door behind them.

The space inside was dominated by Jadrell's launch, a long rowing boat with raised covered decks to fore and aft. It rested on struts a few feet off the floor, suspended from the ceiling by a cradle of ropes and pulleys. It was brightly painted in the green and yellow of Jadrell's house, and there was a crest at the bow with leaping fish, prowling wolves and castles displaying his family's heritage and their connections to other notable powers. It was a Krodan affectation that made Garric sneer when he saw it.

'Aren, Cade, get the gates open. Keel and I will see to the boat.'

Keel was already working the winch that operated the overhead pulleys, tightening the ropes until they took the vessel's weight. The others set to pulling the struts aside, to allow Keel to lower it onto the slipway.

Aren and Cade ran to the end of the boathouse, where they unlatched the wooden gates and shoved them open. The wind howled in and around them, and they found themselves over-looking the torrid grey-blue waters of the Cut. Cade leaned out and peered down the slipway.

'Don't reckon this is entirely safe,' he opined.

'Am I hearing you right?' Aren shouted over the wind. 'Is this the same Cade that faced a savage she-warg and lived to tell the tale?'

'It was a wild pig,' Cade pointed out.

'It was a *big* wild pig,' Aren replied. Cade laughed, and for a moment it felt like they were boys again, back in Shoal Point, and adventures still ended at dinner time.

Then something huge and heavy crashed against the door to the street and Grub jumped back as the chain rattled wildly through the handles.

'Grub think it's time to go,' he said.

'Get in the boat!' Garric barked at them. 'Harod, Grub, Keel – help me push!'

'Why Grub always have to do the hard wor—'

'*Now!*'

Keel had lowered the boat onto the slipway and was hacking

away the ropes that held it while the others clambered in and Ruck was hoisted up. Garric sliced through the anchor rope, which was meant to ease the boat slowly down to the water. They wouldn't be going slowly this time.

A second blow hit the door and the head of Ruin's hammer smashed through it, almost taking it off its hinges. The dreadknight wrenched the hammer free, and Aren glimpsed Plague and Sorrow behind him.

'Push!' Garric roared, and they put their shoulders to the boat. It slid forward easily on greased rollers, and Aren felt the nauseating anticipation of the drop at the end as the boat gathered speed. Once the momentum was too great to stop, the four men who were pushing began to scramble into the moving boat. Grub was nimble enough to climb over the side without aid and Keel had little trouble, either, but Harod was wearing splint mail and needed help. Garric got his arms over the gunwale and Aren and Cade, who were nearest, reached over and started pulling him in.

The door burst apart in a blast of spinning timber as Ruin charged into the boathouse. Plague and Shadow darted in behind him. The boat, accelerating fast, jolted against a jammed roller. Harod fell into the boat, crushing Fen and Orica against the side. Cade stumbled, lost his grip on Garric and tripped over a rowing bench. Suddenly Garric was sliding back over the side of the boat, feet trailing on the ground. Aren, who had one of his arms, lunged forwards to grab the other. The muscles of his back wrenched as they took the strain.

The boat had almost reached the boathouse gates. Ruin thundered after the escaping fugitives, clanking and thumping as he ran alongside the slipway. Plague raised his bow and drew.

Garric was trying to find his feet, tripping along beside the boat as it pulled away from him. Only Aren's grip kept him from falling behind. He looked into the eyes of the Hollow Man, the man who'd sworn to kill his father, and who, in a way, had done so. After all, the Krodans only killed Randill to get to Garric.

All Aren had to do was let him go, and the dreadknights would have their prize. It would all be over, and Cade would be safe.

Without Garric, the rest of them were insignificant, not worth the chase.

In a moment of wild temptation, he thought he might do it.

But it was a moment only, and it passed. He planted his feet against the side of the boat and hauled with all his might. Garric found his footing and launched himself upwards, and then Keel was there, grabbing Garric by his belt, adding his strength to Aren's. They all tumbled into the boat in a heap. Somewhere among the knocks and bruises and the tangle of limbs, Aren heard the snap of a bowstring. Vika grunted, folded up, fell back against the gunwale. Then the world began to tip.

'Grab something!' Keel yelled. Gravity took hold and the boat slithered into a headlong plunge, to the terrifying tempo of the slipway's wooden ribs clacking past faster and faster. Fen screamed as they plummeted towards the waves, her voice drowned out by the wind.

They braced as best they could, but it was never going to be enough. As they crashed into the water, they were flung violently forward. Aren slammed against something wooden and painfully solid. He saw Cade go skidding past him, his head caroming off a supply chest, leaving him in a limp heap, unconscious or worse. Aren tried to get to him but was blinded by a wash of salty water which exploded over the bow, stinging his face and soaking him. Suddenly the boat was turning wildly, black rocks looming above it.

'Get to the oars!' Keel bellowed. Then he went scrambling towards the stern, stepping over Vika, who lay in a heap of hides and tangled trinkets.

Aren, too disorientated to think for himself, did as he was ordered. Others clambered onto the benches around him and fumbled oars into place. Garric yelled 'Pull!' and they did, clumsily at first but tightening the rhythm with each stroke. Orica was to Aren's right, her hair a wet draggle, arms straining. Fen worked ahead of him. Grub's biceps bulged as he applied himself to his task with the determination of the desperate. Waves surged over the side, swilling round their feet and the sliding, rolling bodies of Cade and Vika. Ruck barked in a frenzy, skidding about as she tried to summon help for her fallen mistress.

Lightning flashed, thunder boomed and the wind screamed. The horizon tilted and tipped until Aren had no idea which direction they were going. He could hardly see through the tempest. He wanted to go to Cade but didn't dare let go of the oar.

From out of the chaos came laughter. It was Keel, hauling on the tiller atop the stern deck, skin glistening and his head thrown back.

'Come, then, Joha!' he screamed, madness in his voice. 'I dare you! Crush us if you can!'

'Pull!' Garric shouted, and they did, hauling their way another few feet through the waves. The boat yawed and bucked. Aren's arms and back ached and his hands sang with pain.

'Pull!'

Again they drew on their oars, and again, until it was all Aren knew. The agony of effort became a background haze. He was taken by the same mulish trance that had got him through endless hours chipping stone in the mine. Only Garric's voice mattered. Only the next pull, and the next.

'Hold!'

The break in the rhythm brought Aren back to himself. He blinked and looked about. They were out on the channel now, far from either shore, and though waves still tipped and crashed over the boat, there were no rocks to dash against. Wracken Bay was a distant cluster of lights through the rain and they were speeding westwards, carried along the coast by a fast current.

Freed from the oar, Aren staggered unsteadily across the boat to Cade. He hauled his friend from the water and sat him up against the chest. Cade had a darkening bruise on the side of his head, but he half-wakened at Aren's urging, and though groggy he could focus his eyes with effort. Aren was relieved. He'd taken a knock, but Cade was hard-headed.

'You'll be alright,' he said, more to reassure himself than Cade. 'You'll be alright.'

Vika wasn't faring so well. The others had propped her up against the gunwale, her face a streaked mess of black and white paint, her eyes closed and her hair in soggy ropes. A black-feathered arrow was buried deep in her shoulder.

'Will she live?' Orica asked.

'How would I know?' Garric snapped. 'She's the one with the healing arts!' He put his hand to his forehead in evident distress. 'Let's make her comfortable, at least.'

Ruck barked wildly as they set about it, out of her mind with anxiety. Aren looked back to the tiller, where Keel had fallen silent. His gaze was distant, turned towards the lights of the town, his expression a bleak mix of shocked grief and emptiness.

His wife, Aren thought. *His son.*

The boat sailed on through dark and the tempest, heading for the sea.

63

'Which of you has the answer? Come on, speak up!'

Mara waited before the blackboard, sweeping the room expectantly with hard eyes. She was lean, with short hair the colour of brushed steel and a sharp-featured face creased with the wrinkles and folds of fifty years. Some of her pupils stared furiously past her, avoiding her gaze, trying to make sense of the sums and diagrams. The others looked down, hoping someone else would declare a solution so they wouldn't have to.

There were nine girls in the class, aged between twelve and sixteen, some from wealth and some from nothing but all of them fabulously bright. She'd given them uniforms in the hope of erasing their differences, but they came through anyway. The rich ones arrived immaculate, dresses pressed and hair neat. The canal girls had dirt on their hems, and brought runny noses and lice.

'You all know how to do this,' she told them. She pointed to a simple diagram, representing an open-topped barrel sitting inside a larger vat. 'You have some of the proportions of the two chambers, and you know how much water is being poured into the barrel. Work out how much you can fill the barrel before it overflows. Then you can work out how high the water will rise in the vat. If you do it step by step, it's quite straightforward.'

It wasn't straightforward. It was difficult, and that was the point. She'd left out vital information to hamper them, and it was easy to forget the barrel's displacing effect when calculating how much had overflowed. She hadn't told them how to account for that, so they'd have to stretch themselves to succeed, to reach into the unknown a little. In her lessons, as in life, they'd often find themselves dealt a hand that was less than fair. She'd teach them to overcome a disadvantage any way they could.

The silence of urgent thought filled the classroom. Outside, the sun was shining, but inside it was cool. The walls were panelled with heavy dark wood, and the air smelled of libraries and learning. Mara watched her charges and fought down a familiar frustration. Making them understand was the easy part. Getting them to raise their voices was the real battle. She wanted them to be reckless, to theorise wildly, to guess at what they didn't know. Mostly they only answered when they were certain they wouldn't risk disapproval. Kadelina had been with her three years and still didn't dare to be wrong.

Jinna flung up a hand. Keen little Jinna was always the first to puzzle things out. Mara looked past her to Kiri, the youngest, sitting quietly with her tangled brown hair half-hiding her face.

'Kiri,' she said.

'I don't know,' Kiri said.

'Yes, you do. Try.'

She did try, and she figured it out in the end, but it took some time and Mara had to walk her through it. Jinna kept her hand up throughout. With every new hesitation, each mistake and misstep that Kiri made, Mara saw Jinna becoming more impatient. She had the solution. She couldn't understand why no one wanted to listen to her.

Get used to it. There's a lot more of that ahead of you.

When their lessons were over, the girls made their way out of the classroom, laughing and chattering. Jinna still wore a scowl, but she said nothing as she passed Mara, who was sitting at her desk reading some paperwork. Mara would rather she complain than suffer in silence, but she could only expect so much. A lifetime of submission and low expectations could not be quickly undone.

'Kiri. Stay behind a moment.'

Kiri froze, her eyes full of terror. She was a gawky and gangly twelve-year-old, caught up in the first rush of adolescent growth, and she walked with the manner of someone expecting a beating.

'Don't be alarmed, child. It's nothing bad.'

That scarcely seemed to reassure her. She glanced enviously at the others as they left. They gave her sympathetic looks and began to speculate about her detainment as soon as they were out of sight. Mara waited until the clamour of footsteps on the stairs had receded, then beckoned Kiri to stand before her.

'It's come to my attention that your father has been unable to find work for some weeks.'

Kiri looked at her feet and nodded uncertainly. 'He's a builder, Mistress. All the new buildings, they want them Krodan-style. My da don't know how to do that.'

'*Doesn't* know,' Mara corrected automatically.

'Doesn't know,' repeated Kiri.

Mara produced a folded letter, sealed with her mark, and held it out. 'Take this to Marron the butcher at the Shacklemarket. He'll give you meat and groceries for your family. I won't have one of my pupils coming to class too hungry to work.'

Kiri took it, bewildered. 'Thank you, Mistress,' she said.

Mara returned her attention to the papers on her desk. Kiri belatedly realised she'd been dismissed, and slipped away.

Her paperwork done, Mara straightened the desks and set the classroom in order, then left and locked it behind her. The room was a hired space in a building otherwise filled with clerk's offices, a printmaker's and an artist's studio on the top floor. The setting was conveniently central, near enough to the canals that the poorer girls could get there on foot, far enough away that the wealthy families wouldn't balk at sending their children there. She taught here nine days a week; Jorsday and Festenday were rest days. She had little to thank the Krodans for, but she did admire their work ethic, and the Krodan week – five days work, one of rest, four of work, one of rest and worship – appealed to her more than the old Ossian week of four-two-three-two, which had always struck her as excessively lax.

Outside in the street, the noise and bustle of Morgenholme were waiting for her. Carts creaked by and birds fluttered among the gabled roofs of South Heights. A pie-seller had parked his cart on the corner, hawking his wares to passers-by. A group of laughing

Krodan men emerged from their lunch at the beer-hall down the road. Two finely dressed ladies browsed a confectioner's window, shading themselves from the afternoon sun with parasols. Clia was waiting with the carriage on the other side of the cobbled street, hunched in the driver's seat. Mara looked for a gap in the traffic, but before she could cross she was hailed by a man nearby.

'Your pardon! Be you Mara of Whitherwall?'

She regarded him with immediate suspicion. He was a man of low means, ragged at the edges and smudged with dirt, though he'd evidently done his best to smarten himself up. That and his deferential tone told her he wanted something. Her eyes went to the young boy at his side, waifish and wide-eyed.

'I am,' she said stiffly. Over the road, Clia sat up, alert and ready to intervene.

'Your pardon, your pardon. They say you've a school, that you teach children rich or poor, an' you don't ask no coin for it; but you only teach them's what's they call exceptional. My boy Lud, he—'

She held up a hand, interrupting him. 'I think you've been misinformed.'

The man looked confused. 'You don't teach no school?'

'I don't teach boys.'

A desperate look passed across the man's face. 'But Lud 'ere, 'e's gifted! Speaks four languages and he ain't yet eleven! Reads better 'n anyone. Ask him anything and he'll recall it, clear as if it were a moment ago.'

'Well, good! With such talent, no doubt he'll rise above the circumstances of his birth,' she told him. 'At worst he'll find work as a translator, but likely he'll do better than that. Many masters would be glad to take on such a prodigy, and he may even find his way to the Glass University.' She couldn't help the harsh tone that crept into her voice as she went on. 'Meanwhile, fully one half of the population will never go to the Glass University, never be schooled to their potential, never be allowed a job with any status outside of a narrow few allowed them because they are seen as suitable to their nature. Your son, Ossian and lowborn though he be, has the world at his feet by comparison, and there is a long line of children more disadvantaged who will pass through my doors before he will.'

The man stared at her, confused. He was dimly aware that he'd been told off but he wasn't sure why. She'd never had the knack of talking to uneducated folk.

'I wish you good fortune,' she said. Then, without looking at the boy again, she crossed the street.

'All well?' Clia asked, eyeing the man and his child, hand near her sword. It crossed Mara's mind that she needed to renew the permit soon. Just another thing to add to the calendar she kept in her head.

'Peace, Clia. He's no threat.' She watched the man walk away dejectedly, his hand on the boy's shoulder. The sight made her sad for a moment and she wondered if she'd been too hasty, but she brushed the thought away. Sympathy was a finite commodity in a world such as this.

'I will take a walk, I think,' she told Clia. 'Meet me by the Arcolid at twelfth bell o' day. The time until then is yours.'

Clia didn't have a face made for gratitude. She smiled little and always looked serious. Mara liked that about her.

It was a fine autumn day, the sun was pleasantly warm and the Sisters were waxing in the west. Lyssa was a pale pastel marble made paler by the bright blue sky; Tantera loomed ghostly and glowering.

Mara strode briskly – she did everything briskly – the heels of her shoes clicking on the cobbles as she headed through the streets of South Heights. Her mind was busy, thinking over tomorrow's lessons, plotting the best route to her destination, worrying about what she'd say when she got there. As she walked, she observed how the shadows thrown by chimneys onto rooftops became distorted by the angle of the sun, and wondered how to turn shadow-casting into an experiment for her pupils. A fat pigeon scudded past and she decided to obtain one to learn how such a bulky bird flew. A man sneezed nearby, and Mara wondered why sneezing made her feel so good afterwards, and if that feeling could be replicated chemically without the inconvenience of spraying mucus everywhere.

Her mind turned and turned, never quiet. Even in sleep – which she needed little of – she dreamed vividly and often woke determined to investigate something she'd imagined while unconscious. Long ago, she'd come to realise that not everybody was like her, that the minds of most were not full of restless curiosity and calculation but rather with bovine meanderings interspersed with lengthy periods of vacancy. She pitied and envied them at the same time. There were moments when she thought it might be a relief to be so benighted, to be free of the frustrations and cares of intellect. But she might as well have wished she were a cat.

The traffic thickened as she approached the bridge and she was forced to the side of the street by carts and carriages. At the mouth of the Promise Bridge, the denizens of the Canal District swarmed up from below. They were poorer folk than the occupants of South Heights, living in the rank alleys at the foot of the hill. There, streets of tumbledown houses were mazed with narrow waterways that flooded whenever the river burst its banks, and rats were as numerous as flies.

Mara joined the crowd, threading through the crush towards the bridge. Merchants in finery mixed with toothless hags and book-keepers walked with sewer-men. She looked around and wondered if there was a similarity between the way crowds moved and the way swarms of insects did.

Finally the bridge came into sight. Broad, long and high, it stood on great pillared arches of stone that strode down the hillside into the water and over to the narrow green island that rose from the Cay like the ridged spine of some slumbering riverbed leviathan. Sovereign's Isle had been the seat of Ossian monarchs for centuries, but no monarch ruled there now.

At the entrance of the bridge, standing to either side, were two towering statues: King Farril the Sound and his queen Elidia of Trine. Farril was holding his hand out towards his wife and looking across at her, as if to direct the viewer's attention that way. Elidia was bent slightly, arms spread in a gesture that said *This is yours*, for the Promise Bridge had been her gift to the people of the city.

And what will I leave? Mara thought as she passed beneath the statues, and a shadow fell on her heart. *Who will remember my name when I'm gone?*

The story of the Promise Bridge was well known among the poor folk of Morgenholme. Farril was but a prince when he fell in love with Elidia, daughter of the High Thane of Trine, who was visiting Farril's father at the palace. Elidia had observed on her visit that there was a bridge linking the north side of the river to Sovereign's Isle, but those on the south side had to cross the river by boat. The rich occupied the north bank, living in orderly beauty among the imposing ruins of the Second Empire, while the south bank was chaotic and dangerous, the province of the poor. Elidia was kind of heart and ever a champion of the weak, so when Farril asked for her hand in marriage, she agreed on one condition: that he build a bridge to the south, so all might cross to Sovereign's Isle. Farril was horrified at the idea of common folk tramping past the royal palace in their hordes, but Elidia said it would do him good to be reminded how the meanest of his subjects lived. So Farril promised her the bridge, and when they were married, he kept that promise. Elidia had become one of Ossia's most beloved queens.

One day, Mara said to herself. *One day they will build a statue to me, too. And I will leave something greater than a bridge behind.*

But she'd become gloomy, and her bravado did little to cheer her. Every day the sands of her life ran thinner and the window of opportunity narrowed. While the Krodans ruled Ossia, her voice would never be heard. And there was no sign of that changing any time soon.

Unless, she thought. *Unless ...*

A banner had been hung across the bridge, displaying the crests of Prince Ottico and Princess Sorrel of Harrow. Tomas and Toven stood to either side, one holding a book, the other a blade. A feverish excitement had gripped the city as the impending celebrations neared. A week's holiday had been declared to welcome their Lord Protector, eleven whole days of revels, beginning on the day of the wedding. It was a level of generosity unheard of under the Krodan regime.

They were buying Ossian hearts with a celebration while they put a Krodan in place of their murdered queen and the Ember Blade in his hand. It was cynical and obvious, and Mara was depressingly certain that it would work. People had short memories and thirty years was long enough for the complacent to get used to anything. But Mara hadn't forgotten, and she wouldn't celebrate. The day the Emperor's son was welcomed as their Lord Protector would be the day Ossia embraced her own slavery.

Across the bridge, Sovereign's Isle was festooned with flags and banners. The plazas were aswarm and a festival was setting up in King's Park, which would be opened to the public for the celebrations. Mummers performed before the gates of the royal palace and vendors peddled exotic sweetmeats in the shadow of the House of Aspects, the greatest shrine to the old gods in all of Ossia. The Krodans hadn't dared to tear that one down yet, but it was only a matter of time.

Mara passed them all with barely a glance, heading across the island to Pastor's Bridge, and thence to the north side of the river. At the top of the hill were the Uplanes, where the rich dwelled among the towering edifices of a lost empire. Her business was lower down, in Clockcross, the craft district. There, artists and artisans toiled beneath the Horolith, the mysterious ancient timepiece which had somehow survived the ruin of its makers, and still kept perfect time a millennium after it was built.

Braden's cooperage was a plain wooden building on a street facing out over the river. Mara paused at the door, gathering herself. *I will not ask*, she told herself. *I do not wish to know.* Then she pushed the door open and went inside.

The workshop was busy and cluttered, stacked with staves and metal hoops, apprentices working at tables in between. A barrel was being toasted by the open window, the interior dancing with firelight thrown by the brazier inside it. The air smelled of warm wood, sweat and sawdust.

'Braden! Customer!' one of the apprentices yelled as he saw

her. At the far end of the workshop, a thickset man with a bushy black beard looked up. He laid aside the hammer he'd been using to knock dents from a hoop and came over, dusting his hands.

'Mara,' he said gruffly, with a respectful nod.

'Braden.'

A moment of awkwardness. The big cooper was always uneasy at the sight of her these days. It brought his loyalties into conflict. 'This way,' he said at last, gesturing towards the back.

She followed him through the workshop and out into a small yard which held a cart, a tiny stable and a few storage sheds. He unlocked the smallest and opened it, inviting her inside.

She stepped into the shed. There in the gloom were a dozen barrels standing on end. Each of them was set with a carved crest: two wolves rampant to either side of a spreading tree. The emblem of the Amberlyne vineyards. Mara inspected them critically.

'Finest oak from the forests of Trine,' Braden said. 'Carthanian iron on the hoops. The crests are copied perfectly. It'd take a master craftsman to spot the difference.'

'A fine job,' Mara agreed. 'And at such short notice. My heartfelt thanks.'

'The boys did some, but I finished them on my own. Didn't want them knowing what we were making. Any of this comes back to me, they're not involved.'

'It won't,' Mara assured him. 'I've told no one.' She circled one of the barrels, peering at it as if she could see inside. 'They're exactly as I asked?'

He moved over to show her. 'Two separate compartments inside. The central compartment is about one-third the volume. That's where you put your wine. There's a bung in the bilge so you can taste it, another in the head for the spigot when you're ready to serve.' He slapped the barrel with his palms on either side. 'The other compartment sits against the sides, two chambers, connected across but sealed off from the central part. That one you can't pour from.'

'So how do I fill it?'

'There's a tiny bung behind the Amberlyne crest.' He tapped

the emblem on the head of the barrel. 'I've left 'em loose so you can get to 'em. You'll need to glue 'em down when you're done.'

'So if the first compartment is full of Amberlyne, anyone drinking from this barrel will suspect nothing amiss?'

'Aye, till it runs out and they realise the barrel is still more than half full. Reckon that'll raise their suspicions right enough.'

A question hung at the end of his words. She didn't answer it. He gave her a long look, then asked it aloud.

'So what's the game, Mara? Fill the second compartment with water? You buy one barrel of Amberlyne, sell it as three?'

What's the game? she thought, studying the barrel. *I'm not entirely sure.* But she said nothing.

Braden scratched his beard. 'Not my business, but you're a rich woman. What need you got for ripping off merchants?'

'You're right,' said Mara. 'It's not your business. And you've been very well paid for your trouble.'

If that hurt, it didn't show. Mara felt guilty anyway. He was doing her a kindness and didn't deserve to be treated sharply.

'I appreciate your help, Braden,' she told him. 'And your concern. But I know what I'm doing.' Even as she said it, she wondered if that was true.

Braden grunted and fell silent. Mara spotted her cue to leave, but something was keeping her here. *I won't ask. I won't ask.*

'You didn't tell Danric about this?'

Braden tensed at the name. He was uncomfortable around other people's emotions. No doubt he'd hoped to avoid this conversation.

'Course not,' he said. 'It's between you and I.'

'But you feel bad, having to keep it from your oldest friend. I'm sorry I put you in that position. There was no one else I could trust.'

Braden shrugged it off. 'We're friends, too, ain't we? What passed between you and Danric don't affect that.'

Except that it does, she thought. *So I'll ask no further. I won't.*

'Is he well?' She tried to sound nonchalant, but neither of them was fooled.

'Well enough.'

'And his family?'

He gave her a pitying look. *Don't do this to yourself.*

'Are they also well?' she prompted.

Braden let out a heavy sigh. 'Aye. Thriving. Little Jad never stops running. He wants to be a smith like his da. Minda's three now, charming all who see her. Ariala's heavy with their third.'

A third? Mara kept the shock from her face and forced a smile to cover the ache of grief that followed. 'I'm happy to hear that,' she said. 'Please pass on my congratulations.'

'I'll do that,' he lied.

'I must go. Appointments to keep. Can you deliver the barrels tomorrow?'

'Tomorrow it is. You take care of yourself, Mara.'

'You too.'

Mara stared listlessly at the Uplanes through the carriage window. The skeleton of the old city reared above the great houses, built taller and bolder than they could ever manage now. Great arches of pink stone, some still intact, spanned Victory Way. The crumbled bowl of the Mummery held up one windowed wall to the sun, casting shadows across a sandy floor where the greatest actors of the Second Empire once trod. On the battlements of the Old Wall, outlined by the falling day, stood the Lost Colossus, broken off at the shins, its identity never to be known.

The works of their ancestors loomed everywhere in Ossia, but in Morgenholme they were inescapable. Only Carradis, capital of the Second Empire, was greater; but Carradis was a cursed and haunted place now, where only the mad or desperate went.

How can we ever move on, when we won't let ourselves forget the past?

She shouldn't have asked after Danric. What foolish urge made her probe old wounds that way? What did it bring but pain?

Truth, she told herself. The truth was always worth the consequences. Knowledge was to be faced, never evaded, and she wasn't capable of being wilfully ignorant. That was for the weak-minded, the kind who'd toast the arrival of a Krodan prince to crush their last hope of freedom. It wasn't in her nature to shy away from the reality of things. Her feelings were always secondary to that.

What would it be, this third child of theirs? Boy or girl? She thought of Jad, with his curly, corn-coloured hair, and Minda with her dimples and plaits. She'd never seen them, but they'd lived in her mind a long time. She indulged herself in fantasy for a while, playing with them in the snow on a winter's day, relishing the sweet hurt of it.

Gods, she was tired. Tired of the struggle, tired of the anger and disappointment, tired of battling through the years. She'd been swimming against the current for so long, and she felt her losses keenly today.

Perhaps she'd been too hard on that man. She taught only girls, that was the rule; but perhaps, if the boy was all he said, she could bend the rules just this once. She didn't want to be so inflexible. At her core were kindness, care and love. It was the world that had made her tough.

Why not? she thought. *Teach the boy. You have his name, so Clia will find him easily enough. You can make time for one more, can't you?*

The carriage rattled round a corner, and as it turned, Mara saw a smartly dressed man in black velvet with a polished oak walking stick and an artificial leg. It was an ingenious contraption of leather and metal and wood, with a hinged, locking knee and a flexible heel and ankle, allowing him to walk without a crutch. A Malliard Limb.

Mara only saw him for a moment, but when she drew back from the window, her face was grim and all kindness had withered in her heart.

She didn't teach boys, that was the rule. She'd stick to it. To soften was a betrayal of herself. To flex was weakness.

No compromise. Never again.

She stared at nothing as the carriage rolled on, her thoughts bitter as acid.

Mara's house was on a broad avenue on the edge of the Uplanes, set back from the road, with a ruined section of the Old Wall rising behind it and the grey peaks of the Catsclaws in the distance. Another wall, considerably smaller and newer, surrounded the house and its gardens, setting it apart from its neighbours, who claimed similarly grand and spacious territories.

The wheels of the carriage crushed rust-coloured leaves into the cobbles as it approached the wrought-iron gate and clattered to a stop. Tied through the bars of the gate was a black handkerchief. Mara gazed at it as Clia climbed down, untied the handkerchief without comment and put it in her pocket.

So it begins, she thought.

'Have Laria prepare the house,' she told Clia. 'We will have visitors tonight.'

64

They carried Vika into the bedroom on a litter of wooden poles and sailcloth, Harod in the lead and Garric behind. Ruck howled from down the corridor, where she'd been locked in another room by Grub and Aren. Mara closed the door on the racket, but Ruck howled nonetheless.

'Gentle now. Gentle,' Garric murmured as they lifted her from the litter onto a bed finer than they'd seen for months. He had no need to. Harod was a careful and precise man, and he treated her like porcelain.

'Let me examine the wound,' said Mara as soon as Vika was safely on the bed. 'Garric, help me undress her.'

'I should return to milady,' Harod said quickly, alarmed by the prospect of nudity. He gave Mara a stiff bow and left the room as fast as he decently could.

'How long?' Mara asked as they unfastened her blouse.

'Thirteen days. She's been out since the arrow hit.'

'Thirteen days?' Mara said in amazement.

'Aye,' he said grimly. Thirteen days since they'd left Wracken Bay in the storm. They'd made it upriver as far as Jurlow where they caught the first passenger ship to Westport, arriving just in time to catch another heading to Morgenholme. That one went at a leisurely pace with several stops on the way, delivering them to Morgenholme a day before the cargo promised by Katat-az was due.

Garric didn't mind. He was glad they'd got here at all. The Iron

Hand were swift, and they'd been looking over their shoulders every moment they'd been in port.

They pulled off Vika's shirt. They'd taken out the arrow on Jadrell's boat – Garric had some experience treating battle injuries – and afterwards washed the paint from her face and removed all signs of her faith. Transporting an injured woman was suspicious enough; were it known she was a druidess, the Krodans would surely have found them. Lying there, eyes closed and injured, she was no longer the imposing figure who'd first emerged from the darkness on a windy mountainside. Garric thought it wrong to see her so diminished.

The wound in her shoulder was a puckered red circle, edged with putrid black tendrils that extended some way under her skin. Mara made a noise of faint disappointment as she saw it. She examined the wound closely, stretching and prodding it, sniffing the clear, rancid fluid that wept out.

'It was an arrow?'

'A dreadknight's arrow. There was some kind of poison on it, we think.'

'Help me lift her.'

They half-turned her so Mara could see the exit wound. 'She's not woken at all?'

He shook his head. 'We pour milk and honey into her mouth and she swallows it. She rants in her delirium, sometimes in Ossian and sometimes in another tongue.' He felt a coldness settle on his heart. 'She speaks of Kar Vishnakh, the Citadel of Chains, and converses with the Torments.'

Mara *hmm*ed at that, and said no more. Garric stepped back while she finished her examination, taking a moment to look around the room. Silver candelabra pressed back the dark, spilling soft light across embroidered pillows and sumptuous drapes newly hung in advance of the winter. There were thick rugs from Caragua in the Far West, and the furniture was crafted with a delicacy and elegance rarely seen in common houses. In his younger days, he'd often visited places like this, but decades on the run had hardened him and he distrusted luxury now.

'The prognosis is not encouraging,' said Mara at last. 'See these black tendrils around the wound? Her blood has turned bad and it will only get worse. The rot is too close to her heart to cut out. By all means, send for an apothecary, but I have studied medicine and—'

'I'd be a fool to doubt your knowledge, but you haven't heard all of it. Five days ago, the corruption was all over her chest and back.'

'That's impossible.'

'I saw it with my own eyes. That arrow would have killed any one of us, but she has fought the poison back, and she is healing.'

Mara gave him a sceptical look. Ruck was calming down at last in the other room, her howls fading to sorry whimpers.

'I swear it, Mara. She's a druidess.'

'Oh, that explains it, then!' said Mara sarcastically. 'I expect the Aspects themselves are looking after her.'

'Scoff if you will. If you'd seen what I have, you'd sing a different tune. None of us would be here if not for her.'

'I thought better of you,' she said, with undisguised scorn. 'Taken in by parlour tricks and imaginary gods.'

'There's more in this world than can be measured by your experiments. You say it's impossible that she will heal. I say you've always used that word too readily.'

Mara sniffed, dismissing his observation. She wasn't one to take criticism or advice from her intellectual inferiors. 'Be that as it may, there is little that can be done for her. I will have Laria change her dressings and feed her. She will die, or she will not.'

'She will not die,' said Garric. 'I'll tend her myself.'

Mara gave him a strange look. 'As you wish.'

Once they'd made Vika comfortable, they left her to rest and went to Mara's study. There she poured them glasses of rich red Carthanian wine, and went to stand by the tall arched windows, looking down onto the gardens where the others wandered in the moonlight, stretching their legs after so long aboard ship.

'You've lost many,' she said. 'And gained others.'

Garric sipped his wine and the exquisite taste sent guilty pleasure flooding through him. 'We've travelled a hard road,' he said.

'How are they?'

'The Sard and the Harrish I don't know; we just needed their cart. We can't trust them, but they know too much to send them away.'

'Keep them close, but not too close?'

'It's only for a short while. Perhaps you can persuade them to accept your gracious hospitality?'

'I'll see what I can manage,' she said wryly.

'Fen wavered, but I think she'll stay. Helps that there's some her own age with us. She's tough, but she's young, and not as grown up as she thinks. I wouldn't trust the Skarl as far as I could throw him, but he's in too deep to dislodge, and the boy won't let him go anyway.'

'Which boy?'

'Aren.'

'Who is he?'

Garric's pause was a beat too long. 'Just a boy.'

'Can we trust him?'

'As much as we can trust anyone.'

'How reassuring. And Keel?'

'Keel's falling apart. After what he saw in Skavengard ... and now his family ...' He sighed. 'He's not faring well.'

'What do you intend to do about that?'

'Nothing I *can* do. He'll stand firm till Hammerholt. That's all I need.'

He let his gaze roam the study. It was cosy and dim, lit by wall lamps, with Mara's desk in the brightest spot. An angular iron candelabrum of urdish design, from the days when humans were slaves in this land, stood in one corner. Shadows gathered between laden bookshelves, and at the feet of pedestals that held stuffed birds and the skulls of foreign animals. An architectural plan was framed on the wall, Mara's work, describing a building that only existed in her mind.

He took another mouthful of wine. Gods, it was good. Maybe he'd have another after this. What harm in a bit of pleasure, after all? He took little enough of it.

'You got my letter?' he asked.

'The barrels are coming tomorrow,' said Mara. 'The cart is already here, an exact copy of the kind the Master Vintner uses, with the requisite alterations. I had a friend make the barrels; the cart was built by an artisan on the other side of the city.'

'Never let the right hand know what the left hand is doing,' Garric said.

'I find it's usually wise. Speaking of which, how do you plan to switch your cart with the Master Vintner's?'

'Wilham the Smiler will handle it.'

'Ah,' she said, communicating boundless disdain in a single syllable.

'Question his motives if you will, but he's yet to let me down.'

'He doesn't fight the Krodans because he believes in Ossia. He fights for the love of chaos and discord.'

'Chaos and discord are what we seek, are they not?'

Mara conceded him the point with a flick of her wrist and an irate moue.

'And what of Yarin?'

Mara sipped her wine and turned away from the window. 'There we have a problem. Yarin has disappeared.'

Garric's grip tightened on his glass. 'What happened?'

'The Krodans moved into the ghetto a week ago and began clearing everybody out. They packed the Sards onto trains of prison carts going east. Yarin was taken with them.'

Garric felt a hot ball of rage growing in his belly. Not now! Not when they were so close! Why couldn't the Krodans have waited one more week? Why did the Aspects always conspire to foil him?

'We need those plans!' he barked angrily.

'Yarin would be touched by your concern,' said Mara sarcastically. 'However, there is hope yet. Before he was taken, he found the information we need and stashed it in a secret location in the ghetto. I can only presume it is still there.'

'Then we must go and get it!'

'Easier said than done. The Krodans have sealed it off to keep looters out while they search for hidden Sards. There are patrols day and night.'

'We'll risk it. We have no chance without those plans.'

'Agreed.'

Garric drained his glass. 'Where did the Sards go?'

'I don't know. Nobody does.'

More clearances, more Sards taken east. The Krodans were up to something, but he was gods-damned if he knew what, and he had no time to investigate. He couldn't afford any distractions.

An image of Yarin appeared in his mind, that wily old Sard with his seamed face and gnarled hands, his green eyes paled by the years. He'd been their contact among the Landless, many of whom were as eager as Garric to see the Krodans driven from Ossia. Garric never knew how extensive Yarin's network was, whether he was the mastermind or the agent of some hidden operator, but he'd been a valuable ally. Garric regretted the loss of a useful resource, but no more than that. They hadn't been close, and it was hard to care about anything now beyond what had to be done.

'What's going into the barrels?' she asked.

The question caught him off guard. He sensed her watching him keenly and avoided her gaze. He poured himself more wine instead.

'Amberlyne,' he said. 'And water. We'll swap a dozen barrels that are only one-third full of wine for a dozen full ones. Eight barrels profit. That's Wilham's payment for his services.'

'I could have just paid him the money and saved myself the considerable trouble of having them made. Not to mention the risk.'

'Never let the right hand know what the left hand is doing,' said Garric, raising a newly full glass to her.

'I see,' she said. 'And this mysterious cargo arriving on a Xulan ship that I'm to pay for?'

'That's the Amberlyne to go in the casks.'

'Thirty falcons for a few barrels of Amberlyne?'

'Only the best for the prince, and at such short notice the price was high.'

Mara didn't believe him for an instant. 'What an incredibly convoluted way of doing something very simple,' she observed. 'Give me my due. I play castles a lot; I see you moving your pieces into place for the endgame. What do you really intend?'

Garric swigged his wine. 'Shouldn't have picked such a smart right hand,' he grumbled.

'I'm no one's right hand, Garric, and I won't be kept in the dark. Not if you want that shipment paid for.'

Garric stewed on that for a moment. She had him, it seemed; but why shouldn't he tell her? If there was any among them who might see things his way, it was Mara. She prized sense over sentiment and understood the need for sacrifice. Besides, it would be a waste of time trying to convince her that ignorance was for her own good. He never knew anyone so loth of ignorance as she.

'I will tell you, on your oath of secrecy,' he said. 'The others wouldn't understand.'

'I'll make no such oath. But I'll not tell the others, unless what you propose forces me to.'

He had to be content with that, so he told her his plan, staring into his glass as he did so, his face mirrored red in the wine. When he'd finished, he looked up and was alarmed to see tears in her eyes, this woman who wasn't given to crying.

'This is no time for weakness, Mara!' he warned quickly. 'It has to be this way. You see that, don't you?'

A smile broke over her face at his foolishness, her eyes creasing, dislodging tears. She wiped them away. 'You never could read hearts, Garric. I am not sad or horrified. I weep because you give me hope of a day when my pupils will be considered the equal of men, and Ossia is ruled by Ossian laws again. I knew you were a man of conviction, Garric, but I did not realise how far you would go.'

'Then you agree it must be done?'

'Entirely,' she said. 'And you may rely on my discretion.'

Relief chased the tension from his shoulders. It felt good to share the burden, and to know that she approved.

A few more days, that's all. A few more days to hold the course.

'We must gather the others,' he said. 'I promised them answers when we got to Morgenholme, and I cannot put it off any longer. They have been sorely taxed and I fear their loyalty is rubbing thin. I need them to believe.'

'What will you tell them?'

'What they need to know. The rest, they'll understand afterwards.'

'Afterwards,' said Mara, with something like reverence in her voice. 'Everything will be different afterwards.'

65

They gathered in the drawing room, pulled the drapes closed and locked the doors. When the room was secure, they settled themselves and looked towards Garric, who stood at the centre of attention. Wall lamps cast conspiratorial shadows across their faces.

'Here we are, then,' he said.

Aren felt the thrill of treachery. This was how it was in the stories. They were plotters now, meeting to discuss secret plans. Cade, who was sitting next to him on an ornate and uncomfortable settee, was practically jigging with excitement.

There were seven of them present. Besides Garric and Cade, there was their host Mara, a stern, wiry woman with wolf-grey hair. Grub lounged in a chair with one leg thrown over the arm, gnawing a turkey wing he'd salvaged from the dinner table. Fen leaned against a wall, arms crossed, her body language aloof and defensive. Aren's gaze lingered on her face for a moment, then moved on to Keel, who sat slumped in a wooden seat. The Bitter-bracker's shoulders sagged and his eyes were hollow. He'd hardly spoken since they left Wracken Bay. Aren had never seen a man so laden with care.

Four were absent. Vika was abed, with Ruck no doubt sleeping at her feet; the hound had been let into her room once she'd been made comfortable. Aren was worried about her – they all were – but the improvement in her condition had given them cause to hope. Harod and Orica were not invited, and had chosen to remain in the gardens while Orica practised her lute. Aren felt vaguely bad about that, for they'd travelled together long enough that he considered them companions; but he understood the need for secrecy. They were not part of this.

'I've asked much of you all,' said Garric. 'More than I had a right to, I reckon. After Salt Fork, all seemed lost. Then we had news of the wedding, and the return of the Ember Blade. Some of you have followed me since then, through great loss and trial. Others have joined along the way, despite my best efforts to the contrary.' He gave Aren a pointed glare. 'Through it all, I've asked you to journey in the dark, not knowing the details of our mission. I make no apologies for that. All of us know how good the Krodans are at loosening tongues and twisting men's loyalties.' His face darkened then, and Aren knew he was recalling past betrayals. 'But there comes a time when faith must have its reward, so I'll tell you now what I intend.'

Cade sat up, bright-eyed, and gave Aren a nudge. Aren grinned at him. They knew Garric was after the Ember Blade. They'd waited a long time to find out how he planned to get it.

'Nine days from now, Prince Ottico of Kroda and Princess Sorrel of Harrow will be wed,' Garric began. 'Kroda's alliance with Harrow will secure the northern border of Ossia, leaving them free to consolidate their hold on our land until it is unbreakable. This is our last chance to make the people of Ossia stand up for themselves. There won't be another.'

'The Ember Blade!' Grub cried through a mouthful of meat, thrusting the bone in the air. Aren thought it curious that he, of all of them, should be the one to call its name.

'The Ember Blade,' said Garric. His face became grim. 'Aye, the Ember Blade. Our symbol of the right to rule, the standard of Ossia itself, stolen from us thirty years ago. Now it's coming back, to be put in the hands of our new Lord Protector, the Emperor's heir. I'll be gods-damned if I'll let that happen.

'We need to show our kinfolk they weren't meant to be ruled. That blade is the sign of the Aspects' favour, and if we had it, they'd flock to us. We could take our country back!'

The passion was plain in him now, and it awoke an answering passion in his audience. Aren felt a surge of pride in his breast, and this time he didn't try to quell it. The Ember Blade! It represented the opposite of everything Krodan, an idea of freedom and liberty bred into the fibre of his people. Even a boy raised to ape their masters, as Aren was, had a deep-seated veneration for the Ember Blade. Now he embraced it, claimed it as his own.

He was a child of Ossia, after all.

'Hammerholt is six leagues from here. That's where the wedding is to be held,' said Garric. 'It is the most formidable fortress in Ossia, and it will be more heavily guarded than the most precious trove. But the wedding will bring chaos: hundreds of artisans, guests and servants moving in and out. Most of the Krodan high command in Ossia are arriving over the next couple of days, to meet their new Lord Protector and to organise the smooth handover of our country. We believe the Ember Blade is already there, brought in secret from Falconsreach some time ago. As the wedding approaches, the Krodans will be at their most alert, looking for any attempt to disrupt the proceedings. That is why we will steal the Ember Blade several days *before* it takes place.'

'But how do we get inside?' asked Aren, unable to contain himself.

'*You* don't,' said Garric. 'None of you are going inside. Only me.'

Aren felt that like a slap in the face. He'd assumed he'd be part of the adventure when it came, whether it was to be a daring theft or a breathless battle. The boy in him still believed he'd be the hero of the tale Cade would one day tell. With a few words, Garric killed that dream and humbled him again.

'The Master Vintner of Morgenholme is the only one licensed to supply wine to the Imperial Family,' Garric continued, heedless of the hurt writ plain on Aren's face. 'It's well known the prince will have no sweetwine but Amberlyne with his dessert. It's one of the few things he likes about our country. Several cartloads of Amberlyne will therefore be travelling from the Master Vintner's cellars to Hammerholt. I intend to be on one of them.'

'How?' Aren said, spurred by dismay to bloody-minded obstructiveness. 'They'll search every cart top to bottom, and you'll never hide that scar on your throat.'

'They will indeed search every cart,' said Mara, her words crisp and perfectly enunciated. 'But they will not find him. We have constructed a replica of one of the Master Vintner's carts, identical but for a single detail: a secret compartment, just big enough for Garric to squeeze inside. He will be transported by an unwitting driver, who will be a trusted member of the Master Vintner's staff and unlikely to draw suspicion. Once past the guards and inside, Garric will emerge wearing the livery of a Krodan servant, whose uniforms – as fortune has it – incorporate a high collar. That, and a good shave, will render him all but unrecognisable.'

'She knew, and I didn't?' Keel said, stirring from his misery to shoot Garric an accusing glare.

'I wrote to her from Wracken Bay so she might commission everything we need,' said Garric. 'She worked the rest out herself.'

Keel gave her a sullen look and shook his head angrily.

Aren's mind worked fast. A childish desire for vengeance made him want to poke holes in Garric's plan.

'You wrote from Wracken Bay?' he said. 'Even by fastest post, it couldn't have been nine days since it arrived. Nine days to have a copy of a particular cart built, with a secret compartment to boot?'

'And replica barrels of Amberlyne commissioned, and more besides,' said Mara. 'Pay enough and you can get anything done in a hurry. Your point?'

'Why didn't he send that letter a month ago? Or two? Why not right after Salt Fork, when the wedding was announced and he set out for Hammerholt?'

That piqued Fen's interest. She turned her eyes expectantly to Garric, waiting for an answer. Mara raised an eyebrow at Aren in approval.

'Because he didn't have a plan till then,' said Keel sourly. 'He led us all the way from Salt Fork to steal the Ember Blade, but it took him till Wracken Bay to work out how.'

Aren was taken aback at the tone of his voice. Garric and Keel had always been close as brothers, but he heard the raw edge of resentment now. Did Keel blame Garric for the fact that he had to leave his family behind? That hardly seemed just. If anyone was to blame, it was Aren, for joining the fight at the Reaver's Rest.

'Is that true?' Fen asked in surprise.

'Hollow Man not know what he was doing all along!' Grub

exclaimed. 'Ha! Should have followed Grub. Grub *always* have a plan.'

'Oh, aye?' said Cade. 'And what's your plan now?'

'Eat turkey,' said Grub, and proceeded to do so.

'I told you we'd seize the Ember Blade for ourselves, and I told you I'd explain the plan when we got to Morgenholme!' Garric said bullishly. 'Would you have followed me elsewise? Keel? Fen? Or would you now be wandering the land, watching forlornly as the Krodans crush the last of the spirit from your countrymen?'

Aren's gaze went to the castles board set up by the empty hearth, and he heard Master Fassen's voice in his mind. *Never let your opponent see you uncertain. Behave as if you have a strategy, even when you do not. Act as if your opponent's every move is playing further into your hands.*

'You said the driver won't know you're there,' said Aren. 'How?'

'The Amberlyne will be delivered to the castle some days before the wedding,' he said. 'Before that happens, we'll break into the vintner's yard and switch our cart and barrels for one of the real ones. When they set off, I'll be inside.'

'Grub good at breaking into things!'

'Alas,' said Mara, 'that job has already been entrusted to another.'

'Aye,' said Garric. 'A man who knows Morgenholme and our cause, and is best placed to get it done. I have been fighting the Krodans thirty years now, and I have travelled the breadth of this land. The faces you see here are not the limit of my allies.'

'I *knew* you were a Greycloak!' Cade exclaimed.

'There's no such thing as the Greycloaks,' Keel told him wearily.

'Then what *are* we to do?' Aren cried, frustrated. 'What's our purpose here, if you already have all you need?'

Garric rounded on him. 'Do you think it all ends with Ottico's wedding, boy?' he snarled. 'Do you imagine the Krodans will leave once we've taken the Ember Blade? If I succeed, it will be the *beginning*. All of you will be needed, and many more besides, if we are to carry the flame forward. Do not be so hungry to rush into danger. It will find you soon enough.'

Aren slumped back in the settee, scowling. This wasn't what he'd imagined when he chose to stay with Garric at the Reaver's

Rest. He was nothing but a support player, a footnote, condemned to watch while another man wrote himself into legend. He didn't crave adulation or excitement, but when bards sang of the day Ossia reclaimed the Ember Blade, he wanted to at least get a mention.

'Grub not happy about this,' said the Skarl, his turkey wing now laid on the arm of his chair where it oozed onto the fabric. 'Mudslug not happy either, he thinks. Dumbface doesn't mind, but Dumbface not brave like us.'

'*Dumbface?*' Cade nearly screamed.

Garric raised a hand to silence them. 'Once I'm inside, I'll have to make my way through Hammerholt without capture. For that, I need a map of the castle and information about the preparations so I can work unobserved. No doubt I will have to pass through areas where servants are not allowed, and to find the Ember Blade I first need to know where they are keeping it. All this was entrusted to a Sard named Yarin, an acquaintance of Mara's and mine and no friend to the Krodans. I sent to him immediately when the wedding was announced, and he'd been investigating ever since, through whatever secret channels he knows. But now Yarin is gone, the Sards in the ghetto cleared out and taken—'

Aren sat up in alarm. 'They're gone?'

'Aye. To what destination, no one knows.'

Aren's eyes went to the mark on his wrist. *Sardfriend.* His whole life he'd been told to treat them with suspicion and scorn, when he thought of them at all. Without that mark, he might not have helped Orica in her time of need. He'd certainly have turned a blind eye to what was happening in his land, as many of his countryfolk had. The Sards were little loved and many people were just glad to be rid of them.

But things were different now. Aren's promise to Eifann was fulfilled, but that scarcely mattered. He'd been made to care, and he couldn't undo that.

Who's going to tell Orica? he thought, but he already knew the answer. It would have to be him. It was his duty, as a Sardfriend.

'Yarin did obtain the information,' said Mara. 'He stashed it inside the ghetto, but no one is allowed inside and it is heavily patrolled.'

'Tomorrow night I'm going in to get it back,' said Garric. 'And now you know as much as I do. I've trusted you with the details of our plan, so I want you to trust me. Maybe this business with the Ember Blade won't give you the chance to wet your blades as you'd like. Maybe you think there's little glory in it for you. But hear you me, there'll be plenty of glory to come, and plenty of chances to prove your worth in the revolution. Till then, I need to know I can count on you to do what needs to be done. Even if that's to wait.'

There was silence in the room. Their faces were thoughtful and grim in the lamplight. Finally Fen stirred.

'Whatever needs to be done,' she said.

Cade instinctively looked to Aren for a cue, then decided he didn't need one. 'Aye,' he said. 'We've come this far. I'm with you.'

'Grub don't think any of this is going to get him a good tattoo,' he grumbled. 'He still help, though.'

Aren fought down the urge to sulk and forced himself to swallow his pride and disappointment. Angry as he was, this choice had already been made. He told himself that retrieving the Ember Blade was what mattered here. It was bigger than him, bigger than his resentment of Garric. But still he felt the sting of it.

'I'm with you,' he said, his voice flat. 'Whatever needs to be done.'

'Keel?' Garric asked.

Keel looked up. His eyes refocused. 'Yes,' he said, but it was clear he hadn't been listening, that his thoughts had been elsewhere, with his family.

Garric's gaze lingered on him uncertainly. Then he drew himself up and addressed them all. 'Get some sleep,' he said. 'Speak of this to no one. In a few days, we make our move.'

66

'Daddy!'

Klyssen was hardly inside before Lisi and Juna came charging along the corridor, drawn by the sound of his key in the lock. He knelt down and they flew into his arms in a giggling, wriggling tumble of blonde curls, frills and sweet breath. He kissed them both, laughing with delight.

'How you've grown!' he told them. 'You'll be taller than your mother soon.'

'Silly!' they called him, for they were hardly half her height yet; but they squirmed with pleasure at the thought.

'Ah! Is that Baron Pickles?' Klyssen exclaimed as a fat white cat, sour-featured and groomed to within an inch of its life, wandered out from a doorway to investigate the commotion. 'Come here, you soft old thing!'

Baron Pickles regarded him blandly for a moment, then drifted back into the room he came from, unimpressed by the return of the master of the house.

'Baron Pickles! Come and say hello to daddy!' Juna demanded with the comical sternness of a four-year-old. She was about to go and retrieve the cat, willingly or not, but Klyssen stopped her.

'Wait, Juna. I've brought presents.'

'Presents!' They attacked immediately, squealing at ear-shredding pitch, their excitement spilling over into violence as they tugged at him. 'Presents, presents!' they sang, whirling around in his arms.

'Peace, children!' he cried. 'What is the credo of the Sanctorum? Can you recite it for me?'

'Diligence, temperance, dominance,' they chanted together.

'Yes, *temperance*,' said Klyssen. 'Be calm and moderate in your passions. Can you be calm?'

'Yes, Daddy,' they muttered grudgingly. They put their hands behind their backs, barely able to contain their anticipation.

He dug into his bag and found the dolls he'd bought from a dollmaker on Kingsgrove Street, exquisitely fashioned and eye-wateringly expensive. Privately, he thought that two girls of four and six couldn't tell the difference between a finely made doll and a five-decim toy from the Shacklemarket – and wouldn't care if they could – but Vanya didn't want cheap dolls in the house. She said they made the place look tawdry.

The girls snatched them out of his hands, gasping at their good fortune.

'Mine's Princess Sorrel!' Lisi insisted.

'No, *mine's* Princess Sorrel!' Juna said crossly.

'They can *both* be Princess Sorrel,' said Klyssen, though neither looked anything like her if her portraits were true. This, according to the unique logic of children, was an acceptable solution. 'What do you say when you receive a gift?'

'Thank you, Daddy!' they yelled in discordant chorus.

The sight of his wife at the end of the corridor brought him to his feet. She'd been watching him with their daughters. Now their eyes met, and she smiled. Klyssen felt himself go momentarily weak, his will lost in the glare of admiration.

Vanya was a tall woman, taller than him, with grey-blue eyes, a lion's mane of blonde curls and a face so beautiful and unflawed that it seemed she'd been cut from some other material than fallible flesh, forged without corruption by the Primus himself. He didn't have an artistic bone in his body, but she made him believe in poetry.

'Marius,' she said. 'Husband.'

He went to her, and they kissed, a brief press of the lips, too quick to account for the months they'd been apart. She left him elated and frustrated, but that was how her kisses were. He always wanted more.

'I have a gift for you, too,' he said. He reached into his bag again, adjusting his spectacles with one hand as he rummaged inside with the other. Finally he drew out a small leather-bound box and offered it to her. Her eyes betrayed a flicker of hungry interest as she saw the filigreed emblem there: Axus and Thrane, her favourite jewellers.

'Marius, how thoughtful,' she said, with the slightly wary tone of someone who wasn't entirely sure she'd like what she found inside. She opened the box with elegant and perfectly manicured fingers. Klyssen watched her face in the grip of an excitement that was more than half fear. When he saw her light up with genuine, unfeigned pleasure, he felt a little cascade of joy tumble through him.

'Oh, it's *beautiful*!' She sighed as she lifted the necklace from the box.

He could hardly stop himself from grinning. 'The diamonds are from—'

'Helica, yes, I see that,' she murmured appreciatively. He marvelled at her near-supernatural ability to identify the provenance of gemstones at a glance. He'd have picked the sapphires, which glittered more brightly, complemented her eyes and were significantly cheaper. This necklace looked rather simple and plain by comparison, barely distinguishable from others one-tenth its price. But he'd learned not to trust his own judgement in matters of fashion, so he'd wisely asked the jeweller's wife for advice.

'Breathtaking, my love,' he said, after he'd put it round her neck. She kissed him. This time he felt passion in it, and flushed.

'Ewwww!' cried Lisi. They broke apart to find the girls giggling at them, their dolls forgotten in their hands.

'What are *you* giggling about?' Klyssen demanded playfully. He lunged at them with his hands made into claws. 'Come here, you scamps!'

The girls squealed in delighted fright, and their father chased them from the room, snarling like a monster as he went.

They dined together after he saw the children to bed with kisses and a story. Marla, the housekeeper, served them platters of good Krodan fare: pork brisket in sour apple sauce, butterflied potatoes, steamed cabbage and roasted turnip, washed down with rich, heavy red wine from the homeland. Candlelight glittered on cut-crystal glasses, sparkled from silver knives and Vanya's new necklace.

A portrait of the Emperor and his only son overlooked the table. Kelssing IV, bald, bejacketed and sporting a bushy beard, had his hand on Prince Ottico's shoulder. Ottico was fourteen or thereabouts, his short, curly hair black as his father's beard, pale eyes gazing out with all the arrogance and hauteur of a young man born to rule. Above the portrait, rendered in iron, was the symbol of the Sanctorum: a blade laid point downwards across an open book.

The Emperor and the Sanctorum, the twin pillars of modern Krodan society. Klyssen had put them there as a reminder of what he was fighting for, what they were *all* fighting for. The Ossians dreamed of the past, but Krodans rejected it, for these were their days of glory.

Kroda was an ailing country once, beset by barbarians and menaced by its neighbours. Its ancestral territories in Ozak and Brunland had been lost to independence movements they were too weak to oppose. Then came Tomas and Toven, one a charismatic and radical preacher, the other a young war hero. They brought word of the Primus, and the people listened, for the Aspects of old hadn't served them well. At last they were brought before the Emperor, Steppen III. He was convinced by them, and declared them heralds of the true god. He outlawed all other religions and gave his support to the nascent Sanctorum, the followers of Tomas and Toven, so they might spread their credo of discipline and martial order throughout the land.

Kroda had never looked back. In the two centuries since, they'd reclaimed their lost lands, annexed Estria and invaded Ossia. Even mighty Harrow would rather make alliance with them than oppose them, and Klyssen was confident that they'd one day become part of the Empire in their turn. If they were not conquered by force of arms, they'd collapse from within. Ossified by tradition and heritage, they were a culture incapable of change. They'd crumble like the ruins of the Second Empire, or be crushed in the fullness of time beneath the wheel of Krodan progress.

Kroda was the chosen land, meant to rule its weaker neighbours by divine mandate. Anyone who didn't believe that was a fool.

'How goes your search for the fugitive?' Vanya asked. She kept to small portions, mindful of her figure.

'He is shy prey, but I will catch him in the end,' said Klyssen. 'He has eluded me twice, but only by good fortune, and luck is a poor ally, apt to desert you when you need it most. I am ahead of him again. He will not escape a third time.'

'It is suspicious that such a dangerous criminal should be headed to Morgenholme so close to the prince's wedding,' she observed.

'I thought the same thing. No doubt he has some mischief in mind, though I have little confidence in his ability to execute it. The men we caught at Salt Fork revealed the truth about these "rebels". They're a ragtag band, no more than opportunistic bandits. Ossians are incapable of cooperating for long enough to organise themselves.' He pushed his spectacles back up his nose. 'Still, one zealous renegade can do a lot of damage if given the chance. I will have him before the wedding bells ring, do not fear.'

'Unless Harte sabotages your endeavour,' she said bitterly.

'He has been quiet since Wracken Bay, when I put him in his place.'

'Good,' she said, with a firm nod of approval. She liked it when he was assertive and commanding.

He chewed thoughtfully on his brisket. 'In truth, I'm no longer sure he *is* trying to sabotage me. At first I was certain he was sent by Commander Gossen, but of late I've begun to believe the truth is simpler. I think he's no more than an odious man who enjoys dispensing brutality in the guise of justice.'

There was a clatter as Vanya put down her knife and fork. 'Do not be fooled!' she told him sternly. 'The Commander is jealous of you; they all are. If it were up to them, all positions of authority would be filled with men like Harte. Oh, they may project an image of Krodan superiority to impress the world, but they possess none of the intelligence which made us superior in the first place! They are arrogant, dull, entitled men who will weaken the Empire with their feeblemindedness. It frightens them to see a man of ability, who has climbed the ranks by virtue of hard work and a keen mind. They will do all they can to stop you. Be vigilant, Marius; be ruthless. The Commander's post is yours by right.'

'Take care, Vanya. Guard your words. I am an overwatchman of the Iron Hand, after all,' he said; but he smiled to show he was joking. Her words pleased him, even though he knew she was only echoing his own complaints, which she'd heard many times before. It didn't matter. He had her support, and it made him feel strong.

'An overwatchman now, but a Commander soon. And then ...'

'Then, back to Kroda,' he said, because all conversations with his wife led that way eventually. 'Back to Falconsreach as soon as we can, my love. I have no more affection for this land than you do.'

She sighed and took up her cutlery again. 'I do so long for home,' she said, cutting a tiny slice of turnip. 'The balls, the theatre, the fashions, the food. This place is a decade behind in every way. A cultural wasteland. And the *society*! The same faces, over and over! If I have to attend *one* more gathering at the Daner's ...'

'There are opportunities here,' he reminded her. 'I am working towards our return with all haste, but—'

'I can't even invite my friends over any more! Marius, you don't know how lonely I am when you're away.'

'You can't? Why not?' he asked, and immediately regretted it.

'Because our parlour is so detestably shabby! Nobody has pale blue walls any more! The seats are all but worn through—'

'I don't think they're quite that bad—'

'They *are*, Marius. And the settees and curtains are so out of date. I tell you, our guests would laugh at us! The whole room needs updating before I would dare let anyone see it.'

'When I'm Commander—'

'That could be *months* away! What am I to do while you are off seeking the enemies of the Empire? I cannot go to balls without my husband. Am I to be a prisoner here?'

He wanted to say that there were plenty of diversions she could occupy herself with, plenty of people to visit, plenty of places to go. He wanted to say that she scarcely seemed to be at home even when he *was* there; she was always off to this or that social occasion, sporting a new hat, new shoes or a new dress. But he said nothing. He knew the futility of such arguments.

He was only likely to be home for a week at most, and he wanted it to be a pleasant week. Granting her this would see her compliant, attentive and energetic in bed. Refusing it would damn him to cold wrath until his departure. He could hardly afford it, but it didn't seem like he had much choice.

'Kerin will have to design it!' she warned, pressing the advantage as she saw him falter. 'I'll trust no other! No one has his taste.'

'Kerin? Again?' Klyssen protested feebly.

'He's the best,' she said.

And the most expensive. The Nemesis take that popinjay! It feels like half my wealth has gone into his pockets over the years.

'Very well,' he said, mentally counting the damage. 'Kerin it shall be.' He was beginning to sulk, but she broke into a smile and came round the table to kiss him.

'Thank you, Marius. You're so generous, so kind to me. I don't know what I'd do without you. You make me so happy.'

'To see you happy is my heart's desire,' he told her, and meant it. She kissed him again, and after that the money didn't seem to matter so much.

After dinner, Klyssen went to his study on the top floor of the townhouse. From there, shutters opened onto a cramped balcony with wrought-iron railings. There was a single chair at one end and a brass telescope on a tripod at the other.

He sat with a sigh, a Caraguan cigar smoking between his fingers. He look a long draw, savouring the hot, herbal smoke, and blew out a luxuriant cloud from his nostrils. He'd pay for it with a bellyache in the morning – cigars irritated his delicate stomach – but he felt reckless tonight.

The city spread out beneath him. His home was in South Heights, and from his vantage he could see all the way down the hill to the river, where Sovereign's Isle was a lacework of lights in the void. There were no moons in the sky, but the tangled city illuminated the night with a soft yellow glow. To the east, the Catsclaw Mountains were dark waves in the distance.

Morgenholme had none of the ordered beauty of Falconsreach, the Imperial City, with its magnificent boulevards stretching long and straight beneath triumphal arches. Yet if a man looked hard enough, he might find order in the most bewildering chaos. Their cultures were worlds apart, but Ossians and Krodans had the same needs, the same capacity for love and hate, jealousy, kindness and greed. Once you understood a person's needs and fears, you could bend them to your will. These people would learn discipline in the end, and so lift themselves out of the mire of decadence and criminality. With the Emperor's guiding hand, they'd be great again, part of the most powerful Empire the world had ever known.

Baron Pickles ambled onto the balcony. Spotting a likely-looking lap, he hopped up and settled himself there. Klyssen absently scratched the cat's ears, took another draw on his cigar and looked at the stars overhead. There was the Hangman, there the Crayfish, there the Path of Jewels, the bright smear in the night that the Ossians called Joha's River. The locals claimed that every star was a glittering shard of an unknowable creator god who shattered into a million pieces to give light and life to the empty void, with nine facets of his being set to watch over creation: the Nine Aspects. Klyssen knew better. His father had shown him the hand of the Primus in the sky, the clockwork dance of the universe, impossibly complex but perfectly ordered. Night after night they went out into his parents' tiny garden to look up at the stars through the very same telescope he shared the balcony with. Klyssen was a man without imagination, but he found wonder in those cold, distant lights.

Would that you could see me now, Father. Would that you had lived to know what beautiful granddaughters you have, what a wife your son has caught. Ugly little Marius, whom the girls laughed at and the boys bullied. Nobody is laughing now.

In truth, he'd had little interest in women before Vanya found him, having long considered them unobtainable. It hadn't escaped his notice that the ladies began to pay him more attention as his rank increased, but by then he'd learned to do without them and paid them little mind. It was only when he was passed over for a promotion he surely deserved that they became suddenly important.

'The Empire likes a married man,' a colleague told him. 'You look a little strange, and you ignore women. It's suspicious, that's all.'

Klyssen didn't want to be suspicious. Suspicion was a dangerous thing in the Krodan Empire. So he badgered his colleague until he agreed to invite him to a ball, and let it be known – subtly, of course – that he was available.

His memories of the early hours of the dance were excruciatingly awkward. He wasn't adept at small talk and he didn't know how to dance. As he stood against the wall, drinking too much to cover his nerves, he was approached by a woman more captivating than any he'd ever seen. She talked to him as if he were a normal person, an equal, not some piteous wretch far beneath her notice. He made a hesitant joke and she laughed. They talked all night, and he left the ball feeling dizzy. Six months later, they were married.

Before Vanya, nothing meant anything. He treasured nobody and had no lust for luxury. He only cared for his position and the satisfaction of serving the Empire. Afterwards, it was different. Vanya became his obsession, and in time she bore him two daughters whom he'd lay down his life for.

The things we value make us weak, he thought.

Keel's wife needed little persuasion to betray him. Her love for her son far outweighed her frayed and lamentable devotion to her wayward husband, and she was desperate to spare him any suffering. Klyssen assured her they wouldn't be punished if she was open and honest.

In her terror, she was eager to help. Though Keel had kept much from her, she told what she knew of his companions and their movements. She gave him the name of an inn, the Burned Bear, where Keel had begged her to send him a letter.

'Send the letter,' Klyssen told her.

'What should I put in it?' she asked.

'The truth,' he said.

She couldn't read or write, so she dictated her letter to a scribe. Even now it waited at the Burned Bear for Keel, and a dozen Iron Guardsmen waited with it. The jaws of the trap were set. All that was left was for Keel to walk in.

'Husband?'

Vanya was at the door, a silk nightgown clinging to her curves. 'Will you come to bed?' she asked softly.

Baron Pickles jumped off as Klyssen levered himself up and went into his study, grinding out his cigar in an ashtray on the desk as he passed.

'You'll bathe and clean your teeth first, though,' she told him. 'I can smell the smoke all over you.'

The things we value make us weak, he thought. *But a man who values nothing is hardly alive at all.*

67

The next morning, Mara had a class to teach and Garric had some unspecified business in the city. He'd go to the ghetto after nightfall, he told the others. They were to stay inside and lie low.

No sooner had he left than Aren and Cade began lacing up their boots.

'Didn't Garric tell us to stay here?' asked Fen.

'Pffft,' said Aren. 'He's no liege of mine.'

'We're in *Morgenholme*!' Cade said, alive with excitement. 'Ain't no chance I'm missing this! You coming?'

'Grub is!' cried the Skarl, bounding in from the other room with flecks of his breakfast still stuck to his face.

Fen wavered, inexplicably nervous. Cade couldn't understand why someone so brave and capable would hesitate at adventure, but then he didn't understand a lot about women. They operated by some mysterious logic that was incomprehensible to him, their moods swept here and there by secret currents of meaning and implication he wasn't capable of detecting. It was annoying in those he didn't like, alluring in those he did.

'I'll come,' she said at last. Cade favoured her with his widest grin, which for some reason always made her look perturbed.

In the end, Harod came with them, too. Since the Krodans had cleared the ghetto, it was too dangerous for Orica to be outside, but they'd left almost everything behind when they fled Wracken Bay and there were several things she needed, not least new strings for her lute. Against his will, Harod was forced to leave her side to seek them.

It was a bright, clear day and the chill of autumn was in the air. The city was abuzz, restless with anticipation. Banners hung everywhere and all the talk was of the wedding. Cade and Aren wandered wide-eyed, drinking in their surroundings. They marvelled at the strange fashions and languages, and studied exotic wares in shop windows. Here stood a crumbling fountain, there a fragment of an ornamental wall. The ruins of the Second Empire surrounded them, towering over the streets or hiding round corners, quiet hints of former magnificence.

Cade's chest swelled with triumph. Look where he was! No longer was he some carpenter's boy, damned to a small life. He'd endured hardship and terror, but through it he'd found fellowship, a bond forged from shared danger and shared purpose that was altogether different from the knockabout friendships of the dockside boys in Shoal Point. His companions were his brothers and sisters in rebellion. Whether the Greycloaks were real or not, he felt like one now.

What a story he'd have to tell when he returned home, after the land was free again. Wouldn't Da be proud of him then?

They'd set out with no particular destination in mind, but it soon become clear that Harod, at least, knew where he was going.

'Have you been here before?' Aren asked him.

'In my youth,' said Harod. 'The Shacklemarket is this way.'

'Why's it called the Shacklemarket?' Cade asked. Half his attention was taken up with watching Fen, who had a habit of drifting away from them.

'Because that is where your ancestors sold slaves,' said Harod, with obvious distaste.

'Eh? When did Ossians keep slaves?' Cade asked Aren. Aren had some schooling, even if most of it was Krodan.

'From the middle years of the Second Empire,' said Aren, 'till Queen Vambra outlawed it.'

Cade was appalled. 'After we were all made slaves by the urds? I thought Jessa Wolf's-Heart said there'd never be slaves after that?'

Aren shrugged. 'What's history but a series of lessons we didn't learn?'

Harod gave a haughty sniff. 'Harrow has never allowed slavery,' he said.

'You don't need it. You've got tradition,' said Aren witheringly. 'And half your country are *still* slaves.' With that, he walked off ahead.

Grub cackled. 'Ha! Bowlhead got his mouth shut by Mudslug. Maybe your sweetheart write a song about *that*!' Pleased with himself, he swaggered off after Aren, leaving Harod alone with Cade, taut with indignity.

Cade felt sorry for the big knight. He was over-proud, easily offended and entirely without charm. In Harrow, his noble birth might have shielded him from abuse, but he'd clearly never met anyone like Grub. Highborn wit was no defence against the Skarl's thuggish mockery, and Grub, for his part, enjoyed having someone even less popular to pick on.

'He's just a bit touchy, that's all,' Cade offered as an excuse for Aren's behaviour. 'Doesn't like it when people criticise his homeland.' He thought for a moment, then added, 'Probably feels guilty for doing it himself all these years.'

'There is no need to apologise,' he said. 'Your friend is correct. The low folk are little more than slaves in my land, without hope of freedom. Their chains are invisible, but no less secure for that. I have nothing to boast of.'

That surprised Cade. He'd never heard Harod admit he was wrong before. Encouraged by this unexpected indication of humanity, he pressed further.

'And how did your sweet— Er, how did *Orica* find life in Harrow?'

'Well enough. Better than Ossia, I daresay.'

He meant to end the conversation, but that only made Cade more determined to keep him talking. Cade took silence as a snub, and he hated nothing more than the thought that someone disliked him.

'Because of the news about the ghetto?' Cade prompted.

He gave Cade a sidelong glance. 'The ghetto, and Tatterfane, and Maresmouth and more besides. She grieves for her people and her family. She cannot even walk the streets of this city. East of here, the roads will only get more dangerous as we near Kroda; but east is where the Sards have been taken. She must choose whether to follow her family to almost certain capture, or abandon her search while she still can.'

'And go back to Harrow with you?'

Harod kept his eyes stiffly forward. 'We cannot go back to Harrow.'

They walked on for a short while, till Cade could bear it no longer.

'Er ... why not?' he prompted.

Harod's head whipped around and he gave Cade a look of angry disbelief. No one in Harrow would be so impertinent. But they were not in Harrow now, and Cade was nothing if not tactless and intrusive.

'Well ... Because ...' he stammered.

'You might as well tell me,' said Cade affably. 'I'll only get it out of Orica if you don't. She's quite happy to talk about that kind of stuff.'

Harod looked like a man being slowly and gently strangled. 'You Ossians are quite brazen, aren't you?' he observed, his voice weak.

'Shameless,' Cade agreed.

Harod swallowed, his larynx bobbing up and down his long neck. 'Well,' he said, defeated. 'Then I suppose I have no choice but to tell you. I am, as you know, a scion of High House Anselm. I was *Sar* Harod once. I still am, I suppose, but now it seems ... inappropriate.' He took a moment to firm his resolve, and went on. 'I was betrothed to a daughter of another High House. Our marriage would have secured vital access to a mountain pass for my family, which would have halved the transportation costs of our goods from the coast. The lady was ... an admirable woman, intelligent and pleasant of face.'

'Aye, but did you love her, though?'

Harod visibly flinched at the word. 'That is not necessary for marriage,' he said. 'In Harrow, marriage is a matter of highest political importance, the glue that holds our society together. Only death can put man and wife asunder and even to break a betrothal is unforgivable. It shames the whole family, a crime rank with disgrace that demands compensation.' His voice wobbled a little at the last.

'Then Orica came to your father's house and played for you,' Cade said, beginning to understand now.

'A song of such beauty ...' Harod stopped himself as his voice threatened to betray him again.

'So you left your family and broke off your marriage contract to go with her,' said Cade in wonderment. 'You knew you'd be disgraced and exiled. You gave up everything for a song.'

Harod said nothing, his eyes fixed on the middle distance, braced for mockery. But Cade didn't want to mock him; he was in awe. It was like one of his ma's tales, a story of heroism, sacrifice and glory such as they told of the old days. He'd never suspected that beneath Harod's stuffy, solemn exterior beat the heart of a romantic.

'I hope I hear a song like that one day,' he said. Then he gave Harod a pat on the arm and walked on ahead to catch up with Aren. Harod watched him go, faintly surprised by the boy's reaction.

Unseen by anyone, a small smile of pride touched his lips.

The Shacklemarket was aswarm, a bewildering churn of people of all ages and races milling beneath a webwork of bunting and banners. It was held beneath the coral-coloured roof of the Parthena, a shallow dome standing on a dozen pillars that still bore the memory of thousand-year-old murals. Statues worn to lumps rested on corbels projecting from the dome's interior, aloof from the chaos below. Sparrows darted restlessly in the heights.

'Grub need some time to himself,' Grub told them, eyeing the crowd hungrily. His fingers wriggled in anticipation. 'He find you all later.' He slid off into the market, oozing nefarious intent. Harod excused himself, too, and went to seek the items Orica needed.

Fen hovered on the edge of the market, shuffling from foot to foot and looking less than enthusiastic.

'Come on, let's go in,' Aren urged her gently.

Cade frowned at his tone. There was some meaning there that he was missing, something in the way he said it. With an unpleasant shock, he realised there were private signals passing between them, right under his nose. Fen gave Aren a look that Cade couldn't read, then she nodded and they went inside. Cade trailed after them, his mood souring.

They went from stall to stall, amazed at what they saw. A swarthy Carthanian sold caged cats of many breeds. A Xulan chimericist showed off a live feathered snake that he professed was his own creation, and charged passers-by a decim to touch it, or a half-guilder to have it draped around them. One stall was piled with fruit they'd never heard of before; another offered antique urd jewellery dug from the earth.

They found a vendor selling carvings of elaru whitewood. Fen, who was keen on whittling, stopped to admire them, turning them over in her hands. Aren picked one up and showed it to her. She gasped in delight, and Cade felt a bitter slither of envy in his gut. How had he missed it? Now he remembered Aren comforting her in Skavengard; the way he stayed back to help her along that ledge; the two of them creeping off into the woods to 'hunt'. A dozen other moments sprang to mind. He'd suspected something was up, but he'd never really let himself believe it.

Perhaps it was his talk with Harod that had opened his eyes, turned his thoughts to romance. Now he looked with a sharper gaze at the object of his affection, and he saw what should have been obvious all along.

They moved on. Fen flinched as she was buffeted in the press of people, shying away from an elderly woman who shoved past with vigour belied by her years. Presently they came to an open space that was less crowded, away from the centre, where stalls sold clothes and knick-knacks and sweetmeats. Her eye was caught by a fletcher's stall, and she headed over to see about some arrows. Aren made to go with her, but Cade stopped him.

'Hoy,' he said quietly. 'Why's she acting weird?'

Aren couldn't resist a final glance at Fen's back as she went. 'She's not used to crowds,' said Aren. 'She grew up in a cabin in the woods. Before she left the forest, the biggest town she ever saw was smaller than Shoal Point.'

How easily that knowledge tripped off his tongue. Why had

she told Aren that, and not him? Didn't he entertain her with his stories? Didn't he make her laugh?

Aren's eyes had strayed to her again, checking on her. The fletcher was trying to engage her in conversation as she perused his wares, without much success.

'Have you two done it?' Cade asked suddenly. The question welled up out of him, unstoppable as vomit.

Aren looked puzzled. 'It?'

'*It!*' said Cade, making an obscene gesture with his fingers to demonstrate.

Aren gaped. 'No!' he cried. 'No, of course we haven't. Why are you even asking that?'

'Huh. Why? Reckon you know why,' Cade said. He sounded sullen and didn't care.

Aren was bewildered. 'Cade, she's not interested in me. Not like that.'

Cade pounced. 'So *you're* interested in *her*?'

Aren opened his mouth to form a denial, but no words came out. Maybe he didn't know the answer himself, then. Cade could see him formulating something diplomatic, the kind of meaningless response he was good at, so he decided to get in first.

'I love her,' he said hotly. 'Laugh if you like, but it's true. I love her, and she's going to love *me*, once she gets to know me well enough.'

He waited for Aren to make a joke, to call it one of his fleeting crushes. He was ready to respond with anger. But Aren just sagged, as if a great weight had settled on him.

'Well,' he said sadly. 'Then there it is.'

It wasn't the reaction Cade had expected. Too late, he realised what he'd done. He'd laid claim to her, and by doing so he'd forbidden Aren from ever acting on his feelings. It was an ultimatum: *choose her and lose me.* He hadn't meant it like that, but that was what it meant. He wanted to take it back, but he didn't know how.

At last he understood the feeling that had been growing inside him ever since that day when the Iron Hand came to Shoal Point, and two boys were taken away from home for ever. 'Everything's changing, ain't it?' he said.

'No,' said Aren, wearing the smile of a brave liar. 'No, it's not.'

'It is,' Cade said, and he wanted to cry. 'But the worst thing is, I can't seem to stop it.'

Cade saw in his eyes that he'd been thinking the same thing. The uncomplicated loyalty of youth couldn't survive outside the sheltered lands of home and childhood. Something else was taking its place, something fraught with doubt and conflict. He wasn't sure they'd ever again be the friends they once were, and it frightened him.

Once, Cade had been happy to be led by Aren in all things, but no longer. He wanted to be his own man, he wanted to be a *Greycloak*, and he wasn't sure Aren really did. Aren's heart was set on finding the answers to his father's death, not revolution. He was obsessed with Garric, and Cade was starting to find his anger tiresome. Garric was a hero who'd saved their lives over and over. It was the Krodans that killed Randill, not him. The worst Garric had done was hit Aren a few times, and it was hard for Cade to see what the fuss was about there, since he was no stranger to a clouting from his da. He knew Aren's feelings on the issue were complex and all, but couldn't he just let it go?

Then there was Fen. The only girl in their new world. She divided them just by existing.

'I wish we could go back to how it was,' Cade said.

'Nothing's changed, Cade,' Aren assured him; but there was something desperate in his voice. 'It's still you and me, always.'

Cade nodded glumly. 'Aye. You and me,' he said, his heart slowly sinking.

'You and me and *Grub*!' said Grub, slinging an unwelcome arm round their shoulders. He gave them a hideous grin. 'What we talking about?'

Cade shoved him off, annoyed. The smell of him up close was like an ambush.

'Dumbface not want to be friends?' Grub asked, pooching out his lower lip in a parody of sadness. 'Grub's heart is broken.'

'Find anything interesting?' Aren asked, before Cade could come up with a snappy retort. He'd always had more patience with the Skarl than Cade did.

'Grub find many things! Ossians leave all sorts of valuables lying around. Lying around in their pockets,' he added with a smirk.

Aren sighed. 'You'll bring the Watch down on us.'

Grub shrugged. 'You didn't want Grub to steal, shouldn't have brought him to a market.'

Cade rolled his eyes. 'No one *brought* you anywh—'

'Ho! You there!' A neat young Krodan man in an expensive waistcoat pushed through the crowd. 'Yes, you! The Skarl!'

Grub adopted an expression of comical innocence, ruined by Aren's obvious look of alarm. Cade gave Grub a furious glare. Trust that fool to attract trouble now, when they needed it least!

But the highborn man didn't seem angry. 'Please, if you would wait a moment. My wife is just coming. We saw you in the crowd and she's very eager to meet you. It's rare that she comes across someone from her homeland. Ah, here she is!'

Grub's expression went from innocence to fear. 'Grub has to go,' he said, but it was too late. A Skarl woman appeared next to her husband, flustered from the chase. She was tall, square-featured and striking, her hair in a complex arrangement of plaits. An elegant band of tiny tattoos followed her jawline and hairline, and curled around the socket of her left eye. She wore an excited smile, which froze as she laid eyes on Grub, and then drained slowly from her face.

'Aye, he's no looker, is he?' Cade joked; but nobody laughed, and he knew he'd misjudged the situation. The woman's eagerness turned to hate and disgust, and Grub shrank before her.

'Is something wrong, my love?' the Krodan asked.

'*Khannaqut!*' she snarled in the angular language of her homeland. 'Skin-thief!' And she hawked and spat in Grub's face.

'Alenda!' her husband cried in surprise, but she'd swept off into the crowd. He offered them a look of embarrassed apology and chased after her.

Fen returned from the fletcher's stall to find Grub trembling, his face burning red and a wad of greasy phlegm inching down his cheek. He turned and blundered away, pushing shoppers aside.

'Hoy, Grub!' Cade called after him. 'There's still something on your face!'

Aren gave him an angry look, which surprised and hurt Cade. 'I'll go after him. You stay with Fen.'

'Eh? What are you going after *him* for? He spends his whole life mocking everyone else. Let him be upset. Do him good to know how it feels.'

'I'm going after him because he's one of us,' said Aren sharply. 'And that's what we do.'

With that, he left. Cade felt something leave with him, some butterfly-light emotion too vague to be named, fluttering out of his grasp. But he'd never been good with that sort of thing, so he shook off his unease and gave Fen his best fake smile instead.

'Well, then,' he said. 'Looks like it's you and me.'

68

Skin-thief!

Grub's blood beat in his ears, throat hot, teeth gritted. He'd wiped away the woman's spit with his sleeve but he still felt it there as he hurried through the streets, dizzy with rage and shame, barely aware of the people he was pushing past.

Skin-thief!

Memories swarmed up, of another woman who spat at him. The one who found him in the longhall feasting with heroes, who accused him and brought him down. His former friends dragged him to the priests' black stone halls and threw him before the Sombre Men to answer his accuser.

Skin-thief!

The Sombre Men had listened, shaggy-haired and rancid, mouldering furs piled about their shoulders beneath sagging wide-brimmed hats. Their eyes were hidden behind bands of rag, and on each rag was daubed a new eye: the eye of Urgotha, the Bone God, who saw all lies. Beneath their blind gazes he told his story, protesting his innocence till the end.

When he was finished, the foremost of the Sombre Men leaned forward, skinned back lips over rotten teeth and spoke the word that would damn him.

Khannaqut.

They held him down as the skin-scribe came for him. *Erase him!* they said. *Wipe the lies from his body!* But the skin-scribe didn't. He leaned over Grub, a tattooed skull-face in the torchlight, and dragged the heel of his hand across Grub's eyes. Grub screamed as a pain like fire blazed in its wake. When it faded, an ugly black crescent remained, arcing from cheek to cheek. The mark of his shame; the sign of exile.

Khannaqut.

He fled the Shacklemarket with no direction in mind, his only desire to escape. He took turnings at random, his thoughts circling inwards, and only came to his senses when he reached a dead end. Before him was a low wall. He laid his hand on it and looked over. Some way below, cut into the slope of the hill, was the entrance to Patron's Bridge, busy with traffic heading from the north shore of the river to Sovereign's Isle.

On a whim, he sat atop the wall with his feet dangling over the edge. It was a long way to the ground. Far enough to kill.

A crow flapped down from the heights, alighting a little further along. It strutted back and forth, watching him with a beady eye. Grub watched it uneasily in return.

Bone God's watching, he thought. *Bone God's waiting.*

How long had he been exiled? He couldn't even remember. A long time, anyway. A long time to be without friendship or a kind word. He'd shared rough camaraderie with the lowlifes of many Ossian ports over the years, but they didn't really count as friends. They were alliances of the moment, made out of shared need for shelter, or to carry out a scam. A Skarl couldn't ever really be friends with a foreigner. They were not Skarls. Their feelings were worth no more than a horse's or a cat's.

But his own people had cast him out. There were only foreigners left to him now.

He heard footsteps coming up the street behind him. It was Mudslug. The boy clambered up on the wall alongside, dangled his legs next to Grub's and peered down at the crowd milling onto the bridge.

'Who are you aiming for?' Mudslug asked.

'Huh?'

'Well, if you're going to jump, you have to land on someone. Might as well make it count. Me, I'd go for that soldier there. He's got a look about him I don't like. And he's Krodan.' He glanced over at Grub. 'What about you?'

549

Grub thought about that, and pointed. 'Woman in red dress.'

'The pregnant woman?'

'Yes. Grub get two for the price of one.' He grinned. 'Might as well make it count.'

Mudslug shook his head in amazed disgust, but Grub reckoned he was reluctantly amused all the same.

'Remember the first time we met, in the camp?' Mudslug asked.

'Heh. Grub beat up Mudslug.'

'You ever think we'd find ourselves here, sitting on a wall in Morgenholme, deciding who best to squash with our falling bodies?'

Grub gave him a look. 'Course not, stupid. If Grub could see future, he wouldn't have been in camp in first place.'

'How *did* you end up in there, anyway? You never told me.'

'Got caught pickpocketing. When Grub explain to Krodans how mighty he is, how many foes he vanquish, they not hang him. Send him to mines instead.'

'You got caught pickpocketing?' Mudslug was thinking about the market.

Grub produced an onyx figurine from his pouch, which he'd swiped from an inattentive vendor. 'What did Mudslug say? History just a series of lessons we didn't learn.'

Aren gave a wry smile and brushed tangled brown curls back from his forehead. 'You want to tell me what a skin-thief is?' he asked.

Grub sniffed and wiped his nose with his sleeve. Did he *want* to tell him? Funny way to say it, but then Ossians talked in a funny way, and he'd never really got his head round the language. He wouldn't usually dream of sharing his shame, but Mudslug wasn't the kind to use it against him, and he felt low and lonely enough that it didn't really matter any more.

So maybe he *did* want to tell Mudslug. It seemed the sort of thing that friends did.

He put the figurine back in his pouch. 'Mudslug heard of the Scattering?'

'I've heard of it. Don't know much about it, though.'

'Skarl rite of passage. Firstborn of every family sent out into the world to do great deeds, bring back glory and riches. The rest stay at home, look after things. They say firstborns lucky ones! They get to be heroes. Ha!'

He began rummaging through his pockets and produced a silver hip-flask with a delicate floral design, which he handed to Aren to hold. Then he dug out a tinderbox and two fine cheroots which he put between his lips.

'Not easy to be a hero. Not in Ossia.'

He packed the tinderbox, struck sparks into it and lit the cheroots from the glowing wad. Then he handed one to Mudslug, who took it without much enthusiasm, eyeing the soggy end where it had been in Grub's mouth.

'Grub owes you some cheroots. From back in the camp.'

'So you do,' said Mudslug. 'I'd forgotten.' He took a drag and coughed hard.

Grub cackled. 'You get used to it,' he said and clapped him on the back, almost pushing him off the wall to his death. 'Have a drink, make things better!'

Mudslug unscrewed the lid of the hip-flask, took a swig and began to cough harder. 'What's in that?' he wheezed, handing it back.

'Whatever was in it when Grub stole it.'

Mudslug took a moment to regain control of his lungs. 'So you left home and came to Ossia,' he said. 'What did you do then?'

'Nobody trust Skarls here. Not much work. Grub look for ways to do great deeds, but soon he get hungry.' He shrugged. 'What did Grub do? He wander. Do this, do that. Meet people, leave people. Smoke a lot of clawfoot root. Steal, fight, keep food in belly and breath in body. But great deeds? No. Years pass, nothing. Nothing worth putting on skin.'

He took a draw on his cheroot and swigged the liquor in the hip-flask. It was foul and herbal and tasted like the forest floor, but Grub wasn't particular, so he drank some more of it.

'Then one day, big change. Revolution in Durn. Priests and king and nobles all in trouble, pay plenty for mercenaries. Grub go. Maybe he do something great there. Maybe he die with a rusty sword in his arse.'

He glanced over at the crow, further down the wall. He wished it would flap off. It was hard to tell the tale with the Bone God listening.

'On way, Grub find site of recent battle. Two hundred dead, maybe more. Many crows; Bone God looking for stories among the bodies. We look, too, for coin and riches. Dead men don't need fine things.' He took another swig of liquor to keep him going, then handed it back. 'Grub find body. Skarl man. Half his body all tattoos. Grub read them, become amazed. That man, he a hero!' He sighed then, lowered his head, felt the shame seep through him on a wave of alcohol warmth. 'Then Grub realise. That man's name, nearly the same as Grub's. Just have to add one character and it *exactly* the same. Feel like omen to Grub.'

'What *is* your real name?'

'Don't have one. Name lost now. See?' He pointed to the spot where his left cheek met his eye socket, now entirely black. 'Here where Skarls have name, tribe, place of birth marked. Mine gone. Grub is Grub now, from nowhere.'

'You're always from somewhere. It doesn't matter what's written on your skin.'

'Matters to Bone God. Memories die. Flesh rots. Only what's written lives on.' He waved it away. He didn't want to talk about that. There was no greater hell than to be Unremembered.

'But why, er, Grub?'

'That what they call me when I was part of Nuk's gang back in Karaqqa. Grub like the sound of it in Ossian. Sound very elegant.'

Mudslug had a dubious look on his face, but he held his tongue. Grub could tell he had questions about Nuk and Karaqqa and all of that, but he found he wanted to finish his story now he'd started it.

'Grub decide to take warrior's story for his own. Everyone think *he* do those things. Grub will be hero, feast in longhalls with other heroes, treated with respect till the end of his days. Grub can go home! So Grub take the story and he head for the coast.'

'You copied it from his skin?'

'Mudslug stupid. Only skin-scribe can copy skin-scribe tattoos.'

'So you ... carried him?'

Grub snorted. 'No. He already starting to stink. Skinned him, smoked it, left the rest for the crows.'

Mudslug's appalled stare was genuine this time. Grub didn't care. Mudslug didn't even know the worst of it yet. 'Grub go to a Needler. Used to be skin-scribes, but they break laws, get exiled. They still know the secret arts, though. Best tattooists in the world, sell their skills for money, get rich. Grub not rich, but he beg, and this man help a fellow Skarl. All that warrior's great deeds written on my skin. Then I go to Skarl sailor and say, "Take me home!" And he honoured to. *Honoured*.'

Grub dragged bitterly on the last of his cheroot and flicked it into the air, where it tumbled down into the crowd. Mudslug ground his out on the wall with some relief.

'Worst thing one Skarl can do to another is make him Unremembered,' said Grub. Hard even to say this, but he had to. 'Law says, you find a dead Skarl, you bring them home so their deeds can be recorded. If you can't, leave them for the crows. Crows peck out eyes, see what they saw; peck out tongues, learn what they spoke; read the writing on their skin. All this they take back to the Bone God, and he record it. Don't bury, don't burn. Leaves nothing for the crows to read.' He let out a breath. 'But when Grub was done with the skin, he burned it. Thought no one could prove what Grub did if they never found that skin. But they proved it anyway.'

Mudslug looked at him like he understood, but he didn't understand. Only a Skarl could. 'How long before they caught you?' he asked.

'Few months. Life good. Women, feasting. Young men listen to my tales, buy me drinks. Then one day, old friend turn up. Old friend of *his*. They fight together on mainland. She track him down, and she know my face is wrong. *Khannaqut*, she call me. Then they take me to the Black Triad.'

His voice faded. He didn't really want to talk any more, but he had to say one last thing, if only to dull the barb a little. 'They copied his story from me, before they sent me away. At least Grub did that. Stonesingers put it on wall of mausoleum somewhere. He not Unremembered in the end.'

Mudslug contemplated the crowd for a time. 'So you didn't kill an ice bear?'

'No.'

'Or ambush a shipload of Boskan smugglers?'

'No.'

'Or fight the urds in the Sixth Purge? Or slay ten elaru all on your own?'

'Grub did none of those things.'

'But you did escape the camp at Suller's Bluff. We couldn't have done that without you.'

'Yes.'

'And you did save us at Skavengard. If you hadn't found a way round that collapsed room, we'd all have been killed by the beast, instead of just...' He saddened visibly at the memory of Moustache. 'Well... you know.'

'Grub did that. Still, it not enough.'

'What *will* be enough?'

Grub puffed out his cheeks. The crow had flown away at some point; he hadn't noticed it leave. 'Skarls have tale. Hero called Hagga. He slay his own brother, steal his skin. Caught and exiled. Rest of his life, he do things so heroic, such feats, it hard to believe. Return with treasure. Sombre Men listen to his tale, call it true. Say he repaid his debt to the Bone God. So skin-scribes take away the mark of *khannaqut*.' He passed a hand across his eyes, as if he could wipe away the stain there. 'Grub must do something so great Bone God will forgive him. No faking this time. Then maybe he go home.'

There was silence between them for the span of a dozen heart-beats. Then Grub straightened and pointed. 'Bitterbracker,' he said.

Mudslug followed his gaze. The Bitterbracker was just stepping onto the bridge below them, heading across the river to Sovereign's Isle. He was easy to spot with his distinctive hair, grown long in a strip down the centre of his skull and shaved elsewhere. He moved in a furtive hurry, glancing over his shoulder.

'Bitterbracker told us he staying inside today,' Grub said. 'Grub think he up to something.'

Mudslug's frown deepened. 'So do I,' he said, climbing down off the wall. 'Coming?'

'Grub *better* come. Remember last time Mudslug tried to follow Grub? Grub taken dumps that were subtler.'

'Let's go, then.'

Mudslug headed off to find a path down to the bridge and Grub went after him. He felt better after their talk. Mudslug was good blood, as they said back in Karaqqa. A trustworthy sort. Someone you could rely on. Grub had even developed a sneaking fondness for him.

Shame, then, what he planned to do once Garric had retrieved the Ember Blade. For if that sword was all they said it was, it was worth a king's ransom to Ossians and Krodans alike. What would the Sombre Men say if he were to bring it home as a present for his tharl? Wouldn't that be a deed out of legend?

Grub would let Garric steal it, if he could. Then he'd steal it from Garric. He felt a little regretful about it, but not much.

A Skarl could never really be friends with a foreigner, after all.

69

Aren and Grub had to run to have any chance of catching up with Keel, so run they did. Luck favoured them, and they came across a stone stairway in the next street that led sharply down to the level of the bridge. There they fought their way through the festive crowds heading for Sovereign's Isle, searching for Keel as they went.

Out on the bridge, the traffic cleared somewhat and they sprinted across. The River Cay sparkled beneath them, the painted sails of merchant ships moving in stately progress towards the sea. A pair of Krodan soldiers eyed them suspiciously as they raced past and Aren felt a sudden thrill of alarm.

If we're stopped...

He halted at the end of the bridge. Grub lumbered up behind him, barely out of breath. He was slow, but apparently he could run for ever.

'Mudslug tired?' Grub grinned.

Aren tried not to look at the guards, who were watching them. 'We can't draw too much attention,' he panted. 'We don't have permits for Morgenholme. If they ask to see our papers, we'll be arrested.'

'Didn't Mudslug think of that this morning?'

He hadn't. He hadn't travelled much beyond Shoal Point. Excited by the prospect of exploring and eager to defy Garric's command, he'd taken a foolish and reckless risk. With the wedding coming up, the guards would be on high alert. All it took was one check and this would all be over.

'Didn't *you* know we needed permits?' Aren retorted, angry at himself for his idiocy.

'Grub knew. He just didn't care.' He slapped Aren on the arm. 'Come on, Mudslug. Walk. Try not to look like a criminal.'

'*Me?*'

They proceeded on to Sovereign's Isle, and to Aren's great relief, the guards lost interest in them. Thereafter they went at a quicker pace, but no faster than a hundred other shoppers and harried clerks. Aren scanned the grand square at the end of Patron's Bridge as they crossed it, searching for Keel among the faces that surrounded him.

'Bitterbracker could be anywhere,' Grub said.

He was right, and perhaps it was pointless trying to catch Keel, but something in the way he'd been walking troubled Aren. He was about some secret business. Aren would be eaten by suspicion until he knew what it was.

An idea occurred to him. 'There's another bridge on the far side of Sovereign's Isle. We crossed it when we came from the docks.'

'So?'

'So that's where we're going,' he said, setting off in that direction. 'If his destination is on Sovereign's Isle, we've lost him; but if he's heading for the south bank we can catch him on the other bridge.'

Aren's instincts proved right. They arrived at the Promise Bridge just in time to see Keel stepping off it.

Grub cackled. 'Mudslug make good spy yet. Now follow Grub. Don't get too close.'

Aren followed Grub's lead as they trailed Keel off the bridge and down the hill towards the Canal District. The streets took on a seedy look as the alleyways narrowed and steepened, and there was a faint scent of rot in the air, rising from the lichen-slimed inlets further down the hill where the land met the water. Houses leaned out over the street and the people began to look crumpled and unhealthy.

Grub kept a far greater distance from Keel than Aren would have done. Every time Keel turned a corner, Aren was anxious they'd lose him, but Grub had an instinct for where he was going next and found him again immediately. There was clearly a skill to it, but it was a mystery to Aren.

Keel had stopped looking over his shoulder and was walking with purpose. Aren guessed he was nearing his destination. Grub closed in a little, perhaps fearing he'd disappear into some anonymous doorway. When Keel finally came to the end of his journey, they had him in sight, and Grub pulled Aren behind a corner to watch.

The Burned Bear was a faintly unpleasant-looking inn that stood at the end of a terrace, with a dank thoroughfare running alongside it. Its timbers were painted with flaking pitch and latticed windows of cheap glass turned its patrons into smeared ghouls. The sign showed a bear with ugly red burn wounds, chained to a pole, fighting dogs. Presumably there was a story to that name, but Aren had another story to follow right now. They watched Keel go inside.

'Perhaps he just wants to get drunk,' Aren suggested, though he didn't for a moment believe it. 'After Skavengard—'

'No need to sneak, then.'

'He might be ashamed.'

Grub shook his head. 'Bitterbracker meeting somebody.'

Aren hovered uncertainly, weighing his next move. He was sick of secrecy. Part of him wanted to storm in there, seize Keel and demand some straight answers. Even if it got him another beating, it would be worth it. But he'd learned the futility of asking for truth; it was not freely given. It had to be dug out bit by bit, like chips of elarite from mountain rock.

'Let's go in and see who he's meeting,' said Aren decisively. 'Stay out of sight.'

He was about to set off when Grub hissed at him. 'Wait,' he said. 'Look.'

Two men were approaching the Burned Bear from the other direction. They were straight-backed and tall, with the stern blond good looks of well-bred Krodans. Their clothes were unremarkable, but their arrogant stride gave them away. These were no passing citizens. The swords at their hips were fine and well cared for, and they entered the inn with solemn purpose.

'Grub reckon we not the only ones interested in Keel.'

Aren felt himself go cold. If these were the men Keel had come to meet, they clearly meant him no kindness. He hurried up the alley towards the inn.

'Where Mudslug going? Krodans got swords!' Grub said, scampering behind him.

'Yes,' said Aren. 'And Keel doesn't know it. Want to do something heroic, or are you going to stay out here?'

Grub swore in the language of his homeland and followed.

The inn was cramped and busy, hot with bodies and heaving. Laughter, smoke and threat hung in the air. Sailors and locals of half a dozen races ate and drank at the tables, and whores slid between them. A ship must have come in recently; the docks were not far from here.

Aren pushed his way in, his stomach tight with nerves. Ordinarily he'd steer clear of an establishment like this. The clientele were hard-eyed and gruff, nothing like the friendly faces at the Cross Keys in Shoal Point. He was a boy again here, not the man he'd started to become.

He spotted the Krodans heading through the common room to a doorway on the far side. Grub hissed in his ear, having spotted two more Krodans sitting at a corner table, out of place among the roguish patrons. They exchanged a glance with their fellows as they passed.

'Grub think Bitterbracker in real trouble,' he murmured.

They could do nothing but follow the men through the doorway into a larger room with a bar at its centre, where they found Keel in conversation with a big-bellied man in an apron who Aren took to be the innkeeper. Keel passed him a coin and received a folded letter in exchange, which he tucked inside his jerkin. He didn't notice the Krodans approaching him from behind, eyes fixed on him. There was no doubt left in Aren's mind now: they meant to arrest him, or kill him.

'Come on,' said Grub. 'Outside. We follow, see where they take him.'

Aren felt suddenly, overwhelmingly grateful to the Skarl for that suggestion. Yes, that was what they should do! Intervening would bring the Krodans down on their heads; doing nothing would be cowardice. This was the middle ground that would allow him to live with his conscience while staying out of danger.

And if Keel was slain first, or if they couldn't save him from whatever torture the Krodans had in mind? Well, at least he'd have tried. What more could he do, really? Where was the sense in pitting himself against overwhelming odds? What was the point in getting them all killed to save one?

Some window of understanding gaped in his mind, and he heard those words on the lips of a thousand Ossian nobles as they laid down their arms before the Krodans. Heard it on Randill's lips, too. For the first time ever, he saw into his father's heart, and thought he knew him.

But he wasn't his father.

'Keel!' he screamed at the top of his lungs. 'It's a trap!'

The Krodans at the bar whirled. Keel did, too, and he registered the danger in an instant. His meat knife appeared in his hand, and as the Krodans belatedly drew their swords he threw himself into them, driving his blade into the eye of the nearest as they all went crashing to the floor.

The crowd erupted into chaos. Men scrambled back from the combatants, shoving their fellows before them, who tumbled over stools and barged into others. Drinks were knocked to the floor and punches thrown in blind reaction. In seconds, the fragile peace inside the Burned Bear collapsed.

Aren was pitched this way and that in a churning sea of limbs, fighting to keep his balance. The corner of a table hammered into his thigh. Grub had disappeared in the melee. He caught sight of Keel through the crowd, struggling on the floor with his surviving assailant, his face spattered with blood. The Krodans had swords, but at such close quarters a short blade was better. He saw Keel raise the reddened knife again, his face a savage rictus of hate. The Krodan screamed in fear, and then the crowd closed in and Aren mercifully saw no more.

Rough arms seized him. A square-jawed face loomed in his vision, eyes dull with authority: one of the Krodans who'd been waiting inside. He struggled, but he was pinned against a table which gave way beneath him, sending him and his captor to the ground in a rain of mugs and platters.

Frantically he fought to get out from underneath the Krodan. Booted feet stamped and thundered all around him, inches from his nose. Suddenly the Krodan rocked sideways as he was kicked hard in the head. He rolled off Aren, dazed, and Grub lunged down, stabbing. The Krodan jerked twice and lay still.

Grub pulled Aren up as the bar went from brawling disorder to panic. The hot scent of murder was in the air.

'More Krodans coming. Go!' Grub shoved him into the crowd and was quickly lost to sight.

Aren stumbled towards the back of the room, where most of the patrons were disappearing through a rear door. He couldn't find Keel anywhere. Handbells began ringing outside, the same alarm call he'd heard before the road patrol caught them at the Reaver's Rest. Men with swords pushed in and the rear door was blocked. The main door would surely be covered by now, too.

He saw a booth next to a window. With no better idea, he shoved towards it, slipped into the booth and wrenched at the latch. It didn't move. Painted shut.

Desperately, he snatched up a stool. His first blow bounced off the lead lattice and didn't even crack the glass. It took two more blows before the cheap glue gave way and the window fell out of its frame in a rain of diamond-shaped panes. Someone shouted 'Halt!' in Krodan, and he knew it was meant for him, but he wasn't to be halted now. He wriggled out through the window and tumbled into the dirty gutter beyond.

Panting, he got to his feet. A short distance to his left, standing at the corner where he could see the entrance to the inn, was a man he recognised. He wore a black coat, showing the double-barred cross of the Iron Hand, and there was a long, thin sword at his belt.

Harte.

Their eyes met, and for the briefest of instants a flashfire swept across Aren's mind. He wanted to throw himself at Harte, knock him down, strangle him with his bare hands. But it was an instant only, and then cold sense took hold, and he ran.

'Get back here, boy!' Harte cried and launched into pursuit.

Sailors were still milling about the rear entrance of the Burned Bear, trying to see what was going on inside. Aren dodged past them at a sprint. A Krodan reached out to stop him – an Iron Guardsman in disguise, like all the rest – but Aren jinked away and his fingers only brushed Aren's arm.

The street ended where it was crossed by a sloped and busy road. Aren ran out onto it, darting in front of a cart. The horse reared with a snort, scraping at the air with its hooves, and the driver's curses followed him downhill.

He glanced over his shoulder and saw Harte catching up with him through the traffic. The Krodan who'd tried to grab him had also joined the chase, arms pumping as he ran in the watchman's wake. Tall, athletic men, perfect specimens of Krodan manhood. Aren was quick and nimble, but not as fit and his stride was shorter. They'd run him down, given time.

Aren redoubled his speed, boots pounding, blood thumping in his ears as he searched for an escape. The crowded street descended sharply before him. To his left were rows of houses and shops; no shelter there. To his right, a low wall guarded against the drop to the next street, which ran parallel to this one but much lower, almost at the level of the river. He could see onto the roofs of the buildings there, which rose almost to the height of the wall, but there was no obvious way down.

'Stop that boy!' Harte cried. People slowed to look for him, but Aren had already raced past. Then he saw the soldiers ahead and realised who Harte had been shouting to: two stern men in the black and white livery of the Krodan army appeared in his path, standing low and ready to catch him.

With only a moment to act, he dug in his heels, ran to the side of the road and vaulted the wall.

Terror seized him as he swung his legs over the edge. If he'd miscalculated, there'd be nothing but a hard drop to the street several storeys below. But when he cleared the wall, the rooftop was there, only a half-dozen feet below him as he'd hoped it would be. He landed with a jolt and kept running.

The roof was bare but for a pile of decaying crates and a rickety old jib. He fled towards a door on the far side. Risking a look over his shoulder, he saw Harte jumping down after him, closer on his heels than he'd imagined. The other Iron Guardsman followed, but the soldiers, clad in armour, were too heavy to risk the jump.

The door was little more than a few planks nailed together, held shut by a rusty padlock. Driven by fear of the men at his back, Aren shoulder-charged the door at a run. It smashed open before him, rotten wood splintering, and he found himself at the top of a bare stone stairway.

Shoulder smarting from the blow, he pelted down the steps and into a spacious room, musty with long emptiness. Old blankets and rat-eaten sacks had accumulated in the corners. Once it had been a small warehouse, but it was abandoned now and had fallen into dilapidation.

Aren ran for the first door he could see. Harte was too close behind to do otherwise. Birds exploded in a flutter from the sill of a window as he passed. A floorboard split beneath his feet, sending him stumbling. He fell, landed hard on his hands, scrambled up again. The door was there in front of him, its lock broken and hanging ajar. He shoved it open.

Unexpected daylight brought him to a halt and he found himself at the top of an exterior staircase. Once it had run down the front of the building, but it had long since rotted in the dank air of the Canal District, and all that was left was a precarious landing projecting out over an alley.

He cursed and turned to seek another route, but Harte had already run into the room and was between Aren and the exit. He slowed as he saw Aren's predicament; an ironic smile slid across his face as he drew his sword. His companion appeared and began to circle round to prevent Aren from getting past them.

Cornered, Aren took a step backwards onto the landing. It creaked alarmingly beneath him as he peered over his shoulder. There was no chance of climbing down the wall, but the alley was narrow and the building opposite leaned close. There was a small balcony jutting out from it, one storey below him, surrounded by an iron railing with a shuttered door leading inside.

Could he make that jump? No, that was desperation talking. He'd fall short and break his legs for sure.

Nails pinged and wood groaned as the landing threatened to come away from the wall. Aren lurched back into the room.

'No way out?' said Harte. 'That's a shame. That's a real shame.'

Aren pulled his knife from his belt. One of Rapha's men had given it to him in the bathhouse of a Krodan work camp. Now he held it out before him, a feeble ward against the swords of his enemies. It felt like the only thing to do.

'You want to resist arrest?' said Harte. 'Please do. I'm sure you remember how well that worked out for your father.'

Aren's knuckles whitened on the hilt of his knife. He saw again his father struggling amid a mass of Iron Guardsmen; Harte holding a dagger to his throat; the look in his father's eyes as the blade was driven home. Rage surged through him, sweeping aside all possibility of surrender. To submit to his father's killer was something he could never do.

He flipped the knife in his hand and flung it spinning through the air towards Harte's forehead. It flew harmlessly past his shoulder and clattered to the floor on the far side of the room.

Harte let out a surprised laugh. 'My. You're quite the formidable assassin, aren't you?'

Aren felt a stab of impotent fury. There was no way he could beat this man today, no matter how much he wanted to. Instead he turned and ran out onto the landing. He clambered up on the wooden railing, braced himself and, before he could think better of it, he jumped.

Arms wheeling, he dropped through the air, throat locked shut with the terror of the plunge. He crashed down hard on the balcony, knees buckling, and slammed into the shuttered door with such force it turned his vision white.

Dizzily, he struggled to his feet and rattled the door. It was securely locked, but that didn't matter. The balcony was only two storeys high; he could hang off it and drop down into the alley.

Harte appeared in the doorway of the warehouse landing and

564

let out a cry of rage as he saw Aren on the balcony. Aren gave him a defiant grin. Ignoring the pain of his bruised muscles, he clambered over the rail and dropped to the cobbles below.

'You're claimed, you little bastard!' Harte roared, his oily sarcasm replaced by bald fury. He stepped out onto the landing, climbed up on the railing and readied himself to spring. But the rotten wood had been tested enough; it broke beneath his weight and Harte, unbalanced, lunged forwards as the landing fell apart beneath him. Aren dodged away from the falling wood as Harte plummeted through the air with a yell, but the watchman had put enough strength into his jump to clear the alleyway and landed on the balcony in a helpless tumble.

Aren stood where he was, staring. He knew he should run, but he had to see if his father's killer was dead.

It was too much to hope for. Harte stirred with a stifled groan of pain. His companion appeared in the warehouse doorway, but now the landing was gone he had no way down except back through the building.

'I'll kill you, boy!' Harte snarled, levering himself up with the help of the balcony railing. 'I swear to the Primus, I'll kill you!'

Aren fled. Behind him, Harte climbed over the railing and dropped down into the alley. His leg gave way as he landed and he screamed and collapsed; but by the time Aren reached the corner of the alley, he was getting up again, unstoppable in his wrath.

'*I'll kill you!*' he screamed again, and came limping after Aren, wincing and wheezing whenever he put his weight on his damaged leg.

Aren sprinted out of the alleyway into a small cobbled plaza where a canal dead-ended to form a miniature harbour. A dozen boats were moored haphazardly around a stone quay, and the waterside was cluttered with nets waiting to be repaired and piles of lobster pots. Stalls sold whelks and cress to the men and women who idled nearby, waiting for the next cargo to arrive. Their conversations faltered as Aren burst through, running for his life.

'Stop!' cried Harte as he limped to the mouth of the alleyway.

Small chance of that, Aren thought. Harte had been injured in the fall and his companion was far behind. There was no way they could catch him. A fierce smile spread across his face as he crossed the plaza. He'd outrun them. He'd escaped. He'd—

Something caught against his foot and he fell and smacked hard against the ground. The shock of the impact stunned him and he tasted blood. Dazed, he tried to raise himself. He'd tripped. Somehow he'd tripped.

Rough hands pulled him up, twisting his arms behind his back. He saw the grizzled faces of the men of the Canal District, set hard as they held him.

He hadn't tripped. He'd *been* tripped. Disbelief rendered him speechless for an instant. When he found his voice, it was strangled and mewling.

'You're *Ossians!*' he cried, appalled. He struggled, but they had him fast. Harte was limping across the plaza towards him, a knife in his hand and murder in his eyes. 'Why are you helping *him?*'

His answer was a punch in the gut, driving the wind from him. He sagged in their arms, wheezing and helpless. When Harte reached him, he seized Aren by the throat and propelled him backwards, out of the hands of his captors and up against a wall.

The Ossians fell away, cowed by the sign of the Iron Hand and the blade Harte pressed to Aren's throat. The watchman's face was inches from Aren's, eyes bulging and teeth gritted. Aren could feel the heat of his anger as the knife edge bit into his skin. That crazed stare promised death, and he was taken by a terror he'd never known before. He couldn't die like this, killed by the blade that killed his father, betrayed by his own people. He squeezed his eyes shut. *Meshuk, Joha, anyone, please!*

A drop of blood trickled down onto his collarbone. He heard Harte's heaving breath, smelled his hate and tensed for the final cut.

'No,' said Harte.

The knife withdrew. Aren opened his eyes, trembling, confused.

'No, that's exactly what he'd want me to do. It's just the excuse he needs.' His voice was thoughtful, sly. 'One last black mark on my record.'

Harte took a shuddering breath, smoothed his damp hair back across his scalp and made a visible effort to control himself. Then he grabbed Aren, turned him around and slammed him up against the wall again, cheek-first. Aren was too weak with shock to resist as manacles closed around his wrists.

'Don't think it's your lucky day, you vile little rat,' Harte hissed. 'You'll wish you were dead by the time we're done with you. By the Primus, I'm going to see you suffer. But first ...' He grabbed a fistful of hair, yanked his head back painfully and leaned in close to his ear. 'First, you'll talk.'

70

Ropes creaked, pulleys squeaked and sailcloth flapped in the wind. Gulls wheeled high over the granite-flagged docks of Morgenholme. Swifts darted between the ratlines of towering ships while sailors smoked and cursed happily on the quay, and stevedores unloaded cargoes from across the known world to be sold in the shops and dens of the capital.

Garric stood in the shadow of a Xulan merchant vessel, its gunwales carved with cavorting nudes and the Pradap Tet as its figurehead. Nearby, handlers were loading a cart with four large barrels and a dozen smaller ironbound ones, moving them slowly and with extreme care. Garric wondered if he should be standing further back in case of an accident, but on reflection he supposed it didn't matter. Without that cargo, all was lost anyway.

Katat-az had delivered on time, but that was no surprise. Xulans were a trustworthy folk by reputation, because reputation was what they lived and died by. In a culture that had elevated gossip and rumour-mongering to a martial art, what was said about somebody was more important than any truth. Xulan merchants cultivated a reputation for honesty and reliability by being honest and reliable, and they charged accordingly. Anyone who didn't like it could take their chances with a Carthanian.

The merchandise was here, at least. One more piece in place. But there was so much more that needed to go right before the end, and so many things that could go wrong. He pushed the thought aside. Doubt was a luxury he couldn't allow himself. His course was set, whatever the consequence.

'Laine of Heath Edge, by my breath,' said a voice at his shoulder.

Wilham the Smiler was a small, slight man; freckled, baby-faced, his hair orange as a carrot. He had the innocent grin of someone comical, pitiable and harmless. Never had Garric known anyone whose appearance so belied the person behind it.

'It's Garric now, as well you know,' said Garric. 'Laine died at Salt Fork.'

'As did many who shared our cause,' said Wilham, 'and all for the cowardice of weak men too afraid of their rulers to resist them.' He bowed his head. 'It was a brave try. There are not many left who dare such bold moves.'

'Not many willing to bear the cost,' Garric replied.

'The wheels of change are greased with blood,' said Wilham. 'You know it, as do I. Always surprises me how many think they can win their freedom without doing anything unpleasant.'

Garric grunted and they stood in silence a moment, watching the Xulans load the barrels into the hired cart. If the Iron Hand came sniffing, they'd left no trail to Mara's house.

'They say General Dakken himself will be at the wedding,' said Wilham. He smiled when he said it. He smiled a lot, even when there was nothing to smile about. It didn't always mean he was amused.

'I don't doubt it,' said Garric.

'The very man who stole the Ember Blade from our lands, thirty years ago, when he was nothing but an upstart captain. He's going to present it to the prince. Quite an honour.' His eyes were shrewd behind the shield of his grin. 'Think you could take a detour and kill that bastard while you're about your business in Hammerholt?' He was only half joking.

'Who says that's not my reason for going there?'

Wilham grinned wider. 'Because I know you, Garric. Murdering Dakken would serve no purpose but your own satisfaction. You always thought bigger than that.'

'Reckon I should kill the prince, then.'

'Ha! If only you could get close enough.'

'I'll poison him.'

'All you'd do is to kill his wine-tasters. No, it's the Ember Blade you're after, and don't say otherwise. If you should get it, though, and you need a place to hide it...' He spread his arms. 'None know the city like I do.'

'I'll keep it in mind,' said Garric. 'How goes the struggle in Morgenholme?'

'Well enough. We intercepted a shipment of weapons meant for the garrison and now we have more sword and armour than we know what to do with. There was a Krodan judge getting too free with the noose, started hanging Ossians for his own amusement by the end, so we hanged him for ours. And then there are the informers. Always them.'

'Informers,' Garric echoed, disgusted. There was no lower creature than an Ossian who sold out their kinfolk for coin or advantage.

'Seems our current range of discouragements still aren't getting through to some,' said Wilham. 'Reckon we need to up the ante. Target partners and families, too.'

'Children?' Garric said. That sat ill with him. 'It's a fine line you tread, Wilham.'

'People have to learn. Lie with the Krodans and there are consequences. A man will risk his own neck if he thinks he can get away with it. He'll think twice before risking those he loves.'

Garric said nothing. This was Wilham's city, Wilham's choice, and sacrifices had to be made. But he thought the smiling man should take care, if he went that route. Resistance was a dirty business, but it was all for nothing if they became worse than those they resisted.

'When do we move?' he said.

'Tomorrow night. I have a man on the inside at the vintner's yard who can let us in through the side gate.'

'Good.' Wilham was vicious, but he was clever and thorough. Garric had faith that the plan was sound.

'We'll collect the cart from Mara's in the morning, with the fake Amberlyne barrels—'

'They're being delivered today.'

'Perfect. Once we have everything ready, you'll meet us shortly after seventh bell o' dark. We'll get you into the false compartment in the cart, then exchange it for a real one. In and out, quick as that. But you should be prepared. It won't be comfortable, and you'll be in there a long time. A night and day, at least.'

He'd planned for that. Water to drink. Towels to stuff into his underclothes for when he wet himself. Herbs to cause constipation. Maybe Vika could give him something for cramp if she woke in time; the corruption round her wound was almost gone.

It would be an undignified, painful ordeal, but when the odds were not in your favour, you had to be ready to do what other men wouldn't. History would forget the sordid details, as long as he triumphed in the end.

'I'm ready,' Garric said. 'And you'll be too busy enjoying your stolen Amberlyne to worry about me.'

'Ha! You think I'd *drink* them? Their sale will go towards the cause, my friend. I already have a buyer champing at the bit.'

'You're a man of principle and sobriety, Wilham. I always admired that about y—' His eyes widened in alarm. '*Careful, you fool!*'

One of the Xulan handlers, distracted by something on the docks, bumped against his companion, who was coming up behind him with the last of the small barrels. The man carrying the barrel teetered for a moment, wide-eyed with alarm until the other man grabbed it and steadied him. He looked equally afraid and relieved as he stepped out of the way. His companion gently loaded the barrel into place on the cart and gave the other a lethal glare as they hinged up the tailgate.

Wilham cast a sly glance at Garric. 'Mind telling me what's in those barrels?'

'I'll see you tomorrow night, Wilham,' Garric said.

Wilham smiled. 'I can't wait.'

71

The Iron Hand's headquarters was a terrifyingly innocuous building, tall and plain, hoarding its secrets within. It bore no indication of its purpose, yet still people quickened their step as they passed. Violence at the hands of urds or foreign armies was one kind of fear, but this was something else. It was death made bland, murder in plain sight.

Aren sat on a bare wooden chair, his wrists manacled and chained to a ring in the floor, lit by the wan, shivering light of a lantern. His head hung and his chest was so tight it hurt to breathe. They'd marched him past the torture chamber on the way to his cell and he'd glimpsed what was inside. Cages, hammers, a rack. Blades laid out as if for surgery. He knew they'd done it on purpose, to show him what awaited, but he couldn't put it from his mind. If they were trying to scare him, it had worked.

You'll talk, Harte had told him. And he would, in the end. Everyone did. It was only a matter of time.

Footsteps approached down the corridor, moving with the swift clip of authority. He heard low voices outside. The awful anticipation almost made him retch, and he fought to control his breathing.

Who else had they got? Keel? Grub? Who else was talking right now?

The key turned in the lock. The door was opened by the stern captain who'd previously escorted him to his cell; his name was Dressle. He moved aside and Overwatchman Klyssen stepped in.

Aren's eyes widened in recognition. It was the first time he'd seen him close up since the day his father was killed. He was small and unassuming, with weak, watery features, but none of that mattered when he wore the black coat and double-barred cross of the Iron Hand. Aren hated him and feared him in equal measure.

Dressle closed the door, leaving Klyssen alone with Aren. The overwatchman stood before him, assessing him, his eyes lizard-calm behind his spectacles. He didn't speak. The silence dragged out until Aren was hardly able to bear it. He was desperate to know what Klyssen intended to do with him, and was about to ask, but he spotted the trap and held his tongue.

He wants me to babble and plead, to give myself away. He wants me to tell him things I shouldn't.

'What did he say to you?' Klyssen asked at last. 'What did Garric say to make you follow him? You must have realised you were of no interest to the Iron Hand after you escaped Suller's Bluff. You could have gone anywhere, started again. Instead, because of him, here you are.'

He began to walk around the cell, circling behind Aren. It made Aren nervous to have him where he couldn't see him, like losing track of a spider in a room. He half-expected a blow from behind.

'Garric was your father's sworn enemy,' Klyssen went on. 'He would have hunted him down and killed him like a dog if he could. What could he possibly have said to make you betray your own blood?'

Aren couldn't help tensing at that. He hadn't considered that joining Garric's cause might be a betrayal of his father's memory. Gods, he'd not only joined him, but on occasion he'd found himself looking up to him, the way he'd once looked up to Randill. Somehow he'd avoided thinking about it, with the same wilful ignorance he'd practised back when he admired the Krodans. But Klyssen had put it in his head now, and it gnawed at him.

'I knew something of your father,' said Klyssen, tapping the lantern to steady the flame.

You knew nothing of him, Aren thought venomously, but already he wondered if that were true, if Klyssen knew more than he himself did.

'Men like him are the reason Ossia thrives today,' Klyssen went on. 'You've seen this city, its shopping districts and boulevards. You've seen the people celebrating, eager for the wedding to come. Do they look unhappy to you? Because if you think that is slavery, if you think that is *oppression*, then you have not seen Brunland. Your father saw the futility of resisting and wanted to save his countryfolk. The Brunlanders fought to the bitter end, and the end, when it came, was bitter indeed.'

He returned to stand before Aren, who watched him warily. He wanted to know what Klyssen knew, but wouldn't give him the satisfaction of asking.

'It takes a strong man to accept loss with grace,' Klyssen said, 'and a clever man to make best advantage of it. Your father and others like him were strong and clever. They lost the war, but won the peace.' Then his expression darkened. 'The man you call Garric did not agree with their philosophy. He has, to date, personally murdered six Ossian highborns whom he believed complicit in Ossia's surrender. He has been involved in the deaths of five more.'

That was a cold shock to Aren, but he kept it off his face. *It's a lie*, he thought, but was it? How much did he know of that man, really?

'And, of course, he was very eager to kill your father,' Klyssen added.

'Garric didn't kill my father,' said Aren. 'You did.'

He saw a flicker of triumph in Klyssen's eyes and cursed himself silently. He hadn't intended to engage with his interrogator, but Klyssen's questions had got under his skin.

'We did not want him dead. Watchman Harte was forced to execute him only after your father slew several members of the Iron Guard.' Klyssen spread his hands helplessly. 'We had only intended to arrest him.'

Again, sowing doubt. Everything he said had the ring of truth to it, and Garric had kept him in the dark so much that Aren didn't have any solid grounds to disbelieve him. But Klyssen was a Krodan, and Krodans lied.

'Whatever dream Garric sold you, it is just that: a dream,' Klyssen said. 'Ossia is part of the Krodan Empire, and most Ossians are

574

happy about it. We brought you order and prosperity. We protect you from the elaru across the sea and Harrow to the north.'

Aren snorted. That small defiance gave him courage.

'You don't believe me,' Klyssen said. 'Well, we were all young once, idealistic and naïve. We all thought we could change the world. But civilisation is a structure too massive and rigid to be altered. You may knock down a pillar here and there, but new ones will replace them. You may repaint the façade, but what lies beneath remains the same. Attacking it is futile. You may as well attack a mountain.' He took off his spectacles and polished them with the sleeve of his coat. 'It's time to grow up. Time you learned to deal with the way things are, not the way you wish them to be.'

He put his spectacles back on and gazed gravely at Aren.

'Tell me where he is.'

Aren looked away; he couldn't meet Klyssen's eyes. He saw the torture chamber in his mind again, the instruments of agony, and tried not to think about how they'd be put to use. There had to be some way out of this, some way he could avoid what was to come. His mind raced, searching for an escape.

'I have interrogated many prisoners in my time,' said Klyssen. 'They all feel the need to put up a fight, if only so they can live with themselves afterwards. But I always find out what I want to know.' He leaned closer. 'I think you're smarter than that. Tell me willingly and you will be set free once we have him. Or you can try to keep silent, and be tortured, and afterwards you will be hanged. Either way, I will have my answer.'

Aren closed his eyes, forcing calm upon himself. Klyssen was right: Aren would talk in the end. Garric had already cost his father his life. Should Aren give up his life, too, out of loyalty to a man he hardly knew?

There's something I'm missing, he thought. He fought to see past the uniform, the cell, the terror of it all, to see Klyssen as he was. *To overcome your enemy, you must first understand him.*

'What about Cade?' he asked. 'I won't give you Cade.'

'I'll see he escapes punishment,' said Klyssen. 'You have my word, you can go free together.'

'And the others?'

'They are traitors, and shouldn't concern you. Tell me where Garric is. Now.'

You're in a hurry, aren't you? Aren thought, and suddenly he realised what he hadn't seen before: Klyssen *needed* him. He tried to hide it, but there was urgency in his questioning. So maybe the Iron Hand didn't have Keel or Grub after all. Maybe Aren was the only lead they had. Knowing that, Aren's fear receded a little. That was a lever with which to push back.

'What's Garric's real name?' he asked, out of nowhere. If Garric and Keel wouldn't tell him, perhaps his enemy would, and he had to stall Klyssen to give himself time to think. He was gratified to see a spasm of fury cross the overwatchman's face at the delay. A small victory, but a victory nonetheless.

He saw Klyssen considering whether to answer. *Give me a little*, Aren thought. *Help me trust you.*

'They called him Cadrac of Darkwater.'

Aren was disappointed. He'd hoped for a revelation, but that name meant nothing. 'Who are *they*?' he asked.

Klyssen shook his head. 'You have his name. I will tell you who he is, and who your father was, after you have given me what I want.'

Silence. The flame flickered and twitched in the lamp. Aren felt the chill of the cell, seeping from the walls. Klyssen's offer hung between them. Freedom for Aren and Cade, in return for Garric. But if he told Klyssen where Garric was, everyone at Mara's would be arrested. Fen, Orica, all of them. He wouldn't die for Garric's sake, but he couldn't sell out the others.

No solution. No way out. Only bad options.

'Where are your dreadknights?' he asked, playing for time. 'I suppose the Emperor doesn't want them in the city during the wedding celebrations. It wouldn't give the right impression to the Harrish. I mean, why would you need to employ abominations when we Ossians are all so *happy* with our lot?'

Klyssen's patience was at an end. He leaned close, his voice soft with threat. 'If I have to ask you again, there will be no mercy. For you or for Cade. Do you understand?'

But Aren heard what was behind the threat, heard the fear of failure which the overwatchman didn't even admit to himself. He saw into him then, this small, strange-looking man, beset by enemies on all sides, both real and imagined. Every day he was forced to prove himself against men who were more handsome, richer, better favoured than he, driven to succeed because success was the best vengeance against them. To that end, he had to capture Garric at all costs, and fast. Anything less would prove his detractors right.

Aren knew what he must do then, and his own fear vanished.

'I'll tell you what I understand,' he said. 'You didn't catch Keel, or you'd be talking to him, not me. Keel saw me at the inn, but he doesn't know if I got away. Unless I turn up very soon, he'll assume I've been arrested. Then Garric will know he's been compromised, and he'll disappear, and you'll have lost your chance.' He fixed Klyssen with a look of calm determination. 'So you're short on time, Overwatchman. And you need to make a better deal.'

Klyssen barely managed to keep the amazement off his face. He'd thought he was dealing with a scared boy, whose fragile adolescent truculence would be quickly overcome. Somehow that scared boy had just gained the upper hand.

'I'll give you Garric,' Aren said with a confidence that belied his years. 'Just him, though. I won't give up my friends, but then, you don't care about them. In return, you give me back my father's lands, property and wealth. Cade and I will return to Shoal Point with a public pardon, and we'll never see you or the Iron Hand again. In addition, after I've delivered you Garric, you'll tell me everything you know about who he is and who my father was.'

'And if I agree to this, you'll tell me where he is? Right now?'

'And have you arrest Cade and the others, too? Forgive me, but I have a hard time believing you'd let them go again. My faith in Krodan promises isn't what it once was.'

It was all Klyssen could do not to grind his teeth. He wasn't supposed to be negotiating with a prisoner. 'Then what do you propose?' he said.

'Set me free. I'll tell them I was lying low in the city; they'll believe that. Tonight, Garric intends to go into the ghetto.'

'Why?'

'It doesn't matter. He's going. You'll have men waiting. I'll lead him to them. Only Garric. The others won't even know what happened.'

And Cade will never know what I did for him. Because if he did, he'd never speak to me again.

'You have a couple of hours at most before they decide I've been captured,' said Aren. 'That's not counting the time it would take to assemble your soldiers and get there. I can't hold out against your tortures for ever, but I reckon I can hold out long enough.'

'Can you?' asked Klyssen. 'Would you like to find out?'

'Would *you*?'

There was steel in his gaze, enough that Klyssen believed him. When Aren set his will to something, it wasn't easily broken.

'Let's say I release you,' Klyssen said. 'Why would you not simply go back to them, warn your friends and disappear?'

'You'll just have to trust me. As I will trust you not to hang me when this is done.'

'Not good enough.'

'It'll have to be.'

'No. I'll have Garric one way or another. If not today, then some other day. But I won't have you run off and make a fool of me. So you need to convince me, otherwise you stay here, and there is no deal. You will not like our hospitality, I guarantee.'

Klyssen's gaze bored into him. Aren shifted in his chair. The overwatchman was determined that he wouldn't have it all his own way, and Aren saw he wouldn't flex on this. Now it was his turn to give something up.

'I hate him,' Aren said at last, and it felt so very true. He'd have died rather than give up any of the others, but Garric was a price he could pay, if that would save the rest.

'Why?'

'I hate him for causing all of this. I hate him because he hates me.'

'And you don't know why he hates you, and that makes it worse,' Klyssen surmised. 'Yet still you follow him. So I must ask again: what did he say to you?'

'He didn't say anything,' Aren murmured. All the confidence

578

had gone out of him now. In its place was naked resentment, the burning thwarted anger of youth. 'He showed me instead. Made me believe. I hate him for that most of all.'

'You admired him.'

'I thought he could make a difference. I thought *I* could.'

'And now?'

Aren looked away. 'Your man didn't catch me. Ossians did – my own people. So what's the point? You said it yourself: the smart player wins the peace. I want to go home. I want it back how it was.'

'And Garric?'

'Damn him. Enough lives have been lost on his account, my father's included. He's not worth mine.'

Klyssen nodded to himself, a finger against his lip, considering.

'If you deliver Garric,' he said at last, 'your lands will be restored and the stain wiped from your family's name. You and Cade can live in peace. But listen hard, Aren: if you betray me, I will catch you, and I will take the price of your treachery out of your friend's hide. You will watch as he is tortured to death over many days. Then I will start on you.'

He paused to let that sink in. Aren was in no doubt that he meant it. They'd ridden their luck too far already. Death and failure were all that awaited them if they carried on. The Iron Hand were everywhere, and they had not only dreadknights on their side, but most of Ossia, too, bound to them by fear. What could two boys from Shoal Point do against that?

I wish we could go back to how it was, Cade had said to him in the Shacklemarket. Well, Aren had found a way. They'd go back to the time before Fen, before Garric, before they were imprisoned and disgraced. Back to simpler days, when they were friends without conditions or complications, and they had no notion of the hells the world held in its hollows. They'd go home.

'Do we have an accord?' Klyssen asked.

Aren held up his hands, raising his manacles until the chain was taut against the ring in the floor. A gesture that said *Free me*.

'Your father would be proud of you,' said Klyssen, and he drew a key from his pocket.

72

Orica's fingers shifted and slid across the fretboard, searching for the right shapes to frame the melody her voice described. Her eyes were closed, words drawn up from a well of sadness and anger deep within her, emotion given form by lips and lungs and tongue.

He said, 'I see no clouds, and the waves are not high.
Your omens mislead you, your bones fall awry.'
But the seer said, 'Sire, not all storms come from the sky.
There are depths to which you cannot see.

'The tide is returning, and coming right soon.
It brings with it those you have sent to their doom.
There's a wolf in the waves who yet howls from its tomb
And the fallen keep long memory.'

Then the king said 'You lie! For this land is my land!
Passed on to me by fate's bloodied right hand.'
'But sire,' said the seer, 'though you think you command,
Your rule is but fleeting here.

'There are elder things yet than the god you obey
And none may lay claim to this soil, try you may.
For this land will be here after you pass away
And its children will still persevere.'

As she reached the end, she faltered, the spell of the music breaking. Something wasn't right, something didn't ring true. She let the notes fade and tried to determine what it was.

'That is a dangerous song to sing,' Mara observed.

Orica opened her eyes. She was sitting cross-legged on a stone bench in a granite-flagged nook amid Mara's expansive gardens. Harod was at her side, as ever, companion and guardian both. Orica hadn't heard Mara approach. Behind her, the house towered against a blue sky grilled with cloud.

'If someone were to overhear you, they might mistake it as something other than a ballad of a long-dead king. They might think it a warning to our new rulers,' Mara continued. 'A call to arms, even.'

'Can a bard be blamed if her words are misinterpreted?' Orica asked, with a small smile. She put out a hand as Harod drew breath to come to her defence. 'Peace, Harod. I suspect a call to arms would not find disfavour in this house.'

Indeed, after two weeks with their mysterious saviours, it would take a blind woman not to see they were plotting against the Empire. She'd guessed it from their furtive conversations even before the dreadknights appeared. But Orica was comfortable with secrets, and she let them have theirs.

Harod had urged her to leave them behind as soon as they reached Morgenholme, saying they were risky company to keep. He believed that no one else could be trusted, that he alone could protect her. Since the events at the Reaver's Rest, Orica wasn't sure that was true.

Just a few days, she said, so as not to wound his pride. *Let us see how the land lies.*

Since then, she'd learned that the ghetto had been emptied of Sards, and the land lay bleak and bare indeed.

'I think my song has become too melancholy,' she said, and she knew then why it had felt wrong to her. 'It was intended to inspire. Somewhere in the crafting, it has lost its hope.'

Mara considered that, studying her thoughtfully. 'Do you play castles?' she asked.

'I know how, though I've no great skill.'

'Will you play with me? It's something of an obsession of mine.'

'It would be my pleasure,' said Orica. She looked up at Harod, who understood at once.

'I will practise my forms,' he said, laying his hand on the blade at his hip. Then he bowed to Mara. 'You have an excellent garden, milady. My thanks for your kind hospitality.'

'Honoured guest, thy presence is thanks enough,' Mara replied in flawless Harrish.

'And thy knowledge of the tongue of my homeland does thee great credit,' Harod replied, and bowed again, deeper this time. Then, with a last glance at Orica, he left.

Orica packed up her lute and they walked back to the house together. A cool wind rustled the trees and stirred the flowers lining the paths. Birds hopped and fluttered in the afternoon sun. Orica sensed that Mara had something to ask her and was intrigued. It might help her choose which way she should go next. The world had a way of providing new paths, if you knew where to look for them. The Aspect who watched over her people was Prinn the Ragged Mummer, and she was a trickster, apt to disguise opportunities as setbacks and vice versa.

They made small talk as they headed to the parlour, where the castles board was waiting. Mara didn't make for easy conversation at first – unlike most Ossians, she found the art of speaking about nothing a little difficult – but she warmed up when Orica got her onto the subject of her school. Orica couldn't help but admire her passion, or notice the anger underneath. She spoke of the girls as if they were her daughters, taking pride in their achievements and bearing the blame for their failings. She reminded Orica of the *cwellith*, the teacher-mothers who travelled among the caravans of her people.

Mara's housemaid Laria – a sallow young woman with a red birthmark across much of her face – served wine while Mara reminded Orica of the rules. As they set to playing, it soon became clear that Orica was outclassed. She lost half a dozen of her best pieces in an ill-advised assault across the river. Her attempt at a counter-attack was met with a wall of archers and trebuchets occupying the high ground, and she was decimated.

No matter. Her defeat had been inevitable, and it wasn't about the game, after all. This was only a stage for Mara to play out the proposal to come. It was the way of Sards to look beneath the surface of things. To her people, face value held no value at all.

'Garric told me how you met,' Mara said as she slid an assassin into an area of the board where it would serve no purpose that Orica could see.

'Harod and I owe him much for his aid,' Orica said. 'Without him and his companions, we would have been arrested by now, and likely killed.'

'I understand you let him use your cart to get to Wracken Bay, and you lost it there, along with many of your possessions.'

'The Ragged Mummer plays her tune and we cannot but dance,' said Orica. 'The Aspects give and they take away.'

Mara said nothing to that, her eyes on the board as Orica pondered her next move. 'He also told me why you were travelling to Morgenholme.'

'It was no secret. I sought my relatives, and now I learn they have been moved on again, if they were ever here at all. I despair of finding them.' She didn't try to keep the disappointment and grief from her voice. A Sard was never ashamed of honest emotion.

Mara looked sympathetic. 'What will you do?'

'That is the question I've been asking myself,' said Orica, sliding her remaining giant towards an unoccupied castle on the far left of the board, where there was a break in the line of blue counters that signified a ford in the river. 'Should I head east in search of them, with few supplies and no transport, while all around me Sards are being plucked from their homes in their hundreds? Likely I would not last a week. Should I go elsewhere, then? Perhaps to Galtis, where we could live off my music and I could forget the plight of my people?'

'Except, of course, that you wouldn't.'

'No,' said Orica darkly. Because how could she live with not knowing? Her whole *race* was being rounded up and removed from Ossia, taken east to an unknown destination and an uncertain fate. Slavery? Death? Her mind shied from the possibilities. It beggared belief that this could happen in a civilised land, that thousands of people could just disappear, with hardly a murmur from those they'd once lived alongside.

The thought made her furious. Didn't Sards belong to Ossia, too? Didn't they walk the same earth, breathe the same air? The people of this land enjoyed their craft markets and performances, stole Sard fashions and fantasised about the mysterious lives they imagined Sards had. No doubt there were plenty who were concerned and sympathetic, Ossians and Krodans alike. But when it came to it, no one spoke up for them.

Mara moved a piece and took one of Orica's. 'If you choose to leave the country, I can provide transport and safe passage to the border. If you choose to go east instead, I can at least give you a cart and horses, and supplies to replace those you have lost.'

'You are very generous,' Orica said neutrally, keeping the suspicion from her voice.

'Generosity is giving what you cannot easily afford. Garric's debts are mine, and you should be compensated for your losses.'

'Tsss. He saved our lives. But I accept nonetheless, with thanks.'

'I would ask only that you both stay with me until I can make the necessary arrangements. You will, of course, be well looked after.'

'I see,' said Orica. 'Until after the wedding?'

Mara smiled wryly. 'It would not be safe to travel until then. The roads are heavily patrolled.'

'How could I refuse such hospitality?' said Orica, and wondered if she was really being offered a choice. Mara had just confirmed that whatever the plan, it would happen at the wedding, and Orica and Harod knew enough to sell them out to the Krodans if they chose to. Mara didn't need to worry on that account, of course, but Orica understood the need for caution. Trusting strangers was an idiot's game.

Mara picked up an ivory draccen and flew it across the river. 'There is a third way. Stay and fight with us.'

Orica met Mara's eyes across the castles board. 'I am no warrior,' she said.

'Nor I, but not all wars are won by force of arms. I have heard your song, Orica. We share the same dream.'

Orica sat back, the game forgotten for a moment. She hadn't expected this. Until now she'd avoided prying, but if she was to make a choice here, she needed to know what manner of people they were.

'Why do you fight, Mara? You have wealth and comfort. The occupation has been kind to you.'

It was meant to provoke. Mara almost rose to it, but caught herself at the last moment. She gave Orica a tight smile. 'I was born to privilege, it's true, but my family's wealth was modest. I will tell you how I bought this house and obtained such riches as I have. Maybe then you will not think the occupation has been so kind.' She sipped her wine and waved at the castles board. 'But take your turn, please. I can't bear to leave a game unfinished.'

Orica moved another piece, and Mara talked as they played.

'I was considered something of a prodigy in my youth. I devoured books and learned languages so I could read more. Knowledge came easily to me. I had read Tekaput's *Disquisitions* by age seven, mastered Ith-kilian's *Uncertain Formulae* by nine. I built things, and designed what I could not build. I ran rings around my tutors in rhetoric. And I played castles, a lot. It was my unquestioned destiny to go to the Glass University, to invent wonderful things and to solve the insoluble. My name would echo through the ages, as loud as Tekaput or Chalius or Jessa Wolf's–Heart herself.'

She paused, and her eyes narrowed.

'Then came the Krodans. I was no longer allowed to study, or to take meaningful work. For years I suffered this and sought to work within their system. I was special, I thought. Surely if I tried hard enough, they would notice? But they did not. I am a woman, after all. The Acts of Tomas and Toven says that a woman of ambition is a greedy thing, a malcontent unwilling to play her role in society. But still I designed and invented, still I calculated and dreamed. I had no choice. Only death would have stopped me.'

Orica was barely paying attention to the board any more, but Mara's conversation didn't appear to distract her from the game one bit. She moved with the same precision and speed of thought whether she was talking or not.

'Finally I could bear it no longer. I had a friend who lost his leg below the knee fighting the urds during the Sixth Purge. He was a fool, caught up with dreams of joining the Knights Vigilant, but that is by the by. He came home wounded, with a crude peg in place of his shin. I saw how he suffered with sores from that ill-fitting peg; I saw how people treated a proud man like a beggar just because he walked with a crutch. So I designed a new leg for him, from leather and metal, that imitated the movement of the bones and muscles in a human foot. With a little practice, he could walk again unaided.'

'That is miraculous,' said Orica. 'I have seen such devices. Rare and expensive, but amazing nonetheless.' She frowned. 'But—'

Mara raised a finger. 'Ah. There you see. He urged me to show my invention to the world, to help others like him. But I knew no one would *allow* such an invention, if it came from a woman. I would be cried down and shamed, and a year later an identical device would appear, built by a man. Yet I could not just keep it to myself. My workshop and study were already crowded with discoveries I had been forced to hide away. I had thought of publishing some anonymously, but …' She spread her fingers helplessly. 'But I was still that little girl who dreamed of being immortal.'

'That is no bad thing to dream,' said Orica. 'It is something we have in common, I think. I would have my music played in a hundred years, a *thousand*. That would be my immortality. But, like you, I face certain obstacles of birth.'

'Then don't make my mistake. I was determined to take what control I could, so I approached a man I knew well – a man I trusted implicitly – and put a proposition to him. He would pretend to have invented the device and take a cut of the proceeds, but the lion's share – almost all of it – would come to me. I swallowed my ambition for the good of my fellow folk and gave the credit to a man.'

'You invented the Malliard Limb?' Orica asked.

She saw how the name pained Mara, and just for a moment the older woman faltered in her demolition of Orica's forces. 'The Malliard Limb,' said Mara. 'Yes. Originally it bore another name, but the community had its way in the end. They fell over

586

themselves to celebrate the new inventor in their midst. What genius! What a service he'd done for the lame and unfortunate! How they toasted him.'

'But he paid you, yes?'

'Oh, in that he was as good as his word. And he still is, hence my fortune. *He* has done me no wrong. That I did to myself.'

'You couldn't bear seeing another take the credit,' Orica said.

'I couldn't bear seeing a *man* take the credit!' Mara snapped. 'Even a good man like him! I couldn't bear to see other men make him a hero, to see him laughing among them, all content in their own cleverness while I languish with my riches, unknown and forgotten! And all because of the Krodans! Because of a damnable book scribbled down by some ill-educated preacher! They took our futures away from us, they made us *nothing*, and Ossian men let it happen!'

In her fury, she'd raised her voice. Now she calmed again, took another sip of wine and glared through the tall windows to the patio outside. 'I wish they'd invaded twenty years earlier. At least then I would not have grown up with hope. That is the worst of it.'

Orica surveyed her meagre forces on the castles board. She was heavily outnumbered now. Not even the best player could fight their way out from that.

'I grieve for your plight. I do. But I am a Sard before I am a woman. My people have been nothing for a long, long time.'

Mara looked back at her, her face frosty. 'Let them treat you like nothing for long enough, they'll start to think it's true. Look what's happening to your people now. Vanishing from the face of Ossia, and who will stop it? Not the Sards: you have too long accepted your lot. Not the Ossians, who can barely raise themselves to throw off their own shackles. Who is fighting for you?'

'Are *you* fighting for my people, then?' Orica asked sarcastically.

'We are fighting the Krodans,' said Mara, 'and a common foe makes allies of the wariest strangers.' She picked up the assassin that Orica had forgotten about. 'Or you can go east and be arrested. Or you can turn away, and go north.' She slid the assassin across the board through a hole in Orica's lines and tapped it against Orica's king, knocking him over. 'Game.'

Orica finished her wine in a single swallow. 'I will think on what you have said,' she told Mara as she got to her feet and picked up her lute. 'I must return to my song now.' She looked down at the board. Mara had barely lost a piece. 'My apologies. I didn't offer you much of a challenge.'

'That's quite alright,' said Mara. 'Nobody ever has.'

73

It was early evening by the time Aren reached Mara's house and the shadows of Morgenholme's ancient ruins lay long over the reddening city. He hurried up the tree-lined avenue to the gate with a rolling nausea in his stomach. His skin felt clammy and, despite the mild day, he couldn't seem to get warm. As he approached the gate, he checked over his shoulder, intending to walk on by if he saw anybody.

There was no one in sight. That was a little reassuring, but not much. The fear of the Iron Hand was deeply rooted; they were near-mythical forces of dread, like the Hollow Man who'd once stalked his nightmares. Even if he couldn't see them, they could still be out there, following him.

He'd insisted on being taken back to the Burned Bear, so as to offer no clue as to his friends' whereabouts. From there he'd set off in the opposite direction to Mara's. Klyssen was canny enough to have him tailed, and if he led them back to Mara's house, the Iron Guard would be on them before nightfall.

It had been a fraught few hours trying to shake off the men he knew must be there. Sometimes he thought he'd identified one, a cold thrill of recognition as he glimpsed a face he'd spotted a few streets earlier; but then they'd head off a different way, and he'd be left doubting again.

In the end, he had to accept that if the Iron Hand were tailing him, he wasn't skilled enough to know it. As a last resort, he slipped into an inn, left through the rear door and clambered over the wall of the yard. Once he'd found his way back to the street he felt a little better and, having done all he could to shake his pursuit – if there had ever been any – he headed to Mara's.

Now he was here, he took a moment by the gate to collect himself. He needed to calm down or the others would suspect something. His hands still trembled when he thought of his encounter with Klyssen. He could hardly believe what he'd said in there. Only now did he realise what a gamble he took, how high the stakes were. Only now did it start to sink in, what he'd done, what he'd committed to do.

He'd come terrifyingly close to the end today. He still had the scratch on his neck where Harte's blade had nicked it. Somehow he'd talked himself into a second chance, but there wouldn't be a third. Not for him, and not for Cade.

He rang the bell outside the gate and Clia, Mara's dour bodyguard and driver, emerged from the house. She approached along a short path that ran across the front lawn and unlocked the gate to let Aren in.

He was halfway to the house when Cade burst from the doorway and came running towards him. He barely had time to brace himself before his friend swept him up in a crushing hug.

'You made it! Gods, you had me worrying! Keel just got back, he told us what happened!'

'You know it's possible to hug someone *without* using all the strength in your body?' Aren said, with what breath he had left.

Cade dropped him back on his feet with a grin. Clia had gone into the house, passing Fen as she came hurtling out with relief writ plain on her face. She halted awkwardly as she reached them, hesitated a moment, then plunged forward and threw her arms round Aren, too.

Aren was surprised enough that he didn't react at first. Then, gently, as if she were a fragile thing, he put his arms around her. Her thin body was pressed against his; he felt the rise and fall of her ribs. A pleasant flush of warmth spread through him.

Over her shoulder, he saw Cade struggling to keep his smile. He gave his friend a helpless look. *What could I do? She hugged me.* But the guilty pleasure of her touch made it hard to feel any honest regret.

She pulled away abruptly, brushed a frond of ginger hair behind her ear. 'I'm glad you're back,' she said, without looking at him.

'It took me hours to make sure they were off my tail,' he said. 'Have you seen Grub? He was there, too.'

'Not yet,' said Cade. He was still looking suspiciously from Fen to Aren, deciding if he had grounds to sulk. She'd never embraced *him* like that.

'Did you see him get away?' Fen asked. Their eyes went to the gate now, as if expecting him to appear at any moment.

'It was chaos in there,' said Aren. 'But if any of us could give them the slip ... Well, surely it's him?' He didn't sound confident, and he wasn't.

'Aye, he's a slippy one, alright,' Cade agreed. Then, with a note of unexpected worry in his voice: 'You don't reckon they got him, do you?'

'Got who?' asked Grub, who'd appeared behind them and was craning his neck to see what everyone was looking at.

'That mudheaded Skarl who keeps following us about,' said Cade, without missing a beat.

'Pretty sure they didn't get him,' said Grub.

'Was there something wrong with the gate?' Aren asked.

'Grub thought we were trying not to be seen. Came over the wall. Is Bitterbracker back?'

'He's back,' said Fen. 'Shut himself away in his room.'

'Then all of us back!' said Grub happily, spreading his arms. 'Ha! Stupid Krodans can't catch us! Come here, friends!'

Horrifyingly, they found themselves corralled in his arms, pressed close to the sour stink of him while they squirmed and fought to get away.

'Get off me!' Cade cried. 'Ugh, you reek like the back end of a hog! Enough friendliness!' But he was laughing through his outrage; the Skarl's joy was infectious, and relief had made them all giddy. None of them had been lost, none of them condemned to the unspeakable tortures of the Iron Hand. Even Fen was laughing now. She was less wary these days, more involved. Her defences were lowering; she was becoming one of them.

Aren tried to laugh, too, but an icy cramp in his stomach turned it to a sickly smile. He saw the burgeoning happiness in her, the new light in her eyes, and it was beautiful. *She* was beautiful. But that light would be smothered soon, that happiness would die because of him. In that moment, he could hardly bear to be himself. He wanted to blurt out what had happened, the deal he'd made with Klyssen, the betrayal hidden in his mind.

But it had gone too far for that. He'd made his choice. He'd chosen Cade.

They laughed, and it was an alien sound, strange and grating. He felt himself apart from them, a stranger in the circle. Only he knew the truth here. Only he could see their adventure was doomed to fail. Only he knew there was a traitor in their midst.

'You addle-headed idiots!' Garric snapped as he came storming from the house, towering in his rage. 'Get inside, all of you! You can still be seen from the street out here!'

The laughter died in their throats as he seized Cade by the collar and propelled him towards the door. With his other hand, he grabbed Aren; but Aren, with a surge of fury, knocked his arm away hard.

Garric rounded on him, fists bunched, eyes blazing. Aren met his gaze without fear. He was long past fear of this man.

'Don't you dare to test me,' Garric warned. Aren could see the effort of will it took not to punch him. 'I told you to stay here. Instead you all went wandering into the city *without permits*, and walked right into a Krodan ambush! If just one of you had been caught, you'd have ruined everything we've worked for!'

'Well, then,' said Aren, churlishly defiant, 'it's lucky we weren't.'

Garric stared at him, unable to believe his ears. Then the rage drained out of him, and he chuckled bitterly and shook his head.

'You're something, boy. You bleat and mew about how you want the truth, how you deserve to know everything. Well, I trusted you with knowledge of our mission and you repaid me by endangering the lives of everyone here. You are all children and fools, and you don't deserve to be part of this. Now get inside.'

The force of his scorn withered Aren to silence. Cheeks hot, he lowered his head and slunk towards the house. Garric was right, and Aren hated him for it. He'd been holding back information for good reason; by treating it carelessly, they'd squandered his faith in them.

'Yes, my lord. Inside, my lord. Right away, my lord,' Cade muttered sarcastically, once they were safely out of Garric's earshot.

'Don't worry,' Aren murmured sourly. A quote came to his mind. '"Let each humiliation be paid back a hundredfold, and let no slight pass unavenged."'

It was only once he'd said it aloud that he remembered where he'd heard it. It was from the Acts of Tomas and Toven, and he'd spoken it in Krodan.

Cade gave him an uncertain look, perturbed by a tone in Aren's voice he'd never heard before, and said nothing more after that.

Aren gave Garric an hour to cool off, then sought him out again. He found him beside Vika, sitting on a stool by her bedside, dabbing her mouth with a damp cloth. A jug of honey mixed with milk stood on the side table.

He entered the room warily. Not for the first time, he noted the reverence and respect with which the old warrior treated the druidess. What did she mean to him? he wondered. A remnant of bygone days, before the Krodans came, when Ossian gods still ruled the land?

'How is she?' he asked.

'Healed, as far as the eye can tell,' said Garric, without turning around. 'When she will wake, I do not know; but I reckon it must be soon.'

Aren came closer. She'd lost weight, face gaunt and collarbones stark in the red light of evening that spilled through the window. There were more threads of grey in her long black hair than before. Her lips moved as she muttered inaudibly.

'Does she still speak of Kar Vishnakh and the Torments?'

'She speaks of nothing else. Once she spoke in a voice that wasn't hers, in a language which I swear was no human tongue. Godspit, I wish I could unhear that.' He put the cloth aside with a sigh. 'What do you want?'

Aren's eyes were still on Vika. He'd been fretting about her since Wracken Bay, but he was glad she wasn't awake to hear him now.

She had a knowing way about her, and she'd always seemed kind. She might have seen through him, and her disappointment would have been hard to endure.

'I want to apologise,' he said. Even insincere as he was, it was hard to say it.

Garric looked up at him. The scar at his throat gaped as the ruined flesh stretched. *That's where his throat was cut. That's where his soul fled his body. The Hollow Man.*

'Aye,' said Garric. 'You should.'

'I …' Aren found himself unexpectedly fighting for words. 'I was angry at you. I'm *still* angry at you. But what I did … that's not …' He cursed. He'd had a plan of what to say but it had deserted him, and he found himself saying something else instead, closer to the truth. 'I was always the leader, back home. It's hard to be kept in the dark, hard to obey without knowing the reason. I didn't … I didn't realise the trust you were putting in us, telling us about the plan. Thought I was entitled to it. I suppose … I've always had a hard time knowing my place.'

Garric grunted. 'Aye, well, sometimes that's no bad thing. And there was no harm done, this time. But you came damned close, Aren. Damned close. You could easily have been caught.'

'I know! And I want to make it up to you. Let me come with you tonight, into the ghetto.'

Garric snorted. He got up from his stool, flexing stiff knees. 'After what you just did? I reckon not.'

'I want to prove that you can trust me.'

Garric shook his head. 'You'd be dead weight in there. You can barely handle a sword.'

'I can handle one well enough. I've killed men, you know that. And I'm fleet of foot. I escaped the Krodans once today. Besides, who else would you take? Keel? He's a mess. Fen can draw a bow, but she's no use in a close fight, and in those alleys—'

'I don't *need* help,' Garric said.

'Then why are we all still here?'

'As I recall, you didn't give me much choice. I tried to send you away. You got us into a fight and brought the Iron Hand down on us.'

'That's an excuse. You could have sent us away any time after that. But you didn't, because you can't do this alone. You said it yourself: we'll all be needed when you have the Ember Blade. To carry the flame forward, spread the word, inspire the people.' Aren was breathlessly earnest now, caught up in his own argument. 'So let me show you, Garric! Whatever you thought of my father, he and I are not the same. There shouldn't be bad blood between us if we're bound to the same cause. Let it be over.'

A strange light had come into Garric's eyes as Aren spoke, something Aren couldn't read. Sizing him up, perhaps. Assessing him anew.

Trust me, he thought at Garric. *Trust me.*

At last, Garric sighed. 'Aye,' he said thoughtfully. 'Let it be over. Come with me.'

He led Aren from the room and down a corridor to Mara's study. Aren gawked at the multitude of books while Garric brought down a scroll from a shelf and flattened it out on the desk. Printed in faded ink was a crescent-shaped tangle of curving streets and alleys enclosed within a meandering wall. The legend beneath, written in Krodan, read: *A Map of the Sard Quarter of Morgenholme*. Aren studied it with amazement. Seeing the extent of the ghetto gave him a sense of how many must have lived there, how many had been taken away.

Garric jabbed a finger at the map: an unremarkable street on the east side. 'There. Third house along. That's Yarin's place. That's where he's stashed the information we need.' He straightened, surveying the ghetto critically. 'We'll find somewhere dark and quiet to climb the wall and make our way in. It's too long for the Krodans to watch all of it. There'll be patrols on the other side, watching for looters and any Sards still in hiding, but we'll be on our guard. If we're seen, we run, or fight if we have to. Get yourself killed, by all means; just don't get yourself captured. Clear?'

Aren nodded. Just like that, he had their destination; now he could take it to Klyssen. He was dazed by how quick it was, how easy. Usually Garric kept his cards close to his chest until the last minute.

Fortune favoured the treacherous, apparently. The thought made him feel sick.

'Study the map,' said Garric. 'Memorise it as best you can. If we have to run, you should know these streets.'

'I will,' said Aren.

Garric grunted. 'I have other things to arrange now. I'll come for you after sixth bell o' dark. Be where I can find you.'

He made to leave, but Aren's voice stopped him at the doorway. 'Thank you,' he said gravely. 'For giving me this chance.'

Garric regarded him with a grim face, his eyes cold. 'It's your last,' he said. 'Tonight, you'll show me what you're made of.'

The click of the latch was loud in the silence as he closed the door behind him.

Aren tried to commit the map to memory, but his thoughts were too turbulent for anything to stick. Still he couldn't get warm. Fear had chilled him bone-deep. Fear of getting caught, fear of what would happen if he *didn't* get caught, fear of being discovered afterwards. Fear of what he had to do.

Finally, he could stand it no longer. He found a quill and some blank paper and wrote a quick letter, his ears straining all the time for sounds of Garric's return. When it was complete, he folded it up and put it in his pocket, where it weighed far more than a single sheet of paper should.

Do it, he told himself.

His mouth was dry. He should burn the letter, forget the deal he'd made with Klyssen. He didn't know how he could live with himself afterwards.

He closed his eyes, saw the torture chamber again and heard Klyssen's voice: *If you betray me, I will catch you, and I will take the price of your treachery out of your friend's hide.* It was a threat Aren believed absolutely, and it terrified him.

But hadn't Aren always protected Cade, even when he didn't want to be protected? *I'll never leave you behind*, he'd said, and he meant it. So he'd take his friend home, keep him safe from the horrors that lurked just out of sight. With Garric gone, Cade would have to give up his childish dream of being a Greycloak. They'd live in his father's house in comfort, drink ale at the Cross Keys and talk about girls, and all would be as it was, or as close as he could make it. All it would cost was one man's life. One man he hated, and admired, and whom he'd just tricked into trusting him.

He was dirt. He was lower than dirt. But he'd smear his soul with all the filth the world had to give if it would keep Cade from Klyssen's clutches.

When the coast was clear he slipped out, heart pounding, and walked through the house as nonchalantly as he could. At the top of the stairs he encountered Laria, who was carrying a pile of freshly laundered bedsheets. He tensed as she spotted him, sure that she could see the guilt written on him; but she paid him no mind and he made his way downstairs.

He could hear Cade's voice from the parlour, telling Fen a story. Garric was elsewhere. Keel, as far as he knew, was still locked in his room, where he'd retreated without a word of thanks to Aren for saving his life, nor any clue as to content of the letter he'd received.

He slipped through the house, seeing nobody on the way, and left via a side door. He could hear Orica's lute faintly, coming from the garden. Harod would be with her. It was a short distance from the side of the house to a row of vine-tangled trellises fixed to the outer wall. Satisfied that nobody was in sight, he climbed the trellis and went over the wall, landing on a patch of common land on the far side.

The tension in his chest eased a little. He was out. With the looming shadow of the Old Wall behind him, a darker black against the gathering night, he made his way into the streets.

The lamplighters were out, dim and furtive figures moving through the Uplanes, shrouded in shadow. A cart clattered past, making Aren jump. There was an eerie tint to the last light of day. It was a blood moon night and Tantera held the sky alone, a black, dead eye lined with burning veins.

Well, Tantera's watch was a time for ill doings, and fitting for a night like this. Aren screwed up his courage and pressed on, keeping an eye out for anyone he recognised. If he was seen, no excuse would save him.

A few streets away was a Krodan beer-hall he remembered passing that morning. It was better appointed than most, for this was a rich district. Moneyed Krodans usually drank in their own private parlours, in an endless round of soirees; but beer-halls were men-only, and many Krodans loved the convivial warmth of their traditional watering-holes, rich or not. As in Shoal Point, there were soldiers on the door to keep the peace, in black and white livery and polished armour.

Aren paused at the corner as the beer-hall came into sight. The chill had seeped deeper into him now he was outside, and the tightness in his chest made it hard to draw a full breath. He felt like he'd been poisoned, but he'd done this to himself.

Collaborator. Traitor. Turncoat.

He remembered the men of the Canal District holding him, pulling him up, delivering him to Harte. The watchman had come within hair's breadth of murdering him and the Ossians had just stood and watched. He'd dreamed of being Krodan most of his life, until he rejected them. He'd only just started to feel proud to be Ossian; but now he knew what that was worth, too.

His teachers had been right all along. He was born of weak stock. This was no heroic legend, no bard's tale of victory. The world was more complex than that. Life and death couldn't be boiled down to a few verses.

A Krodan boy was making his way along Aren's side of the street, spinning a rattle in his hand. 'Hail to the Emperor,' Aren called.

The boy came to a stop. 'Hail to the Emperor,' he replied warily, making a closed-fist salute across his chest.

Aren took the letter from his pocket, and three decims with it. 'I have a very important task for you,' he said in Krodan. 'For the Empire. Do you understand?'

The boy straightened. You could get far with a Krodan by appealing to their sense of duty. 'What is the task?' he asked.

Aren pressed the letter into his hand, along with the coins. 'Take this letter to those soldiers there. The coins are for your trouble.'

'That's all?' the boy sounded confused and disappointed.

'That's all,' said Aren. 'Now go, in the name of the Emperor!' He shooed the boy away and retreated round the corner, where he waited long enough to see the boy hand the message to the soldiers. By the time the boy turned and pointed to show the soldiers who'd given him the message, he was already out of sight.

Let it be over, he thought darkly. The blood moon shone down on him as he hurried back towards Mara's house, and the treachery ahead.

74

The barn behind Mara's house lay in red darkness, lit only by Tantera's baleful light spilling through the cracks in the boards and an open hatch in the loft. The air, usually dry and powdery with hay husks and mouse droppings, smelled sharp and acrid and somehow threatening.

Resting at one end of the barn was an elegant cart, bearing the crest of the Master Vintner of Morgenholme. Several barrels of Amberlyne were already upon it. The rest stood on the floor next to other, smaller barrels of plainer design: the Xulan delivery brought from the docks that morning.

Garric laboured in the gloom, alone, a kerchief tied around his nose and mouth to block out the alien smell which had begun to make him light-headed and dizzy. With great care, he tipped one of the Xulan barrels and poured a viscous liquid into a funnel placed in an upright Amberlyne barrel, in a hidden hole behind the famous crest. The Xulan barrels were only two-thirds the size of the Amberlyne casks, but they were still heavy enough to make his arms tremble. It would have been steadier and safer with two, but sharing his burden wasn't a luxury he'd permit himself. This task was his alone, as it had ever been.

Once the secret compartment was full, he gently put his burden on the ground and replaced the bungs. Six done, six to go. Then he had to glue down the Amberlyne crests to complete the illusion before Wilham arrived to collect the cart and its newly prepared cargo. Later, Garric would head to the ghetto with Aren.

It would be a busy night. A hard night. But things were moving now, things were getting done, and he was full of febrile energy.

He shook out his aching arms and was about to resume work when he heard movement at the other end of the barn, a soft sound in the poisonous dark. He lifted his head and peered into the gloom.

'Mara?'

It wasn't Mara who emerged from the shadows by the door, but Keel. Garric hardly recognised him at first. He'd always walked tall, like he owned all he surveyed. Now he slunk into sight, shoulders slumped.

'I knew you were up to something,' Keel said. As he came closer, Garric saw his eyes were bloodshot and red. He was drunk, and he'd been crying. 'Knew it. All those secret trips you were making. You never used to be secretive. Not around me.'

Garric pulled the kerchief down from his face. 'What are you doing here, Keel?'

'Came looking for you. Came to talk, eh?' He sniffed. 'It reeks in here. Why are you working in the dark?'

'Wouldn't be wise to have a light,' said Garric.

Keel's eyes skated across the cart and the barrels arranged around Garric's feet. 'What's in the barrels?'

Garric would rather he'd never have known, but now Keel was here, there was no avoiding it. 'Elarite oil,' he said.

Keel frowned, too drunk to grasp it at first.

'Remember what the boys told us, back in Skavengard, about when they were down in the mine? They said they saw fire in the air and heard a thunder loud enough to wake the Aspects from their slumber. I knew then what I had to do. That was when I made my plan.' He laid a hand on one of the Xulan barrels. 'These barrels are full of elarite oil. Come near them with a flame, they'll destroy the barn, and likely half of Mara's house with it.'

Keel smoothed his hair back along his skull, shifting his weight from one foot to the other as his balance wavered. Slowly the seriousness of the situation dawned on him. 'Godspit,' he breathed. 'How did you get it?'

'Osman talked about Xulan chimericists who made fire and

thunder such as the boys had spoken of. I wondered if our friend Rapapet might know something. Seems Krodan engineers pump it out of elarite mines when they find it, and the Xulans buy it up and send it home to their chimericists, or to the Glass University for whatever they get up to there. They say the Lord Marshal of the Knights Vigilant in Mitterland has started looking into it. They're planning a new Purge, did you know? The seventh. They want to use chimericist arts to crack open the underground cities and blow the urds from their holes.'

Keel came closer, staring at the barrels, half awed and half horrified. 'And what do you mean to do with it?'

Garric met his gaze flatly. 'I'm going to kill every high-ranking Krodan in Hammerholt.'

Keel shook his head, as if trying to dislodge something in his ear that had prevented him from hearing Garric correctly. 'You're going to do *what*?'

'These barrels look like Amberlyne. If anyone tastes them, they'll find Amberlyne inside. But they're mostly full of elarite oil. Once they're delivered to Hammerholt, they'll be taken to a storeroom – I'm hoping Yarin found out which. When I get inside, I'm going to find them. Sealed, they're safe enough, I reckon; but break them open, put a torch to them … Fire and thunder like you've never seen.' His eyes glittered in the faint red light. 'The prince of Kroda will be there, Keel! The heir to the Empire. The whole of the Krodan high command in Ossia will be with him, and who knows how many barons and counts? *General Dakken*, the man who stole the Ember Blade!'

'Princess Sorrel of Harrow,' Keel breathed.

'No. I doubt she'll be at Hammerholt till the day before the wedding, and it will all be over before then. But she doesn't matter. Ottico is the Emperor's only son, and the King of Harrow has only daughters. There can be no marriage if Ottico is dead, and Harrow is so bound by its own traditions that only marriage will do.' Garric's hand became a fist. 'The alliance will collapse, the Emperor's heir lost, the Krodan chain of command in Ossia thrown into chaos.'

'And the Ember Blade?' Keel asked weakly.

'I'll not see the Ember Blade in the hands of a Krodan,' said Garric. 'I told you that.'

'You told me you were going to steal it.'

'The Ember Blade will be heavily guarded and locked in a vault that only the Master of Keys has access to. I'll never get near it, much less get it out afterwards. Stealing it was always impossible. I mean to *destroy* it.'

Keel leaned against the cart as if all the strength had gone out of him. Learning of Garric's plan hadn't filled him with excitement, as it had Mara; instead it seemed to have drained him.

His voice was quiet. 'You're not coming back, are you?'

There was something final in that, something which hit Garric in the heart. He'd known it for a long time, but to hear it said aloud, so baldly, drove the truth of it home. Hammerholt was the last place he'd ever see. No more grass, no more trees, no more fireside ales or sunlight. Never again to be touched by a woman, or to laugh, or to hear an Ossian bard tell tales of the old time in his mother tongue.

'It takes a fire to make a fire,' he said. 'Someone has to carry the flame.'

Keel was silent as he digested that. Finally he lowered his head in despair. 'I always knew you were a callous bastard, Garric, but till now I had no idea of the depths of it. You're going to start a war, aren't you? You're going to start a war and you won't even be here to see it out.'

Garric wasn't sure what he'd expected from his oldest friend, but it wasn't this. Anger flared in him. He'd just declared that he was willing to give up his life for his country! Didn't he deserve a little more than bitter disapproval?

'They're killing us by stealth,' Garric said. 'The Krodans are comfortable in occupation, and we're comfortable being ruled. Bit by bit they're erasing us, until one day there'll be no difference between us and them. So we have to hurt them! *Really* hurt them. We have to show them they can't take our land without consequences. Let the Emperor know how it feels to lose a loved one, the way so many Ossians have!'

'And then what? They'll stamp on Ossia in retaliation! They'll crush us! It'll be like Brunland all over again!'

'Good!' cried Garric. 'They'll hang people in the street in their frenzy to hunt down subversives! They'll imprison us in our villages and take away our luxuries! Families will be torn apart! Innocents will die! And then, *only* then, will Ossia realise it has to get up and *fight!*'

He was suddenly furious, thirty years of coiled rage driving the words out of him. 'We outnumber them ten to one, for Joha's sake! Just like when the urds had us under the yoke! They've divided us with fear and self-interest, setting countryman against countryman until we're so busy looking out for ourselves that there's no time to fight the *real* enemy! We need to show the people that their overlords aren't invincible, that they can be toppled if we all pull together! Because who's next after all the Sards are gone? We're sleepwalking into slavery, and somebody has to wake us up!'

'And that somebody has to be you.' The sneer in Keel's voice brought Garric up short. 'I was there in your darkest days. I walked by your side when no one else would. I know who you are even when you don't. Lie to the others if you like, but not to *me*! Don't keep your secrets from *me*!'

'And if I had told you? You would have tried to stop me!'

'That's not the point! We're supposed to be friends!'

'You wouldn't have understood. You don't understand now. I'm not *starting* a war – we've been at war for thirty years. Did you dream that change would come without sacrifice?'

Keel sagged, and a shadow fell across his face. 'And so Garric will decide, alone, the fate of uncounted thousands. Perhaps you *are* chosen of the Aspects. Only with their approval could a man act with such arrogance.'

'You're drunk,' said Garric. 'Spare me your sarcasm.'

'And when the war reaches Wracken Bay? What then?' Keel drew a letter from his jerkin, holding it loosely between two fingers. 'Mariella sent me news from home,' he said.

Garric's mood darkened further. Now he knew why Keel had sought him out. Mariella had always been a thorn in his side, ever wanting, needing, demanding. For years she'd been his opponent in the tug-of-war for Keel's affections, always trying to pull his only true friend away from him. He hadn't known the details about the Burned Bear, for Keel had locked himself away upon his return, but the letter made it all plain. That was why Keel had gone to the inn. He'd told Mariella how to contact him, the Krodans had got it out of her and they'd been waiting. She was always his weakness.

'Whatever's in there, it's a lie,' he warned. 'The Krodans wrote it for her. How else would they have known to ambush you there?'

Keel shook his head and tears gathered in his eyes. 'This is truth, I know it. Fluke is dead. The Iron Hand killed him when they went to his farm. Looking for you.'

It was something Garric had half-expected, but hoped never to hear. Fluke was no friend to him – he may well have sold them out, in fact – but it was hard news for Keel all the same.

'He was the one putting food on the table for Mariella and Tad,' Keel said. 'The money I gave them will last the winter, perhaps, but then ...' He tailed off. 'What choice do I have, Garric? I have to support them. It's what a man should do.'

Garric fought down a rising tide of irritation. In other times he'd have lent a sympathetic ear, but here? Now? Surrounded by barrels of elarite oil, with Wilham on his way and dark business tonight? Keel had been singing the same song for years, ever since he'd first left Wracken Bay. Garric knew how it pained him, but his constant indecision was galling.

'Jadrell will arrest you the moment you set foot in Wracken Bay,' Garric told him. 'The note is a trap. You know it and I know it. But if you would go, Keel, here's my blessing, for I'm tired of trying to talk you out of it. Take a ship tonight. Be with your family, for the few hours you'll get before they arrest you and you're hanged.'

Keel swayed away from the cart, gazing at him with moist, hurt eyes. 'Am I worth so little to you, now you can see the end? After all this time, you'd send me away so easily?'

At that, Garric was overwhelmed with disgust. This puling wreck of a man wasn't the warrior brother he'd fought beside these many years, against seas and whales and the might of the Krodan Empire. Skavengard had unhinged him; losing his family had broken him. Garric had given up this way once. He'd been as pathetic as Keel was. Perhaps that was why it was so unbearable to witness his best friend's fall. All he wanted was to cast him away.

'What would you have me say, Keel?' he cried. 'Go if you must, stay if you want, but whatever you do, trouble me no more! I have more important things to do than to coddle your feelings.'

Keel flinched at his words, stung. Garric almost hoped he'd respond with fury, the way he would have, once. He shrank back instead.

'I will stay,' said Keel. 'At least until tomorrow night. I'll come with you to the vintner's yard and say farewell there. At least allow me that.'

'Aye,' said Garric gruffly, pulling his kerchief back over his mouth. 'We'll say our farewells on the morrow, then.'

Keel waited, perhaps expecting something else, perhaps wanting to say more. In the end, he walked away without a word, heading unsteadily for the door of the darkened barn.

Garric watched him go, his anger fading as quickly as it came. He didn't want to deal with his friend tonight, but he couldn't let him leave on such a sour note. Before Keel reached the door, he called his name again.

'I've no craft with words,' Garric said. 'Never had. I lied to you, and I'm sorry for it. I'm sorry for Fluke and your family. I'm sorry for it all.'

Keel lowered his head. 'I'm sorry, too.'

Garric waited till he heard the barn door close, then he put Keel from his mind and returned to his task. There was much yet to do before he could rest.

75

In the deeps of the night, the temperature plummeted and the first breath of winter brought a thin ground mist to the moon-reddened tangle of the ghetto.

The wall built around the Sard quarter was more symbolic than secure, being only twice the height of a man and not even thick enough to merit ramparts. Aren and Garric were over it in moments. They dropped down to a roughly cobbled street, and at once it was as if they'd fallen from the bright living city into a silent, empty world abandoned by human life.

Aren stared at the dilapidated buildings surrounding him. Sewage, sodden and reeking, choked the open gutters. The wet, curled corpse of a dog lay nearby, rats busy about it. He'd never seen such dank and dismal squalor. Hard to imagine people had lived here, a little over a week ago. It looked like it had been left to rot for years.

'Stop gawking,' Garric snapped, and led him across the street into an alleyway. Behind the main thoroughfare was a warren of flaking brick tunnels that wound between piled hovels where Sards had once been packed, whole families to a room. Aren saw strange graffiti in an alphabet he didn't know, which reminded him of the mark on his wrist.

It was cold, but the chill in the air was nothing to the chill of treachery in his bones. His stomach ached hollowly; he'd been unable to eat at dinner. Since he'd sent his message to Klyssen, his thoughts had stampeded in an endless circle. He was terrified by what he was doing. He dreaded the look in Garric's eyes when the

Krodans fell on him, the shock and disbelief as he found himself betrayed.

But the alternative was worse. He remembered the torture chamber in the Iron Hand's headquarters. The thought of Cade's screams gave him strength to carry on.

The passageway opened into another maudlin street, cramped and mean and dripping. Garric stopped at the end, looked out and then waved Aren back into hiding. From the street ahead they heard footsteps and a lantern brightened the mouth of the passageway.

'Want one?' a voice asked in Krodan.

'Have I ever wanted one?' came the reply.

'Thought I'd ask, nonetheless. My mother raised me polite.'

'She wasn't so diligent in teaching you to follow regulations, though, eh?'

'Ah, who's to see? A small reward for a miserable duty.'

A low chuckle was his response. 'Go on, then. Give me one.'

'Really?'

'Cold as coffins out here tonight. Anything that'll warm me will do.'

Two soldiers, taking a rest from patrol. The aromatic whiff of cheroot smoke reached them.

Aren stared at Garric's back. *Cadrac of Darkwater*, he thought. Garric's true name; Klyssen had told him that. It was what he'd been waiting for all this time, the key he could use to unlock the secrets he craved.

'Saw you got a package today,' said the first voice. 'Your wife again?'

'Yes,' said the other man. 'Five pairs of good socks. She knitted them herself. My toes sing her praises.'

'Wish I had a woman who'd send me socks.'

'Socks are a poor substitute for seeing the woman I love. I haven't been back to Kroda since the spring. At least you have no one to miss.'

'Ha! That's cold comfort if ever I heard it. What fortune, to have no one who cares about me.'

Aren barely heard them. He was gathering his courage, ready

to do what had to be done, what he'd told himself he must do tonight. This would be his last chance to know the whole story, to hear it from Garric's lips before they reached Yarin's house, where the ambush waited.

'You'll find someone. You're not a bad-looking fellow. Women love a uniform.'

'Why do you think I became a soldier?' joked the first man. 'Come on, we can smoke on the hoof. Standing still's not keeping me warm, and I don't have socks like yours.'

Aren and Garric stayed hidden until the soldiers were long gone. Finally, Garric relaxed and made ready to move again. If there was any moment to force the issue, it was now, but when it came to it, Aren feared the answers he might get. Would he be better keeping his illusions, leaving his father's memory undisturbed? And yet he couldn't let this opportunity pass. He *couldn't*.

'Cadrac of Darkwater!' he blurted, in that dark tunnel in the ghetto.

There was something in Garric's stillness that was terrifying. 'Where did you hear that name?' he said, his low voice carrying the words like a threat.

'Keel told me,' Aren lied. 'He thought I deserved to know.'

'Did he now?' Garric's tone was deadly. Then, suddenly, he changed the subject. 'The patrol is gone. We've got business yet.'

He slipped up the alleyway and into the street. Aren hurried after him. Rats scurried towards the gutters, lit red by the maddened eye of Tantera. As they reached the far side of the street, Aren caught Garric up and grabbed him by the arm.

'You owe me, Garric,' he said through gritted teeth. 'My father died because of you. I loved him, and he's gone, and however it happened, some of that falls on you. Keel told me who you are, but he wouldn't speak of my father. I would hear that tale from you.'

Garric's eyes blazed. He looked up and down the street. The patrol was gone, but they were still dangerously exposed. 'Godspit, boy, you pick your times! We'll talk after!'

'It's Aren. Not *boy*.'

Garric held his gaze. Something in the way Aren said it impressed him, apparently, for there was a decision made in his eyes.

'Aye. Perhaps it is a tale you ought to hear, before it's too late to tell it. You know my shame, then; no reason to keep the rest from you. But you'll hear nothing if we're caught, so get moving.'

Garric led him along the street until they found a way into the back alleys and passageways on the other side. Aren was excited and afraid all at once. His bluff had worked; Garric assumed that if Aren knew his name, he knew the whole tale. But what was this shame he spoke of? And what story would he tell of his father? After so long wondering, he was suddenly aware he might have best left this stone unturned.

'Your father's name was Eckard when I met him,' Garric told him quietly as they hurried through the narrow ways. 'Eckard the Quick. I'd never seen anyone so fast with a blade, and never since till I saw that dreadknight at the gates of Skavengard.'

Aren felt a hole opening up inside him. Eckard the Quick. His father's true name, given him at last. The syllables landed on him like stones. His whole life, he'd never even known his father's name.

'When he came to us, he was young and full of fire,' Garric went on. 'Drunk on his own skill, getting into fights he shouldn't. He needed a direction; he'd have destroyed himself elsewhere. But Kesia found him, recognised his qualities, brought him into the fold. Would that she had not. The world might be a very different place.'

Aren brimmed with questions: who was *us*? Who was Kesia? He forced himself to keep silent. Interrupting would display his ignorance.

'I was new then, too, and of similar age,' Garric said. They reached a junction where broken pipes dripped foulness and rags hung from a windowsill. After a moment of indecision, he picked a direction. 'We became friends first, then close as brothers. Perhaps I should have been the first to see the signs, but I loved him too well. He was a man who changed his skin to suit his surroundings. When he joined us, he threw off his old life, forgetting everyone he knew, and he never looked back. I took that for devotion, but I was wrong. He adopted the role and became it. It never crossed my mind that he might change again as fast, and as completely.'

It was strange to hear his father spoken of that way. Aren had never conceived of him as a person with wants and needs, only as a parent, a myth of a man. He didn't recognise the chameleonic figure that Garric described.

'We all swore an oath to fight until death for the Ember Blade,' Garric said. 'But to Eckard, they were just words.'

Aren came to a halt as he realised what Garric had just said, braked by the shock of it. Garric, noticing that he was no longer following, turned and frowned at him down the shadowed brick tunnel. 'Keep moving! We don't have much—'

'My father was a *Dawnwarden*?' Aren blurted.

Garric was puzzled. 'Of course,' he said. 'Surely you had guessed that, since you knew that I was also a ...?' He trailed off, and a grudging respect crept onto his face. 'I see,' he said. 'Well played, Aren.'

Aren could hardly believe his ears. 'You were *both* ...? But I thought ... There have been no Dawnwardens in Ossia for centuries!'

'Not since the days of King Garam Hawkeye. But it takes more than the word of a king to break a Dawnwarden's oath. They were outlawed and forgotten by the people, which was how they liked it. They operated as a secret society after that, working behind the scenes for the good of Ossia. Rooting out conspiracies, spying on other lands, doing the things our kings and queens couldn't. When they did it best, our rulers didn't even know they were being helped. That's how it was when I joined them.'

He looked around a corner and went on. Aren followed, reeling from this new information. *Garric is a Dawnwarden.* It was impossible to square that thought with the brutal, bitter man who'd once beaten him to a pulp on a mountainside. The Dawnwardens were the stuff of legends.

Were the Dawnwardens great heroes, then? Sora had asked him once, on the night of the ghost tide when he was a boy flush with love.

Yes, he'd replied. *They were great heroes. Back when we had any.*

And here one was before him. A man Aren could never decide whether to despise or admire, a sour and grim-faced warrior with ready fists and a scornful tongue. A man who'd saved them from soldiers and dreadknights, who'd seen them through cursed Skavengard and faced down a servant of the Outsiders. A man who'd kept them one step ahead of the Iron Hand while devising a daring plan to infiltrate a heavily guarded fortress, so he could single-handedly retrieve the Ember Blade.

'We saw the invasion coming,' said Garric, his voice so low that Aren was forced to keep close to hear him, 'but Queen Alissandra was too fond of making peace to rush to war, and the lords and ladies were too concerned with their own squabbles to listen to our warnings. Still, the speed of it came as a surprise. We barely got the Ember Blade away in time.'

'I thought the Ember Blade was lost when Queen Alissandra was taken?'

'Aye, that's the story. Truth is we stole it away before the Krodans could lay hands on it. We took it to a secret keep in the forest, planning to use it to rally the country. We'd lost Morgenholme, but the Krodans didn't have the west, and the Rainlands were still free. The nobles were slow to react, but they were mustering. Losing the queen had rocked them, but we always were a country fond of changing our royalty; for some it was the best chance at the crown they'd ever have. Whoever took up the Ember Blade would have united the country, I know it. They'd have fought back. They might even have *won*.'

Aren could hear his voice darkening, filling with hatred.

'Your father had other ideas.' Aren saw his hand flexing on the pommel of his sword as he went on.

If you ever see the Hollow Man, you run. You run and you don't stop. For he's come to kill you.

'The Krodans promised we would be well treated if we surrendered. The nobility would keep their lands and wealth. If they resisted, they'd be executed, and the common folk would be enslaved. We all knew what Brunland was like when the Krodans were finished with it.

'Your father argued for surrender. He said the Krodan armies were too strong, too well organised, and we were unprepared. He was shouted down, humiliated by the others. We had taken an oath to keep the Ember Blade in Ossian hands. Surrendering it was out of the question. He left angry; he was convinced surrender was the right thing for Ossia. If we fought back, he believed it would be a ...' He trailed off as they rounded a corner and his gaze fell on what lay beyond. 'Bloodbath.'

Three dozen corpses lay there in the red moonlight, maybe four. It was hard to make numbers from that multitude of limbs and torsos. The mannequin faces of the dead stared out from the slumped pile of greying flesh. Those whose lips and eyes hadn't been eaten by rats were puffy and swollen, cheeks bloated with blood that had pooled there after their hearts stopped pushing it. They'd been slain and left naked in a heap at the corner of this tiny tumbledown square criss-crossed with washing lines. Merciful shadow hid the worst of it, but Aren could still see pinpricks of green shining amid the horror: the dead eyes of the Sards, still gleaming unnaturally bright even in death.

'Reckon they didn't go as quietly as the Krodans hoped,' Garric rumbled. 'Or they tried to hide, and failed.'

'But ...' Aren couldn't find the words. 'They just left them out here ... like animals ...'

'Aye. Our beloved overlords behave less admirably when there's no one else to see. But you knew that already.'

Aren had no response to that. The inhumanity of such slaughter, the indignity of it, took away his breath. The flies were at rest now, but no doubt the maggots were at work, and the rats scampered and gnawed restlessly. The stench made him sick.

Then his eyes narrowed and his heart jumped. He leaned forward to see. There, in the shadow, among the dead. That face! He knew that face!

Eifann.

Panic bloomed in his breast. How could the boy be here? Had the Krodans found him? Had he been dragged to Morgenholme and killed?

He ran to the bodies, rats scattering at his feet, his arm across his mouth. Where he thought he'd seen Eifann was an elderly man instead. Had it been over there, then? Hard to tell in the tangle of corpses.

He cast about desperately. He'd *seen* him! He knew it. That wild hair, that dirty face.

'What's got into you?' Garric said, dragging him back. 'There's no time for this!'

'I saw someone! A boy I knew!'

'You saw nobody,' Garric said. 'And better not to find them if you did. You've already proved more trouble than you're worth tonight. Keep your mind on the job!'

Aren, still unable to find anyone who looked even vaguely like Eifann among the hellish mass, let himself be drawn away. As he went, he looked down at his wrist and the curling symbol there. *Sardfriend*. He'd been marked by that boy, claimed by him. Perhaps his mind had merely conjured him from the frightful dark.

Sardfriend. He was anything but. There was only one man he knew who could hurt the people that committed this atrocity, and Aren meant to betray him.

'What did he do?' Aren said, pulling free of Garric's grip. 'Tell me now, before we go further. What did my father do?'

Garric cursed, torn between the desire to spit up the rest of his tale and the desire to keep moving. But Aren wouldn't let him go now. He'd hear the end of it, in this dripping, blood-fouled yard behind the squalid ghetto tenements, witnessed by the dead.

'Very well,' Garric said at last. 'For both our sakes, you'll know it all. One night your father came to me, in my rooms in the keep. He was fevered with nerves and wanted me to go hunting with him right then, in the dark. I refused. It was a ruse to get me away, and I knew it. Then he told me what he'd done. The others couldn't see past their oath, he said. They'd damn Ossia to slavery. So he'd taken matters into his own hands, made contact with a young Krodan captain named Dakken and told him where the Ember Blade was. They'd be upon us at any moment. As my friend, he wanted to spare me.'

Aren had sensed it was coming, but it still felt like a punch in the gut. 'My father? My *father* gave up the Ember Blade?'

Garric didn't seem to hear him. His eyes were far away, his jaw tight as he spoke. 'He thought I'd see it his way. I didn't. I should have run him through on the spot, but my first thought ... my first thought was to warn the others, to save the Ember Blade. I cursed his name, shoved him aside and made for the door, but... well, there was a reason they called him Eckard the Quick.'

He lifted his chin, showing Aren the horrific scar running across his bearded throat.

'This is your father's mark,' he said, his phlegmy voice low with loathing. 'He drew his blade across my throat from behind.'

Aren shrank from the sight. Now at last it made sense, why Garric hated him so. And gods, Aren didn't blame him. Didn't blame him at all.

'He did that?' Aren asked weakly.

'Aye, he did. Left me bleeding out on the cellar floor. But your father was a swordsman, not a footpad. Didn't know how to do it right. Lot of muscle in the neck; you need to really saw to get through it. He cut my throat, but not deep enough. I tied a cloth round my neck to staunch the blood as best I could, then went to warn the others, or to get help ... I don't know. I blacked out, I reckon, maybe more than once. Doesn't matter. By the time I got downstairs, the Krodans were already there.'

He glared into the middle distance as he spoke, struggling to keep the pain of the memory in check.

'I heard the others being slaughtered. Dawnwardens are worth five Krodan soldiers, but we're no dreadknights. They had numbers far beyond ours and surprise on their side. I couldn't fight, could barely stand. All that was left was escape. So I staggered out into the woods, and when I could go no further, I fell. That's where I thought it would end.'

He took a shuddering breath. Aren was shocked to see how his tale wracked him. *He survived. That's what's killing him. That's why he couldn't speak of my father. Because if I knew the truth of that, he'd have to tell me all of this. That he was a Dawnwarden. That he failed in his duty. That he lived while the others died.*

When Garric had steadied himself, he spoke again. 'I woke in the care of a druidess. She found me, healed me, brought me back from the brink. She said the Aspects still had a task for me, and they were not willing to let me go just yet. When I was healed, she sent me back into the world again.' His troubled brow eased as he remembered her. 'Her name was Agalie-Sings-The-Dark.'

He lowered his head then, and shadow covered his face. 'Your father changed his name and hid, took on a new life paid for with Ossian freedom and Krodan riches. No doubt he heard that I'd survived, and knew I'd swear to kill him, but I never found him and he'd put the Ember Blade far beyond my reach. I did what I could to fight for Ossia, as the Dawnwardens' oath compelled me. Then I got word that the Ember Blade was coming back and was to be placed in a Krodan hand. That set me on the course that brought us both here.'

He raised his head and squared his shoulders, and Aren thought he looked taller somehow.

'So now you know, Aren. Who I am, and who your father was.'

So now I know. The man he'd loved and worshipped was also a cut-throat and a coward, who'd given up Ossia's greatest treasure and tried to murder his best friend. It sounded impossible, and yet there was no lie in Garric's voice, and it made sense of everything where there had been no sense before.

Answers will come in their own time, Vika had told him once, *and when they do, you may wish you'd never asked.*

'You see now why I kept it from you?' Garric asked.

'I do,' he said. 'And why you despise me. You see my father in me.'

'More than you know,' said Garric. 'The good and the bad. For I loved him well, before I hated him utterly.'

'I was never highborn,' Aren said. His mouth tasted like ashes. 'All I had was given me by the Krodans, for what my father did to *you ...*' He looked up at Garric with amazement dawning on his face. 'And yet after all that you still came to my aid when I was in danger.'

'I swore an oath. I keep my promises.'

As simple as that. As if it hadn't been torment.

'And ... the other Dawnwardens? Did any of the others ...?'

'I am the last of them,' he said. 'For more than a thousand years they have guarded Ossia and kept watch over the Ember Blade, but they will die with me. Perhaps it is for the best. Too long the people of this land have relied on others to fight their battles. They wait for heroes to save them, when they ought to be saving themselves.'

'No!' Aren cried, louder than he'd intended. Garric made an irate gesture to hush him. 'No,' Aren said again, more quietly but with no less force. 'This land *needs* heroes. It took Jessa Wolf's-Heart to lead the uprising against the urds. Our people have the will to fight, I know they do, but they need someone to show them how! If we had the Ember Blade ... if *you* had it ...'

Aren trailed off as he realised what he was saying. Garric's eyes were dark beneath his brows, his gaze penetrating.

'Aye, well,' he said at length. 'There's a long road to *if*, and we still have business tonight. Enough talk. Yarin's house is just down the way.'

With one last glance at the pile of bodies, Garric slipped out of the square and down another alleyway. Aren almost reached out to stop him, but he hesitated and the chance was gone. He followed instead, plunging back into the tight brick passageways, where Tantera's nightmarish light only penetrated at slanted angles. Garric was moving at speed now and Aren could barely keep up.

Stop him. Take it back. Tell him.

But he couldn't. To do so would cost him Cade. Even his best friend would shun him when he knew what he'd done. Aren would be cast out at the very least, if he wasn't killed by Garric in his rage. He'd lose it all.

All he had to do was nothing. So much easier to do nothing than something. And then he and Cade would be free, and all would be as it had been. Except that Garric would be caught and tortured and killed. The last Dawnwarden of Ossia, Vika's champion, shown to her in a vision by the servants of the Aspects themselves.

Garric was a hero. Maybe Ossia's only hero. Blinded by his anger and resentment, he hadn't seen it till now.

So what did that make Aren?

'Down this way,' said Garric, disappearing into a gap between buildings. He paused outside a narrow wooden door, hardly visible in one of the walls. 'That's Yarin's place.'

Aren's chest tightened. There was no more time to deliberate. The Iron Hand were beyond that door. Garric had survived one act of treachery, but he wouldn't survive this one. It would take two generations of betrayal to lay him low.

Like father, like son.

Garric put his hand to the door.

Stop him!

His throat had closed up. He couldn't bring the words of warning to his mouth, couldn't condemn himself to that disgrace, that pain.

Quietly, Garric turned the handle. The door wasn't locked.

Stop him!

He dared not. It would mean the ruin of him.

Stop him!

'Are you ready?' Garric asked, and he pushed the door.

Aren's hand clamped around his forearm. The door stopped moving, a finger's width from the jamb. Aren was white-faced and sweating, but his eyes were steely.

'Close the door,' he whispered.

Slowly Garric closed the door, slowly released the handle. Never once did he break Aren's gaze. When he spoke, his voice was a wolf's growl. 'What's in there, boy?'

Aren let him go and swallowed down the urge to be sick. 'Krodans,' he said. It was all he could manage.

Garric loomed over him in the dark, filling the passageway. His eyes were cold as coal in the red shadow, his hand on the hilt of his dagger. 'You made a deal,' he said.

It took every ounce of Aren's willpower not to turn and run for his life. 'They caught me,' he said. 'I had to ... I did it for Cade, I ... I didn't want anyone else to be hurt ...' But they were weak excuses, and he knew it. He lowered his gaze. 'I made a deal.'

'Small wonder you were so eager to come with me tonight. Fool that I am, I told you exactly where we were going. Were I to step through that door, I'd find a dozen Iron Guardsmen with crossbows ready, is that it?'

'I ... I suppose ...'

'Then perhaps they'll find you a better target!' Garric snarled.

With that, he seized Aren by the front of his jacket, pulled open the door and shoved him into the dark room beyond.

Aren stumbled inside with a shocked cry, his arms reflexively thrown up in front of his face, instincts screaming in expectation of the volley of bolts punching into his torso. But he only staggered to a halt, and nothing struck him. When he lowered his arms, the room was empty but for a few pieces of furniture tipped on their sides against the wall. He stared in bewilderment.

'In thirty years I've seen a lot of traitors and turncoats, boy,' said Garric from the doorway. 'You're not half as subtle as you think.'

'You *knew*?' Aren gasped.

'Suspected. Enough not to credit your sudden desire for atonement this evening. I thought it wise to give you a false address for Yarin's place. Had you memorised the map as I told you, you'd have known we were nowhere near the spot I pointed to.'

He stepped into the room, pulling his dagger from its sheath, and closed the door behind him. 'It's just you and me now. I knew you'd show your true colours sooner or later, Aren son of Eckard.'

Aren's eyes went to the blade in Garric's hand. Every fibre of his body urged him to flee or draw steel to defend himself. He did neither. He'd dreamed of being a man of honour, but he'd shamed himself instead. For all his airs, he was a wretch lower than Grub. The least he could do was face his end like a man. Wild with fear though he was, he lifted his chin and put his arms down by his sides.

Garric approached until they were face to face, the dagger point between them. 'Well,' said Garric. 'There's courage in you after all.'

'I ... I was wrong,' said Aren. He was trying not to cry, but tears gathered anyway: the final humiliation. 'As my father was wrong before me. I didn't understand. Please keep Cade safe. He had no part in this.'

A handful of heartbeats passed, each one an agony, until Aren could have screamed for the thrust to end it. Then Garric seized his left hand and drew the blade across it in one quick, searing stroke.

Aren hissed with pain, staring in confusion as a line of blood welled in his palm. Garric slowly, deliberately drew the dagger across his own left palm, then sheathed it.

'In thirty years I've seen a lot of traitors and turncoats,' Garric said again. 'And I've seen a lot of people make mistakes, and make up for them. You were tempted, but at the last you stayed strong. You could've let me step through that door, but you didn't. That's who you are, Aren. You're a better man than your father was. And I reckon you won't make a mistake like that again.'

He clapped his bloodied hand into Aren's, and gripped it there.

'Swear to me!' he said fiercely. 'Swear you'll fight for Ossia for the rest of your days, that you'll never rest till this land is free. Swear, as I give your life back to you, that you will give it for Ossia when the time comes! Swear!'

Tears rolled down Aren's cheeks. At last he recognised the purpose he was meant for. The pain of his stinging hand was nothing in the white heat of that. 'I swear,' he whispered. 'I swear it!'

Garric clasped his other hand round the nape of Aren's neck and pulled him into a rough embrace. Aren clutched him and sobbed, and Garric held him like a father as all the spite and hate and anger came tumbling out of him, carried on scalding tears.

When his crying had calmed, he felt emptied and pathetic, raw and new.

'Reckon the others don't need to hear about any of this, do you?' Garric said. 'Wouldn't serve our cause any.'

Aren nodded mutely. Garric let him go and he stepped away, wiping his nose with the back of his hand.

'Well, then,' said Garric, gruff again. 'Let's get to it.'

Aren followed him up a creaking set of stairs, walking in a haze of unreality and disbelief. He'd believed Garric would kill him; instead he found acceptance. He understood in some dim way that Garric's loathing of him had been waning since he beat him on the slopes of the Ostenbergs, but he'd never expected this.

Garric had tested him. Had he failed, he would have been slain. But Garric would rather have his loyalty than his blood, and Aren was bound to the cause now, by ties which no promise from the Iron Hand could break.

This is the man I was about to betray, he thought.

They came to a tiny bedroom. Garric pulled aside a wooden pallet bed and searched the floor beneath. With a grunt of satisfaction, he found a loose board and lifted it. From the hole beneath he drew out a large tin, which he opened with his thumbs and looked inside. Aren saw his shoulders slacken, but whether it was relief or disappointment he couldn't tell.

'Is it there?' Aren asked from the doorway, his voice still thick with the memory of tears.

Garric turned to him with the face of a man who'd stumbled upon treasure beyond his wildest dreams. 'It's all here,' he said. He put his hand into the tin, turning over papers. 'Plans, schedules ...' He tugged out a ring of keys and held it up in amazement. 'God-spit, Yarin. You did it!'

He gathered the papers together, shut the tin and slipped it in his pack. When he got to his feet, there was fire in his eyes.

'That's the final piece, Aren! We need nothing else. Before the sun has risen thrice more, we will deal the Krodans such a blow that the bards will sing of it till the death of days! Back to the others, quickly! There are preparations to be made!'

He strode to the doorway, where Aren was standing, and stopped before him. 'Are you with me, Aren?'

Aren straightened, firmed with fresh conviction. No more uncertainty, no more questioning. He knew his answer now.

'Yes,' he said. 'I'm with you.'

76

When Aren woke, the sun was already bright beyond the curtains. He'd slept late, having gone to bed at dawn, and he lay there for a while, his eyes tracing the pattern on the curtains, thinking of nothing. His mind was at ease, more so than it had been for a very long time. Today, he knew exactly who he was.

He turned in his bed, soft sheets rustling, and found that a cold breakfast of ham and hard-boiled eggs, pastries and fruit had been left for him on a side table. The sight of it made him ravenous, and he wolfed it down before heading to the door to seek Garric out. He had to know if the change he felt was real, if the oath he'd sworn last night meant as much to Garric as it did to him.

He found him with Mara in her study, poring over the plans they'd obtained last night. The door was open and Aren could hear them as he approached.

'Incredible,' Mara was saying. 'They've only just begun to explore what's down there. Look, that's where they broke through!'

'It was the urds' seat of power in the First Empire. Their greatest fortress.'

'I know that, Garric,' she said testily. 'And the new one was built on its foundations. But urds build underground more than they do over it. I'd give anything for a map of *that*.'

'There's an engineer's diagram here. Is that what you're looking for?'

'No. That's a cave system. It comes off a mountain lake, I think.

Maybe how they get their water in? But look at the mark – this must be two hundred years old! How did Yarin obtain all this?'

'Perhaps one day you'll get the chance to ask him.'

Garric saw Aren in the doorway and beckoned him in. 'Come and see,' he said. 'It's only right, as you had a hand in finding them.'

Aren glowed with pleasure. Where before he'd found secrecy, now he was included. He saw the slightest look of puzzlement in Mara's eyes, but she said nothing.

The amount of information was bewildering. He saw timetables, accounts ledgers and strange diagrams which Mara explained were floorplans. Some were original documents, some laboriously hand-copied, others little more than scrawled notes. It was a muddle to Aren, but Mara had made some sense of it. She only had to read something once to remember it verbatim, and Aren marvelled at her ability to connect the details in her mind. Having studied the papers, she knew when and where feasts were to be held, and who was attending, and what was to be served; she knew the schedules of cleaning staff, and the names of the various valets, butlers and mistresses who ran each division of the complex network of staff. Krodans were notorious organisers, and for an event as important as a royal wedding, everything had been planned out on paper far in advance.

'This is where the cart will be unloaded once we enter the keep,' said Garric, pointing to a courtyard inside the main wall. 'The barrels of Amberlyne will be taken to a storeroom. We suspect it will be this one, near the kitchens and just below the feasting halls, where it will be convenient to serve the prince. But even with all the information we have, some things are far from certain.'

'Why do you care where the wine is going? Where is the Ember Blade?' Aren asked impatiently.

'Every detail is important, Aren,' said Mara.

'I'll slip out in servants' livery during the unloading,' Garric said. He pointed to a room on another map. 'Then I'll head to the vault, and the Ember Blade.'

'So how will you get there?' Aren asked. He didn't fully under-stand how the floorplans fitted together, but he knew enough to realise that there were many chambers and levels between the vault and the courtyard.

'That's what we're working out,' said Mara. 'Come back later, and it may be we have an answer for you.'

Aren took the hint. His curiosity was slowing them down, and it was best not to outstay his welcome, when welcome had come so rarely till now. He thanked them both and headed downstairs, looking for Cade.

Last night in the ghetto, Overwatchman Klyssen and his men had lain in wait for a fugitive who never arrived. At some point, Klyssen must have realised that his gamble hadn't paid off, that the boy he'd released wasn't going to bring him Garric. He'd have been made to look foolish in front of his men, and he'd be murderously angry.

Aren took no satisfaction in humiliating the man. He'd made a mortal and powerful enemy last night, who'd show no more mercy or compromise to him, or to any of the others. Klyssen wouldn't rest until he had his revenge.

If you betray me, I will catch you, and I will take the price of your treachery out of your friend's hide.

There were many reasons he'd made that deal with Klyssen, but foremost among them was Cade. His desire to save their friendship, to save *him*, had almost caused him to make a tragic mistake.

This time, he was determined to do it the right way.

Aren found him out in the garden, sitting with Fen in one of its many nooks, whittling. Orica's voice drifted up through the autumnal trees as Aren made his way towards them.

Said the king, 'For this heresy, I'll see you burn.
I say destiny's charge is not easy to turn.'
But the seer shook his head. 'Sire, you have much to learn,
For the urds said the same in their day.'

Now the king stands at his window and watches the sea
And he knows that his castle's no sanctuary
As he waits for the truth of the seer's prophecy
And the storm that will sweep him away.

Occupied with their work, they didn't see him approach. Cade made a noise of frustration as he hacked at the piece of wood in his hands; Fen looked over at it and stifled a laugh.

'I thought you were a carpenter's son?'

'Aye, I am. And never has an apple fallen further from the tree, I reckon.'

'Apparently not,' she said, amused.

Aren couldn't help a pang of jealousy at the easy way they had with each other. Cade looked up and saw him. 'Hoy, Aren! Come see what I made.'

Aren took the puzzling lump of wood. He looked at it from all sides. 'Is it a horse?' he asked.

'It's a she-warg!' Cade said. 'Like the one we hunted that time.'

'Oh! A wild pig, then.'

'It was a wild pig?' Fen cried, turning to Cade. 'You told me it was a she-warg!'

'It was a *big* wild pig,' Cade said sheepishly.

Aren smiled, but their casual joviality felt forced. 'Cade, will you talk with me?'

Cade had that half-joking smirk on his face he got when he was nervous. 'That sounds serious.'

Fen slid off the bench and picked up her bow. 'I should practise. I'm getting rusty.'

Aren gave her a grateful look as she slipped away. Cade shuffled awkwardly in his seat. 'So ...?'

'So,' said Aren. It was always hard to start these things. 'I had a close call yesterday. Really close.'

'Aye,' said Cade. 'You said. You only just gave that watchman the slip. Sounded pretty hairy.'

'It was,' said Aren, though that wasn't the close call he was talking about. 'And it got me thinking about what we said in the market. If I'd died jumping off that building, or been killed by a watchman ... Well, I wouldn't like that to have been the way we left it.'

Cade nodded. 'I've been thinking the same,' he said. For once he wasn't making a joke of it, which Aren was grateful for.

'After we escaped the camp at Suller's Bluff, I thought we had the whole world in front of us. We could go somewhere, make a new start. But then we got caught up in Garric's cause, and I wasn't sure if I wanted that, but I *did* want to know about my father so I stayed and … And then I thought we might be able to go *back* to Shoal Point so it really could be like it was, but …' He trailed off as he saw the bewildered expression on Cade's face and realised he was rambling. 'What do *you* want?' he said at last.

Cade looked surprised. 'Can't remember the last time you asked me that.'

Aren felt a pang of shame. 'I'm sorry, Cade. I always called all the shots, didn't I? Sometimes it's hard to shake off old habits. But we're not children any more.'

'Reckon we ain't,' Cade said. He seemed thoughtful for a moment, then raised his head and said firmly 'I want to see this out. That's what I want. I want to be part of something. These people are our friends now. Aspects forgive me, I'm even getting fond of Grub, for all that he smells like a donkey's arse.'

'You know what that means, though?' Aren said. 'You know the Iron Hand will be after us every step of the way, and if they catch us they'll do worse than kill us? Have you thought about that? *Really* thought about it? Because this isn't one of your tales where you know the hero will win because they're the hero. There's a good chance we'll all end up like Osman.'

'I've thought about it,' said Cade. 'Thought about it a lot.'

'Doesn't it scare you?'

'Course it scares me. But the idea of ending up back in Shoal Point scares me worse. People like Garric are fighting for something *true*. Even if I were an actor, like I dreamed, I'd just be telling stories other people wrote down. Here, we're writing our own!'

Aren couldn't help a smile at that. Cade was only ever this eloquent when he'd rehearsed it in his head. He *had* been thinking about it, then, and he made this choice with open eyes. That was all Aren needed to know.

'I should have listened to you from the start,' he said.

'*Now* you realise,' said Cade, with a grin.

'Things are changing, aren't they? Like you said. But that doesn't have to be a bad thing. Maybe … maybe things will be better?' He was frustrated at how clumsy it sounded when spoken aloud. Why was it so difficult to put feelings into words? 'All we have to do is stick together. You and me.'

'Aye,' said Cade. He was rummaging for words himself, as awkward as Aren when it came to making up. 'What I said in the market, about Fen … That ain't fair. Shouldn't have done that.'

'It's all well. You love her.'

'It ain't that simple, though. I don't know if I do.' Aren had reached across the gap between them, and now Cade was eager to reach back. 'You don't say it, but I know what you think. I get caught up in a girl and throw myself at her, like with Astra, and Perla before her, and Chenny, and—' He saw the smile growing on Aren's face. 'Aye, I know, I'm a hopeless case. And how many of them did I kiss? Not a one.' He shrugged. 'I was jealous of you and Sora. Didn't even like her much and I was still jealous. Maybe I just wanted a girl to be mine for once. Reckon sometimes I get tired of being the funny one.'

'People *like* you, Cade. You don't need to try so hard.'

'Ain't so easy to shake old habits, though, is it?'

Aren had to give him that.

'Point is …' said Cade. 'Point is, if you like Fen, too … well, may the best man win, that sort of thing.'

Aren laughed. 'She's not a prize to be won, Cade. I'm not sure she likes either of us as anything more than friends. If she does, I reckon she'll tell us.'

'You know what I mean, though.'

'I do. And I'm grateful to you for saying it. But listen: it's you and me, alright? First and always. Let's not allow a girl to get in the way of that.'

They clasped forearms and shook, and that was an end to it. Aren felt the happy relief of resolution. Apologies started hard, but more often than not they turned out to be easier than expected.

A thought occurred to Aren then. 'Hoy, did you ever write to your da and ma? To let them know you're safe?'

Cade looked guilty. 'Never had the chance. Suppose I could have posted from Wracken Bay, but … you know, me and letters.'

'Want to do it now? I'll help you write it. And maybe Mara can post it.'

'What if the Iron Hand are still watching Shoal Point, though? I mean, they might see the letter.'

'So? They'll only know it came from Morgenholme, and I'm pretty sure they know we're here already.' In fact, he was certain of it. 'Come on. You can tell your da you've joined the Greycloaks, if you like.'

'There's no such thing as the Greycloaks.'

'Your da doesn't know that.'

A smile spread across Cade's face as he considered it. 'Aye, why not? It ain't like it matters. I mean, we're never going back, are we? Not till the Krodans are gone.'

'No. We're never going back. Only forward.'

Cade slapped him on the arm, and in that moment, it all felt just as it ever had. 'Ha! Well, then. Let's go and write that letter!'

77

'To our great venture,' said Mara, glass held high, 'and to freedom!'

They all raised their glasses to that, and Aren and Cade cheered. Mara sat down and they fell back to eating, except for Grub, who'd never stopped. Tonight was for celebration, and they ate and drank as if their victory was already assured. Tonight, they were seeing off two of their own; one to go to glory, and one to go home.

Mara's dining room was spotless, grand and thirty years out of date. There were none of the stern, clean Krodan lines here. The curtains were heavy and rich, the walls hung with tapestries and papered with busy designs. A fire burned in an oversized inglenook hearth and the tableware was a mismatched mix of wood, stone, glass and pottery. It was a thoroughly Ossian room, frozen in time on the eve of the country's fall to the Krodans.

Aren, wine-warmed and full, leaned back contentedly and surveyed the table. Fen was poking fun at Grub, with Cade egging her on. Mara, usually cool and stately, looked excited. Orica and Harod sat side-by-side, Harod eating with precise formality, Orica laughing and joking with everyone around her. Even Keel appeared to be in good spirits; quieter than usual, but more like himself. His choice made, Keel had found some peace.

Garric was across the table from Aren, the man he now knew as Cadrac of Darkwater, the last Dawnwarden. He was drinking little, for he still had work ahead. The revelations about his father had given Aren a lot to think about; but where Garric was concerned, he'd forgiven all. The wrongs visited on Aren felt petty compared to the wrongs Garric had suffered, and yet he'd still risked everything to save the son of his mortal enemy. All because he'd made a promise.

Would Aren have done the same in his shoes? He didn't know. But he wanted to be the kind of man who would.

'A moment, if you please!' Harod called. 'Milady has something to say.'

'A song!' cried Cade as Orica rose from her chair. His cheeks and nose were red with wine.

Grub groaned. 'If Grub hear that song about whatever it's about one more time, he going to stab himself in the eye with his fork.'

'Tsss. Not a song,' Orica said, smiling at them both. 'Though you may be out of luck if you want to silence me, my Skarl friend. Neither my song nor I are going anywhere.'

Grub, who was back to gnawing on a ham bone, raised his lip and snarled at her like a dog.

'Strange fortune brought us together, yes?' said Orica, addressing them all. 'But the Ragged Mummer's ways are often strange. My people are being taken from this land, and none know where or why. I cannot learn any more without help; nor can I turn my back on what is happening here. We do not know what you intend, but we know we must see the Krodans thrown from Ossia if there is to be any hope of helping my people. Your cause has become ours, and so we humbly ask: will you have us?'

'Aye!' Cade cried excitedly, then wilted as he realised it probably wasn't his place to decide. 'Well, that's my vote, anyhow.'

Mara was on her feet again. 'I believe our overenthusiastic friend speaks for us all. There is much work ahead, and we have need of stout hearts and strong minds, sharp wits and sharp swords. You are welcome.'

The others cheered and thumped the table, except Grub. Even Keel clapped. Orica bowed with a flourish, then Harod got up and gave a considerably stiffer bow of his own.

'Nobody cheered for Grub when Grub joined,' Grub grumbled, rolling his eyes.

'Don't reckon anyone actually asked you to,' Cade said.

'Oh!' said Grub, brightening. 'Well, that explain it then.'

At last they were all seated again, and Aren smiled at Orica across the table. She smiled back, and her eyes went to his wrist, where Eifann had left his mark. *Sardfriend*, it said; and so he was.

'My father used to tell me "After every greeting comes a good-bye,"' said Keel. He'd drunk a lot, though he wasn't yet drunk. 'He never did take much joy in life. I'm not one for farewells, but we've seen too much together for me to leave without a word.' He gathered himself; it wasn't easy for him to speak like this. 'My family needs me,' he said. 'I have to do right by them, and that means leaving you behind. I'll see Garric to his destination tonight, and after that I'll be sailing on the morning tide to Wracken Bay. I won't be coming back.'

'One last journey,' said Garric. 'We'll end it side-by-side, as we began.'

Keel nodded gravely and drained his glass.

They offered their condolences and support, and the conversation gradually moved on. The one thing they couldn't talk about was Garric's mission, for even though Harod and Orica were with them now, it was too soon to trust them with everything. They'd know it all in a few days, when Garric returned with the Ember Blade.

So Garric would go to Hammerholt alone, and it was Garric's name that would be sung in years to come. Once that thought had enraged Aren, but no more. The battle ahead would be long and there'd be many opportunities to distinguish himself. He'd have to earn his glory. This was Garric's tale, not his.

The door to the drawing room opened and Laria hurried in to whisper in Mara's ear. Her urgency alerted them all, and they looked to Mara for the news.

'Peace,' she said as she saw their worried faces. 'It is nothing ill. Quite the contrary, actually. It seems your druidess friend is awake.'

There was a moment of shocked delight; then, with a screech of chairs, Aren, Cade, Fen and Garric hurried out of the room. Grub, who'd demolished his meal already, reached across to scrape the remains from Aren's plate onto his own.

78

Aren and Cade burst into Vika's room to find her sitting up in bed, ruffling the fur at Ruck's throat, looking thinner than before but otherwise entirely well. Aren cried out with joy at the sight. Only now did he realise how keenly he'd missed her.

They rushed over to hug her, and she laughed in surprise while Ruck whirled about the bed barking. Finally, the hound jumped up on the bed and shoved her muzzle into the circle of their embrace, so as not to be left out.

'I would have come back earlier if I'd known I'd get such a welcome!'

'We're just glad you're back at all,' said Aren. The uncertainty of her condition had worn on them these past weeks. Osman's death was still fresh in their minds, and losing Vika would have been harder still. Her return now felt like a good omen.

Fen had arrived and was standing just inside the doorway, with Garric behind her, a rare smile on his lips.

'And how are you all?' Vika asked them. She looked from Aren to Garric and, in that uncanny way she had, she knew something had changed. 'Much has happened, I see.'

'You'll hear it all in time, no doubt,' Garric said. 'But we're all well, more or less.'

'It's good to see you, Vika!' Cade said, and squeezed her again until Ruck licked his cheek and he let her go, flailing at his face with a groan of disgust.

'She's just being affectionate,' Vika told him.

'I wish her affection didn't come with so much dribble.' Cade wiped his cheek on his sleeve.

Fen approached the bed awkwardly. 'I made this for you while we were on the ship.' She held out an expertly carved wooden figure, the size of a thumb. It was a likeness of Sarla, the Red-Eyed Child, with her hood far back on her bald head. Even at that small scale, Fen had managed to capture the menacing stare of the Lady of Worms.

'I asked her to spare you, many times,' Fen said, embarrassed.

Vika smiled as she took the figure with both hands. 'And so she did. For Sarla brings mercy as well as death, and sometimes both together.' She nodded to Fen. 'My thanks. I will wear it among my charms, to remind me.'

Fen blushed and stepped away.

'You spoke in strange tongues while you slept,' Garric told her. 'Where have you been, in your dreams?'

'Where have I been?' Vika said, becoming distant. 'Aye, there's a tale. I roamed further into the Shadowlands than ever I've gone before. I saw castles in the air that crumbled to rubble even as they rebuilt themselves in new forms. I saw lakes of fire and ice, and beasts that held no shape. I saw cities under a black sun, aswarm with ghosts, and streets that parted before me like waves before the bow of a ship. In time, I came to the gates of Kar Vishnakh, the great citadel that guards the Outsiders in their prison, which hangs suspended by chains over an abyss without end. I knocked upon the gates and was given entrance, to where the Torments walk in clinking robes, and the screams of the tortured echo from the depths.'

'And what did you learn there,' Garric asked gravely, 'among the Torments?'

'Much and more, and none of it good,' said Vika, her eyes intense behind her curtain of hair. Ruck whined and put her head on her mistress's lap. 'The Divide between this world and the Shadowlands is thinner than it has been since the days of the Second Empire, and it is thinning by the day. This is no natural waning. Something, somewhere is causing this. Chaos grows, and grows close. Urd shamen are uncovering lost arts in the lowlands. In the south, the chimericists, so long only charlatans and fakes, have learned how to breathe life into their creations. The Theocracy of the Incarnate tightens its grip to the west and the witches of Skara Thun find their scattered bones tell the truth more often than ever before. I fear the dreadknights are only a glimpse of what is to come. Something stirs, and brings the doom of the world with it. We are no longer fighting for Ossia. We are fighting for *everything*.'

Aren felt a chill seep through him as she spoke, and it seemed to him that the lamps in the room darkened. There was a fervour in her voice and a look of madness in her eye; yet it was impossible not to believe her.

There was a knock at the door and the spell was broken. Laria came in with food and wine for Vika. 'With compliments of the lady of the house,' she murmured, eyes downturned, her voice a soft lisp. 'She hopes you regain your strength soon.'

'Please send her my thanks,' said Vika, bright and polite, as if the dire warning of moments before had never been spoken. Laria bowed and hurried out while Vika fed a piece of chicken to Ruck.

'What does it all mean?' Fen asked, when Laria was gone.

'I do not know,' said Vika. 'But I know this: the dreadknights must be stopped. The Krodans are meddling with forces they do not understand. They are fools to believe they can control them.'

'Is there no good news?' Aren asked.

'Do not despair,' said Vika. 'The battle is far from lost. We have been warned, and forewarned we are forearmed. I have been touched by the taint of Plague's arrow, and learned from it. I know the nature of our enemy now. The Ember Blade is within our reach, and we still have our champion, who will seize the bright blade and lead us to victory.' At this, her eyes went to Garric, and Aren saw a zealot's light there.

Garric grunted. 'I know nothing of visions,' he said. 'But I will bring ruin upon the Krodans, I promise you that.'

They heard footsteps on the stairs and Garric, still in the doorway, looked away to find their source.

'We must go,' they heard Keel say. 'It's time.'

Garric nodded and turned back to Vika. 'Farewell, Vika. I'm glad I got to see you safe before I left. Farewell, Cade, Fen ... Aren.' Aren heard the unspoken meaning in the way Garric said his name, a reminder and an acknowledgement of what had passed between them. 'I go now to take the first step to a free Ossia. Aspects go with me.'

'Aspects go with you,' Cade and Vika said together. Fen echoed them quietly.

Garric headed downstairs with Keel, leaving Aren staring at the empty doorway. How different things might have been between them if he'd known the truth about the Hollow Man. When Garric returned, he was determined to begin again, properly this time.

But Vika had a suspicious look on her face, and he knew she'd noticed something that Aren hadn't.

'What is it?' he asked her.

'Nothing,' she lied.

79

There were no moons that night, and racing streaks of cloud obscured the stars as the carriage clattered across the sleeping city, passing through islands of light cast by streetlamps. Where the Uplanes ended in the equally exclusive streets of Consort's Rise, Clia pulled the horses to a halt. They'd walk from here.

Hooded and cloaked in the driver's seat, she waited silently while Garric and Keel climbed out, swords at their hips. There was no point carrying their weapons wrapped up. They clearly had no business in such an exclusive district at this hour, and no passes would spare them if they were seen. Between a fight and an arrest, they'd take their chances on the former. Stealth was the watchword now.

Clia shook the reins and the carriage rolled away, leaving the two of them in the shadows. In the distance they heard the great bell of Braw Tam began to clang, ringing dolefully across the hills.

'Seventh bell o' dark,' said Garric. 'Let's be about it, then.'

They set off into Consort's Rise, where wide, leafy avenues gave way to winding paths and steps as the land steepened sharply. The houses were narrow but imposingly tall, piled up alongside one another behind stone-walled gardens. Those windows that were lit revealed glittering chandeliers and elaborate plaster cornices, harpsichords and dining tables, pastel walls in the Krodan style.

They hurried upwards, heading for their rendezvous with Wilham and his men, and the vintner's yard beyond. Keel had spoken little on the journey and said even less now, for which

Garric was thankful. There'd be dark business tonight, and he was eager for it to be over.

It saddened him that his friend had become a liability, but there was no denying the truth. Keel had been used up in service of the cause, his nerves shredded and his bravery gone. He'd become erratic and indecisive, and he was drinking too much. His decision to go home was no less than suicide, and worse, it would endanger everything they'd worked for. He'd be taken by the Iron Hand, they'd torture him, and he'd give them Mara's name and address. At the very least, his decision to return to his family would cost the resistance its richest benefactor. She'd be forced to go into hiding and her assets would be seized.

Garric couldn't risk that, so there'd be extra men at the rendezvous to seize Keel and keep him safe, in chains if necessary, until his departure was no longer a threat. He wouldn't be going home tomorrow, or any time soon.

Garric had made Wilham swear that Keel wouldn't be harmed, although he wasn't sure how long his word would hold. Wilham liked the surety of death's silence a little too much. But Keel had backed them into this corner, and there was more at stake here than one man's feelings for his family. He'd never understood the need for sacrifice. Not like Garric did.

'You remember old Crackjaw?' Keel said, rousing him from his thoughts.

Garric frowned. A strange subject to bring up now; but perhaps this was the moment for reminiscing. It was the last time they'd see each other, after all.

'Course I remember,' he said. 'He was a monster whale. Bit Rallen's launch clean in two and crunched him down. Terrorised the Cut for a year.'

'Remember the day we saw him?'

'Aye, I remember that, too.' Garric was only half-listening, more concerned with keeping an eye out for soldiers. They could walk right into a patrol in these tight, high-walled lanes.

'There was a storm coming in fast,' Keel said. 'The waves were already climbing when Jad sighted him. There he was, some way off to starboard. The torn fluke, the markings on his flank … the *size* of him!'

Keel's words conjured the memory and a faint smile touched his lips. 'That was old Crackjaw, no doubt,' said Garric. 'Right till that moment we were going to head for port, but you turned us into the storm instead.'

'Godspit, I was a madman back then,' said Keel. 'I hungered for Sarla's embrace. Went up against the worst the sea could throw at me. Anything to feel free. Anything rather than going home.'

'We all knew it, too,' said Garric, warming to the tale. 'Only the wildest sailed with you. We were all reckless, scornful of living. There was kinship in that.'

'The storm came upon us, howling like the thwarted dead.' Keel had a fierce grin on his face. 'Rain like needles of ice, thunder fit to burst your ears! And we saw old Crackjaw again, and again after that, always before us, always just out of reach. Like he was leading us into the heart of the tempest.'

'Keb went over, taken by a wave,' said Garric, excited now, caught up in the memory. 'The boat heeled and tipped till we weren't sure she'd stay afloat. We couldn't have dropped a launch if we tried, but we didn't care. You had us stand ready to harpoon that monster from the gunwales. You said it was only a matter of time before it turned and came at us.' He stopped then, and the fire in him waned. 'But then you changed your mind. You told us to turn around, give up the chase and return to port with our lives. So we did, and old Crackjaw swam on, and this tale comes to nothing.'

Keel drew back suddenly, holding up a hand. He peered round a corner, then motioned for Garric to come and see. In the lane beyond, some way distant, four Krodan soldiers loitered, talking quietly among themselves.

Garric cursed under his breath. Wilham had only a narrow window of opportunity and they'd agreed to be there shortly after seventh bell. The patrol was blocking their route to the vintner's yard and showed no sign of moving.

Keel pulled his shoulder and pointed at the mouth of an

alleyway a little further up the hill. 'Reckon we can go around them that way.'

Garric grunted in agreement. With a last glance at the soldiers, they slipped into the alley and found themselves on a winding path between high-walled gardens, so narrow they had to go single file.

'Not nothing,' said Keel, from behind him.

'What's not nothing?'

'You said my tale comes to nothing. It doesn't. We never caught Crackjaw, but we lived instead, and we forged many new tales together that would not have been told elsewise.'

Garric was having trouble seeing his point, and was beginning to find the conversation irritating. The sight of the Krodan patrol had reminded him that there were more important things to do tonight than indulge in nostalgia.

'You know why I turned us around that day?' Keel asked.

Garric didn't care, but it seemed easier to hear him out. 'Tell me.'

'Because it hit me, all in a flash,' Keel said. 'We'd already lost Keb. I thought of Halger's sons, and Caffey's wife, and all the men on that ship. Thought of you, too. You didn't all deserve to die just because I wanted to. I was ready to take you all down with me, just to get that whale.' His voice became hard. 'The cause wasn't worth the cost. Reckon that's a lesson you never learned.'

Garric's mood darkened. So that's what this was about. One last argument, before they were done. 'I'd see every man, woman and child in this land dead before I'd see them live as slaves,' he growled, 'and I'll give my life to stop it happening. Freedom has no price.'

The alleyway came to a crossroads ahead. Garric guessed that a right turn would bring them back to their path, with only a little delay.

'Every man, woman and child might disagree with you,' said Keel. 'Is it really their freedom you're after? Or is it atonement? Still making amends for that day thirty years past when you failed in your duty? You say you're doing this for Ossia, Garric; but maybe you were just doing it for you, all along.'

Garric quelled a surge of anger. They were only words. Let the coward talk; he'd not be moralising when Wilham's men got hold of him. 'Some things are worth any cost,' he said as he reached the junction.

'Not to me,' said Keel, and he pulled Garric's sword from its sheath with a ring of steel.

Too late, Garric saw the armoured men hidden to either side of the junction. They lunged, seizing his arms, driving him against the wall and cracking his head against the bricks hard enough to split the skin. He roared in rage and disbelief, kicked away from the wall to dislodge them; but now the gates of the surrounding gardens burst open and Iron Guardsmen flooded out, swords at the ready.

'No!' he shouted in wild denial as the reality of Keel's betrayal set in. 'No! No! No!'

He thrashed in their grip, but there were too many hands on him, and his dagger was pulled from his belt. Through the blood that ran into his eyes, he caught a glimpse of Keel beyond the melee. He was backing down the alley, Garric's sword in his hand, an expression on his face like a little boy aghast at a prank gone wrong.

'Keel!' he screamed, spittle flying. 'You son of a whore! Traitor! *Traitor!*'

Stars exploded behind his eyes as someone smashed the pommel of a dagger hard on his crown. His legs turned to water and the soldiers bore him to the ground. Someone knelt on his neck and his arms were wrenched up behind him. Before he could struggle free, there was a click of manacles and a soldier booted him in the belly, hard enough to drive the wind from him. When his attackers drew back, they left him gasping on the floor like a fish.

The blow to his head had him seeing double, and the man who approached him was little more than a dizzy blur. As he neared, the two images slowly merged. He was small and balding, with weak eyes and a wide, wet mouth, wearing the black coat of the Iron Hand. He hunkered down before Garric. A soldier yanked his head up by the hair.

'Cadrac of Darkwater,' he said. 'My name is Overwatchman Klyssen. I've been looking forward to meeting you for some time.'

639

80

Most nights Fen dreamed of falling, and tonight was no exception. She jerked awake in bed, heart lurching in her chest. Panic gave way to sweet relief as she found herself in a guest bedroom in Mara's house, in a bed softer than she'd ever slept in before. She lay there a moment, breathing hard, her head thick with wine and a faint ache in her knees and shins, more remembered than real.

There were urgent voices downstairs. Men's voices. Doors banging, hurrying feet.

She sprang up, pulling on her clothes, a new panic driving her. Someone was barking orders below, the words muffled through the floor.

They've found us!

She snatched up her bow and arrows, her only thought to escape. Someone ran past in the corridor outside. Not that way, then. The window! She struggled with the catch, pushed it wide and leaned out. It wasn't a long drop to the garden. She'd be over the back wall before anyone could stop her.

Go. Run. Survive.

She hesitated with one foot up on the sill. Aren and Cade were still in the house, and if the Krodans hadn't found her yet, maybe they hadn't found them, either.

The need to flee was an almost physical pull. She heard her father's voice: *Don't lean on anyone or anything, Fen. Not no place or person. Elsewise, when they fall, you'll fall with 'em.*

She had to cut them all loose. She should have done it a long time ago, but Aren and Cade held her back. They were the first people near her own age she'd ever grown close to. There had been others at Salt Fork, like Otten and Dox, but they hadn't liked her and she hadn't liked them. Aren and Cade were her friends; perhaps the first real friends she'd ever had.

Beyond the window was a wide, wild world, empty and frightening. Beyond the window, she'd be alone. She didn't want to go back to that.

With an exasperated curse, she climbed down and darted to the door. She heard nobody nearby, only a clamour of rough voices below. Cracking the door open, she peeped out. The lamplit corridor was deserted.

She could make it to their bedrooms, if she was quick. Maybe they hadn't woken yet; they'd all been drunk, after all.

She opened the door and hurried down the corridor, an arrow nocked to her bow, heart thumping. A short way along, she reached a landing overlooking the foyer. She pressed herself to the wall and peered down. The front door was wide open, letting in the night air.

Movement below. She sucked in her breath as a man in a cowled cloak strode into view from another room. Fright made her draw and aim. If he should look up, if he should see her . . .

'Fen! No!'

Aren's voice made her start and she almost let fly. The man below whirled, showing a black-bearded face she didn't know.

'They're with us,' said Aren, stepping onto the landing from the other direction. 'Listen.'

Fen lowered her bow. Of course: they were speaking Ossian. She'd been frightened, muddled with sleep, and their voices had been muffled by the floor, but still she should have realised. The two languages sounded nothing alike.

The man she'd almost shot gave her a baleful glare, then hurried on.

'What's happening?' Fen asked.

'I don't know,' Aren said as he reached her. 'But I think we have to leave. Go wake Cade and Grub and Vika; I'll find out what I can. Meet me in the parlour. That's where they've gathered, by the sound of it.'

Cade was bleary and slow to rouse, though his eyes lit up when he saw Fen at his bedside, at least until he heard why she'd come. Vika was already heading out by the time they got there, Ruck at her heel. Together they went to Grub's room and found it empty. It was only when they called his name that he emerged from behind the door, holding up two daggers with an apologetic look on his face.

The parlour was crowded with strangers, the atmosphere tense. Fen pushed inside to join Aren. Mara was in the centre of the room, deep in conversation with a small, baby-faced man with hair a fierce shade of ginger. He was pacing angrily back and forth.

'That's Wilham the Smiler,' Aren told her, though he wasn't smiling now. 'He's the leader of the rebels in Morgenholme. Garric and Keel were supposed to meet them, but they didn't show up. Wilham smuggled the cart in without them and then came here.'

'Why smuggle it in without Garric?' asked Fen.

'They only had one chance to get it inside,' said Aren. 'Garric might be able to slip in later – easier to sneak in one man than a whole cart.'

'So it's sitting in the yard with a secret compartment and no one inside it? What happened to Garric and Keel?'

'Wilham's men are trying to find out. Tapping all their contacts in the area. We know they were dropped off by Clia, and they didn't have far to go after that.'

'If they don't find them soon, we have to leave,' Cade interjected. He'd squeezed through the crowd to join them, along with Grub. 'If they were captured—'

'Garric would never talk,' Aren said firmly.

'Reckon Keel would, though. Ain't like he's at the peak of mental stability these days, is it? Feller looks like he'd have a breakdown if you slammed the door too loud.'

'We ought to go now,' said Fen. She was feeling edgy, and this uncertainty troubled her.

'Freckles say something smart, for once,' said Grub. 'Hollow Man gone. Bitterbracker, too. Krodans on the way, Grub thinks.'

'They might have been delayed,' said Aren, with forced optimism. 'Chased off by a patrol. Maybe they're lying low till it's safe.'

Grub snorted sceptically. 'And maybe Grub have the gateway to a magic kingdom hidden in the crack of his arse.'

There was a commotion at the door of the parlour and a young man elbowed his way in, cheeks flushed. 'Wilham! I have news!'

They crowded in closer to listen as he spoke with Wilham and Mara. Only Ruck was disinterested, occupied as she was with sniffing everyone in the room.

'We found someone who saw it all from their window,' he panted. 'The Iron Hand were waiting in ambush and they've taken Garric.'

A murmur of shock went round the room. Aren blanched.

The man held up a sword. 'We found this nearby.'

Mara inspected it. 'It is his,' she said at length, her voice dull.

'And Keel?' Wilham asked.

'They let him go. It seems . . . It seems he was in league with the enemy.'

There was uproar at that. Fen felt as if she hadn't quite woken from her dream of falling. Garric had given her direction when she had none. Even after the rout at Salt Fork, he'd made her believe. Now he was gone, betrayed by his own, and his grand plan lay in ruins.

When they fall, you'll fall with 'em.

Vika looked stricken. 'He is taken?' she said in disbelief.

'This house is no longer safe!' Wilham shouted over the hubbub, silencing them all. 'Gather the guests, take them to the safehouse in Riverside. Go in small groups and use different routes. Mara, you have carriages?'

'Two. Clia can drive one. The servants must come, too – I'll not leave them to the Iron Hand.'

'Well enough. The rest go by horse.' Wilham's soft face was screwed up in anger as he addressed the room. 'Gather anything the enemy could use against us. Burn what you can't take. Leave no trace. *Move!*'

81

The mood was bleak as the carriage jolted and bounced through city streets. They were packed in close: Aren, Cade, Fen, Vika and Grub, with Ruck at their feet. Passing streetlamps showed glimpses of drawn faces. Nobody spoke. Even Cade had the sense not to attempt one of his uplifting monologues.

Aren looked at the floor and despaired. How could it have turned so fast? How could it be over, when it had just been about to begin? Garric was gone, betrayed by his closest friend for the second time in his life, and with him went all hope of seizing the Ember Blade.

Aren picked through the rubble of the night, looking for hope and finding none. There was no telling how much Keel had revealed to the Iron Hand. They couldn't even send someone in Garric's place. The whole plan was compromised.

Were they already strapping Garric into a chair in some torture chamber? Would his thirty years of struggle be rewarded with agony and death?

For Keel, whom he'd once thought a good man, he felt only black loathing. No wonder Klyssen had been willing to let Aren go. He knew he had a second traitor in his ranks if the first one failed. Aren had believed himself clever in escaping the Iron Hand, but the overwatchman had another card up his sleeve the whole time. It made him sick to think of how effortlessly he'd been outplayed.

How could Keel have done that to Garric? *How?*

But then, Aren knew how. He'd been a hair's breadth from doing it himself.

'I thought...' Vika began, and then stopped. There was desolation on her face. 'He was the champion... The one to seize the burning blade...' Ruck folded her ears down and whined as Vika shook her head in disbelief. 'Were the Torments ever talking to me at all? Or was I talking to myself all along?'

'Grub talks to himself sometimes,' the Skarl offered helpfully.

'Oh, shut up!' Cade snapped.

Aren sat in a window nook in an empty room, his knees drawn up to his chin, hugging himself. There was no lamp or lantern here, no rugs or hangings, nothing but a stack of battered mattresses in the corner. He was on the top floor of a tall old house, high above the street. Beyond the window was the river where Sovereign's Isle glittered in the night, as did the lights of the south bank beyond. He gazed through the glass, seeing nothing, in a state of perfect misery.

There were voices below: Mara and Wilham arguing. Wilham's people thumped up and down the stairs, banging doors and holding urgent conversations. Garric's capture had stirred them up like an ants' nest. Aren and the others were ignored in the chaos, so Aren had slipped away, hoping to clear his head.

Alone at last, he'd stilled the clamour in his mind, but in its place he found a void, a numb vacancy of thought. Garric was gone. The Ember Blade was gone. Even his father was gone; it was as if he'd died all over again last night. Doggedness was a part of Aren's nature, but he'd been knocked down one time too many. This time, he felt like staying there. Because what was the point of getting up again?

He heard the door squeak open, casting a lopsided oblong of lamplight across the floorboards from the corridor. By the shadow it contained, he knew it was Fen. She came in, closed the door and sat at the foot of the windowsill, her back to the wall beneath him.

'What are they saying?' he asked.

'Some talk of staging a rescue,' Fen said. 'Wilham won't allow it. We don't have the numbers to storm the Iron Hand headquarters, even if we could be sure he was there. Others want to hunt down Keel, to find out what he told them and make an example of him. Mara frets about the girls in the class she can no longer teach, and the servants she can no longer protect.'

'And the Ember Blade?'

She shrugged. 'No one's mentioned it. It was Garric's plan, not theirs.'

Aren felt nothing. Her words tumbled into the space inside him and were swallowed. For a long time, there was silence.

'You probably noticed I'm afraid of heights,' Fen said at last.

'I noticed.'

'I never told you why.'

He waited. He had the sense that she was gathering herself.

'After Ma died,' she began, 'my da was different. You never saw any two people who loved each other more. Losing her broke him, and there was never joy in him again. The day we buried her, he told me I had to learn to look after myself. He'd take me out into the forest and up into the mountains, and leave me to find my way home. I had to survive on my own for days at a time. I was eleven or twelve ... I don't know. It went on for a few years. Once I got sick out there and nearly died. Once I was almost caught by a bear.'

Her tone stirred Aren from his despair. Fen had never spoken so openly before. It was like that night in the sanctum in Skavengard, waiting for the beast. In her darkest moments, she reached out.

'*Don't lean on anyone or anything, Fen. Not no place or person.* That's what he used to say. *Elsewise, when they fall, you'll fall with 'em.* He really meant himself. Don't lean on me, because I don't plan to stay. But I never heard what he was saying. After Ma was gone, he was the only person I knew. All the tasks he set me, I did only to please him. I lived for the times when we'd do things together.'

'He was your father,' said Aren. 'You just wanted to be with him. I know how that feels.'

'One day, we headed out east towards the mountains. Where the land steepened, he chose hard routes and we had to climb. He went ahead of me each time, and at the top, he'd reach down to help me up. Twice he did that. The second time, I saw the disappointment in his eyes, the *grief*... But I didn't see it for what it was... I had no idea...'

Her voice wobbled. She might have been crying, or trying to stop herself. Aren couldn't see her face; she was sitting below him with her back to the wall. Without thinking, he let his hand dangle down next to her. She reached up and took it just as absently, her fingers folding around his, gripping tight.

'The third time...' she said, her voice dull with remembered pain. 'The third time he dropped me. He did it on purpose, to show me. Sometimes we're so casual about putting our lives in each other's hands, and he... He wanted to show me the danger. So he let go.'

Her grip tightened on his hand, and he knew she was falling again, that she'd always be falling.

'I broke both legs,' she said. 'Lay there screaming. I thought it was an accident, expected him to save me. But he never came. So after a while, I stopped screaming, because there was no point. I'd only attract wolves and bears.'

'How did you survive?' Aren asked quietly.

'I crawled home.'

I crawled home. Aren couldn't imagine the agony contained in those three short words. The pain of dragging two shattered legs behind her, for hours, for *days*, perhaps; the kind of pain that made it easier to lie down and die. All the while knowing that her father had dropped her on purpose, and that she had no choice but to go back to him. Where had she found the strength to carry on?

'He was there when I got home,' she said. 'Drunk, but not so much that he couldn't put me on a cart and take me to town. The healer set my legs so they wouldn't mend crooked, and I had to rest at home for a long time. A long time. My father fed me. He owed me that, I suppose. But I never spoke another word to him in his life.'

She sniffed. So she was crying, then. He imagined the tears he couldn't see and his chest tightened. His feelings of betrayal towards his father must have been nothing compared to hers. Yet still she hadn't given up, still she'd kept on going, until one day her path crossed his. That thought shamed him. What right had he to wallow in misery, when she had a greater claim to it?

'What happened to him?' he asked.

'He stayed till I was fit again, able to walk and hunt. Then one morning he walked out into the forest with no pack, no supplies and no weapons. He never came back. I never looked for him.'

She wiped her cheeks with her free hand. Her voice was steady now.

'He'd wanted to end himself ever since Ma died, but he couldn't go till he knew I would survive on my own. In his way, I think he tried to make it easy for me. So it wouldn't hurt so much when he was gone. He did the best he could...'

Aren stared out at the city, a heavy weight on his heart. No longer was he numb. It was impossible not to feel, with her hand in his. He wondered how much cruelty the world could hold. How many other stories like hers were out there, hidden behind darkened windows, kept secret by doors and walls? How many men who beat their wives near to death, how many starving and neglected children, how many who planned treachery against those they professed to love? Weighed against that, his own despair seemed a small thing. He had life, strength and liberty. If his dreams had come tumbling down, well, at least he'd been allowed them in the first place.

He found himself becoming furious. How could Fen's father give up on his child like that? Perhaps he thought it an act of love to delay his suicide, but to Aren's mind it was cowardice. He'd always intended to abandon her, and had only instilled that lonely philosophy so he could die with a clear conscience and avoid the harder road of carrying on.

Now she'd been let down again. She'd put her faith in Garric and his cause, and Garric was gone, betrayed. Just when she was learning to trust others, her father's ghost had returned. He didn't think she'd trust again, after this.

His despair felt false and indulgent now. He was angry, and he turned that to strength. He wasn't giving up today, nor was anyone else.

'Come on,' he said, pulling her up. 'On your feet.' He swung his legs off the sill and dropped to the floor.

'Where are you going?' She sighed wearily. Her eyes and nose were red, but they were dry. 'It's done, Aren. Garric was the one with the plan.'

'Then we make a *new* plan!' Aren said. 'We still have Yarin's notes, don't we? And we still have time till the wedding. Garric saved my life more than once, and I'm damned if I'll count him lost just because the Iron Hand have him! Damned if I'll give up this chance to take back the Ember Blade!' He put his hand on her arm and held her gaze, so she could see he was in earnest. 'And I'm damned if I'll let you think your father was right. There are people in this world you can believe in, Fen. You can believe in me.'

He burst through the door, carried on a wave of new conviction, and as he stormed downstairs, he found courage in his certainty. Consequences meant nothing in his mind. He'd do anything rather than passively accept his fate.

'Aren?' It was Cade, coming up the staircase from the first floor with Grub behind him. Aren swept past, too focused on his purpose to stop. Cade and Grub exchanged a glance and followed him.

'Mudslug mad about something,' Grub said with a grin as Fen caught them up.

The safehouse was chilly and sparsely furnished, all bare boards and stone. It was a temporary place for people passing through. The largest room was the basement, where a plain wooden table was scattered with jacks of ale and heels of bread. A dozen men and women sat around it by lanternlight, more standing against the walls. Vika was among them, leaning dejectedly on her staff, Ruck at her feet. Orica and Harod were there, too. She looked worried while he showed nothing at all.

Mara and Wilham, both seated, were arguing as Aren came in.

'At least send someone to the vintner's yard to take Garric's place!' Mara said. 'If Keel had told the Iron Hand about the cart, the ambush would have been at your rendezvous and they'd have arrested you, too. Whatever his reasons, the evidence suggests he was careful to betray no one but Garric. The risk is worth taking to get somebody inside Hammerholt.'

'And who'd go?' Wilham asked, with a smile that was more of a sneer. 'None of my people. Garric knows little of our operations in Morgenholme, but even a little is too much. I will not send someone who could supply the Krodans with the rest of it. No. We cut our losses and retreat. There will be other chances to strike at the Krodans.'

'But not like this! Never again like this!' There was desperation in Mara's voice.

'I will not retreat!' said Aren as he walked into the room. 'Nor will I leave Garric to the Iron Hand. Thirty years ago, the people of this land refused to fight because they were too afraid of losing what they had. We must not make that mistake again. This is our best, perhaps our *only* chance to knock our overlords from their pedestals.'

He swept the room with his gaze, meeting scornful amazement with defiance. Most looked amused; they saw only a self-important boy with a surfeit of opinion. But he was their equal, and he stood his ground.

'Do any of you even know who Garric is, this man you're so eager to abandon?' he demanded.

'A man who should choose his friends more carefully,' somebody quipped, to general laughter.

'He is Cadrac of Darkwater!' Aren shouted over their mirth. 'He is the last Dawnwarden, the only living guardian of the Ember Blade. *That* is who you would cast aside!'

Vika cried out in anguish, and it was her reaction, more than his words, that sobered the room. But while the others were shocked, Aren saw Wilham's grin turn angry, and he realised that Wilham had known.

Murmurs ran around the room and he saw doubt on some faces. Aren was loth to reveal another man's secrets, but he hadn't been sworn to silence, and he couldn't think of another way to save Garric. Secrets had got them into this mess. It was time for a little honesty.

'Is it true?' one of Wilham's men asked.

'Ask him,' Aren pointed at Wilham, whose smile was now a rictus of hate.

'Wilham?' said a woman at the table. 'You knew?'

'I didn't know for sure,' Wilham told them, but he wasn't firm enough to be convincing. 'I heard tell the Krodans were hunting the last Dawnwarden, and that he'd been at Salt Fork, but I didn't pry further. If Garric had wanted us to know, he'd have told us.'

'If he's a Dawnwarden, we *must* save him!' said a man at the back of the room, and there was a chorus of agreement around him.

'No!' said Wilham, surging to his feet and slamming his hand down on the table. 'Do you think the Krodans would take a Dawnwarden to some shabby local jail, with drunken guards we could bribe or overpower? He's a great prize for the Empire! Likely he is halfway to Hammerholt by now, where he will languish in the most secure dungeon they have until such time as they decide to execute him! Would you dash yourselves against the walls of that fortress to get him back?'

'I would,' said Aren. His mind was racing but his voice was calm. 'Mara, you have Yarin's plans. You said there was an urd structure underneath Hammerholt, and waterways that lead from the lake. Can you find us a way in?'

'If there is a way inside, I will find it,' said Mara.

'And if there is none, we will enter by the front gate. There will be hundreds of people going into and out of that fortress every day. There must be a way to smuggle ourselves in. And not just one of us this time. *All* of us!'

He was excited, and saw an answering excitement in his friends. He might not know how they'd do it yet, but he knew they *could*, and the others were beginning to believe it, too.

But Wilham laughed in contempt. 'Brave words and heroic fantasies. This is life and death, not some game of knights with wooden swords. Leave the thinking to the adults, boy.'

'And who are you to me?' Aren replied with equal contempt, killing the smirks on the faces of their audience. 'Where were you when we defeated the beast of Skavengard? Where were you when we faced Krodan dreadknights, not once but three times?

Were you hiding away then, as now? You're not one of us. If you don't want to help, stand aside.'

What remained of the mirth in the room was gone, replaced by cold silence, and a touch of fear. No one spoke to Wilham the Smiler that way.

Wilham's smile turned murderous. 'You've quite the mouth on you, whelp,' he said. There was a ring of steel as he pulled his dagger from its sheath. 'You need to learn some manners.'

Aren's courage faltered at the sight of the blade. Swept up in his own enthusiasm, he'd misjudged the danger, failed to see the killer's heart inside this baby-faced man. And here in Wilham's safehouse, surrounded by his people, the only law that applied was his.

Perhaps Wilham meant to cut his throat, or take an ear, or merely give him a scar on his cheek for his impertinence. Aren never found out. Wilham lunged forward, his blade flickering in the lamplight, and his arm was caught by a strong hand around the wrist.

'I think not,' said Harod, towering over the smaller man. 'As the young master says: you are not one of us.'

Wilham's eyes blazed and his cheeks flamed red, but Harod was immovable, projecting such fearless strength that it was impossible not to be intimidated. Wilham looked around, expecting someone to come to his aid, but not even his own people wanted to see a young man hurt for the crime of being passionate. He'd lost the room in his rage, and he saw it. He snarled and pulled free with a curse, throwing his dagger point down into the table.

Look at them, Aren thought. *Look how the mere mention of a Dawn-warden inspires them. What, then, could the Ember Blade do?*

Wilham's men were torn between fear of their leader and their desire to go to a Dawnwarden's aid. Aren believed some of them would join him if he asked, but that would be a direct challenge to Wilham, and he'd pushed far enough.

'Wilham,' he said, holding up his hands. 'I spoke hastily, and I apologise. Fear leads to careless words, and I am scared for my friend. You are right to be cautious, and I know there is much at stake. I do not ask you to risk your people, only that you do not hinder us, and perhaps you'll be gracious enough to render us what aid you safely can. We are all on the same side.'

Furious as Wilham was, he was canny enough to see the way out Aren offered him, which would allow him to retreat with his pride mostly intact.

'Would that Keel was as loyal to Garric as the rest of you,' he said. He glowered at their audience, reasserting his authority over them. 'Be about it, then. It's foolishness, but your lives are your own. We will give you what help we are able, but we will not go to Hammerholt with you, for you go to your deaths.'

'So be it,' said Aren. 'You have our thanks.'

Wilham pulled the dagger from the table, staring at Harod as he sheathed it again. Then he walked from the room and his people followed him uneasily, leaving only Aren and his companions behind.

'Ha! Mudslug showed Carrot-Top who's boss!' Grub crowed.

'I don't know if I just made an ally or an enemy,' Aren said. The tension of the confrontation was leaving him and he was light-headed with victory. 'Thank you, Harod. It would have gone the worse for me if you had not been here.'

The knight merely nodded.

'You spoke well,' said Vika, stepping forward. 'And Dawnwarden or not, Garric deserves more from us than to be abandoned. Whatever the odds.' Ruck barked in agreement.

'I will not abandon him, either,' said Mara as she rose to stand with the others. 'There is still hope.'

Cade spoke up next. 'You're sure he really is a … you know, a Dawnwarden?' he said in awe.

'I'm sure,' said Aren.

'Then count me in!'

'We are with you,' said Orica, speaking for Harod, too, as she laid a hand on his arm.

'Hammerholt is impenetrable fortress, heavily guarded, very dangerous?' Grub rubbed his hands together. 'Good. Grub needs new tattoos!'

Aren looked last to Fen. She smiled at him and dipped her

653

head in a nod, and the look she gave him kindled a hot glow in his chest.

'There is one matter outstanding,' Mara said. 'What shall be done about Keel?'

Aren's mood spoiled at the thought of the Bitterbracker. He mastered himself before he could let bitterness take control. There were greater things at stake. 'Vengeance is not our business here,' he said. 'Keel will be gone with the tide and can harm us no further. Even if we could find him in time, punishing him would serve no purpose.'

'Grub punish him for fun?' the Skarl volunteered, raising a dagger.

'Aye,' snarled Cade. 'We agree on something for once.'

'No,' Vika said. 'Our time is short; we cannot waste it on point-less retribution.'

'He is not worth the hunt,' Fen said. 'If we want him, we know where he'll be.'

'I concur,' said Mara. 'If we are to save Garric and retrieve the Ember Blade, we must work with all speed, and work together. Are we all committed to this course?'

'Aye!' they shouted in response, and even Harod, nodding grimly, had a new glint of fire in his eye.

82

Keel sat swollen-eyed, watching through a narrow window as morning stole over the docks. Two empty bottles stood on the table before him and he'd nearly finished a third. It had been a long and lonely watch by candlelight, here in the poky garret of a tumbledown inn. Many shadowed hours had dragged by with only his liquor for company, his thoughts circling like sharks round a kill. But soon it would be over. Soon.

The room was bare and draughty, holding little more than a table, a chair and a mean bed. Chill air seeped down from the rafters. Keel relished that small suffering. He didn't deserve comfort, or joy, or love ever again.

The inn had a good view of the waterfront, where drunken sailors on their way back to their hammocks weaved between stevedores loading cargo. Among the forest of masts was the ship he was due to leave on, a fast clipper called the *Merriweather*, headed for Wracken Bay and other towns up the Cut. He'd met the captain and paid for a berth yesterday in anticipation of a swift departure. He wouldn't survive long in Morgenholme once news of his betrayal spread. Wilham the Smiler would see to that.

He swilled his liquor, welcoming the burn in his throat and belly. Blearily he saw that the *Merriweather* was moving now, slipping away from the jetty, out into the Cay. He watched it head downriver, Sovereign's Isle rising steep and green in the background. When it passed beyond his sight he let out a sob, surprising himself. He hadn't known there were tears on his cheeks.

He wasn't going home. He was never going home.

His eyes fell to the document beside the empty bottles. He couldn't read Krodan in his current state – even reading it sober was like wading through mud – but he knew what it said. It was a promise. A lifetime income for Mariella and Tad. A grant of ownership to Fluke's farm. A pardon for his crimes. And, most importantly of all, an instruction to Lord Jadrell to secure the best medical attention for Tad, with all costs paid by the Empire.

Drunken tears spilled afresh. *My boy. You'll live, my boy. You'll live to see wonders, just like you did at the Marisport fair. I promised you that.*

Secured to the foot of the document was a small silver disc, imprinted with a complex pattern around its edge and the double-barred cross in the centre. It was the work of a master craftsman, highly valuable and almost impossible to duplicate. The seal of the Iron Hand. No one would argue with a message that came with that seal attached.

Next to it was the tight, neat signature of Overwatchman Klyssen, the bespectacled demon who'd forged this contract. He'd met Klyssen in the headquarters of the Iron Hand, after they caught him outside the Burned Bear. If Klyssen had made threats, if he'd urged him to give up the others as well, Keel would have dug his heels in; but somehow Klyssen knew that. Instead, his proposal was as simple as it was cruel: Garric's life for Tad's.

And godspit, it wasn't as if Garric had long to go anyway. Even before they'd talked in the barn, Keel had known Garric was headed for destruction. His plan was half-formed, making no provision for escape, and his obsession with ending the Krodan occupation bordered on madness. Everyone was expendable in service of his quest, and it had already claimed many lives. He was hurtling eagerly towards his end.

Yet even after Keel had made his deal, he'd held on to a last shred of faith. He'd gone to find Garric, still wanting to be persuaded, to be shown the wisdom of his path. Looking for a reason not to betray him.

The truth, when it emerged, was worse than he'd imagined. Barrels full of elarite oil! A plan to murder Prince Ottico and the entire Krodan high command in Ossia! Garric wasn't just seeking death, but war as well, and if he succeeded he'd plunge them into a brutal state of occupation which Mariella and Tad would surely not survive.

But what hurt the most, what cut deepest of all, was that he'd decided to do it without Keel.

He folded up the document, took a stick of wax and held it unsteadily in the candle flame. He made a clumsy seal and pressed it with his thumb as a makeshift mark, then turned it over and wrote an address on the blank side, one eye closed as he carefully scratched the letters. That done, he pushed it away, sat back and took a bitter swig from his bottle.

Garric had cut him out. That was the crux of it. If he hadn't, perhaps Keel wouldn't have betrayed him. But Garric had grown remote and secretive, careless of Keel's concerns. He dismissed Keel's dilemma over his family as if Mariella was a nuisance and Tad was worth nothing. Fluke's death lay at his door, but he barely acknowledged it, let alone admitted his responsibility.

Keel felt betrayed, so he'd betrayed Garric in return. For his family. For the good of Ossia.

He felt a wrench in his guts and sucked down another swallow of liquor to quell it. He wanted to kill all thought, but the thoughts kept coming, swarming up towards him like

black tentacles reaching from the dark and waiting behind them mouths within mouths within

He started back to reality with a jerk, gasping. He took another hit from the bottle. It didn't work. Nothing worked.

A knock at the door made him jump again. Heart bumping against his ribs, he stared at it fearfully. Wilham's men? Already? Garric himself, escaped and returned for vengeance?

'Imperial courier,' came the voice from beyond the door.

His muscles unclenched. In his drunken haze he'd forgotten he'd sent for a courier. 'Come in.'

The door creaked open and a clean-cut young Krodan peered through, dressed in a neat uniform. He looked around the small, miserable room, clearly wondering if he'd come to the wrong place. 'You have a message?' he asked.

Keel tapped the document on the table. 'Imperial post, eh?'

'Of course,' said the courier as he approached. 'It will be

delivered by hand. There is no way more sure or secure, short of delivering it yourself.'

'That won't be happening,' Keel slurred. He took out a pouch of money and emptied it onto the table. It was all the money he had left in the world.

The courier raised an eyebrow. 'That's far too much,'

'It's yours,' said Keel. 'But listen close. I want you to open it and read it to her. She doesn't have letters. Don't... *Don't* put it in her hands without reading it to her first. Understand? It's life and death. She'll destroy it.'

'You may rest assured,' said the courier, 'it will be as you ask.' He picked up the letter and read Keel's drunken handwriting with some difficulty. 'Mariella-from-Arianne of Wracken Bay. Do I have it aright?'

'You do.'

The courier scooped the money off the table into his pouch, straightened and gave Keel a look of concern. 'Your pardon, but... Are you well? Is there someone I can fetch for you?'

'I'll be fetched soon enough,' said Keel. 'Go on.'

'As you wish. Hail to the Emperor,' said the courier. He saluted and left.

So it is done, thought Keel. He'd finally made his choice. Garric had always called him indecisive, but how was a man to decide when all choices left him wretched? Stay in Wracken Bay in misery, or abandon your family for adventure? Die in pain on a Krodan rack with your family condemned to starve, or save your loved ones at the expense of your only true friend? He was neither the husband he should be, nor the man he aspired to be. He was a failure and a traitor, and now he could never go home. Everyone would know he was a collaborator, including Mariella and Tad. To return would be to trap himself in the life he'd so desperately wanted to escape, despised by all those he'd once called friends. Every coin that came to his family would be stained with Garric's blood. Mariella deserved more than him in a husband. Tad deserved more in a father.

Could he have chosen a different path, in the end? Was there any right way? Or did all routes lead here, to this meagre garret, with no options left?

No options but one.

He walked over to the bed and picked up the rope that lay coiled there. Easy to find rope on the docks. He set to work, fashioning himself a noose. He was a whaler; he knew knots. It was a relief to be doing something honest again. When he was ready, he dragged his chair over beneath the thick rafter overhead.

mouths slavering mouths exhaling dread and how they wanted him with such hideous lustful need

He stumbled away with a cry, back towards the table, where he drained the bottle. When he was done, he leaned there panting, face drawn and shiny with sweat in the cold morning light from the window.

No more.

He was driven back to the noose by that thought. He could suffer no longer the horror of what he'd seen, what he'd done, what he'd become. The darkness that had always stalked him had returned, and consumed him. He'd stayed ahead of it for a few years, on the road with Garric, but it had never lost his trail. Now there was only cold emptiness, and there'd be no laughter again. That was a hell worth escaping at any price.

Up on the chair he went and tied the rope round the rafter, working with grim efficiency. When it was done, he put his head through and tightened the loop.

No going back. He had not a coin to his name, nor a friend in the world. The future held nothing but starvation or murder at the hands of Wilham's people. Only by shutting off all ways out could he take this way forward.

He closed his eyes, silent tears of relief running down his face. It was so simple now. So simple.

He kicked the chair, and dropped.

83

'Are you all listening?' said Aren. 'This is the plan.'

Cade could hardly suppress his excitement. There were nine of them round the table, in the light of a lantern hanging from a chain overhead. Before them were jacks of ale and leather goblets of wine. Their faces were shadowed and grave and full of purpose. They'd come to learn how they might do the impossible, and write themselves into legend.

The safehouse basement had been transformed since Aren's confrontation with Wilham. Now every wall was covered with nailed-up pieces of parchment showing diagrams, lists of dates, schedules, maps and other things incomprehensible to a slow reader like Cade. On the table were several plans showing the various floors of Hammerholt. Mara and Aren had spent the last two days in a frenzy of plotting, comparing staff rotas and consulting moon charts, wading through the mind-boggling complexities of a royal wedding. Neither had slept much, and it showed; but though Aren looked drawn, there was a fierce conviction in his voice.

'Wilham's people have learned that Garric is to be executed at dawn on Scorsday, the day before the wedding,' he said. He was leaning over the table, his hands spread across the floorplans. 'General Dakken – who destroyed the Dawnwardens thirty years ago – will wield the blade himself. They mean to tidy up the last loose end before the new era begins. The princess and her considerable retinue will arrive after the execution, which will cause chaos among the staff, so most guests have been instructed to arrive the day before, on Chainday. Hundreds will be coming, and all of them will need to be fed, entertained and accommodated. Even for such efficient organisers as the Krodans are, it will be pandemonium. That's when we will strike.'

He cast his gaze around the table. 'If we are to triumph, we must be like the workings of a clock, everyone doing their part, acting in perfect harmony. We work as a team, or we fall together.' He glanced briefly at Fen. 'Are we all of one mind in this?'

'Tell us what must be done,' said Vika, scratching behind Ruck's ear. She seemed recovered from her poisoned wound, but the need to rest had kept her from joining in the planning as much as she'd wanted.

Aren pushed away from the table and pointed to a faded and ancient-looking diagram on the wall that showed nothing Cade understood. 'Hammerholt gets its water from Lake Calagria, in the mountains nearby,' he said. 'It passes through a series of caves into a tunnel, probably built by the urds in the First Empire.' He returned to the table and stabbed the floorplans with a finger. 'We think that this door in the sewers underneath Hammerholt opens into a cave at the end of that tunnel. A secret escape route, perhaps, or a way for engineers to access the caves in days gone by when the lake was lower. It's possible the Krodans don't know about it; the fortress is vast and most of it lies unused. Either way, a small boat can make it through the caves to that door. But there are two significant problems.'

Mara took over. 'First of all, we can't open the door from the cave side, and it will certainly be too thick to break down.'

'Grub can pick any lock!' the Skarl boasted.

'There will likely be no lock at all, only a handle. According to my calculations, the cave is submerged when the lake is high. This door will have been built to withstand that, and I suspect it will be barred on the other side to prevent Hammerholt from flooding.'

'So how will you open it?' Wilham the Smiler asked. He'd insisted on joining them tonight, to hear their plans. Since they were here on his sufferance, he wanted to know what they were up to, and they had little choice but to let him listen.

'One of us will have to open it from the other side,' Aren said. 'Only five of us will be in that boat, six if Ruck is coming—'

'She is,' said Vika. Ruck put her paws up on the table and barked, as if offended at the possibility she might be left behind. 'Do not fear; she can be stealthy when she needs to be.'

'Six, then,' said Aren. He gave Ruck a tired smile. 'Harod, Orica and Mara will get inside another way.'

Cade sat back in his chair, a jack of ale in his hand, marvelling. All his life, Aren had just been Aren: strong-willed and full of plans, but still a small-town boy for all that, no more remarkable than Cade was. Now here stood a different Aren, who spoke with clarity and command, and bore himself with a presence beyond his years. In Ossia, adulthood wasn't an age but an attitude; their history was littered with child queens, young generals and precocious scholars. Aren was barely sixteen, but the last few months had made him a man worthy and willing to take the lead in Garric's absence. They listened to him, though he was the youngest here.

Cade grinned. He'd never been more proud to be Aren's best friend.

'Earlier this afternoon, Wilham and his people located Morgenholme's most eminent lutist in an inn,' said Aren. He nodded at Wilham; he'd been careful to keep him sweet since their encounter. Cade would never have forgiven him so, but Aren had a way of making enemies into allies.

'There was an unfortunate accident,' Aren went on. 'A passer-by gracelessly spilled her drink. Of course, being polite, he bought her another one, this time laced with one of Vika's potions.'

Grub, who'd been squirming with glee in his seat, could no longer contain himself. 'It was Grub! Grub did that!'

'Right now she is beginning to feel very ill indeed,' said Vika solemnly. She'd painted her face again and wore all of her trinkets, including the effigy of Sarla that Fen had whittled for her. In the lanternlight, she was shaggy and feral and strange. 'There will be no lasting damage, but she will not stray far from a bucket for the next few days.'

'The leader of the troupe is desperate,' said Aren. 'They were due to perform at one of the many feasts in Hammerholt, but now their star musician cannot play. They will be forced to miss the wedding and the generous payment for their services.' He held out a hand towards Orica. 'Luckily he will soon cross paths with a wandering minstrel who happens to be prodigiously talented and familiar with all the songs they are likely to play.'

'Tsss, you are very kind,' Orica said with a smile.

'I still say it is too dangerous,' Harod said. 'This city is unsafe for Sards.'

'Peace, Harod,' said Orica. 'We must all bear our share of the risk.'

'She will be under the troupe's protection until the wedding is done,' said Aren. 'There will be honoured guests from across the near world in Hammerholt, so a Sard won't excite much notice, and they are not officially outlaws yet. The Krodans haven't even admitted they're rounding them up. They won't start trouble at a royal wedding.'

Cade found it hard to tell if Harod was mollified or not; his face was rigid. But he said no more, so Aren moved on.

'Once inside, Orica's job is to get away from the troupe and go to the lower levels, which should be relatively empty. She will make her way to the sewer door and let us in.'

'And what if it is sealed shut? Or needs a key? Or she is seen and turned back?' Wilham asked.

Mara met his gaze calmly. 'Then Orica will have to use her initiative. Additionally, if Harod or I have completed our tasks then we will also make our way to the door. It is vital enough to merit a certain level of redundancy.'

'Let us be clear about the risks,' said Aren. 'The margins here are very narrow. The lake is tidal and we will only be able to access the caves at the lowest tide. By the time we reach the door, the lake will be rising again and our way out will be cut off. The cave will fill up. If Orica cannot get that door open in time, we will drown.'

Cade felt the enthusiasm drain out of him. Suddenly the plan didn't sound so good.

'I warned you,' said Aren, seeing his face fall. 'If one part fails, we all do. Those of you who don't want to be on that boat, speak now. No one will judge you.'

'Is there no other way?' Fen asked.

'Not if we want to smuggle in weapons and enough people to do what has to be done.'

There was a grim silence around the table.

'How long would I have?' said Orica.

Mara replied. 'The tides are complicated. Thea has two moons that follow irregular orbits and only repeat their cycle every two-and-a-quarter years. On top of that, it is necessary to calculate the volume of the water, correcting for any choke points which will slow the flow and the time it takes for ...'

Her words became a jumble to Cade. Why did she need to explain so much? He wished Aren would talk again; at least he was direct.

'Given all that,' Mara finished at last, 'I have calculated that we will have about an hour before we drown. Orica, you will need to open the door by first bell o' dark, or last light, which fall together this time of year.'

'By fair means or foul, I will do it,' said Orica.

Cade swallowed, thinking of the freezing water rising around them as they gasped for the last pockets of air, but his fright quickly faded. He found it hard to be afraid of something that hadn't happened yet, and the future didn't bother him overmuch, as a rule. It all felt beyond his control, so it wasn't worth worrying about. Let tonight be tonight, and tomorrow be tomorrow.

'Harod and I will enter through the front gate,' said Mara. 'Harod is a scion of High House Anselm of Harrow and, despite his disagreements with his family, his rank entitles him to an invitation to the wedding of a Harrish princess. It was not easy to secure one at such short notice, but I do have certain ... connections.'

It was hard not to notice the bitterness that crept into her voice, but Cade didn't understand it and she didn't elaborate. Harod was looking as uncomfortable as Cade had ever seen him. He clearly disliked trading off his family name, after the disgrace he'd brought upon them. Cade wondered how many more unspoken sacrifices, how many quiet agonies, he'd endured for Orica's sake. Putting up with Grub's abuse was an act of heroism in itself.

'I will pose as Harod's wife,' said Mara. A half-smile twitched at the edge of her mouth. 'I'm a little old for the role, but there have been stranger matches.'

'Ha! Bowlhead got married!' spluttered Grub, spraying ale.

Mara ignored him. 'We will join the other guests for the entertainments.'

Grub's face fell. 'That about right,' he grumbled. 'Bossychops and Bowlhead get to watch jugglers and stuff their faces while we all drown.'

'No one is going to drown,' said Aren. 'Harod and Mara will take care of Jarrit Bann, the Master of Keys. He alone can access the vault, where the Ember Blade will be kept.' He pointed again at the floorplans to show them. 'His name is not on the list for any feast, so we assume he will head to his chambers after the pre-dinner entertainments are over. This presents a problem, because that's likely to be where the key to the vault will be kept, and we need him not to be there.'

'Would he not keep such a key with him at all times?' Orica asked.

'Yarin's spies think otherwise,' said Mara. 'He locks his most important keys in his study. It would be too easy for a thief to pilfer them if he carried them on his person.'

'Grub could just kill him?' Grub suggested.

'We're trying to do this without leaving bodies,' Aren said.

Grub harrumphed and drank his ale.

'Once we are in, some of us will head to the cells to free Garric, but Grub will go to the Master of Keys' office while Harod and Mara delay him elsewhere. He will need time to search the place because, for all Yarin's comprehensive information, we know almost nothing about the vault door or how it is opened. Mara and Harod will learn whatever they can from the Master of Keys.'

'Grub will get you in, Mudslug. Don't worry.'

'And no one will notice a Skarl running around the corridors of Hammerholt?' Wilham asked sceptically. 'Or, for that matter, a druidess with a dog?'

Cade flashed him a look of annoyance. His purpose here appeared to be to poke holes in Aren's plan, and there were holes enough in it already.

Aren didn't seem to mind. 'We thought of that,' he said. 'Hammerholt is so big that whole areas are disused or have fallen into disrepair. Yarin has provided us with keys to those areas, so we can make our way around the celebrations rather than through them. As to Grub, he will go in through the window.'

'Grub climb up outside wall. Grub better than anyone at climbing. One time, Grub climb into a maiden's tower, and he—'

'What of Garric?' said Vika. 'How will we free him?'

Aren traced a route through the plans with his finger and tapped on the dungeons. 'Those of us not working to secure the key to the vault will make our way to the cells, subdue the guard and leave them in Garric's place. There's usually only one man on duty, but we will have the numbers and the weapons to deal with more if we need to. The shift doesn't change over till sixth bell, by which time we will be long gone.'

'Maybe Orica can get away from the troupe. Maybe she can open the door,' said Wilham. 'Maybe the Skarl can steal the key to the vault. Maybe Mara and Harod can keep the Master of Keys distracted. Maybe there'll only be one guard. Maybe you won't be seen.' He raised an eyebrow. 'There's a lot that could go wrong with your plan.'

'Or it may be easier than we think,' Aren replied. 'There's no way to know until we're inside.'

Wilham shook his head with a despairing smile and sat back, arms crossed.

'Once we have Garric,' Aren went on, 'we head to the vault, where Grub will meet us with the key. We will take the Ember Blade and return to the door in the sewers while the Krodans are busy feasting. By this time, according to Mara's calculations, the water will be falling again. We may have to hide awhile before we can enter the cave again and take the boat back to the lake, but if all has gone to plan, the Krodans will have no idea anything is amiss until much later.'

'What if all does *not* go to plan?' asked Fen. 'What if the alarm is raised and we can't wait an hour or two to escape?'

'There is another way out,' said Mara. 'But we do not want to go that way, if we can help it.'

'An urd underkeep lies beneath Hammerholt,' said Aren. 'It was built over when the original fortress was destroyed, but it's still down there, and we think the Krodans have broken through the foundations and begun exploring. We don't know why, and we have no maps of it. But it's reasonable to assume there are other exits down there, even if we don't know where they are.'

'There will be no light, and no telling what we might find,' said Mara. 'I have studied urd architecture and culture extensively, and read reports from Delvers who have explored their ruins. The urds were masters at constructing traps, some of which might still be operational after all this time. It would be far better to leave through the caves.'

'And after that?' said Fen. 'If we do manage to get away with the Ember Blade?'

'If luck is with us, the Krodans will never even know who stole it. If not, it may be necessary to disappear for a while. We will leave ourselves maps and supplies in case.'

There was a moment of silence, and then Wilham clapped his hands, making Cade jump. 'Excellent!' he said brightly. 'I think you are mad, and you will all die; but it's audacious, I'll give you that.'

'A little audacity is what we need if we hope to free our country,' said Aren. 'Look where playing safe has got us.'

Wilham shrugged to concede the point, then finished his drink and stood up. 'Regardless, I wish you the Mummer's luck. If you can pull it off, they'll sing of you for ever. Any who decide not to go, you'll be welcome to join my people instead. We need brave folk, and if you're even considering going along with this ... Well, then you really *are* brave.'

The moment he was gone, Aren turned to them, his eyes flashing with determination. 'Did you hear?' he said. 'They will sing of us for ever! *That* is what the Ember Blade means to our people. Yes, there is risk – *great* risk; but it is worth the prize. I fear death, as do we all, but I would do this alone if I had to.'

'You will not go alone,' said Vika. 'Ruck and I are with you. If there is still hope for the champion to seize the blade, we must not falter.'

'Grub going, too! No one singing any songs that don't have Grub in them!'

Cade couldn't keep down a grin. The Skarl was obnoxious and annoying, but his reckless bravery was strangely inspiring. 'Well, I certainly ain't staying behind with Smiler and his miserable lot!'

Mara agreed, too, and Harod, and when it came to Orica, she smiled at them all, her face lighting up. 'I know how my song ends now,' she said. 'I hear it at last – I must find my lute, and some paper to mark it down!'

'Hold, hold,' said Mara. 'We are not finished.' She nodded at Fen, who hadn't yet spoken. All eyes turned to her, and she looked fearful and hunted in the lanternlight.

'How easily you put your lives in one another's hands,' she said quietly. Then she lowered her head. 'But we must stand together, or we will fall alone. I will come.'

'Don't worry,' Cade told her. 'We've done plenty of stupid stuff in the past, but Aren's never got me killed yet.'

'Then we are agreed,' said Aren. 'We go to make history. We go to take back our destiny!' He lifted his jack high, sloshing ale over the rim. 'For Garric, and the Ember Blade!' he cried.

In their answering cheer, Cade heard the sound of victory, and his chest swelled with pride as he roared his approval.

Look at me now, Da. Look at me now.

84

Oars creaked and water lapped against the rowing-boat as it slid across the lake towards a broken wall of grey cliffs. The sun was golden on the mountains and the air was crisp with the bite of coming winter. Grub leaned forward and pulled again, and the boat drew on, the small sounds of its passage swallowed by the enormous, lonely quiet of the lake.

Ruck sat at the prow like a figurehead, shaggy and straight-backed, tongue lolling in the wind. Vika hunkered beside her, patched furs and painted face, one hand on her hound. Aren and Cade were jammed in close, their eyes on the rearing cliffs and what lay beyond. Grub took up the middle bench and Fen was at the back, her green hood thrown up over her head. Her expression was dour and her eyes faraway, the better to conceal her fear, but Aren sensed it anyway. He knew her well enough by now.

'Why Grub always end up rowing?' the Skarl grumbled.

'You volunteered, you idiot,' Cade told him. 'After boasting how much stronger you are than all of us.'

Grub considered that. 'Still not seem fair,' he muttered.

Aren barely heard their bickering. His eyes were on Hammer-holt, a league distant or less, its upper reaches visible through a break in the cliffs. Even the mellow afternoon light and the hazy streamers of mist couldn't soften it. It was a sloped pile of walls and angles, dizzying in scale, crouched formidably among the peaks. Battlements piled upon battlements with parapets like teeth and square towers guarding every corner. There was hardly a curve on it, and nothing of glamour or glory. It was as solid as the mountains, a blunt statement of power. This was the keystone of Ossia, the point upon which all the country's might rested. Had Queen Alissandra Even-Tongue made her stand here, had she not been caught by surprise in a lesser fortress, the invasion might have gone very differently.

Aren felt a chill of nervous excitement at seeing their destination. Like Fen, he was afraid, but he had a ferocious certainty that she lacked. So much could go wrong, there were so many bad ends to this adventure, yet he believed in his heart they'd win out. He believed it with the kind of brash confidence he'd felt when he faced down Rapha, Klyssen and Wilham. He may have cast aside the Krodan god, and the Aspects had yet to convince him, but he was a man of faith nonetheless.

A man, not a boy. Not any more.

Sometime in the last few days there had been a change. He was centred, calm, self-possessed. No more was he his father's son, no longer a burden to others. His choices were his own now, and if they went to their deaths tonight, at least he'd die free.

Grub brought the boat into the shadow of the cliffs that edged the lake. They'd purchased it with Mara's money from a village on the far shore, hardly visible now in the mist. Fishing craft bobbed in the centre of the lake, but they didn't see a soul as they made their way along the barnacled feet of the cliffs, searching among the folds of rock. Somewhere here was an entrance to the caves, promised by the old map that Yarin had left them. By now the water should have lowered enough to reveal it.

If the map was right. If Mara's calculations were correct. If.

Aren tilted his head back. Lyssa was above them, ghostly in a rich blue sky. His mother's moon. Tantera would be along with the dark, pulling the water with her, battling Lyssa for her father's affection; for Joha was the Aspect of Sea and Sky, and the water remembered.

Had his mother known who his father was? he wondered. Was she complicit in his crimes, or was she deceived? And in the end, did it matter? Perhaps, he thought, it only affected him if he let it. His parents' choices were not his responsibility, and he didn't need to atone for decisions he had no hand in making. His mother, like

670

his father, was as distant and remote as the moon for which she'd been named. On some level he'd always be drawn to them, but they had no real power to change his course.

He'd get the Ember Blade back. Not to make up for his father's treachery, or to impress Garric, but because it was the right thing to do.

'Is that it?' said Cade. He was pointing off to port, where a narrow opening was half-visible in the darkness between two projecting rocks.

'It may be,' said Vika. 'Grub, bring us closer.'

Grub muttered something in Skarl as he hauled on the oars and steered them towards the opening. They had to duck as they entered, for the ceiling was low enough to hit their heads, but once inside they saw that the passageway headed on into darkness. It was chilly and dank beneath the rock, and cold water dripped on them.

Cade lit a lantern and held it up. Grub took the oars from the rowlocks, handed one to Aren, and they used them as poles, pushing against the sides of the passageway to propel the boat along. It was an awkward job in the crowded space, but the cave was too narrow to row.

They left the light of the afternoon behind. Glistening stone closed in, pressing down on them, and noises echoed eerily. Ruck whined and flattened her ears against her head.

Aren was pleased when the passageway branched: it matched the map of the caves, which Cade was holding. Cade directed them left. The ceiling got higher, or the water got lower, and soon they could sit up straight again, and everyone felt better. Aren took them down another turn, reassured that they were making progress. There'd be another junction ahead, according to the map.

Except there wasn't. There was only a wall of stone, blank and impassable. Aren and Grub poled them to a halt.

'Did I miss a turn?' Cade wondered.

'There shouldn't be a blockage here,' said Aren, puzzled. He'd been following the map with Cade, and there had been no mistake.

'The map is very old,' said Fen.

'Not as old as that rock is,' Cade said testily.

'Dumbface navigate like a drunk cow,' Grub opined.

'He's reading it aright,' said Aren. 'As am I.'

He peered more closely at the map, trying to see if there was some mark, some clue he'd missed, but this was the only way through. If they couldn't pass, then they'd fall at the first hurdle and the whole plan would lie in ruins. They'd placed their trust in him and his ideas. Failure here would crush him.

Then Vika chuckled. 'Peace,' she said. 'We are early, that is all. The water is still too high.'

Aren groaned in relief. Yes, she was surely right. The ceiling ahead was below the level of the water. They'd simply have to wait.

Wait they did, in the chill tomb of the waterway, as the black water lapped at the stone, each wave visibly lower than the last. It was dropping fast. Aren dreaded the moment when that downward creep would be reversed, when each little wave would be higher than the one before it, rising up to claim the caves once more.

To pass the time, they speculated on how Orica, Harod and Mara were faring. Orica had been hired on the spot, as they'd expected, and they'd left Harod and Mara in the safehouse, getting dressed up in clothes befitting guests of the Krodan Empire. Yet though their companions were entering by the front gate, they faced dangers every bit as real as those in the boat. How much had Keel told the Iron Hand? Did they have names and descriptions? Was Mara's invitation reliable? If they were caught, or refused entry, Aren and the others would never know.

He became aware of an irritating drumming noise: Cade's fingers on the gunwale of the boat.

'Ain't hardly the breathless charge into peril I was imagining,' Cade said as inch by inch the cave ahead was revealed.

At last they sank to a level where they could move forward by ducking down and pushing themselves along the ceiling with their hands. After a few uncomfortable minutes, the ceiling lifted again. The passage widened out into a cave and the light of the lantern barely reached the walls. They began to joke among themselves, feeling more cheerful now they were not so confined. Then they heard something splash in the dark, something that sounded larger than a fish, and they quieted again.

'The way through should be just over there,' Cade said, pointing.

'Grub feel more like rowing now,' the Skarl said. He took up the oars in haste and put his back into it, scanning the waters to either side as they went.

Lantern light played over the wall of the cave, brightening it steadily as they approached. It took Aren only a moment to find the mouth of the next passage, right where the map said it should be. As they got closer, he saw there was something inside it, throwing the light back wetly. He squinted to see, and when he realised what it was, his heart sank.

Bars. Vertical bars, set firm into the rock a short distance along the passage, with a gate allowing access. Grub brought them up to the gate and they pulled the boat in against it. The metal was rusted but sturdy, and a huge iron lock held the gate closed. Aren gave it an experimental tug but it didn't move.

'Let Grub see! Grub can pick any lock!' said Grub, clambering towards the front of the boat while the others fought to stop it from tipping. He muscled Ruck aside and peered into the keyhole, then sat back and thought for a moment.

'Grub can't pick that lock,' he announced firmly.

Cade let out a sigh of exasperation. 'One day we really ought to talk about your overconfidence.'

'It rusted solid!' Grub protested. 'Nobody put a key in it for a hundred years. Cade can't pick a lock if the parts don't move!'

'This gate's not on the map ...' Aren said, as if by pointing that out he might make it go away.

'I told you – the map's old,' said Fen. 'Someone put this in since it was drawn.'

Aren threw her an angry glance. She was being sullen as a defence against nerves, but it didn't make her unhelpfulness any easier to swallow.

'If I may?' said Vika, who was squashed behind Grub. She pushed past and Grub reluctantly moved aside. He began working his way back from the prow, threatening to tip them again.

'Don't know what Painted Lady can do that Grub can't,' he muttered. 'She going to pray it open?'

Ruck snarled at him, and he aimed the back of his hand at her before thinking better of it.

Vika studied the lock for a time while Aren chewed his lip, his confidence eroding. Another unforeseen problem, and they'd barely started. How many more were waiting? He'd been a fool to imagine this would go like clockwork, with so many uncertainties involved. Perhaps it was best if they were turned back now, before they got themselves killed. Wilham might have been right to call his plan a naïve fantasy.

Vika reached into her patchwork coat, pulled out a phial and emptied it over the top of the lock. It contained some kind of thick, glutinous liquid. She replaced the phial, took out another and unstoppered it.

'Push us away from the gate when I say,' she said. 'Do it gently, so I do not fall.' She poured the contents of the second phial on to the first. 'Now.'

They pushed away, Fen steadying Vika, and the boat slid backwards in the water. They watched the lock. Nothing happened.

Cade, as usual, was the first to state the obvious. 'Nothing's happeni—'

He was interrupted by a sharp hiss from the gate, growing louder till it was like a nest of snakes. A wisp of smoke rose from the lock, and then a tiny, furious white glow squirmed out of nowhere, growing in size and intensity until it was blindingly bright. Aren had to shade his eyes and look away until the noise and light faded again, leaving a smell of sulphur and tin.

'Now,' said Vika. 'Let us try again.'

They paddled closer. The passage was murky with a thin, toxic-smelling mist which obscured Aren's view until they were very close. When they bumped up against the gate, he was amazed to see that the lock had melted into a thick black sludge, shot through with specks of glowing red.

'Push,' she urged them, 'before it hardens.'

They pushed. The metal groaned and the lock stretched and pulled apart, but still the gate didn't give. They tried again, but the harder they pushed, the more the boat wanted to move away from the gate. Then Fen had the idea of propping the oars against the tunnel wall to brace them. They shoved once more, and this time the gate screeched open, suddenly enough that Vika had to grab Cade to stop him falling in.

'Yes! Grub knew he'd get through! He is unstoppable!' the Skarl cried.

They laughed and Aren grinned at the sight, ashamed of his doubts. *Who says Ossians can't work together?*

Vika caught his eye. 'How much sweeter the victory when it is shared, hmm?' she said quietly.

He smiled at her. 'I'm really glad you're back, Vika.'

'I would not be anywhere else,' she said. 'Now, onward, and may the Aspects go with us.'

Aspects go with you. Her words triggered a hint of a memory, which bothered Aren as they passed through the gate. The rough passageway was quickly becoming wider and higher as the water lowered, and he let Cade navigate as he tried to remember when he'd heard those words last. Finally it came to him.

'Vika,' he said.

'Aye?'

'Just after you woke, when Garric said his farewells and set off with Keel … You realised something, didn't you? I remember seeing it on your face. Did you suspect Keel then?'

'Keel?' she said. 'No. No, I am sorry to say I had no idea about him. It was Garric who concerned me.'

'Why?'

She weighed her words, her face thoughtful. 'When he said farewell … and I could be mistaken, Aren, though I am not often … When he said farewell, I believe he knew it was the last time he would ever see us. He did not intend to come back. I heard it in his voice.'

'But how could he bring us the Ember Blade if he didn't mean to return?'

'That, I do not know,' she said. Then she shook it off. 'It matters not, Aren. Our task is unchanged.'

But her dismissal was too brusque to be convincing. The news settled uneasily on Aren, and the dark seemed a little darker after that.

★

At length, they neared the tunnel promised by the map, the waterway built in days gone by to link this network of caves to the caves underneath Hammerholt. They'd emerged from the passageways into a large cavern, and as they rounded a bulge of stone they found the tunnel entrance before them. Cade sat up a little straighter, raising his lantern.

'Nine,' he breathed. 'Now ain't that a sight to see?'

The mouth of the tunnel was wide enough for five of their boats, and was flanked by two thick pillars cut from the mountain rock, their surfaces carved with huge leering faces, cavorting figures and strange beasts. The centuries had worn the detail from them, but they still possessed an unsettling primal savagery, and the faces – heavy of jaw and brow, small-eyed, subtly inhuman – unnerved them all. The massive lintel overhead bore an inscription, still visible after all this time, but the message held in those stark, jagged runes was a mystery to them.

'Urds,' said Vika, in a low voice. 'Once they were the masters of Ossia, over the earth and under it.'

Grub studied the pillars as they slid past. 'Grub think they not as ugly as the new lot.'

Cade snorted with laughter.

The tunnel was a wide, square channel, walled with immense mould-streaked bricks and supported by more pillars and lintels along its length. Glaring faces loomed and receded to either side, craggy and shadowed. Some were urds, brutish and fierce, but others were more monstrous, with huge teeth and bulging eyes. They wore necklaces of ears or sported manes made of swords. Aren sensed the malevolence of old gods here, angry at being robbed of their might, and it made him feel small.

'Do not fear,' said Vika, responding to his unspoken thought. 'They cannot hurt us now.'

'They can if they decide to stop holding up that roof,' said Cade.

The tunnel was long, and seemed longer, but at last they rowed out into another cave, higher than it was wide, its upper reaches in darkness. Before them was a metal ladder fixed to the cave wall, rising to a ledge overhead. Running alongside it was a vertical mooring pole.

'Can you see a door?' Aren asked, craning.

Cade raised his lantern high, but the projecting ledge obscured his view. 'Reckon we need to go up there and look,' he said.

They tied the boat to the pole, leaving the knot loose enough that it would slide up as the water rose. Then they clambered out one by one, except for Vika, who stayed with Ruck. Cade was first up the ladder, climbing awkwardly with the lantern in one hand and Aren close behind him. The ledge was broad and naturally formed, and there they found the door, as promised.

The two of them exchanged a grin. It was a relief just to have got this far. Even this small success encouraged them.

They examined the door. It was narrow and low, made of metal, and it looked thick. Aren doubted even Vika's concoction could burn through it, assuming she had any left. There was no lock on their side, but a crank extended from the centre, lying flat against the door. Aren tried to turn it downwards, and then up, but no matter how he pulled or pushed, it would only move a fraction. Something was barring it on the other side, as they'd feared.

By this time, Fen and Grub had got up the ladder. Grub insisted on trying himself, with no better luck. Aren looked over the ledge to Vika and Ruck.

'Are you coming?'

'The tide has turned, I think,' Vika said, her particoloured face eerily bright against the dark mass of her coat. 'I will wait for the water to lift us higher. Easier than carrying Ruck.'

Aren stood back and looked around at the others. He was eager to act, to move on, but the next step was out of his hands. He didn't like that feeling.

'I suppose we must wait, then,' he said. 'Let us hope our friends in the fortress are successful.'

'That, or better learn to breathe water,' said Grub grimly.

Fen hugged herself and gazed into the dark. Cade noticed and forced a jovial tone.

'Hoy! Does anyone know the story of how Hallec Stormfist

677

fought his way through the hordes of the Revenant King and slew him in single combat?'

'It rings a bell,' said Aren wryly, 'though the version I heard was about a Krodan warrior called Hokke storming the castle of the Lich–Lord.'

Cade cackled. 'I reckon you'll like this version better.' His face came alive in the lanternlight as he turned his attention to his audience, and the performance began.

'So there was Hallec, alone, having lost all his faithful companions on the trek across the Plains of Poison Fire. All his companions but one, which he was never without: a sword that glowed red as molten rock as the dawn sun struck it, an unbreakable weapon, sharp as time's teeth. The Ember Blade, they called it, and he carried it with him into the lair of his greatest enemy, the herald of the Outsiders: the Revenant King himself!'

They listened, eager for distraction, as Cade told his tale. Below them the water lapped hungrily against the stone, creeping higher with every little wave.

85

I'm late. I'm late. I'm late.

Orica tapped her foot nervously against the floor of the cart, her lute – safe in its case – clutched to her side. Sards, like Ossians, were not generally concerned with punctuality, but tonight was an exception.

The troupe and their instruments were crowded into two carts, roofed with canvas but open at the sides. Towering before them was another massive gatehouse, the third they'd encountered. At each there had been queues, checks and searches, driving both Orica and their harried leader to distraction. Delays, delays, delays, and with every wasted moment the water in the caves rose higher.

The road through the mountains was clogged with traffic by the time they reached it. Guests and their retinues jostled with merchants delivering last-minute supplies and teams of soldiers borrowed from the Morgenholme garrison. They'd seen signs of the Iron Hand, too: an outsized black wagon with huge wheels, the double-barred cross emblazoned on its flanks. Its contents were a mystery, but Orica felt the cold touch of dread as it passed, which didn't lift until it was gone.

Soon the road had narrowed, passing between two shoulders of rock topped by squat guard towers, and they'd been funnelled into the shadow of Hammerholt. Some of the musicians gasped at the scale of it as it sprawled up the slope where the mountains met, a forest of square towers penned behind tiered walls that rose steep and angular against the evening sky.

Once inside, their pace had slowed even further. The best

organisation in the world couldn't cope with so many people arriving at once, and the fortress was designed to repel rather than welcome. They inched along walled corridors intended to hamper invaders, beneath rows of murder holes through which arrows could be fired and boiling oil could be poured.

At last, they'd reached the final obstacle, the gatehouse that gave access to the inner fortress, where the night's festivities would be held. Already the eleventh bell o' day had sounded. She had less than two hours left; more like one-and-a-half by now. They were scheduled to perform at twelfth bell, providing half an hour of entertainment before the guests headed to their feasts. There'd be a break before the post-dinner performances, which was the perfect moment to slip away. But if they started late, or if the proceedings went on too long…

Surely not. These were Krodans, the most diligent timekeepers in Embria.

'Don't worry,' said Olin. He was an elderly Bitterbracker who played the idra, a traditional Ossian ram-skin drum. 'Nobles or peasants, an audience is an audience, eh?'

Orica looked down at her tapping foot, stilled it and gave Olin a smile of gratitude. He'd misunderstood the source of her agitation – she could play for the Aspects themselves and not worry – but it was kind of him. A few of the others were visibly displeased to have a Sard among them, but most, like Olin, treated her like anyone else, and the harpist eyed her with obvious lust. Musicians were travellers, always on the move, and less apt to hold the cosy prejudices enjoyed by small-town folk who were never exposed to any but their own sort.

Edgen was the leader of the troupe, a fractious middle-aged Rainlander with a flowing moustache and a mane of glossy black hair that he played with constantly. He was speaking to a gate guard, trying to keep his temper as he ran through the same answers he'd given at the last two gatehouses. Krodan soldiers passed up and down the carts, eyeing Orica with particular suspicion. She kept her gaze on the floor of the cart and said nothing.

She wished Harod were here. It was a new feeling, this sense of need. She was bereft without him, and that thought didn't make her comfortable. She'd always been independent, even for a Sard, who prized freedom higher than most. How quickly she'd become accustomed to Harod's tall, solid presence at her side. How easily she trusted him to guard her, when once she'd guarded herself.

How absurd that she was jealous of Mara, for being on his arm tonight.

The Ragged Mummer liked her tricks, but it was Sabastra, Aspect of Love and Beauty, who made fools of them all, and the two of them loved to work together. At first, she'd thought Harod a strange fish, but she knew the ways of Harrow and she was impressed by his awkward declaration of loyalty the night she played at his father's court. For the Harrish, who considered showing emotion to be the mark of an unschooled serf, it was madly romantic, impossibly gallant.

Of course she'd refused, for he was already betrothed and she wanted to save him from himself. But he'd persisted, and when she left for Ossia he'd followed, catching her up on the road. By then, he'd already spoken with his betrothed and destroyed himself in the eyes of his family and peers. She talked with him long enough to ensure he understood her circumstances, and that the most she could offer was friendship. He was undeterred, so she accepted him. It wasn't the Sard way to reject willing company.

She knew he burned with love for her, but he was ever chaste, polite and restrained, and after some time together, she came to trust that he'd never act on his love, or even speak of it, unless she invited him to. And she couldn't help being flattered by the force of his attention. Sard passions burned bright and were rarely hidden, but this was of a different order, a level of sacrifice she'd never expected. He was a good and admirable man who'd fallen for her at first sight and given up everything for her. It was hard not to be a little intoxicated by that.

How slowly Sabastra worked her art, and how the Ragged Mummer must have laughed behind her hand. As their friendship deepened, Orica began to see the man beyond that wall of Harrish reserve. She found kindness, a passion for justice, unexpected warmth and humour. She came to admire his morals and his discipline, and to understand what he'd done when he turned his back on his family. To follow your heart was the ultimate rebellion in Harrow, but he'd chosen dishonour rather than to betray his, even with no hope of reward.

He was so different to any man she'd loved before, so far from what she thought she wanted, that she didn't recognise what was happening until it was too late to avert the heartbreak that had to follow. They were together, yet they could never be together, not as lovers should be. The risk was far too great.

It was well known that Sards were forbidden to bed anyone other than a Sard. But only they knew the real reason why.

'Get on with you, then!'

The voice stirred her from her thoughts. The gate guard was done with Edgen and the first cart was moving through. A soldier slapped the side of Orica's cart and they jerked into motion, rattling under the arch into a crowded courtyard where a dozen other carts were being unloaded.

No sooner had they stopped than they were spotted by an angry man in fine velvets and a bearskin cloak, who came hurrying over.

'Edgen! By the Primus, where have you been?'

The Master of Revels was a red-faced, bespectacled man with a white moustache and mutton-chop whiskers, wearing a rabbit-fur hat to cover his bald pate. He'd evidently had a long day, and what patience he possessed had been used up some time ago.

'My deepest apologies,' Edgen said. 'We set off early but we shed a wheel on the way and—'

'Get your people ready! I want you tuning up in the West Gallery in ten minutes! Do you—' He stopped as he noticed Orica's bright green eyes. 'Is that a *Sard*?'

Edgen paled. 'Madilla fell ill and this is her replacement. I had no other choice. I assure you, she is an exquisite musician—'

'Toven's blood! I don't care how she plays! She's—' The master closed his eyes and pressed his fingers to his temples, where the veins were beginning to throb. 'No matter. It's too late to switch you around. For your sake, you'd better hope the prince doesn't take exception to having a Sard in his presence.'

'The *prince*?' Edgen squeaked.

'I promised him the best *Ossian* musicians to play the finest

682

songs of the land he is soon to rule. That would be you. At least, I thought it was.'

'She *is* from Ossia,' Edgen said weakly, but the master's glare warned him to go no further.

'Don't disappoint me,' the master said venomously and clicked his fingers at a servant who was hovering nearby. 'Take them to the West Gallery!' he said, and then he was off, shouting at someone else.

'You heard him!' said Edgen, hurrying to the rear of the cart. 'Ten minutes!' He gave Orica a barbed look, as if it was her fault he'd been snapped at.

Orica said nothing, just as she'd said nothing to the Master of Revels. Once, she'd played in the highest courts of Harrow, for the king himself, and been treated as an honoured guest. There were few Sards in Harrow and they were not numerous enough to be despised, unlike here where she was talked down to, sneered at or discussed as if she wasn't there. Yet she'd swallow their insults, as she always had. She'd keep her mouth shut and her head down, and she'd fight for her land. Because whatever they said, she *was* Ossian, and this was her home.

'Prince Ottico!' Olin was saying excitedly as he gathered up his drum. 'We're playing for the prince!'

No, thought Orica as she stepped down from the cart with the lute under her arm. *We're playing for my friends' lives.*

86

The great hall of Hammerholt echoed with hundreds of voices speaking in a dozen languages. Harod and Mara, having been shown in moments before, stood at the edge of the sea of faces and looked out over the remarkable gathering before them.

Crowded together beneath the towering stone arches were representatives of many countries, from Embria and beyond, even as far as Caragua in the uttermost west. Here were black-skinned Xulans, elegant as water; red Helicans from the arid south, painted and pierced; desert-dwelling Boskans like beetles inside their rigid hoods; Carthanians, richly clad and raucous; tall Trinish from the mountain forests; Lunish, arguing as ever; Shangi, calm as always; drab grey Galts; Ossian nobles; haughty Harrish; sober Krodans; and more, and more besides, from all across the lands. They'd come to witness a historic union, the joining of the two most powerful forces on the continent, and to jockey for position in the new future ahead.

'There are some here that shall know me,' said Harod, showing none of the unease Mara knew he felt. 'They will know of my disgrace.'

Mara looked at him. He was dressed in a green velvet jacket, dark purple hose and soft doeskin boots they'd picked up on Chandlery Lane. A short cloak covered one shoulder, pinned there with a silver brooch in the shape of a draccen *sejant*: the emblem of Harrow. She'd hardly seen him out of his armour until yesterday and the clothes of his homeland suited him well.

'Knowing, they will not speak to thee,' she said. She spoke

in Harrish, as did he. 'And they will not dare to question thy presence. So let them gossip among themselves. They can do us no harm.' She held up her arm for him to take. 'Let us find our quarry.'

He took her arm and they made their way into the crowd, where they were offered wine. Harod refused, but Mara accepted a glass. It was a Carthanian white, dry and woody and delicate. She savoured it while she listened to the sixteen-piece orchestra playing at the far end of the hall, smoothing the tempest of conversation with the sweet harmony of strings. The Carthanians might make the best wine – only Amberlyne was comparable – but the Krodans made the best music. Nothing equalled the mathematical grace of the Krodan maestros.

Shrill, breathless laughter caught her ear as two fair-haired Trinish children darted through the crowd, a brother and sister chasing one another, drawing scowls and indulgent chuckles. They passed Mara, and were gone.

The joy of their game brought a smile to Mara's lips for a moment, but it faded fast as blissful imaginings gave way to cold reality. The children she longed for were someone else's, as was the man she might have had them with. That had been her choice. She'd seen children as the end of life, not the beginning. She'd believed that to be a wife and mother would be to submit to the Krodan way, to forfeit her power and independence. After that, there was only the slow decline into domesticity, giving up the extraordinary for the mundane.

Would that have really been her fate? She didn't know. But she'd been younger then, fiercer, more certain of things. So she'd refused Danric his dearest wish, and it had broken them, and he found another. To the end of her days, she'd never be sure if she'd had a lucky escape or made a colossal mistake; but in moments like this, she knew which one it felt like.

A terrible thought struck her. She saw a flash in her mind, a roar like thunder, fire billowing through the doorways. Children screaming; wounded, burned, dead. Little girls, just like those she'd once taught. She'd known there might be children in Hammerholt when Garric had outlined his plan, but it had been easy to dismiss it then, when she couldn't see their faces. Easy to say they were a necessary sacrifice when she hadn't heard them laugh.

Danric had never liked the way she could wall off her heart with logic, separate herself from her feelings with facts. But it was a skill that only went so far. She could never wall herself off from him.

Peace, she told herself. *Garric's plan will not come to pass now. Nobody will die.*

It hadn't seemed necessary to tell Aren and the others about Garric's plan to destroy Hammerholt with barrels of elarite oil. Let them keep believing he was trying to steal the Ember Blade. Aren had impressed her with his mind and his character, but he was still idealistic, not ready to see Garric as he truly was. If they managed to rescue him, Garric might well lead them again, and it would only harm the cause if they knew the truth.

She didn't know where the barrels were now, whether they'd been delivered or not, but it hardly mattered. They had a new plan, which Mara and Aren had cooked up between them. It was best to let sleeping dogs lie.

'The Iron Hand,' Harod muttered, directing her attention to two black-uniformed men standing together at the edge of the room. One was short and balding, with spectacles and a somewhat froggy look about him. The other was stern, blond and handsome in a Krodan sort of way.

'They are on their guard,' Mara said. 'They suspect something, perhaps.'

'Garric cannot have talked or we would have been arrested at the gate.'

'Likely thou art right. Certain, the security has been no stricter than we expected. Perhaps the Krodans imagine the danger is over now that Garric is in irons.' She watched as the men scanned the room. 'I do not think those two share that view.'

Mara kept an eye on them until they left, the taller one limping as he went. Their presence made her tense. It was a reminder that torture and death awaited them if they failed.

'There he is,' said Harod. 'The Master of Keys.'

He wasn't hard to recognise from his description. The Master of Keys was imposing in size, broad-shouldered and big-bellied. His face was soft and jowly, and a roll of flesh sat between his chin and his collarbone. His jacket was stitched with the crossed keys of his office, and he wore a golden medallion on a heavy chain around his neck.

'We should introduce ourselves,' said Mara.

Before they could do so, the orchestra stopped and a bell rang for attention. Conversation petered out as all eyes turned to the servant with the bell.

'Honoured guests!' he called. 'It is my pleasure to inform you that performances of traditional Ossian folk music are about to begin in the West Gallery, the Blue Room and Stoker's Hall. Please consult your programmes and make your way to your assigned rooms; otherwise you are welcome to stay and enjoy yourselves here. Thank you for your attention.'

There was a general murmuring as the guests found the printed papers they'd been given upon arrival, each one a schedule dictating where they were supposed to be and when, personalised according to their importance.

'Leave it to the Krodans to throw a party and then organise the guests to within an inch of their lives,' Mara muttered. Even for her, an orderly woman by nature, this was taking things a little far.

'It is not dissimilar to how we do it in Harrow,' said Harod, puzzled at the scorn in her tone. 'How else is one to control so many people without inviting chaos?'

'This land could use a little chaos,' said Mara. 'Come.' She headed off across the hall.

'The Blue Room is that way,' said Harod, looking up from his schedule and pointing in the opposite direction.

'We're not going to the Blue Room.'

Harod had to hurry to catch her up. The crowd was beginning to thin out as the guests drifted to their designated rooms. Mara kept her eye on the Master of Keys. He was the target; schedules be damned.

They were carried after him on a tide of excited chatter and exotic perfumes, down stone corridors where servants waited to guide them onwards. Soon they came to a long chamber set with dozens of portraits on one wall. Tapestries hung on the other, showing parables from the Acts of Tomas and Toven in the Krodans' distinctive geometric style.

Seats had been laid out in rows for the guests. The Master of Keys had already taken his place when they entered and the seats around him were filled, preventing them from getting close. They were shown to seats several rows behind him by an usher, and they had to be content with that.

'Yonder is Prince Ottico,' said Harod as they made their way along the row.

Mara, not so tall as Harod, took a moment to find him. He was sitting at the front, his head turned to the side as he joked with a neighbour about something. She recognised him from his portraits, though the artists had flattered him, making him look more regal than was true. In life, he was dough-faced, with long sideburns and a wispy moustache on his upper lip. He had the milky look of one who'd been spoiled and indulged so long that they knew no other way.

He will soon rule this land, Mara thought. *But he will not have the Ember Blade when he does.*

A bell began to toll in the heights as they seated themselves. Mara didn't need to wait for it to finish to know the count. Last bell o' day. Outside, the sun was slipping behind the mountains, and in the deeps below Hammerholt, the water was climbing the cave walls, black and freezing.

'After the performance has begun, if thou canst do so without drawing attention, excuse thyself,' said Mara quietly in Harrish. 'Feign that thou art ill, if necessary, and find the door. I shall attend to the Master of Keys.'

Harod nodded and they settled in their seats. For the first time, they looked at the stage and the musicians assembled there. Harod stiffened. Mara had no need to ask why.

There, hidden at the back, was Orica.

87

Quietly, relentlessly, the water stole higher. Vika watched it with flat eyes over the side of the boat. Beneath the broken glimmers thrown back from Cade's lantern, it was utterly black. An abyss rising inch by inch to claim them.

Is this how it will end? she thought to herself. *With all consumed by darkness?*

She thought of Agalie, so warm and wise. In Vika's mind, she was sitting owlishly by a campfire, her hands clasped round a steaming wooden mug, a knowing half-smile on her face. *You will find us a champion*, she'd said. And perhaps Vika had. Or perhaps she'd misread the signs and they'd all die here. Perhaps the only voice she'd ever heard was her own, and the gods she'd met merely the conjurings of a damaged mind.

Ruck lifted her head and whined, sensing her mistress's doubts.

The boat had almost reached the stone ledge where the others waited in grim silence. Even Cade's good cheer had faltered in the pressing dark as the chill set in. Now they watched the door, and each other, the passing of time measured by soft drips from the ceiling.

'The water will be around your ankles soon,' said Vika. 'Come back to the boat.'

'Should it be rising this fast?' Cade asked. 'What if Mara got her calculations wrong?'

Aren stirred. 'I don't think she ever gets her calculations wrong.'

'She was working off a two-hundred-year-old map and a bunch

of moon charts,' Cade argued. 'Even *she* would have a hard time being accurate with that.'

'Door will open,' said Grub. 'Bowlhead or Tonsils open it. Grub is very confident.' But Vika heard fear in his voice, fear of a death he wasn't yet ready for.

'We have time yet,' Vika agreed, though she'd lost all sense of what time it was.

One by one, they climbed back into the boat. Ruck reluctantly got up and moved to the stern, grumbling low in her throat. When they were all in, Vika passed round a phial.

'Drink this,' she told them. 'A sip each.'

Grub sniffed it. 'Booze?' he asked hopefully.

'No. But it will warm your bones deeper and for longer than any liquor can.'

'Painted Lady hasn't tried witch-tear rum from Skara Thun,' said Grub. 'Drink that, then roll in fire to cool down.'

'Sounds good to me right now,' said Cade.

When they'd all taken a sip, she did, too, and let Ruck lap a little from her cupped hand. Heat spread through her, making her fingers tingle and bringing a flush to her face.

'That ain't bad,' said Cade. 'Nine, I feel like I should take my coat off.'

'You may need it yet,' said Vika, thinking of the killing cold of the lake water.

She untied the rope that tethered the boat to the mooring pole and cast it free. It would only drag them under when the water rose higher. Slowly they drifted away from the ledge, out into the cavern. She looked up at the ceiling, not far above them now.

Joha, hold back your waters, she prayed. *Our people will come for us. Give them time.*

88

Orica played. It was all she'd ever wanted to do, since she first laid hands on her mother's lute in the warm summer shadows of the communal caravan. Music, like blood, was life to her.

Every significant moment in her past was linked to a song. Her earliest memory was her mother humming a lullaby while Orica sat in her lap, drowsy in the warmth of a fire. She remembered the tumbling drums of *Llach Na Thuun* playing nearby as she and her first love lost themselves in a twist of blankets beneath an ash tree. The delicate arpeggios of a Trinish lament healed her heart after the same boy rejected her, for nobody told tales of heroic sorrow like the bards of Trine. Then there was the song that was played when her mother remarried; and the one that so impressed her master he said he had no more to teach her; and the song that made Harod fall in love with her.

Music surrounded her, shaped her, underpinned her world. When she played, she tuned herself to the key of Creation.

Yet as the troupe ran through Edgen's selection of Ossian folk songs, Orica couldn't feel the music. Her mind was elsewhere, with her companions in the cave, and worry gnawed at her. Her fingers knew their places on the fretboard, but she played mechanically, without passion.

Few in the audience noticed. An average performance from Orica was still head and shoulders above what most bards could manage. But Edgen scowled at her, because she'd been better in her audition. He scowled more deeply when Orica began the next song at a brisk clip, faster than it ought to be played, forcing the rest of the troupe to follow her tempo.

Orica didn't care. The quicker they finished, the quicker she could leave.

She glanced at Prince Ottico as they launched into their final tune, a jaunty number about women and wine. The songs had been picked for their inoffensiveness. There was nothing about the Aspects, for these were the Primus's lands now; and nothing of Jessa Wolf's-Heart, Ossia's most beloved rebel. It had been a wise decision on Edgen's part, for the prince appeared to be enjoying himself immensely. His foot tapped to the beat of Olin's idra and he had a broad smile on his face. If he had an issue with a Sard being onstage, it didn't show.

Everything was still going well as the troupe drew the last song to a close and the crowd began to applaud. The grin on Edgen's face was one of profound relief as he bowed to the prince, who was applauding loudest of all.

'Wonderful!' he cried, and he rose to his feet, forcing everyone to rise with him. 'Encore! Play another!'

Edgen beamed with delight at the honour. He bowed low and turned back to the troupe. '"The Mountain Man's Jig"!' he cried. 'One, two, three—'

Orica struck her chord and the pipes began to play, but horror was growing in her heart. Her fellow musicians' smiles were nightmarish rictuses, the tune jarring and discordant to her ear.

He wants more? How many more? How long will he have us play?

Somewhere in the dark, the water was rising.

Mara saw their chance when the prince got to his feet. 'Now,' she said to Harod.

Harod had been watching raptly, his eyes fixed on Orica. He shook out of his trance as the audience around him rose, clapping enthusiastically in imitation of Prince Ottico. Even those who didn't care for the music were pretending to be impressed. Mara gave Harod a gentle shove to get him moving, and he began to blunder his way along the row, squeezing his large frame between the applauding guests.

Then Mara heard the prince call for more, and the troupe struck up another tune. The applause died away and the audience began to seat themselves again, stripping Harod of his cover before he reached the end of the row.

Seeing him leaving, a servant hurried to intercept him. Mara couldn't hear what was said, but the servant's raised hands and urgent muttering didn't bode well.

Let him pass, Mara thought fiercely. It was imperative that they stayed beneath the notice of their hosts, and every moment Harod was delayed drew more eyes towards him.

But the servant wouldn't let him pass. Mara saw Harod put his hand on his belly, miming sickness, but the servant only gestured back towards Harod's empty seat, apologetic but insistent.

Everybody behind them was watching their quiet argument. People nearby scowled and tutted, distracted by their voices. One of the guards stationed at the side of the hall stirred at his post, wondering if he needed to intervene.

Let him pass! Mara thought again, more urgently. She knew what the encore meant. Their already fine margins were narrowing fast, and Orica was still tied up with her performance. Harod *had* to get to that door in the sewers. But if any more fuss were made, then some officious attendant would be forced to take him aside and deal with him, reducing his chances of slipping away to nil.

In the front row, the prince turned and looked over his shoulder, an irritable frown on his face. The servant saw him and blanched. 'Please, Sar, you must!' he said, almost begging now. The guard began to walk over and Harod was forced to concede. With one last indignant comment, he made his way back along the row, running the gauntlet of disapproving stares and tuts. He must have been mortified by the ordeal, but his face was rigid and he didn't so much as blush as he sat down.

'They would not let thee leave?' Mara whispered.

'Nay,' he said. 'The prince considers himself a great patron of the arts, it seems, and believes that to leave in the midst of a performance shows disrespect to the performer. No such disrespect is permitted in his presence.'

Mara cursed herself silently. How had she not known that? It wasn't in Yarin's notes, but that was no excuse; she should have researched it herself. It was only a small detail, easily overlooked amid the mass of other information she'd absorbed, but small details could topple empires and cost lives. She thought she'd considered every angle, but she'd missed this one. Now all three of them were trapped in the same hall, and still the music played on, counting out the remainder of their companions' lives beat by beat by beat.

Fen hunkered down low in the boat. She had no choice. The roof of the cavern was so close, she couldn't sit up any longer.

Black water below them, hard rock above, the six of them sandwiched in the thinning layer between. Cade's lantern rested on the floor of the boat, casting its light over their frightened faces. There was desperate hope in their eyes, each of them alert for any intervention which could save them; but it was becoming ever clearer that there might not *be* any salvation. And soon there wouldn't be any air.

Don't lean on anyone or anything, Fen. Not no place or person. Elsewise, when they fall, you'll fall with 'em.

No. She wouldn't let herself believe that. Orica and Harod and Mara would come through. They had to.

Vika was praying to Joha, bent over in a forced bow, her mouth moving and her eyes closed. Ruck huddled beside her. Cade was praying, too, but Grub was becoming panicked, his eyes wild, palms on the ceiling as if he could fend it off.

Aren's hand sought Fen's and gripped it. She met his gaze. Scared as he was, she found strength there.

'They'll be here,' he said.

She loved him a little for that, for making her believe. There was something indomitable in him which wouldn't lie down and die. Sometimes she was amazed by it. Amazed by *him*. She wanted to kiss him, hold him frantically tight, push away the terror of death with passion. But the thought paralysed her, and she could do nothing but offer a wan smile of thanks.

'Nobody's coming,' Grub muttered. Then, louder: 'Nobody's coming!' His voice became a shriek. 'Grub not ready to meet the

Bone God! Grub not want to be Unremembered! Grub sorry for what he did! Grub sorry!'

'Pipe down, you noisy bastard!' Cade snapped angrily, lashing out with his own fear.

But Grub wasn't listening. He tried to get to his feet but only pressed up against the ceiling, rocking the boat alarmingly. 'Can't stay here! Grub swim for it! Swim back to the lake!'

'Don't be a mudwit! You'll never make it!'

'Grub can't stay here!'

He lurched towards the edge of the boat, pushing Vika aside as he went. The sudden shift in weight tipped them. Fen gave a scream of surprise as the boat flipped underneath her and she was plunged into freezing water, soaked to the bone, shocked by the cold of it. Even with Vika's potion warming her, it took her breath away. She flailed, searching desperately for the surface, but the lantern had gone out and in the darkness she couldn't tell which way was up.

Lost in the abyss, clutching to the last moments of life, one thought broke through her panic.

Da, you were right. I should have listened. You were right.

Harod's attempt to leave the hall hadn't escaped Orica's attention. She knew his posture so well, she could identify him at any distance. She felt the thrill of contact as she saw him, the illicit shock of two saboteurs crossing paths. Until that moment, she hadn't known he was in the room.

She watched as he argued with the servant, her heart sinking, hands moving mechanically through the chords of the jig. She saw him turn back to sit down next to Mara. Now she guessed what Mara had already realised: none of them could leave until the music stopped.

The jig wound down to its close and the audience clapped again. *That's it, let us go!* Orica thought. *It's time for the interval.* But the prince was still seated and showed no sign of getting up. A servant whispered in his ear, but was waved away impatiently. Prince Ottico still expected more.

Edgen turned to his troupe, looking a little panicked now. 'Quick!' he said. '"The Maven's Respite"!'

'I don't know it,' Orica said, before anyone could strike up the song. It was a lie, but it was all she could think to do.

'You don't know it?' Edgen said, aghast. 'Everyone knows it! "Lord Lusty and the Swan", then.'

'I don't know that one, either,' said Orica. She was trying to stall them, but she couldn't do it for long. Sooner or later, Edgen would think of a piece that could be played without a lute.

'The prince wants another song!' Edgen said, his voice quiet and strangled, his eyes boring daggers into Orica's skull. 'What *do* you know?'

And then it hit her, a thought so wild and *right* that she could do nothing but act on it. It was as if all the convolutions of her life had played out in order to place her here, at exactly this moment.

'I have a song for the prince,' she said, and walked to the front of the stage.

Edgen goggled at her, aghast, but the whole audience had seen her intention and he couldn't send her back without embarrassment. All he could do was move aside, with a sickly grin, and pretend this was planned.

'You'd better know what you're doing,' he said through gritted teeth.

Then Orica was alone at the front of the stage, with only her lute between her and Prince Ottico and a hundred dignitaries behind him. Some of them – Ossians and Krodans, mostly – murmured at the gall of a Sard presenting herself so brazenly to the prince. But she only thought of one man as she played the introductory arpeggio, and her heart swelled as the music found her. Her voice carried across the hall, husky and haunting, taking all her worry and fear with it.

The king stood at his window in his castle on the shore.
His family were sleeping, his foes were no more.
As he looked o'er the sea he heard knuckles on the door.
'Twas his seer, white as a ghost.

> *'Sire, please beware, for a storm does draw near*
> *That will tear down your walls and take all you hold dear.'*
> *But the king laughed and knew he had nothing to fear*
> *And he turned his old eyes to the coast.*

The murmuring had died away; her voice always had the power to surprise a crowd to silence. Even the prince looked up at her with something like awe.

> *He said, 'I see no clouds, and the waves are not high.*
> *Your omens mislead you, your bones fall awry.'*
> *But the seer said, 'Sire, not all storms come from the sky.*
> *There are depths to which you cannot see.*

> *'The tide is returning, and coming right soon.*
> *It brings with it those you have sent to their doom.*
> *There's a wolf in the waves who yet howls from its tomb*
> *And the fallen keep long memory.'*

She saw suspicion dawning on him now, the sense that something was wrong. This tune wasn't harmless, like the others. His face fell slowly and hardened, and Orica felt nothing but triumph at the sight.

> *Then the king said, 'You lie! For this land is my land!*
> *Passed on to me by fate's bloodied right hand.'*
> *'But sire,' said the seer, 'though you think you command,*
> *Your rule is but fleeting here.*

> *'There are elder things yet than the god you obey*
> *And none may lay claim to this soil, try you may.*
> *For this land will be here after you pass away*
> *And its children will still persevere.'*

Prince Ottico's face was a picture of sullen anger. He knew he was being defied, perhaps laughed at, but he didn't understand how or why, and that made it worse. Many in the audience looked

697

appalled while others listened happily, their command of Ossian too weak to read between the lines.

Orica raised her eyes and found Harod in the audience. Even at this distance, she saw his eyes sparkling with tears, his face slack with admiration and fear for her.

This is for you, my love, she thought.

Said the king, 'For this heresy, I'll see you burn.
I say destiny's charge is not easy to turn.'
But the seer shook his head. 'Sire, you have much to learn,
For the urds said the same in their day.'

Now the king stands at his window and watches the sea
And he knows that his castle's no sanctuary
As he waits for the truth of the seer's prophecy
And the storm that will sweep him away.

As the final chord rang out into silence, she felt herself blissfully empty. After so long, her song was complete, and it was perfect. Let them do as they would with her now. Her music had been heard.

Scattered applause faltered and died in the audience as the prince glared up at her. Edgen squirmed in an agony of exquisite humiliation, desperate to salvage the moment, not knowing how. Orica stood alone, the focus of it all, and held her head high.

'I have heard enough Ossian music,' said the prince at last, and stalked out of the hall. His attendants hurried after him.

'Honoured guests!' cried a servant. 'Please make your way to your assigned rooms for dinner, which will be served shortly!'

The tension broke and the audience all began to talk at once, rustling and gossiping and scraping chairs as they got to their feet and began flowing towards the exits. Orica walked past her stunned fellows to the back of the stage, her heart hammering, and returned her lute to its case. She didn't dare look over her shoulder, afraid that some agent of the Iron Hand was already making their way to the stage to arrest her. If she didn't look, she might stay beneath their notice for long enough to leave the hall.

A hand fell on her shoulder before she could pick up the case.

'What was *that*?' Edgen hissed. 'What in Joha's name did you *do*, you little Sard bitch?'

The hate in that word was like ice down Orica's back. Edgen had never shown any signs of prejudice against her race, but how quickly the veil fell now she'd displeased him.

She pushed his hand off her shoulder and turned, such fury in her gaze that he took a step back, surprised by the force of it. Elbowing her way past him, she headed for the small door behind the stage.

Edgen followed her. 'Where do you think you're going?' he demanded in an angry whisper.

'Next performance is third bell o' dark, yes?' Orica said over her shoulder. 'I am taking a break.'

She left him fuming. Belatedly she realised that she'd forgotten her lute in her agitation, but she dared not turn back for it now. She couldn't risk being detained; there was too much at stake.

A Krodan guard at the door watched her approach, clearly wondering if he should stop her. Everyone in the hall had seen her performance; everyone had witnessed the prince's bristling displeasure. But he probably didn't know enough Ossian to understand her song and he had no orders to detain her. When it came to it, he stood out of her way.

She sighed with relief as the door closed behind her. She was in a narrow service corridor used mainly by servants and there was nobody in sight, for the staff were all busy herding guests to their various feasts. She'd have to hurry; first bell o' dark couldn't be far off now, and she had some way to go to reach the others.

She set off quickly, keen to put some distance between her and the hall before any watchmen should hear of what she'd done and come looking. She had her excuses ready in case anyone questioned her, and the best route to the sewers was fixed in her mind, along with several alternatives besides. Her memory had been sharpened by years of training; it had to be good to remember her arsenal of music.

My lute, she thought. It had been her companion for many years and she was sad to leave it behind. But Sards didn't place much value on objects, for they travelled light and possessions could easily be stolen and lost. Feelings were all that counted. An instrument could be replaced. Her companions' lives couldn't.

She began to tremble as she walked. The recklessness of what she'd done was beginning to sink in. She hadn't felt the fear on-stage, but it came now, and with it the cold terror of discovery. She found no thrill in trespassing. Her bravery was confined to her art.

Prinn, Ragged Mummer, lend me your gift of disguise. Let me go unseen.

But no sooner had she sent her prayer than she heard hurrying footsteps behind her. She turned a corner, hoping to evade whoever it was, but the footsteps kept coming at a pace just short of a run. She'd have to run too if she wanted to avoid them, and that would damn her.

At least Harod could save the others now. At least there was that.

'You!'

She stopped. It was Edgen. He stood at the corner, breathing hard, his hair falling in disarray around his face. 'I'm not finished with you,' he told her.

'I've nothing to say to you, Edgen,' she replied, though the look on his face made her afraid. He wasn't an intimidating man, being of no great size, but alone with his anger in an empty corridor, Orica found him intimidating enough.

'Well, I've something to say to you,' he told her, advancing. 'And your paymaster Errel!'

Her brow creased as she backed away. 'I don't know who that is.'

'Lying slut!' he spat. 'Who else would profit from my humilia-tion but my rival? Did he make my lutist ill, I wonder?'

She had no idea who he was talking about, but she'd stopped listening anyway, his words becoming a jumble in the rolling wave of fear that swept her up. He seized her wrist and she wanted to slap him, but didn't dare in case it made things worse.

'Do you know what you've done to me with that little ditty of yours? To my *reputation*?' His face was close to hers now. She could smell his breath, scented with lavender and fury. 'It's lucky the prince's Ossian isn't up to much. If he'd been able to decipher all your little wordplays, we'd both be hanged already!'

'Let me go!' was all she could think of to say. It came out weak, and sounded pathetic. A few moments ago, she'd dominated an entire room, but he'd robbed her of that in an instant.

'Let you *go*?' he cried. 'No, you're coming with me! You can explain yourself to the Master of Revels. I'll be gods-damned if I'll be ruined over one gold-digging green-eye ghetto whore!'

She tried to pull away but he dragged her roughly after him.

'Unhand that lady,' said a stern voice.

Harod. She could have wept with joy.

'I told you to unhand her,' Harod said when Edgen hesitated. He began walking towards them. 'Otherwise, you'll deal with me.'

Edgen was transformed, becoming peevish and whiny in the presence of a bigger man. 'You don't understand! She's an impostor sent to ruin me!'

'I understand that you still have not released her, and I will not ask a third time.'

Edgen dropped her arm as if it were a burning log. Harod loomed over him, chillingly impassive, a wall of threat.

'It would be best if you made yourself scarce,' he advised, 'before I bring dishonour on us both by beating you soundly.'

Edgen hesitated, caught between his desire for revenge and his fear of Harod. Harod flared his nostrils slightly. Edgen jumped as if he'd been shouted at, and fled up the corridor.

The instant he turned the corner, Orica threw herself into Harod's arms, clutching tight to him. Only the fast thump of his heart revealed the anger and worry he'd kept from his face.

'Did he hurt you, milady?'

'No,' she said. 'Thanks to you.' Then she pulled away, eyes wide, remembering their mission. 'We must go. Now!'

A bell tolled in the heights of Hammerholt, a solitary note reverberating through the corridors. The doleful sound of doom.

'First bell o' dark,' said Harod.

'We're too late,' said Orica in horror. Then, breaking into a run: 'We're too *late*!'

89

Darkness. Terror. The icy clutch of black water.

Aren broke the surface with a gasp and hit his head painfully on the cave roof. Dazed and panicked, he flailed about with his hands, trying to make sense of the space around him. His knuckles burned as he skinned them on the rough rock. His palms found stone, splashed into water.

'Hoy!' he shouted. 'Hoy!'

'Aren!' It was Cade, somewhere nearby.

Aren could hear Grub gasping and grunting off to his left. 'Are we all here?'

'Aye,' said Vika. 'And Ruck, too.'

'I can't see!' Fen cried.

'I know,' said Aren, trying to keep calm. 'Nor can I.'

The water was up under his chin and the top of his head bumped against stone again. The water level was rising so fast that they'd resurfaced into a sandwich of air mere inches thick. His swords were dragging him down – he carried Garric's as well as his own – but he couldn't let them go without giving up all they'd come for. Kicking his feet, he fought against their weight as the water tried to drag him down.

Something hard and heavy nudged his shoulder and his hand found the side of the upturned boat. It had become wedged against the ceiling, pressed upwards by the water, and it didn't move when he pushed it.

A memory flared in his mind, of a bright, hot day in the class-room back in Shoal Point. Aren had been struggling to concentrate as his tutor droned on about mathematics and how to calculate volume. The master had demonstrated how you could put an upturned glass tumbler in a beaker of water and it would remain empty. Aren had marvelled at that. How could the glass stay empty even though it was underwater?

Because it wasn't empty, said the master. It was full of air.

'The boat!' Aren cried. 'Get under the boat! There's air underneath!'

'Where are you?' Cade called.

'Swim to my voice!'

There was bumping, gasping and splashing in the dark. Ruck barked right by his ear and paddled past.

'Everyone found it? Everyone found the boat?' Aren called, but if there was any reply he couldn't hear it now. The water was around his ears and he had to tilt his head right back to find air. Taking as big a breath as he could, he closed his eyes and ducked under the water, feeling his way under the gunwale and into the forest of kicking legs beyond. Someone booted him in the chest as he ascended but he hardly felt it in the flurry. He came up and hit his head hard on one of the bench seats. Blindly, he hooked his arm around it. His relief at being able to breathe outweighed the pain.

'Help me with Ruck!' Vika pleaded. The wet animal smell that engulfed him could have been her hound or her cloak of furs.

'Where is she?'

Vika pushed Ruck against his body. Paws scrabbled at him as Aren and Vika each got an arm under her.

'Peace, Ruck. Do not struggle so,' said Vika. Ruck did as she was told and allowed herself to be held above water.

Cade was whimpering close by. 'I don't want to die! I don't want to die!'

'We're not going to die,' Aren told him. Reassuring him was a reflex. 'Fen?'

'I'm here,' she said, quietly.

'Grub?'

Grub swore in Skarl.

'He's here,' said Cade, with a burst of shrill hysterical laughter.

'Cade,' said Aren. Then, more sharply: '*Cade!* We're *not* going to die.'

Cade's laughter subsided to a muted sniffle.

'They'll come for us,' said Aren.

No one said anything to that. The boat bumped and scraped against the roof of the cavern. Water sloshed around their shoulders.

'Do you know the story of Red Asp, the desert Dawnwarden?' Cade began.

'We need to save our breath,' Aren said gently.

They all hushed after that, and only their breathing told of the private terrors they suffered as they waited in the dark. Aren became detached from the beat of time, floating in a black eternity. The cold crept deeper into his body, overwhelming the warm glow of Vika's potion, slowing his thoughts. Webs of blue, green and red flashed before his light-starved eyes.

They'll come for us, he told himself as his teeth began to chatter. *They will. They will.*

After a while, the cold began to recede and he started to feel drowsy. Then, suddenly, he was underwater. The shock of it jolted him awake, sent him spluttering back up to the surface, Ruck scrabbling against him. He secured them both again, arm around the bench overhead, but no sooner had he done so than he felt sleep coming again, pressing in at the edges of his eye sockets. His head ached and the sound of breathing around him had turned deep and slow, as if everyone was on the edge of slumber.

'Crows,' Grub slurred. 'Why Grub hear crows?'

'What crows?' Aren mumbled thickly. He was surprised to find his own voice was slurred, too.

Grub didn't answer. Instead there was a quiet slithering splash. 'Grub?'

It was hard for Aren to concentrate. He'd already forgotten what he'd meant to ask. Something about crows? Next to him, Cade gave a drowsy snort.

'Grub?' said Fen from the far end of the boat. He heard more splashing as she felt around. 'Grub?' she cried. 'He's gone! Grub's gone!'

It took a moment for the news to penetrate the fog in Aren's head. When it did, it threw him back to wakefulness. He pushed Ruck towards Vika, filled his lungs as best he could and plunged under the water.

He heard someone cry out, telling him not to do it, their voice muffled by the roar of blood in his ears. But all he knew was that Grub was sinking into the abyss, and he refused to let that happen.

With one powerful stroke, he propelled himself down. His next stroke was leaden, muscles aching. The next was like pulling through treacle. His weakness terrified him but he still reached outwards with his hands, casting his arms wide, trusting to luck to make contact with Grub.

No good. He pushed down again, head buzzing, chest aching. The breath he'd taken had lasted a pitifully short time. He cast out again, waving blindly at the water, and his wrist hit flesh. Desperately he snatched at Grub, found an arm, seized it.

Now up! Up!

He hardly had the strength to move himself, let alone the hefty Skarl, but he forced his dulled and throbbing muscles to move to the engine of his will, and he swam.

One stroke. Another. Now his lungs were twin balls of fire and his vision writhed with sparkling worms. In a lash of mad panic, he thought *Where is the boat?* and realised too late that he had no idea. It could be anywhere above him, and that tiny island of air was no easy target to hit. If he missed, he'd find only the roof of the cave, and death.

There was a third swimmer in the water with them. He knew it as clearly as if he could see her. The Red-Eyed Child floated in the dark nearby, her hood wafting in the water around her bald head, her gaze fixed on him.

One more pull. One more.

The water parted and sweet cold air burst into his lungs in a rush, dousing the blaze in his chest. He reached back with his free hand, numb fingers clenched around Grub's collar, and pulled him up into the darkness and dripping silence.

They were not inside the boat. Dizzy, not understanding, Aren looked about as if he could penetrate the endless dark. His splashes echoed back strangely, telling him the story. There was air here, filling the space all around him, but that was impossible; the water had filled the cave.

It could only mean one thing. The water level was dropping. Dropping *fast*.

Something pulled at his leg, a force that quickly grew to surround his lower body, gathering strength with every moment. In his mind's eye he saw Sarla, cheated of her catch, her arms wrapped round his legs to drag him down to the depths. He gave a shrill cry as the force became irresistible and he was sucked under again, still holding on to Grub as the water closed over his head.

They were dragged into a swirling torrent of invisible currents, tumbling through the thundering dark. Something smacked Aren's leg, sending him spinning; Grub was ripped from his grasp. He flailed as a light rushed towards him at terrifying speed and he was disgorged into the air. For one sickening instant he was flying, then he splashed down onto his side and was shunted helplessly along a stone channel, arms waving in search of a grip.

His hand was caught and he was hauled bodily from the water and dumped onto a path, where he lay gasping like a landed fish, clutching his belly as he coughed and retched.

'There's Grub! Catch him!' Orica shouted over the bellow of the water.

Aren, too weak and battered to raise his head, could only listen to the chaos around him, his ribs rising and falling in desperate relief. He heard Grub hauled out and dropped alongside him, heard Orica thump his back until he gagged up water. Harod hunted along the waterside, snatching up their companions as they tumbled through the doorway.

'Is that everyone?'

'There's still no sign of Cade.'

Cade.

'Hold!' Harod cried immediately. 'Here he comes!'

'Grab him!'

Cade's distressed wail as he was belched forth from the doorway brought an exhausted smile from Aren. If he had breath to scream, he had breath to live. Harod grabbed him and Aren at last let himself believe they were not going to drown.

He heard the slapping of wet paws and a warm tongue slurped across his cheek. He rolled onto his back as Ruck barked in his face.

It was hard to ignore a summons like that. Slinging his arm around the hound's neck, Aren hauled himself up, fighting off a wave of nausea. He was in an ancient vaulted tunnel, cold and rank-smelling, lit by a pair of lanterns resting nearby. The stone path he lay on was above the level of the water, which burst from the doorway to race down the sewer channel in a torrent. Arranged along the path were his companions, all as bedraggled as he. Squatting among them was Harod, shoulders heaving with effort, his hair plastered to his head and his fine clothes drenched. Orica was kneeling by Vika, helping her to sit up.

All safe. Thank Joha for that.

Fen was curled up next to him, tangled in her bow, which had miraculously stayed on her back. Perhaps half a dozen arrows remained in her quiver. She let out a groan and raised her head.

'Told you they'd come for us,' Aren croaked, and gave her a grin.

Fen huffed with laughter. 'I hate you sometimes,' she said, meaning the opposite.

90

The Lords' Parlour of Hammerholt was busy with guests. They chattered in clusters, smoked cheroots and played cards and castles while a musician struck up a jaunty tune on a harpsichord. Mara drifted among them, her wine glass never far from her lips, eyes restless. Hunting.

It was a narrow chamber with a low ceiling, more intimate than imposing, warmed by a crackling hearth set into one wall. Brass candelabra hung from elaborate ceiling roses along its length. Frescoes softened the fortress's stern design, depicting scenes from Ossian folk tales which the Krodans must have thought harmless or obscure enough to escape erasure. One showed Haldric and his companion Bumbleweed trudging dejectedly out of the sea after Haldric's ill-fated attempt to woo the kraken's daughter. It was one of Mara's childhood favourites; the sight gave her a twinge of nostalgic delight.

A rousing guffaw drew her attention to the Master of Keys. He was standing with a group of men, trading anecdotes. Mara watched them as she picked at the buffet table, and the taste of wine soured in her mouth.

How she loathed those braying Krodan highborns and the Ossian nobles who aped them. How she hated their clubs and societies that divided the world into who was in and who was out. Every joke and gesture were part of a secret code she wasn't privy to, meant to exclude anyone who wasn't connected enough, successful enough, *male* enough.

Were they discussing Orica? Possibly. Her exceptional performance in the West Gallery had caused much gossip. What were they saying, then? Mocking her, most likely, or speculating what they'd do to such a beauty, given half a chance.

She felt herself becoming angry on Orica's behalf. Orica's song had touched her, and Mara wasn't easily stirred. Her daring and quick thinking might have saved the lives of their companions down below; she deserved admiration, not belittlement. But Orica was a woman, and a Sard, and it wasn't in the nature of men like these to admire women, except as objects of desire.

Peace, Mara, she told herself as she felt the old poison oozing up inside her. *You have a task. This is a time for intellect, not passion.*

After the performance, the guests had dispersed to various amusements before dinner. Mara had followed the Master of Keys. If Yarin's intelligence was correct, he wouldn't be at any of the feasts, so Mara had to ensure he didn't go back to his chambers, to give Grub time to find the vault key.

She'd need to engage him somehow, but to do that, she had to draw him from his circle. For an unaccompanied woman to approach a man was brazen behaviour in Krodan high society, and she'd lost her escort when Harod left her. Alone, these men would ignore her at best, patronise her at worst. Even if her pride could suffer it, that was no way to impress him.

As she was considering her strategy, she felt a touch at her elbow. She knew who it was before she heard his voice.

'Mara.'

The Ossian by her side was broad-chested, his proportions bear-like, with hairy hands and a neat brown beard. His Krodan jacket and trousers were cut from expensive cloth, but he was ill at ease in such finery. She supposed all the money in the world would never change that.

'I am Lady Harforth of Harrow, if it please you,' Mara told him.

He looked even more awkward. 'And where is your lord?'

'On some nefarious business elsewhere,' she said. 'But I believe I know you. Aren't you the famed Malliard, inventor of the Malliard Limb?'

'Mara ...' he said again, his tone somewhere between pleading and warning. *Mara, don't torment me. Mara, don't embarrass yourself. Mara, don't get out of hand.* He was Ossian but his words were flattened by Galtic inflections: a gift from his father, as was his surname.

She took a breath to say something caustic, then checked herself with a sigh of resignation. She was imagining conflict when there was none. He wasn't her enemy – quite the opposite – but she'd been caught off guard.

'I did not think you would be here,' she said, as an apology of sorts.

'I'm leaving soon. I came as a favour to the man who arranged your invitation.' He had the grace to look shamefaced. 'He asked me to meet his son. The boy wants to be an inventor.'

'Inspiring the next generation. Admirable.'

'Don't. I'm only here for your sake.'

'And now you're checking on me. For my sake.'

'Yes,' he said. 'Exactly. "Lady Harforth"? What are you up to?'

'Merely trying to advance my position in society,' she said. 'We women must do what we can to get ourselves noticed in these challenging days.' She smiled without humour. 'But you've heard my thoughts on that subject many times.'

'Please be careful, that's all. The Iron Hand are everywhere. I don't know what you're doing, but as you're under a false name, I assume it isn't good.'

'Good is a relative concept, don't you think?' she said. 'It rather depends on your point of view. I wonder if the Krodans consider themselves villains? Or the elaru? Or the urds?'

He checked no one was close enough to overhear, then gave her an exasperated glance. She took some small glee in that. She hoped he'd argue the point with her, but he didn't rise to it. Once he'd enjoyed their sparring, the cut and thrust of argument. Now he found it tiresome, and that grieved her.

'I hear congratulations are in order,' she said. He gave her a puzzled frown. 'Ariala is with child again.'

The horror on his face would have been amusing if she hadn't been dying inside. 'Oh, Danric, it's quite alright. I didn't want children, remember?'

But she'd never been a good liar, and her fragile smile did

nothing to conceal the hurt of old wounds reopening, all the more painful because his had long since healed. She hated herself for wanting him, hated the wistful need she felt in his presence.

'I should go,' said Danric as he saw the turn things were taking.

'Not yet!' she said, more urgently than she'd intended. She composed herself and spoke more calmly. 'One last favour. Please.'

'This was a mistake,' he said. 'I didn't mean to—'

'Danric,' she said, growing flinty. 'Your new baby will be delivered by the best Krodan doctors. They will have the finest education, eat good food and live in a safe neighbourhood. You and yours have health and security and want for nothing. You owe me for that.'

His eyes lost their softness. He didn't like to be reminded that his wealth and success came from her, not earned but given. Perhaps that was her goal, when she approached him with the idea in the months after they broke up. She'd thought there was still hope for them then, and meant to chain him close with bonds of obligation, to prove he could never do better than her.

In the end, it had the opposite effect, fostering resentment in them both until they had no choice but to cut off contact altogether. She saw that same resentment in him now.

'What do you need?' he said coldly. The sullen anger in his voice wounded her afresh, but she'd suffer the scars if it brought them the Ember Blade.

'Introduce me to the Master of Keys,' she said, nodding towards her quarry. 'Tell him I am fascinated by his work and wish to hear all about it. I am Lady Harforth, a dear friend of yours from Harrow.'

'Very well,' he said. 'Whatever plan you have in mind, I am already damned by inviting you.'

He walked away without waiting for reply, brusque enough to be insulting. She followed him. In the weeks and years to come – if she lived to see them – she'd pore over this meeting and relive the chill agony of his anger like hollow icicles in her guts. But there was more at stake than her feelings, so she built her walls, bricking up the hurt inside. By the time they reached the Master of Keys, she was composed and ready to play the game.

'Your pardon,' said Danric as he reached the group.

'Malliard!' said the youngest of the men. He was an acquaintance of Danric's, and obviously quite impressed and excited by the fact. 'This is Danric Malliard,' he told the others, 'inventor of the Malliard Limb. A fine fellow, be assured.'

Greetings were exchanged, friendly smiles and handshakes. When the men were done with their welcomes, Danric gestured to Mara, whom no one had acknowledged till now.

'May I introduce Lady Harforth of Harrow? She is a dear friend of mine, and she is so full of questions about the Master of Keys that I thought you two should meet.'

'Oho!' cried the master, preening. 'Questions, is it? I shall be glad to answer! Jarrit Bann, Master of Keys at Hammerholt, at your service.'

'So kind of you to take the time to indulge my curiosity,' said Mara, affecting a Harrish accent. 'Tell me, is it true you have the Ember Blade here in Hammerholt?'

The other men chuckled and exchanged indulgent glances. Mara seethed inwardly but she kept her tongue still. She knew the role she must play if she wanted to keep him busy. Intelligence was disconcerting. Assertiveness meant she was uppity. Pleasant deference was all that remained.

'It is indeed true,' said the master, his thick-fingered hands folded over the large gold medallion that rested on his belly. 'The Ember Blade is secured in a vault in the heights of this very fortress, waiting to be delivered to Prince Ottico on his wedding day.'

'Ossia's most prized relic,' she said. 'It is a great responsibility you carry! What if some thief should pick the lock?'

'My lady, I welcome them to try!' He guffawed. 'They would have a hard time finding a lock to pick!'

'I don't understand,' said Mara, with a confused smile.

'The vault door is quite unbreakable and there is no keyhole in it. The mechanism that secures it is a wonder of Krodan craftsmanship, installed to replace the inferior Ossian version after Hammerholt was taken. But to say more would be indiscreet, and I am nothing if not discreet!'

The men laughed at this; some shared joke she was excluded

from. Before the conversation could turn away from her, she asked him another question about his duties in Hammerholt. The Master of Keys was flattered by her interest and happy to describe his day at length. Soon his companions lost interest and began to talk among themselves. Danric excused himself with a last warning glance at Mara. She ignored him, though her heart felt him go.

Now that she had the master to herself, she feigned fascination in order to learn more. He talked readily about things of little importance but became cagey if she pressed him for details. It was good to have confirmation that the Ember Blade was in Hammerholt and being kept exactly where they thought, but his cryptic hints about the vault door bothered her. If there was no key, then how was the door to be opened? She needed to find out, but she dared not press too hard for fear of arousing his suspicions. Time and again she was forced to dance away from the subject, and time danced away from her.

They were interrupted by a servant ringing a bell, asking those guests who were dining to take their places.

'Madam,' said the master. 'It has been a pleasure, but I really must retire.'

'Oh, you are not dining?' Mara asked.

'I am not,' he said. He patted his stomach and gave her a rueful smile. 'My doctor advises I stay away from feasts and strong drink, and I fear my will is weak. I will take a small meal in my study, with my books for company.'

'Ah.' She gave a regretful sigh. 'I am no lover of raucous feasts, either. Would that we could continue our conversation in some quiet spot instead.'

It was a desperate ploy, and she was ashamed of it, but she'd never had the art of light conversation. The Master of Keys looked a little embarrassed on her behalf. Krodans thought it unseemly for a woman to go off alone with a man at a party, unless she was a certain sort.

'I would like nothing more,' he lied, 'but I'm sure a lady of such grace would be missed at the dining table.'

He was attempting to get away with as much elegance as he could muster. Mara felt a flutter of panic. She couldn't let him go.

This was her task, and she was failing it, and she wasn't used to failing anything. She snatched for an idea and blurted it out.

'Do you think a woman could ever be the Master of Keys?'

Her question stopped him, and several of his cohorts turned back in the act of leaving. Suddenly everyone was interested in their conversation. Mara saw one man hiding a smirk behind his hand.

'I ... well ... Whatever do you mean?' the master floundered.

'You must forgive my pestering you with questions, but they were all for a purpose,' Mara improvised frantically. 'It has been something of a foolish desire of mine to one day call myself Mistress of Keys in some wondrous old castle.'

One of the men snorted down a laugh and was quietly struck by his companion, who was also trying to keep his composure. It was so absurd a wish that Mara blushed.

'And why not?' she asked them defiantly. 'Why should it not be so?'

'Well ... There are many good reasons, I'm sure ...' said the master.

'Name some,' one of his companions urged, enjoying the master's discomfort. The other man snorted again.

The master shot him a venomous look. 'It's just ... Well, the post of the Master of Keys requires an immense capacity for *organisation*, you see. I am in charge of the security and care of many precious objects. I see to the safety of a large number of important individuals. With so many considerations to account for, it requires a level of logical and tactical thinking that, I'm sorry to say, is beyond the capacity of a woman. A lady's mind is more inclined towards nurture and care, the conversational arts and certain crafts at which they exceed.'

Mara smiled sweetly to conceal the fact that her blood was boiling. 'Logical and tactical thinking, you say? Such as might be employed in a game of castles?'

'Exactly so!' said the master triumphantly. He threw his arms wide, appealing to his fellows. 'I have played castles since I was at my father's knee. Hundreds of games, against all manner of opponents! And never once, not *once* have I been beaten by a *woman*!'

Mara raised an eyebrow.

91

Klyssen hurried through the corridors of Hammerholt, Harte limping at his heels. By his side was a young underwatchman called Oslet, freshly blooded, lean and eager. Oslet might have been guiding them but Klyssen set the pace, keeping it brisk enough to make Harte struggle. Tormenting his subordinate had begun as a necessity but ended up as a habit.

'The prisoner is just down here, Overwatchman,' said Oslet.

They passed doorways that rang with the sound of cutlery and conversation, pulsing waves of sweaty heat out into the cool corridors. The formal dining rooms were on the floor above; this floor was for the guests' retinues: their footmen, servants and guards. Their feasts had all the noisy ruckus of a beer-hall.

Worry put speed in his step. The royal wedding was a prime target for every dissident in Ossia and the Iron Hand was on high alert, but despite the danger they had strict orders to conduct their business out of sight. Whatever happened behind the scenes, the prince wasn't to be troubled.

Yet Klyssen heard that he *had* been troubled, by a Sard lutist with a seditious song.

A Sard lutist. It cannot be a coincidence.

At least Oslet had come to him with the news, and not the Commander. Klyssen had already been chewed out by that senile old fool once today. It wasn't enough to capture the most wanted man in Ossia, apparently. He should have brought in the whole Morgenholme network with him. Commander Gossen had demanded to know why he'd let Aren go, why they hadn't re-arrested

Keel when they had the chance and tortured him to make him talk. When Garric hanged at dawn, the Iron Hand would lose their only link to the Morgenholme rebels. So why had he done it?

Because I know my job, you withered old bastard. Because neither Keel nor Aren would have talked in time if I'd tried to make them sell out the whole group. Because I made a deal, and I honour my deals, for I represent an Empire which is fair and just. Without their Dawnwarden, they're a headless rabble not worth the effort of hunting, and the most they'll manage from now on is some mildly offensive graffiti. Also, it's hardly my fault if the higher-ups would rather hang Garric for show than give us the time to interrogate him.

But there was a worm of doubt in his mind. He'd misread the boy, he had to admit that. He'd waited in a dark, cold house in the ghetto with his men, but Aren had never come. The humiliation of ordering his men home wasn't one he'd soon forget. He wouldn't make the mistake of being merciful a second time.

When Garric swung from a rope tomorrow at dawn, Klyssen would be there to collect the glory. The Chancellor could hardly refuse him the position of Commander then. Gossen would go back to Kroda to live out his twilight years in the motherland, and his lickspittle Bettren would be out in the cold.

Unless the Commander was right. Unless Garric's companions managed to make trouble without him.

Oslet led them to a small, disused room on the edge of a vacant wing of the fortress. Captain Dressle was there, with another grim-faced guardsman and a watchman second class, of equivalent rank to Harte. The prisoner, who'd been seated in a chair, sprang to his feet as Klyssen entered.

'I didn't know!' he cried. 'By the Primus, you must believe me! The Sard bitch was sent to ruin me!'

Dressle moved to intercept him, but Klyssen held up a hand. The prisoner was an angry dandy and Klyssen despised him on sight; but he was desperate to talk, and Klyssen was of a mind to let him.

'I am Edgen, leader of the finest musical troupe in Morgen-holme,' he gushed, relieved that someone was finally listening. 'Yesterday our lutist fell ill, likely to a poison administered by my rival, and that very day I met a Sard with the skills to fill her place. I should have known then, but alas! I was too eager to perform for the prince to see the trap. I had no idea she would play such a scandalous song for his Highness! I tried to arrest her myself, but I was stopped so I reported her to the Iron Hand. I had *nothing* to do with—'

'Stopped?' Klyssen interrupted him. 'By whom?'

'A Harrish, a noble sort. Tall. His hair was cut in that ridiculous style they favour, as if a dome had been placed upon his head and a blade passed around it—'

Klyssen felt his guts tighten. A Sard lutist and a Harrish noble. The same couple that had been at the Reavers' Rest. There was no question, then.

'Captain Dressle, take some men and go to the dungeons at once. Secure the prisoner. No one sees him until I tell you otherwise.'

'Yes, Overwatchman. Hail to the Emperor.' He saluted and left, taking the other guard with him.

Klyssen looked at the watchman standing by the door. 'You did well to bring this to my attention. Keep this man here, out of the way. I'll deal with him later.'

'But I—' Edgen began. A sharp look from Klyssen persuaded him of the advisability of silence. He sank fretfully back into his chair.

'Watchman Harte, find the Sard and the man called Harod. Use whoever you need, on my authority, but for the Primus's sake, be discreet about it.'

'What will you do?' Harte asked.

'There are two here we know of,' said Klyssen. 'There may be others.'

He pulled open the door and headed up the corridor, fear nipping at his heels.

They're a rabble, he reassured himself firmly. *Tie two Ossians to a cart and they'll pull in different directions. They're harmless without their leader.*

But he was going to find the Master of Keys, just in case.

92

The sewers beneath Hammerholt were a maze of tunnels, where narrow stone paths ran alongside reeking waterways criss-crossed by crumbling bridges. The water was restless and high, lapping over the path in places. Grub's boots splashed in the puddles as he lumbered along, lantern brandished before him to fend off the dark.

The others were heading for the dungeon and Garric, but Grub's mission took him elsewhere. He had a map with him, sketched out and kept in a sealed, watertight tube, but he hadn't needed it yet, preferring to navigate by instinct and memory. He went with haste, spurred on by the desire to keep ahead of the rising water and the terror that followed him in his mind.

He couldn't forget what had happened in that cave. The feeling of his strength draining away, that final sigh before the water closed over his head and he went slipping into the dark. As his senses faded and his thoughts went still, he'd reached the borders of death and glimpsed what waited for him there.

Nothing. Emptiness. No Bone God to welcome or damn him. He wouldn't even be afforded that grace. Not for him the ice fields of Quttak, where heroes hunted mighty shabboths and battled giants in the snow. He wouldn't see the halls of Vanatuk, where there was feasting and merriment and hearths that burned eternally. His fate was the Forgetting, where the Unremembered went when they died. He'd seen it as he sank into the black abyss, and it struck fear into him such as he'd never known.

But Mudslug had saved him. Dumbface told him so. Mudslug went after him and pulled him out of the water. Mudslug had spared him the Forgetting, given him a second chance. A chance he meant to seize with both hands.

Only the Ember Blade could keep him from that bleak hell. Only the Ember Blade could buy him forgiveness from the Bone God. He *had* to have it.

The water was lapping around his ankles by the time he found the stairway. Mudslug said the sewers would keep flooding until the water level fell in the cave, and it was impossible to push the door shut against the force of the water gushing through it. The cave would drain out again in time, but it didn't much matter as their boat would likely have sunk by then. Untying it from its moorings had allowed them to survive, but it might also have shut off their best route out. Without some kind of boat, they couldn't escape back to the lake. They'd resolved to keep their original rendezvous for now, banking on the slim chance that the boat had managed to stay afloat, but if the alarm was raised, they'd have to take the alternative option. They'd head for the excavation site on the far side of Hammerholt, and the unknown depths beneath.

Grub grunted to himself. He'd take some urd ruins over going back in that water. Skarls didn't fear the deep earth; they lived half their lives underground and could keep their bearings without sun or sky to guide them. Besides, there was more chance for adventure there.

He came to a sturdy door at the top of the stairs and found it locked. Listening at the keyhole, he heard nothing, so he drew his lockpicks from a soggy pouch. He was cold and his fingers were numb, but no Skarl paid much mind to such small discomforts. In short order, he heard the lock click.

'Grub is the greatest,' he muttered to himself. In absence of anyone else to boast to, it made him feel better.

He pushed the creaking door open into an unlit corridor, chilly and austere. Faint moonlight made its way through the windows. Grub grinned in satisfaction. Deserted, as he'd hoped. This part of Hammerholt was being rebuilt in the Krodan style, having long fallen into disrepair. It wasn't trafficked by anyone but workmen, who'd all been sent home till the wedding was over.

He blew out his lantern and slid into the corridor. The chambers of the Master of Keys were several levels above him, according to the map, but he'd never get to them by passing through the busy area that surrounded it. His was a more direct route, straight up the wall outside.

He drew out his map and frowned over it for a short time. Once he had the route set in his mind, he headed off again, down lonely ways where tattered strands of spiderweb waved in the breeze and the dry bodies of mice lay in corners among the dust and pebbles.

As he went, his mind turned to Mudslug, and he felt a pang of guilt sharp enough to surprise him. Guilt wasn't an emotion he was used to, at least not where foreigners were concerned. He knew Dumbface would curse his name when he stole the Ember Blade, and Painted Lady would spit and Freckles and the others would all hate him; but it was the thought of Mudslug's disappointment that stung. Mudslug had been on his side when no one else was. Mudslug had saved him from the Forgetting. Stealing the blade felt like a poor way to repay him.

He'd had loyalty once, and honour of a sort. Back in Karaqqa, he was part of an orphan gang. They'd all looked after each other, comforted one another when they were beaten, mourned when one of them got hanged. The camaraderie of thieves made them strong. Even when you didn't like someone, you backed them up because they were one of yours. The old man taught them that. He was a poor father figure, but he was what they had.

Maybe he'd always been trying to get back to those days, the warmest he remembered in a cold, hard life. Maybe that was why he'd stolen another man's skin. But his own motivations were murky to him; he'd always been driven by forces he didn't understand. His instinct now was to save himself.

The Sombre Men would forgive him. The skin-scribes would erase his crimes. The stonesingers would carve his deeds on towering obsidian stelae. And he'd be a hero again, this time for ever.

So why did he feel bad about it?

A door opened ahead of him. Hurrying footsteps. A light approaching.

He was caught in the open, halfway down a corridor, and the stranger was coming too fast to find good cover. Next to him was a door in a recessed alcove. He tried it, but it was locked and he had no time to pick it. Instead he pressed himself up against the stone of the alcove and went still.

She came towards him on soft feet: a girl, by her breath and the weight of her. She moved with haste, late for something, or on some urgent errand. What was she doing here, in these abandoned parts? It didn't matter. All that mattered was that she wasn't allowed to raise the alarm.

Grub drew his dagger, the blade whispering against the sheath.

The light brightened as the girl passed him. She was plump, with blonde hair in a long braid, her cheeks flushed and her eyes fixed forward. In her hurry she didn't see him, and she headed off and up the corridor.

Then, suddenly, she came to a halt.

Grub gripped his dagger harder, his muscles tensing, ready to spring. If she turned, she'd spot him.

If she turned, he'd kill her.

She was looking down at the floor, her lantern held up for a better view. Grub followed her gaze and saw what had stopped her.

Water. Fat spatters of water in a trail along the stony floor. Coming from ahead and leading away behind her. Leading to Grub.

He heard the change in her breathing. There was fear now, the fear of strange things happening in dark places. Perhaps she sensed his eyes on her. Perhaps she felt some premonition of his hand clamping round her mouth, his blade piercing her back.

If she turned…

He saw her shoulders hunch. A child afraid of phantoms, suddenly vulnerable in the dark. She dared not look behind her, dreading what she might find there. Whatever that water meant, she didn't want to know. She hurried off down the corridor and never turned.

And so she lived.

Grub put his knife back in its sheath and waited till she was gone. Then he emerged from the alcove and walked away.

He counted doors until he reached the one he wanted. It wasn't locked. Peering through, he found a grey room, stark and empty in the moonlight, with a rumpled bed of rugs and ram-skins laid in the corner.

The air swam with the smell of sex. Grub leered as he realised why the girl had been down here. A secret tryst before heading back to her duties. Where was her partner, then? Gone another way, with luck. Otherwise they might find themselves on the point of his dagger.

He crossed the room and found another door there. Cold air blew in around the edges. It was locked, so he knelt down and picked it, alert for movement behind him.

The hall beyond was open to the sky, the stars glittering overhead. Tantera hung high above, with Lyssa beside her. One wall was mostly in ruins, with scaffolding all along its length. Through an archway, Grub could see another hall in even worse repair, the walls held up with iron props.

The scaffold was an easy climb for someone of Grub's rare talent. When he got to the top, he manoeuvred himself out onto the broken wall. Hammerholt towered overhead, enormous in its might. All around, the jagged tips of the Catsclaw Mountains shone like frozen waves in the moonlight. He crouched there, the wind chilling him in his wet clothes, and sniffed back a runnel of watery snot.

He'd lived in Ossia longer than he'd lived in his homeland. Funny to think about that. Neither country had been kind, but Ossia, at least, hadn't rejected him. From this vantage point, he could see for leagues about, and it brought an odd contentment.

Winter would come soon, but here in Ossia there'd be no deadly blizzards of ice shards, no fanged predators raiding the villages, no sacrifices to the blood-witches. Ossia was a gentle place compared to the land of his birth. For the first time, he began to wonder why he was so keen to go back.

He shrugged off the thought with a grunt. There was work to be done. He wiped his nose with one wet sleeve and looked up. Several stories above him was the window he wanted.

Maybe he hadn't killed an ice bear. Maybe he hadn't ambushed a shipload of Boskan smugglers. But nobody could climb like he could.

He flexed his fingers and rolled his shoulders. Time to earn another tattoo.

93

The dungeon was quiet and all but empty, far from the celebrations on the floors above. The only sounds were the prisoner
shifting in his cell, and the steady snap of the jailor's cards as he
played One-Up with himself next to a glowing brazier.

Snap. Snap. Snap.

He sat at the head of a short, shadowy corridor with several
cells running along one side. Various doorways led off it, leading
to a privy, a storeroom, and a small torture chamber which was
nevertheless large enough to accommodate great magnitudes of
pain. The prisoner was in the cell at the end, slumped in the
shadows.

Snap. Snap. Snap.

The jailor was a thickset man with a flat, broken nose, his hair
shaved to disguise the fact that he was losing it. He scooped up
the two piles of cards, shuffled them together and started turning
them again.

Snap. Snap.

An animal whine and a scratch at the door made him look up.
He put down his cards and made his way over to investigate. The
door was thick wood reinforced with iron, with a barred window
at face-height. As he was about to look through, a hound's face
appeared there, grey and lean and bearded like a ragged old man.
Standing on its hind legs, it was taller than he was.

Ruck woofed in a friendly manner.

'Hey, boy,' said the jailor. 'Where's your master?'

Ruck's tongue lolled and she panted. The jailor put his hand up to the window, and she sniffed and licked it. He was pleased with that.

'Anyone out there?' he called, but the corridor was empty. 'Huh,' he said. 'Lost, are you? All kinds running around up there, eh? Surprised you didn't find your way to a feast.'

He took out his keys and unlocked the door. 'Come on in, then. It's warmer in here and you'll make better company than my prisoner. Better conversation, too, I reckon.'

Ruck dropped away from the window as he opened the door, but she didn't come in. Instead, she loped off up the corridor to the T-junction at the end and looked back with a whine.

'You coming in or not?' the jailor demanded.

Ruck whined again. A look of dawning comprehension crept over the jailor's battered face.

'Something you want to show me?' he asked.

Ruck barked.

The jailor sighed and looked over his shoulder at the prisoner. His legs were visible; the rest of him was hidden in a fold of dark.

'Sorry. Ain't supposed to leave my post,' he said.

Ruck barked again, with dumb insistence. The jailor rolled his eyes. 'Just to the corner, then. I ain't going further than that.'

He lumbered up the corridor to Ruck, but as soon as he came close, she barked and darted out of sight.

'Oi, come on!' the jailor groaned as he turned the corner after her.

Standing there, bow drawn and an arrow aimed at his chest, was Fen. The jailor stared at her in blank surprise as Vika lunged from the shadows behind him and clamped a wadded rag over his nose and mouth. The paint on her face had smeared and run, turning her into something primal and horrific, a fearful demon from an elder age. The jailor gave a muffled cry and shoved back against her, crashing her up against a wall; but Vika was tough as a root, and she held firm until his eyes rolled up and he crumpled to the floor.

Fen lowered her bow as Aren emerged from an alcove behind her, his sword ready in his hand. Cade, Harod and Orica came with him. Cade squatted down by the jailor and prodded him in the nose with his forefinger.

'That's incredible!' he said. 'Is he asleep?'

'He is unconscious,' said Vika, 'and will remain so for some hours.'

'All because he smelled that potion?'

'It's remarkable what a few herbs and a little woodcraft can achieve.'

The druidess was being modest. Aren knew she'd spent hours preparing her potions in the safehouse, locked away with her strange rituals. He'd seen the orders she'd sent to the city herbalist, calling for rare ingredients she usually collected by hand. Vika's art paled in comparison to the sorceries of the Second Empire, if the legends were true, but there was power in her concoctions far greater than any apothecary could muster.

Aren took the keys from the jailor's belt. He was glad they hadn't needed to kill him. Krodan or not, he was just doing his job.

'Lock him in a cell,' he told the others as he hurried towards the dungeon, his sword in his hand and excitement in his step. He knew it was selfish and silly, but he wanted his face to be the first Garric saw. He wanted him to know who'd rescued him.

'Garric?' he called as he entered the dungeon. The light from the brazier made it hard to see to the back and he passed several empty cells before he saw the figure stirring in the last one. 'Garric, is that you?'

The prisoner surged clumsily to his feet, his hands gripping the bars. When Aren reached him, there was a look of such disbelief and amazement on his face that Aren could do nothing but grin breathlessly. Neither of them knew what to say. He was tattered and sallow, wearing roughspun prison garb, his hair and beard shaved off; but he was here, and alive!

'*How?*' he managed eventually, looking Aren up and down. Aren was still sodden, his clothes sticking to him in places.

'That's a long story,' Aren said. Then, because he couldn't think of anything else: 'Are they keeping you comfortable in there?'

'Not really.'

'Let's get you out, then.'

Aren unlocked the cell door and pushed it open as the others came up behind him, dragging the unconscious jailor. Garric moved to the door of the cell. His features looked all wrong without his hair and beard to frame them, and the deep scar across his throat was stark and repulsive, but his eyes were as fierce as ever. In a rush of relief, Aren stepped forward and hugged him hard.

Garric's hiss of indrawn breath sent him stepping back quickly, uncertain whether he'd overstepped the mark. Then he saw the new scars peeping out from the collar of Garric's shirt and his torn sleeves; the raw, seeping pads where the fingernails of his left hand used to be; the weary, injured way he held himself.

'They cut you where it won't show,' Garric said, his voice low and grim. 'Cut you, and worse. Wouldn't do their image good to have my face all bruised up when the crowd come to see me hang.'

'They tortured you?'

He grinned. There were two teeth missing on the right side. 'They tried,' he said. 'Reckon Klyssen would have loved to keep me longer, but the powers that be want me in a noose before the princess arrives. I gave them *nothing.*' He spat it with furious pride.

The others had crowded up behind Aren in the corridor. Aren unstrapped Garric's sword from his belt and held it out. Garric took it, turning it this way and that, studying it as if it were something unfamiliar.

'Keel?' he asked.

'We don't know. He's gone.'

Vika stepped up beside Aren. 'Are you ready to take back the Ember Blade, Garric?'

'You're going to steal the Ember Blade?' Garric asked in surprise.

'Of course,' said Aren, puzzled. 'Weren't you?'

His gaze fell on Aren. 'And all this was your idea, I take it?'

'Mine and Mara's,' he said, suddenly worried he'd done something wrong.

But there was pride, not anger, in Garric's eyes. 'Shades, I'd never have believed it,' he said quietly. 'If Ossia has more like you, let her enemies beware! It's almost enough to give a man back his faith.'

Happiness filled Aren like the light of a dawning sun. To win such praise from a Dawnwarden, from *Garric*, made him feel invincible! He fought to keep the smile off his face. 'Almost?' he asked mischievously.

'Aren!' It was Fen, from the dungeon doorway. 'Men coming! A lot of them, in armour!'

Aren was serious again in an instant. 'Move!' he snapped. 'We can't face them here, we'll be trapped!'

They were quick to obey, leaving the jailor on the floor as they ran for the door. Aren turned to Garric, brusque now, all business. 'Can you fight?' he demanded.

'Against Krodans?' Garric drew his sword and let the sheath clatter to the floor. 'Always.'

94

Mara picked up an ivory trebuchet from the castles board and hovered it over the battlefield, pretending to dither. Across from her was the Master of Keys, wearing a smugly indulgent smile on his face. She had his measure entirely. He was monotonously aggressive and easy to predict. With a swift break for the high ground and her knights sweeping in from the side, she could ruin him.

'There are so many factors to consider, aren't there?' oozed the Master of Keys. 'It's enough to muddle anybody. Do take your time.'

Taking her time was exactly what she was doing. She agonised over every action, feigning indecision. She picked up pieces and put them down again, humming and hahing all the while. The master endured it all with the patience of a father teaching an infant, having been confident of victory from the very first move. As long as he was beating her, he was content.

'Tactical and logical thinking, remember?' said the master as she wavered again. 'Now imagine having to do this every day. That is what it takes to be a Master... forgive me, a *Mistress* of Keys.'

He gave a knowing glance to one of his companions, a moustachioed young Krodan called Tallen. Several more people were observing the game. One, an Ossian, had brought his wife to watch, too. Some were supposed to be feasting, but they wanted to see how this turned out. Men enjoyed a wager, even if it was only pride at stake, and Mara's challenge had intrigued them. She guessed that no one would be sad to see the master lose – everyone liked to see a braggart taken down a peg – but it would be equally satisfying to see a mud-headed woman with delusions of grandeur learn the error of her ways. It was win–win, as far as they were concerned.

She looked over the board. Her pieces were few, and getting fewer. If she lost many more, she wouldn't be able to win the game, and she'd delayed him a good while already. She could begin to fight back by moving her trebuchet to that hill, overlooking the river of counters which divided the board.

She moved it backwards instead, withdrawing it to defend one of the two castles she still held.

'Ah! A defensive move. Very wise,' said the master. 'But perhaps you did not see how it leaves your eagle exposed to my assassin, thus?' He slid his piece across the board and tapped it against her eagle.

'Well, we must all make sacrifices,' she said, with a tight smile.

It was good that she'd had a few glasses of wine. She'd need a couple of bottles later to wash away the shame. Sacrifices? She'd made more than her share. A lifetime's potential sacrificed on the altar of Krodan belief. Her genius smothered, her voice silenced, her only great contribution to the world credited to her former lover. So many times she'd bitten her tongue, bowed her head, dimmed her light so as not to outshine a man. And now she was forced to do it again. For Grub's sake. For the cause.

'Might I suggest reinforcing your left flank? You're rather exposed there,' said the master helpfully.

'So I am!' she said in mock surprise. 'Thank you for your advice. Hmm ... Perhaps a swordsman would bolster my forces?'

'Ah ...' The master sounded uncertain.

'You have another idea?'

'Have you considered that the giant might offer better protection?'

'Of course he would,' said Mara. 'Thank you.' *Thank you for telling me how to play my own pieces against you, you patronising bastard.*

'Here, allow me.' He reached across the table and moved her piece for her. It was all Mara could do not to slap him.

'I see,' was all she could manage, almost choking on her rage.

'Now ... Ha ha! I seem to have stymied my own next move!' he chuckled. 'There's a giant in the way now! I'd better think again.'

'Don't despair. There is a way through every barrier.'

'Oh, not *every* barrier,' the master replied. 'Otherwise I'd have no job!'

'I must disagree. Surely there must be someone out there clever enough to get through your mysterious vault door.'

'You *are* worried about thieves, aren't you?'

'Well, the Ember Blade is quite a target, and I've heard Ossians have a rebellious streak. Look at Salt Fork.'

'Salt Fork! Ha! The average Ossian can't get on with his neighbour long enough to borrow a pair of shears! Present company excluded, of course,' he added, nodding to the Ossians in the audience.

'No need to apologise, Jarrit. You're quite right,' said Lord Hewit, a lanky man with a sharp nose. 'Weak stock, that's what this country has. No discipline or willpower in the common folk. Half of them are barely better than animals. Only bloodlines worth a damn are the nobility.'

Mara was finding it increasingly difficult to contain herself. She wanted to rain righteous truth down on these insufferably superior fools. She met the eyes of the only other woman present, Lady Hewit, a raven-haired Ossian who'd once been swan-necked until age loosened her skin. Did she feel as Mara felt? Did she burn inside daily at the injustice?

'Still,' she said, returning her attention to the master, 'if *you* can open the door, is it not possible someone else could?'

'Not without the key. There is only one, and I keep it safe.'

Mara's face was a picture of innocent puzzlement. 'But you said there was no key?'

'My lady, I said there was no key*hole*.' He absently moved a piece and took her other eagle. 'There is, however, a key, if not in the conventional sense.'

'How intriguing! But a key can be stolen, surely?'

He gave a slightly exasperated chuckle. 'If the key to the vault were taken, I am quite sure I would notice in *very* short order.'

There. She'd caught him; he'd finally dropped one hint too

many. Distracted, unguarded, it never occurred to him that a woman approaching her elder years posed any kind of threat. Even her probing questions about the vault were dismissed as harmless curiosity, where a man would have been met with suspicion.

Of course you would notice if the key was gone, she thought. *Because you're carrying it on your person.*

Grub's mission was destined to fail. There was no key to be found in his chambers because the master had it with him. Yarin's spies had been wrong on that score. Whatever the nature of this key, the master sounded confident there was no chance of a thief making off with it.

She didn't need to keep the master from his chambers any more. In fact, she should send him there as soon as possible. It was a dangerous ploy, but if anyone could get the key away from him, it was the light-fingered Skarl.

No need to humour him further, then. No need to smile and defer and lose with grace to pamper his ego. It was time to show him who she really was.

'Are you stuck?' he asked with that oily tone that felt like a pat on the head. 'Might I suggest you move your arch—'

'No, I think I'll do this,' she said, shifting a piece out to the edge of the battlefield.

'Hmmf,' said the master. 'Well, of course it's your choice. But then I shall simply do this.' He slid his assassin across the board and took her piece. 'You must always think three moves ahead,' he advised.

'I really just needed you to move your assassin,' she told him as her knight captured his trebuchet on the high ground between two of his castles.

'Oho! Didn't see that one coming, did you, Jarrit?' crowed Tallen, who was more than a little drunk.

'Be assured, it was all in the plan,' said the master uncertainly. He scanned the board and his eyes lit up. 'As you see.' He swooped his eagle in, adding its value to the adjacent swordsman, and took the knight. 'There!'

'Oh, very good,' said Tallen. 'But I think you'll find—'

'You've exposed your giant,' Mara finished, and took it.

731

'Exactly so,' said Tallen.

'The lady has claws!' one of the audience commented, enjoying Jarrit's increasing discomfort.

'Nonsense! She's merely realised at last that attack is the best defence! A little too late, though. As you can see, I have more than double her pieces.'

'Battles have been won with worse odds,' said Mara calmly. 'Assandra's stand at Gudruk during the Third Purge. Rennau's rout of the Royalists at Durn, which turned the tide of the revolution. The Battle of Ravenspear, when the gnawls turned on the urds and ogren. Tactics trump superior numbers every time.'

'You know your history,' said the master, staring at her in worried amazement. Suddenly he didn't recognise the woman in front of him. Then he shook himself and his face firmed, as much as was possible with the excess of flesh that surrounded it. 'However, it will avail you nothing. I have superior numbers *and* superior tactics.'

'Then make your move,' said Mara, 'and we shall see.'

Stung, he threw his forces into a reckless attack. Mara caved before it, skirmishing along his line, picking off the weakest – and fastest – pieces as his forces were stretched thin. He took a castle at considerable sacrifice, then while he was gloating, Mara slipped across the river and assassinated his draccen.

Over the next few turns, the master began to understand what she'd done. Almost all his highly mobile pieces were gone, leaving him with a powerful but lumbering army, most of which was on the other side of the river from his king.

'Jarrit, I do believe she's beating you!' said Lord Hewit with delight.

'She is *not* beating me!' he huffed. 'I still have my most powerful pieces, while she is reduced to the rank and file.'

'Better get them back across the river fast, though,' said Tallen, chuckling.

The master was flustered now, the colour rising in his cheeks and his temper with it. His moves became hasty, striking out at anything he could hit. Mara dangled bait in front of him, sacrificing pieces to draw his troops away from their king's side, and he took it again and again.

By the end, he even believed he was winning.

'Ha!' he said as he reached for an archer. 'Did you forget that this hill increases my archer's range? I can hit your swordsman from there.'

A snort of laughter from the audience stopped him and he glared at Tallen in irritation. 'By the Primus, you are getting on my nerves!' he complained.

'Haven't you noticed she's beaten you?' Tallen told him.

The master's face went slack. 'No, she hasn't!' he said.

Tallen leaned over the board, tracing lines with his finger. 'Assassin here. Swordsman here. Knight here. Your king doesn't have enough moves to get up to that high ground, so there's nowhere he can go. Next turn, her archer moves to the high ground your king can't reach, and he's dead. No escape, no matter what you do.' He straightened and applauded, slowly but earnestly. 'Bravo, my lady. Bravo.'

The master was still furiously searching the board, seeking some way out, unable to understand how he'd come to this predicament. He wanted to cry 'Cheat!', she saw it. It would be so much easier than admitting he'd been bettered.

'It would appear that some women have more logical and tactical minds than you give us credit for,' she said, unable to resist twisting the knife.

The men in the audience guffawed and the master went beetroot with anger. His chair screeched as he surged to his feet. He was being mocked now, and he didn't like it at all.

'A very fine game,' he managed to say through a strangled grimace. 'Excuse me. I must take my supper now.' With a stiff bow, he stormed away, the laughter of his fellows ringing in his ears.

Mara got to her feet, a smile of raw satisfaction on her face. She basked in the glow of victory, and it was all the better for having rubbed his arrogant face in it. That had felt good; so very, very good.

'My lady,' said Tallen, full of boozy gallantry, 'I must apologise for Jarrit's lack of grace. Perhaps you'd join us in a discourse on the great battles of history, among which your game of castles will no doubt soon be reckoned.'

She caught the eye of Lady Hewit, hoping to see a glimmer of satisfaction there, some appreciation that Mara had struck a small blow for their kind. But she was clearly appalled at Mara's behaviour and looked away when she met her gaze.

Mara should have expected no better, but still she was disappointed. Just as Ossians policed themselves, their self-interest keeping them under the Krodan boot, so women policed each other more thoroughly than men ever could.

Well, damn her. It'll all be different, one day. We'll make it different.

'I thank you for your invitation,' she said to Tallen, 'but I'm afraid I have somewhere else to be.' She swiped a glass of wine from a passing servant, raised it to them and took a swig. 'Good night, gentlemen. Madam.'

With that, she swept away across the parlour and out through the door, buzzing with a feeling sweeter than any drink could deliver.

95

They crowded up the torchlit corridor, shoulder to shoulder, swords in hand. Aren, Harod and Garric were in the lead, the others behind. Aren's mouth was dry with excitement and fear, muscles trembling with the anticipation of combat.

You can do this, he told himself. *You can do it.*

The enemy had their swords drawn by the time Aren and the others hustled into view, warned by the sound of approaching footsteps. Aren saw the double-barred cross of the Iron Hand on their armour and recognised the man at their head: Captain Dressle, who'd escorted him to the interrogation room after Harte captured him. Dressle's eyes hardened as he saw Aren and then flicked to Garric.

'For Ossia!' Aren cried, unable to contain the tension inside him. They charged and met their opponents in a jagged crash of steel.

All of Aren's training went out of his head the moment the fight began. What was left were the reactions and responses drilled into him by Master Orik, as familiar as instinct. In the confines of the corridor, he was jostled from all sides, battling for space to swing his sword. Before him was a pug-nosed, black-bearded man with a scar across one eye. Just another face, meaning nothing. He wasn't a person but an obstacle. All Aren needed to do was kill him.

There was only space for three abreast in the corridor, but the Ossians had Harod on their side, the calm force holding the centre. Dressle could barely get a blow in on him. His blade flashed here and there as he blocked and feinted, his stance rigid and his back stiff.

Dressle quickly realised the way things would go in an even fight and barked an order to fall back. Behind them, the corridor opened up into a wider room where the rest of his guardsmen could lend their swords.

Aren's opponent stepped back and swung. Aren moved to block it, but Harod's blade was there first. He turned his block into a thrust, driving his blade into the man's armpit. The soldier gaped and coughed blood. Aren put his foot to his chest and sent him sprawling into the man behind him. Another soldier pushed in to fill the space, but there was the thump of a bowstring and he fell with one of Fen's arrows protruding from his mouth.

Aren glanced to the right and saw Garric smash through his opponent's weak guard before hacking deep into his shoulder. The soldier screamed and blood spurted from the wound as Garric yanked his blade free. Where Harod was calm, Garric was possessed, teeth gritted, fuelled by a furnace of rage. Without his beard and hair there was a raw, lean savagery to him, the look of a starving wolf.

They pressed their advantage and Dressle retreated under a rain of blows. He tripped over a fallen soldier and tumbled into the room behind him, his attackers spilling in after. Two more soldiers closed ranks to protect their captain before Harod could impale him. One of them found themselves impaled in his stead.

Aren took a moment to size up the odds. There were half a dozen including Dressle, spread across a square chamber that Aren guessed was an unmanned guard post. He saw an empty weapons rack on the wall, a table and chairs, sacks piled near a battered supply chest. A torch burned in a rusty sconce and a narrow staircase led upwards.

The combat spread out inside the room. Ruck pushed past Aren and pounced on a soldier, knocking him down in a tumble of fur and claw to savage his exposed face. He screamed in horror and pain as his cheek was ripped away from the bone beneath. One of his companions tried to break off from the fighting to help him, and Aren took advantage of his distraction to press the attack. A lucky blow sheared the fingers off his opponent's sword-hand, causing him to drop his weapon, and he stared at the stumps in shocked puzzlement before Aren ran him through.

Garric, a ragged agent of vengeance, cut down another guard to Aren's left. Angry as he was, he had a Dawnwarden's skill and his blows were cunningly placed. He stepped past the fallen man, stalking Dressle, who was scrambling back on his elbows, yet to find his feet. Dressle saw him coming and reached for a sword that had landed near him, but he was too late. Garric executed him with an overhead swing so hard that it chipped the stone beneath his body.

The discipline of the last two guardsmen faltered and broke. One of them ran for the stairs and was shot through the back by Fen. Vika flung a handful of red powder in the other soldier's face. He stumbled away, gagging, and Garric cut him down.

A handful of heartbeats after it had begun, it was over. Aren stood among the carnage, panting, both hands on his sword hilt as if expecting more enemies to appear. The only sound was huffing breath and the wet, desperate gargle of Ruck's victim as he tried to draw air through a torn-out throat. Soon his eyes glazed and he fell silent. Ruck, her muzzle bloody with gore, began to lick her paws.

Harod sheathed his blade. He looked absurd. His velvets and hose were splattered with blood and his hair had dried in a jester's mop, but his face was impassive and serious as ever and no one felt like laughing at him. Orica and Cade crept into the room now the fighting was done, Cade holding a sword out before her like some brave defender.

Garric surveyed the bodies scattered around the room. The tinny-sweet smell of fresh blood was thick in the air. 'Reckon anyone heard us?'

'The guards are all on the floors above, protecting the guests,' said Aren, 'and these walls are thick. We may have been lucky.'

Garric began moving between the bodies, examining them, searching for something. 'They came down here for me. That means they know we're here.'

'Not necessarily,' said Aren. 'Only that they suspect something. Maybe they were just being cautious. We don't know, so we go on.'

737

Garric gave him a look, half-amazed. 'You don't give up, do you?'

'Tires you out, doesn't it?' Cade commiserated.

'Grub's out there somewhere,' said Aren. 'He's relying on us to be ready when he gets to the vault. I won't let him down. So that's where we're going.'

'Not I,' said Garric. He knelt down next to the guard that had been shot through the mouth and began unstrapping his armour.

They stared at him in silence. 'What do you mean, "*Not I*"?' Aren asked at last.

'You think you'll even *get* to the Ember Blade?' Garric replied, tugging off the guard's trousers. 'You're going to climb all the way up through this fortress, bedraggled and covered in blood, while the Krodans are on the alert and looking for you? Good luck with that. If I thought you'd listen, I'd tell you to turn around and get out of here while you still have your lives.'

Aren was aghast. The man before him had suddenly become a stranger. 'We can make our way through the empty parts of the fortress, you *know* that!' he argued, hurt and shocked. 'You planned to do it yourself!' His face slackened as a dreadful suspicion settled on him. 'Didn't you?'

'No,' said Vika, who'd reached the same conclusion. 'He didn't. Whatever he planned, he never meant to come back at all.'

Garric met her eye briefly then looked away, busying himself with stripping the armour. 'If I learned one lesson from Salt Fork, it was this: a man who overreaches cannot long keep hold of what he grasps. We were brave and eager and swift, but all we gained was death. The Ember Blade was always out of reach, Aren. I don't know how you plan to break into the vault, nor how you plan to escape, nor how you mean to keep the Blade if you get it; but I reckon you'll die if you try.'

His words fell on them like stones, and Aren wanted to punch him for saying them. They were a betrayal, after all they'd been through to free him.

'But one man …' he went on. 'One man, disguised as one of the Iron Guard … He might be able to move among them.' He pulled his roughspun shirt over his head, showing the criss-cross of welts on his torso, the burns, the crudely stitched line where a nipple had been. 'One man might get close enough to strike a blow the Krodans won't soon forget.'

'And the Ember Blade?' Vika asked.

'The Ember Blade is not enough!' Garric snapped. 'It was *never* enough! Our people are too far gone. They collude with their masters against their own kin. They do not have the courage to risk what they have and fight! The Ember Blade belongs to the days before the Krodans came, and those days have already been forgotten. Hope will not inspire them. But fear might.'

'Hope inspired *me*!' Fen said, and Aren could hear she was as hurt as he was.

'You promised us the Ember Blade and we followed you,' Aren told him. 'We were once a great people, and we still are! I know it! The blood of the wolf still flows in Ossian veins. They will rally to the Ember Blade!'

'You don't have it yet,' said Garric. 'And even if you did, they won't.'

The cold certainty in his voice numbed Aren. Nobody had expected this. Nobody knew what to do.

'When did you stop believing?' Aren asked him, his voice small.

Garric was pulling on the dead man's clothes and armour. 'You're young,' he said. 'And I admire your newfound patriotism. But it *is* newly found, Aren, and hardly tested. I've been fighting this battle a lot longer than you.' He paused for a moment, pulled an undershirt over his head. 'You want to know when I stopped believing? When my closest friend sold me out to torture and death, just like thirty years ago. All that struggle and I'm right where I started, with a knife in my back.' Garric sighed wearily. 'I'll not chase false hope any more.'

'You are not the champion in my vision,' Vika accused, her voice sharp with disgust. Ruck growled at him.

'I never claimed to be,' said Garric, fixing on the greaves.

'What about your oath?' Cade cried. 'You're a Dawnwarden!'

'Aye. I'm a Dawnwarden, for what that's worth. And I swore never to see the Ember Blade wielded by any but an Ossian. But if we're all killed trying to get it, as we likely will be, then it will be

739

in Prince Ottico's hands two days from now. You have my thanks for saving me, but my mission remains unchanged.'

'What is your mission, then, if not to steal the Ember Blade?' Orica asked.

Garric ignored her as he finished strapping on the breastplate and threw the cloak over his back. The fit wasn't perfect, but it would pass. He pulled up his shirt till it sat tight under his chin and covered the scar at his throat.

'Milady asked you a question,' said Harod.

Garric straightened, his face grim in the torchlight. 'I'm going to kill the prince,' he said. 'I'm going to kill General Dakken, who slaughtered the Dawnwardens. I'm going to kill every high-ranking Krodan I possibly can. And then I'm going to burn this place to the gods-damned ground and bury the Ember Blade under so much rubble it will lie in these mountains till time's end.'

'The barrels on the cart,' said Aren. He remembered Garric had been interested in which storeroom they'd be taken to. 'There's something in them, isn't there?'

Garric stared at him levelly, and that was answer enough. 'I'm leaving now, to do what I must. Any man or woman who wishes to stop me, make your play. Elsewise, step aside.'

No one spoke. Even if they had sure grounds to oppose him, none of them wanted to. They hadn't forgotten the man who'd led them all this way. They heard the dull conviction in his voice and saw the sword in his hand. He'd kill them if they tried to stop him, and they had enough enemies without fighting among themselves.

He snatched up a helmet and pushed past them, back the way they'd come. Aren held his gaze as he passed.

'You're not the man I thought you were, Cadrac of Darkwater,' Aren said coldly.

'Nor are you, Aren of Shoal Point,' said Garric, and there was no hatred but rather a rough tenderness in his voice that made Aren's heart hurt. 'I've never been so glad to be wrong.'

Then he was gone, up the corridor and out of sight.

Vika was the first to recover. 'We should not dally. Time is against us.'

'We're still … er … We're still going for the Ember Blade, then?' Cade asked.

'Of course we're going for the Ember Blade, mudwit!' Aren snapped. 'Why else do you think we're here?' He stalked off towards the stairs, his mind swirling with black thoughts.

'Alright, good,' said Cade, a cheery grin springing to his face. 'Just checking!'

96

The quiet of the Master of Keys' study was punctured by the delicate tinkle of breaking glass.

A desk stood in the moonlight next to a window set deep into the stone and covered by miniature curtains. From behind them came the soft sound of a bolt sliding back. The window squeaked open and cold air blew in, stirring the curtains. There was grunting, scraping, a muffled curse. Tattooed fingers dashed the curtains aside.

There, squashed in the tiny window recess like some grotesque frog, was Grub, his face stretched in a sour grimace.

'Mudslug never said... window was... so *small*,' he huffed as he forced himself by stages through the gap before finally slithering to the floor like a particularly recalcitrant turd.

He got to his feet, rubbing his hands together to chase away the icy chill. His fingers were numb and the muscles in his arms and back ached. He glanced at the hearth, prepared but unlit, and wished for a fire there.

No time to waste. Bossychops was supposed to be keeping the Master of Keys busy, but who'd want to talk to her for long?

There was a door on the far side of the study, which Grub reckoned led to the corridor outside. A quick scout through the other doorway revealed a bedroom with a shrine to the Primus. From there, a small door opened into a privy, with a bench of polished wood and a nosegay of pungent herbs and flowers to mask the faint scent of night-soil.

The study seemed the most likely place to start. In short order, he found a reinforced lockbox on the mantelpiece and set to work with his picks. His fingers were clumsy with the cold, but he got it open in the end.

Inside was a bewildering assortment of keys arranged in stacked wooden trays. Each had a small paper label attached, with the door that it matched written there in tight, neat Krodan.

Grub frowned as he pawed through them. Mudslug had made him memorise the Krodan word for 'vault', but he didn't see it here and even without the labels, Grub's instincts said none of these were right. Even the largest keys didn't look, well, *vaulty* enough.

Somewhere else, then. This key was too important to keep with all the others. He began to search the desk, but the sound of approaching footsteps stopped him and he froze as he heard voices outside the door.

'Can I help you, er ... ?'

'Overwatchman Klyssen,' said a moist voice. 'You are a hard man to find, Master Bann.'

'I was ... I went to the kitchens to fetch myself a dish. Is there some problem?'

'Let us in, please.'

Grub felt a jolt of alarm as he realised that Klyssen had been standing outside the door the entire time, waiting. Frost and bones, if he'd been heard ...

'Um, of course. Can you ... Could one of your men hold this while I get my key? Careful, it's hot. Am I ... Am I in some kind of trouble?'

'Just open the door.'

One of your men. There were more of them outside.

Grub rushed over to the window with its broken pane, closed and bolted it. He'd never be able to squeeze back into that recess in time, but he could pull the curtains and cover it up, sweep the glass under the desk with his boot. The window had a lattice design, so he'd only needed to knock out one small square to reach the bolt. The architects hadn't anticipated burglars clinging to the wall high above a fatal drop, but those architects hadn't met Grub.

The key rattled in the lock as he hurried into the bedroom,

searching for a place to hide. Under the bed? Too obvious. In the wardrobe? Just as stupid. There was nowhere a cursory search wouldn't reveal him.

The door in the study opened. With no other choice, Grub darted into the privy and pulled the door shut behind him. Maybe they wouldn't look in here.

'Search the place,' said Klyssen.

Grub rolled his eyes and swore under his breath. He heard armoured men clump into the study, the screech of a chair as it was pulled aside. The Master of Keys' chambers were small; they'd only take moments to find him. In desperation, he went to the privy-hole, stared down into the blackness as if it might offer him escape, but there was no way he'd fit in there.

They were in the bedroom now, opening doors, looking into the wardrobe and under the bed. His heart thumped against his ribs as they came closer. He cast about for some way to avoid discovery, hoping for a miracle to present itself. But he was in a tiny room not much wider than he was, with only a narrow bench of polished wood and a hole for the master's doings. There was nowhere to go.

A thought struck him. *Unless...*

'Look in there!' said a voice from outside.

The door was pushed open. An Iron Guardsman, sword in hand, poked his head into the room. He lingered there a moment, perhaps tickled by some sense that something was wrong, but it was an empty room with no corners to hide in. He grimaced and pulled the door shut.

'Privy,' he said. 'There's no one here.'

Grub listened to their footsteps move back into the study, then let out his breath through lips drawn taut with effort. He was pressed against the ceiling above the door, having jammed his feet against one wall and his shoulders against the other. Silently, he dropped down to the floor.

'Heh, heh, heh. Grub is the greatest,' he whispered to himself, and made an obscene gesture at the door and the guards beyond.

'Now perhaps you can tell me what this is all about?' The Master of Keys' voice was shrill with worry.

'When did you last examine the vault?' Klyssen asked.

'At sixth bell, as usual.'

'And everything was in order?'

'Of course.'

'Where is the key?'

Grub pressed his ear to the privy door. This he was eager to hear.

The master began to bluster. 'The location and nature of the key are closely guarded secrets!'

'Is it safe?' Klyssen demanded.

'Assuredly!'

'Show it to me.'

'Overwatchman, I cannot! It's simply that—'

'The Iron Hand take a dim view of those who impede their efforts to protect the Empire,' Klyssen said. 'Are you a loyal subject, Master Bann?'

Grub felt a grin spread across his face. That was a nice piece of bullying. He had to respect a fellow artisan.

'Um . . . Perhaps I could just show *you*?' the master wheedled.

'Very well. You two, guard the door. No one comes in or out but me. The Master of Keys is confined to his chambers until further notice.'

'But I . . . But—'

'You have a meal, don't you? Books?'

'Well, yes—'

'Then you should be well entertained.'

The door opened and closed as the guards left. No escape that way, Grub thought. Lucky that was never the plan.

'Now,' said Klyssen. 'Show me the key. I want to know that the Ember Blade is safe.'

'Why is everyone so concerned with the Ember Blade today? Nobody can reach it in the vault.'

'Who *else* has been concerned?' Klyssen asked sharply.

'An odious woman who latched on to me. She was obsessed that thieves might steal it. A terrible bore. Rude, too.'

'What was her name?' Klyssen's voice was like creeping frost. 'And what did she look like?'

'Lady Harforth of Harrow. Tall-ish, I suppose. Grey hair, short, you know how women cut it when it gets straggly? Sad when they go to seed that way.'

Grub's grin widened. Even in his predicament, it was fun to hear somebody abuse Bossychops behind her back.

'Here is the key,' said the master.

'*That's* the key?' Klyssen sounded surprised.

'Indeed. You see, if I twist it like *this* ...'

'That is like no key I have ever seen.'

'It fits in a recess in the door, and you turn it. There is only one and I wear it at all times, hidden in plain sight. It cannot be taken without my knowledge, and no thief would recognise it for what it is.'

'Ingenious,' said Klyssen, reluctantly impressed. 'Your medallion is the key. I never would have guessed it.'

'That is precisely the point,' said the master. 'I trust you are reassured, Overwatchman.'

Klyssen made a concessionary noise, already focused elsewhere. 'Stay in your chambers,' he said. 'Lock the door. I will speak with this Lady Harforth.'

Grub heard the door open and close, and the key turned in the lock.

'Yes, Your Spectacled Magnificence,' the master sneered venomously as soon as Klyssen was safely out of earshot.

Grub heard the master muttering to himself as he lit the fire in the study. He arranged his platter and cutlery to his satisfaction on his desk. Then he came striding into the bedroom, straight to the privy, where he opened the door.

Grub stabbed him in the throat, bearing him backwards onto the bed. With his hand pressed over the master's mouth, he stabbed him again and again, his knife darting in and out. Flabby flesh ran with blood, sliced into gory blubber. The master's eyes gaped comically wide. The only sound was Grub's heavy breathing, the creaking of the bed and the thud of the knife.

When the master went still, Grub took his hand away from his mouth. The silk sheets were sodden red and he was waxen now, his mouth in a slack gape and his eyes faraway. Grub snorted. If

746

ever proof were needed that men were just mannequins of meat constructed by the Bone God, it was there in death. All that mattered were the stories you left behind.

The master's medallion was on a heavy chain around his neck. Grub tugged it over his head and wiped away the blood with his palm. He had no eye for design but didn't think much of it. A falcon – the Krodans liked that bird – was set inside a border decorated with the motto of the Sanctorum. He'd seen it about enough to know it.

Diligence. Temperance. Dominance. Well, the last one sounded good to him, at least.

He turned it this way and that, examining it with his clever hands. He found one hidden clasp, and another, and then he pulled it apart, separating the medallion into a pair of thin discs. One had two dozen metal teeth, like the teeth of keys, protruding from its flat inner edge. The other had holes to accommodate them.

'Huh,' he said. He'd found the key to the vault. It wasn't quite what he'd expected, but it would do.

He tucked it into his pocket and went into the study. The guards hadn't looked behind the tiny curtains during their search, which was sloppy work. He pulled them open again, revealing the broken window beyond. He was just readying himself to squeeze back outside when his eye fell to the platter of food still on the desk.

Roast beef. Crispy potatoes cooked in goose fat. Quail on truffled aspic. Bull's brain pie. Candied fruits on the side, and a jug of heavy red wine.

He licked his lips and glanced at the door. Well, it was locked, wasn't it? And the only key was on the dead man in the bedroom. No reason for Klyssen to be back any time soon, and Mudslug was likely nowhere near the vault yet.

The fire was growing in the hearth and the room was getting warm. He thought of the climb ahead, and the bitter wind blowing through the broken pane.

It was no decision at all, really.

Grub wiped his bloody hands on his trousers, sat down at the desk and jammed a chunk of roast beef in his mouth. Being a hero was hungry work.

97

What about your oath?

Cade's question whispered in Garric's mind as he walked through the hive of scampering servants beneath the main feasting halls. Scrubber-boys hurried this way and that, butlers snapped orders at their subordinates and cooks sweated over cauldrons of soup, all in the light of a huge fire that cast the shadows of turning hogs across the grey brick walls. Those who noticed Garric looked away at the sign of the double-barred cross. Nobody hindered the Iron Guard.

What about your oath?

What if Aren was right? What if they *could* spirit the Ember Blade away? Wasn't that slim hope worth the gamble? Didn't he have to try?

Perhaps, perhaps not. The wording of the Dawnwardens' oath was muddy and archaic, updated piecemeal over the centuries as the language evolved. It had been interpreted many different ways. The Dawnwardens' decision to depose King Danna the Moon-Touched was only taken after some masterful rhetoric from Kalen the Rhymist persuaded them they were not breaking their oaths by doing it.

But Garric was no scholar, and there were no other Dawn-wardens to advise him. All he knew was that he couldn't risk the Ember Blade falling into Prince Ottico's hands. Let Aren try for the grand prize, flush with the naïvety and enthusiasm of youth. Garric would hedge their bets in case he failed. He'd protect the Ember Blade by returning it to the bosom of the land from which it sprang, to lie beneath an incalculable weight of stone for future generations of Ossians to unearth. If the legends were true, it was indestructible. And if they were not, it was still better than the alternative.

The Krodans wouldn't have it. At all costs, never that.

He tugged his collar up over his throat and strode on. The memory of torture stabbed him with each step, the pain in his body as nothing next to the pain in his mind. His jaw set hard as he thought of Klyssen, the bright tip of a burning poker reflected in his round spectacles. That soft, breathy voice asking questions, questions, questions. Promising to stop the agony if he gave up the others, if he'd betray all he was and all he'd ever been.

Garric's mouth twitched in a bitter smile. Small chance of that. He'd welcomed the pain. *Wanted* it.

He passed through the sweltering kitchens into the corridors beyond, which led to pantries and storerooms. Racks of meat hung in cold chambers, and there were shelves lined with hundreds of jars of honey and jam, bread and cheese. He counted the doors until he reached the one he wanted. Behind it, he expected to find a dozen Amberlyne barrels, each of them two-thirds full of elarite oil. Enough to destroy a sizable chunk of Hammerholt and burn the rest. Certainly it would kill everyone in the feasting halls above, including the prince and General Dakken. Maybe the chaos would ease Aren's task, or perhaps the blast would bring down a tower on their heads. Either way, it wouldn't stay Garric's hand. He'd been too long on this course to change it.

Unless the barrels had never made it out of the vintner's yard. Unless they'd been delivered to a different storeroom. Unless he was too late, having been delayed too long in his cell, and they'd already been moved elsewhere.

Aspects, if you ever had any love for this land, if you're there at all, be with me now. Azra, Lord of War, let those barrels be where I need them to be.

He opened the door. A servant emerging from a pantry down the corridor gave him a curious look and Garric glared at him until he hurried off.

Beyond the door was a chilly stone chamber lit by a lantern

hanging near the entrance. Racks of bottles ran along one wall and ale barrels were stacked wherever they'd fit, with a narrow, winding aisle left between them.

He shut the door behind him, took up the lantern and made his way in, searching for the telltale crest of the Amberlyne vineyards. Walking through a crowd of servants disguised as an Iron Guardsman hadn't worried him in the least, but anxiety tightened his guts as he cast his light about and saw no sign of what he was looking for. But those barrels *had* to be here. They *had* to!

There! A dusty blanket had been thrown over a small stack of barrels against one wall. Amberlyne didn't like the cold; they must be the barrels he sought. He hurried over, took up the corner of the covering and ripped it away with desperate hope.

His face fell slowly as he looked on what was beneath.

More ale barrels. That was all. The Amberlyne wasn't here. Maybe it never had been, or maybe it lay in a different storeroom, one of a dozen scattered throughout the keep. It didn't matter. He'd never find them now. He had no map, and had only memorised the small part of it that he needed. He could search all night and find nothing, and when his escape was discovered – as it would be soon – no disguise would save him.

Black despair turned to boiling rage. All his planning, all his *life* had come to naught, thwarted by a friend's betrayal and a twist of fate. All he wanted was to free his people. All he wanted was to make them stand up for themselves.

Damn you, Azra! he thought furiously. *Damn you, and the rest of the Nine. Your people cry out for you, and you do nothing. Well, if you will not, then I will!*

Nothing left. No grand destruction, no heroic end. No escape. Just like Salt Fork, he'd been undone by the fears of weak men. But he knew where the prince and General Dakken feasted, and he still had his sword. If he couldn't have victory, then he'd still have red vengeance.

His eyes dark coals of hatred, he stalked from the storeroom, his mind set on murder.

98

'Klyssen!'

Klyssen's shoulders tensed as the Commander's brandy-roughened bark stopped him in his tracks. He took a moment to compose himself, relaxed his scowl and turned. The Commander was standing by a doorway, a cigar in one hand and a glass in the other. Next to him, as ever, was that greasy snake Bettren. Evidently they'd stepped out of their feast to discuss some secret matter. Just Klyssen's luck to bump into them.

The Commander switched his cigar to his other hand and crooked a finger at Klyssen, summoning him like a naughty child. Klyssen kept his expression bland, letting the indignity slide off him. The Commander could play his power games if he wished. His days were numbered, and that number was small.

'Commander,' he said politely as he came over, masking his loathing with an ease born of years of practice. 'Head Adminis-trator Bettren.'

The Commander was once a square-jawed, athletic man who'd become fat and saggy with decades of rich food and soft living. He had the sour, sharp scent of the aged and his hands were speckled with liver spots. An eyepatch covered one eye, which had tended to wander since the stroke.

'A Sard singing treasonous songs to the prince?' he hissed angrily, keeping his voice low. 'Isn't that exactly the sort of thing you're here to prevent?'

Bettren smirked at that. He was dark-haired, slender and book-ishly handsome with his pencil moustache and his immaculate jacket. He was also a shameless flatterer. Pull out his tongue and you'd find it black to the root with boot polish. Klyssen would have loved to pull out his tongue.

'I am looking into it, Commander,' Klyssen said.

'The prince is incensed!' the Commander continued. 'And I see your moronic subordinate is blundering hither and thither with a group of watchmen in tow, questioning all and sundry! We're meant to be invisible, Klyssen! Behind the scenes! There are representatives of half the civilised world here tonight! At least try to maintain an *illusion* of competence.'

'It's all in hand, Commander,' said Klyssen. *Or at least it would be if you'd shut up and let me get on with my job.*

'While you're here, Overwatchman,' said Bettren, in that fey, airy manner that made Klyssen dream of signing his execution warrant, 'I have a question.'

Oh, you do, do you? 'And what is that?' he said wearily.

'Some of my men were turned away from the north tower earlier. Apparently you ordered that nobody be allowed inside. I wonder what you're doing in there?'

'I wonder what business your clerks had in such a remote and unoccupied part of the fortress,' Klyssen replied.

'Answer the question, Klyssen!' snapped the Commander. 'What's in the tower?'

'Insurance,' said Klyssen. 'Something only to be used in the direst emergency. The prince's safety is more important than preserving the image of the Empire.' *And because I'll end my days in a work camp in Ozak if a hair on his head is harmed. Which will be a pleasant fate compared to what you'll suffer.*

The Commander's expression faltered as he realised what Klyssen had done. He knew what was in the tower, but he couldn't say a word so he would be able to feign ignorance if anything went wrong. *On such hypocrisy rests our Empire.*

'You disgust me, Klyssen,' the Commander said. 'You've always disgusted me.'

'Your honesty is as commendable as it is rare,' said Klyssen with a hateful smile. 'But it's what the Chancellor thinks that's important, isn't it? I imagine he'll be quite impressed when he hears I caught the last Dawnwarden. Now you must excuse me, I'm busy protecting the Empire.'

With that, he made his escape, leaving the senile old fool and his pet seething in his wake. Such open insubordination was reckless and ill-advised, but by the Primus, it felt good. Besides, the Commander had already made his feelings about Klyssen clear to anyone who'd listen, and it hadn't stopped him yet. Once Garric swung from the gallows, he'd be untouchable.

Unless Garric's followers managed to foul up the prince's wedding. Then the blame would fall squarely on Klyssen, and the Commander – who was ultimately responsible for the Iron Hand's operations in Ossia – would go down with him. Only Bettren would escape unblemished. The administrative arm of the Iron Hand had nothing to do with security, so a catastrophe here would virtually guarantee his succession. If that happened, missing out on promotion would be the least of Klyssen's worries.

He thought of Lisi and Juna, his golden-haired daughters. He thought of his beautiful wife and the fine home she'd curated at vast expense. He thought of silly old Baron Pickles. He'd lose it all if he couldn't root out whatever plot was afoot tonight. The idea quickened his heart and made him desperate, so he crushed it down again.

The things we value make us weak. Now is not the time. Now I am authority.

He found Harte near the armoury, limping fast towards his next destination with a harried underwatchman trailing behind him.

'A few servants saw the Sard and her companion heading for the lower levels,' he reported as soon as he saw Klyssen.

It was a refreshing change to have Harte be efficient instead of sulky and obstructive. 'Did you search down there?'

'We did and found no sign. But there is something else – all the privies on the lower levels are backing up.'

Klyssen gave him a dry look that communicated exactly how many seconds he had left to explain himself.

'The sewers are flooded!' said Harte. 'I don't know what it means, but the servants say it's never happened before. They don't think the prince's guests will notice since they're all on the higher floors, but it's out of the ordinary.' He gave Klyssen a challenging look. 'I thought you'd want to know.'

It *was* out of the ordinary, like too many things tonight. 'Have you heard anything from Dressle?'

'No. I thought he was meant to report to you.'

'He was,' said Klyssen. He shook his head in frustration. So many signs, not enough evidence. Well, damn what the Commander said. There was something going on.

He snapped his fingers at the underwatchman. 'You. Find Watchman Tull in the barracks and tell him to double the guard on the prince. I don't care how it looks.' He snapped his fingers again at Harte. 'Check the dungeons and come straight back to me. I want to know why Captain Dressle hasn't sent word. I'm going to get the key to the vault. I want half a dozen men guarding the Ember Blade until it's safe in the prince's hands.'

'Hail to the Emperor,' said Harte, fist clenched, arm across his chest in salute.

'You might make watchman first class yet,' said Klyssen approvingly.

'Master Bann! Master Bann! Open the door!'

The guards were hammering on the door now. It made no difference. There was no answer from inside.

'Break it down,' Klyssen told them, but his guts were a ball of ice.

He's choked on a bone and died. He's overdosed on feathermilk. He's hanged himself for fear of the Iron Hand. Anything, anything but what Klyssen suspected they'd find within.

The guards barged and battered at the door until the lock gave way at last. They rushed in, swords drawn. Klyssen came after.

The room reeked of blood. Klyssen took in the empty platter on the desk, the open window with the broken pane. Through the doorway, he could see the Master of Keys' bloody carcass lying on the bed. He didn't need to enter the room to know the medallion had been taken from around his neck.

'This has gone too far,' he said to the guards, his voice flat. 'Come with me.'

'Where are we going?'

'The north tower,' Klyssen said. 'It's time to release the dreadknights.'

99

Aren and his companions approached the vault by a circuitous route, through empty halls and corridors rarely trodden. Using Yarin's keys, they had access to whole sections of Hammerholt where the furniture was draped with cloth and their feet left prints in the dust. In this manner, they bypassed the celebrations entirely and reached the heights of the fortress without encountering another soul.

The vault was in a squat, square tower, far from the heart of the keep. They hurried up spiral stairs, following their map, and went through a door halfway up to find themselves in a short corridor, which soon turned a corner and led them to the vault at the end.

Aren had hoped to find it unguarded, but there was a single sentry on duty before the door, sitting on a stool, bored witless. His eyes widened in shock as he saw them, and he scrambled to his feet and drew his sword. Aren took a breath to tell him to surrender, but Fen shot him through the eye.

'He might have given up!' Aren cried.

'He was in our way,' Fen said coldly. 'And he was a Krodan.'

Aren let the matter drop. Perhaps he was naïve in wanting to keep the killing to a minimum when they were about such deadly business as revolution, but he didn't believe all Krodans were culpable for their masters' crimes. That man's death felt needless.

'Grub wondered how he was going to get rid of that sentry,' said Grub, melting out of the darkness behind them.

Cade jumped out of his skin. 'Gods, but you nearly stopped my heart, you sneak!' he snapped. 'What's that stuck to your cheek? Is that roast beef? Have you been *eating*?'

For an answer, Grub plucked the fleck of meat from his cheek, popped it in his mouth and smacked his lips.

'Do you have the key?' Orica asked him eagerly.

Grub held up a golden medallion on a chain.

'Um...' said Cade, raising a finger.

'This the key,' Grub told them, before Cade could say what they were all thinking. 'Trust Grub.'

'Two words I never thought to hear together,' Cade said. He clapped his hands. 'Well, then, who wants to see what's on the other side of that door?'

The vault door was hard to recognise as a door at all. There was no handle to be seen. It was a slab of metal set into the wall between two pillars, eight feet high and five broad. Etched into its surface was a dramatic, angular bas-relief showing the parable of Tomas and Toven and the mad ogren. Toven was locked in combat with two hulking brutes, jaws agape in primitive faces, features stylised into geometric shapes in the Krodan fashion. Tomas stood in the background, his hand raised, preaching aloud from a book. In the story, Tomas calmed the crazed ogren with the message of the Primus, and they went away meekly to spread the word among their people. Aren thought that more than a little fanciful. The ogren were the hammer of the elaru, brutish shock troops whose savage strength put even the urds to shame. They weren't much given to religious introspection.

'Reckon I expected something bigger,' Cade said, eyeing the door uncertainly. The lanternlight stirred shadows across the design and the figures appeared to move. 'Big double doors, twenty feet high, that kind of thing.'

Aren stepped over the sentry's body. 'When you tell the tale, you can make it whatever size you like.'

'Oh, no,' said Cade. 'I'll tell it like it is. Ain't no *need* to exaggerate this one.' He frowned. 'Hoy – there's a bit missing in the middle.'

Aren looked closer and saw a circular depression hidden among the ogren's limbs, with a multitude of tiny slots cut into it in a curious pattern.

'Grub?' Aren said, inviting him forward. 'You found the key. You should be the one to open it.'

'There is blood on the medallion,' Vika observed as Grub stepped up to the door.

Grub snorted. 'Last owner didn't want to take it off,' he said.

He fiddled with the medallion and separated it into two discs, one with a series of projecting teeth sticking out of the inner side. He held it up to show them. 'Key,' he said, and placed it into the depression. The teeth fitted perfectly into the slots there. Grub turned it with his fingertips, and they heard the crunch of a lock disengaging from within.

He turned and bowed with a flourish. 'Grub will accept congratulations and praise now,' he informed them.

'How in Prinn's name did you work out *that* was the key to the vault?' Orica asked, amazed.

'Because Grub is a genius,' he said matter-of-factly.

They hauled the sentry's body out of the way. Harod pushed at the door, which did no good, then found that there were handholds cunningly crafted into the scene. He seized them and slowly pulled the door open. Aren's fists clenched in anticipation and he felt a wave of angry triumph.

You were wrong, Garric. We did it. We're here!

Ruck slid inside as soon as the gap was wide enough to admit her. The others followed more carefully, raising their lanterns to push back the darkness. Beyond the door was a circular chamber with pillared alcoves around the edge. Like the door that led to it, it was surprisingly small. Aren had imagined a great treasure chamber; instead he found a neat, solid room of grey stone.

In they went, searching the shadowed corners. Grub's eyes grew large and hungry as the lanternlight fell on the prince's treasures, arranged among the alcoves. They saw a suit of exquisite witch-iron armour, polished to a mirror sheen, and a jewelled necklace in a glass display case. There was a copy of the Acts of Tomas and Toven bound with gold hinges, the sword-and-book symbol of the Sanctorum crafted from silver and set with a blood-red ruby.

They saw strange gifts from faraway lands: precious reliquaries and caskets, a gnawl skull set in amber, a long coat made of iridescent scales.

Yet for all the treasures that surrounded him, Aren's eyes were locked on only one. Set upon a pedestal, lying next to a scabbard on a cloth of blue silk, was the Ember Blade.

His breath became short. For all the tales told of it, he'd thought it only a sword, a symbol they might use to unite his broken people. He hadn't expected it to have such presence, such magnetic power. The others watched as he approached it reverently, recognising his right to take it. Even Grub seemed impressed enough that it temporarily overwhelmed his instinct to steal whatever he could get his hands on.

Its hilt was a masterpiece of craftsmanship, forged from polished witch-iron. Upon the pommel were inscribed words in Old Ossian, a tongue now lost to all but the scholars. Black leather had been newly wrapped round the tang and the quillons flowed like water to either side of the ricasso. But it was the blade that mesmerised Aren: a length of pure embrium, the rarest metal known. It threw back the lanternlight with a sullen red tint like the glow of a dying fire, and the sight of it kindled a fire in his own breast.

Everything had brought him to this: his father's death, the escape from the camp at Suller's Bluff, the flight through Skavengard and all that followed. He'd been forged, as surely as this blade had been forged, fashioned into a man capable of breaking into Hammerholt, of entering this vault, of seizing the sword. It was Garric who'd planted the idea in his head, but Aren who'd followed it through. The Ember Blade had called to him, and he'd come.

His hand closed round the hilt and he lifted it. It might have carried the weight of ages, but it was impossibly light. He understood now; the stories were true. He had no doubt that this sword, forged from the bones of Ossia, would inspire his countryfolk. Just to see it was to believe.

He was so absorbed that at first he didn't notice the itch in his hand. Only when it became maddening did he tear his gaze away, and his joy turned to horror. A rash of blisters was spreading up his sword-hand, swelling and bursting, oozing pus. His hand began to burn, and he cried out as the skin under the blisters split and he saw something white and maggoty moving beneath. He staggered away from the pedestal, the Ember Blade still in his hand, but now a new pain was tormenting his scalp. He put his hand to it, felt something wet there, and a chunk of his hair sloughed free.

The room was full of screams. He whirled and found the others clawing at themselves, pulling at their skin, eyes bulging with horror. There were no marks on them that he could see, yet they acted as if they were all touched by the same nightmarish affliction that was spreading throughout Aren. He tried to speak, but his tongue had swollen and his eyes were swimming with tears.

Then he saw them, standing in the doorway, two figures he'd hoped never to see again. Klyssen, bespectacled, quietly malevolent; Plague, wrapped in belts and straps with a black spiked bow in his hand, his face a stitched mask of dead skin. Behind them stood a half-dozen Iron Guardsmen.

The Ember Blade dropped from Aren's hand, ringing loudly on the stone floor as he was seized by a cramp strong enough to bring him to his knees. They were all helpless; even Ruck was writhing on the floor biting at herself. This was the dreadknight's work, it *had* to be! But the knowledge brought him no respite.

'Aren of Shoal Point,' said Klyssen. 'Now, isn't this a surprise?'

100

The head butler had a ladle of soup to his lips, ready to judge its quality, when he saw the Iron Guardsman approaching through the chaos of the kitchens. He lowered the ladle and straightened his uniform as a frightened scrubber-boy led the guardsman to him.

'He asked for the man in charge,' the boy mumbled, desperate to escape. The double-barred cross had a way of making even the innocent feel guilty.

'Thank you, Malek. You may go,' said the butler. Malek needed no second prompting.

The guardsman was unusually unkempt for his rank. He was coarsely shaven and hollow-eyed, his lips chapped and red marks at the corners of his mouth. Momentary puzzlement creased the butler's face, but it wasn't his place to question.

'How may I help you, Guardsman?'

'I've been sent by Overwatchman Klyssen. The prince may be in danger and I need your help.' His voice was a growl of command.

The butler stiffened. 'Of course!' he said. 'Anything.'

'He is at the feast now?' the guardsman asked.

'We have just served the main course.'

'How many swords at his side?'

'Only his bodyguard's. No one else may carry a sword in his presence.'

'Thank the Primus for that. Entrances and exits?'

'Two. The main door, and a side entrance for servants.'

'Are they stout?'

'Very.'

The guardsman scanned the kitchen restlessly as he considered that information. 'And who holds keys to these doors?'

'I do. And the Master of Keys, of course.'

The guardsman held out his hand. 'Give them to me.'

The butler hesitated, but only for a moment. He picked two keys off his ring and handed them over.

'Delay the next course until I return,' he said, and then saluted briskly. 'Hail to the Emperor.'

'Hail to the Emperor!' the butler replied, making a salute of his own; but the guardsman was already on his way.

Krodans! Garric thought scornfully as he strode through the clattering, steaming kitchen. His untidy appearance, his inauthentic accent, his unusual request, all these should have raised suspicion. But they were conditioned to obey authority without question, and so long as he was dressed as an Iron Guardsman they'd do as he said. Whatever failings the Ossians had, they didn't share that one.

When nobody was looking, he snatched up a knife and slipped it beneath his steel arm-guard. When it came to murder, the fast blade trumped the sword.

He made his way upstairs quickly. Time was against him, and when his escape was discovered, Klyssen really *would* send reinforcements. Perhaps he already had, since he'd been suspicious enough to send Captain Dressle to the dungeons. But Hammerholt was vast, and orders took time to travel, and the butler had only mentioned the bodyguard. If reinforcements were coming at all, Garric had to hope he'd get to the hall before they did.

Ifs and buts and maybes. It didn't matter. A hundred swords or one, his course was set. He'd die today. The only question was how many he could take with him.

Following the map in his mind, he found the main door to the feast hall. The sounds of conversation and clinking glasses came from within, the restrained, formal revels of Krodan high society. Garric locked the door from outside, then went up a side passage to the servants' entrance. He grasped the handle, closed his eyes and took a breath.

Now to death, and darkness, and glory.

He opened the door and stepped through.

The feast hall was long and high-ceilinged, with lamps burning on the walls and glowing wrought-iron braziers standing in the corners, radiating heat and light. The walls were draped with thick tapestries depicting hunting scenes. At one end stood the main doors, while at the other, a few steps led up to a raised dais separated off from the festivities with green velvet curtains.

Garric, unnoticed at the edge of the feast, closed the door behind him and surreptitiously locked it.

Tables ran the length of the hall, arranged in a hollow rectangle. Diners laughed and gossiped, drank from glittering crystal glasses, cut meat with shiny silver knives. The light of a candelabrum reflected in a lady's eyes as she gazed with veiled lust upon her neighbour; a red-faced Krodan guffawed, drunk on wine and company; a nervous young man pulled at his food, waiting for an opportunity to join the conversation surrounding him. The air smelled of roast venison, buttered leeks, hot coals and perfume.

All this Garric noticed, and more besides. He wasn't observant by nature, but he drank in every detail now. His senses had opened up, absorbing as much of the world as they could before the end. This was the last room he'd ever see, these the last faces. He was alive now as he'd never been before.

The servants' door was near the head of the room, where Prince Ottico sat with his back to the curtains. Garric briefly wondered what was behind them – spare chairs, rolled-up tapestries, a grand dessert ready to be unveiled with a flourish? – but once he found his target, the thought went out of his head.

Prince Ottico was disappointingly mundane in the flesh. For all his power, for all that he represented to the people of Kroda, he was just a man, and an unimpressive one at that. He was pale and soft, barely able to grow a moustache despite being in his thirties. The bodyguard was the threat here: tall, shovel-nosed and keen of eye. He stood a short distance behind the prince, his hand resting on his sword. He was the one Garric would have to reckon with first. Further along the table he saw the hated General Dakken, his white hair cut short, looking robust and vigorous despite his three-score years. Dakken would be third to die; he owed his fellow Dawnwardens that. But it was all for nothing if Prince Ottico lived. The prince was the priority.

Garric strode around the edge of the room with the purposeful air of a man who was meant to be there. A few diners spotted him, but they thought him a messenger and saw no threat. Dakken was one of the few who would recognise him, armour or no, but he was deep in conversation. The bodyguard was more alert and he moved to meet Garric, positioning himself in front of the prince. Garric saw the flicker in his eyes as he noted the sword at Garric's hip and the dishevelled look of him. This wasn't a man to be cowed by a uniform.

Garric stopped before him and saluted smartly, fist clenched, arm across his chest. 'Hail to the Emperor!' he said in greeting.

'Hail to the Emperor,' said the bodyguard, and saluted automatically. The instant his sword-hand moved away from the hilt, Garric pulled his knife from inside his arm guard and buried it in the bodyguard's throat.

The bodyguard gargled, clawing at his neck, eyes turned up to the ceiling. Blood fountained from the wound, spattering the food and faces of the prince and his neighbours. Garric pushed him aside, toppling him to the floor in a clatter of armour, and drew his sword.

Now he was surrounded by screams as people scrambled to flee. Hot blood pulsed at his temples as he bore down on his target. Prince Ottico had the terrified glaze of a child seeing a bogeyman in the flesh.

I am the Hollow Man, and I've come for you.

Garric reached for the prince, but Ottico went boneless and slid off his chair and under the table like an eel. It was such an un-manly act of cowardice that it took Garric completely by surprise. Garric lunged for him but the prince was already crawling away, scrambling between the feet of the panicked diners. Garric tried to grab him but guests and fallen chairs got in his way. Finally he shoved a shrieking lady aside and vaulted over the table, scattering plates and candelabra. There were no chairs on the other side to hinder him, and he caught the wriggling prince by the boot and

764

pulled him out from beneath the table. Some of the guests were pounding on the doors or screaming, while others watched in horror as Garric raised his sword to kill the prince.

A battle-cry sounded to his left and he heard running feet. The blade that was meant for the prince's skull turned to meet the attack instead, clanging against the sword that swung down towards him.

It was General Dakken, wielding the bodyguard's weapon which Garric had failed to take. He cursed himself for the oversight.

'Dog! You will not murder an unarmed man!' Dakken spat.

Seeing his chance, the prince kicked wildly, catching Garric in the thigh. In the same moment, Dakken attacked and Garric lost his grip on the prince as he was forced to defend himself. Ottico scrabbled under the table again and was hauled out on the other side by a few guests who hadn't tried to flee.

Garric turned a dark gaze on to Dakken. He'd been a heartbeat from killing Ottico and the prince had escaped. But it would only be a temporary stay of execution.

'You were next anyway,' he snarled.

'I think not,' said the general, circling around, poised in the stance of a trained fighter. 'Thirty years I've been waiting to finish the job I started.'

His blade flicked out. Garric knocked it away and retaliated, testing his enemy's guard, finding it solid. Bad to worse. He didn't have time for a drawn-out fight. Already the doors were being battered from the other side as servants and guards tried to get in. They'd break in the end, or a key would be found. He glanced at the prince, but he was hiding behind his nobles; Garric would never reach him before Dakken cut him down.

Let's make this quick, then.

They prowled around each other, searching for an opening. The tables had become the limits of their private arena. Age hadn't slowed the general, but Garric – who wasn't much younger – twinged with pain from a dozen injuries sustained on the torture table. His skin pulled over new scars, his bruises hampered him and his ruined gums had begun to bleed again. The unfamiliar weight of the armour was sapping his strength, and he'd already been weakened by the Iron Hand's ministrations.

He blocked out the pain as best he could, and remembered that night when his best friend had slit his throat and he'd crawled into the forest to die with the sound of slaughter in his ears.

'You didn't destroy the Dawnwardens, Dakken,' he growled. 'Eckard the Quick did that. You were just a lowly captain in the right place at the right time, who forged his career from that happy chance. Must have pained your betters to see you climb so high without merit.'

He moved fast, bringing a flurry of blows down on his opponent. Dakken, wearing no armour, was faster still. He knocked them away one by one and made no attempt to return them, keeping his distance instead.

He's playing for time, Garric thought in frustration. *Waiting for reinforcements. Wearing me down.*

'Some might say that being in the right place at the right time is the very essence of war,' Dakken said. 'And here I am again.'

A lunge, a parry. The doors thundered under renewed assault from the other side. Garric caught another glimpse of the prince, shielded by his barons and dukes. So close, and yet Garric couldn't get to him. It made him want to howl with fury.

'Nothing to say?' Dakken taunted. 'Then let me tell you how my career will end, which you think so free of merit. After I have killed you, I will retire in glory to the motherland and be remembered for ever as a hero of the Empire. You, on the other hand, will not even have the honour of an Ossian burial. We will burn you on a pyre, the Krodan way, and you will be cleansed with the light of the Primus.'

Garric gave him a bloody grin. 'See, there's the difference between us, Dakken,' he said. 'You're planning to have a long and happy life. But I came here to die.'

He threw himself forward, swinging wildly with no thought for defence. Dakken was taken off-guard by the suicidal force of it. He barely parried the first blow and only just managed to turn the second aside. As Garric brought his blade around again, Dakken swung frantically into the gap. Garric threw up his left arm and cried out as the blade smashed into his armour with enough force to break the bone beneath. His own blade took Dakken horizontally in the side of the head, smashing through cheek and teeth and skull before coming to a jarring halt in the centre of his face.

Horrified screams filled the room. With an animal bellow of rage, Garric tore his sword free from the mangled ruin of the general's head. His body spun away and crashed to the floor, oozing brain and blood onto the flagstones.

Garric turned, panting, his face spattered red and one arm hanging limp. There was a mad hatred in his gaze, the savage anger of a dying animal. He pointed his sword at Prince Ottico.

'Now you,' he said.

The door to the hall exploded inwards in a shower of splinters and spinning wood. Garric staggered away, his sword-arm up before his face. When he lowered it again, he felt the cold touch of despair on his heart.

Stooping through the doorway was a mountain of a man clad in tarnished black armour, an enormous warhammer held in both hands.

Ruin had come.

101

Vika clawed at the stone floor of the vault, crawling horrors on her tongue, skin itching with burrowing worms. Around her, the others retched and pawed at themselves, helpless before Plague.

He stepped into the room, making a soft, wet clicking sound like bones rattling in his throat. Klyssen followed with his troops, but they were insignificant ghosts to Vika's eyes. She didn't see them as the others did. The foul shock of the dreadknight's power had triggered a reaction in her mind. Beneath the skin of reality, something swarmed, and chaos bled through the weave of the world as the Shadowlands pressed close.

Her battle with the beast of Skavengard and the days she spent fighting off Plague's corrupting poison had taught her things that Agalie never could. She'd been changed by the touch of the Abyss and hadn't known it till now. For the first time, Vika touched the Shadowlands without need of a potion to help her. Her senses teetered, and madness loomed.

She had to fight the demon. He was a blasphemy to the Aspects and she was compelled to destroy him. But though her instincts demanded it, her body refused to comply. Her skin split and festered, and her mind was a wild whirl of panic.

'You should have run, and kept running.' Klyssen was talking to Aren, who was writhing at his feet. 'You might even have got away. But to come *back*? What were you thinking?'

The light! Where was the sacred light that shone from her at the gates of Skavengard, which had driven the dreadknights back? How had she done that? She fought to remember, but her fingernails were splitting and flaking away, and she was choking on a throat filled with maggots.

'I will torture Cade to death,' Klyssen said, 'and you will watch. It will bring me no pleasure, but I must keep my word. The Iron Hand are the conscience of the Empire. And, you must admit, you were warned.'

Aspects, save us! Vika begged, but the Aspects were silent. She moaned in desperate frustration. Why set her on this path if they refused to help in her time of direst need? Why show her the end of the world if they wouldn't help her avert it?

Doubt swarmed in. Agalie always said she doubted too readily. But the Aspects had shown her a champion wielding a blade that shone like the sun, and he'd abandoned them! What was she to think, then? She'd let herself be guided by visions, but the mad saw visions as clear as the holy.

Visions. The thought gave her an instant of clarity through the fog of nightmare. Her companions were wracked with pain as she was, but she saw no sign of affliction upon them. The worms and boils and blackening flesh were visions, put in their minds by Plague's dark power. They were only as real as she believed them to be.

Then I don't believe!

She *knew* this demon. She'd cured herself of his poison, and she'd learned him. He'd tried to kill her once and failed, and she was stronger for it.

This isn't real.

The pain began to draw back. Only a little, for she couldn't entirely quiet the shrieking in her mind; but she doubted these terrors now, and her doubt weakened them.

'Shackle the prisoners,' Klyssen was saying, dimly heard at the edge of her consciousness. 'We'll take them for questioning. Between them they will give us the rest of the rebels in Morgenholme.'

'What about the dog?' one of the Guardsmen said.

Klyssen sniffed. 'Kill it.'

No! Panic shot through her like a bolt. She raised her head, fighting to clear her mind. The others thrashed on the floor of the vault, backs arching and eyes rolling, howling at their private torture as the guards began to spread out between them. One was making his way towards Ruck, sword drawn. Plague stood at the edge of the room, his dead-skin mask impassive.

Get up! Fight him! she told herself, but it was beyond her. She wasn't strong enough to face down that thing alone. She needed the Aspects with her, and the Aspects wouldn't come.

Why aren't you here with me now? Why?

A memory came to her then, clear and vivid, a pool of calm in the chaos. She stood in the light of a fire, staring into a stream that ran through a forest clearing and past her feet. Agalie-Sings-The-Dark was standing behind her.

'Five times I was visited by the gods,' Vika had said. 'Five times, and then no more. Can you imagine that? To be so blessed and then ... not to be?'

'I have never seen them,' said Agalie. 'Only their signs and agents. Be grateful for what grace was given you. We are each tested in our own way.'

She heard the rank ingratitude in her words, to complain that she'd *only* been visited five times by the Aspects, when Agalie kept iron faith on much slimmer evidence. *We are each tested in our own way.*

'If the Aspects are silent,' Agalie had said, 'it is because we have forgotten how to listen.'

The soldier walked closer to Ruck, his step heavy with doom, blade ready in his hand. Ruck gnawed her own foreleg and whined, oblivious to her impending death.

Vika's staff lay next to her. She reached for it, but was hit by a fresh spasm which collapsed her again. Tears sprang to her eyes as she lay, cheek to the ground, looking at her beloved hound. So close, and yet she couldn't save her. She couldn't rise up and fight.

Not real. It's. Not. Real.

But if she felt it so keenly, did it even matter whether it was real or not?

A glint of red caught her eye, like the bloody light of a new dawn. The Ember Blade, which had fallen from Aren's hand. The standard of their nation.

Another memory hit her, from moments before. Aren lifting the Ember Blade, holding it aloft. The triumph and joy on his face.

Her eyes widened. *The champion with the bright blade.*

Her vision had been clear all along, it was just that she failed to understand it. She'd been so certain Garric was the champion that she'd forced all the evidence to fit that theory, and then blamed the Aspects when he'd disappointed her. But it was her mistake. They hadn't shown her Garric.

They'd shown her *Aren.*

If the Aspects are silent, it is because we have forgotten how to listen.

The revelation tumbled through her like an avalanche. She'd thought she was listening, but she hadn't been. Instead she'd fashioned herself a champion and appointed herself his protector: Vika, chosen of the gods, tasked with the sacred duty to save the world. She'd made herself special, as she'd been when she was a young girl, as she'd wanted to be ever since the Aspects stopped visiting her. And all along, she'd demanded clearer signs, more help, intervention from the Nine.

We are each tested in our own way.

She'd been arrogant. And now she recognised that, she remembered how she'd felt at Skavengard, when she'd driven the dreadknights back. She hadn't defeated them through any power of her own. Instead she'd let herself be used, becoming a channel for the Aspects' will. All she needed to do was to submit.

I am your instrument, she thought. *Use me as you see fit.*

And with that, she found the light.

She felt it first in her breast, a blazing star of wrath, bursting into existence. It blasted away the corruption that clung to her mind and body, driving out the foulness. A tide of strength crashed through her. She snatched up her staff, planted it in the ground and rose to one knee.

'Back!' she cried, throwing out a hand towards the soldier standing over Ruck, ready to impale her. 'You will not touch her!'

The guardsman faltered, halted by the power in her voice. The prisoners were meant to be incapacitated. He looked at Klyssen uncertainly, who looked to Plague in turn. The dreadknight stepped forwards, gaze fixed on her, and the clicking in his throat became louder. Vika felt his terrible will bear down on her again, but the light was growing in her now, and nothing could hold it back. The air seethed and swam as the chaotic stuff of the Shadowlands pressed close. Angles stretched impossibly; faces shifted as if viewed through water; lanterns flickered, waned and grew fierce again.

'You are a creature of the Abyss!' she accused, and she pulled herself to her feet, dragging herself up the length of her staff. 'You are unhallowed, and your Krodan masters are damned for treating with you! Spawn of the Outsiders, these are Joha's lands, and the Nine rule here!'

The light flared in her, filling her up, and it was impossible to contain it any longer. She lifted her staff in the air. 'Down, beast!' she cried, and it shone with a blinding glow. Plague cringed from the light, throwing a hand up to shadow his stitch-riven face. 'Down!' she shouted again, and thrust the staff towards him. Plague staggered back, rattling like an angry snake.

'Kill her!' Klyssen shouted at the soldiers.

At his order, the guardsmen overcame their uncertainty and advanced on Vika. Either they didn't see the light or were not affected by it. Vika was so focused on Plague that she didn't notice them coming. The nearest guard, who'd been about to kill Ruck, drew back his sword to stab her in the ribs.

A snarling mass of teeth and fur knocked him to the ground before the blade could find its mark. Suddenly the vault was alive with confusion and movement as the fallen companions, freed from Plague's influence, surged to their feet and took up their weapons. Harod's sword was first to his hand; he clashed with two men, then three, holding them off until Aren could bring his own blade to the fight. Grub leaped onto a soldier and tore away a piece of his chin with his teeth, then knifed him as he screamed.

Vika was only half aware of it, locked in her own battle. The light was too fierce to bear, burning her from the inside out; she couldn't sustain it for much longer. Plague cowered before her upraised staff, but she could only repel him, not destroy him, and when her strength failed, he'd kill her. She began to claw inside her patchwork coat, her fingers brushing over the clay phials there.

'Kill that Ossian witch!' Klyssen demanded again, but in all the disorder he went unheard. Seeing that nobody would do it for him, he drew his own knife and circled around Plague. Vika was still fixated on the dreadknight, unarmed but for her staff, and his hands flexed on the hilt of his knife as he prepared to stab her.

He was an instant too slow. Vika found the phial she needed and drew it out.

'Down!' she screamed again, and she flung it into the dreadknight's face. It shattered as it hit, covering his head and upper body with a viscous jelly which burst into flame the moment it was released. Klyssen was caught at the edge of the splash, his arm and face spattered with blobs of the stuff. He wailed in pain and horror as it ignited, dropping his knife and flailing backwards, beating senselessly at his own face and arms.

Plague went up like dry tinder. He reeled away with a frenzied clattering coming from his mouth. Black smoke boiled off him and the air filled with the choking stench of burning flesh, and something foul and bitter underneath.

Then she could hold the light no longer, and somehow – she knew not how – she shut it off. The strength flowed out of her like water and she sagged, but she was caught by Cade before she could fall and he dragged her upright again.

'Come on!' he cried as he led her round the edge of the room, stepping over bodies, hurrying past treasures of uncountable value. To their left, Harod and Aren fought with several guardsmen, their backs to the door, keeping the soldiers occupied in the centre of the chamber while their companions made their escape. Klyssen was on his knees in an alcove, his back to them, hands beating frantically at his face.

'The Ember Blade...?' Vika gasped.

'Orica has it,' said Cade.

Plague's thin, ragged body had become a torch. He staggered across the chamber and fell against the guardsmen's backs, sending them into agonised panic as they were burned from behind. While they were distracted, Aren and Harod slipped out behind Vika and Cade. In the corridor were Ruck, Grub and Orica, who had the Ember Blade in one hand and its scabbard in the other. Fen fired her last arrow through the doorway, killing a guardsman who tried to follow them out. Grub put his shoulder to the vault door and shoved.

As the door swung closed, Vika caught a glimpse of a frightened face, lit by the burning slumped heap that Plague had become. It was Klyssen, his spectacles gone and his eyes full of fear. One gloved hand held his cheek as he stumbled towards them, the other reaching out in supplication.

'Don't close the door! Don't close the—'

The vault boomed shut. Grub twisted the Master of Keys' medallion to lock it, then spat on the door.

'Grub like to see you get out of *that* any time soon,' he sneered.

They slumped against the walls, panting, drained by the horrors they'd endured. There was no triumph, just the shock of survival. A great weakness lay on Vika, bone-deep, so heavy she could hardly stand. Ruck flurried around her, licking at her fingers, and she could have wept with relief at the touch of that slobbering tongue.

From behind the door they heard the faint thumping of Klyssen's fists, his howls as he begged for escape.

It was Aren who spoke first. 'We make for the underkeep,' he said. 'It's our only way out.'

Orica offered him the Ember Blade and its scabbard. He took the sword and sheathed it. A faint and weary smile touched Vika's lips as she looked at him.

'Lead on,' she said.

102

Ruin's hammer swung high and hard, smashing apart the table in front of him. Nearby guests huddled and shrieked as they were pelted with splinters, glasses, food and wine. The dreadknight heaved the sundered table aside and stepped past, into the make-shift arena where Garric stood with one arm hanging limp, the body of General Dakken at his feet.

Soldiers hurried into the feasting hall behind him. Some ran to surround the prince, others spread out around the room. Seeing their chance, many of the guests fled through the broken door, but some, mostly Krodan, stayed. They were reluctant to abandon their prince, or they didn't want to be branded disloyal. That, or they just wanted to see what would happen next.

Garric backed away from the monstrous figure, his legs trembling with weakness. Torture had sapped his strength and fighting Dakken had tired him, but the final blow was despair. The prince was beyond his reach now. Even if he could beat this dark giant, there was a forest of blades between them.

He hefted his sword, which was now so heavy he could hardly lift it. Men with crossbows were moving into place for a shot and the prince was being hustled away.

Thirty years a rebel, and he may as well have been a flea for all the trouble he'd caused the Empire. Thirty years of failing. They spoke true who said that one man couldn't make a difference against such might. He'd been arrogant to dream he could.

Let them kill me, then, he thought as he saw the crossbowmen set their sights. *But there will be no surrender.*

'Stop!' cried Prince Ottico.

His voice brought the soldiers to a halt, and the dreadknight, too. All eyes went to the prince, who was irritably shrugging off one of his barons.

'Unhand me!' he snapped.

His gaze met Garric's across the room, over the shoulders of his guards, and there was a glitter of hungry malice there. He'd been scared and humiliated, but the tables had turned now and he wanted vengeance.

'This man, this *assassin*, was once counted among the greatest of Ossian warriors,' he declared, red-faced. 'Let us see how he fares against a *Krodan* warrior, then! Crossbowmen, stay your triggers. Let the dreadknight have him.'

'Your Highness, let us take you to safety,' the baron beseeched, but Prince Ottico waved him away.

'There are a dozen men between us. I will stay, to see the last Dawnwarden fall.'

Ruin stepped closer, his hammer ready. Garric kept out of his reach. For all his courage in battle, he knew fear now. It radiated from his opponent, setting his skin crawling. If any heart beat beneath that armour, it belonged to no ordinary man.

'Death to the enemies of the Empire!' cried some enthusiastic patriot in the audience, and Ruin lunged forward.

Garric was ready for the attack and jumped out of the way as the hammer came down, shattering the flagstones. He hacked at his enemy's outstretched hand, but he was off balance and his blow rebounded from the armour. The agony of sudden movement almost made him faint as the two halves of his broken bone ground against each other. He staggered away, retching up bile.

There were cheers from the audience and shouts of abuse. 'Eeleater scum!' 'Die, traitor!' 'The Nemesis welcomes you!' Garric barely heard them through the red mist of pain. His vision had narrowed to a tunnel, at the end of which he saw Ruin advancing again, hammer cradled in his massive hands. Instinct told him to attack, but he held himself in check.

Wait for it. Wait...

The hammer came from the side; Ruin was quicker than his

size suggested. Garric dropped to one knee and ducked as it whistled over his head, then he thrust forward, aiming for a chink in the dreadknight's armour. But Ruin shifted his weight and the gap closed before he could reach it. For all its brutish design, the armour was a masterpiece, an impenetrable carapace of witch-iron.

The next swing came from overhead, so fast that Garric barely dodged it. He sprang up and back as the floor exploded in a stinging flurry of stone chips. Unbalanced by his dead arm, he tripped over his heels, stumbling backwards till he crashed into the edge of a table. Plates smashed, spraying food; cutlery bounced away across the floor. Someone reached over the table and shoved him from behind, sending him reeling back towards Ruin.

He saw the hammer coming to meet him and dug in his heels, his sword raised automatically in defence. The hammer blasted past his face, missing his nose by inches. It caught the blade instead, ripping it from his grasp and sending it spinning away. It slid under a table and was snatched up by a Krodan who raised it in the air, to the cheers of the audience.

'How unfortunate,' sneered the prince. 'It seems you've lost your blade.'

Ruin lumbered towards him. Garric, dizzy and weaponless, tried to back away, but there was no strength left in his legs. He was helpless as he was seized by the throat and lifted off the ground. The dreadknight's armoured hand was cold enough to burn, and its touch carried a creeping foulness that horrified him. Garric kicked uselessly at the air, choking. His ears roared with blood and the triumphant cries of the audience.

The world tipped and spun as he was thrown bodily across the room. He smashed down onto a table, skidded across it in an avalanche of goblets and furrowed cloth and flew off the other side to crash into a brazier. Hot coals scattered as it tipped over.

He lay there gasping in agony, his broken arm screaming at him. He'd snapped at least two ribs in the impact, and they sawed at his back with every drawn breath. He was bruised and torn, and there was blood in his mouth.

He was dying, of that he was certain. But still he clawed at the ground, dragging his knees beneath him. Still he fought to stand.

'Fetch water! Water!' he heard somebody cry. Fire was blooming at the edge of his vision: a tapestry, ignited by the coals.

'My prince, we must leave!' the baron pleaded.

'Nobody leaves until justice is done!' Prince Ottico yelled in fury.

Ruin filled Garric's vision, a faceless monster of dirty iron. He tried feebly to fend him off, but he was seized by the throat again and lifted up.

End it, he begged silently, because he wouldn't beg aloud. *End me.*

There was no such mercy. He was thrown, high and far, flailing through the air towards the curtained alcove at the far end of the room. Plush fabric swallowed him. There was a moment of excruciating impact as he crashed into something unforgivingly hard. Blackness took him, but all too briefly.

When he opened his eyes, he was tangled in a green velvet curtain, which had fallen across his face. It was sodden, and there was an acrid stink coming from it. His head pounded and there was a ferocious knot of agony at the base of his skull. Below that, he felt nothing at all.

A deep calm came over him. He was disembodied, helpless in an ocean of fabric. That last collision had broken his neck.

No more, then, he thought, his mind clear and serene. *I strived and failed, but none can say I did not give my all.*

Footsteps, slow and heavy, coming closer. The curtain was pulled from his face and Ruin stood over him. Behind him, Garric could see the hall, where soldiers were beating at the fire that had spread to a nearby tablecloth. His eyes were dimmed and everything was blurring. It all seemed like a strange play, viewed as from some far distance.

There was the prince, surrounded by nobles imploring him to retreat from the smoke and growing flames. There was General Dakken, sprawled out on the flagstones in a pool of gore. And there was a little girl, too, a little girl wearing a black hooded robe, her forehead high and white. He couldn't focus well enough to see her clearly, but he knew she was watching him, standing eerily still at the edge of the room while others flurried around her.

His eyes rolled in their orbits; they were the only thing he could move now. He lay among the shattered remains of a barrel rack which had been hidden behind the curtain, where the servants could draw drinks for the guests. His body was twisted and limp, tangled in bloody armour and splintered shards of wood, and his face was wet with spilled wine. Wine, and something else that gave off a sharp reek which he recognised.

'Stop playing and finish him!' the prince ordered.

Ruin lifted his hammer, ready to bring it down on Garric's skull. But Garric wasn't looking at him. He'd caught sight of a broken crest amid the folds of curtain: two wolves rampant, flanking a spreading tree. The emblem of the Amberlyne vineyards.

The prince will have no sweetwine but Amberlyne with his dessert. It's one of the few things he likes about our country.

He knew that smell. He'd smelled it in Mara's barn as he filled these very barrels with elarite oil. His gaze flicked from the crest to the burning tablecloth, and the thick, clear liquid spilling down the stairs towards it. Finally he looked up at his enemy, into the darkness behind his visor. A smile of triumph spread across his bruised and discoloured face.

'For Ossia,' he croaked hoarsely.

Then all was fire and force, and nothing after.

103

They hurried by lanternlight down silent ways, faces grim with the memory of what had gone before and the thought of what lay ahead.

Aren would never forget the sight of his skin bursting with boils, nor the taste of diseased flesh in his mouth, but it was already losing the power to terrify him, fading like a nightmare. Plague's touch had humbled them all, and Aren was ashamed at how completely he'd succumbed to it; but they'd defeated him nonetheless, thanks to their druidess.

He looked back over his shoulder. Vika was catching them up, staff in hand, Ruck trotting protectively at her side. She'd plainly been exhausted by fighting Plague, but after swigging a concoction from one of her phials, she'd found strength to move again.

What secret battle had she fought with the dreadknight, while he was occupied with his own agonies? Had there been a light, or had he imagined that? All he knew was that Vika alone had overcome Plague, driven him cowering before her and set him aflame. She'd proved stronger than the foul sorcery of their enemy. It was enough to make Aren wonder if the Aspects were real after all, and on their side. Anything felt possible with the Ember Blade in his hands.

He clutched it close to his chest as he hustled through dusty rooms, passing covered furniture and walls empty of tapestries or decoration. The sword was sheathed now, but its nearness heartened him and made him brave.

Their route took them back to the lower levels by the same

way they'd come. With luck, Mara had anticipated their decision and would meet them at the entrance to the underkeep. If not, she'd head there when the alarm was raised, which couldn't be long now. Once in the underkeep, there was no telling what they might find, but whatever it was, Aren had faith that he and his companions could handle it. They'd claimed the Ember Blade. There was nothing they couldn't do.

They came to a shadowy hall, huge and echoing, grey in the moonlight. Aren went first and the others came behind him: Grub, his eyes glittering with dark excitement; Orica, fearful, watching for enemies; Harod, stoic as ever, with Vika labouring at his side and Ruck loping at hers. Fen's expression was cold, yet even so, Aren found it hard to take his gaze from her face. Last was Cade, holding the lantern, his jaw set.

They were strung out in a line, halfway across the hall, when a deafening boom of thunder sounded from the heart of the keep and Hammerholt shuddered. The floor shook beneath them and they staggered this way and that. Chunks of masonry plunged from the ceiling, smashing around them and driving them to the walls, which seemed less dangerous than open space. But the walls were shivering, too. Great cracks appeared in the masonry, jerking and branching like black lightning.

At last, the sound faded, leaving the hall quiet but for their terrified breathing and Ruck's wild barks as she spun in circles, snapping at phantoms. A haze of dust hung around them, and a long, ominous groan sounded from overhead. They looked to the ceiling, newly conscious of the immense tonnage of stone above them. In the distance, they heard faint screams.

'He did it,' Aren whispered, half in horror and half in awe. 'Shades, he did it.'

Far above, a rumble of stone and a dull crash sent a tremble through the hall. It shook harder as another crash came, closer now, then another, loud as the end of the world.

'Run!' Fen screamed, and they fled for the exit. Aren tripped and sprawled as the ceiling burst, spewing a torrent of rock and dust which smashed through the floor behind him. The Ember Blade jolted free from his grip as he fell. He reached to snatch it back, but a stone smacked off his arm and he withdrew it quickly, folding it over his head in a futile attempt to protect himself from falling masonry. Something punched his thigh with numbing force, making him jerk and curl up. The noise was overwhelming, drowning his senses in a blare. He could do nothing but cower and wait for his fate to find him.

The tumult died as rapidly as it had come, leaving a loud ringing in his ears. He raised his head and blinked dust from his eyes. The rocks had stopped falling, and somehow he was still alive.

The hall had become a netherworld of drifting grey, where lumps of shadow loomed at the limit of his vision. He heard a sob from Orica and tried to find her. One of the lumps, which he'd thought was a fallen rock, unfolded and separated. It was Harod and Orica, together. The knight had thrown himself across her.

'Are you hurt?' Aren called.

'Grub is here! Grub is alright!' came the Skarl's voice from somewhere.

'She is not hurt,' said Harod.

Aren pulled himself upright, wincing as his leg protested. He tested his weight on it, but it was only bruised and not broken. A trickle of blood ran down his temple from his hairline; he couldn't feel the cut. Still dazed, he looked around with a growing sense of alarm. Orica, Harod and Grub were all accounted for. He heard Ruck barking and saw Vika moving nearby, a shambling silhouette amid the destruction. But he'd lost sight of the Ember Blade in the murk, and where were Cade and Fen?

'Aren!' It was Fen's voice, filled with such fright it made his blood freeze. 'Aren, where are you? I found Cade!'

'*Aren!*' Cade's terrified cry set him running, all thoughts of the Ember Blade forgotten. The far end of the hall had completely disappeared, leaving only a ruined hole above and below. He could see its near edge dimly, ragged and torn, with broken timber beams thrusting out.

'Where are you?' he cried.

'Aren!' Cade wailed again. 'Oh, shades, Aren!'

'Over here!' Fen called.

Aren saw her now, crouched near the edge of the hole. He ran to her. Green eyes stared from a face caked with grey dust. She pointed at the swirling haze above the hole. Aren tried desperately to find Cade, but to no avail.

'Out on the beam,' she said, her voice tight.

Aren's stomach upended. Cade was sprawled awkwardly across the end of a splintered beam that projected horizontally over an unknown drop. His arms were flung across it, fingers locked to the far edge, legs dangling. 'Oh, Nine! Oh, Nine!' he was whimpering.

'I can't go out there,' said Fen helplessly. 'I can't. I'll fall.'

Aren ran to the beam. It was perhaps two feet wide, with a jagged split where it emerged from the stone. Cade was a dozen feet away, his upper body spread across the beam, legs hanging in space.

'I can't hold on!' he cried.

'Can you move along the beam?' Aren called.

'I'm stuck! I can't hold on!' He was panicking. Aren tried to keep his own panic in check.

'I'm coming to get you.'

'Hurry!'

Aren lowered himself onto the beam with clumsy haste. The murk was thinning a little now, enough to see the far end of the hole. The wall of the hall had been destroyed and the rooms beyond exposed. Below him, he saw the orange glow of fire blooming through the dust. Cade's lantern must have smashed and ignited something down there. Over the ringing in his ears, he could hear distant screams drifting through the fortress. There was a dull rumble as another section collapsed and he held tight to the stone at his back as Hammerholt shivered in response.

Orica, Harod and Vika arrived, with Ruck at their heels, drawn by Fen's cries. He heard them frantically discussing ways to rescue Cade, but Aren couldn't wait for them. He dropped to his hands and knees and crawled out along the beam.

A low, sinister creak sounded beneath him, followed by the stealthy sound of wood peeling apart. He froze.

'The beam is too weak, Aren,' said Vika. Her voice was grave and flat.

Aren sucked in a breath, bit his lip and inched forward again with his eyes on Cade. A loud crack beneath him made him start, and the beam tilted fractionally downwards.

'Stop! Stop! You'll break it!' Cade pleaded. Aren could see his face now, powdered with grime, his eyes wide and glistening with terror.

'We're making a rope!' Orica called. Harod was pulling off his jacket, Vika her cloak, but it was a hopeless effort driven by the need to do something. All their clothes together wouldn't make a rope long and strong enough to save him, and the moment Cade let go to take it, he'd fall.

The only chance was to get to him. Aren moved forward again. The beam creaked and sagged.

'Stop!' Cade begged.

'I'm coming,' Aren said relentlessly. 'Hold on.'

'*You'll kill us both, you mudwit!*' Cade screamed.

The hysteria in his voice halted Aren. Cade had never screamed at him like that before. Tears of frustration welled in his eyes. He could almost reach out and touch his friend. Going back now was impossible.

Just a little further. The beam would hold. It *would*.

'I have to try,' he said.

'No,' Cade said. His eyes became clear, terror replaced by firm purpose. A decision had been made. 'You don't. No sense both of us dying today.'

'I told you,' Aren said, his voice thick with tears. 'I'll never leave you behind.'

Cade gave him a sad smile. 'You ain't,' he said softly. 'You ain't, Aren. I'm leaving *you*.'

He loosed his grip, and fell.

Aren screamed and lunged forward to catch him, but he was too late. Cade plummeted like a stone, the dust and smoke swirling around him as he dropped out of sight.

'*Cade! Cade!*' Aren shouted into the gloom. He was laid out flat on the beam, reaching down as if he could stretch far enough to bring his friend back. The world rushed in on him like a torrent. His senses roared with shock.

Cade was gone.

It wasn't true. It *couldn't* be.

Dimly he realised the others were shouting at him. He felt the beam shift beneath him and heard a long, tortured creak. Suddenly focused, he scrambled backwards along the beam, but his dive to save Cade had taxed it too far. It jerked and tipped forward as it broke away from the stone. He shrieked in fear as the beam slid out from under him and he fell, head-first and flailing, into the same abyss as Cade.

A hand closed round his ankle, arresting his fall with a jolt. Looking up, he saw Harod there, holding fast to him. Fen seized his other foot and, grunting and groaning, they hauled him up. When he was near enough, Orica and Vika took hold, too, and between them they pulled him to safety. No sooner did he have the ground under his feet than he was up again, staring over the edge, yelling Cade's name.

'We have to go down there!' he insisted, tears cutting paths through the dust on his cheeks. 'He might still be alive! We have to look!'

But he knew by their expressions that they couldn't, they didn't have the means. Cade was lost to them. Fen turned him away from the edge, put her arms around him and laid her head against his shoulder. The tenderness of her touch was almost unbearable. He wanted to throw her sympathy back in her face. Cade *wasn't* dead, he *wasn't*! He was down there somewhere and they had to *rescue* him!

Hammerholt rumbled again. A fresh crack ran across the ceiling and a slab of masonry tumbled down, smashing to pieces nearby. Vika looked up, her hand shielding her eyes from the dust.

'The ceiling will not hold for long,' she said. 'If we stay, we will all die. We have the Ember Blade – we can save that, at least.' Her face fell as she realised Aren was no longer carrying it. 'Aren, where is the sword?'

'Grub got it,' said Grub, emerging from the dusty haze. He was holding it before him, staring at it with a strange gleam in his eyes. 'Mudgrub very careless to lose something so valuable.'

'He's still down there!' Aren snapped, pushing Fen away.

'Aren,' said Fen softly. 'He let go so you wouldn't kill yourself trying to save him. Don't waste the chance he's given you.'

He loathed her for saying that. Hated her for being right. He knew how near this hall was to collapse, knew he was risking all their lives by arguing. He just didn't want to face it.

But the truth was the truth. Cade was gone.

He stalked away from the edge, pushing angrily past them and out of the hall. The others followed. Behind them, stonework creaked and groaned, and it sounded like the voices of damned spirits, calling him back to share his best friend's doom.

104

Aren was hardly aware of the rest of the journey through the abandoned reaches of Hammerholt. His mind felt like it had suffered a physical blow; his brain throbbed with loss. An aching hole threatened to open inside his chest, and it was only by furious effort that he could hold it closed and keep the void from consuming him.

The others struggled to meet his eye. There was nothing they could offer to salve his grief.

In time, they emerged from the empty chambers into the lower reaches of Hammerholt near where they'd entered. The fortress shuddered periodically and they heard distant collapses and screams. A thin smoke drifted along the ceiling. A pair of servants spotted them as they ran past, but though they were ragged and bloodstained and carrying swords, the servants were too interested in escape to care.

They made their way down as far as they could, reasoning that the lower they went, the fewer people they were likely to find. They only stopped when they reached a level flooded ankle-deep with foul water. Below them, the sewers were still submerged. It would be a long time before they could access the caves, and they didn't have time to wait. They were heading for the underkeep.

'Aren, you have the map?' Vika said.

'That way,' said Grub, pointing along the corridor.

'Are you sure?'

'Grub was born underground. Grub knows.'

They took his word for it and let him lead. He still had the

Ember Blade jammed in his belt, its magnificence a ridiculous contrast to the man who wore it. The sight stirred faint concern in Aren – the Skarl wasn't the safest choice to carry Ossia's most prized treasure – but he was too numb to do anything about it.

The water rose around their legs as they went, and soon they had to climb up a level for Ruck's sake, and for Vika's. The druidess was weak, and she was finding it hard to labour through the water even with Harod supporting her. The smoke thickened as they went on and they could hear the crackle of flames. Distant footsteps hurried away from them. Voices called for the lost and fallen.

None of it felt real to Aren. Their predicament reached him through a haze. The others wore worried expressions, wary of fire or collapse or guards, but such concerns were meaningless now. He knew they had a destination, and he followed his companions towards it. More than that was beyond him, in the ringing aftermath of Cade's death.

Their route took them towards the fire and past burning rooms. Once they found their way blocked by rubble and smouldering timbers and were forced to backtrack and go around. They heard the cries of trapped people and encountered several who were trying to find their way out. An armed guard blundered coughing from a smoky corridor right into their path; he looked them over and staggered the other way.

Then, as they passed a doorway, Aren saw a man on the other side. He was hurrying through the blazing room towards an exit, his arm across his face. It was no more than a glimpse through the smoke, but it brought everything sharply into focus, and the fog lifted from Aren's senses.

Harte. That was Harte!

Suddenly he couldn't hold back the emotion any more, but it wasn't sadness he felt; it was rage. Rage was safer, easier, better. His back teeth clenched hard enough to hurt. He needed to destroy, to *kill*, to have his revenge on a world that had ripped his best friend away.

'Aren?' Fen asked. He'd come to a halt in the doorway, glaring like a madman.

'I'll catch you up,' he heard himself say.

'What? No, we must stay togeth—'

'There is something I must do,' he told her flatly, and he headed into the room before anyone could object. 'I will catch you up! Go!'

He was gone too quickly for them to follow. They had the mission – and Mara – to think about, and his tone didn't allow argument. By the time he was across the room, he'd forgotten them, and the Ember Blade with them.

In the midst of his blackest hour, he'd found his father's killer, as if the Aspects themselves had put him there.

The heat of the flames beat at his skin and smoke clawed at his throat. At the end of a corridor, he saw his quarry again, a darting figure in a black overcoat disappearing through another doorway.

The fortress rumbled around him, but Aren ignored it. His sword sang from its scabbard as he ran, now bright, now dark as he passed the scattered fires.

Beyond the doorway was a short hall. One wall had partially fallen, leaving a heap of burning rubble blocking the far door. The timbers overhead sagged and creaked, thick wood smoking in the heat from below.

Harte was at the end of the hall, searching for a way through the rubble. His hair was red with blood and he still limped heavily on one ankle. The sight of him ignited a flame in Aren. His fury was so wild that he trembled on the edge of tears.

'*Harte!*' he roared.

The watchman started at his name and whirled around. When he saw Aren standing there, wet and bedraggled and blood-spattered, his face changed from shock to mocking incredulity.

'You can't be serious?' he said.

'Draw your sword,' Aren told him.

'Get out of my way!' he said dismissively. 'The castle's coming down around our ears!'

'Draw your sword,' Aren told him, 'or I'll run you through unarmed. It's more of a chance than you gave my father.'

Harte had to think for a moment to remember who he was talking about, and that small hesitation brought Aren's blood to a boil.

'*That*'s what this is about?' Harte asked, as if it was something so petty it was amazing Aren would trouble him with it.

'Fight me or die, murderer!' Aren screamed.

Harte rolled his eyes, pulled his blade and strode along the hall towards Aren. 'You really want to do this now? Here?' He tutted. '*Ossians.*'

Aren had never felt such hate for the Krodans as he did then. The gods-damned *arrogance* that oozed from him! They were all responsible, all those squarehead bastards that had brought him to tragedy. All Krodans, and one other. He felt his hatred condense into a hard knot around one man, one he hated above all now, but who was forever beyond retribution.

Garric. Garric, the author of all this destruction. Garric, whose suicidal quest had claimed Cade's life along with his own.

He charged, his sword raised and ready. Harte met his first swing, knocked aside a second, then slashed at his ribs. Only Aren's training saved him; it was a textbook manoeuvre, and his dodge was an instinctive response.

Undeterred, Aren pressed the attack, hacking at the watchman's guard. Harte, the stronger of the two, deflected the blows with ease, then struck with his free hand. Aren's vision flared white as a gloved fist lashed across his face, sending him staggering. He barely got his sword up to parry the thrust that followed.

They broke apart, panting. Blood trickled from Aren's split lip. Harte's hair was mussed and he wore a fixed grin.

'Last chance, boy. Whether you live or die is neither here nor there to me. But I'm getting out of here, one way or another.'

There was too much anger in Aren to permit compromise. He knew Harte was the better swordsman, even with an injured ankle, and he was taller and stronger, too. But he'd dash himself against this enemy, even if it meant his death. It was all he could do.

He flew forward again with a cry, blade swinging. Harte, infuriatingly calm, stepped back before the assault. He parried, parried, and struck. Aren felt a sharp pain as the blade nicked his shoulder. His next swing was more savage still, born of frustration. Harte dodged and feinted; Aren fell for it, and the watchman struck at his throat. Aren pulled back, but not fast enough to avoid a stinging cut along the underside of his jaw.

He broke away again. His fingertips went to his face and came back wet. By now the fire had spread, the wallpaper running with flame. The heat was rising and the ceiling timbers fumed and glowed. Blood trickled over Aren's collarbone and his head was becoming light. Smoke seeped into his lungs and he coughed hard.

'It's not going how you imagined, is it?' Harte sneered. 'You thought that feeling of righteous vengeance would be enough to guarantee victory. Do you think the world owes you justice? Ask the women and children, crushed and maimed and burning right now, if your resistance is worth it. Most of the servants here are Ossian, you know. You call me a murderer, but I've not killed one-tenth the number you have. And my victims, unlike yours, were all guilty of something.'

Doubt crept into Aren's heart as he understood the cost of what he'd committed to. Destruction was always Garric's plan, never Aren's; but Aren had broken him out, freed him to complete his task. He bore the responsibility for that.

But there was no retreat now, no route back to the boy he was before this all began. It was far too late for all of that. So he squared himself, aimed his sword and took his stance.

'To the end,' he said.

'As you like,' said Harte, and struck.

Back and forth they went, swords blurring. Aren had sobered a little now, and he'd gained proper respect for his opponent's skill. He tried to force himself to be calm, to study his adversary. *To overcome your enemy, you must first understand him.* But his thoughts were awhirl, and he hated too much. He saw nothing but that Harte's injured ankle was hampering his footwork. If not for that, Aren would likely have been dead already.

But Harte was impatient and distracted, too. The heat was becoming difficult to bear and it was hard not to cough in the gathering smoke. The fire was moving to cut off their exit, timbers were bulging and splitting overhead, and though Aren couldn't win, still he wouldn't give way. Harte's attacks became more purposeful, more risky. He needed to finish Aren off.

You're getting careless, Aren thought.

But that moment of confidence made him careless himself, and he mistimed his thrust. Harte twisted his wrist and knocked Aren's blade from his hand. With a quick movement, he brought his own sword back across and drove the pommel into Aren's temple. Aren fell, stunned, a blinding pain in his skull.

Harte stood over him, shoulders heaving, sword pointing at Aren's chest.

'So,' he said. 'That's that. You did know your father was a traitor to his people, didn't you? That he sold your country out for his wealth? I hope he was worth dying for.'

There was a sudden crack from above. Harte looked up in alarm and Aren drove a vicious heel into the watchman's injured ankle. Harte bellowed in pain and collapsed to one knee, clutching his leg. Aren planted his other foot in Harte's chest and shoved him away with all the force he could muster. Harte staggered across the room, his leg folded under him and he fell onto his back.

Aren scrambled over to his sword, snatched it up and jumped to his feet. Harte, a short way from him, was struggling to rise. Aren headed towards him, lured by the red temptation of vengeance, but stopped as he heard a groan from the ceiling and it began to bulge downwards. There were mere moments left before it caved in, but maybe moments would be enough to do what had to be done. And if they were both buried in flames, so what? Wasn't that a better end than facing what waited on the other side of his rage? The only desire he had left was to plunge his blade into the breast of the man who killed his father.

But Garric had taken that path, and Cade had died for it. Aren owed it to his friend to make that mean something. With a savage effort of will, he tore himself away from his helpless enemy, and the satisfaction he felt he deserved. He'd take the harder road, and live.

The groan of the timbers overhead reached a crescendo as he ran through the closing flames towards the exit. He heard Harte's rising scream as he dived through the doorway, and then the ceiling gave way and the watchman was silenced in an avalanche of rock and blazing wood.

Aren lay gasping in the corridor outside, his mind blank with shock. Now that it was over, it felt like madness had taken him for a time. A few more moments and that hall would have been his tomb. In avenging his father, he'd have joined him.

But he'd chosen otherwise. He chose to carry on.

He pulled himself to his feet and looked back through the doorway. From beneath the pile of rubble, a black-clad arm protruded, a hand lying limp and bloody at the end of it.

'He was a traitor,' Aren said quietly. 'But he was still my father. And I loved him.'

It wasn't much of an epitaph, but it was what he had. Eyes tearing from more than the smoke, he sheathed his sword and set off after his friends.

From somewhere in the depths of the burning fortress came a thin, inhuman shriek: the voice of Sorrow, chasing him towards the dark.

105

Fen stood against the railing, thin hands gripped tight round the cold metal, and stared fearfully into the shaft below. A cage lift waited at the top, suspended by a winch, with gatefold doors on two sides. A vertical metal track ran down the wall into the depths. There was a substantial gap between the lift cage and the shaft's far wall, which had been ribbed with timbers. Beyond the range of the lanternlight, Fen could see nothing. It might have been thirty feet to the bottom, or thirty thousand.

Grub chuckled by her ear. 'Long way down,' he said, enjoying her discomfort.

It had been a long way down for Cade, too.

Don't lean on anyone or anything, Fen. Not no place or person. Elsewise, when they fall, you'll fall with 'em.

She shut her eyes. It didn't stop her seeing it.

'Where *is* he?' Mara hissed. She was standing by the door to the cellar, looking out into the corridor. The others waited anxiously among the mess of the excavation: rubble, stacked pickaxes, lanterns and oil. Some of the lanterns had been put to use, their light reflecting from the damp bricks of the barrel-vault ceiling.

Grub brandished the Ember Blade, still in its scabbard. 'Grub not worried. Grub ruler of all Ossia!'

Vika surged towards him, staff clicking on the stone, and snatched it from his hand. 'Show some respect!' she snapped and shook the sword at him. 'This is not for you.'

Grub glowered, and Fen saw real anger in his eyes then, a glimmer of pure malice, quickly cloaked. He gave Vika a wide smile, as if it had all been a big joke. 'Grub just keeping spirits up!' he said lightly.

But it would take more than that to lift the gloom over them. Even Ruck whined uneasily and didn't seem herself. Cade had been liked by everyone, and he was gone. Fen hadn't been attached to Osman – she hadn't let herself get close – but Cade was her friend. Had been.

She couldn't stop seeing him fall.

No. He didn't fall. He let go. Just like Da.

Garric was gone, too, and though he wasn't so pleasant or kind, he'd loomed large in all their lives. They'd suspected that the explosion was his doing, and Mara confirmed it when they found her. She'd made her way to the cellar before the chaos began, reckoning it the safest place to be when the Iron Hand started searching for her. She'd revealed that she knew of Garric's true plan when they rescued him, but she'd never believed he would be mad enough to still attempt it.

Halfway through, Fen realised she wasn't giving an explanation, but a confession. 'There are children here,' Mara had said, her voice going thin. '*Danric* was here, though it's my hope he left in time. I just didn't *think*…'

No one was in the mood to judge her, and she lapsed into a prickly silence. Fen's only concern was Aren, who'd taken a bewildering detour before anyone could stop him. She wouldn't dare to guess at his state of mind.

Come back. I can't lose you, too.

Hammerholt shuddered and grumbled overhead, loud enough to make Fen tense her shoulders. Dust sifted down from the ceiling and she saw cracks spreading in the bricks.

'We must go,' said Mara.

'Not yet. He will be here,' said Fen, her voice dull and flat.

'Or the guards will. Or this fortress will come down on our heads!'

'No guards will come while Hammerholt burns,' said Harod. 'Not even the Krodans are so fanatical as to seek us out now.'

From somewhere above them, they heard an anguished shriek. Orica hugged herself at the sound.

'There are other things than guards abroad tonight,' said Mara.

'Grub knows that sound,' said Grub, his tattooed brow creasing in puzzlement. 'From the mountains round Suller's Bluff.'

'It is the sound of Sorrow,' said Vika. 'He comes for us.'

Mara held up a hand, listening. 'I hear footsteps!'

'Aren!' Fen breathed, for the hooded dreadknight made no such sound. She hurried to the doorway in time to see him approaching down the corridor. His chin and neck were smeared with blood and there was a huge bruise developing next to his eye, but he was alive. Swept up in a flood of relief, she moved to embrace him; but something in his grim manner made her hesitate, and the moment was lost.

'About time Mudslug got here!' Grub called.

'Where have you been?' Mara demanded.

'Mara. You're safe,' Aren said, dismissing her question with a brusque air of command. 'Where is the Ember Blade?'

'I have it,' said Vika, walking over. 'And now you shall have it. You are its keeper, at least for now.'

Aren met her gaze gravely. He took the sword and strapped it to his belt while Grub watched with weasel's eyes.

'Hold still,' said Vika. 'That cut will keep bleeding until it is salved.' She took out a small pot from inside her cloak and smeared a paste on his chin. He endured it impatiently and shook her off when she was done.

'Sorrow has our trail. We shouldn't delay. Vika, can you stand against the dreadknight if he comes?'

'I cannot,' she said bitterly. 'I do not have the strength.'

'Then you go down first. Mara as well. How many more can it fit?'

'Grub staying with Mudslug!' Grub announced.

'Harod and Orica – you, too,' said Aren. 'You might need Harod's blade down there. You have lanterns? Go!'

They crowded into the lift with Ruck. It seemed sturdy, supported by thick ropes from above and fixed to the vertical track on one side of the shaft by metal wheels. Fen still didn't like the look of it. She hated to be confined, and her first instinct was mistrust. The thought of climbing into a tiny cage hanging over an unknowable drop made her sick with fear.

At the top of the shaft was a winch and a brake, and there was another inside the lift. Aren and Grub set to work and managed to get it turning. Ropes squeaked through pulleys and the lift began to descend, rolling down the track. Fen stood at the railing and watched the anxious faces of those inside disappear from sight.

The light of their lanterns illuminated the sides of the shaft as they were lowered. It occurred to Fen that she could climb down the shaft by using the timber planks as a ladder, for they were set close and would offer good hand- and footholds. But that felt scarcely less terrifying than the lift, and a great deal slower.

You will get in that cage, she told herself sternly. *You have to, or Aren will not.*

It was that thought, rather than any of safety, that gave her heart. He'd be there beside her, just like he was in Skavengard. Sombre as he was now, she took strength from his company.

The rope slackened and they heard a cry from below. 'We're down!' Mara called.

'How far?' Aren shouted back.

'Ninety feet, no more!'

'Shades, you must see this!' Vika yelled up to them, her voice full of wonder. She didn't go so far as to tell them what she'd seen.

'We're out. Bring it up.' Mara called.

'Send it down, bring it up, send it down, bring it up,' Grub carped as they reversed the direction of the winch and started hauling.

In the distance, there was a grinding noise which grew to a rumbling avalanche. It shook the walls hard enough that they stopped winching and covered their heads, fearful of the roof caving in. But though bricks fell from the ceiling and new cracks grew, the cellar held and the sound faded.

'Reckon that was a whole tower coming down,' Aren said as he straightened. He'd just set his hand back on the winch when they heard Sorrow shriek again. He was closer now.

'He won't stop, will he?' said Fen, remembering the pursuit

through the mountains. 'He doesn't rest. Once he has our trail, he'll keep coming.'

Aren said nothing and turned the winch. At last, the lift rattled into place at the top of the shaft and Grub put the brake on. 'It's time,' Aren said to Fen.

She walked around to the door, hesitated a moment, then stepped inside. It was easier than she thought. Fear of the dread-knight on their heels was a powerful motivator. Aren told her to put on the brake in the lift, and then he released the one at the top of the shaft. The small lurch as the weight shifted made Fen swallow hard.

All you have to do is stand still, she told herself. *You can do that.*

Grub and Aren crowded in with her and Aren pulled the gate-fold door shut behind him. Fen closed her eyes and concentrated on breathing steadily. Grub's sour smell was hard to bear this close up.

'Heh. Freckles doesn't like heights,' Grub said.

Fen couldn't manage a retort. She just wanted this to be over.

'Down we go,' said Aren. He released the brake and began turning the winch inside the lift.

Their descent was painfully slow. The toothed wheels of the lift squealed like restless mice as the cellar dwindled to a lit square overhead and the stone closed in around them. Fen pressed against the side of the lift and tried to forget there was only a half-inch of metal between her and the drop into the dark beneath.

All you have to do is stand still.

There was a loud boom from overhead and a shiver passed through the rock. Fen's eyes flew open and she clutched the bars of the cage as the distant rumbling grew louder, closer, louder still. In moments, the whole lift was shaking and she had to bite her lip to keep from whimpering.

Please let it stop please let it stop please let it stop

But Meshuk, the Stone Mother, was in no mood to listen to pleas. Pebbles and then stones bounced off the roof of the lift as the frame rattled and timbers creaked. There was a crash of masonry, a shriek of bending metal, then the lift was struck hard from above, making Fen scream in terror. She held fast to the sides of the cage, fingers wound through the metal bars, as a chunk of stone bounced past them and plunged down the shaft.

Finally, it was over, and there was quiet again, but for the plangent groan of stressed metal coming from all around them.

'Aren? Fen? Are you hurt?' Mara shouted from the bottom of the shaft.

'Yes, Grub is well, too, thank you for asking!' Grub yelled back.

Aren put his hand on Fen's arm. She opened her eyes, found him gazing at her with concern on his face.

'Get us down,' she said. 'Just get us down.'

Aren nodded. He put his hand to the winch and tried to turn it, but found that it wouldn't move. He tried again, harder.

'Let Grub try,' said the Skarl, muscling him aside. He strained at the handle for a moment, then stood back and harrumphed. 'Stuck,' he declared.

'The winch must be damaged,' Aren said, looking through the roof of the lift. He peered down the shaft. 'I can see the lanterns at the bottom. It's not more than forty feet. We can climb it.'

Fen shook her head. She didn't want to move. If she moved, she'd fall.

'It's easy! Grub go first!' Grub said.

Fen winced as Grub clattered over to the other side of the lift and pulled the gatefold door open. Beyond, there was a gap of about eight feet to the far wall, where the timber planks formed a makeshift ladder. Grub launched himself without hesitation, springing through the air to catch the other side.

He looked over his shoulder at them. 'See?' he said, and climbed down the shaft as if it were nothing at all.

Another shiver ran through the earth, the death throes of the fortress above. It had been cored by Garric's bloody farewell, and now it was collapsing in on itself. Aren glanced up, worried.

'We can't stay here,' he told her

'I can't do it.'

'You can. You can do it. It's a short jump and a simple climb. I bet you used to climb mountains that made this look like nothing.'

'I'll fall,' she said, and hated herself for saying it, hated the way her voice sounded.

'I'll make sure you don't. I'll—'

The lift tipped forward, its top edge coming away from the wall with a screech. Fen clung to the bars but Aren went stumbling sideways towards the open door of the cage. She screamed his name as she saw him lose his balance, but then, at the last moment, he half-turned, planted his foot and jumped out into the shaft. It was clumsy, but luck was with him. His hands snagged a timber plank and he crashed against the wall and hung there, panting.

Once he'd caught his breath, he found a foothold and checked that the Ember Blade was still safe at his hip. That done, he looked back at Fen, who was still pressed against the side of the cage, breath short with panic.

'Jump,' he told her.

There was a slow shriek of warping steel and the lift gently bowed forward, tipping her towards the open door.

'I'll fall!' she cried, and though she wanted desperately to move, she couldn't. She was locked in place, already falling in her mind as she fell in her dreams, her da's hand opening and pitching her out into empty air.

'You won't. I'll catch you.'

'You'll let me go!' she accused.

'I won't let you go, Fen. I promise.'

His voice was calm, strong as iron, and she believed him entirely. Cade had let go, but Aren never would. No matter what.

Move. Jump. Move.

'Trust me,' he said.

Something snapped overhead and the lift lurched. The rope began thumping and slithering in coils onto the roof of the cage.

'Look out below!' Aren barked. 'Fen! *Now!*'

The new note of fear gave her the spur she needed. She ran two steps forward and launched herself out into the air an instant before the arm of the crane smashed down into the cage with terrifying force and both plunged away, taking their lantern with it.

Fen flew through the sudden dark, caught in an instant of perfect terror. She hit the timbers shoulder-first, missing her catch, and bounced off with a scream; but a hand clamped onto her wrist, and before she could fall she was jerked back up, hard enough that

800

her arm almost came out of its socket. Aren held her, dangling, his other arm anchored around the timbers.

'I've got you,' he said through gritted teeth.

She seized the edge of a plank, pulled herself to the wall and got a foothold. When she was safe, he released her wrist and she pressed against the wood, feeling its roughness on her cheek, breathing in the dank scent of it.

'Fen? Aren?' Orica's worried voice floated up the shaft.

'We're alright!' Aren called. He looked down at Fen, his eyes shining in the faint light from above and below. 'We're alright?' he asked her softly.

'We're alright,' she agreed.

Then, to her surprise, she smiled at him. It was a smile of relief and gratitude and something more than that, some strange and foreign feeling which she didn't recognise and wouldn't admit. Her own reaction perturbed her, so she looked away and began to climb down.

For some reason, the drop didn't seem quite so terrible now.

106

The base of the shaft was a mess of bent metal and rope, the remains of the crane arm and the crushed lift. Harod had climbed the heap and was waiting there to guide them through the tangle to safe ground.

They climbed down into a small square chamber, damp and cold with long, empty centuries, half of it buried under debris from the shaft. The others were gathered near a stone doorway, anxious faces softening in relief as they saw that Aren and Fen were unhurt. Something about the sight of them clustered in the lanternlight gave Aren a pang. All the people that knew him, all those who cared, were right here. After losing Cade and almost losing Fen, they felt unutterably precious. Here was the sum total of his world now. Without them, he had nothing.

'Aren, Fen,' said Vika, beckoning. 'You should see this.'

They followed her through the doorway and the others trailed in after. Vika held up a lantern and the light swelled, but still it didn't fill the great hall they found themselves in; only just enough to illuminate the face of the monster.

The sight of it emerging suddenly from the gloom made Aren step back. An enormous statue towered over them, a seated figure on a throne of bone and tusk, its leering face horrifying to behold. A fat tongue lolled greedily over blade-like teeth and its three eyes were bulbous and crazed, the largest in the centre of its forehead. It wore a necklace of ears and its clawed hands rested on two draccen skulls. The whole of it exuded a primal, carnal savagery, a lewd animal lust for meat and slaughter.

'*Ganakh-ja-varr,*' said Mara, her voice echoing in the hollow hall. 'Chieftain of the urdish pantheon. For many long centuries, he has waited here in the dark.'

As they stood there, unsettled by the presence of an abandoned god, Aren felt a new understanding come over him. Once, the people who'd built this statue had been masters of Embria, makers of wonders. Their gods had ruled and their ways were the ways of the land. They told their own stories, in their language, and humans were savage, uneducated slaves only fit for servitude.

All his life he'd been taught that the urds were mindless primitives, vermin to be exterminated in the Purges; yet this wasn't the work of the mindless. How had the urds felt when plague had taken so many of them? Did they grieve as humans did? Did they weep when their children were slain by the ignorant masses that rose up behind Jessa Wolf's-Heart? He knew that story as a triumph, but an urd would speak of tragedy, betrayal and an upturning of the natural order.

What would his own tale be if a Krodan told it, then? One of theft, regicide and indiscriminate slaughter. An underhand plot to destroy the decency and order the Krodans had built in this backward land. The ungrateful act of malcontents who held to blasphemous gods and didn't know their place.

Right and wrong were just a matter of perspective. Stories and histories changed depending on the teller. Justice was an illusion. All that mattered was what you believed.

His hand went to the Ember Blade at his hip. *I believe in this*, he thought to himself. It was a solemn dedication, made with every fibre of his being. He believed in the Ember Blade, and his friends, and the rebellion he hoped would come. He believed with angry passion, and he knew now why Garric's quest had consumed him. Like Aren, Garric had needed one absolute to cling to, a cause to make all the loss mean something. Otherwise all their suffering was just chance and chaos, the random thrashings of an uncaring, godless existence. And he couldn't accept that. He wouldn't.

From somewhere above, they heard Sorrow howl.

'Let us make haste,' said Aren. 'We have no maps now. We'll have to find our own way out.'

'Lake is that way,' said Grub, pointing. 'Maybe we get back into caves we came in by. Maybe find some other way out.'

Mara made a noise of agreement. Grub had an uncanny sense of direction underground and his logic was sound. 'Water makes its own openings, even through rock. We are much more likely to find an exit near a lake than by heading further into the mountain.'

'Water makes openings. That what Grub meant,' said Grub, though it was evident he didn't know what she was talking about.

'Have a care, though,' Mara said to them all. 'When the urds were driven east, they left many traps and tricks behind for their enemies. Even now, the Delvers fear what lies in wait in the ruins. The urds were the greatest engineers of their day, and their craft has stood the test of time.'

'Ha! Grub not afraid of stupid urds. He will go first, because he is the bravest. Follow Grub!'

He took up a lantern and lumbered off across the hall, the others following in his wake.

They made their way through the cold, silent hollows of the underkeep, a world built by people whose thoughts moved by different tides. Every edge looked jagged or sharp. Horrible faces, violently angular, lunged from the darkness. Strange creatures sprawled across lintels and down square pillars. Everything the urds fashioned was a display of power and intimidation, and to Ossian eyes it was unbearably harsh. Yet to an urd, there must have been comfort here, just as Krodans took comfort in their piously austere houses and the rigid order of their society.

But that is not my world, Aren thought. *No more than this is.*

The underkeep was a maze of tunnels and halls, interconnected chambers linked by stairways and passages. They found complex junctions set over many levels, with multiple exits hidden among a knot of steps. There were rooms of all shapes and sizes, some with obvious purpose and some entirely mysterious. Empty of life, it was a sarcophagus for a vanished empire.

They passed through circular rooms with deep pits in the centre, and later crossed a square arena surrounded by stone tiers that might once have been benches. Aren wondered whether battles had been fought here, or if it was in fact a theatre, or a forum.

Then the walls closed in again and they were hurrying through narrow corridors once more, glancing over their shoulders as they went. The dark ahead and behind was oppressive, and though they hadn't heard Sorrow for some time now, they couldn't shake the sense that they were being hunted.

It was there, in the tight confines of the corridors, that they sprung the trap.

Aren, following just behind Grub, was the one who triggered it. A slab shifted beneath his foot, dropping an inch with a loud click and causing him to stumble. Grub went rigid at the sound, then suddenly darted forward. With a thunderous screech, two metal barriers sprang from recesses in the walls, slamming across the corridor in front and behind them. The rest were taken completely by surprise, but Grub, quick as a cat, slipped through the gap a moment before the barrier cut them off.

Seven of them were left on one side, Grub on the other. The barriers were solid slabs of metal, carved with leering faces and symbols of death in the ugly alphabet of the urds. Ruck barked angrily at the faces as the shock wore off, and they took stock.

The barrier in front of them wasn't quite closed. It had shunted a piece of rubble before it, and was now held a hand's width from the wall by a trembling chunk of stone.

'Grub?' Aren called.

Grub's eye appeared in the gap, a lantern held up above it. The barrier was still straining to close, driven by some great force from behind. The rock quivered and shifted, threatening to crack at any moment.

'Can you find a lever?' he asked Grub. 'Something to jam this open?'

Grub looked him over, and there was something calculating in his gaze which Aren didn't like. He grunted and disappeared, and Aren heard him moving around in the corridor. The rest of them watched one another, packed close in the small space between the barriers, each hoping that someone else had a solution.

'If that barrier closes—' Orica began.

'We'll be trapped here, yes,' Mara said tersely. 'And our lanterns will go out and we'll starve in the dark. We're all quite aware of that.'

'Vika, your staff?' Aren suggested. 'You can fit it in the gap.'

'It would shatter,' Vika said.

'Do you have a potion? Can you do anything?'

'If I could, I would be doing it.'

'Nothing out here!' Grub called from the other side.

'Is there any kind of mechanism?' Mara said. 'These barriers did not move by sorcery. There must be some way to retract them.'

'Grub will look.'

There was a click behind the wall where the barriers had sprung from and a rough grinding noise began, frighteningly loud in the silence.

'Grub?' Aren said. 'Did you—'

'Grub didn't touch anything!' came the irritated reply.

'Well, something happened!'

'The wall is moving!' Harod said.

And so it was. Narrowing the corridor inch by inch. Moving to crush them.

'*Grub!*' Fen cried as she put her shoulder to the wall in a futile attempt to slow its progress. Harod joined her, and Orica, too, while Ruck ran in tight circles, barking in distress.

'Wait! Something here!' said Grub.

'We don't have *time* to wait!' Aren yelled through the gap.

There was a crash of breaking stone on the other side of the barrier. 'Grub found it!'

'Found *what*?' Aren cried in frustration. The wall was pushing them together now, gathering them up before it. Aren couldn't help imagining the steady, relentless squeeze before the end, the cracking of ribs and bones, the pressure on his trapped skull building and building until—

'*Grub!*' he yelled again. 'What is it?'

'*Grub doesn't know!*' Grub shouted back in exasperation. 'Behind slab in wall, moving things, spinning things! No lever! No switch!'

'Do something!' Fen shouted, her heels skidding on the stone floor as she was forced backwards. 'Do it now, or we're going to die!'

Grub's eye appeared in the gap again. 'Ember Blade,' he said to Aren. 'Give Ember Blade to Grub.'

'Don't!' said Vika. 'He desires it – I hear it in his voice. Long have I suspected, but when I saw him with it, I knew. He means to take it. He has meant to take it all along.'

Grub's eye darkened in anger. 'No time for this, Painted Lady. Give!'

'Save us first!' Vika demanded. 'Or the Ember Blade will be lost to you for ever!'

Grub ignored her, his gaze fixed on Aren. The rock holding the gap open cracked under pressure from the barrier and a chunk of it skittered away. What remained would only hold for a few instants more.

'Mudslug,' said Grub, his voice hard. 'Give Ember Blade. Last chance.'

Aren pulled it from his belt, scabbard and all, and thrust it through the gap. Grub snatched it and yanked it the rest of the way out. A moment later, the rock exploded in a shower of powder and the barrier slammed shut, cutting them off entirely. Aren had a horrible feeling that he might have just made a terrible mistake; but it was done now, and couldn't be undone.

The wall had closed off half the corridor and there was hardly space to move as they were jammed up against one another. He smelled sweat and sewer-water and heard the frightened breath of his friends. Wild, wide eyes darted desperately, searching for salvation. The wall kept coming, oblivious to prayers or wishes.

They began to whimper and gasp as the space between them closed. The crush would worsen, tighter and tighter. Unimaginable pain was coming and they were helpless to prevent it. Aren fought to keep the scream inside him, but he wasn't sure how long he could.

'Grub! Help us!' Orica cried.

'He has his prize,' Vika said bitterly. 'He has already fled. Skarls have no conscience when it comes to foreigners.'

'No,' said Aren, through gritted teeth. 'He's out there. He's trying. I know him.'

But the wall came grinding onwards, and now they were so

807

tightly packed they could no longer move. Fen was pressed up against him, Vika on the other side, Ruck whining somewhere near his feet. Still the pressure increased. Aren shut his eyes and braced himself as best he could for the agony to come, but the mere thought of it turned his bowels to water.

No, no, please! Meshuk, Joha, Primus, anybody, no!

There was a shriek of metal from behind the wall and a *clunk-clunk-clunk* from some thwarted mechanism. The grinding fell quiet.

They waited, squeezed together, their faces inches from each other's, underlit ghoulishly by the lantern resting on the floor. None of them dared to breathe.

'The wall has stopped,' Orica whispered. She let out a little chuckle that was halfway to a sob. 'It stopped!'

Metal squealed and the barrier between them and Grub drew back a fraction. Fingers appeared in the gap and it was hauled open further, until it was wide enough to squeeze through. The Skarl's tattooed face appeared on the other side.

'Not squashed?' he asked in faint surprise.

They crowded past him, spilling out into the corridor beyond, gasping and panting in relief.

'Yes, thank you, Grub!' Grub griped sarcastically as they caught their breath. 'Thank you for saving our—'

He was cut short as Aren hugged him, and then Fen, too, and he was showered with pats on the back and exclamations of gratitude. Even Ruck barked and slobbered on his hand. By the end of it, Grub was equal parts pleased and embarrassed.

'Well, then,' he said, blushing. 'That a bit better.'

'How did you stop the wall?' Orica asked.

Grub pointed, and Aren blanched as he saw what the Skarl had done. There was a square hole in the wall of the corridor and a broken slab of stone on the floor where it had been pulled away. Beyond were toothed cogs, metal bars and counterweights like the workings of some ancient and enormous clock. The Ember Blade's elegant scabbard lay on the floor, while the sword itself had been jammed between the teeth of two large cogs.

Aren gaped. 'That's . . . That's the *Ember Blade*?' he managed.

'Mudslug rather be paste?' Grub asked. 'Dumbface said it was indestructible.'

'It's *supposed* to be...'

'Shouldn't say things if they're not true.' Grub sniffed. 'Let's see.'

He walked over, took hold of the hilt and yanked the Ember Blade free. Unblocked, the cogs came to life again, and there was a heavy boom as one wall met the other. Aren cringed.

Grub held up the Ember Blade and inspected it. 'Not a scratch,' he said, and sheathed it in its scabbard. 'Dumbface was right.' Then he held out the sword to Aren and snorted back a nostril full of snot. 'Here,' he said, with a pointed gaze at Vika. 'This not for Grub.'

Aren took it. 'Thank you,' he said earnestly. 'For more than just this.'

Vika stepped up beside him, shamefaced behind her smeared mask. 'I apologise, Grub. I wronged you,' she said.

'No, you didn't,' he replied breezily.

'Er...You mean you *were* going to steal it?' Aren asked.

Grub nodded. 'Grub made a choice tonight,' he said. 'Grub could have taken Ember Blade, gone home, made himself legend. Maybe Sombre Men judge him good then, maybe skin-scribes take away *this*.' He motioned to the black swipe across his eyes, the sign of the exile. 'Grub *khannaqut* no more. Bone God welcome him then.'

'But you chose otherwise,' Harod said. They were all listening now.

'Yes. Because being thief not enough. Leaving friends to die, not enough. Ember Blade? Not enough.' He poked a finger at Aren's chest. 'You start something here. Something bigger than stealing some stupid sword. Your people going to throw off Krodans. Going to fight an impossible fight and win. Know why? Because you have Grub with you. And when skalds tell of Grub a thousand years from now, when people read what the stonesingers write a hundred feet high, they not read about a thief who stole a sword. They read about a hero, like Jessa Wolf's-Heart! First Skarl they ever built a statue of in Ossia! Grub don't just want to be famous in Skara Thun. He want to be famous *everywhere*!' He thought for

809

a moment. 'Except maybe Kroda,' he added. 'His chances there, not good.' He shook his head, dismissing the thought. 'Anyway, you got Ember Blade now. Do something with it.'

Aren was half awed and half intimidated by the responsibility. 'That's a heavy weight to put on my shoulders,' he said.

'You trusted Grub. Grub trusts you. Don't let Grub down.'

'I won't,' said Aren. Then, more firmly: 'I won't.'

Grub harrumphed and fidgeted, suddenly awkward. 'Grub sorry about Dumbface,' he said. 'Going to miss him.'

The unexpected sympathy brought tears to Aren's eyes. 'Me, too,' he said quietly.

Grub took up the lantern and looked around at the others. 'You lot alright as well,' he told them. 'For foreigners, anyway. Just watch your step next time. Grub likes you better when you not crushed to bloody ooze.'

With that, he strode off down the corridor, his lantern swinging at his side. Fen and Aren exchanged a glance, then Fen shrugged and followed him.

107

There was vengeance in Sorrow's cries. Aren could hear it. Somehow he'd sensed Plague's death. Until now, the dreadknights had kept up some semblance of humanity, but that was all over. They were servants of the Outsiders, and his angry, haunting screams were the voice of the Abyss.

They went deeper into the underkeep, maintaining a punishing pace despite the threat of more traps. Sorrow sounded like he was almost on top of them, but they could only keep moving, and hope. They didn't have the strength to stand against him. Vika was their only weapon, and she was spent.

The darkness bore down on them as they hurried through abandoned chambers, their lanterns lonely flickers of light. They headed towards the lake, following Grub's lead, but they kept hitting dead ends and were forced to backtrack many times. Stairs took them up and down, tunnels split and split again, and the more detours they took, the more Aren began to despair of ever finding an escape. All the time, Sorrow drew closer.

Eventually, they emerged from the maze of tunnels and halls and found themselves on an ancient bridge over a breathtaking chasm that extended far beyond the limits of their lanterns. At the edge of the light, they could dimly see other bridges crossing theirs, both overhead and below, some straddled by squat, silent gatehouses with empty black windows. There were other buildings along the side of the gorge, angular dwellings descending into the dark. A great stone promontory held up a huge structure that had the look of a temple, but which was more intimidating and awesome in its setting than any Sanctorum building Aren had ever seen.

'How far do these tunnels spread?' Mara exclaimed. 'We must have left Hammerholt far behind by now.'

'The Knights Vigilant of Mitterland spoke of finding underground cities during the Purges of the lowlands,' said Harod. 'It is thought that they are pale shadows of those built across Ossia when the First Empire was in its pomp.'

The bridge ended at a gaping portal leading to another cave, where they found a bewildering tangle of steps and platforms spreading out before them. There were half a dozen exits they could see, and probably more they couldn't.

Aren's heart sank a little. 'Which way?' he asked.

Even Grub's confidence waned, faced with so many options. He surveyed the scene helplessly, trying to guess the route onwards. Then Ruck barked, and Vika stepped forward and laid a hand on her back.

'That way,' she said, pointing to a doorway high above them with her staff.

'How can you tell?' asked Orica, her green eyes shining bright in the gloom.

'Ruck can hear night birds, calling on the lake.'

'Fleabag tell you that, did she?' Grub asked, eyeing Ruck suspiciously. Ruck growled at him.

'In a way,' said Vika, and offered no further explanation.

Aren was in no mood to turn down any offer of hope. 'Lead on, then,' he told Ruck, who loped off ahead. They followed her, Grub grumbling under his breath about the indignity of being replaced by a hound.

The prospect of escape spurred them to new speed. Though they were tired and footsore, they pushed past gruesome carvings, through grim halls thick with shadow and chambers full of pillars and pits. The scowling craft of the urds oppressed them, and with every step they feared to trigger some new trap; but whether by luck or divine favour, they made their way unhindered.

At last, they emerged through a doorway into another cavern. Before them was a gorge spanned by a narrow bridge. They could hear water running somewhere below. At the far end of the bridge, rough steps zigzagged upwards, ending in—

'Light!' Orica cried. And it was: the cool glow of the moons, knifing through some unseen gap at the top of the stairs. Ruck barked joyfully and went running ahead, Vika running with her.

'Wait for Grub!' said Grub, bounding after them onto the bridge.

Aren was no less eager, chasing the others towards the moonlight. He knew haste was foolish, but he couldn't help himself. It was only when he was some way across that he remembered Fen's fear of heights and stopped to check she was coming.

To his surprise, she was right behind him. The bridge wasn't wide, but it was wide enough that she was in no danger of falling, and there were crumbling parapets to either side. Her face was alight, and the sight of it warmed him, a small comfort in the vast, numb waste left by Cade's death.

He looked past her to the others: Mara was close on Fen's heels, then Harod, with Orica just behind him.

And behind her, swirling like ink from the dark mouth of the doorway, a shadow in a black cloak, his metal face frozen in an anguished howl.

'*Look out!*' he screamed; but already he knew that no warning would be enough.

The dreadknight lunged from the doorway. Orica's eyes went wide as she was enfolded from behind. A blade flashed in the blackness, and plunged.

Time slowed to a crawl. Orica went stiff, caught inside that tangle of darkness, her gaze drifting far away to something they couldn't see. Sorrow drew back his blade and released her, and she crumpled in a heap on the ground.

Harod stood at the end of the bridge, frozen in place. He'd turned in time to see Orica stabbed, but too late to intervene. Now he quivered like a plucked string, his eyes filling with horror, his Harrish composure peeling away before the heat of his emotion.

Sorrow raised his paired swords, the short blade and the long, and took his stance. His first strike had been murder; now he meant to do battle. A scream of rage and grief ripped from Harod's throat. He drew his sword and charged, and Sorrow ran to meet him.

They met in a storm of blades, a flurry of strikes almost too fast for the eye to see. Sorrow's swords were everywhere, and at first Harod was equal to it. Though he wasn't so inhumanly quick, he anticipated every blow and was ready when it came. Back and forth they went, but Sorrow's speed gave him the edge in the end, and Harod was driven steadily onto the bridge and further from his fallen love.

Shock had stayed Aren's hand at first, but now he drew his sword, intending to run to Harod's aid. Fen grabbed his arm before he could.

'Don't,' she told him. 'You can't win.'

It was truth, and he knew it. He couldn't even beat Harte in a straight fight; walking into that whirlwind would be suicide. But he couldn't stand by and do nothing. It wasn't in him to do that.

'Come on, Mudslug!' Grub was back with them now, tugging him towards the stairs. 'Bowlhead buying us time!'

Aren shook him off. 'Vika! Help him!'

'I want to,' said the druidess, her painted face tortured in the lanternlight. 'I can't.'

'Fen has no arrows,' Mara said. 'Only you and Grub can help, and the bridge is not broad enough for you both.'

'And Grub isn't stupid. He not fighting *that*!'

'We must save the Ember Blade!' Mara urged. 'Out in the open, maybe we can escape him.'

Aren watched the battle raging on the bridge and knew that Harod couldn't win it. The dreadknight was tireless, and Harod wasn't. He'd be worn down and killed eventually, and if they were still here when that happened, they'd be killed, too.

But he was one of them, and that meant more than any sword did.

'Wherever we go, Sorrow will find us,' Aren told them. 'We stand united, or we fall apart.' So saying, he ran into the fray.

It took all of his courage to cross swords with the dreadknight. It was a thing of shadow, the only bright points its witch-iron blades and twisted mask. Terror surrounded it like a mantle. Yet for all his fear, Aren moved alongside Harod and took his place in the fight. They'd both lost someone they loved today, and there was brotherhood in that. Aren wouldn't lose Harod, too.

He expected to be outclassed and fought accordingly. He wasn't there to kill the dreadknight but to divide his attention. If he could defend himself awhile, he might give Harod the chance he needed; but even that was almost beyond him. The dreadknight's blows came so fast that he was barely able to fend them away. Were it not for the fact that the dreadknight was focusing on Harod – clearly the more dangerous opponent – Aren would have been cut down like wheat.

To overcome your enemy, you must first understand him. But how could he possibly understand what lay beneath Sorrow's mask?

Harod let out a high, raw scream that sounded wrong coming from a man who'd once seemed a stranger to emotion. Yet even taken by purest fury, he was in control. Still he didn't overreach, still he kept his straight-backed stance while his blade flickered here and there. Perhaps Sorrow had hoped to unbalance him by attacking Orica first, but Harod was too skilled a swordsman for that.

Hard and quick they fought, by the light of the moons and their lanterns. Aren wasn't aware of what the others on the bridge were doing, if they'd fled or not, and he had no space to care. All his focus was on this battle, every fibre of his being dedicated to the fight.

It wasn't enough. Sorrow's blade whipped out, and as Aren pulled his head out of reach, his leg was kicked from under him. He fell backwards and crashed against the parapet, which broke beneath his weight, ancient stone giving way to pitch him into the black gorge.

Harod grabbed him by the scruff of his jerkin, lightning-quick, and hauled him away from the edge. Instead of falling over the side, he tumbled onto the floor of the bridge. But that distraction was what Sorrow had been counting on. The instant Harod took his eye from his opponent, Sorrow hooked his shortsword around Harod's weapon. There was an instant of struggle, then both blades went spinning into the void.

Harod stepped back from his opponent, weaponless now, without armour. Sorrow drew himself up to his full height, his long blade hanging from his gloved hand, that anguished face gaping. A snake about to strike.

'Harod!' Aren cried.

Harod whirled in time to catch the sword Aren flung towards him. Sorrow lunged in the same moment, thrusting for the kill, but Harod spun back to face him, the sword singing free from its scabbard as he turned, and it wasn't Aren's sword he held but the Ember Blade, a streak of sullen fire in the dark which smashed the dreadknight's blade to shards.

Sorrow stared in surprise at the sundered weapon in his hands, and in that moment of hesitation, Harod swung again. The dreadknight gave an unearthly shriek as the Ember Blade clove into him, the force of it sending his body over the parapet. Still shrieking, he tumbled raggedly into the gorge, and kept falling till they could hear him no more.

'*Orica!*' The Ember Blade clattered to the ground, forgotten, as Harod raced to Orica's side and gathered her up in his arms. '*Orica!*'

The sound of his grief pierced them all. Aren stood wearily, gathered up the bloody Ember Blade and sheathed it. The others were clustered uncertainly at the far end of the bridge. They hadn't run, but nor could they celebrate Sorrow's death. All sense of triumph had been swept away by the loss that came with it.

Aren approached Harod, drawn by the need to see if Orica lived, but he stopped at a distance. This was Harod's tragedy; he didn't want to intrude.

'Speak to me,' Harod begged, holding her head up. Her eyes found him and focused, and he broke into a smile of desperate hope. But there was no coming back for her. Aren knew it, and he saw Harod's face fall as he realised it, too. Sarla was here to claim her.

'I love you,' he told her, gasping the words, tears dripping from his eyes. 'I love you. I should have said it all along. Don't leave me, Orica. I love you!'

Orica's hand lifted, trembling. Her eyes stayed fixed on his as it slid inside her clothes, searching for an inside pocket. Her gaze was fierce, as if to break connection with him would be to lose the last thing anchoring her to the world.

'I love you,' he sobbed, as if by saying it again he could undo what had been done to her. 'Don't go.'

From out of the pocket she drew a folded sheaf of paper, wet at the edge with her blood. She took his hand and pressed it there. He hardly seemed to notice.

'I love you,' he whispered again.

Her lips parted as if to speak, but giving him the paper had taken the last of her. Her face went loose, and her body relaxed with a long sigh.

Harod's desolate scream cut Aren to the heart, and he had to turn away. Nothing he could do would make anything better. All he could do was leave, and let Harod have his grief.

He walked across the bridge to the others and passed without looking at them. Above and ahead, close enough to smell it, was freedom. With the Ember Blade in hand, he trudged towards the light.

108

A mossy stone door stood ajar at the top of the zigzag stair. By the looks of it, it hadn't been moved for centuries. The work of some forgotten Delver, perhaps, or an old escape route lost to time. Aren didn't care. He just wanted out.

Beyond was a narrow cave passage, moonlight shining through a gash at the end. Aren stepped out into the speckled night.

He found himself on a ledge on a mountainside, the moons hanging side-by-side in the sky before him. Behind him, out of sight, Hammerholt burned bright enough to light the undersides of the clouds. Spread out below was Lake Calagria, the black water glowing with the fire's reflected rage. Scattered lamps picked out the towns on the shore.

He breathed in, smelling the smoke on the wind, and let it out again. He was alive. Just to exist was enough in this moment. He dared not think beyond that, to what life without Cade would mean. He was here, breathing, and that was victory of a sort.

The others followed him onto the ledge, sank to the ground and rested, looking out over the vista or leaning against the rock. None of them spoke. No one had the words.

Harod was the last to arrive. He walked with Orica cradled in his arms, his blood-smeared face puffy and red with tears, his ridiculous hair in a mess. Silently, they got to their feet again and Fen led them off the ledge, picking a way down the mountainside for them to follow.

At Mara's suggestion they'd buried maps, weapons and supplies in some woods by the lake the day before. A contingency plan, in case they had to escape cross-country. Fen guided them back to the spot and they unearthed their stash, washed the blood from themselves in a stream and changed their clothes. Harod put Orica's body down next to the water and cleaned her face and hands with a cloth, wiping it carefully across her skin, murmuring to her as he did so. When he was finished, he lifted her again.

'She will not lie here beneath the trees,' he said, his voice dull. 'She always loved the open sky.'

'We will find a place for her,' said Vika.

They laid her to rest beside a shallow tarn in a reedy mountain meadow as dawn broke over the mountains. In the distance, visible between the peaks, Hammerholt still burned, a torch that could be seen as far as the Krodan border.

As was the Ossian way, she was placed in the ground with no marker, given to the mercy of the Lady of Worms. She'd go back to the earth she'd come from, dissolving into the land she'd loved. And as they grieved for Orica, they also grieved for Cade. While the others threw soil over her still body, Aren's eyes were on the burning fortress that had taken his best friend.

Vika prayed to Sarla, for Orica and Cade, and Garric, too. Aren couldn't even muster any anger at that name, even though he still blamed him for Cade's death. He'd been emptied by the past few hours. In the end, Garric wasn't the villain Aren's father had warned him about, nor the hero he'd once appeared. There were no heroes or villains here, or anywhere. He was just a man, flawed as the next, and he made his choices like the rest of them. Whether they were good choices or bad was a matter of perspective.

When Vika was done, she stepped back from the grave and looked to Harod.

'Will you speak?' she asked him. 'You, who knew her best?'

He moved to the foot of her grave and looked down upon it. He was wearing his armour again, his velvets discarded, a knight once more. At last, he lifted his head, and in a high, frail voice, he sang.

The king stood at his window in his castle on the shore.
His family were sleeping, his foes were no more.
As he looked o'er the sea he heard knuckles on the door.
'Twas his seer, white as a ghost.

'Sire, please beware, for a storm does draw near
That will tear down your walls and take all you hold dear.'
But the king laughed and knew he had nothing to fear
And he turned his old eyes to the coast.

His voice was weak and he could hardly hold a tune, but it didn't matter somehow. Aren felt something stir inside him as he listened, a shred of defiance and battered pride amid the empty sadness. He couldn't let Harod continue alone, and after hearing it so many times from Orica's lips, they all knew the words. Aren lifted his voice with Harod's, and one by one the others did, too.

He said, 'I see no clouds, and the waves are not high.
Your omens mislead you, your bones fall awry.'
But the seer said, 'Sire, not all storms come from the sky.
There are depths to which you cannot see.

'The tide is returning, and coming right soon.
It brings with it those you have sent to their doom.
There's a wolf in the waves who yet howls from its tomb
And the fallen keep long memory.'

Then the king said, 'You lie! For this land is my land!
Passed on to me by fate's bloodied right hand.'
'But sire,' said the seer, 'though you think you command,
Your rule is but fleeting here.

'There are elder things yet than the god you obey
And none may lay claim to this soil, try you may.
For this land will be here after you pass away
And its children will still persevere.'

By now, all of them were singing, even Grub. Despite everything, Aren's heart swelled at the sound. His hand went to the Ember Blade at his hip. For all it had cost, they'd done something miraculous tonight. Cade would have appreciated that.

Said the king, 'For this heresy, I'll see you burn.
I say destiny's charge is not easy to turn.'
But the seer shook his head. 'Sire, you have much to learn
For the urds said the same in their day.'

Now the king stands at his window and watches the sea
And he knows that his castle's no sanctuary
As he waits for the truth of the seer's prophecy
And the storm that will sweep him away.

Tears were running down Harod's cheeks as the final line faded, and he stood trembling for a time. Finally, he reached inside his splint mail and took out the folded papers Orica had given him. He opened them up, revealing scribbled verses and pages of staves marked with musical notation.

'Here is her song,' he said. 'Her masterpiece. It is all that is left of her. I say it will be the anthem of your revolution. I say we will spread it throughout this land, until her words are on the lips of every bard, and all who hear it will know it as her call to arms. The Krodans will say, "Death to all that play it! Death to all that hear it!" And they will play it anyway, in secret, in back rooms and behind closed doors. It will be a beacon of hope in the red days to come, when the Krodans bear down upon this land in vengeance for what we have done this night, and Ossian tears wash the streets. And when all is over, when you have driven the occupiers from your land, her name will be remembered for ever, revered for all time in your histories.' He waved the papers before them. 'A song for a new Ossia, written by a Sard. For this was her land as much as yours, and she has given her life for it.'

'The anthem of our revolution,' said Aren. 'Well spoken. It shall be so.'

'Then my sword is yours,' said Harod. 'Until the day your land is free and the Sards are returned to it. That is my quest, taken in her name.'

He bowed his head and stepped away from the grave. Birdsong fluted in the lightening sky and wind stirred the long grasses.

'You know my mind,' said Vika to them all. 'The Aspects set me on this path. A great darkness gathers and the demons we faced tonight were the merest part of it. Whatever evil is coming, the Krodans are somehow involved; and so I will resist them to my last breath.' Ruck barked in agreement.

'My home is lost to me,' said Fen, 'and it always will be while Krodans rule in Ossia. Until they are gone, my home is here, with you.'

'My home is lost, too,' said Mara. 'But there is liberation in that. No longer will I live in a society that limits and forbids me. I will set my discoveries and inventions to use at last, for the good of the resistance. My pupils may have lost their teacher, but I will see a day once again when no woman of this land will have her talents stifled and her thoughts curtailed by the Sanctorum and their damned kind.'

'We all have our reasons for revolution,' said Aren, 'but *this* is our common cause.' With a sharp ring, he drew the Ember Blade and brandished it before him, its blade touched with red in the first light of day. The sight of it inspired him, and made his words reckless and brave.

'Some will say the last Dawnwarden died tonight,' he said. 'But we will make liars of them. For though we hail from different lands and different stations in life, though we believe in different gods or none at all, tonight we reclaimed that which the Dawnwardens lost. Tonight, we earned the right to take on their mantle.' He raked them all with his gaze, his face alive with conviction. '*We* are the Dawnwardens now!'

'Dawnwardens? Us?' Mara looked bewildered, but as the idea sank in, a light kindled in her eyes. 'Yet, why not? We *did* win back the Ember Blade.'

'And who were the Dawnwardens but the guardians of the Ember Blade?' said Vika, a wry smile growing on her face. 'Long have our people wished for their return. It would not do to disappoint them.'

'Grub want to be a Dawnwarden!' Grub cried eagerly, bouncing up and down.

'We are *all* Dawnwardens!' Aren said, swept up in the moment. He held the sword before him. 'I swear I will protect the Ember Blade with my life, until such a day when it can be put into the hand of one who deserves to rule this land. I pledge myself to any who share this purpose, an unbreakable bond, unto death. Will you swear with me?'

'I will,' said Harod, grimly.

'Aye,' said Vika, her eyes creasing with approval. Ruck barked happily at her side. 'I think the Aspects would be pleased. I swear it, for the Ember Blade, and for each other.'

'Me, too!' Grub said, and then cackled. 'Ha! Now you *all* have to be friends with Grub!'

'I am not given to grand gestures,' said Mara, 'but I have kept my silence all my life, and my name has gone too long unrecognised. I will be a Dawnwarden. I swear with you.'

'And you?' Aren asked Fen. 'Would you stand with us, knowing what's to come? Knowing we might all fall together?'

'Yes,' she said softly, and there was that look on her face that Aren was coming to know, the one that sent fire through his veins. 'I'll stand with you.'

'It is done, then,' said Aren, and he thrust the sword back into its scabbard. 'Let us spread the word. The Dawnwardens have returned, and they have the Ember Blade.'

Grub cheered then, and they looked at each other with new eyes, and a new sense of beginning. A shadow fell across Aren as he thought of Cade, who should have been there with them; but it couldn't entirely darken the moment, and he still found it in himself to smile.

'These mountains will be crawling with Krodans soon,' Vika said. 'Whither now?'

'We can find shelter near Gallenpeak. I know people sympathetic to our cause,' Mara said. 'You don't mix with traitors for years without picking up a few contacts.'

'We'll stay off the roads, take the wild paths,' said Fen. 'These lands are new to me, but I'll get us there unseen.'

Aren shouldered his pack and took one last look around the meadow, where the risen sun had turned the waving reeds to gold.

'Then show us the way, Fen,' he said. 'We've work to do.'